The Sword Brothers

Peter Darman

I would like to thank the following people whose assistance has been integral to the creation of this work:
Julia, for her invaluable help and guidance with the text.
'Big John', for designing the cover.
Donald Gruener, for the cover image via iStock.

Those marked with an asterisk * are known to history.

The Order of Sword Brothers

Aldous: Master of Lennewarden Castle
Anton: novice at Wenden Castle
Berthold: Master of Wenden Castle*
Bertram: Master of Segewold Castle
Bruno: novice at Wenden Castle
Conrad Wolff: novice at Wenden Castle
Friedhelm: Master of Uexkull Castle
Gerhard: Master of Holm Castle
Griswold: Master of Kokenhusen Castle
Hans: novice at Wenden Castle
Henke: brother knight at Wenden Castle
Jacob: Master of Gersika Castle
Johann: novice at Wenden Castle
Lukas: brother knight at Wenden Castle
Mathias: Master of Kremon Castle
Rudolf: brother knight at Wenden Castle and deputy to Master Berthold*
Thaddeus: chief engineer at Wenden Castle
Volquin: Grand Master of the Order of Sword Brothers*
Walter: brother knight at Wenden Castle
Livs
Caupo: king of the Livs and ally of Bishop Albert*
Daina: daughter of Thalibald
Rameke: youngest son of Thalibald*
Thalibald: Caupo's chief warlord*
Vetseke: prince, former ruler of Kokenhusen*
Waribule: eldest son of Thalibald*

Germans

Albert: Bishop of Riga*
Albert, Count: crusader*
Helmold of Plesse: crusader*
Stefan: archdeacon, Governor of Riga
Theodoric: Bishop of Estonia*

Estonians

Alva: Chief of the Harrien
Edvin: Chief of the Wierlanders
Eha: wife of Kalju
Jaak: Chief of the Jerwen
Kalju: Chief of the Ungannians
Lembit: Chief of the Saccalians, Grand Warlord of all Estonia*
Nigul: Chief of the Rotalians
Rusticus: Lembit's deputy

Russians

3

Domash Tverdislavich: Mayor of Pskov*
Gleb: *Skomorokh*, follower of the old religion
Mstislav: Prince of Novgorod*
Vsevolod: Prince of Gerzika*

Lithuanians

Arturus: Duke of the Northern Kurs
Butantas: Duke of the Samogitians
Daugerutis: Duke of the Selonians and Nalsen, grand duke of the Lithuanian tribes*
Gedvilas: Duke of the Southern Kurs
Kitenis: Duke of the Aukstaitijans
Mindaugas: son of Prince Stecse*
Rasa: daughter of Daugerutis and wife of Prince Vsevolod
Stecse: prince, chief warlord of Duke Daugerutis*
Ykintas: Duke of the Semgallians

Maps

The following maps relating to the lands and peoples described in 'The Sword Brothers':
1) Livonia in 1210
2) The Estonian tribal kingdoms
3) The Lithuanian tribal kingdoms
can all be found on the maps page on my website:
www.peterdarman.com

Chapter 1

Lübeck, 1210.

Now that it was spring the city seemed a much more agreeable place, the weather warmer, the streets less muddy and the people happier. Not that Conrad saw much of it or them each day, save for the customers who came into his father's bakery to purchase his bread. It had been a hard winter but pray God the spring and summer would be better for him and his family. His father was reckoned one of the best bakers in Lübeck, not only among his customers who tasted his produce but also within the guild that controlled the city's bakeries. But life for him and his family was still hard. For all of them the working day began before dawn and did not end until the evening. Hours spent making dough and baking bread to fill the bellies of the city's increasing population, should have meant an increase in the family's income. But Lübeck's laws regarding the production of bread were numerous and strict, chief among them being that such a vital food source should not be over-priced. The price of flour was also strictly controlled, at least in theory, but the bakers' guild was forever complaining that unscrupulous millers were always over-charging for their goods.

'Conrad, make sure the mark is on every loaf.'

Dietmar Wolff was pointing at a row of loaves in front of his son that had yet to be branded.

Conrad smiled and shook his head. 'Yes, father, of course.'

His father was not smiling. 'Make sure you do. I don't want to pay any more fines for selling unmarked bread.'

It had been a cause of great celebration when Dietmar Wolff had first been issued with his own baker's mark by the city authorities, for it meant that his bakery was considered to be one of Lübeck's finest. The mark itself was a simple wooden die that was used to stamp the underside of loaves before they were cooked, Dietmar's bearing the letter 'W' for Wolff to indicate where the loaf came from. Marks were also used to identify bakers who sold underweight loaves or those made from inferior flour, but those bearing Dietmar's brand were fast becoming known for their taste and quality, something that he was keen to encourage. Loaves bearing no mark were not only lost opportunities to advertise his talents as a baker, they also incurred fines imposed by the authorities. It was no exaggeration to state that the wooden die was the family's most prized possession.

Conrad had served his father for nearly seven years as an apprentice and regarded himself as a talented baker in the making, notwithstanding that he sometimes forgot to mark the loaves before they were placed in the oven.

His mother stopped kneading dough on the table in front of her.

'Leave him alone, Dietmar. This summer will be a good one, I can sense it.'

Dietmar ran a hand over his balding crown. 'It needs to be. The price of flour keeps going up and I cannot pass on the increase to my customers because of the ridiculous city laws.'

Conrad began pressing the die into the underside of each loaf. 'Your brand is becoming well known in the city, father. Soon we will be able to move to a larger house in the west of the city.'

His mother smiled at him but his father's forehead creased into a frown.

'A larger house? Four mouths to feed, increasing flour prices, not allowed to work on a Sunday and a further fifty saints' days each year? I think not.'

'It is important to give thanks to God for our good fortune,' his wife rebuked him.

Dietmar ran a hand over his head once more and went back to his work. He did not need to go to church to thank God for giving him such a wife, and the truth was that he praised the Lord each and every day for blessing him with his wife. Eight years his junior, Agnete Wolff was a beautiful woman who should have been married to a rich merchant or perhaps even a richer knight. That she had somehow ended up marrying a stocky baker shorter than she was a mystery that he had never been able to fathom.

Agnete's father was a miller who supplied Dietmar with flour and that is how he had first met his bride, the tall, slender beauty who trapped him with her blue eyes and soft smile. He had fallen in love with her on sight but it had taken a while for Agnete to reciprocate the sentiment. But over time she came to respect the hard-working, stubborn baker who presented a stony exterior to the world but who underneath was kind and loyal. And so they married and Agnete bore him two children – Conrad and Marie – and never complained about the days of unceasing toil that filled their lives. God was good and would ensure that their piety and hard work would be rewarded, of that she was certain.

Their home was a small two-storey half-timbered house with a thatched roof in the eastern side of the city: one of a myriad of tiny abodes positioned either side of the warren of narrow streets that made up the poorer quarter of the city, a home to Lübeck's small traders and artisans. They all slept in one room above the ground-

6

floor shop where the oven was located, to the rear of which was a dirt patch where the pigs were kept. Many kept pigs. They were released in the daylight hours to consume the rubbish that was thrown into the streets by householders – human and animal excrement, animal entrails and rotting food. That was the theory at least. The reality was that the earth streets were always full of filth that a traveller had to pick a path through. The pigs just added to the general noise and unpleasantness of the streets, which today were more crowded than usual.

The city authorities sometimes attempted to clean the streets, hiring muck-rakers to clear away the filth, especially when the cankerous smell reached the rich houses in the city's western quarter. But hiring muck-rakers meant expenditure and Lübeck's city fathers were notoriously parsimonious. And so as the temperature rose the stench increased so that by high summer everyone was praying for the cooler air of autumn.

But today the smell was hardly noticeable as the bakery that fronted the shop was filled to bursting as Conrad and his father toiled to produce the loaves that everyone wanted to buy. Agnete served the customers with a smile as Marie ferried fresh loaves from the oven. Two years younger than Conrad, she had inherited her father's frame. A happy-go-lucky, cheerful child, her round face always wore a smile, especially when she was rounding up her beloved pigs at the end of the day, to be confined in the pen that she called their home.

Conrad often thought that he could produce bread in his sleep so adept had he become at it. He could create all the varieties produced in his father's bakery – white bread, brown bread, black bread and horse – with ease, and in their two main types: trenchers and table bread. The former were long, flat loaves turned over and over in the oven until hard, flat crusts were formed on both sides. They were usually cut horizontally and filled with cooked meat whose juices soaked into the bread, a delicacy largely denied to Conrad and his family who could rarely afford meat – save if Dietmar slaughtered one of Marie's beloved pigs. The most common type of loaf consumed by Conrad's family and indeed most of the city was table bread: a simple round loaf.

Conrad loved his parents and looked forward to the day when he would follow in his father's footsteps and become a master baker, producing white bread for the rich, brown bread that was sold for half the price of white, black bread that was cheaper still, though hopefully not horse bread, made from the lowest quality flour and not fit for human consumption, though it was eaten by the poor when times were hard. This then was his life: working from dawn till dusk to help his

7

father feed his family with the expectation, God permitting, that he would eventually work in his own bakery to feed his own family. Every working day was the same, year in, year out.

Until today.

During the preceding weeks a regular visitor to the bakery had been a scullion, a lowly servant who worked in the home of one of Lübeck's richest merchants. In an effort to ingratiate himself with Conrad's mother he never failed to mention this fact, along with leering at her every time he purchased a white loaf. Dietmar disliked him and bristled with anger every time the man looked at his wife in an inappropriate way. Agnete brushed aside the man's ogling, though always maintaining a polite disposition as she relieved him of his master's money. The scullion may have looked like a beggar but his master's coins were a valuable addition to the Wolffs' income, as Agnete always reminded Dietmar.

For his part the scullion rarely saw his master, Adolfus Braune, though he talked incessantly about the beautiful woman who worked in a bakery in eastern Lübeck. Eventually word reached Braune of this woman and he became curious and decided to pay her a visit to see if the rumours were true. If they proved false he would have the scullion's tongue bored. Being the richest merchant in Lübeck meant he could dispense justice almost at will. What use was power if it could not be wielded?

It was late afternoon when he left his three-storey brick building sited near his harbour-front warehouses. As usual he took his entourage with him – half a dozen burly thugs he had recruited in the aftermath of his father's death a year earlier. It was his father who had built up the Braune fortune, establishing a trading network throughout the Baltic region, only to be stabbed to death on the island of Gotland by a creditor with a grievance. So at the age of thirty-five Adolfus inherited his father's fortune and his fleet of trading vessels, which at a stroke made him one of Lübeck's wealthiest citizens. His mother had died of a pestilence during his early years and his father had largely ignored him, leaving the young Adolfus to develop a sly, manipulative character spiced with a high degree of resentment against first his father and then the world in general. Being overweight, prematurely bald and unattractive meant he preferred the company of sycophants and lackeys to polite society and equals, which would not have mattered had not his father been murdered. His father's demise at a stroke made him both rich and powerful and thrust him into Lübeck's highest echelons.

His guards had been recruited from harbour workers: brutish, uneducated men who would obey commands unquestioningly as long as they were paid. Adolfus never went anywhere without them, not least because he feared suffering the same fate as his father.

The crowds were insufferable, a sea of stinking bodies, disfigured faces and raucous individuals, and after a while Adolfus was beginning to regret leaving his spacious, elegant and sweet-smelling house. His temper began to fray as his progress to the eastern quarter was slowed by simple-minded idiots who barred his path rather than bowing and getting out of the way. He ordered his men to clear a path, which they did by shoving aside anyone in their way. Adolfus recoiled in horror when a beggar extended his grubby, calloused hand to him, earning the poor unfortunate a heavy thwack on the arm with a baton carried by one of his men.

Eventually they reached the street of bakers, which also contained shops selling pies and vegetables. The air was filled with different accents for Lübeck was a rich trading city that attracted people from all over Germany, as well as from Denmark, whose king also ruled Lübeck, Norway and Sweden.

'This is the place, lord,' remarked one of the bodyguards.

Adolfus, who had been paying careful attention to where he placed his feet in an effort to avoid stepping in a pile of rotting vegetables or pig dung, stopped and looked up at a sign hanging over an open-fronted shop from where the pleasant aroma of freshly baked bread was emanating. The sign displayed a poorly painted loaf of bread on a red background.

Adolfus screwed up his face. 'This had better be worth it. I fear I may catch some sort of pestilence just breathing the same air as these people.'

Just then a squealing pig raced past him, pursued by a young girl in a russet dress.

'Quite intolerable,' sniffed Adolfus, who waved his men forward into the shop.

The early morning bustle, the busiest time of the day, was long gone and now the bakery's shelves and counter were largely empty. However, Agnete always kept a loaf of table bread for a regular customer who always visited the bakery late in the afternoon. Roger the Putrid knew he stank, his neighbours knew he stank and so did anyone unfortunate enough to pass by him in the street. As a fuller he spent most of his days walking up and down on wool in huge vats of urine. Wool was essential to the lives of rich and poor alike but no one wanted to wear clothes that were itchy and stiff. Therefore the wool was soaked in stinking, stale urine to draw

9

out the grease in the material and pounded by feet to interlock the fibres. The end result was wool that was kind to skin thanks to Roger and his fellow fullers. Everyone knew that fullers were crucial to the manufacture of clothing; they just did not want them anywhere near them.

Roger earned a good living but his was a solitary life. That is why he looked forward to his daily visit to the Wolffs' bakery. In truth he was a little in love with Agnete, though he would never admit it. But who wouldn't be entranced by the angelic beauty with the soft voice who always had a kind word for him? It was the same today as he passed her the money for his loaf.

'Are you well, Roger?' she enquired as he dropped the coins into her palm.

'Well, thank you, praise God.'

She smiled and nodded at him. 'Praise God indeed.'

Roger looked past her to where Dietmar was removing the ashes from his oven.

'And good day to you, Dietmar.'

Agnete's husband turned and raised his hand to his customer whose aroma was slowly filling his bakery. 'Roger.'

Agnete's smile slipped as a group of men led by a richly attired overweight man with pale skin entered the shop. Their leader may have been dressed in a long scarlet tunic with a bright red trim round the neck and cuffs, but his companions were all covered in black and had a menacing air. They were also all armed with daggers and two were carrying batons. The man in the fine belted tunic suddenly recoiled from the smell coming from the man standing in front of him.

'What is that smell?' he said loudly before covering his nostrils with a thumb and forefinger.

Roger sighed resignedly and turned to leave the bakery before he upset the new arrivals further, only to be grabbed by the collar and thrown into the street by one of the ruffians. Agnete was appalled as Roger crashed to the earth outside the shop, spilling his loaf, which was immediately seized by a grunting pig that scurried away. Adolfus and his companions laughed and mocked the smelly individual as he tried in vain to retrieve his loaf.

'That's much better,' said Adolfus who walked up to the counter and studied Agnete.

She may have been the wife of a low-born baker but even with her hair covered by a white wimple and the arms of her blue tunic being dusted with flour her beauty was apparent. Her flawless, fair skin contrasted sharply with her clear blue

10

eyes and even though her gown was loose fitting he could see that she had a slender figure.

'Can I help you, sir?' Her soft voice only added to her attractiveness.

Adolfus' piggy eyes opened wide as he beheld her.

Dietmar stopped his cleaning and moved to stand beside his wife. His instincts told him that something was untoward, not because Roger had been treated poorly – the rich always behaved badly towards those less fortunate than themselves – but more because this man of importance was leering at his wife.

Adolfus smiled lasciviously at her. 'Indeed. I am here to convey my gratitude to you for furnishing my table with your fine bread.'

Agnete was confused. 'I have not served you before, sir, I think.'

Adolfus brought his puffy hands together in front of his chest. 'No, indeed, but I have a servant, a base fellow, who purchases your bread for my table every week and so I thought it only proper to visit your bakery myself to convey my congratulations.'

Agnete smiled but Adolfus did not see it as he was now staring at her chest. 'My husband, Dietmar, makes the bread, sir, not I.'

Adolfus looked at the non-descript stocky man beside her. 'Mm? Yes, of course.'

While this was going on Conrad was standing beside the oven observing the scene, catching the eye of one of the burly men who were preventing anyone else entering the shop. The man, a swarthy individual with a scar on his right cheek, regarded Conrad with contempt.

The others looked bored as the atmosphere in the shop became more strained as Adolfus continued to stare at Agnete's chest.

'Did you want any bread, sir?' said Dietmar slowly and purposely.

Adolfus averted his gaze. 'Bread?'

'We are a bakery, sir,' replied Dietmar, 'so people come here to buy bread.'

Adolfus nodded slightly and leered once more at Agnete before turning and walking out of the shop, his men following. Dietmar followed them and stood in the doorway to watch the fat rich man and his rogues disappear among the now dissipating throng of people who filled the narrow street.

'That was most odd,' remarked Agnete.

Dietmar may not have been an educated man but he knew lust when he saw it in someone's eyes and he felt both angry and helpless at the violation, albeit mild, of his wife that had taken place in front of him. He ambled back into the shop, anger rising within him.

'Conrad, stop idling and get that oven emptied.'

Conrad jumped at the severe tone in his father's voice and began brushing the oven's ashes into a sack.

Dietmar went to his wife's side and placed an arm around her waist.

'Are you all right, my love?'

Agnete smiled warmly at him. 'Of course. You think that my head would be turned by a lecherous overweight man with money?'

'What? No, but his behaviour was not right. Who was he, anyway?'

Agnete shrugged. 'I have no idea but he obviously likes your bread.'

At that moment Marie ran in from the street and stood in front of the counter, hands on her hips.

'Fritz ate Roger's loaf,' she announced.

Conrad smiled and Agnete laughed.

'Who is Fritz?' asked her father, still annoyed at the earlier episode.

'One of our pigs, of course,' answered Marie.

Agnete smiled again at her lovely daughter while Dietmar shook his head and returned to his oven. Outside Roger the Putrid was loitering, maintaining a safe distance to ensure the rich man and his brutes did not return before entering the shop. He took off his hat and sidled up to the counter. Marie turned up her nose at the smell. He went to reach into his purse but was stopped by Agnete's voice.

'There is no need, Roger,' she said, taking a fresh loaf from the shelf and handing it to him.

He grinned to reveal a mouth of discoloured teeth and bowed his head to Agnete, then hurried away. Dietmar could not afford to give away free loaves. He looked at Marie and then at the pigs in the street. Perhaps the family would have pork this Sunday.

In the days following Dietmar and Agnete forgot the fat rich man and their life continued as before. The family rose from its slumbers before dawn and spent their days making and selling bread. Spring progressed and the weather became warmer, though not unbearably so. Agnete took Marie on her weekly visit to the local market and Conrad continued to look forward to the end of his apprenticeship. The Wolff family was healthy and relatively comfortable, for which they thanked God and prayed that He would continue to watch over them. But the Lord was not the only one who was taking an interest in them, and in one family member in particular.

The baker's wife had entranced Adolfus Braune, so much so that in the days following his visit to the dingy little bakery he had ignored his business interests to plan more occasions where he might lay eyes upon her. He had the scullion brought to him and instructed the wretch to spy on her and her family and to report back to him when she left her home. When the man relayed news that she was visiting the market he had hurried to the place so he could admire her once more. He took his men with him as usual, but such was the press of people that it was easy for him and them to melt into the background and remain unseen. The scullion may have been a revolting creature but he knew how to find a face in a crowd and what a face it was. Impure thoughts flooded Adolfus' mind as he stood and watched the baker's wife chatting to a stallholder who was selling furs of rabbits, foxes, cats and squirrels. The marketplace was filled with the din of a thousand voices shouting, arguing, laughing and conversing but Adolfus did not hear them. All he could hear was the beat of his thumping heart in his chest and all he could see was the beautiful wife of the baker in her blue gown and white headdress, a vision as pure as the Virgin Mary herself.

That night, as the servants were serving him and his companions supper, Adolfus began to hatch a plan to snare the tasty dish that was more appetising than the stewed meat before him. His companions sat on a separate table at right angles to his own that he shared with his trusted deputy, the swarthy, scarred Artur, the former mercenary who now killed and threatened for Lübeck's richest merchant. While he and his fellow thugs heaped meat into their sliced trenchers, Adolfus took sips of spiced red wine from his silver-rimmed mazer. Artur noticed his master's lack of appetite.

'Not hungry, lord?'

Adolfus cast him a sly glance. 'Hungry, yes, but not for food.'

'Lord?'

Adolfus took another sip. 'How does a man satisfy his appetite, Artur? I will tell you. By seizing what has been laid out before him, that is how. I have need of your services.'

Artur did not understand what his master was talking about but when he mentioned his services it usually involved breaking someone's bones or actions in a similar vein. Artur shoved a great wedge of bread soaked with meat juices into his mouth.

'I am your servant, lord.'

13

Adolfus smiled to himself. It was a most curious thing how men could be bought so easily. Artur was a perfect example: an individual who had spent his life largely beyond the law who had fought for kings and princes, and who had then taken to smuggling grain from Germany to anyone who would buy it. This was illegal and punishable by the severest penalties, largely because the authorities were fearful of food shortages, especially in times of poor harvests. The more grain that was exported meant less was available for home foodstuffs, which could lead to starvation. But starving people could also revolt and overthrow their masters, hence the ban on exports. Artur's activities came to the attention of Adolfus, who recruited this most ruthless and resourceful individual rather than having him punished. Artur was well rewarded and recruited a group of like-minded individuals from the docks for Adolfus. And as long as Artur and his men were paid they remained loyal, willing to undertake any nefarious activity.

Thus it was that all of them stood at the end of the street that contained the Wolff bakery, their master wrapped in a black cloak with a hood to hide his identity. The curfew bell had been rung an hour earlier and now the streets of Lübeck were quiet and empty, the citizenry all safely confined indoors to ensure a peaceful and crime-free evening. The citizens were also legally required to cover or extinguish all household fires before they went to bed as a precaution against a general conflagration.

Adolfus, being one of the members of the city council, was exempt from the curfew and could travel about the city at all times. Still, he did not want to be identified by the night watch, whose members roamed the darkened streets in search of anyone who was abroad with no legitimate business. So he and his men had donned black cloaks and hoods and had made their way to the baker's street by skulking in alleyways and hiding in shadows. And now they had arrived at their destination. Artur had insisted on silence during the journey but had not informed the others of the objective of the evening's foray. Not that they were interested: they did as their paymaster told them. They had brought the scullion along who was familiar with the route and also knew the layout of the baker's home, which was nothing more than one room above the ground-floor space. He also knew what they were here for and kept grinning dementedly and nodding at Adolfus at every opportunity. The man was an imbecile but had his uses, one of which was to gain entry to the premises.

While Adolfus and the others waited near the end of a street in the dark of a narrow alleyway that provided a shortcut to an adjacent lane, the scullion crept towards the bakery. Like most shops it was secured by means of shutters. But the wood was often old, neglected and weather beaten, which meant there were gaps between the shutters. So it was now as the scullion used a knife to gouge a space that allowed him to move aside the iron bar that secured the shutters.

After doing so he crept back and reported his handiwork to Artur, who informed Adolfus. The merchant could barely conceal his excitement as he frantically waved Artur forward. His mouth began to salivate and he felt a tingling in his groin. His breathing became heavy. The group moved silently as the scullion scampered ahead to gently ease the shutters up to allow the others to enter. He was told to remain near the shop front as two of Artur's men brought down the shutters once more so as not to arouse suspicion. Then he led Artur to the stairs that led to the first floor.

Artur held up a hand when he heard some grunts, but then smiled when he realised that it was the sound of pigs in a pen to the rear of the shop. He drew his dagger and slowly walked up the stairs, Adolfus following and the others trailing behind. It was pitch black and so their progress was agonisingly slow. Artur could hear the heavy breathing of Adolfus behind him and smiled. His master could have any whore he wanted and yet here they were, feeling their way upstairs in the house of a humble baker. Sometimes he preferred smuggling.

But for Adolfus this was one of the most exciting moments of his pampered life. Paying prostitutes to submit to his unnatural demands was at first desirable but then became boring. But this; this was different. Perhaps it was the prospect of having something that was beyond his reach, notwithstanding his wealth and position. Or perhaps it was the thought of contravening the laws of God and man and getting away with it that was the attraction. He could hear the family's relaxed breathing now as he stepped into the bedchamber. The others silently filed in behind him. His forehead was beaded with sweat and he kept licking his lips.

'Hurry, Artur,' he whispered, his lower body tingling like it was aflame. The anticipation was unbearable.

With difficulty Artur identified the sleeping family: the parents in a double bed and two single beds to one side in which their children lay in slumber. The family slept on mattresses stuffed with straw placed on wooden planks under linen sheets and woollen blankets, their heads resting on pillows. Artur clicked his fingers and two of his men rushed forward to hold down Dietmar while he and another man went to the other side of the bed to grab Agnete. It was she who opened her eyes a

15

split second before the blanket and sheet were ripped off the bed and a hand was forced over her mouth.

At first she thought it was a nightmare but then with horror realised that the frantic struggling of her husband beside her was very real. Her linen nightshirt was then roughly yanked up to reveal her naked body and she too began to struggle furiously, to no avail. Adolfus ran his hands over her body as Dietmar, a pillow over his face, wrestled with his assailants like a man possessed. Adolfus fondled her breasts and than placed his hand between her legs to feel her most intimate place.

'Hurry lord,' hissed Artur.

Adolfus was frantically pulling up his tunic and grappling with his braies to set free his hardened manhood, which even in his high state of arousal left a lot to be desired. Then Marie screamed.

Artur turned to squint at the figure of the young girl sat up in bed and instinctively lashed out with his right hand, striking the girl hard with the back of his hand and sending her sprawling onto the floor. Adolfus grunted with satisfaction as Artur turned back to the bed and grabbed Agnete's right leg and pulled it towards him as the man behind the bed who was holding her left arm and had his other hand over her mouth struggled to control her as she thrashed around wildly. The men who were restraining Dietmar were also having problems holding down the baker. Artur was beginning to regret the whole enterprise as Adolfus threw himself on top of Agnete and tried to force his manhood into her.

But Agnete was possessed of the strength of a wild woman and his efforts were to no avail. It did not matter: Adolfus groaned and released his pent-up sexual tension. A split-second later Conrad threw himself onto Artur's back and began punching the man in the face. Taken aback by this unexpected assault Artur let go of Agnete and threw his head back, smashing it into Conrad's nose. The boy felt intense pain in his face and wilted but held on to his target with grim determination.

Marie was lying on the ground sobbing but Agnete used her free arm to gouge the eyes of the man who continued to hold her, also biting his hand for good measure. The man cried out in pain and released her, Agnete kicking wildly at Adolfus who was still fiddling with his undergarments. Artur had had enough. He reached behind him, grabbed Conrad's hair and then yanked the boy forward off his back, drew his dagger and then punched Agnete hard in the face with his left fist. The blow temporarily stunned her and stopped her struggling, before Artur's blade slit her throat and silenced her for good.

16

Adolfus stood open-mouthed, transfixed in terror at the murder of the woman. Artur turned to face the boy in the dimness but then heard a shriek of pain and realised that the baker had broken free. One of his assailants had been preoccupied watching the attempted rape of his wife and had loosened his grip sufficiently for Dietmar to free his arm and smash his fist into the man's groin, causing him to collapse to the floor in pain. He then grabbed the other man and dragged him onto the bed, biting his ear and tearing off a great chunk of it with his teeth. That was the cry that Artur heard.

'Take Marie and get to safety,' Dietmar shouted at Conrad, who was rising to his feet, blood pouring from his nose.

'I will not leave you, father,' replied Conrad defiantly.

'Get out now!' screamed Dietmar.

Three of Artur's men were temporarily disabled and the other two had drawn their daggers and were closing in on Dietmar, so Conrad grabbed his sister's hand and pulled her towards the door. And so he ran, dragging his sister down the stairs.

'Stop them,' shouted Adolfus, whose wits were returning to him.

'You two,' Artur hissed at his two remaining men, 'go and get them.'

Dietmar flew at him as the two men followed the boy and his sister down the stairs. Adolfus was like a mouse trapped by a cat – totally helpless and useless – but Artur's mind kept working despite the exceptional circumstances. He had seen rape and murder many times, had carried them out himself, and thus was thinking ahead. This is what his master paid him for. He saw Dietmar's lunge, moved aside and then hit the baker hard on the side of the head with the hilt of his dagger. As Dietmar crashed to the floor Artur hit him two more times with the blunt end of the dagger, knocking him unconscious. He slipped the weapon back in its sheath and looked around. What a mess.

His other men were now struggling to their feet as he roughly grabbed Adolfus' sleeve.

'Time to go, lord.'

'What about her?' he stammered.

'She won't be going anywhere.' Artur turned to his men. 'Bring the baker.'

One of the men was rubbing his groin, still in pain. 'Why? He's unconscious.'

'Because we need him,' hissed Artur, 'now do it.'

It had been like a bad dream to Conrad as he bounded down the stairs holding the arm of his sobbing sister. As he raced towards the closed shutters he ran into a man squatting by them, knocking him over. Despite the pain in his nose and his wailing sister he still managed to direct a punch at the individual, who curled up into a ball and begged for mercy. Conrad pulled up the shutters and ran into the night, pulling his sister after him.

'Run, Marie,' he shouted, the two of them bounding up the street as fast as their young legs could carry them.

He had no idea where he was heading or what he was going to do, only that he must carry out his father's orders.

'Come here!'

He turned to see two dark shapes exit his father's premises and knew that they were being chased.

'Don't look back,' he told his sister as he increased his speed and tightened the grip on Marie's arm.

They darted into an alleyway and ran along its deserted course, the cool earth beneath their bare feet. Occasionally they would step into something unpleasant but the fear of being caught by their pursuers blotted all other thoughts out of their minds. They entered the adjacent street and Conrad saw glimpses of light from windows and heard laughter coming from inside homes. On they went, not daring to look back at those who were chasing them. Marie had stopped crying now, the only sound Conrad heard being her heavy breathing as she struggled to keep up with him.

It seemed like hours but was probably a few minutes when they ran into the square that fronted the city's magnificent cathedral, its two spires dwarfing the two youngsters as they headed for the building's twin doors. The cobbles beneath Conrad's feet felt hard and cold as he pulled his sister towards the entrance to God's house. Here they would find sanctuary from their pursuers. Conrad could see the large wooden doors ahead as he increased his pace and then tripped over as Marie stumbled.

His sister squealed as she sprawled onto the cobbles and Conrad grazed his knee as he fell. He tried to get up but was kicked back down by one of the men who had been pursuing them.

'You are coming with us, you little bastards.'

The other man grabbed his hair and yanked him up, then twisted his arm behind his back as the other fellow pulled his sister to her feet. Marie began to sob uncontrollably as the man holding Conrad's arm pushed the youth away from the cathedral entrance.

'What is going on here?'

Conrad felt the grip on his arm loosen slightly and he turned his head to see two individuals a few feet away, both of them wearing white sleeveless surcoats bearing a motif of a red cross above a red sword, the white cloaks around their shoulders carrying the same symbol. Conrad also saw that their arms and legs were encased in chainmail and they wore mail coifs on their heads. Both men had neatly trimmed beards and moustaches.

'Nothing to do with you,' spat the brute holding Conrad.

'Everything that happens within sight of the house of God concerns me,' replied one of the white-clad men. Conrad estimated his height to be around six feet.

'Be on your way,' sneered the man holding Marie, who was still sobbing.

'Did you hear that, Henke?' said the mailed man again, 'we are to be on our way.'

The man called Henke was shorter than the one who was speaking, but only marginally. But he was certainly more broad shouldered and powerful in appearance. He now stepped forward and held out his hand to the man who was restraining Conrad.

'My apologies, brother. Will you take my hand by way of atonement?'

The man twisted Conrad's arm once again, causing the youth to wince, and then extended his hand to Henke, who smiled, took it and then head-butted him, splintering his nose. He groaned and collapsed to the ground, releasing Conrad. The other man released Marie and went for the dagger tucked into his belt, but before he could reach it Henke's companion drew the sword that was hanging from his belt and had the point against his neck.

'Pull that dagger and I will spill your blood on these cobbles.'

Henke walked forward and kicked the prostrate man hard under the chin, sending him sprawling.

'I suggest you depart immediately,' said Henke's companion, 'lest Henke becomes angry.'

The man with the sword at his throat raised his arms in a sign of submission and backed away slowly, hauling his bloodied companion to his feet as he did so. They slowly ambled away as Henke watched them impassively, arms folded across his broad chest. His friend sheathed his sword and made the sign of the cross.

'Go with God, brothers.'

19

Conrad, his face and nightshirt covered with blood, put an arm around his weeping sister and attempted to smile at his saviours.

'Thank you, sirs. Those men attacked my family and I beg for your help.'

The man whose name Conrad did not yet know smiled at him.

'We are here to assist pilgrims in need of help, but first I think that we should get you both more suitable clothing and dress your wound, as well as calming the young girl.'

'My sister, sir,' said Conrad, 'Marie.'

Henke's associate smiled, walked forward and knelt before Marie, who was still terrified.

'Do not be alarmed, Marie. My name is Rudolf and I am your friend,' his voice was calm and soft. 'Will you come with me so that we can get you cleaned up?'

She half-nodded, still clutching Conrad's hand. 'My mother is dead.'

Rudolf continued to smile. 'We will wash your face and get you some clothes and then we will go and find her.'

He turned to look at Conrad. 'What is your name, boy?'

'Conrad Wolff, sir.'

The next hour was a like a dream to Conrad. He remembered being taken to the monastery sited next to the cathedral where monks washed his face and gave him a clean shirt, tunic and leggings. Black-robed nuns calmed Marie and took her way. She returned dressed in a long gown and black headdress, and all the while the men who had rescued them stood and watched Conrad, the one named Rudolf occasionally nodding and smiling, Henke staring impassively. Conrad noticed that the monks addressed them as 'brother', leading him to believe that they too were monks. But their dress, weapons and demeanour led him to think they were unlike any monks he had ever seen.

After further pleading Conrad convinced the two monks armed with swords to return with him and his sister to their father's bakery. Rudolf and Henke followed Conrad and his sister as they retraced their steps and headed back to the city's eastern quarter. Accompanying them were half a dozen soldiers of Theodoric, Bishop of Lübeck, who was currently away on a tour of southern Germany. They were dressed in mail hauberks, helmets and carried blue shields bearing the arms of the bishop: a gold mitre over a gold cross. Four of the men carried spears and two held torches to provide illumination.

No one spoke during the journey and as they neared his home a sense of dread began to engulf Conrad. He had a terrible foreboding that his parents were both dead and his dread was soon consumed by an even more tortuous emotion: guilt. He had abandoned his parents in their hour of need to save his own skin. He would forever be known as a base coward who had betrayed his parents, who had laboured hard to provide for him and Marie. What would his sister say when she learned the truth? With these thoughts swirling in his mind he led the small group down his street and halted in front of the bakery, the shutters up and the shop open.

'We are here,' he said to Rudolf.

'Perhaps you should stay here, Conrad,' Rudolf suggested.

Conrad's nose still hurt and he could sense tears coming to his eyes.

'No,' he said.

Rudolf took a torch from one of the bishop's soldiers.

'Well then, let us proceed.'

He nodded to Henke who instructed the guards to wait outside while he, Henke and Conrad entered the shop. Marie made to accompany them but he took her hand and placed it in the grasp of one of the other soldiers.

'Keep her here.'

Conrad followed Rudolf into the shop, the torch illuminating the empty shelves and oven. He had lived here all his life but it suddenly felt cold and alien to him, the violation it had suffered having snuffed out all the happy memories he had of his home. He placed a hand on Rudolf's arm.

'They might still be here, sir.'

Rudolf turned his face to the youth.

'I think they have long gone.'

The three walked slowly up the stairs, Rudolf and Henke having drawn their swords just in case anyone was still loitering on the first floor. But they sheathed their weapons when they entered the bedroom and saw the lifeless body of Agnete lying on the bloody mattress. Conrad cried out in anguish and rushed forward to cradle his dead mother, sobbing as he held her head to his, kissing her forehead and rocking to and fro in anguish. Henke looked at Rudolf and shrugged. Rudolf made the sign of the cross as Conrad Wolff sank into black despair.

Rudolf left the boy to his grief as he went back downstairs and informed the young girl that her mother had been taken to heaven and was now with God.

Marie looked up into the night sky. 'Will she be able to see me?'

Rudolf smiled. 'She is looking at you right now, child.'

Marie began waving at the sky. Rudolf was glad that her childish innocence protected her from the brutal reality he had just seen.

21

Minutes later Conrad joined them in the street, his face ashen and haunted. 'Where is my father?' he asked forlornly.

Rudolf ordered that the body of the children's mother be taken back to the nunnery to be washed and dressed in a white gown. The next morning he stood with Conrad and Marie as an abbot recited prayers at the graveside and they said farewell to their mother. Rudolf had reported the murder to the church authorities that had in turn relayed it to the *vogt*, the judge who administered the city's laws. Because Lübeck was a commercial centre of great importance it had been granted the right to administer itself through a city council. This was made up of thirty burghers drawn from the most powerful and influential members of the citizenry and which was responsible for the daily government of the city.

Conrad and Marie were taken back to the monastery as a gravedigger began shovelling earth on Agnete's corpse. But the question remained: where was her husband? The answer came that afternoon when a messenger sent by a city councillor to the monastery brought news that Dietmar Wolff had been arrested for the murder of his wife and attempted murder of one of the city council: Adolfus Braune. His trial was set for the next day, as Rudolf told Conrad.

This made no sense, and as Conrad filed into the packed courtroom located in the city's town hall, an imposing structure constructed from black bricks, he was certain that his father would be found innocent of this preposterous charge. The guards standing at the entrance to the large, spacious hall carried shields that bore an eagle motif – the symbol of Lübeck – for this was a city rather than a church court. They looked bored as Conrad passed them and tried to squeeze through the press of people who stood near the entrance. Rudolf and Henke had brought him here after learning of the crimes levied against his father. He was confident that he would be back home with his father by the day's end but they knew differently.

The hall may have been spacious but it soon became hot from the heat of dozens of bodies. A clerk called for silence as the judge entered the hall via a door at the far end and took his place in his ceremonial chair, which was placed on a dais next to the hall's end wall. Conrad was three rows back from the front of the crowd and had to continually crane his neck to see what was taking place. As the spectators fell silent the black-robed judge sat in the chair and nodded to a sombre-looking priest standing to the side of the dais. The latter said 'let us pray' and everyone bowed their heads as he called upon God to bless the city of Lübeck, these proceedings and to ensure that justice was done.

Directly in front of the judge was a desk where his notaries and clerks were sitting on a bench. The 'advocates learned in law', those representing the accused and those prosecuting, sat to the right and left of the judge on elevated benches in their order of seniority. Expected to dress in a way that befitted their social status and the dignity of the court, they were all attired in dark-blue sleeved robes. The hall itself, as befitting an official building in Lübeck, was decorated with tapestries, shields and banners, with wood panelling lining all the walls.

A clerk began the proceedings by reading a list of those accused of minor crimes, the defendants being escorted from a holding pen located to the rear of the building. Guards ushered them roughly into the hall where their crimes were read out and they gave their plea. If they were wealthy enough they had an advocate, who rose from his seat and descended to the floor of the courtroom where he stood facing the judge and stated his client's case. A young man pleaded guilty to being drunk in public – a day in the stocks; an overweight middle-aged woman with rosy cheeks was convicted of idle gossip – two days wearing the brank, a metal cage that fitted over the head that placed a metal curb in the mouth to prevent the sufferer from speaking; and so it went on. Not everyone had a lawyer and so those who had no one to plead their case tended to receive harsher sentences, including being branded and losing fingers. Once convicted the punishments were carried out immediately.

They were bundled out of the court to where men with whips and branding irons were standing ready to tear and cut flesh. Those who were sentenced to the stocks at first appeared to have got off lightly, but once confined people were free to pelt them with rotten vegetables, rub excrement in their hair and faces and, if they were particularly disliked, hurl stones of varying sizes at them. A few hours in the stocks could be a potentially lethal experience.

The next group of prisoners to be brought before the court were those accused of more serious crimes. Conrad saw his father and waved at him, Dietmar catching the eye of his son and smiling faintly. Conrad thought he looked terrible: unshaven, his shirt torn and his shoulders sunken. He looked visibly drained, his eyes red and puffy, his face bruised.

'That is my father,' Conrad said to Rudolf, who placed a reassuring hand on the boy's shoulders.

Henke looked at Rudolf and shook his head for he knew that, barring a miracle, the boy's father was a dead man. Trials were rarely a venue to decide guilt or innocence, more a forum whereby justice could be publicly served upon the convicted. And so it was now as the judge pronounced sentence upon the unfortunates brought before him. A wife found guilty of petty treason, the murder of her husband: death; an old woman who poisoned her younger and more attractive niece: death; a talented young smith revealed to have indulged in coining, the manufacture of counterfeit money: death; and a terrified teenage girl found guilty of strangling her newborn baby: death. And then Dietmar Wolff was standing before the judge with head bowed while the prosecutor revealed what he was accused of: the murder of his own wife and the attempted murder of Adolfus Braune, one of Lübeck's most esteemed residents.

'That is a lie!' shouted Conrad, who pushed his way through those standing before him to reach the front of the crowd.

The advocates looked at each in disbelief and the judge sat open mouthed at this severe breach of etiquette.

'Silence!' he bellowed, pointing at Conrad. 'Whose child is this?'

Dietmar looked at the judge. 'He is my son, sir.'

The judge smiled savagely. 'He will be flogged for his insolence.'

Rudolf came forward and grabbed Conrad's arm to force him behind where Henke could keep an eye on him.

'My humble apologies, lord,' said Rudolf, 'the boy's wits have temporarily deserted him. I beg the court's mercy.'

The judge saw Rudolf's white surcoat and the sword and cross motif. 'A Sword Brother. You speak for this disrespectful boy?'

Rudolf nodded. 'I do, lord. I would ask you to show mercy towards him.'

The judge leaned back in his chair and stroked his pointed chin. 'You are in Lübeck on what purpose, brother?'

Rudolf bowed his head ever so slightly at the judge. 'To enlist recruits for God's crusade against the heathens in Livonia, lord.'

The judge smiled. 'A most noble calling, brother, and one that the citizens of this great city support with all their hearts. For myself I pray daily that Bishop Albert and the Sword Brothers vanquish their enemies speedily.'

There were murmurs of agreement in the hall and the judge smiled at Rudolf once more. 'As long as you keep that urchin under control I release him to your care. And may God smile upon you and your fellow warriors of Christ.'

Rudolf bowed his head at the judge and stepped back to stand beside Conrad.

'Do not speak out again,' he hissed, 'unless you want to be standing beside your father to receive punishment.'

'But it is a lie,' hissed Conrad despairingly, 'I was there and saw what happened.'

But Rudolf knew that children, along with Jews and women, unless they had the consent of their husbands, were not allowed to testify before a judge.

'You must trust in God, Conrad.'

Henke grunted but said nothing as the advocate related to the court how Dietmar Wolff had killed his wife in a jealous rage, suspecting her of having illicit relations with Adolfus Braune, who had visited Wolff's premises to do nothing more than compliment the baker on his goods. After killing his wife Dietmar Wolff had journeyed to the merchant's home under cover of darkness, intent on killing him also. The advocate relayed to the court that fortunately the Braune home was defended by a number of guards who had managed to overpower Wolff before he could complete his heinous plan.

Two things sealed Dietmar's fate. First, he was found unconscious outside Adolfus Braune's house in the west of the city. When asked to explain this, Dietmar stated that he had been knocked unconscious in his bedroom before being carried across the city. The judge asked him why anyone would wish to transport him to the other side of the city, to which Dietmar replied that it had obviously been Braune who had broke into his home and attacked his family. There was a stunned silence after he had spoken these words, not least among the advocates. Adolfus Braune was one of the most respected leading citizens of Lübeck, a man renowned for his generosity to both the church and the city. The idea that he would break into the home of a lowly baker to assault his wife was preposterous. Worse, it was insulting.

The second thing that condemned Dietmar was the testimony of the imposing Artur, the commander of the men who guarded the property of Adolfus Braune. The judge rubbed his chin once more as he listened to Artur tell of how he had with great difficulty prevented Dietmar Wolff from entering his master's home, the baker wounding two of his men in the process. The merchant had been too shaken to appear in person but had sent Artur to testify in his place, who handed a notary a letter prepared by his master. The notary passed the letter to the judge who read it and then looked at Dietmar Wolff with narrow, merciless eyes.

'The sentence is death. Take him away.'

'No!' wailed Conrad, who was quickly bundled out of the room by Rudolf and Henke to save him from being flogged or worse.

Outside the town hall he angrily wrestled himself away from his two guardians and made to go back into the courtroom. Henke stood before him.

'Don't be a fool.'

'My father is innocent,' he shouted, and then held his head in his hands. 'Innocent,' he said quietly.

'There is nothing to be done,' said Rudolf. 'I am sorry.'

They took Conrad back to the monastery. He wanted to see his father but the authorities would not allow that. Too many instances of relatives smuggling weapons to the condemned on the eve of their executions had resulted in a spate of fatal injuries to gaolers. They could see their errant loved ones when they were brought to the scaffold. Conrad trudged back to the south of the city with his head hanging low, not really believing that his father had been sentenced to death for a crime he did not commit. In his innocence he believed that the truth would surface and his father would be released and then they would be a family again. And that is what he told Marie after he had returned to their new home. Despite his father's gaunt and dirty appearance Conrad went to bed convinced that they would soon be reunited with their father.

'The boy's father will go to his death an innocent man,' remarked Rudolf, placing the silver goblet on the table in front of him.

The hour was late and silence permeated the bishop's lavish quarters, the candles flickering in their holders, their fire illuminating the chiselled features of Bishop Albert who sat opposite him. In Livonia Rudolf and his brothers always seemed to huddle round the half-light produced by their cheap tallow candles. But in the cathedral palace in Lübeck the expensive beeswax candles gave off much brighter light.

'The court found him guilty,' replied Bishop Albert.

Rudolf traced a finger round the rim of the goblet. 'The influence of Adolfus Braune weighed the scales of justice against the baker.'

'Braune is this city's wealthiest merchant, brother,' said Bishop Albert, 'and much respected.'

Rudolf smiled. 'Wealth and respect always seem to be close relations, bishop.'

Bishop Albert shrugged. 'The fact is that Braune has been most generous concerning supplying ships to transport those crusaders who are at this very moment marching from Saxony to Lübeck to fight for the cross against the heathens.'

'Your uncle has been most fervent, bishop.'

Bishop Albert was the nephew of the Archbishop of Bremen and Hamburg, who did much to encourage lords to undertake crusade in the Baltic to support

Bishop Albert's efforts against the pagans. The bishop himself often travelled throughout Germany to enlist recruits to his cause, but he was based in Riga whereas his uncle was stationed permanently in Germany.

'Indeed. Concerning Adolfus Braune, I cannot afford to alienate him so I would appreciate it if you did not provoke him.'

Rudolf looked hurt. 'Provoke, bishop?'

Bishop Albert wagged a finger at him. The lighted reflected off the gold ring carrying an amethyst that he wore on the fourth finger of his hand, which had been given to him by Pope Innocent III himself. 'The Sword Brothers are not titled thus for nothing.'

Rudolf spread his hands. 'I would not dream of disturbing the peace, bishop.'

Bishop Albert nodded. 'You will still return to Riga early?'

'I will, bishop. Wenden needs strengthening before winter comes. To that end I will be taking stonemasons and mercenaries back with me.'

Wenden was a former pagan hill fort that had been captured two years ago by the crusaders. It was now a major stronghold of the Sword Brothers who were building a stone castle in place of the wooden ramparts. But progress was slow, not least due to a paucity of funds. Rudolf welcomed the annual influx of crusaders into Livonia but they usually only stayed for the summer; when they departed the forces left behind were greatly overstretched. At this time the number of secular German vassals resident in Livonia was small. Mercenaries were a useful addition to Christian forces and they stayed all year round, as long as they were paid.

'I hope to bring several hundred men with me when I return to Riga,' said Bishop Albert.

'We will need them,' said Rudolf, taking a sip at his wine. 'We stand a Christian island surrounded by an ocean of pagans.'

'God is our armour, Brother Rudolf. We must have faith. Returning to the matter of the baker's children, what do you suggest Bishop Theodoric should do with them, seeing as God has seen fit to entrust them to his keeping?'

'I will take the boy back with me to Wenden,' answered Rudolf. 'If he stays here he will be in danger from Adolfus Braune, either that or he will attempt to kill the merchant and will thus follow his father to the scaffold.'

'And the girl?'

'The nunnery will offer her security and safety,' Rudolf answered.

'Why do you take such an interest in these children?'

It was a good question and Rudolf had to think for a few seconds before he replied. 'Perhaps because they came to me, two frightened, lost souls who were in need of aid. Besides, the boy might make a useful soldier.'

Bishop Albert laughed. 'Ever the realist. It may interest you to know that I have more lost souls for your care. One boy, a beggar, was caught stealing a loaf of bread. Fortunately for him he was brought before a church court that sought fit to show clemency.'

'As long as he devoted his life to the church,' said Rudolf.

'Better than swinging from the end of a rope,' Bishop Albert rebuked him. 'You can take him back with you as well. Another soldier for the army of God. The baker will be executed tomorrow, I believe.'

Rudolf nodded.

Bishop Albert frowned. 'Perhaps it would be best if his children did not witness it.'

'The girl I agree,' said Rudolf, 'but I will take the boy so he can bid farewell to his father. He deserves that at least.'

Bishop Albert raised an eyebrow.

'The boy should see death in all its grisly glory, bishop, the more so if he is to become a soldier. He will see enough of it in the years to come.'

Bishop Albert smiled. 'I am hopeful that we will baptise the pagans rather than subdue them with the sword, Brother Rudolf.'

Now it was Rudolf's turn to smile. 'If that were true you would not have created the Sword Brothers.'

Conrad rose early the next morning, before the first rays of the sun were lighting up the eastern sky, just as he had done every morning while working for his father. He was still in a state of shock caused by the events of the past few days. A part of him still did not believe that his mother was dead and his father sentenced to death for her murder. He had been in the room when the criminals had broken into his home. It was they who should have been in that courtroom, not his father. But Brother Rudolf and his stern companion Henke would be taking him to see his father today so all would be well. He was confused as to exactly who they were. The black-robed monks of the monastery had told him that they were Sword Brothers and were warrior monks, knights who had taken holy orders, but he did not understand. All he knew was that they were taking him to see his father and all would be well.

Marie was full of questions to which he had no answers, not least why she was not allowed to sleep in the same room as him. He told her that she should obey the nuns and not cause trouble, but that this evening they would all be back together at home. Tears came to his eyes and he looked away when she stated that she missed her mother.

After a simple but fulsome breakfast of thick soup in a bowl and ample portions of bread Marie was taken back to the nunnery and Rudolf and Henke came to collect Conrad. As before their arms and legs were covered in chainmail and they both wore white surcoats bearing red crosses and swords. Around their waists were brown leather belts holding swords on their left sides and long daggers on their right hips, while their heads were encased in mail coifs.

The day was sunny and mild as the three made their way in silence to the city's cobbled market square where the executions were to take place. Conrad walked between Rudolf and Henke, the latter keeping a tight grip on the hilt of his dagger. From experience he knew that public executions were rough, boisterous affairs and already there were a great many people heading for the square. They spoke in loud and eager voices, many already inebriated from drinking copious amounts of ale and boasting of wanting to be close to the 'stage'. Henke had seen this type of bloodlust before – the desire to get as close as possible to where death was being meted out. He also knew that crowds could turn ugly if executions were botched or presented a poor spectacle.

'Are you sure this is a good idea?' he said to Rudolf.

'Not frightened of a few townspeople are you, Henke?' replied Rudolf, smiling. He knew that Henke was not afraid of anything but also knew that his friend regarded most civilians with a cool contempt at best, believing them to be cowards at heart. The fact that they revelled in public executions only increased his disdain for them.

'We must hurry,' said Conrad, still convinced that his father would be freed.

Henke looked at him and sighed while Rudolf said nothing.

The market square was teeming with activity when they arrived, the vendors who had arrived hours before to set up their carts and booths doing a brisk trade selling food, drink and souvenirs. The scene had a carnival air as minstrels and jugglers entertained the crowd, which for the moment was good-natured. Rudolf nodded towards the large wooden scaffold that had been erected on the northern side of the square.

'Come on.'

He led the way through the crowd that thickened as they neared the platform, upon which had been arranged tables holding swords, axes, knives, branding irons, tongs and ropes. Two braziers stood beside the tables and in front of them, fixed to the scaffold, were two large, thick wooden beams arranged in an 'X' shape. On one side of the scaffold was heaped a pile of large spoked wheels with iron rims. Henke pushed people out of the way, who turned angrily to face him but then cowered away when they saw the size of him, his weaponry and the insignia on his surcoat. Rudolf, in contrast, gently tapped individuals on the shoulder and asked if he and the boy with him could get to the front of the crowd, making the sign of the cross as they moved aside.

Conrad looked around the square and saw that some of the rooftops were filled with spectators, while below them people were hanging out of windows to get a better view.

'Crows,' sneered Henke.

On the higher rooftops were real crows, great fat beasts that were beginning to assemble in anticipation of a tasty feast. Conrad was perplexed by the whole spectacle. He had never been brought to such events before, though there were some children in the crowd, most on the shoulders of their parents who were pointing at the scaffold and the various devices on it. In the windows of the houses positioned immediately behind the scaffold were persons of quality, noble men and women who had paid for the privilege of being close to the executions.

'Will my father be arriving soon?' asked Conrad, who began to suspect that something was not quite right with what he was seeing.

Half a dozen individuals entered the square, all dressed in black leggings, short-sleeved tunics and hoods over their heads. They were skinners, men who made a living from skinning dead animals and disposing of the carcasses. But they also assisted the executioner in a number of ways, from torturing prisoners during interrogations to assisting him on the day of executions itself.

'Yes,' said Rudolf, 'he will be here soon.'

People began to jeer and hiss as the skinners made their way to the scaffold. Not for nothing did they wear hoods to conceal their identities. The church absolved executioners of any personal responsibility for the deaths they caused because they were carrying out the judgement of just and godly authorities, but the citizenry largely despised them. So they hid their identities to prevent public opprobrium and out of fear of retribution from friends or family of the condemned. Once on the scaffold they placed the branding irons and tongs in the coals of the braziers. The chatter among the crowd became more agitated and excitable. There was a frisson in the air, the anticipation of blood and suffering. Rudolf looked at Henke and shook his head, then glanced at Conrad.

There were more boos and hisses as the executioner himself slowly made his way to the scaffold, a hulking brute of a man attired in knee-length black leather boots, tight black hose, waist-length short-sleeved grey tunic secured by a black leather belt and a black leather face mask that encased his large head. Members of the crowd moved back as he ambled to the scaffold, not daring to look this agent of death in the eye.

'There's father,' shouted Conrad as a wagon pulled by two horses entered the square from the northeast entrance, a great cheer erupting from the crowd when they saw it. Driven by a skinner wearing a hood, a pale, nervous priest attired in a white gown walked beside it, reading from an open Bible he had in his hands. On the back of the wagon was a large iron cage, in which were half a dozen prisoners – three male, three female – one of whom was Dietmar Wolff. Without thinking Conrad rushed forward to be near his father, who sat disconsolately on the floor of the cage. His fellow male prisoners were standing at the bars of the cage, staring wide-eyed at the crowd and then at the scaffold that was rearing into view as they contemplated the final minutes of their lives.

'Father, father,' called Conrad, who reached the wagon and began waving at his father.

Dietmar looked up and saw his son walking beside the wagon. He rose unsteadily and went to the bars, stretching out a hand to his son.

'It will be all right, father,' said Conrad, grasping his father's hand, 'I have brought friends who will get you released.'

Tears streamed down Dietmar's face as he held his son's hand.

'Where is your sister?'

Conrad smiled. 'She is safe at the nunnery, father. The nuns have been very kind to her.'

'You must leave this place, Conrad.'

Conrad was shocked. 'Leave? Why? We will leave together, father.'

Suddenly the crowd began pelting the cage with rotten vegetables and stones, a piece of flint hitting Dietmar above the eye, causing him to flinch and let go of Conrad's hand.

'Come with me,' said Rudolf as he pulled Conrad away from the wagon that was now being struck from all directions. Those inside cowered and sank to the floor in an effort to make themselves smaller targets, shielding their heads with their hands as best they could. The crowd was engulfed in rapture at their plight and the filth-covered priest who had been unwittingly caught in the barrage.

'Father, father!' screamed Conrad as Rudolf and Henke dragged him back to a safe distance.

'It is too late, Conrad,' said Rudolf, holding his shoulders firmly and looking directly into the boy's eyes.

The realisation that his father had been brought to this place to die finally dawned on Conrad. The colour drained from his cheeks and his knees buckled from under him. Henke caught him before he collapsed and held him upright.

'No,' said Conrad faintly.

But his anguished cry was drowned out in the tumult as the crowd warmed itself up pelting the now terrified prisoners. After a few minutes one of the skinners blew a short trumpet, its high-pitched sound resonating across the square and silencing the crowd. The executioner also raised his hands to still any other noise. A silence charged with expectation hung over the throng like a thundercloud.

The executioner nodded to one of the guards ringing the scaffold and he and two others went to the wagon where the priest was rubbing his now dirty robe with his hands. The skinner was unlocking the cage door and opened it when the guards arrived. One called a name that Conrad thought he had heard before and one of the male prisoners walked gingerly forward, to be roughly seized by the guards and manhandled down the steps at the back of the wagon. He was pushed forward to the scaffold and up the steps to where the skinners were waiting. The priest followed him, reciting prayers as two skinners grabbed his arms and a third pulled off his white gown, now smeared with filth.

Executions were always held three days after sentencing – the same length of time between Christ's death and resurrection. During this time a priest would hear a prisoner's confession, grant absolution and offer the Eucharist.

Now the prisoner, wrapped only in his braies, was spread-eagled on the X-shaped cross and secured in place by leather straps around his wrists and ankles. The tension among the crowd was unbearable. A skinner approached the secured coiner with a pair of red-hot tongs and began to nip the flesh on his chest with them, causing the man to scream and convulse as the pain shot through him. The crowd erupted into wild cheering as the skinner began to dance round the victim, stopping to tear at his white flesh with the tongs. The priest standing to one side on the scaffold was now visibly shaking as he tried to pray for the man, who shrieked every time his flesh was singed. He thrashed around on the cross in an effort to set himself free but the straps were too thick and his efforts were in vain.

Conrad saw the man's chest rise and fall as he gasped for air as the shock of his ordeal gripped his body. The executioner waved the skinner away who replaced the tongs in the brazier, and then went to the table and picked up a thick iron bar some three feet in length. The priest was now talking in gibberish as he stared down at his prayer book. The executioner walked forward to stand beside the right leg of the prisoner, who was now groaning. He raised the iron bar above his head and smashed it down on the man's shinbone, a sickening crunch resonating across the square as the limb was shattered.

The coiner emitted a high-pitched scream as the crowd shouted.

'One!'

The executioner moved to stand on the other side of the prisoner and once more brought down the iron bar, this time on his left shin. The man squealed in pain and the priest threw up on the scaffold.

'Two!'

The executioner shattered the man's right thigh.

'Three!'

Then his left thigh.

'Four!'

With each blow the victim's screams became fainter until they were nothing more than weak groans by the time that the executioner had smashed his forearms and upper arms. He walked back to the table and replaced the iron bar on its surface, then filled a cup with water from a jug beside it. He drained the cup, refilled it and walked over to the priest, offering it to him. Conrad stood open mouthed, both horrified and fascinated by what he had just witnessed: a man reduced to a bloody pulp that was now being unfastened from the cross by four skinners while a fifth rolled over one of the wheels and laid it flat on the scaffold. The mutilated prisoner was then lifted off the cross, placed on the wheel and his shattered limbs then braided through the spokes of the wheel. He and it were then carried to the rear of the scaffold where six tall poles were positioned in a row. Ladders were placed against the pole on the far right end of the line and the wheel hoisted onto its top – directly in front of the noble spectators who applauded politely. The still living victim, his body a writhing mass of lacerated gore and shattered bones, was left to become a feast for crows when the crowds had departed and the scaffold disassembled.

The executioner, his tunic now splattered with blood, nodded to the guards once more for them to bring another of the condemned to the scaffold. The custom was for a woman to follow a man and so the guards went to the rear of the cage and ordered the poor wretch who had been found guilty of petty treason to come forward. The woman, dressed in a white linen gown, screamed and refused to move as the crowd began jeering. The guards entered the cage. One grabbed her hair as another hit her hands with the butt of his spear shaft. They dragged her out and handed her over to the skinners.

They ripped off her gown and spread-eagled her on the blood-coated cross, fastening the straps round her limbs. The dancing skinner took a pair of red-hot tongs from the brazier, these having four claws on the end that he proceeded to clamp on one of the victim's breasts. She squealed in agony as he twisted the tongs to rip the breast from her chest. The crowd, delighted, erupted into rapturous applause as he held the grisly trophy in the air and tiptoed back to the brazier.

The ashen-faced priest, now in a state of shock, babbled incoherently as the executioner proceeded to smash the woman's limbs with his iron bar as the crowd once more counted down the strikes. When it was over the squirmy pile of flesh and bone was threaded through another wheel and hoisted into position beside the first victim. And then the name of Dietmar Wolff was called.

'No!' shouted Conrad and lurched forward, only to be restrained by Henke's tight grip. Rudolf grabbed the boy's shoulders.

'There is nothing you can do, Conrad. I am sorry.'

Conrad, tears welling up in his eyes, looked forlornly at Rudolf as his father stepped from the cage and walked to the scaffold. He knew the horrible death that awaited him but to his credit did not flinch in the face of terror. He may have been a lowly baker but he walked to his death unfalteringly and with his head held high. The crowd fell silent as Dietmar Wolff ascended the steps to the scaffold and pulled the robe over his head and handed it to one of the skinners.

The executioner's other apprentices grabbed the baker and forced him back on the now bloody, slippery cross as the priest, who had at last managed to compose himself, stepped forward and made the sign of the cross over Dietmar. One of the skinners took a pair of tongs from the brazier but the executioner waved him back. A ripple of excitement went through the crowd – the executioner wanted to have some fun with this one. He took the iron bar from the table and wiped the blood from it with a cloth, then swung it in the air a few times. People in the crowd nodded and smiled to each other. This should be worth watching. Conrad, horrified but

34

unwilling to abandon his father by averting his gaze, saw his lips move as he prayed to God, the priest likewise reading from the blood-splattered Bible in his hands.

The executioner stepped forward, raised the iron bar above his head and brought it down savagely on Dietmar Wolff's neck. There was a loud crack followed by a stunned silence from the crowd. What nonsense was this? The executioner had killed the baker with a single blow. He had administered mercy and thus deprived the spectators of witnessing the torments of a man being smashed to pieces. Conrad covered his face with his hands and began to sob. Henke looked at Rudolf who nodded back at him. The previous night they had visited the executioner in his home and paid him to ensure that Dietmar Wolff would have a swift death.

'We should leave this place of death,' remarked Rudolf, who caught the eye of the executioner and made the sign of the cross.

Henke led Conrad away as the executioner proceeded to smash the limbs of the baker prior to his corpse being hoisted aloft on a wheel. He proceeded at speed for the murmurs among the crowd told him that they were not best pleased to have been deprived of their fun. He knew that it was not uncommon for executioners to be ripped to pieces by an angry crowd for either failing to fulfil their expectations or botching the killing of prisoners. When he had finished he barked orders at the skinners to fix the mangled corpse to the wheel and ordered the guards to fetch the next prisoner. Fortunately it was a woman. Once she had been stripped and her torture started the crowd would soon forget their displeasure.

On a balcony behind the scaffold Lübeck's judge sipped at his wine and waited for the young boys who were serving custard dyed with sandalwood. He leaned to his left where Adolfus Braune was watching the executions.

'That fellow was the baker who tried to kill you, I believe.'

Braune nodded. 'Yes. I am not happy that he was not put to the tongs first. Very poor showing by the executioner.'

The servant refilling his goblet jumped as the woman spread-eagled on the cross below them screamed as one of her breasts was torn from her body. Braune licked his lips and once more began to feel his loins stir with excitement as he witnessed a helpless woman being degraded and mutilated.

'Have no worry,' replied the judge, 'I will have stern words with him. He is paid well for his work and will be reminded that justice must be seen to be done.'

But Braune was not listening, so engrossed was he in the slow and agonising death being meted out to the naked woman on the scaffold.

Conrad left the square in a daze, unaware of his surroundings or time of day. It felt as though his insides had been gouged out. He was numb. The tears had stopped because he had none left. He suddenly stopped.

Rudolf looked at him quizzically. 'Conrad?'

The boy looked at him with puffy red eyes. 'Kill me. Please.'

Rudolf smiled kindly. 'It is an offence against God to take an innocent life, Conrad.'

'My father and mother were innocent but their lives were taken.'

Henke nodded thoughtfully, earning him a frown from Rudolf.

'Sometimes we cannot fathom God's plans, Conrad,' said Rudolf, 'but there is a plan and we must not question it. Suffice to say that your parents are together in heaven and you should be grateful for that at least.'

'Grateful,' murmured Conrad without emotion.

Rudolf placed an arm around his shoulders and moved him forward. 'Come. You will feel better with some food in your belly.'

The monks at the red-brick monastery were kind and brought Conrad and his sister large bowls filled with a thick chicken stew. The monastery had its own cattle and chickens that provided the monks with milk and food all year round, though they were not allowed to eat meat from four-legged animals. But he could not eat it and so sat and watched his sister devour the meal, scooping up mouthfuls of stew with pieces of the loaf that sat on the table between them. The nuns of the convent had covered Marie's curly hair with a white veil, which framed her face and made it appear even rounder. She stopped eating and looked at her brother with her large grey eyes.

'Why aren't you eating?'

'I'm not hungry. Our parents are in heaven, Marie.'

She dropped her spoon in the stew. 'Father is dead?'

'Yes.'

'Why?'

'I do not know why,' he answered.

She began to cry. He stood up and went to comfort her.

'Do not cry, Marie. Please,' he implored her, tears coming to his own eyes.

'What is to become of us, Conrad?'

But that question had already been addressed by Rudolf and that very evening the warrior monk escorted Conrad to the monastery's chapter house, located in its east range. He was still pained by his father's death and his sister's distress but had calmed down a little. He was now possessed by a strange indifference as he walked beside Rudolf from the west range of the monastery along stark stone floors. Despite its austerity Conrad liked the monastery. There was an ordered calm within its walls, with no raised voices, filth or bad odours. The monks went about their business quietly, contentedly and with a sense of purpose. He had given no thought to what would happen to him but thought that perhaps he could make a life for himself here within its walls. Perhaps that is why he had been summoned to the chapter house.

The walled monastery was located next to the cathedral and adjacent to the nunnery. Conrad had been lodged in the west range where guest rooms were provided, the monks sleeping in a dormitory on the building's second storey. They walked along the west range's corridor before going through a door that led to the cloister and then across the garden where flowers to decorate the cathedral were grown. These all had a religious symbolism: violas that represented the humility of the Virgin Mary, white roses associated with her purity and red roses that were linked with the blood of Christ. Conrad looked up into the moonlit sky and saw the imposing black shapes of the cathedral's twin spires towering above the monastery.

They walked through the garden to the east range's cloister and then through a door that led to the chapter house. This was positioned in the centre of the east range and was a place where the monks assembled each morning and where the abbot decided the day's business. Though the cathedral was the fief of the bishop of the city who technically ruled the monastery, his many religious and secular interests meant he was away a lot. Thus he delegated authority to the abbot.

When Conrad entered the chapter house he was impressed by its size and rich decoration. Candle stands arranged around the spacious circular room illuminated the interior and the glass in the tall windows, constructed high enough to prevent anyone outside spying in. He noticed that around the edges of the room was a series of stone benches, while opposite the door they had entered was the abbot and two of his monks, one of whom was sitting at a table with a quill in his hand. Rudolf ushered Conrad forward and they both halted in front of the abbot, a portly, middle-aged man with a tonsure and a white habit. Chosen by the other monks for his goodness and authority, he ruled the monastery and also had power over the many tenants who lived on church lands in Lübeck and the surrounding area.

Conrad noticed that above the benches were beautiful stone carvings of heads, animals, birds and flowers. He was staring at them when the abbot cleared his throat and Rudolf gently jabbed him with a finger.

The abbot smiled. 'Well, Conrad. Brother Rudolf has brought you here so that your future may be decided.'

The monk with the quill began taking notes of the meeting.

The abbot brought his hands together in front of him. 'It would appear that you have three courses of action open to you. I believe that God brought you to us for a purpose and to that end Brother Rudolf would like you to go with him when he returns to Livonia. There you will be instructed in the ways of the Sword Brothers to become an agent of the Lord against the heathens. This is your first option.'

Conrad looked at Rudolf who nodded at him.

'Alternatively, you may remain here and become a novice in the monastery and thereby devote your life to the Lord within its quiet confines. Your last option, and in my view the least desirable, is to leave these walls with your sister to live on your own wits. This I would advise against.'

He gestured to the other monk sitting beside him who handed him a note.

'I have been notified by the city authorities that your father's premises and all tools and fittings pertaining to his business as a baker have been confiscated as a consequence of his conviction. So you see, you have no means to make a living.'

He leaned forward and fixed Conrad with his eyes. 'What do you intend to do?'

What choice did he have? He had no home, no means of making a living and no family members he could lodge with. Apart from his sister he was truly alone. It was the fate of his sister that was uppermost in his mind.

'What of my sister, sir?

'She can enter the convent as a novice,' replied the abbot, the sound of the monk's scribbling beside him filling the chamber. 'She will be clothed, cared for and perfectly safe within its walls.'

Conrad felt relieved. The safety of Marie was what his parents would have wanted. Better a nun than a starving beggar on Lübeck's streets. He was tempted to stay at the monastery. At least he would be close to Marie and they would be able to see each other as they grew up. But in his heart he did not want to stay in Lübeck, the site of his parents' murders. He had a strong desire to flee its narrow streets and its base citizens. He could leave Marie behind and depart on his own, of course. But to what end? He had never been outside the city and knew nothing of the world that existed beyond its confines. At least if he went with Rudolf he would have food in his belly and would learn to be a Sword Brother, whatever they were. His mind was made up.

'I will go with Brother Rudolf, sir.'

Chapter 2

Lübeck's docks were heaving with activity. The city was now a commercial centre of great importance for the Baltic region and for trade with the German Empire to the south. The city was situated on an island enclosed by the River Trave and was thirteen miles inland from the Baltic Sea. Its strategic location meant that its merchants and their ships controlled the fish trade in the Baltic itself and the North Sea and the grain trade to Norway. Lübeck grew rich dealing in salt, herring, grain, timber, honey, amber, hides and ships stores. Fish, amber and hides entered the port and were then transported by land to southern Germany, while merchandise from the Mediterranean – jewellery, weapons and tools – were brought to Lübeck and shipped elsewhere. But it was the herring trade, the fish caught and then salted in their tens of thousands, that had made Lübeck rich. So numerous were Baltic herrings that it was said that a man could scoop up the fish with his bare hands.

Conrad had risen early to eat breakfast with Marie, the last time he would see her in a long time, perhaps the last time he would see her ever. The thought weighed heavily upon him and he ate little, picking at the rye bread and taking small sips of the cup of milk. Marie devoured her bread and drank greedily from her cup.

'I have to go away,' he said to her.

She put down her cup, milk on her top lip. 'Go where?'

'To a place called Livonia. Brother Rudolf is going to train me to be a Sword Brother.'

The names meant nothing to Marie, who continued to smile at her brother in ignorance.

'When will you be back?' she asked.

He avoided her gaze and turned away. 'I do not know. You like it here, with the nuns, I mean?'

'Yes, they are kind to me.'

That was something at least. 'You will be safe here until I get back.'

The abbess appeared, a middle-aged woman in a pure white gown with a large silver cross hanging over her habit. Marie saw her and smiled.

'It is time to say goodbye to your brother, Marie.'

Conrad tried desperately to stifle the tears that were welling up in his eyes as he left his bench to embrace his sister.

'Promise me that you will take care of yourself, Marie.'

Not realising that he was saying a last farewell, she smiled. 'Of course I will. I will see you when you get back.'

'It is time,' said the abbess softly.

Conrad released his sister and looked at the abbess. 'You will take care of her, won't you?'

The abbess looked at him with sympathetic eyes. 'You can be assured of that, Conrad. And may God go with you.'

He kissed Marie on the cheek, turned and walked to the door of the dining room. He stopped and looked back, raised a hand to his sister and then walked briskly into the corridor. Rudolf and Henke were waiting for him in the garden and they walked in silence from the monastery north to the city docks. The spring days were getting warmer and there was a pleasant breeze blowing but Conrad was dejected and walked with his head down. Rudolf noticed the boy's demeanour but said nothing. Hard work would soon occupy his mind and he would be too tired to be morose.

At the docks their progress was slowed by a mass of sailors, port officials, wagons, cattle, horses and dockers. The quayside was filled with the aroma of salt and fish and cawing gulls hovered above. The harbour area was crammed with boats of all shapes and sizes. The largest, the single-masted cogs, were nearest to the quay, their cargoes being unloaded by cranes for storage in the great warehouses that lined the docks. These impressive brick-built structures comprised three storeys, the ground floor being the venue where buying and selling took place and the second floor the space where goods were stored. The top floor was filled with offices and living quarters.

Around the cogs were aged byrthings – short and broad boats with a single sail and rudder – and even older boats called busses that had slender hulls and one mast and sail. There were also a great number of cobles: flat-bottomed, open-decked, high-bowed, clinker-built fishing vessels. The high bow was necessary for sailing in the rough waters of the Baltic. Further upstream the riverbanks around the villages were littered with smaller vessels. These included punts with flat bottoms and square bows – ideal for fishing in shallow waters. The villagers also used coracles, stringing nets between two boats to catch fish.

Rudolf and Henke pushed their way through the crowd until they reached two cogs moored by the quay flying pennants bearing a red sword below a red cross from the top of their masts. Standing on the stone quay was a collection of soldiers and civilians, including a handful of women and young children. Conrad noticed a

41

group of youths standing with a man in his twenties dressed in mail over which he wore a white surcoat. He was armed with a sword and carried a wide shield in his left hand. His helmet was on the ground before him and he had removed his mail coif from his head. He had a handsome if serious face topped by trimmed brown hair.

Henke nudged Rudolf. 'Behold. Walter the Penitent.'

Rudolf frowned at his grinning friend who pointed at the young knight. 'You see that handsome young knight, Conrad? That is Walter, a young noble from one of Saxony's richest families. Killed a friend in a duel so I heard, and now he is full of remorse and wishes only to absolve his sins by seeking a heroic death fighting the godless heathens. He might get his wish, but it won't be heroic.'

'Thank you, Henke,' Rudolf rebuked him. 'The bishop welcomes all those who volunteer to fight the pagans.'

'His enthusiasm will cool when he experiences the reality of our cause,' sniffed Henke.

The youths standing with the handsome young knight were an unprepossessing sight: all but one dressed in poor quality, ill-fitting shirts and leggings. One in particular caught Conrad's eye, a painfully thin boy at least six inches shorter than him with sallow skin and greasy brown hair. He looked as though he could be broken in half with ease.

Rudolf walked over to the group and spoke to the knight first.

'Welcome Walter. I am Rudolf and this is Henke. The bishop informed me that you would be travelling to Livonia before him and the other crusaders.'

Walter bowed his head to Rudolf. 'Thank you, Brother Rudolf. I am eager to get to grips with the heathen to do God's work.'

Henke smirked but Rudolf nodded his head and placed a hand on Walter's shoulder. 'With a fair wind and a calm sea it shall be so.'

Rudolf next placed an arm around Conrad's shoulders and spoke to the four youths behind Walter.

'This is Conrad Wolff, who like you has volunteered to join the holy crusade in Livonia. You are brothers in the service of God so conduct yourself as such and you will prosper.'

Conrad had little opportunity to get to know his young companions as the next hour was spent assisting the captain and his crew stowing the supplies for the voyage. The two ships were over seventy feet long and over twenty feet wide with a single unfurled sail tied to each mast's yardarm. At the stern was a 'castle' that contained the captain's cabin.

The decks were being loaded with cages containing chickens, crates and spare timber for repairs at sea. The casks holding water, wine and ale were stashed below decks along with spare anchors, sails and rigging. The chickens would be eaten during the voyage but the main food source would be the salted fish, dried meat and biscuits that Conrad and his comrades helped to load.

Conrad and the thin youth began ferrying the chicken cages from the quayside to the first boat under the supervision of an evil looking sailor with a thick beard and filthy clothes. He barked orders at the pair to stack the cages neatly against the starboard side of the boat, spitting after every sentence.

'We'll be eating these,' the stick-thin boy said to Conrad, nodding at the cage they were carrying, 'but first they will be laying eggs for us to eat. Lovely.'

He grinned triumphantly at Conrad. 'What did the brother say your name was?'

'Conrad Wolff.'

They placed the cage holding two hens on top of another that also held a brace of poultry. They stepped away and the sailor inspected their work, shifting the cage slightly to align its edges so they were flush with those of the one beneath. He spat over the side of the boat and ordered them to go and fetch another cage.

'I am Hans.' He looked around at the supplies being stowed on board the two cogs. 'Don't think we'll starve on this trip. Where is this place we are going to, Livonia?'

Conrad shook his head. 'I do not know.'

'How long do you think it will take us to get there?'

Conrad pursed his lips. 'I do not know.'

Hans rubbed his hands together. 'Well, at least we won't starve.'

Conrad smiled, the first time he had done so in days. This boy seemed obsessed by food. Conrad also noted the large amount of supplies being loaded onto each cog and also thought it unlikely that they would starve. He counted thirty-five casks of water that were stowed beneath the deck in the hold, with a further ten casks of wine and ten casks of ale that followed them. There were also a great number of crates holding salted fish, dried meat and biscuits that would be consumed on the journey. The sailors were bemused to see Walter the Penitent lending a hand loading the cog with supplies. Noble knights usually did not get their hands dirty doing such work.

The other passengers were also lending a hand save for the handful of women who were minding their children. Each vessel had a crew of twelve men

43

including the captain and could accommodate up to thirty passengers, who slept in the hold in hammocks. However, because of the food, ships stores and other supplies crammed into the hold there was only space for twenty hammocks, which meant that everyone had to share their sleeping space.

As time wore on the two captains, who both shared a remarkably similar shabby appearance, began to get more irritated and scolded their men and those assisting them for their tardiness. They wished to catch the tide and be away. Conrad was also eager to leave Lübeck and so he and Hans worked hard to get everything on board. The civilians and their families, who Conrad discovered were stonemasons and blacksmiths, were carried in the second cog, along with some of the mercenaries. The balance of the latter, along with Rudolf, Henke, Walter the Penitent and the five youths, travelled in the first cog.

Just as Conrad believed that the head of the captain would burst, so flustered had he become, all the supplies had at last been loaded and the anchors were weighed. As the passengers gathered at the sides of the ship sailors threw a rope to a waiting buss, whose oarsmen began rowing as soon as it was secured to the stern. Conrad felt the cog move as the longship pulled it away from the quay and towards the middle of the Trave. The captain kept a keen hand on the cog's rudder for the harbour was full of vessels that he had to thread a path through.

Their progress seemed agonisingly slow as they passed by other boats moored in the harbour, the second cog behind them was also being pulled by a buss. But as the minutes passed the quay diminished in size and they left the harbour to enter the wide waterway that was the Trave. Conrad gripped the side of the boat and spat in the direction of the spires and buildings of Lübeck, the city that had killed his family and cast him as an orphan into the world. Then he remembered Marie and said a silent prayer to God that she would be safe and protected for he suspected that he would never see her again.

After two hours the cogs had reached the estuary of the river and the longships cast them adrift, the captain ordering the sail to be unfurled as he sought to catch the breeze. Everyone looked up in excitement when the great canvas sail billowed as the wind filled it and they began their journey across the Baltic. Conrad noticed that the sail carried the red sword and cross emblem that Rudolf and Henke wore on their surcoats. He also noticed that Walter was kneeling on the deck praying, which Conrad took comfort from. God would not sink their vessel with such a pious man on board.

Once under way the ship's cook began roasting fresh fish over a brazier positioned near the bows of the boat. Soon a queue had formed as sailors and passengers alike waited to satisfy the appetite they had built up during the loading of the ship. Hans was near the head of the line, eagerly waiting with his wooden eating bowl. Rudolf had ensured that the ship's food supplies were more than sufficient for the journey and had purchased fresh meat and fish on the morning of their departure so the bellies of all the crew and passengers would be full at the start of the voyage and during the passage. From bitter experience he knew that empty bellies bred mutinous spirits and lethargy. There was little point in arriving at Riga with a ship full of half-starving people.

Hans was eating greedily from his bowl when Conrad sat down beside him beneath the gunwale, using his fingers to shovel cooked mackerel into his mouth.

'I told you we would not starve,' he grinned.

'That depends on how long we have to stay on this boat,' said Conrad, who had to admit that the mackerel was most appetising.

Hans emptied his mouth and scooped up some more fish. 'Just over three weeks. I asked one of the sailors.'

The prospect seemed daunting but the days following were filled with work that kept Conrad's mind occupied. When helping to clean the deck with buckets of seawater he occasionally glanced at the distant horizon, the endless ocean making him and the boat he was on appear miniscule and unimportant. He shuddered. He had never seen the sea before let alone sail on it. He gazed at the dark water and wondered what monsters swam below its surface. At night he lay in his hammock and heard the creaking of the ship's timbers and wondered if the vessel would break apart while he slept.

He had counted himself lucky that he had been allotted a hammock to sleep in and wondered why Rudolf, Henke and the mercenaries preferred to sleep in the open on deck. After the first night he knew why. The hold stank of urine and human dung, made worse when several of his fellow youths were seasick. Whereas Hans was talkative and jovial the other three – Anton, Bruno and Johann – were more reticent and aloof. They rarely spoke and kept their heads down, and even the frequent questioning by Hans had little success. However, their bouts of seasickness and Conrad's offer to help them to the deck so they could throw up over the side made them more approachable, even if they nearly always vomited below deck, creating a nauseous stench. Added to the odour of dung and urine it was quite overpowering. Everyone was given a terracotta pot to piss in each evening, which also doubled up as a sick bowl. They were emptied every morning but in the foetid darkness of the hold many were kicked over by accident, especially during Bruno and Johann's desperate attempts to reach the side of the ship before they emptied their stomachs, which invariably failed.

Conrad emerged each morning clutching his piss pot and his nose permanently twisted at the reek that greeted his nostrils when he opened his eyes. Climbing the steps slowly so as not to disturb the contents of his pot, he always encountered a cheerful Rudolf.

'I trust you had a good night's sleep, Conrad?'

Henke grinned evilly as he and Rudolf joined the queue of those waiting to empty their bowels at the bowhead where there were located two seats, one projecting out either side of the prow. It was an undignified and precarious business but absolutely essential.

Conrad noticed that during the voyage most of the crew and passengers became a little leaner, especially Bruno and Johann who took a week before they acquired their sea legs. However, Hans actually gained weight on account of the regular meals he was eating.

'What did you do, Conrad, before this voyage, I mean.'

They were in the hold armed with hammers trying to hunt down and kill the rats that occupied the ship's interior. Hans was clutching a candleholder, the flickering flame barely enough to see by let alone hunt black rats.

'I was an apprentice baker to my father,' answered Conrad proudly. 'What about you?'

'Beggar and thief. There's one, quick!'

Conrad raised his hammer but he only caught a fleeting glimpse of a black shape and then it was gone. This was hopeless. Conrad lowered his weapon.

'A thief?'

'Caught stealing a loaf of bread. They were going to hang me but it was a church court, fortunately, and so they offered me a life serving God or dancing on the end of a rope. So here I am.'

'What about your family?' asked Conrad.

Hans scratched his head and picked a louse from his hair. 'Don't have any. I was an orphan and beggar on the streets of Lübeck. Managed to survive most of the time but I had not eaten in two weeks. I was so hungry that I didn't consider getting caught. I just saw that big fresh loaf and the ache in my belly and took it. What about you?'

'I lost my family,' was all that Conrad would say on the matter.

The voyage was largely uneventful, the waters of the Baltic remaining largely flat and the winds mostly mild. Occasionally they were struck by a thunderstorm that drenched the boat, but not before everything on deck had been covered with canvas sheets. The rainwater was caught and stored in the casks that had been emptied of water and so there was no need to put into shore to replenish what had been consumed. No one washed or shaved and so as the days passed everyone stank and got progressively filthier. Rudolf and Henke discarded their surcoats and chainmail and donned garnache – loose outer garments with short, wide sleeves. The mercenaries similarly stashed their padded coats away and wore their leggings and shirts only.

The mood was relaxed and friendly, the sailors appreciative of Conrad and his companions lending a hand with daily tasks on board and the mercenaries being kept on a tight leash by Rudolf. In their spare time the sailors played dice but Rudolf prohibited Conrad and his comrades from taking part.

'Gambling pampers to our base instincts and leads to resentment and anger,' he told them. 'No good comes of it.'

His words were prophetic as two days later a fierce argument broke out between two of the crew concerning cheating at dice. One of the men pulled a knife and stabbed the other sailor, resulting in his death. He was immediately arrested and placed under guard in the hold while his fate was decided. Rudolf ensured that Conrad and his fellow youths were in attendance as the man was hauled before the captain. The day was warm and sunny with a light breeze filling the sail above them as the offender was brought up the steps. The body of the dead sailor lay on the deck, blood oozing onto the wood. Conrad deliberately stared ahead to avoid looking at it.

Rudolf and Henke, now dressed in their mail armour, though not coifs, and both with swords in their hands, flanked the prisoner. Conrad noticed that Rudolf had some terrible scars on his neck.

The captain wiped his nose and eyed him.

'Have you anything to say?'

The sailor, nervous and pale, clasped his hands in front of him. 'It was just an argument that got out of hand, captain. Nothing more. You know how it is, sir. Nerves and tempers wear thin at sea.'

'That they do,' agreed the captain, 'which is why you should have known better. There is nothing more to say. The punishment is well known. Brother Rudolf.'

Rudolf turned and nodded to one of the mercenaries who was holding a rope.

'No, captain,' pleaded the sailor. 'It was just a flash of temper.'

The mercenary grabbed the man's arms and yanked them back so Henke could bind them behind his back with the cord, then bound his ankles together with another length of rope. The sailor, suddenly aware of what was going to happen, began to struggle violently, falling on the deck.

'No, no! Leave me alone.'

Two more mercenaries grabbed the body of the dead sailor and passed Henke another length of rope. They dragged the corpse to place it next to the thrashing prisoner and then Henke tied the rope around the necks of the prisoner and corpse, thus binding them together. The mercenaries lashed the two pairs of ankles together as the prisoner began to moan.

'No! For the love of God, no!' The rope around his neck was constricting his breathing and he had difficulty talking.

Another rope was passed around the mid-rifts of the prisoner and corpse to tightly secure them together. The sailor was now whimpering. Rudolf began reciting a prayer and made the sign of the cross as Henke and two others hauled the corpse and sailor up and tossed them over the side of the ship. There was a splash and then silence. The captain dismissed the assembly as Conrad and his companions looked at each other. Rudolf came over to them.

'That is why I forbid gambling.'

The next day one of the sailors explained to them that the law of the sea was severe when it came to killing on board ship. Not that it stopped gambling for that afternoon the same man was playing dice with another sailor. Rudolf made sure that all the youths were given daily tasks to stop them becoming bored and restless. Fishing over the side of the boat was one, rather enjoyable, of these tasks. Conrad sat with Hans on empty crates, dangling their rods over the gunwale hoping for a fish to bite the hooks. It was another glorious spring day and the slight breeze hardly rippled the marble-smooth waters of the Baltic. The two ships had hugged the coast to keep the sight of land permanently on their starboard side but the two youths were fishing on the port side of the cog. They were only five days away from their destination.

48

'Where's that?' asked Hans, who had managed to scrounge some dried biscuits and was shoving them into his mouth.

'A place called Riga,' answered Conrad. 'I asked Brother Rudolf.'

'Is it a city?'

Conrad peered over the gunwale at the water below to see if he could spot any fish. 'I don't know. Brother Rudolf said that it had been founded by Bishop Albert nine years ago so it can't be a city.'

Another biscuit went into Hans' mouth. 'Will we live there?'

'I do not know.'

Hans shrugged. 'Anywhere will be better than Lübeck.'

Conrad nodded. 'Yes, it will.'

Hans pointed out to sea, towards the northwest. 'Do you think they are from Riga?'

Conrad looked up and stared in the direction Hans was pointing, to see four small boats on the horizon. They appeared not to be moving but that was only because they were so far away. Conrad went back to peering at the sea, convinced that they would catch nothing today.

Suddenly the ship's bell start to ring and frantic activity broke out on the boat. The sailors began to furl the sail and the mercenaries began donning their mail armour and helmets, the crossbowmen unpacking their weapons from their waterproof crates. Conrad and Hans stood up and looked at each other in confusion. Moments later Rudolf, attired in mail armour, surcoat and helmet in hand, was before them.

'Store those rods and join your comrades at the mast. Be quick!'

'What is happening?' asked Conrad.

Rudolf pointed to the four ships in the distance. 'Those are Oeselian ships.'

The name meant nothing to Conrad. 'Oeselians?'

'Pirates who desire to kill us and take our ships. Now move.'

Conrad and Hans took the rods below deck and then re-emerged to stand beside the other youths at the mast. The sails of both ships had now been furled and the vessels were being lashed together so that they would be side by side. The boys looked at each other nervously. No one spoke but they all knew that danger was approaching fast. Walter, now dressed in his full war gear, was kneeling on deck deep in prayer, his helmet resting on the deck beside him. Rudolf had been organising the transfer of some of the spearmen and crossbowmen from their own cog to the other vessel but now he strode over the boys, Henke following him.

'Can any of you use a crossbow?'

Conrad looked at Hans and then at the others. He certainly had no knowledge of the weapon but Anton raised his hand.

'I do,' he said nervously.

Henke walked forward and handed him one.

'Good. Take this.'

He passed Anton a crossbow and then a quiver filled with bolts made of seasoned yew measuring around a foot in length. Each one was winged with thin strips of leather. Henke watched more of the spearmen and crossbowmen scramble over the gunwale onto the deck on the other boat.

'You denude our numbers, Rudolf.'

Rudolf smiled at his friend. 'I have to protect the stonemasons and their families. They will be no use to us if their loved ones are butchered and we need enthusiastic stonemasons in Livonia.'

He looked at the youths grouped before him. 'Stonemasons are more valuable than urchins.'

Conrad was hardly fortified by Rudolf's words and became decidedly queasy when he was handed a shield and a spear from those brought from below deck by the mercenaries who had remained on their cog. The captain and sailors had also equipped themselves with an assortment of weaponry, including swords, spears and short axes, and stood ready at the stern. The defence of the prow was left to Rudolf, Henke, half a dozen spearmen, the same number of crossbowmen and Conrad and his companions. The spearmen formed a line as the crossbowmen advanced to the bow and knelt down, resting the stock of their weapons on the side of the boat. Their quivers were slung over their shoulders by means of a leather strap, their faces covered my mail coifs and their bodies protected by thick padded coats called gambesons that reached down to below their knees.

While Anton clutched his crossbow Henke showed Conrad and the others how to hold their shields: passing their left arms through two leather straps on the back and grasping a pair of cross-straps further along with the hand, the back of which rested on a stuffed pad. Though large, having a height of around four and half feet and being two feet wide, the wooden shield faced with hide was surprising light, Conrad thought. He gripped the iron-headed spear tightly, hoping that he would not have to use it.

The shields of Rudolf and Henke were shorter and curved to better fit the contours of their bodies, each sporting a red cross over a red sword. Their helmets had flat tops with the face-guards joined to the neck-guards to produce a completely enclosed helmet. Walter also had a similar helmet and as he finished his prayers he picked it up and then strolled over to stand beside the two Sword Brothers, his face a mask of steely determination.

The enemy was close now and Conrad could hear the shouts of the Oeselian rowers as they pulled on their oars to get their longboats nearer to the now stationary cogs. Slim, fast with pointed bows and sterns, each longship had forty pairs of oars to propel it through the water. Two men pulled on each oar and another man held the side-mounted rudder at the rear. Oeselian tactics were simple but effective: board an enemy ship, kill its crew and take it as plunder, along with anything in its hold. Because they were rowed into battle the longships had to approach their target head-on to prevent their oars being smashed against the side of the enemy vessel. This meant that the raiders had only a narrow point of access onto the lashed-together cogs, which sat higher in the water. The oars could, if necessary, be retracted to allow a longship to lie alongside an enemy vessel, but this meant that it could not be withdrawn speedily if things did not go according to plan. Longships were too valuable to risk this. Its crew was expendable; the vessel was not.

Conrad felt his heart pounding in his chest as Rudolf spoke to him and his companions.

'I know that you are frightened and have not been trained in the arts of war. But you are not alone and it is better to stand here on deck and face your attackers side by side with your brothers rather than hiding in the hold. Have faith in God and He will protect you, his chosen warriors. God with us!'

Henke and Walter shouted 'God with us!' and the youths tried to be brave. Hans looked even more gaunt and pale while Bruno and Johann were shaking. Only Anton seemed calm, though the truth was that he was preoccupied with ensuring his crossbow was armed and ready rather that thinking about the enemy.

Henke nodded at the stern-faced Walter who put on his helmet and drew his sword, his shield bearing a black lion on a white background, his white surcoat bearing the same coat of arms. He looked at Rudolf.

'A fine speech. Let us hope that the Oeselians show these lads some mercy.'

'Have faith in our crossbowmen, Henke,' replied Rudolf, slapping his friend on the arm before placing his helmet on his head. Henke did the same and then they waited for the enemy.

The longships had now divided into two groups; the two vessels on either end circling round the cogs so they could direct their bows at the boat containing the civilian workers and their families. The other two attacked Conrad's vessel. He could hear no grunting now as the longships' momentum carried them towards their targets and their crews prepared to board the cogs.

Conrad's heart missed a beat as he heard cracks coming from the crossbowmen kneeling by the starboard gunwale as they shot their weapons and knew that the battle had begun. The spearmen held their shields over the gunwale to provide cover for the crossbowmen who were loosing bolts at the enemy. Their targets were those warriors on the longship who were throwing grappling irons attached to ropes to enable other men to scale the side of the cog.

Conrad heard shouts and screams as Oeselians were felled by quarrels and relief swept through him. This was not so bad after all. Then the air was filled with spears and axes as the Oeselians threw a deluge of missiles against the shields of the spearmen in an effort to clear the crossbowmen from the gunwale. Conrad watched in horror as a spear came over the row of shields towards him, raising his own shield at the last moment to deflect it away from him.

'Use your shields,' Rudolf screamed at them as a single-handed axe thudded into the mast above Hans. Another axe thudded into Johann's shield, splintering the top edge though missing his head. The boys instinctively huddled together and locked their shields as the missiles clattered into them, above them and around them. Conrad's mouth was dry and his breathing was heavy as fear coursed through him. He thought he would foul his leggings as his stomach turned to mush, but then his attention was drawn to the right of the line of mercenaries where a grapping iron suddenly bit into the gunwale. Rudolf, Henke and Walter were preoccupied with dodging the rain of spears and axes that were still coming on to the boat and did not see it. But Conrad did.

'Hans, look!' he shouted.

He looked at Hans and then at the grappling iron and then saw two hands and a helmet appear. They had been boarded. The captain and sailors at the stern had also been under a deluge of missiles from the second longship alongside and had taken shelter beneath the gunwale. The Oeselians in the first ship had been held back by the crossbowmen and had taken refuge behind their shields but the men of the second ship were free to scale the rope attached to the grappling iron.

Walter saw it too and now ran forward to thrust the point of his sword into the eye socket of the first Oeselian. The man screamed and fell back onto the others behind him, temporarily halting the boarders. But then another grappling iron appeared and then another, and suddenly two Oeselians jumped on deck. Both were bearded brutes, one wearing a mail corselet that extended to below his knees and armed with a great two-handed axe, a round shield strapped to his back. The other wore a short-sleeved mail tunic and was armed with a shorter axe, carrying a large, round shield painted red and yellow in his other hand. Walter did not hesitate but immediately attacked them, jumping to the side to avoid a great scything blow from the larger axe and catching a blow from the smaller axe on his shield. Rudolf and Henke also spotted the boarders, who had been joined by two more of their comrades, and went to assist Walter, Henke bringing his sword above his head and then whipping it down to slice the calf of an enemy warrior armed with a spear and shield. The man yelped in pain and then fell silent as Henke thrust his sword point into the man's neck, before falling in beside Rudolf who was fighting on the left side of Walter.

More Oeselians came on board as the crossbowman on the far right of the line spotted a man hauling himself over the gunwale and shot him in the chest, causing him to collapse back onto his comrades. At the stern the captain and his men were also hacking with their swords and thrusting with their spears, keeping the Oeselians at bay but at a price.

An Oeselian armed with sword and shield jumped on deck and approached the line of spearmen and crossbowmen that were still keeping the crew of the first longship at bay. He drew back his sword to despatch the mercenary who had killed his comrade and was shot by a quarrel as Anton released the trigger on his crossbow. The boys cheered and congratulated him as the mercenary turned and raised his hand in acknowledgement. But the battle was becoming fiercer as more and more Oeselians came aboard. Rudolf, Henke and Walter fought with a grim determination, deftly wielding their swords to fend off attackers and cut faces and legs. Conrad noticed that their strikes were concentrated against enemy faces and necks mostly, with low blows being directed against unprotected thighs and calves. He also saw the brute with the two-handed axe bring the massive iron head of his weapon down on Rudolf's shield, splintering it and forcing the Sword Brother on to his knees. The man tried frantically to wrench the metal free of the shield as Rudolf desperately jabbed his sword at him, for he knew that if the Oeselian freed his weapon the next blow would split his skull. And then Conrad charged.

He did not know why he did so. Perhaps it was because God had infused him with courage. Or maybe it was the reaction akin to a cornered animal that fights out of fear and desperation. But more likely it was because he had had been witnesses to his parents' deaths and had been unable to do anything. And now

Rudolf, the man who had shown him and his sister mercy and kindness, was helpless just like his parents had been. Only this time Conrad had a weapon in his hands and somewhere within him came the urge to use it. So he ran forward, screaming at the top of his voice, and stabbed the spearhead into the axe man's mail corselet. The latter was well made and thick and the point hardly pierced it, but the attack was totally unexpected and the Oeselian stopped trying to free his weapon from Rudolf's shield and looked down at his pierced armour. He released his axe and angrily grabbed Conrad's spear blade and threw it aside, then drew his sword and raised it to spilt Conrad's skull, just as Hans shoved his spear through the man's throat.

Rudolf threw aside his shield, jumped up and swung his sword at the man's head, the edge cutting deep into the Oeselian's skull and knocking him to the ground.

'God with us!' he shouted and then attacked the enemy warriors grouped behind the dead axe man. He was their chief, their captain, and seeing him felled made their attack falter. They began to lose heart when horns were sounded from the first longship whose crew had been unable to board the cog, signalling a retreat. Walter killed a man with a thrust into his armpit and then cut down another who was attempting to leave the boat, while Henke barged over a warrior and then rammed his sword into the man's chest as he lay helpless on the deck.

Bruno and Johann were attempting to battle an Oeselian armed with a sword and shield but their efforts were being soundly defeated. The warrior lopped off the head of Bruno's spear and then barged him with his shield, knocking him down. Johann tried to stab the warrior with his spear but the Oeselian was too quick and spun round to face the now very nervous youth quivering behind his shield. Conrad saw his predicament, picked up his spear and threw it at the Oeselian, hitting him in the lower left leg. The man grunted in pain and turned to glare at Conrad. But the strike had the desired effect for the man yanked out the spear point from his leg and limped to the gunwale, sheathed his sword, threw his shield on his back and disappeared down the rope to his longship.

The fighting was over now, the deck littered with half a dozen Oeselians that had been killed. The longships disengaged from the cog as their oarsmen rowed backwards to pull away. Rudolf ran to the opposite gunwale and leapt onto the other cog. But happily that had not been boarded and the extra spearmen and crossbowmen he had assigned to its defence had beaten off the other two longships with ease. The civilian workers and their families emerged from the hold shaken but unharmed. When he returned to Conrad's ship Walter had taken off his helmet and was already on his knees giving thanks for their salvation. Conrad was hugging and congratulating the other boys and thought it the greatest victory the world had ever seen.

Rudolf, now helmetless, came over to them as they were basking in their mutual admiration.

'They might come back,' he warned, instantly deflating their spirits. He pointed at the mercenaries standing at the gunwale.

'Those men are professional soldiers. They will not let down their guard until the enemy has disappeared from view. You all should join them.'

And so Conrad and his companions stood beside the mercenaries and watched the longships disappear into the north, back to the island of Oesel, their lair. Walter finished his prayers and came to Conrad's side.

'Well done,' he said, the first words he had spoken to him during the voyage.

'Well done, indeed,' agreed Rudolf, slapping Conrad on the shoulder, 'and well done to all of you boys. You will make fine soldiers.'

They grinned coyly as the Oeselians disappeared from view and the mercenaries stood down and rested their weapons and shields against the gunwale. Henke was already assisting the sailors throwing the dead Oeselians overboard, having stripped them of anything useful first.

As the captain ordered an issue of ale to be made to everyone Rudolf pulled Conrad aside.

'You saved my life, Conrad. I thank you.'

Conrad could feel his cheeks blush.

'But never throw your only weapon away. If your spear had missed him or if you had been attacked by another enemy soldier afterwards what would you have done? In battle the man who keeps his wits about him stays alive, remember that. All the same, I am in your debt.'

That afternoon everyone assembled on deck to witness the burial at sea of three of the cog's sailors who had been killed in the fighting, two more on the other ship also being consigned to the sea.

The experience of combat, albeit brief, had forged a bond between the boys and afterwards they became much more relaxed in each other's company. Anton, who was from a wealthy family and who had been somewhat aloof and disparaging towards the others, especially Hans, was now much more agreeable and forthcoming. Rudolf encouraged their bond, knowing that it would serve them well when they faced even greater dangers. He had been greatly impressed with Walter who, despite his piety, had shown himself to be an accomplished killer like Henke. The latter thought it hilarious that his friend had nearly been cut in two by an Oeselian axe. But Rudolf was most pleased that his civilian workers had been unharmed in the fight. They would be worth their weight in gold when it came to establishing Christian rule among the heathens.

Two days later they landed at Riga.

*****

Olaf heard the shouts from inside his longhouse, stopped sharpening his sword and slid it back in its scabbard. The increasing noise could only mean one thing: the return of his son Eric. He buckled his sword belt round his waist and went outside to see men, women and children running to the shoreline to greet his oldest child.

'Eric is back?'

He turned to see Dalla, his wife, wearing a smile, her blue eyes sparkling with excitement. She loved all her four boys but Eric was her favourite; indeed, Eric was everyone's favourite. The handsome warrior who would be the future king of his people, if he did not get himself killed first.

He nodded to her. 'So it would seem.'

They walked together towards the gently sloping beach where three more newly built longships stood on wooden frames, carpenters working on their hulls. They had been laid down during the winter and were now nearing completion. Three more ships to add to Olaf's fleet. Three other longships stood moored in the water and there were more in the other settlements that dotted Oesel's coastline, the great island that was positioned off the western coast of Estonia. But this was Kuressaare, the king's capital and the largest community on the island. Nestled at the end of a bay and thus blessed with calm, deep waters, the settlement contained a great many longhouses along with forges, animal pens and a large meeting house in its centre. Beyond the wooden palisade that surrounded the whole town were farms that grew rye and barley, the land having first been cleared of the trees that covered half the island. Oesel was an island rich in oak that provided timber to build homes and ships. Elk, roe deer and wild boar were hunted to provide meat, and pastures provided grazing for herds of cows. Oesel was blessed by the gods, of that Olaf was convinced.

When they reached the shore the beach was filled with cheering people, many waving at the four approaching longships. Two of Olaf's sons had left earlier as part of a hunting party but his youngest, Kalf, now came running up to them.

'Eric has returned,' he beamed.

Olaf stood with his arms folded across his thick chest, attempting to count the number of oars on each ship. His wide forehead creased as they got nearer and he saw that not all the rowing stations were manned. The longships slowed to a halt as they ran aground on the sand and a figure appeared at the prow of the leading boat. Tall, handsome with long blonde hair, beard and moustache, his eyes blue like his mother's and his body powerful like his father's, Eric spread his arms wide to milk the rapturous welcome he was receiving. He then jumped down into the water and waded ashore, followed by the crews of the other longships. Women and children rushed forward to welcome their returning husbands and fathers as Eric gladly received the kisses of young women who threw themselves at him as he walked towards his parents and brother. He really was the returning hero.

Dalla beamed with delight and Kalf grinned with pride, dreaming of the day when he would be like his eldest brother, but Olaf looked past his son to where some women were shaking their heads and weeping as they were told by those who had returned with Eric that their loved ones had been killed.

Eric winked at his mother and bowed to his father. 'Hail Olaf, King of Oesel and Lord of all the oceans.'

Olaf nodded at his son. 'Your sword has been bloodied judging by the tears that are falling from the eyes of my womenfolk to fill the bay.'

Eric twisted his mouth to indicate indifference. 'All warriors desire death in battle.'

Olaf stepped forward and placed an arm round his son's broad shoulders.

'Come, let us speak in private away from your adoring women.'

Eric grinned as his mother kissed him on the cheek and Kalf shook his hand vigorously as he strolled with his father back to the royal longhouse. In truth it was nothing special, aside from being longer and slightly taller than the others. Its roof was thatched like the rest and its walls were made of logs hewn from the great oak forests that covered the island.

'I would speak to Eric alone,' said Olaf to his wife and Kalf when they reach the longhouse.

The crowd had followed them to the king's residence and so Eric turned and raised his arms to them once more, receiving loud cheers in return. He dazzled them with a smile as his father held open the door for him and the islanders' favourite son gave one more wave before disappearing inside.

Olaf closed the door and bolted it and then slapped Eric's face hard with the back of his hand. Momentarily stunned, Eric turned to face his father, his nostrils flared, his eyes filled with fury and a hand went to the hilt of his sword. Olaf said nothing and made no movements with his hands but Eric thought twice before drawing his blade. His father may have been older and shorter than he but even at the age of fifty Olaf was a fearsome warrior known throughout the Baltic for his skill with a sword.

'You are an idiot, Eric,' spat Olaf. 'How many men did you lose during your little expedition?'

Eric, still bristling with anger, turned away from his father. He could taste blood in his mouth from the king's blow. 'An insignificant number.'

'I asked how many,' growled Olaf.

Eric turned to face him. The interior of the longhouse was dim, the only light coming in from the holes in the roof that allowed the smoke from the fire that burned in a stone fire pit to escape the dwelling, but he could see the deadly serious expression on his father's face clearly enough.

'Thirty men killed. We came across two ships carrying Germans to Riga and intercepted them.'

Two rows of wooden posts ran down the length of the longhouse supporting the roof beams. These columns divided the interior into three long aisles, the central one having a packed dirt floor, the two outer ones containing benches for sitting or sleeping on and covered in furs for warmth and comfort. The king and queen slept in a bed in a room at the far end of the longhouse. Olaf rested a hand on one of the posts.

'And where are these German ships?'

Eric scraped at the floor with the heel of his boot. 'They escaped.'

'So thirty men died for nothing,' snarled Olaf.

Eric smiled, blood showing in his teeth. 'An insignificant number compared to the thousands of warriors who serve you, father.'

Olaf considered striking his son again for his stupidity but then thought better of it. He could not batter more brains into his son's head. Instead he walked over to where his wife had left a jug of ale on a small table and filled two wooden beakers. He held out one to his son. Eric smiled and took it, raising it to his father before draining it.

Olaf stared at the drink. 'Every year more and more of these Germans land at Riga to kill and conquer. Twenty years ago there were hardly any of them but now they infest the land like a plague of rats. How long do you think it will be before they turn their attention to Oesel?'

'No barbarian will set foot on this island, father,' boasted Eric, refilling his beaker. 'We are many, they are few.'

Olaf shook his head in despair. 'Have you learned nothing, Eric? Have you not seen with your own eyes the armada of ships that brings more Germans to Riga every summer? This summer will be no different. They have destroyed the power of the Livs, the ancient people who have inhabited their land since the earth was young. And now they have named their newly conquered territory Livonia in mockery of those who originally held it. They push north against the Estonians, east against the Russians and south against the Lithuanians. There is no end to their ambition or greed.'

Eric was unconcerned. 'The Livs and Estonians are farmers. We are warriors.' He glanced at his father. 'If I were king I would take the fleet and burn Riga.'

'If you were king this island would be empty of warriors so blinded are you to the truth. Riga is surrounded by a high stone wall and defended by a large garrison. How will we breach its walls, by flying over them?'

Eric drained his beaker a second time. 'Walls can be broken down, father.'

Olaf raised his eyes to the roof. 'I am considering an alliance with the Estonians to fight our common foe.'

Eric put down his beaker and wiped his mouth on his sleeve. 'An alliance? With those whose lands we have raided since time began?' Why would a wolf seek the friendship of a lamb?'

Olaf smiled and began pacing up and down, pointing at his son. 'The world is a simple place to you, isn't it Eric? You get up each morning, fill your belly and then go in search of a woman to seduce or a man to pick a fight with. You pester me incessantly to give you command of a fleet and when I yield to your pleadings you return with nothing but a tale of Oeselian dead. But the world is changing and if you are to one day be king of my people then you had better learn to recognise the signs. We must change with the times and seek pacts where once we spilled blood. We cannot destroy this German pestilence alone.'

'The Estonians might not see it the way you do,' replied Eric, who saw no merit in his father's plan.

But Olaf thought differently. 'They will. It is their lands that are being plundered and stolen.'

'And the Russians, will they be agreeable to an alliance?'

Olaf toyed with his white beard. 'They pray to the same god as the Germans and view us as pagans. I doubt we will have their friendship. And yet, as the Germans push ever further east they will encroach upon Russian lands. When they do so they may be able to forget their hatred of us, if only for a short while.'

'I will go to the Estonians with an offer of peace,' proclaimed Eric.

Olaf stifled a laugh. Sending Eric would result in perpetual war with the Estonians. He needed someone with diplomatic skills to bring his plan to fruition.

'No. As my direct heir you must stay here. I will send Sigurd.'

Sigurd was Olaf's second son, a thoughtful, resourceful individual who was very different from his thick-headed elder brother.

Eric laughed. 'Sigurd? He is too quiet and accommodating. The Estonians need to know at all times that we do them a great honour by treating with them, and should be reminded that they are bargaining from a position of weakness.'

Olaf's mind was made up. 'Sigurd will go to treat with the Estonians. And now, to celebrate your "victory" over the Germans, I will give a great feast tonight.'

'You honour me, father,' said Eric.

'But it will be many moons before you lead another fleet to sea again. I will need all the warriors I can assemble in the coming months and can ill afford to throw their lives away to satisfy the vanity of my son.'

Sigurd and Olaf's other son, Stark, returned later that day with the boar and deer they had killed and in the evening Kuressaare resounded with laughter and music as Olaf feasted his people. Oesel was teeming with wildlife and timber, while the sea that surrounded it was filled with fish. The great forests on the island were inexhaustible and its iron deposits provided the Oeselians with weapons and armour. And Olaf knew that soon such a rich land would attract the attention of the Germans and their men of iron on their great warhorses.

Chapter 3

Riga was located around five miles inland on the northern bank of the River Dvina, the great waterway that flowed for over six hundred miles from far away Russia to empty into the Baltic. Conrad and Hans stood at the prow with the other youths as their cog entered the river's estuary and made its way upstream. Two small boats with oars had greeted the cogs, having pushed off from a small settlement of log cabins positioned half a mile inland, and now they towed the larger vessels upstream. The captain ordered the sail to be furled as the cog cut through the waters of the Dvina.

The river at this point was over a thousand feet wide and the banks seemed a great distance away. Beyond them was an ocean of greenery – forests of mighty oaks stretching as far as the eye could see. Storks flew over the river looking for fish to pluck and higher up corncrakes circled above the boats.

'There is good hunting in those woods, boys,' said Rudolf, who had come to join them at the prow. 'This land is filled with deer, wild boar, lynx and bears. Lots of bears. A man can never starve here.'

'That is good to know,' smiled Hans who, despite having eaten a fair portion of the ship's food stores, was still as thin as a spear shaft.

Conrad pointed at the men straining at the oars in the two small boats towing their cog. 'Are they pagans, Brother Rudolf?'

'They were,' he answered. 'They are Livs and once worshipped false idols but now follow the true religion.'

'When it suits them,' added Henke, who had wandered over to join his friend. 'They are quick to revert to their old ways when they are of a mind to rebel.'

'Old habits die hard,' agreed Rudolf, 'but they are God's creatures nonetheless.'

Henke curled his lip. 'Creatures is right. I wonder what mischief they have been up to in our absence.'

'We will know soon enough,' answered Rudolf.

An hour later they docked in Riga, the town that had been founded nine years earlier by Bishop Albert himself. German traders had been coming to this spot for fifty years, which was originally a collection of poor villages, but only in small numbers. Now Riga, the name derived from the Latin word *rigata* – meaning 'irrigated' – was a bustling river port surrounded by thick walls. Bishop Albert had named the town thus for he intended to irrigate the dry souls of the pagans with Christianity.

The wooden quays were crammed with boats of all shapes and sizes, from great cogs to small riverboats and barges filled with goods and manned by strange looking men with long moustaches, some with shaved heads, brightly coloured coats, most with shoulder-length hair and fur-lined hats. As Conrad walked down the gangplank following the others, languages he had never heard before – all harsh, guttural and brutal – assaulted his ears. He stared at half a dozen men unloading furs from a single-masted vessel until they noticed him and stopped what they were doing and stared back at him. He saw a cross around the neck of one of them and supposed they must be Christian, but their hard features and strange language made them seem like enemies.

'Russians,' said Rudolf beside him.

'They are Christians?'

He smiled. 'They do not follow the teachings of our church, Conrad, or of the Pope, the voice of God on earth. They are what are called heretics.'

The word meant nothing to Conrad and in truth he was more fascinated by their clothes and fearsome visages than their religion.

'We burn heretics in Germany,' said Anton.

'That we do,' agreed Rudolf.

'Then how is it they are free to go about their business here?' asked the youth.

'They are not citizens of this town or of this land,' said Rudolf, 'and so are free to come and go as they please and trade their goods.'

The boys, mercenaries, civilian workers and their families left the quay to enter the town, passing warehouses filled with fur, flax, timber, tar and hides that would be sent back to Germany for sale. Led by Rudolf and Henke they walked along dirt streets filled with fair-haired men and women dressed in brown and red tunics, leather belts and red sashes, the women also wearing red or brown woollen hats. Conrad recognised men and women dressed similarly to Lübeck's citizens but they were in a minority. As far as he could tell all the buildings in the town were wooden with thatched roofs.

They eventually came to Riga's castle, a square stronghold built of stone with a square tower in each one of its four corners. Set back from the Dvina, it was surrounded by a moat filled by water from the river and accessed by means of a drawbridge. The guards standing sentry at its entrance bore two keys on their shields to symbolise St Peter, the first patron of Riga. The foundations of the cathedral that would be built in his honour had already been laid in the centre of the town.

Inside the spacious castle the new arrivals were lodged in the wing given over to the Sword Brothers, for though Riga was the possession of the Bishop of Riga it was also the headquarters of the bishop's military order. Thus the brothers had their own stables, armoury, offices and quarters in the castle, though their numbers were dwarfed by the size of the town garrison. However, when it came to quality the Sword Brothers were far superior.

Conrad and his companions were shown to a first-floor dormitory in the castle's north wing, while the civilians and their families were quartered beneath them on the ground floor. The mercenaries were lodged in one of the towers. The arrangement was not particularly satisfactory but they would only be staying in Riga for two days at most before leaving for Wenden.

Rudolf left Henke to supervise the youths while he went to see Grand Master Volquin, the head of the Sword Brothers whose office was in the castle's northwest tower. There were only half a dozen brother knights in Riga's castle and a score of sergeants. It was a purely symbolic presence – the Sword Brothers were needed on the Livonian frontier fighting the heathens. Rudolf walked up the steep tower steps to the second floor where two sergeants of his order stood sentry outside the grand master's office. They wore surcoats resembling his own and steel kettle helmets on their heads. The men saluted when Rudolf announced himself and said he wished to see the grand master. One knocked on the door and entered when ordered to do so. Moments later he reappeared and told Rudolf that Grand Master Volquin would see him.

Rudolf closed the door behind him and bowed his head. 'Grand Master.'

Volquin rose from behind his desk and extended his hand. Rudolf took it and Volquin gestured for him to sit in the chair in front of his desk.

'I trust your trip was uneventful.'

Rudolf sat down. 'It was until the Oeselians paid us a visit two days out from Riga.'

Volquin walked over to a small table and poured wine into two silver cups, handing one to Rudolf before he retook his seat.

'Olaf's raiders become ever more troublesome. Did you suffer many losses?'

'None of consequence.'

Volquin placed his cup on his desk and rubbed his thick beard. Some five years older than Rudolf, his fierce stare and black hair and beard made him look much older. He had headed the Sword Brothers for less than a year and the burden of his office was already bearing heavily upon him.

'Unfortunately I have news that is of consequence to our cause. In your absence the Estonians launched a great raid against our northern domains and killed several hundred civilians, together with a hundred local levies, fifteen of our sergeants and two brother knights.'

'The work of Lembit, I assume.'

Volquin nodded. 'Indeed, the scourge of our crusade.'

'He must be dealt with sooner rather than later,' said Rudolf, finishing the most excellent wine he had just been served.

'To which end I have been summoned to the bishop's palace to discuss strategy with the archdeacon tomorrow. I would consider it a favour if you would accompany me. I find his company irksome. That being the case, your calming presence will prevent me saying something that I may later regret.'

Rudolf smiled. 'I might say something that the archdeacon may regret, grand master.'

'He fears an uprising incited by Lembit,' continued Volquin, 'a not entirely unreasonable assumption.'

'The walls of Riga are strong enough,' said Rudolf.

'Though not, perhaps, the faith of our resident archdeacon,' suggested Volquin. 'Now, if you will forgive me, I have letters to write.'

The aim of the Bishop of Riga was to import Christian settlers into Livonia who would eventually outnumber and then supplant the indigenous peoples. Though many of the latter had accepted baptism and been received into the church's embrace, many more remained pagans. Even among the lands controlled by the bishop and the Sword Brothers the newly converted locals could be volatile and untrustworthy. For generations their ancestors had worshipped strange gods and made human sacrifices to appease their deities and though they professed loyalty to the Christian religion, they were apt to waver at the slightest provocation. The news of massacres of Christian priests and settlers had done nothing to encourage the flow of those willing to begin a new life on the Baltic's Christian frontier. Every year a few hundred crusaders came with the bishop from Germany. They stayed for a year, sometimes less, and then returned to their homelands, having dipped their swords in pagan blood. But Livonia needed settlers if it was to survive and prosper.

'Ah, Grand Master Volquin and Brother Rudolf. Please, be seated.'

Archdeacon Stefan held out a hand to the two well-furnished chairs placed in front of his desk and smiled at his two guests. The audience chamber of the bishop's palace was a sumptuous place, its stone windows softened with cushions and fabrics and the walls covered with oak panelling. Behind the archdeacon's desk was a magnificent stone fireplace, above which was a large painting depicting Bishop Albert kneeling on the soil of Livonia and giving thanks to the Lord for his safe arrival. The bishop's palace was located adjacent to the castle and was one of the first stone buildings to have been built in Livonia. It had begun as a modest structure but had been expanded to include a great hall, audience chamber, withdrawing chamber, bedrooms, kitchens, courtyard, stables and storerooms. When the bishop was away his nephew the archdeacon was left in charge.

Archdeacon Stefan was, like his uncle, a member of the Buxhoeveden family, one of the oldest noble families of Europe originally from Saxony. And though he had taken the vows of poverty, chastity and obedience as required by his religious position, he was also very aware of his own and his family's power and influence. Reflecting his position he wore a rich white dalmatic and a gold pectoral cross, with a gold ring on his finger. His eyes darted left and right as he observed Volquin and Rudolf take their seats.

'Some refreshment, perhaps?' he offered, clicking his fingers at a young man, a fresh-faced youth in a white habit standing by a table covered with a linen sheet. He picked up a silver tray holding drinking vessels and brought it over, holding it out to the archdeacon first.

'Thank you, Brother Thomas,' said Stefan, a flash of desire in his eyes.

Brother Thomas then placed silver-gilt wine flagons before Volquin and Rudolf before returning to the table to fetch a jug. He then proceeded to fill the flagons with wine.

'I heard about your unfortunate incident with the Oeselians,' Stefan said to Rudolf, 'but I am glad to see that you are unharmed. You have returned with reinforcements?'

Rudolf nodded. 'Mercenaries and stonemasons, archdeacon, plus a handful of boys.'

Stefan's eyes lit up. 'Boys?'

'Unfortunates and those sent by their families to serve God against the heathens,' answered Rudolf. 'I am hopeful that they will make fine soldiers.'

'We have too few of those, I fear,' remarked Stefan casually. He looked at Volquin. 'To which end, grand master, I have asked you here to ascertain if the Sword Brothers can spare any men to reinforce the garrison of Riga.'

'Impossible,' replied Volquin. 'To strip any garrison of men would be to fatally weaken it.'

'It is as Grand Master Volquin says,' added Rudolf.

Stefan began tracing a finger around the rim of his flagon. 'It is my responsibility to ensure the safety of Riga in the bishop's absence. With the Oeselians ever more troublesome and the Estonians at war with us, to say nothing of the Lithuanians, Riga is threatened on all sides.'

Rudolf raised an eyebrow. 'The Lithuanians?'

Stefan waved a hand at him. 'Just rumours that one of their leaders, Prince Stecse, is raising an army that he intends to bring across the Dvina in order to assault Riga.'

Rudolf looked at Stefan with contempt. The Lithuanians infested the lands south of the River Dvina but mainly kept themselves to themselves. They formed a loose confederation of tribes that were mostly bickering and fighting among themselves, giving the crusaders a free hand to conquer the tribes north of the river. But now river gossip had reached the ears of the archdeacon, who was clearly terrified that Riga would be attacked and his luxurious living disturbed.

'The most pressing threat lies to the north,' said Volquin, like Rudolf unimpressed by rumour. 'Lembit has united all the tribes of Estonia and now seeks nothing less than the conquest of all Livonia to make himself king of all the lands north of the Dvina.'

'To which end, archdeacon,' said Rudolf, sipping his wine, 'it would be more prudent to reinforce Wenden rather than reduce its garrison. I was hoping that I might take some of Riga's soldiers with me when I journey north later today.'

Stefan nearly choked on his drink. 'Take Riga's soldiers? No, no, not at all. That will not do at all. I have barely enough men to defend the town as it is. The great majority of last year's crusaders have returned to Germany. All I have left are the bishop's soldiers and a few mercenaries.'

Volquin sighed. 'Three hundred of the bishop's soldiers in addition to a further two hundred mercenaries that make up the garrison and a hundred remaining crusaders constitutes a more than adequate force, I think.'

Stefan jumped up out of his chair and shook his head with alarm. 'And if a fleet of Oeselian ships sails up the Dvina and the Lithuanians cross the river to attack Riga I will need every one of them. I cannot spare a single man.'

Stefan's eyes narrowed as he looked at Rudolf. 'You said that you have brought stonemasons back with you?'

Rudolf nodded.

Stefan regained his chair. 'Well, then, those combined with the ones already at Wenden will be able to make the castle's walls strong enough to resist a pagan attack.'

'The construction of the castle has been going on for barely two years, archdeacon,' protested Rudolf. 'It will be many more before the work is finished.'

Stefan held up a hand to him. 'The bishop will be here in three months, God willing, and will bring with him a great army of crusaders that he will use to crush Lembit and the rabble that follows him. Of that you can be certain.'

'But if Lembit attacks Wenden before then, archdeacon,' reasoned Rudolf, 'the garrison will be hard-pressed.'

Stefan was uninterested. 'Ill-armed pagans cannot take a Christian fortress, Brother Rudolf. God will not allow it.'

Rudolf was tempted to say that if the archdeacon believed that then there was little need for him to cling to his soldiers at Riga but thought better of it.

Stefan was now in full swing. 'Which brings me neatly to matters of strategy, Grand Master Volquin.' He brought his hands together in front of him. 'The recent, unfortunate reverse at the hands of Lembit was the result of over-ambition and carelessness, of that I have no doubt.'

Volquin's jaw locked in anger but he said nothing.

'So I must ask you, grand master,' continued Stefan, 'to convey to your castellans not to undertake offensive action on their own volition but to remain on the defensive until the bishop arrives with his army. After all, the Sword Brothers are his servants.'

'Are the castellans free to undertake defensive action, archdeacon?' asked Rudolf mischievously.

Stefan was confused. 'Defensive action?'

Rudolf began to enjoy himself. 'Yes. For example, if Wenden is attacked is the garrison free to defend itself or should it wait for the bishop's army before it acts.'

Stefan was not amused. 'I would have thought the answer was obvious. The Lord does not look kindly upon those who treat His work with levity, Brother Rudolf.'

Rudolf restrained himself from laughing. 'No, archdeacon, of course not.'

Stefan frowned at Rudolf before turning his attention to Volquin. 'I would ask you to write to your castellans to remain on the defensive until the bishop arrives, Grand Master Volquin.'

Volquin smiled through gritted teeth. 'I shall despatch letters this very day, archdeacon.'

After the meeting he walked with Rudolf back to the castle. 'Lembit will attack in great strength before the bishop arrives,' he said glumly. He looked at Rudolf. 'And when he does the first blow will fall on Wenden.'

Ever since their establishment the strategy of the Sword Brothers had been to storm the hill forts of the pagans prior to building stone castles on those sites. In this way Christian control of the countryside could be established and expanded. Settlers were then enticed from Germany who cleared the forests to plough their fields and sow their crops while the local garrison of Sword Brothers provided security. As more castles were built more land came under Christian control. That was the theory at least.

'Even though its castle is less than half-built,' replied Rudolf, 'Wenden is strong enough to resist assault. I am more concerned about the loyalty of the Livonians.'

Volquin shrugged. 'They have received baptism and are faithful.'

'As long as we stay strong,' said Rudolf.

'Ever the realist, Rudolf. Please convey my regards to Master Berthold when you arrive back at Wenden.'

'I will grand master. Would that you were in command at Riga instead of the archdeacon.'

'He is the bishop's nephew so I have to tolerate him, much as one would put up with a toothache. But I agree with you concerning the next Estonian attack. It will undoubtedly be against Wenden. Alas I have no forces to send back with you.'

'Then the sooner I get back there the better,' Rudolf replied.

Fortunately for Conrad and his youthful companions they had no knowledge of Estonians or Lithuanians as they helped load the wagons assembled in the castle courtyard with food, tools, weapons and tents prior to their journey to Wenden.

'Where is Wenden?' asked Hans.

68

'I do not know,' replied Conrad as he and his friend finished packing tent poles onto a four-wheeled wagon.

'It is the home of Rudolf and Henke,' said Anton, with Bruno's help heaving a vat of salted meat onto another wagon.

'Hopefully it will be as grand as this castle,' added Johann, struggling with a handful of tent poles.

'As long as its granary and storerooms are well stocked I do not mind where it is or how big it is,' remarked Hans, prompting laughter from the others. Hans had never known a time in his short life when he had had regular meals and he could not have been happier.

They left just after midday, three four-wheeled wagons piled high with supplies, each one pulled by a single horse, and half a dozen smaller two-wheeled carts hauled by mules carrying weapons, armour and crossbow bolts. The wagons, carts and their civilian drivers were in the pay of the Sword Brothers, as were the riverboats that would take Rudolf and his party to Wenden.

The area around Riga was flat and had been cleared of trees so the land could be cultivated. Small settlements of farmers' wooden homes dotted the landscape but as the party trudged north the fields disappeared and were replaced by forests of thick spruce and pine. Everyone walked by the side of the wagons, apart from the children who were allowed to ride next to the drivers, and so the pace was slow. Conrad had never seen so many trees and after a while their towering presence began to unnerve him. Everyone was walking in silence, the only sound being the clanking of cooking utensils hanging from the wagons and the jangling of the harnesses on the mules and horses.

The air was suddenly filled with an unearthly wail coming from the forest and everyone stopped and stared in the direction it had come from. There was another long wail that cut through air, the children began to cry and the mothers ran to their offspring in alarm.

'It is just an elk,' shouted Rudolf, 'nothing to be alarmed about.'

Hans looked at Conrad. 'It sounds like a monster.'

'They are big, boy,' said Henke in front of him, 'but easy enough to kill and they make a tasty meal.'

The women fussed over their nervous children as the elk made another call and the journey re-commenced. Conrad kept glancing at the dark forest on his right. What other monsters were lurking within its forbidding interior?

With the rutted track and the slow pace of the youths, women and stonemasons they made barely ten miles before Rudolf gave the order to halt and make camp in a large meadow sited by an even larger lake filled with crystal-clear, ice-cool water. Rudolf gave instructions that no one was to drink it, as ingesting the standing water would result in diarrhoea, stomach cramps and loss of strength, and there was no room on the wagons to carry sick individuals. The mercenaries erected their own tents but Rudolf and Henke instructed Conrad and the other youths to construct their own shelters and those for the stonemasons and their families. As the shadows lengthened when the spring sun began to dip in the west Conrad and the others learned how to erect central poles, ridge poles, tent canopies, ornamental valances and guy ropes. After they had finished they stood back and admired the half dozen round tents with sloping sides that they had pitched, all sporting a pennant on top bearing the insignia of the Sword Brothers.

Anton pointed to one of the flags hanging limply in the windless late afternoon air. 'That is to indicate whose camp this is,' he said, keen to show off his knowledge of banners and heraldry.

'It is to stop birds roosting on the top of the tent and shitting all over it,' Henke corrected him, causing Anton to blush.

After a day of walking they were beginning to feel tired but Rudolf had another task for Conrad and his companions when he handed them shovels made of oak with iron-reinforced bands on the digging end and mattocks. He then led them a short distance from camp and instructed them to dig latrine trenches. By the time they had finished they were exhausted and it was dusk, the camp illuminated by fires that had been lit. Conrad looked at the black mass of trees that surrounded them on all sides and shuddered. The forest seemed even more foreboding as the light faded and the night began to envelop them. Rudolf organised the rota of sentries to stand guard throughout the night and then said prayers in front of the entire party, everyone kneeling with heads bowed. Afterwards the boys ate a hearty meal of cured meat and bread washed down with ale. Despite his apprehensions Conrad slept more soundly than he had since that dreadful night in Lübeck.

The next morning the camp was dismantled, the tents packed back on the wagons and the journey north continued, everyone walking aside from the children. Despite Hans' attempts to brighten his spirits Conrad remained largely silent, staring down at the dirt track as he trudged along. Had he made the right decision in leaving Lübeck? What future lay in store for him in this strange land of trees and lakes? He had no answer to these questions but comforted himself with knowing that at least

Marie was safe. That was something at least. He pulled his cloak tight around him. Though it was spring the morning had been cool with a heavy dew and the sun was slow to show itself from behind the grey clouds above. But amid the gloom the signs of spring were everywhere: flowers and trees in blossom and the twittering of birds.

After an hour they came to a settlement of wooden huts next to a wide river and Rudolf called a halt. He and Henke went to one of the huts and disappeared inside while a collection of blonde-haired men and women stared at the new arrivals. After a few moments they went back to their labours as Conrad sat on the ground next to Hans, resting against one of the solid wheels of a cart. The women began assisting their children down from the drivers' benches.

'Looks like we will be travelling on the river,' said Hans, grinning. 'No more walking.'

Rudolf and Henke reappeared from the hut accompanied by an old man with white hair and a bushy beard who proceeded to bark orders at a group of sullen-looking men standing near another hut. They slouched off in the direction of the river where Conrad could see the masts of several boats in the water.

'We'll soon have you on your way, sir,' the old man grinned at Rudolf, revealing a mouth largely empty of teeth. 'If you can get the carts to the river we'll load their cargoes first.'

Henke strolled over and pointed at Conrad and his companions. 'Some more labour to prevent your minds from filling with wicked thoughts.'

Five minutes later Conrad and Hans were once again unloading barrels and crates from the wagons onto a rickety wooden quay on the riverbank, to which were moored riverboats. In appearance they were very similar to the ones that had attacked the cogs, Conrad thought, though were smaller and shorter. They were around forty-five feet in length, wide in the middle and pointed at each end. Each one had a mast some thirty feet high to which was attached a furled sail, plus a side-mounted rudder on the starboard side. The hulls were made from overlapping oak planks, which were around twelve feet in width.

The men from the village placed the supplies and stores into the boats and then Rudolf divided his party among the vessels. He assigned two crossbowmen and two spearmen from the mercenaries to each boat and then divided the civilians between the vessels, ensuring that all the families stayed together. Finally he ordered Conrad and Hans to travel in the first boat with him, with Henke keeping charge of Anton, Bruno and Johann in the second boat.

Two hours after arriving at the village the boats were pushed away from the quay with long poles into midstream where their oarsmen heaved at their stations. Each boat had a crew of six rowers – three on each side – plus a captain who stood at the rear holding the rudder. There were no seats or benches in the boat, just crates and chests that the rowers and everyone else sat on. Rudolf sat opposite Conrad and Hans near the prow as the rowers found their stroke and the boat eased its way upstream. There was no wind so there was no point in unfurling the sail. Rudolf was examining his dagger in between glancing at the crew and the passengers to ensure all was well. Conrad leaned forward and whispered to him.

'Rudolf, that is Brother Rudolf, are the men rowing the boat Oeselians?'

Rudolf smiled. 'No, Conrad, though I dare say that their blood is mixed with the sea heathens if you dig deep enough. No, they are Livs.'

Conrad and Hans stared at him with blank looks.

'The people who have lived in these lands since earliest times,' Rudolf continued. 'Pagans whom we have rescued from their unholy ways.'

'What ways?' asked Conrad, casting a glance at the backs of the rowers heaving at their oars.

'Human sacrifice to appease their false gods,' answered Rudolf.

'Barbarians,' said Hans, disgusted.

'What gods?' asked Conrad further.

Rudolf nodded at him. 'You are curious about this land and its people. That is good, for the more you know the better your chances of surviving in this place of great beauty and great savagery. The Livs worship many gods but the chief among them are Mara, the Great Mother, the god who rules over all the others. Then there is Laima, the Goddess of Fate; Saule, the Sky God; and Jumis, God of the Land.

'But now they worship the one true God, the Lord of all the earth and the heavens.' Rudolf winked at them both. 'Or at least they pretend they do.'

Conrad was confused. 'I do not understand.'

Rudolf pointed at the rowers. 'They have been baptised in the river, had their sins washed away and have accepted the love of Christ. But always remember, my young friends, that old ways cannot be erased in a short time. Their fathers, grandfathers and ancestors going back generations worshipped their gods before our holy crusade and old habits die hard.'

'They do not follow God?' asked Conrad.

Rudolf reflected for a moment. 'Some have embraced our religion wholeheartedly and can be counted as loyal. But the majority wait.'

'For what?' asked Hans.

'To see who triumphs. Crusaders or pagans,' answered Rudolf.

Conrad did not really understand but was comforted by the fact that Rudolf was very knowledgeable about this land and its people. His commanding presence was a source of reassurance and Conrad, for the first time since the dreadful events that had brought him to this place, began to relax a little. The motion of the boat as it glided over the smooth surface of the river had a calming effect on him and he began to take an interest in the varied terrain they passed through. Rudolf informed them that this river, the Gauja, and the Dvina were the lifeblood of the crusade in Livonia. Most travel was conducted along these waterways and the Sword Brothers were building stone castles along the length of both rivers to consolidate and expand Christian control over Livonia.

Conrad did not see the two castles they passed during their journey on the Gauja, Rudolf explaining that they were located some two miles inland rather than being on the actual riverbank. Their names were Kremon and Segewold but Rudolf's castle was Wenden, some fifty miles from the village they had departed from. Along the Dvina four castles had been established – Holm, Uexkull, Lennewarden and Kokenhusen – all of them in various states of completion.

'It will take years to finish them,' said Rudolf, 'but the important thing is that with every stone laid our rule in Livonia is strengthened. Stone castles cannot be burned to the ground and nor can they be pulled down. They are the invincible monuments to the power of God.'

'Do not the Livs have castles?' asked Conrad.

'They have hill forts,' answered Rudolf, 'strongholds that have wooden walls and towers. But they have no knowledge of masonry and so their forts can be set on fire and stormed. Not that they fall easily. Much blood is spilt taking them.'

Conrad was fortified by Rudolf's words, thinking that he and his fellow Sword Brothers were more than a match for the local pagans. And they also had God on their side so they were invincible. His boyhood mind had yet to fathom that the world was a complex place that could be cruel and uncertain, but for the moment he felt secure. Rudolf's authority and certainty made him believe that God had brought him to this land for a purpose, though what it was he knew not.

They journeyed on the river for two days, following its course as it meandered through dense forests and lush meadows. They passed white sandstone crags topped by towering pines that looked down on the dark and brooding waters of the river. On occasion they threaded their way through sandbanks and negotiated small rapids of bubbling water. Then the river would widen to reveal steep sides of red sandstone that seemed to take an age to pass through. Conrad observed kestrels hovering above the riverbanks searching for prey and saw fallen trees lying in the water where they had toppled from a great height on the crag above. And stretching into the distance were trees, always trees: huge forests that seemed to have no end. Not only spruce and pine but also mighty oaks, aspen and ash. No wonder the pagans used wood to build their homes and strongholds – there was an endless supply of it.

When they arrived at their destination the boats were run aground on a sandbank at the river's edge and the crews unloaded the supplies and carried them onto the grass of a meadow that extended half a mile from the river. Beyond was the inevitable dark and imposing forest that blanketed most of Livonia. It was now midday and, as there were still eight hours of daylight left the crews opted to take their now empty and lighter vessels back to their poor village. Their enthusiasm rose markedly once the crusaders and German civilians were off their boats and they began to chatter among themselves in a language that Conrad could not understand. They became more excitable when an easterly wind picked up and they unfurled their sails and began their journey home.

Henke stood on the sandbank next to Conrad and Hans and spat after them. 'Heathens.'

'Henke has a low opinion of our newest converts,' grinned Rudolf.

'Thieves and beggars the lot of them,' spat Henke with contempt.

Rudolf put an arm around the shoulder of a sheepish Hans. 'Young Hans here was a beggar, and a thief, and yet you like him, do you not?'

Henke looked at Rudolf and then at Hans and grunted. 'He speaks the same language as me, comes from the same race as me and doesn't want to stick a dagger in my guts. Of course I like him.'

Rudolf asked Henke to walk to Wenden – two miles to the east – to bring back horses and wagons to transport the supplies, and also detailed half a dozen spearmen to go with him. While he was away he gave orders for the boys to serve a meal to the other mercenaries and the civilians. Despite the cool mornings the spring days were warm and long and the air was filled with the sweet aroma of blossom. Everyone was cheerful and some of the children were running around and screaming with delight. Conrad was warming to this land by the minute.

Henke returned two hours later riding a horse that was attired in a caparison: a thickly padded and quilted long cloth robe that covered its body, neck, legs and head. It was white and carried the insignia of the Sword Brothers, as did the other horse that Henke was leading and the ten others carrying sergeants with their distinctive kettle helmets. They all dismounted and walked up to the waiting Rudolf, the sergeants saluting to their senior officer. Behind the horsemen came four-wheeled wagons pulled by horses that looked in far better condition than the ones that had ferried the supplies from Riga.

Once more the children were allowed to ride on the wagons after the crates, chests and barrels had been loaded, Henke and Rudolf riding at the head of the column and Conrad and his companions walking at the rear. The track led from the river, through the forest and then came into a great open space devoid of trees. And directly ahead, sited on the top of a rising piece of ground that resembled a peninsula, was Wenden Castle. The steep slopes on its northern and western sides made an attack from those directions virtually impossible. The eastern and southern sides had less severe slopes but even so the castle was well sited. On the southern side of the stronghold was a perimeter wall comprising horizontally laid wooden logs on top of an earth rampart, with wooden towers at regular intervals. There was also a ditch in front of the rampart.

The column entered this compound via its only entrance, located on the south side. Conrad walked across a wooden bridge over the ditch and through the two open gates. Once inside the compound he saw people – men, women and children – dressed like the civilians who had been in his party, with others in the robes of the native Livs.

'It does not look like a castle,' remarked Hans as they ascended the slope that led to the castle's entrance in its southern wall. Except that there was no wall. There were the foundations of all four walls, the beginnings of three stone towers in the southeast, southwest and northwest corners, and a sizeable number of workers working on these structures, but no walls. There was a timber wall that encompassed empty spaces between the fledgling stonework and a great many pallets stacked with stone, but no stone wall. Conrad and Hans walked across the bridge that spanned the dry moat and entered what would eventually be Wenden Castle.

'It looks as though it has just been started,' remarked Conrad, who was underwhelmed by what he saw. What did impress him was the outlook that the castle's position afforded: uninterrupted views in all directions of the surrounding countryside – forests, clearings and lakes.

As he continued to look around he began to appreciate the extent of the castle's area. On the western side stood a long stable block next to an even longer single-storey dormitory, each of them constructed of wood with thatched roofs. The northern end of the great courtyard area was open aside from the wooden wall and pallets holding stones. The only stone building was a chapel in the northeast corner, a cross mounted on its roof. The hall of the master, dining hall, armoury and smithy filled the rest of the eastern side of the cobbled courtyard. These buildings were also made of wood.

Conrad saw Walter kneeling on the ground, gently elbowed Hans and pointed at the young knight deep in prayer, his eyes closed as he gave thanks for their safe deliverance after their journey. Conrad smiled and shook his head, then felt something sharp and cool against his neck. He froze as Hans' eyes widened as he stared at the man holding the point of a sword against Conrad's neck.

'You think prayer is amusing, boy?' said a deep voice beside him.

Conrad turned his head ever so slightly, the steel point biting into his flesh as he attempted to get a glimpse of his assailant.

'No, sir,' he whispered.

'Otto, leave the boy alone.' Conrad felt relieved when he heard Rudolf's voice and more so when the sword point was removed from his flesh.

He nervously peered to his right to see a tall, thin man with cold, black eyes glaring at him, sword in hand. Conrad's alarm returned when he saw that the man was completely bald, his skull covered in scars, a particularly deep one on his forehead above the right eye. Conrad shuddered. He may have worn the surcoat of the Sword Brothers but he looked like a monster.

Rudolf was tall – at least six foot – but this beast was taller by six or seven inches. The former now stood in front of Conrad and Hans.

'So, what have you two done to earn the displeasure of Brother Otto?'

Hans looked at his feet and Conrad blushed.

'They mock a noble knight for giving thanks to God,' Otto answered for them and then nodded at the praying Walter. 'They should be punished for their levity.'

Rudolf pointed at Otto's drawn sword. 'Unless you are going to chop off their heads I think you should sheath your sword, brother.'

Otto curled his lip at Hans and Conrad, slammed his sword back into its scabbard and stomped away. Conrad breathed a sigh of relief.

'Brother Otto is a fine priest,' said Rudolf, 'though apt to be rash in his actions. He used to be a soldier and sometimes forgets that he is now a man of the cloth. As such he is not allowed to spill Christian blood, or carry a sword for that matter. But he is very forgetful. I would advise caution in your dealings with him.'

Hans was nodding as though he was having a seizure and a pale Conrad was likewise agreeing to Rudolf's suggestion. Rudolf turned but then was stopped by a woman who ran up and threw her arms around him, kissing him on the cheek. Tall like him, she had dark brown eyes, full lips and hair as black as a raven's wing.

'You return is most welcome, lord,' she said, her eyes burning with happiness.

'How is my forest princess?' asked Rudolf, running a finger down her alluring face.

'Filled with joy by your return,' she replied.

Rudolf ignored the boys as he walked away with the mysterious beauty just as a bell began ringing. The mercenaries, Sword Brothers and civilians stood and looked at each other as a stout middle-aged man with a great bushy beard wearing a white surcoat came from the master's hall escorted by four mail-clad Sword Brothers. Walter halted his prayers and rose to his feet. The middle-aged man stepped onto a crate and then the back of a wagon to face the assembly, mothers hushing their children and ushering them to their sides. Conrad saw Rudolf and his black-haired companion with Henke standing nearby and then the fearsome Otto, who glowered at him before looking at the man on the cart. The individual with the thick beard raised his hands as the bell stopped ringing.

'My name is Master Berthold, castellan of this, God's fortress of Wenden,' Conrad looked around at the lack of walls and barely established towers. 'We have been tasked by the Holy Church to bring this wild land under control so that it may bear fruit to feed the word of God and spread His message. The Sword Brothers are the warriors of Christ and defenders of the true religion against heresy, blasphemy and false gods. All of you, soldiers and workers, are engaged upon holy work. So fight and work well and your place in Heaven will be assured, for God is at this moment looking into your souls to discover if you are worthy of the task He has set you.'

The mercenaries stared dead-eyed at this bearded figure while the civilian workers appeared to have been impressed by his words. Walter wore an expression of saintly determination. He had at last found his true home. Conrad and the other youths glanced at each other, unsure what to do, until Henke came over and told them to start unloading the wagons as the mercenaries and civilians were shown to their accommodation. This was sited to the south of the castle, down the slope

77

beyond the moat in the area encompassed by the wooden outer perimeter wall and earth rampart. The civilian workers and their families were located in the eastern part of the compound, the mercenaries in the west, all lodged in simple logs huts with thatched roofs. Despite their rudimentary nature the huts were remarkably snug. Constructed from logs laid horizontally and fastened together with notched ends, they were small, one-room dwellings with a stout roof, one entrance and no windows. A centrally placed fire was used for cooking and provided warmth, the spaces between the logs being packed with moss for insulation. And as the population of Wenden increased so did the number of cabins.

With the arrival of Rudolf and Henke the number of brother knights of the Sword Brothers once more equalled twelve. This number was considered especially auspicious as it equated to the number of disciples that Christ had gathered around him. These holy knights were the most highly trained soldiers in Livonia and were equipped with the best armour and weapons that money could buy. In battle they rode stallions brought from Germany, horses selected for their weight, power and ability to carry a knight on their broad, flat backs. These and the horses used for hauling wagons were stabled inside the castle, as were the mules. Below the brother knights were the sergeants, soldiers who wore kettle helmets and mail coats without sleeves and gloves, over which they wore leather gambesons bearing the insignia of the Sword Brothers. Their clothing may have been inferior to the brother knights but the swords they wore at their hips were of the same standard. Otto the priest was also attached to the garrison but in theory was not trained to fight. There were now fifty mercenaries at Wenden divided equally between spearmen and crossbowmen, plus the civilian workers and their families. These included cooks, clerks, stonemasons, carpenters, blacksmiths and wagon masters – just over sixty individuals in total including their wives and children.

The garrison of Wenden also included four hundred indigenous warriors commanded by a local chief named Thalibald who were raised from the settlements that dotted the area around the castle. These comprised in the main spearmen equipped with shields, no armour and few helmets. As most could use a bow for hunting they could also be used as missile troops but the fact that only a handful of locals were allowed to live within Wenden's settlement indicated that Master Berthold did not trust them, perhaps. They might not have been trusted but all the natives, who now lived on land owned by the Sword Brothers, were taxed to feed Wenden's garrison and its workers, the natives paying their rent in produce that they brought to the castle.

The brother knights and sergeants slept in the dormitory on mattresses stuffed with straw, as did Conrad and his fellow youths who were allotted beds in one corner. Conrad, who had been used to rising at dawn, found the transition to life with the Sword Brothers relatively easy but Hans, who had lived a feckless existence, at first found it difficult to rouse himself in the morning, though the others usually turfed him out of his bed onto the floor. Then, in a semi-daze, he dressed and joined the others for mass in the chapel, after which his spirits were revived by breakfast.

'When and what you can eat are laid down in the rules of the Sword Brothers,' Rudolf informed them on their first morning at Wenden. 'You may eat meat three days a week and fish on Fridays. All your other meals will consist of vegetables, beans, broths, bread and fruit.'

Hans raised a hand. 'Excuse me, sir, but did you say meat?'

'That is correct, Hans,' Rudolf replied, 'but only three times a week.'

Hans began grinning like an idiot at the others. He had hardly ever tasted meat and had grown accustomed to going for days at a time without any food at all. And now he was not only going to be fed regularly but would also dine on meat. Meat! He could have wept with joy.

He had to control his eagerness as the brother knights ate first in the dining hall followed by the sergeants, the boys, who were now designated novices, eating last. But when they did sit down they found ample food to fill their bellies.

'This is easy enough,' remarked Bruno.

'Praying and eating,' added Johann. 'My friends we have fallen upon good fortune.'

And then they met Brother Lukas.

After breakfast Rudolf took them down into the large compound below the castle where mercenaries were shooting their crossbows at targets and spearmen were practising their drills. The day was warm with a slight westerly breeze blowing. They walked to a quiet area where a man of medium height with broad shoulders, thick arms and a powerful neck was standing beside a two-wheeled cart hitched to a mule. Rudolf told the novices to stand in a line and then went over to greet his fellow brother knight.

'This is Brother Lukas,' he told them. 'I will leave you in his capable hands.'

He nodded to Lukas and then took his leave. Conrad looked at Lukas. He looked more like a blacksmith than a knight. Lukas rubbed his neatly trimmed beard.

'My name is Brother Lukas and my task is to teach you how to fight.' His voice was calm but forceful. 'Brother Rudolf has acquainted me with your

79

backgrounds, what he knows of them, and he believes that you can all be turned into soldiers.'

The youths puffed out their chests with pride at this announcement. Lukas scratched the back of his head.

'Though no one is infallible, of course, aside from His Holiness the Pope.'

He walked over to the back of the cart and picked up a bundle of swords, brought them back and handed one to each novice. Conrad grasped the grip of his sword and moved it in the air. He had never held a sword before. It was lighter than he expected and finally balanced. He admired the silver-grey blade and its point and imagined what destruction he could wreak with such a weapon.

Lukas drew his own sword and held it at arm's length before him.

'The sword will be your principal weapon. You will learn to use it to kill an opponent quickly and mercilessly. Pay attention because in a fight if you do something wrong you die. Now give me those swords back, they are far too valuable to be used as training tools for novices.'

He collected the blades and placed them back in the cart and brought back wooden swords, giving one to each boy and keeping one for himself.

'They are called "wasters",' he informed them.

Conrad looked at his replica sword. It had a blade shaped like a real sword plus a grip, pommel and guard.

'These will be your close companions for the next few months. During that time you will learn to use them with knowledge, dexterity and cunning.'

He stepped forward to face Bruno, pointing at his wooden sword. 'Attack me.'

Bruno glanced at Johann standing to his left. 'Now!' bellowed Lukas.

Bruno, startled, swung his sword clumsily at Lukas who blocked the blow with his own waster.

'Wasters are able to withstand use and abuse while leaving the expensive steel weapons for real combat.'

Lukas then stood before Johann and told him to attack him. Johann, thinking to catch Lukas off-guard, thrust his waster forward at Lukas' chest, but the knight deftly moved aside and then struck Johann hard on the top of his right arm with the flat of his waster, causing the youth to drop his own weapon.

'Wasters have all the attributes of a real sword: flat blade, guard, grip and pommel. They are not clubs.'

Johann rubbed his arm and Lukas told him to pick up his weapon before moving to stand before Anton, instructing the youth to strike him with his sword. Anton brought his sword up and shouted as he attempted to bring it down on Lukas' head. But the knight brushed the blow aside with his own waster before flicking his wrist to bring the edge of his wooden sword against Johann's neck.

'With a waster when you make contact the target will not be injured or unduly hurt.'

Conrad was decidedly nervous when Lukas stepped in front of him, expecting to be likewise struck by the knight's wooden sword. But instead he was asked a question.

'Three men stand before you: a rich man, a poor man and a swordsman. Which of them is the wealthiest?'

'The rich man, sir,' answered Conrad.

Lukas stepped back to address them all. 'The rich man has money, it is true, but he has no wealth because he has no strength or skill. The poor man has strength of body but no money or skill. But the swordsman has skill and strength and is thus the wealthiest of all for he can use his sword and preserve his life, the most valuable gift known to man.'

And so their training began. Using their wasters they trained for hours each day under the watchful eye of Lukas. They learned how to use their swords to kill opponents quickly, to sidestep, duck, dodge and feint to avoid an enemy's sword, and to deflect an opponent's sword blow instead of blocking it. Above all they were instructed to keep moving.

'If you remain stationary the enemy can harm you,' Lukas told them, striking anyone who stopped moving.

They returned to the dormitory with aching limbs and bruised bodies and every night slept like the dead. They consumed their generous meals like ravenous wolves and always seemed to be hungry. They attended prayers and then went back to their training, all the time the eagle-eyed Lukas picking up their failings and pointing out mistakes with a sharp, painful blow with his waster.

'Keep moving!' he shouted as the rain lashed them and their clothing became drenched.

Conrad was fighting Rudolf, who parried his every strike with consummate ease. He held his waster in his right hand and let his left hand hang by his side. He was tired, wet and cold. He flinched as a sharp pain went through his left wrist. He spun round to see Lukas behind him.

'How many times have I told you: keep your free hand behind your back. If your free hand is not holding a shield or a weapon it is just another target.'

Lukas hit Conrad again, this time on the back of the thigh with the flat of his waster's blade.

'Keep moving.'

The days turned into weeks and the training was unrelenting. Everything and everyone else became a blur as sword fighting filled the minds of Conrad and his fellow novices. Their first thoughts were about fighting, they spent their days fighting and their dreams were filled with swords and fighting. The days became longer and warmer as spring gave way to summer and still there was no let-up in their training.

At the end of one particularly gruelling day, as they lay in their beds having spent the whole afternoon in duels with brother knights, in which Conrad had received waster blows to every part of his body, he just wanted to close his eyes and forget the pain caressing his body.

'I don't understand,' said Hans beside him, propped up on one elbow.

'Go to sleep,' pleaded Conrad as his eyelids closed.

'Why are we exercising so hard?'

'So we can defend ourselves,' said Conrad, drifting off to sleep.

'Defend ourselves from what?' queried Hans, 'where are these enemy pagans we have heard so much about?'

There was no answer. Conrad and the others had taken refuge in blessed sleep, which would seemingly last an instant before they were called once more to the chapel at dawn.

*****

The warriors were waiting on the bank as the riverboat eased onto the sandbank and two soldiers jumped from the vessel. The warriors, mostly spearmen carrying round wooden shields and armed with spears and axes, stood motionless as Prince Vsevolod was assisted from the boat by two of his soldiers and walked towards them.

The prince's men were more heavily armoured than the hundred or so motionless warriors, being attired in hemispherical iron helmets, mail neck protectors termed *barmitsa*, *kuyaks* – leather vests with overlapping steel plates on the outside – and almond-shaped shields painted blue and bearing red Byzantine crosses. More of the prince's men clustered around him as they got out of the boat, and were reinforced by a score more as another boat ran up on the sandbank and disgorged its occupants. But they were still greatly outnumbered.

There was movement among the warriors facing the prince and his soldiers and a stocky man pushed aside two men in the front rank and marched up to the prince. Their appearances could hardly have been more different. The prince was dressed in a long crimson tunic with narrow wrist-length sleeves and a high-cut neckline, over which was a white *dalmatica* that was shorter than the tunic but which had wide, straight sleeves and was belted at the waist. A rich purple cloak lined with fox fur was clasped on his right shoulder. His embroidered green boots completed his opulent appearance.

The only thing he had in common with the man he faced was that they both sported thick beards, though his was much darker. The fair-haired man wore a simple knee-length green tunic edged with red, brown leggings and boots and a functional brown leather belt around his waist. Only two things indicated that he was a man of standing: his sword in its richly decorated scabbard and his gold, jewel-encrusted belt buckle. He took off his helmet and passed it to one of his men and then stepped forward to embrace the prince.

'Welcome, son.'

His warriors began cheering and banging their spear shafts on the insides of their shields as the prince embraced his father-in-law and then stepped back.

'Hail, Grand Duke Daugerutis, Lithuania's greatest warlord.'

More cheering erupted as the duke's men chanted his name and he led the prince away with his arm around the younger man's shoulders. They walked to where Daugerutis' bodyguard waited on their horses, the grand duke and the prince mounting horses that were being held for them and then trotting down the dirt track with their escort following. They rode for some miles before they came to the duke's stronghold, a great wooden hill fort with an outer wall containing ten towers and an inner stronghold containing a hall, barracks, storerooms and four towers in each corner, flags displaying the bear symbol of the grand duke fluttering from the top of every one.

The visit of Prince Vsevolod occasioned the gathering of all the princes, chiefs and village elders in the grand duke's considerable domain. Lithuania was a tribal land of dense forests, lakes and rivers controlled by a small number of dukes, under which were a greater number of princes who swore allegiance to their duke. At least that was the theory. Weak dukes held little sway over their princes and were often deposed and killed when an upstart prince decided that he should be duke.

Those dukes who were feared and respected had the absolute loyalty of their princes. And the most feared of all was Grand Duke Daugerutis.

His loyal lieutenants gathered in his hall to welcome his gaudily dressed son-in-law who was married to his only daughter. The hall stank of their sweat as Vsevolod took his place on the top table on the right hand of Daugerutis, his bearded, raucous son on his other side. Most of the men sitting on benches at tables were already drunk as women ferried great serving jugs from the kitchens to satisfy their seemingly unquenchable thirst. They swore oaths, just swore, slapped each other on the back and banged their fists on the table as the Prince of Gerzika viewed them with distaste. He had always believed that civilisation ended and barbarity began at the Dvina and every visit to his father-in-law reinforced his belief. That the Lithuanians were strong and free only increased his resentment and jealousy.

Daugerutis rose and spread his arms, calling for silence. The din in the hall died away as every pair of eyes turned to him. He picked up his cup and raised it to the assembly.

'To your health, brothers.' He then drank from his cup and handed it to Vsevolod. Drinks were always passed to the right in imitation of the spring seeding, when the grain was always sprinkled on the right side. In this way the gods would look favourably upon the gathering.

Vsevolod took the cup, rose, toasted the gathered lords and then drank from the cup. There was loud cheering and thumping of tables and then everyone drained their own cups and called for more drink.

The grand duke said nothing to his son-in-law as slaves brought a platter holding a loaf of black rye bread to the top table but he knew why he was here. It had been a year since the Christian Bishop Albert and his army of crusaders had stormed the city of Gerzika, the formerly impregnable fortress on the banks of the Dvina, and captured the wife and daughters of Prince Vsevolod, the prince having escaped, some say fled, from the crusaders and their siege engines. The price he paid to get his family and city back was to swear fealty to the bishop and become his servant. And ever since that time he had pestered the grand duke to lead a great army over the Dvina to destroy the bishop's army.

The slave laid the platter holding the bread before the grand duke and once again the hall fell silent. The cutting of bread held deep significance among the Lithuanians and the drunken men with their beer-soaked beards watched intently as the grand duke took his knife and cut a slice off the black loaf. Vsevolod looked on with barely concealed contempt as he witnessed at first hand this absurd pagan ritual.

The grand duke gave the slice to his married son with wishes that his firstborn would be a son. The duke ensured that the cut end of the loaf was not pointing towards the hall's entrance, for it was widely believed that if it did the aforementioned first son would be born mad. Satisfied that the loaf had been cut correctly the elders and princes went back to their drinking.

Slaves brought cooked meat from the kitchens, mostly huge steaks and ribs of wild boar that had been hunted and killed in the days before the feast. They also brought cauldrons filled with *juka* – blood soup – and ladled it into large wooden bowls. Vsevolod may have believed that the Lithuanians were backward pagans but they knew how to feed their guests. He loved the surprisingly edible black bread and the *juka* containing boar blood, rye flour, bay leaves, salt and mint, dipping the bread in the soup and shoving it greedily into his mouth. And Lithuanian beer was far better than the Russian equivalent.

The morning after the feast, as bleary eyed elders and princes wandered around the hill fort, occasionally supporting themselves against a wall to throw up the contents of their guts, the grand duke requested the presence of Vsevolod in his hall. The latter had also drunk too much the day before and was feeling delicate as guards opened the doors of the hall and he stepped inside. He almost threw up as the foul stench of sweat, vomit and the rancid odour of yesterday's cooking assaulted his nostrils. The grand duke gestured for him to retake his seat at the top table. Slave girls fussed around cleaning up the mess left by the feast, their eyes cast down in deference to their masters.

'Keep the doors open,' Daugerutis shouted at the guards. 'Let some air in.'

Vsevolod smiled weakly at him as he flopped down into his chair and the grand duke ordered a slave to serve his guest some water.

'Or would you prefer beer?' he asked.

A wave of nausea came over Vsevolod again as he waved a hand at the grand duke and nodded to the slave girl holding the jug to pour him some water. He gratefully took a swig and caught sight of a man standing near the end of the top table. Tall, handsome in a rustic way, he had blonde hair and beard, broad shoulders and carried a long sword in a red scabbard on his left hip. One of the grand duke's bodyguard, Vsevolod assumed. The grand duke waved him over. Daugerutis' son was nowhere to be seen. Laid low by a hangover, no doubt.

'You said in your letter that you see an opportunity to attack the bishop's lands, my son,' he said to Vsevolod.

'It is true, lord,' answered Vsevolod, 'if your warriors cross the Dvina at Kokenhusen they will reap a rich harvest.'

Kokenhusen, positioned on the north bank of the river some fifty miles west of Gerzika, was formerly the stronghold of Prince Vetseke, a Liv who had fought the Bishop of Riga and lost. Now he was in exile and his stronghold was in crusader hands.

'The crusaders are building a stone fortress at Kokenhusen,' said the grand duke, 'and we have no engines that can be used to batter down its walls.'

'Those walls are as yet unfinished,' replied Vsevolod, who was curious as to why this blonde-haired warrior was standing before them. 'And the garrison of Kokenhusen is but small. A large force of warriors could take it with ease.'

'You forget,' said the grand duke, 'that soon the bishop will return with an army of crusaders. It has been the same every summer for these past few years. When he does reinforcements can be sent downriver to Kokenhusen easily enough.'

Vsevolod finished his water and smiled. 'The crusaders cannot be in two places at the same time, lord. My spies inform me that the Estonians are about to launch a great war to the north that will absorb the crusaders' attention. The tiny garrison of Kokenhusen is on its own.'

'Your spies are reliable?' asked the grand duke.

Vsevolod smiled maliciously. 'I have paid them well enough and they have many contacts among the Livs who strain under the bishop's rule. When the Estonians attack there are many Livs who will rise up to throw off the crusader yoke. Assailed from the north and from within, the crusader strength will be shattered. It will be the perfect time to strike.'

The grand duke leaned back in his chair as the female slaves began brushing the floor. If what his son-in-law said was true then an attack against Kokenhusen was worth considering. The crusaders were erecting four stone castles along the Dvina – Holm, Uexkull, Lennewarden and Kokenhusen – and he knew it would be only a matter of time before their eyes turned south once they had conquered the people living to the north of the river. He also knew that every year more and more crusaders remained in Livonia to consolidate the bishop's rule. Riga was once a collection of huts but would soon be a great city. He knew that inaction was no longer an option.

He pointed at the blonde warrior standing before him. 'This is Prince Stecse,' he said to his son-in-law, 'one of my best warlords. A man most accomplished at mounting raids against the enemy.'

86

Stecse bowed his head to Daugerutis. 'You flatter me, lord.'

The grand duke waved away his deference. 'Stecse will go back to Gerzika with you, my son, so you both may plan an attack against Kokenhusen.'

Vsevolod smiled at Stecse. 'You are most generous, lord. The loss of one of their castles will be a grievous blow to the crusaders and will give heart to their many enemies. With the crusaders fully occupied in the north there is a possibility that all their strongholds along the Dvina might fall into our hands.'

The grand duke chuckled. 'There is an old saying among my people, my son – easy to say, but not to do. One castle at a time.'

'Before the crusaders came my city was part of the mighty Principality of Polotsk, a kingdom that existed peacefully among its neighbours.'

Daugerutis remembered differently but remained silent.

'Once the crusaders have been evicted from Livonia Lithuanian and Russian will rule all the lands from here to the Baltic,' Vsevolod boasted.

The duke's son-in-law returned to Gerzika the next day, taking Prince Stecse with him so they could plan an attack against Kokenhusen.

Chapter 4

Conrad lay on the ground looking up at the cloudless blue sky, the wind knocked out of him as the others laughed. He had ended up flat on his back courtesy of Lukas during a lesson concerning the correct use of the shield. The brother knight extended his right arm and hauled Conrad to his feet and turned to the others.

'A shield is not just a wall against which an enemy can batter his weapons against. It is a weapon in its own right and can be used to strike, push, pin and trap an opponent.'

Conrad picked up his waster and held it in his right hand, his shield positioned to protect his sword arm but not impede it, just as he had been shown. Lukas turned back to face Conrad and indicated for the youth to attack him again. His shield of wood covered in leather was surprisingly light and was comfortable to wield, his left forearm secured by two leather straps with buckles. He gripped a third, unbuckled, strap with his hand, his forearm resting against a padded leather squab that was attached to the inside of the shield to prevent chafing. Lukas held his own shield in front of him.

'A fighter uses a shield aggressively, holding it forward, ready to move it in any direction.'

Conrad and the others had been training non-stop for nearly four months now and their bodies had grown accustomed to the daily physical exertions. Their generous diets had made them stronger so that their wasters had seemingly become lighter as the time passed. They thus wielded them more freely and with much more aplomb. They had also learned the hard way to keep moving at all times during practice. Conrad and Lukas moved around each other like a pair of wolves involved in a mating ritual. Lukas only had a shield; his sword remained in its scabbard. Conrad jabbed his shield forward at Lukas to draw the knight's attention, then aimed a sword thrust at the older man before sweeping his waster down to strike at Lukas' extended left leg. It was a bold move and against an average opponent it might have worked, but Lukas was not only a knight but also a student of the fighting arts and had noticed that Conrad's initial thrust did not have a lot of force behind it and was therefore a feint. As Conrad's waster swept down to strike Lukas' leg the brother moved back and stepped to his left to avoid the blow. He then barged his shield against Conrad's exposed right arm, knocking him to the ground once more.

'Always look to block or avoid an enemy's strike in such a way as to create an opening for a strike,' he said as the others burst into laughter once more.

Despite being fed like a fighting cock Hans' body refused to gain weight despite his efforts to devour more food than the others combined. He still looked perilously thin though no longer gaunt and Conrad noticed that his friend's strength and stamina were increasing as the days turned into weeks. Of all of them Hans seemed the happiest and most content and though Conrad was settling into his new life with relative ease, in the quiet moments – at night and during mealtimes when all talking was forbidden – his mind went back to those terrible few days in Lübeck that had changed his life forever. At first he viewed the daily services in the chapel irksome but after a while found them comforting. He always prayed for his dead parents and for his sister and believed that the more he asked God to keep watch over her the safer she would be.

The arrival of summer brought with it not only an increase in temperature but also saw the land come to life as flowers and plants bloomed and the forests carpeted the land in a rich green. White wagtails flew overhead. The castle compound was filled with daises. Outside the compound the meadows were filled with edible mushrooms, wild strawberries, wild raspberries, cloudberries, blueberries, cornflower and flax plants. Though the boys sweated under the summer sun as they practised their weapon skills, the nights could still be cool and they required their cloaks. It was also surprisingly rainy, dark clouds suddenly appearing overhead and bursting to drench the land, though rainy afternoons at least meant warm evenings.

The mercenaries and brother knights undertook regular hunting expeditions into the surrounding forests, returning with slain wild boar, elk and roebuck. The beavers that lived in the Gauja were also hunted and killed, Conrad and his companions especially looking forward to when their carcasses were taken to the kitchens to be skinned, as their meat was delicious. The Gauja itself was teeming with life and daily fishing parties were despatched to bring back lamprey, perch, grayling, pike, bream, roach, dace, chub and burbot. Mealtimes were so bountiful at this time that Hans thought he had died and gone to heaven.

The boys were forbidden to go outside the compound and in truth they had no time even if they had permission to do so. In addition to their incessant weapons training they were introduced to the other duties of garrison life, including keeping watch. As the weeks passed they had barely noticed the castle taking shape around them. They had seen the stonemasons going about their work, of course, but had not been aware that Wenden was starting to show signs of becoming a Christian stronghold. Master Berthold had decided that the northwest tower should receive the lion's share of the stonemasons' attention so it would be completed first. In this way, should the worst happen, the garrison would have a place of refuge if the walls of the compound were breached. The circular tower was as yet only twenty feet in height but it still offered excellent uninterrupted views of the countryside for miles around.

Conrad stood on the top of the scaffolding that encased the fledgling tower and pulled his cloak around his shoulders. It might be the longest day of the year but it was still cool. He had started sentry duty this week and had been allocated the night watch. He was not the only one standing guard, the wooden perimeter wall around the compound being guarded by sergeants and mercenaries and the castle itself watched over by sergeants and brother knights. One of the latter accompanied the novices at all times during their guard duties, not least to impress upon them the importance of not falling asleep. Conrad was delighted to discover that his guardian was Rudolf.

'A sentry is the most important man in a garrison,' Rudolf told him, 'for he keeps watch while the others sleep. That is why the penalties for abandoning one's post and falling asleep on duty are so severe. The carelessness of one man can cost the lives of hundreds.'

Conrad looked alarmed and tightened the grip on his spear. Rudolf slapped him on the arm. 'Not that there is any chance of you falling asleep. Lukas tells me that your weapons training is coming along well.'

Conrad was delighted that Rudolf was taking an interest in him. 'I am anxious to receive my own sword, sir. We all are.'

Rudolf nodded. 'I have no doubt but you will have to wait a while longer, I think. A sword is a soldier's most precious item and should stay with him until the day he dies, thereafter to be buried with him or passed on to someone worthy. When the time comes Lukas will present you and the others with your swords.'

'And then we will fight the pagans?' asked Conrad.

'Most likely, as there seems to be an inexhaustible supply of them. Or perhaps they will all accept baptism and become willing members of Bishop Albert's flock.'

The light was fading now as the sun disappeared on the western horizon and darkness crept over the land. Conrad peered to the north and saw the glow of fires in the distance. Turning, he saw that there appeared to be fires in every direction around the castle. He looked at Rudolf apprehensively.

'Do not alarm yourself,' he said to Conrad. 'It is called *ligo*, a ceremony that the natives hold every mid-summer on the longest day of the year. They gather in clearings and meadows, start a fire and then stay up all night, drinking and waiting for the sun to rise the next morning. The women pick flowers to make crowns to wear upon their heads and the men jump naked into rivers and lakes.'

Conrad was confused. 'Why?'

'Why? To ask their gods to make the crops grow and provide for their families during the winter. The farmers have ploughed their fields, sown their crops and now they wait for the harvest. They believe that by participating in the *ligo* their gods will make the crops grow.'

Conrad stared at the myriad of yellow and orange glows around the castle and was frightened. 'The local people who live around Wenden are pagans?'

Rudolf considered for a moment before answering. 'The people who live in the villages around the castle have all been baptised. So in theory they are Christians. But the church has a tenuous hold over this land, Conrad, and cannot easily dispel hundreds of years of myths and rituals, much as it would like to do. It can only prove that it is stronger than the gods that these people worship.'

'How can it do that?' asked Conrad.

Rudolf looked north. 'By crushing those pagans still in arms against it.'

******

Lembit gazed at the embers of the great bonfire that had been burning all night and which was only now entering its death throes. Most of the dozens of people who had gathered round it the night before were now asleep on the ground, having drunk themselves into unconsciousness. He had noticed a few young couples sneak off into the woods to make love, believing that a child conceived during *ligo* would be blessed by the gods, especially Uku, the supreme god. As he sat on the ground with his knees drawn up to his chest and his cloak wrapped around him he wondered if the gods cared about the people who worshipped them. After all, why did they allow the 'Iron Men', the crusaders on their big horses, to desecrate the soil of Estonia?

But then, he had done what no one else had achieved before: he had defeated a party of crusaders encased in their armour sitting on their mighty warhorses. Admittedly there had been only half a dozen of them accompanied by a score of spearmen, and they had been ambushed rather than defeated in battle. Still, a victory was a victory and his had galvanised the whole of Estonia so rare had it been. The tribes of his people had watched the defeat of the Livs and Letts in the south, and although they had no great affinity with these people their demise had been an ill portent for his own kind. He had tried to convince the elders of his own tribe, the Saccalians, that they should not wait for the crusaders to invade their own lands before taking up arms against the foreigners, for to do so would be to invite disaster. He had advised an invasion of their land that they called Livonia but they had been against it. So he took the men of his own stronghold of Lehola and marched south with them. As luck would have it, or perhaps it was the hand of the gods, word reached him of a party of crusaders advancing into Saccalia and he laid his trap. After he had butchered the men in mail the fame of his name spread throughout Estonia like a forest fire fanned by the wind. The elders of his tribe accorded him the title 'Grand Warlord' and the other tribes – the Harrien, Wierlanders, Rotalians, Jerwen and Ungannians – promised him allegiance and men for his war against the crusaders. Such was the magnitude of his victory. He peered at the crackling embers of the fire. Perhaps the gods were assisting him after all.

He heard footsteps behind him and turned his head to see the hulking figure of Rusticus coming towards him. His second-in-command was obviously the worse for wear, having no doubt spent all the preceding hours drinking. Lembit never ceased to be amazed by how much beer his deputy could accommodate, but now even his iron constitution seemed to have taken a battering by the way he trudged towards him with his over-sized head cast down.

Lembit hauled himself to his feet and stretched out his arms. 'I see you have indulged in the *ligo* willingly, Rusticus.'

His deputy grunted a reply under his breath and lifted his head. His eyes were red and puffy and his great beard streaked with what looked like vomit.

'You look disgusting,' Lembit said to him.

'Too much beer,' complained Rusticus.

'Come,' said Lembit, 'time for morning inspection.'

Rusticus looked as though he was going to be sick again. 'What? After *ligo*? All the boys will be asleep. Either that or making babies for next spring.' His ugly face broke into a leer but Lembit was far from amused, pacing away towards the imposing fort atop the great earth mound behind them. He kicked a man who was lying face-down on the grass, then another who was lying on his side with an empty cup beside him.

'Get up.'

Rusticus struggled to keep up with his commander as the latter frowned and shook his head at the open gates of the fort and the lack of guards on the battlement above them.

'Have you ever thought, Rusticus, what would happen if an enemy attacked us during the mid-summer festival.'

Rusticus coughed and spat the foul-tasting phlegm from his mouth. 'Attack? During *ligo*? No one would dare.'

Lembit stopped and faced him. 'Oh? And why is that?'

Rusticus was unsure why because the question was absurd. Everyone was always drunk or making babies during *ligo*. 'Because the gods would be angered and no one would dare anger them.'

'None of our people, certainly,' said Lembit, 'but what of the crusaders? They do not worship our gods. There is nothing to stop them launching an attack during the festival.'

Rusticus belched, the foul odour making Lembit recoil. 'With you and the gods on our side we have nothing to fear from them.'

Lembit looked at his deputy. For raw courage and brute strength there were few men like Rusticus in all Estonia, but he had the brains of a bull and a not very bright one at that. But then perhaps it was better to have a blindly loyal subordinate rather than a scheming and cunning one.

'Come on,' Lembit said to him, 'let us rouse everyone from his or her happy slumbers.'

It took two hours before any semblance of normality had returned to the fort. In that time warriors woke up with burning headaches and had stumbled around as though their wits had deserted them, vomiting in every corner and filling the stronghold with a disgusting aroma, the more so when others voided their bowels into their leggings. Lembit ordered them all to immerse themselves in the nearby lake and burn their soiled clothing before allowing them to return, the slaves being detailed to clean the fort and its compound while it was empty. He then held an inspection of the garrison in the courtyard. The hundred warriors armed with spears, swords and carrying shields bearing Lembit's wolf symbol were made to stand for an hour before they were dismissed. Each of them was informed that they were to drink no alcohol for the next seven days.

'And that includes you, Rusticus,' the chief said as he passed his deputy to go back into his reeking main hall after the inspection.

Lehola, like other great Estonian forts, was sited on a hill and was a very solid stockade with high walls. It was constructed using massive tree trunks buried deep in the ground as vertical supports, around which a framework of interlocking horizontal timbers was laid. Square towers were sited at regular intervals along the walls, each one having a protective roof of shingles. And from every one flew a wolf banner. How he would like to fly his banner from the walls of the crusader capital at Riga. Lembit was determined that his people would not suffer the same fate as the Livs.

'There's a man outside who wants to see you,' said Rusticus as Lembit was sitting in his chair pondering the coming weeks, the slaves having at last exorcised some of the pungent smells from the hall.

'Send him away,' replied Lembit, 'I am not receiving visitors today.'

'You might want to see this one.'

Lembit sighed and looked at his deputy, who appeared to have regained some of his colour after having immersed himself in the lake.

'Why? Is it a messenger with news that the crusaders have boarded their ships and departed, never to come back?'

Rusticus looked confused. 'No. It is Sigurd, one of Olaf's sons.'

For a few seconds the significance of what the big oaf had announced did not sink in, but then Lembit jumped to his feet.

'Sigurd? Of the Oeselians?'

Rusticus nodded.

'What does he want?'

'To speak to you,' answered Rusticus.

Lembit jabbed a finger in his deputy's broad chest. 'Send out patrols to scour the countryside to ensure there are no Oeselian war parties in the vicinity. Get every man of the garrison to his post.'

Rusticus nodded and turned to go but then stopped.

'What about Olaf's son?'

Lembit sat back down in his chair. 'Send him in.'

Rusticus strode towards the door.

'And shut the gates,' Lembit called after him.

He called over the head of the hall, a wiry man in his sixties, and ordered him to bring beer for him and his guest. The man bowed and then scuttled away. Moments later four wolf shields escorted the son of Olaf into the hall, each of them clad in mail shirts and wearing helmets. They were heavily armed with short spears, swords and daggers, the man they flanked having had his weapons taken from him before entering the hall. He would also have been searched to ensure he carried no hidden weapons. When the party halted a few paces from Lembit two of the guards walked forward to stand either side of their chief, leaving the other two to guard the son of Olaf. The latter was a tall, slim man in his twenties, blonde haired with a round, clean-shaven face, which was unusual for an Oeselian. He bowed his head at Lembit.

'Greetings Lembit, Grand Warlord of the Saccalian people. My name is Sigurd, second son of Olaf, King of the Oeselians.'

The head of the hall returned with a female slave carrying a tray holding two wooden cups of beer. Lembit waved her forward to offer one to Sigurd. He took it and then she proffered the tray to Lembit, who took the remaining cup. Without taking his eyes off Olaf's son he lifted the cup to his mouth and took a sip of beer, Sigurd toasting his host before also tasting the liquid.

'My father sends his greetings to you also,' said Sigurd, not knowing quite what to make of the Estonian leader sitting before him.

Lembit smiled wryly. 'That would be the same King Olaf who has spent most of his reign raiding the shores of Estonia, killing, burning and taking away women and children to be his slaves.'

Sigurd looked decidedly uneasy as he took another sip of beer, the unblinking eyes of Lembit upon him, while from behind the great figure of Rusticus entered the hall and sauntered over to stand behind Lembit. With a hand on the hilt of his large sword, he curled his lip at the young man squirming before him.

'What you say is true, lord,' replied Sigurd. 'The Oeselians and Estonians have always fought each other. It is the way of things. But now my father seeks to put aside our enmity so that we may forge an alliance.'

Rusticus laughed derisively but Lembit said nothing as he studied the young man before him.

'Why should I listen to you?' he said at length. 'You state correctly that Estonians and Oeselians have always fought each other. Why should I not kill you now without a second thought?'

'If you did then my father would still have three sons and many longships with which to carry on the war between our two peoples that seemingly has no end. But while we slaughter each other a greater enemy threatens the very existence of our two peoples.'

'What enemy?' asked Lembit, already knowing the answer.

Sigurd kept his eyes fixed on Lembit and ignored the brute standing behind him. 'The crusaders. How long will it be before they are standing outside the walls of this very hall or landing their ships on my father's island?'

'The crusaders may take your island and butcher its inhabitants,' sneered Rusticus, 'but they will never take this fort. Are you so ignorant that you have not heard of Grand Warlord Lembit's great victory over the crusaders? They shit their leggings at the mere mention of his name.'

Lembit held up a hand to silence his deputy and continued to observe Sigurd, who turned up the corner of his mouth at the outburst of Rusticus.

'We have all heard of Lord Lembit's victory and the inspiration it gives to all those fighting the crusaders. But the truth is that every year more and more of them land at Riga and soon more ships will bring this year's crusader army to once more wage war against your people.'

'More victims for our swords and spears,' boasted Rusticus.

'I am sure that is what the Livs believed when the crusaders invaded their lands,' replied Sigurd sarcastically.

Rusticus stepped forward menacingly. 'I will send your head back to your father.'

'Enough!' snapped Lembit, stopping Rusticus in his tracks and pointing behind him to indicate that his deputy should take up his original position. He then stood up.

'Prince Sigurd, you have come here with a bold offer and one that deserves consideration. On the matter of an alliance with your father I will give you my answer after I have had time to deliberate. Before then please avail yourself of my hospitality.'

He waved forward the head of the hall. 'Show the prince to his quarters.'

His servant bowed and then held out a hand to Sigurd, who bowed to Lembit and then followed the old man out of the hall, the guards once more flanking the Oeselian. The doors were closed behind them.

'Do you want me to kill him?' asked Rusticus enthusiastically.

Lembit sat back down and rubbed his beard with his hand. He felt tired after a night without sleep.

'Certainly not. I like him. He has spirit.'

'He's an Oeselian,' growled Rusticus.

'I am aware of that,' replied Lembit. 'But his father is no fool and knows that there is unity in numbers. Whatever the merits of an alliance with our old enemies, there is certainly nothing to be gained from continuing to fight each other while the crusaders consolidate their strength to the south.'

'You are not thinking of an alliance with them, are you?' asked Rusticus incredulously.

'I am not thinking of anything at this precise moment, mainly because your incessant interruptions are giving me a headache. Did you send out those patrols?'

Rusticus nodded.

'Good,' said Lembit. 'We must not trust our young visitor too much. You may go. And close the doors behind you.'

Left alone with the fire illuminating the gloomy interior of his hall, Lembit pondered the course of action he should take during the coming weeks. He knew that a new crusader army would be landing in Livonia soon and would be marching north to avenge the defeat he had inflicted on the Sword Brothers. He also knew that to meet them in open battle would be to invite certain defeat. He knew his warriors armed with their spears and swords were no match for the men of iron on their mighty horses and their accompanying crossbowmen. And they had machines, terrible instruments capable of hurling great stones against timber walls and shattering them. Waging war against the crusaders required cunning not brute strength. He smiled to himself. But not even the mighty crusaders could be in two places at once.

He began tapping his fingers on the arm of his chair. The unexpected visit of Prince Sigurd would not interrupt his plans but might in fact aid them. If the Oeselians stopped raiding Estonia then that would make available more warriors to fight the crusaders. The Rotalians, the tribe that occupied the coastal lands and who suffered most at the hands of Olaf's deprivations, would be especially grateful and would surely be more amenable to increase their aid to him. But the Oeselians would have to earn his trust. His mind was made up.

That evening he asked Sigurd to dine with him. The meal was a modest and sober affair compared to the previous night's festivities. Lembit sat on the top table flanked by Rusticus, who for once refrained from assaulting his innards with vast quantities of beer and food, and Sigurd. His warriors sat at benches that had been arranged at right angles to the top table. Slaves placed large pieces of roasted pork and mutton on platters on the tables along with loaves of rye bread and bowls of salted herring. Others served water and milk from great earthenware jugs. Only Sigurd and his escort were offered beer.

'I have given your father's offer great consideration, Prince Sigurd,' said Lembit, 'and have concluded that it would be prudent to agree upon a cessation of hostilities before we can think of an alliance. If your father keeps his longships away from the coast and rivers of Estonia for six months then I see no reason why an alliance cannot be forged thereafter.'

'I can tell my father that you are agreeable to an alliance, lord?' asked Sigurd.

'You may tell him that if he suspends his raiding against Estonia for a period of six months, prince, then afterwards you may return and we will discuss things further. Let us walk before we attempt to run.'

Sigurd toasted his host with his cup. He seemed pleased with the outcome. At the very least he would keep his head if nothing else. Lembit was doubtful whether Olaf would be able to keep his men from the women and children who inhabited the villages along the Baltic coast. Pillage and rape was in Oeselian blood. Still, better to try than to do nothing.

Sigurd left the next day and once he was far away from Lehola, Lembit and Rusticus rode to the hill fort of Fellin, located ten miles south. A score of warriors accompanied them, all riding ponies. These hardy beasts with their low-lying withers, wide, straight backs, muscular croups, short ears and necks had been bred in Estonia for generations. Their hardy nature and great endurance meant they could live out of doors in the summer and could survive on the minimum of fodder during the long winters.

Lembit's party reached Fellin in two hours and was greeted by the foreign ambassador who had been alerted to the approach of the horsemen by the wolf shields on watch in the towers. Lembit dismounted and clasped the forearm of a tall man in a black tunic, tan leggings and gaiters. He had a red beard and hair that had been shaved from above the ears and was plaited from the crown to the back of his neck. The four men behind him, his escort, all wore helmets, mail armour and carried round shields and spears. Their shields carried the insignia of a black seagull.

'Lord Torolf,' Lembit said, 'apologies for the delay. I had an unexpected visitor. I hope you have been well looked after.'

Torolf placed his left hand on Lembit's shoulder. 'We have been availing ourselves of your land's abundance in game. A most enjoyable time.'

Lembit smiled at him. 'Walk with me.'

They went back into the hall that was similar to the one at Lehola, albeit smaller, and sat in chairs while both groups of warriors were served with refreshments. Lembit and Torolf sat down opposite each other. The latter was an emissary of the Northern Kurs, a fierce people who lived south of the Dvina, in the west of Lithuania. He had been at Fellin for a week, during which time he and Lembit had thrashed out an alliance between their two peoples.

'I leave tomorrow,' said Torolf, 'and hope to be back in Kurland within the month. After I have arrived I will finalise the details of our plan with Duke Arturus and put it in motion.'

Upon hearing of the defeat of the Sword Brothers Arturus had sent Torolf to Estonia to meet with Lembit to suggest an alliance, which the latter had readily agreed to.

'And if the crusaders do not march against me?' asked Lembit.

Torolf smiled mischievously. 'These Christians believe that their god is more powerful than any others. Your defiance is an affront to them and cannot be ignored. But, to assuage any doubts you may have, even if they do not make any moves against you the Northern Kurs will still launch their offensive.'

'The crusaders will march against me,' said Lembit grimly. 'Their most northerly stronghold, at Wenden, lies only seventy-five miles from this very hall.'

Torolf and his men left the next morning. Lembit escorted them east to the shores of Lake Peipus, the great inland sea that marked the boundary between Estonia and Russia. Once in Russian territory they would travel to Pskov and then southeast to Gerzika before taking boat to travel on the Dvina west to Kurland. The land was now covered in cow-wheat, marsh orchids, cotton grass and twinflowers and above them fluttered beautifully coloured butterflies: the Olive Skipper, Woodland Brown, Clouded Apollo and Lapland Ringlet. It was a land of peace and tranquillity soon to be scarred by war.

*****

Conrad stood next to Hans, both of them clutching lances, and watched as Walter the Penitent and Henke rode towards each other. The other boys stood either side of them and likewise held their breath as the two men in mail armour and riding warhorses thundered towards each other, their lances held in the 'couched' position: under the arm to steady them.

'See how they are holding their lances,' shouted Lukas behind the boys, 'to reduce the amount of flex and increase the accuracy of the lunge.'

Both knights were wearing full-face helmets and mail suits, though neither was wearing a surcoat. They both carried shields that protected their left sides and their horses wore white caparisons bearing the insignia of the Sword Brothers.

There was a sharp crack as Walter's lance hit Henke's shield and splintered, Rudolf's friend receiving a heavy blow but remaining in his saddle. The boys cheered as the two riders passed each other and Walter rode over to Conrad, threw down his broken lance shaft and held out his hand to receive another. Conrad passed him one of the four lances he was holding and grinned at Walter, who nodded and then wheeled away.

'Come on, Henke,' called Rudolf, who had ambled over to watch the spectacle, 'make a fist of it.'

It was a glorious summer's day and the castle and compound were bathed in warm sunlight. The air was sweet with the smell of grass and the ground was littered with daisies. The boys had eaten their midday meal after having completed their morning training session and now they stood on the meadow outside Wenden's great compound as Walter and Henke took part in a joust.

Walter and Henke trotted to their starting positions once more as Lukas continued to educate his charges.

'Note how the saddles have a high pommel and cantle that wrap around the riders. This holds the rider securely in the saddle and helps to withstand blows, both in the joust and in battle.'

The two horsemen began to trot towards each other, breaking into a canter as they couched their lances.

'The stirrups are long so that a rider's legs are straight as he sits in the saddle,' shouted Lukas, 'so he will be in a solid position to fight with a lance or a sword.'

The horses broke into a gallop, their riders ensuring they maintained a straight line and did not veer off course or cross in front of the other jouster. Once again there was a sharp crack as the lances struck shields, only his time both weapons broke and because Walter had turned his shoulder away at the last moment he was knocked from his saddle. He was thrown onto the turf as his horse raced off. Henke threw down his lance and rode after the beast – warhorses were far too valuable to be allowed to wander off into the woods. Expensive to purchase and maintain, each one consumed fifteen pounds of oats a day in addition to hay. Fortunately in the summer they could be put out to pasture, though they still required armed guards to watch over them when they were outside the compound. They also needed regular shoeing and daily grooming in addition to the girths, harnesses and other harnessing equipment they required. Every brother knight had his own horse, as did Walter, paid for by the large donation he had given the order before his arrival in Livonia.

As he dusted himself off and offered his congratulations to the returned Henke leading his horse, Walter came over to where Rudolf was talking to Lukas.

'Brother Henke is a most capable jouster,' he said.

100

'He has had a lot of practise,' said Rudolf, 'though in battle rather than on the jousting fields.'

'I hope to be able to fight alongside him against the heathen soon,' said Walter solemnly.

'You will get your wish,' replied Lukas. 'We wait only for the bishop's arrival to continue our campaign against the Estonians.'

'And after them the Oeselians,' added Rudolf, smiling at Walter. 'Plenty of heathens ready to be sent to Hell.'

'God willing,' replied Walter.

Lukas smiled and shook his head. He liked Walter, they all did, not only for his religious zeal but also for his willingness to get his hands dirty. He was quite prepared to muck out the horses, clean his own armour and even assist in the building of the castle, though the stonemasons guarded their domain jealously and would not allow anyone on their scaffolding that was not properly trained. Walter would have liked nothing more than to take his vows and join the Sword Brothers on the day of his arrival at Wenden. But the rules of the order stated that prospective brother knights had to serve a probationary period of twelve months before they were considered eligible for entry.

'I will be a brother knight, of course,' announced Anton a few days later while the boys were cleaning the mail armour of the brothers. 'My family is wealthy and I have had an education. Who among us can read and write?'

Everyone stopped what they were doing and looked at each other. Aside from Anton no one could read or write.

He spread out his hands. 'So you see only I have all the qualities required to be a brother knight. The rest of you will be sergeants.'

'What's wrong with that?' asked Conrad.

They were in the castle courtyard, outside the armoury, each of them in charge of a wooden barrel, inside of which was bran. In each barrel was placed a hauberk, chausses and coif. The barrel was then sealed, tipped on its side and rolled around the courtyard a dozen times, the boys racing each other around the pallets piled high with stone and trays holding mortar. In this way the bran polished the mail and the oil in it coated the metal and protected it against rust.

Conrad won the race and stood panting with his hands on his knees as the others brought their barrels to a halt beside his.

'Brother knights ride down the enemy on the backs of their warhorses,' said Anton, rivulets of sweat running down his face, 'sergeants are servants who attend the knights and do not really fight.'

'If that is true,' queried Hans, gasping for air, 'then why are we being trained to fight?'

Anton had no answer to his question and became irritated when Bruno and Johann insisted on addressing him as 'sir' for the rest of the day.

The bond that had been forged all those weeks ago on the cog grew stronger as the time passed. The things they had in common – young men alone in a foreign land, hard daily training and an all-pervading sense of adventure – outweighed their differences. In another life Anton would have looked down on Bruno and Johann and would have viewed Conrad, the boy whose father had been a murderer, with contempt. He certainly would have had nothing to do with Hans. But in this strange land they were equals, judged on their daily efforts rather than their social status. It was if their lives had been washed clean to be remade in Livonia.

As well as the sword and shield Lukas instructed them in the use of the spear, axe and crossbow, the boys being particularly keen on these items because, unlike tuition in the use of the sword, they were handed real weapons with which to practise. The long days meant they spent many hours training, in the afternoons shooting crossbow bolts at targets of packed straw, wielding axes or learning spear thrusts, but the mornings were given over to the sword and shield. Always the sword and shield.

'Keep moving,' Lukas bellowed at his charges as they practised thrusting with a spear. 'Just because it's a spear does not mean you have to stand still. You stop moving, you die. How many times do I have to tell you?'

Just for good measure he walked among them with a waster in his hand, administering a sharp blow to the hamstrings or back of anyone still stationary.

The boys had been at Wenden for four months now and even in that short time the constant training and hearty diet had made them stronger and more agile. Hans still looked as though he had gone without food for a month but now he had a lithe rather than a gaunt appearance. His eyes were bright and alert and his hair thick rather than straggly.

'They look like a pack of ravenous wolves,' remarked Rudolf who was leading his horse prior to undertaking a patrol with a dozen mounted sergeants. He held the reins of a palfrey, one of a score of such well-bred mounts that were used for patrols and general riding. The great warhorses were used for battle and though they were ridden around the castle to keep them in rude health, they were far too valuable for general-purpose riding.

'They are coming along nicely,' replied Lukas. 'I might let them have their own swords next year. The bishop should be arriving soon.'

Every castle had a loft full of pigeons that were used to carry messages between each castle and Riga. In this way news could be relayed to an outpost in a few hours rather than days or even weeks. Wenden was no different and had been alerted by courier pigeon that Bishop Albert and his army were on their way from Riga.

'Perhaps this year we will finally rid the world of Lembit and his Estonian heathens,' continued Lukas, nodding at the boys thrusting with their spears. 'Perhaps they will need ploughs instead of weapons.'

'You really think that, Lukas?' asked Rudolf.

'Why not? The Livs and Letts have been subdued. Why not the Estonians?'

Rudolf placed his foot in the stirrup and then hoisted himself into the saddle. 'Even if we defeat Lembit there remain the Russians to be dealt with, in addition to the Oeselians. I think these boys will spend a good few years yet holding swords rather than ploughs.'

He raised a hand to Lukas and then trotted towards the compound's entrance, his men following. A week later Bishop Albert arrived.

Conrad and his companions had never seen so much colour and splendour as when the bishop's army made camp at Wenden. A forest of tents sprang up around the castle, many topped by pennants bearing heraldic symbols from Saxony, Thuringia and Franconia where the crusaders had been drawn from. Conrad saw shields and banners sporting eagles, bells, trumpets, lions, wolves, bears, boars, oxen and stags. Horses wore caparisons bearing strange beasts that he had never heard of: white unicorns with a single horn and cloven hooves like a deer; and blue griffins that had the head, chest, wings and forelegs of an eagle with the hindquarters and legs of a lion. Other shields bore the images of fantastic sea creatures: yellow half-fish, half-lions, red half-fish and half-horses. Brightly coloured banners fluttered in the breeze showing black and silver serpents and lizards, with armoured knights bearing fierce red dragons on their surcoats. Other knights had heraldic symbols of three animal heads on their shields, such as bulls, griffins and boars.

The bishop's army was a most impressive sight and the boys were agreed that no force on earth would be able to withstand it. Bishop Albert himself came not as a man of peace but as a scourge of the heathen, dressed as he was in mail armour, full-face helmet surmounted by a metal bishop's mitre painted white and bearing a silver cross on the front, red surcoat adorned with Riga's twin key symbol and a red shield painted with the same motif. He rode a great warhorse whose caparison also sported the twin keys symbol. The twenty knights who formed his bodyguard were armed and attired in a similar fashion, as were his sergeants, though they wore kettle helmets instead of the full-face variety. These were German lords and their vassals who had settled in and around Riga and who willingly joined the bishop in his crusade to rid Livonia and Estonia of pagans. Also recruited from in and around Riga were the bishop's three hundred militia spearmen and three hundred crossbowmen, though the latter were actually mercenaries in the pay of the church who were billeted in the city's castle. Like most German towns and cities Riga was administratively divided into quarters, each one responsible for raising, equipping and drilling a certain number of men. Though prosperous through trade and donations Riga was not yet wealthy enough to raise and equip both spearmen and crossbowmen. A spearman alone required a large shield, mail armour, helmet, sword, dagger and spear, in addition to food while on campaign. The spearmen of Riga's garrison remained in the town to protect the archdeacon.

The two hundred German crusader knights formed the core of the bishop's army. Each knight brought with him two lesser-armoured horsemen recruited from his retainers, plus his squire. The knight and his two retainer horsemen, termed 'lesser knights', were termed a 'gleve' and fought as such on the battlefield. Occasionally a knight was accompanied by two or three mercenary horsemen instead of retainers, who would often dismount to fight on foot in battle.

The Sword Brothers made up a small part of the force encamped around Wenden, the brother knights from the castles of Kremon and Segewold being added to those at Wenden to give a total of thirty-six heavy horsemen. Supporting them were fifty sergeants of the order. Small garrisons of sergeants had been left behind at Kremon and Segewold to ensure a line of continuous communications with Riga. In addition, the garrisons of those strongholds along the Dvina – at Holm, Uexkull, Lennewarden and Kokenhusen – had been untouched to ensure the security of Livonia's southern border.

Finally there were the support personnel, without whom the army could not function. These included farriers, carpenters, cobblers, armourers, fletchers, surgeons, engineers, porters and chaplains. Conrad did not understand why the bishop had brought fifteen minstrels with him but was informed that their music brought him closer to God at the end of a long day.

104

The day of the army's arrival was exciting enough, but as the hours passed and Conrad and his companions watched the encampment take shape from the compound's earth and timber rampart they were struck by the great number of horses and wagons that accompanied the soldiers. There were hundreds of warhorses and hundreds more palfreys and packhorses. The carts and wagons were loaded with supplies for three months' campaigning – grain, wine, beer, dried fish and meat – plus tools. These included axes, planes, augers, boards, spades and iron shovels. Other wagons were loaded with armour, weapons, tents, saddles, crossbow bolts, shields and lances. The carts and wagons were brought inside the compound for security, as were the siege engines that had been broken down into their constituent parts and loaded onto wagons by the engineers. Everyone else save the bishop, his knights and the most senior crusaders were kept outside Wenden's perimeter.

The bishop's companions were quartered in the castle's dormitory, Conrad and the other boys being evicted to sleep in a tent they erected in the compound below the castle. Master Berthold gave up his room so the bishop could sleep in it during his residence at Wenden.

'Our stay will be brief,' announced Bishop Albert as he wiped his mouth with a cloth, Conrad taking his empty bowl from the table in front of him.

The candles in the dining room cast a poor light, making the building's austere interior even more dismal.

Conrad's companions cleared the empty dishes of the others sitting in the company of the bishop: Master Berthold, Brother Rudolf, Grand Master Volquin, the masters of the castles of Kremon and Segewold and two German knights whom the bishop had designated as commander and deputy-commander of the crusader contingent.

'We wait until Caupo arrives and then we will march north into Estonia,' continued the bishop. He looked at Master Berthold. 'What news do you have of Lembit?'

'He sits in his stronghold at Lehola, bishop,' answered Berthold.

'Where is this place?' asked the crusader commander, a swarthy individual with a deep voice and huge hands.

'Around eighty miles to the north,' replied Berthold.

'Six days' march,' said the crusader.

'More like ten,' Rudolf corrected him, 'given the state of the tracks and the number of waterways we will have to go around.'

Conrad filled the crusader's cup with wine and then moved behind him to refill the Master of Kremon's cup.

'Who is this Caupo?' asked the crusader commander's deputy.

'The King of the Livs,' replied Bishop Albert.

The crusader commander looked alarmed. 'A pagan?'

The bishop smiled. 'A *former* pagan. Now a convert to the church and a servant of Christ. Seven years ago he accompanied me on a visit to Rome to see the Holy Father himself. I count him among my most loyal subjects.'

The two crusaders looked at each other in confusion but asked no more questions about Caupo, the former pagan who now provided soldiers to fight beside the crusaders and the Sword Brothers. He resided at the hill fort of Treiden, around twelve miles southwest of Wenden. He may have had the trust of the bishop but those Livonians who were in exile and still in arms against the crusaders regarded him as a traitor. Lembit for his part had promised to kill him and mount his head on a pole on Treiden's highest rampart. The Sword Brothers also did not trust him, less for the fact that he was a former pagan but more because he was a king who could summon several hundred men to his banner at a moment's notice. And in a land where Christian castles were few, widely separated and had small garrisons, a man who commanded such power was dangerous indeed.

He arrived the next day with a retinue of four hundred warriors on foot and a score of men on ponies. Caupo himself led them on a pony and was dressed in a simple grey tunic, mail armour vest, brown leggings and boots. He carried a sword in a red scabbard and a round shield painted red with a huge metal boss in the centre. His simple helmet with its large nasal guard partly obscured his large face but not his beard. Only a few of his men – his mounted bodyguard – wore mail armour and carried swords. The rest were dressed in tunics in varying shades of red, brown and black and grey leggings fastened round the calves with gaiters. All carried spears, round wooden shields and had knives in sheaths hanging from their leather belts. Some also carried axes tucked into their belts. There were at most fifty archers among Caupo's soldiers.

Bishop Albert received the Liv king warmly outside the chapel in the castle courtyard, the crusader leaders and Sword Brother commanders looking on with blank faces. The bishop then put an arm around Caupo's shoulders and led him away while his men were shown to their allocated camping spot, which was well away from the rest of the army. The latter was spread over a few square miles around the castle and its horses had to be taken further out so they could graze on the lush summer grass. On average each acre of grassland could provide enough grazing for twenty-five horses, though the longer the army stayed at Wenden the more the ground would be stripped bare. In addition, every horse required at least ten gallons of water a day and so the squires, porters and Conrad and his associates were detailed to ferry the beasts to the Gauja so they could drink.

Conrad may have been greatly impressed by the army upon its arrival, but his enthusiasm soon diminished when he and the others found that they were given additional daily duties that involved shovelling horse dung into wheelbarrows to keep the camp clean.

The day after Caupo's arrival came ill tidings from Riga.

A courier pigeon brought news that a great fleet carrying Kurs had appeared in the Dvina and had disgorged hundreds of warriors who had attempted to storm Riga. Fortunately they had been spotted in time and the town gates had been closed. But the Kurs had then turned their attention to the surrounding countryside, burning and pillaging defenceless villages and farms in their path. Archdeacon Stefan wrote that it had been a miracle that Riga had not fallen and he implored the bishop to ·return with his army.

After reading the missive Bishop Albert handed it to Grand Master Volquin and sighed. 'I must return to Riga.'

Volquin read Stefan's note and then ordered the bishop's guards to go and fetch the senior Sword Brothers and crusaders.

The bishop sat in Berthold's chair in the Hall of the Master and held his head in his hands. This was a grievous blow indeed. If Riga fell then ten years' work would be undone and the crusade in Livonia might collapse altogether. He felt the weight of responsibility bear heavily upon his shoulders.

'If Riga's gates are closed then it will not fall,' said Volquin, trying to reassure the bishop.

Albert looked up at him. 'That might be. But what about the villagers, farmers and landowners who live beyond its walls? No doubt they have already been killed or forced to flee into the forests. And what of the women and children? Captured, no doubt, and carried off into slavery. Monstrous.'

Half an hour later the hall was filled with mail-clad men as the bishop relayed the news to them.

'We must return to Riga immediately,' he said. 'Give the order to your soldiers.'

The crusader leaders looked most surprised at this and looked at each other in confusion.

'Who are these Kurs?' asked their commander.

'Pirates and robbers who live beyond the southern shore of the Gulf of Riga,' replied Volquin. 'Raiders who plunder and pillage the godly.'

'They have siege engines?' asked the swarthy crusader.

Volquin shook his head. 'Siege warfare is unknown to them.'

The crusader spread his arms. 'Then they will be gone before we reach Riga. Its walls are strong and it has a garrison. It is safe enough, surely.'

'No,' said Bishop Albert firmly. 'It is an insult against me and against God that these Kurs attack Riga and the surrounding area. If we do nothing we will appear weak and helpless in the face of a pagan attack. We must return to rid the land of the Kurs to show that the armies of Christ cannot be defeated.'

'We came here to kill pagans, not to chase bandits,' said the crusader commander, his fellow knights murmuring their agreement.

The bishop glowered at him. 'I hope you came here to serve God rather than your own vanity.'

The crusader commander held the bishop's icy stare for a few seconds and then shrugged disinterestedly. 'We are happy to kill whoever you want dead, lord bishop.'

The other crusaders smiled and slapped him on the back.

'We are fifty miles from Riga,' said Volquin as the bishop retook his seat and continued to study the crusader commander. 'The quickest way to get there is by river but with the amount of wagons and horses that are here that is clearly impossible. Therefore I propose that the crusaders, the bishop's knights and sergeants, together with my own Sword Brothers and their sergeants, will form a mounted column to get to Riga as quickly as possible. The bishop's spearmen and crossbowmen, together with King Caupo's warriors, can accompany the more slow-moving wagons back to Riga in the wake of the mounted column.'

The crusaders looked at Caupo and his four lieutenants behind him and then at each other. Their commander spoke once more.

'You would entrust the wagons and supplies to barbarians?'

Caupo's men bristled at this slight but the king had heard it all before. He knew that he had once been a pagan who had fought the bishop, and would forever have to bear the insults and disdain of the arrogant young men on their big horses who arrived every year to wage war against the unconverted.

He merely smiled at the crusaders as the bishop spoke slowly and purposely. 'King Caupo has my full trust. No more will be said on the matter.'

The crusader camp was dismantled that afternoon, Conrad and the others assisting the porters and young squires who had come from Germany to pack the tents and supplies into wagons. After the meeting in the chapel the bishop and Grand Master Volquin decided that there was little point in hauling the siege engines to Riga, only for them to be transported back north once the Kurs had been defeated. The wagons carrying them and their ammunition would therefore remain at Wenden along with the engineers who operated them. The long summer days meant that the mounted knights and sergeants could depart for Riga that very afternoon, each man carrying sacks of food and fodder behind him on his horse. The squires also rode south with their masters, each one holding the reins of their knight's warhorse as they departed Wenden. The bishop led the way surrounded by his bodyguard, followed by Volquin and his Sword Brothers and Caupo, who left behind his foot soldiers to escort the wagons.

The wagons left the following morning, escorted by Caupo's warriors and the bishop's spearmen and crossbowmen. It had not rained for many days and so the tracks they would traverse would at least be dry, but they were still rutted, full of holes and their surfaces damaged by water erosion caused by downpours and flooding. This meant the rate of advance was tortuous – no more than five miles a day – but at least there was no shortage of fresh water with the Gauja always nearby on the column's right flank. The crusaders might have been disparaging about Caupo's warriors but the bishop's foot soldiers were glad to have them guarding the column of wagons and carts that stretched over several miles.

At Wenden the only indication that an army had been camped around its ramparts was a vast area of flattened grass and great piles of horse dung. The inhabitants of the local villages, who had made themselves scarce during the army's presence, especially the attractive young wives and daughters, returned to tending to their animals, fields, beehives and apple orchards. Master Berthold had issued strict instructions, backed up by the bishop himself, that the crusaders and their attendants were to have no contact with the locals, were to keep their horses away from the fields full of ripening crops and on no account were to slaughter cows and pigs. To enforce this edict Rudolf organised joint patrols with Thalibald's men while the army was around Wenden. But now the army was gone and life returned to normal. Conrad and his companions returned to their dormitory and continued with their weapons practice while the bishop hurried south to slay the Kurs.

*****

Prince Stecse knelt by the water and stared across its perfectly smooth surface at the enemy stronghold. Despite it being summer the nights were not hot, particularly tonight when there was a full moon in a cloudless sky. There was no wind and the stillness was oppressive, or perhaps it was the prospect of the coming assault that gripped his senses. He looked at the objective again; some two thousand feet away perched atop a steep mound of earth. Kokenhusen Castle still retained its original timber walls and towers, the Sword Brothers having taken possession of it less than a year before. Built at the spot where the River Perse entered the larger River Dvina, Kokenhusen had water on its western and southern sides, archers on the ramparts being able to cover the riverbanks in these directions with their missiles. Any attack would come from either the north or east, but on these sides of the castle a ditch had been dug in front of the earth mound on which Kokenhusen sat. It was a most impressive stronghold.

Stecse tapped his lieutenant kneeling beside him on the arm and the man crept away to commence the attack. In the trees around him squatted six hundred of his warriors under strict orders to stay silent. An Ural owl gave two short hoots, indicating he was alarmed. Stecse's blood ran cold. Had the garrison heard? To those who knew of such things it was a telltale sign that something foreign, alien, was moving through the forest. It did not matter: it was too late to call off the attack.

Kokenhusen may have been a formidable fortress but its garrison was small. No more than a dozen Sword Brother knights, perhaps a score or more sergeants, a score more spearmen and perhaps the same number of crossbowmen. There might also be native warriors inside the castle, though the Sword Brothers usually kept the Livs outside their walls in surrounding villages. Whatever their numbers the crusaders were greatly outnumbered by his own men and the soldiers of Prince Vsevolod that were at this very moment approaching the castle from the east. Stecse disliked the prince. Disliked him for his effeminate appearance, cowardly ways and duplicitous nature. Were it not for the fact that he was the son-in-law of Grand Duke Daugerutis he would have nothing to do with him. Still, his five hundred Russian soldiers who would assault the castle from the east would add to the weight of the attack and spread the garrison even more thinly along the walls.

His men had spent three days several miles south of the river, in the forest's interior, felling trees and fashioning assault ladders. These were now loaded onto forty row boats, two in each vessel, that were positioned among the trees a hundred yards from the water. Each vessel resembled a miniature longship with pointed prow

110

and stern, wide amidships, but having no mast. With six oars on each side they would be able to cross the wide stretch of water quickly and silently right under the noses of the garrison.

He closed his eyes and said a silent prayer to Perkunas, the God of Thunder who was also the deity of warriors and the son of Dievas, the Chief God. He prayed that his efforts would be worthy of a Lithuanian prince and if not, that he would die from wounds in his chest and not in his back. Then he rose and walked over to the nearest boat, grabbed its prow and with the other warriors hauled it from the treeline to the water's edge.

The plan agreed with Vsevolod was that the Lithuanians would commence the attack and, once engaged against the enemy, the Russians would assault the east side of the castle where there would hopefully be few if any soldiers manning the defences. The boat moved effortlessly over the sand and then Stecse felt water around his lower legs as it entered the river and he and the others hauled themselves aboard. The oars were speedily shoved through the oar holes and their operators began to apply power to each stroke, propelling the boat through the water. He crouched at the prow as either side of him the other boats cut silently through the water.

Stecse's heart was pounding as the flotilla reached mid-stream and still there was no sound from the castle. He gripped the hilt of his sword and held the wooden handle behind the metal boss of his shield with his left hand. Then the sound of a bell being rung frantically suddenly sounded from inside the castle. They had been spotted. The clang of the bell grew louder as his men strained at their oars to close the gap between them and the opposite bank as quickly as possible. The plan was for half the boats to row into the mouth of the Perse and then veer sharply right to beach on the bank on the western side of the castle, while the rest rowed straight ahead to land on the bank directly beneath the castle's southern ramparts.

Stecse's boat ran aground on the soft sand and he leapt from the vessel, as there was a thud and a low groan behind him. One of the rowers was slumped over his oar, a quarrel lodged in his back.

'Move!' shouted Stecse as there was a succession of phuts around him as crossbow bolts slammed into the ground.

The rest of the boats ran aground as their occupants jumped from them. Stecse scrambled up the earth bank that led to the castle's timber walls, his men following. They and he held their shields above their heads as from above the crossbowmen on the ramparts shot their bolts. The air was alive with deadly hisses as quarrels punched through helmets and splintered shields. Then spears were thrown at the Lithuanians, their points finding flesh as men screamed, clutched their wounds and tumbled back down the bank.

But now the castle was being assaulted on two sides and forty ladders had been hauled up the earth bank and placed against the timber walls, and then like ants the warriors scrambled up them. The defenders managed to push half a dozen away from the walls, screams piercing the air as Lithuanians fell back down to earth, the fall smashing their bodies and sending slivers of broken bones into their hearts and lungs. The crossbowmen managed to slaughter those climbing a further five ladders, Lithuanian bodies hanging limply from the wooden frames. But the defenders were too few to be everywhere and other Lithuanians managed to reach the top of the walls.

Stecse, his shield on his back held in place by a leather strap around his shoulders, clambered to the top of the ladder just at the moment a spearman thrust his weapon at him. He saw it at the last moment and instinctively swung away, holding the top rung of the ladder with his left hand. He grabbed the spear shaft and yanked it violently down. The spearman's thrust meant his torso was hanging over the wall and so it was easy for him to be hauled down to his death. He screamed as he fell to the ground below and Stecse jumped onto the fighting platform and pulled the axe that was tucked in his belt. Another spearman came at him, his large, almond-shaped shield covering his body. Stecse pulled his own shield from his back, grasped its handle and threw the axe at the spearman's head. The man instinctively ducked, giving Stecse time to draw his sword, dash forward and run the blade into the man's guts.

The warriors who had been following him up the ladder now came onto the battlements. He felt a surge of ecstasy flow through him. They were up and over the walls! Then he looked down and saw a line of crossbowmen pointing their weapons up at the walls. Pointing them at him and his men. He glanced over to where the Russians should be assaulting the eastern side of the castle walls but saw no activity. Where was Vsevolod? He saw the crossbowmen again.

'Take cover!' he screamed as a score of quarrels lanced through the air and found their targets.

He had managed to crouch down behind his shield but the others were not so quick thinking. There was another volley of crossbow bolts and at least a score of Lithuanians were killed, some of them toppling from the battlements onto the ground in front of the crossbowmen. The latter shot another volley and more

Lithuanians were cut down. Stecse looked left and right and saw that although some of his men had reached the walls, they were being contained by a combination of spearmen and crossbowmen. And now, from below, they were being shot at by men who should have been fighting Russians on the eastern ramparts.

A crossbow bolt slammed into the top of his shield, the point fracturing the wood. He looked left and saw a spearman charging at him. He jumped up and to the left and barged the shaft away with his shield, then thrust his sword over the top of the man's shield and into his face, driving the point into his mouth and out through the back of his neck. He yanked the blade back as more crossbowmen formed up below to rake the battlements still occupied by Lithuanians with bolts.

'We must fall back, lord,' said his deputy beside him. 'We are being slaughtered.'

Fresh groans and screams heralded another crop of Lithuanian dead as Stecse and his deputy once more crouched down behind their shields.

'Give the order,' said Stecse, his deputy turning to bellow a command at a man nearby, who blew a horn. He blew it again and thankful Lithuanians began scurrying back down ladders to their boats.

Stecse was the last to leave, making sure there were no more live Lithuanians on the walls before holding what was left of his shield above him and climbing back down his ladder. Already boats were pushing off into the black waters as his men beat a hasty retreat. Quarrels kicked up sand at his feet as he ran to a boat that was now in the water and jumped aboard, the rowers groaning as they strained at their oars in order to propel the vessel as far from the crossbowmen as quickly as possible.

*****

In the woods to the east of Kokenhusen Prince Vsevolod sat on his horse and listened as the sounds of battle coming from the castle petered out. Around him his senior officers shifted uncomfortably in their saddles as they waited for him to give the order to attack. They had over five hundred soldiers in the woods, the vanguard equipped with scaling ladders, bows and ropes with which to storm the castle. But Vsevolod gave no command. He just sat on his horse impassively.

Eventually he turned to his general. 'Send some scouts ahead to see what is happening.'

It was half an hour of more waiting before they returned with news that the Lithuanian attack had failed. There were angry murmurs among his officers.

'Silence!' snapped Vsevolod. He turned to his general. 'We will advance to the castle walls.'

He looked at his officers and then Vsevolod, confusion etched on his face. 'I do not understand, highness. Should we not have coordinated our own attack with that of the Lithuanians?'

'We are not going to attack,' announced Vsevolod, digging his spurs into his horse's sides. 'Ensure that the assault parties are withdrawn and sent back to Gerzika forthwith.'

'I do not understand, highness,' said the general who followed his lord's horse.

'That is why I am a prince and you are not,' replied Vsevolod condescendingly. 'See to it that my orders are obeyed.'

Vsevolod smiled to himself. What were the lives of a few Lithuanians to him? He had to tread carefully. If the Lithuanians had taken the castle then he would have thrown in his lot against the bishop's forces. He knew that Lembit was going to attack south and if Kokenhusen had fallen then Daugerutis would have sent more soldiers over the Dvina to support him. But the attack had failed and once more he was in a vulnerable position: an isolated ruler on the northern bank of the river facing the bishop and his considerable forces. His defeat at the hands of the crusaders last year had illustrated the folly of confronting the Germans directly. It was not lost on him that the castles being built along the Dvina – at Holm, Uexkull, Lennewarden and Kokenhusen – had all formerly been the strongholds of pagan lords, now either dead, reduced to vassals or in exile. No, he would bide his time.

He would ride to Kokenhusen and act the part of an ally bringing a relief force after having heard a rumour that the Lithuanians were going to attack the castle. This would endear him to the bishop at least and would lure him into believing that the Kingdom of Gerzika was loyal. And now that his honour had been affronted Grand Duke Daugerutis would undoubtedly wage more war against the bishop's lands, and would perhaps even assault Riga itself. Whatever the outcome a war with Lithuania would drain the bishop's resources, in addition to the not inconsiderable matter of the conflict with Lembit that he still had to resolve.

Vsevolod forgot that he was sitting on an uncomfortable horse as he rode towards the castle with these happy thoughts swirling in his mind. Perhaps that oaf Stecse had been killed in the attack, a most pleasing thought. Vsevolod began to whistle to himself. This night was improving by the minute.

*****

Stecse stood on the riverbank and observed his men disembark from their boats and pull them up the bank and into the trees. The assault had been a disaster. He stood with his arms folded, staring at Kokenhusen across the river, while a roll call was taken. The plan had been simple enough: assault a small garrison on all sides under cover of night and capture it with speed and overwhelming numerical superiority. He had gone to Gerzika where details of the assault had been finalised. Vsevolod's commanders had even built a model of Kokenhusen and the surrounding terrain to acquaint their soldiers with the local geography and its features. He himself had sent spies to the castle to collect information pertaining to the size of the garrison and the location of any forces in the local villages. It was all for nothing.

His deputy cleared his throat behind him. Stecse snapped out of his staring and turned to face him.

'Seventy-five dead and eighty wounded, twenty-five fatally, lord.'

'We will rest for an hour and then row east to get well away from this place,' said Stecse.

'Where were the Russians, lord?' asked his deputy.

'Where indeed?' replied Stecse.

'Perhaps they were ambushed,' suggested his deputy.

Stecse shook his head. 'There are no other crusader forces in this area aside from those in that castle across the water. There was no ambush.'

He was going to say that treachery was a more likely explanation but stopped himself. He would wait until he was back at Grand Duke Daugerutis' stronghold before giving his opinion on the matter.

Chapter 5

Lembit sat crouched beside an aged oak on the edge of the forest, observing the castle. Rusticus was kneeling beside him and behind him over fifty wolf shields crouched low among the foliage to prevent them being spotted. They were in the trees to the north of the castle and could see workmen on the scaffolding labouring on the castle's towers. Lembit had never seen Wenden before; indeed had never been this far south outside of his own lands. The scouts that he had despatched to keep an eye on the crusaders' movements had returned with news that the great army at Wenden had left to return south. The Kurs had kept their word, then, and had attacked Riga. His own army was camped ten miles to the north, well away from the eyes of the locals who were the slaves of the crusaders.

Wenden was strong, that much was certain. The steep sides of the ground on its northern and western sides made an assault from those directions out of the question. Even the slope leading to its eastern ramparts was formidable. Any assault would have to be directed against its southern side.

'What are we waiting for?' complained Rusticus.

'For the crusaders to depart the castle so we can take possession of it,' Lembit replied.

'Well they had better get a move on,' said Rusticus, 'my knees are aching.'

Lembit looked at him in disbelief. The two were contrasting in appearance: Lembit short in stature with quick reflexes, broad shouldered with long, thick hair; Rusticus large, lumbering with shorter hair and a great thick beard. In intellect they were opposites as well: Lembit cunning, intelligent and calculating; Rusticus stupid and cruel but very useful with a weapon in his hands.

'I have seen enough,' said Lembit, 'let us return to camp.'

He and his men moved slowly and stealthily among the trees until they were a safe distance from any of the villages that ringed Wenden. These were the original settlements that had been in existence when Wenden had been a hill fort of a pagan lord, but Lembit knew that the crusaders often sent their priests to live among the locals to poison their minds with their religion. He also knew that the presence of a large body of warriors, if spotted, would be immediately reported to the commander at Wenden.

Camp was deep in the forest. On the way back Lembit walked in silence, deep in thought, his men in single file behind him and scouts ahead and on each flank. He had left nothing to chance. His men had crafted scaling ladders in Estonia and had brought them south with them so they did not have to cut down any trees and thus make a lot of noise. They had moved during the hours of darkness and in the pre-dawn light of the early morning before resting during the day so as to remain unobserved. Even so, despite the crusader army having moved back south, Wenden was still a formidable fortress notwithstanding that it had a small garrison and was only partially built. But if he and his men could breach the outer perimeter wall than surely it would fall.

Later, when dusk was falling and he had rejoined his men at camp, the scouts reported to Lembit regarding the perimeter wall. No campfires were allowed so the men chewed on cured meat and salted fish and drank water. The scouts told him that a ditch surrounded the southern and eastern sides of the castle, behind which was an earth bank with a glacis slope, on top of which was a timber palisade of horizontally laid logs. There was one entrance, on the southern side, with a wooden bridge over the ditch leading to two wooden gates.

'How many guards did you see on the wall?' asked Lembit.

'Six or seven above and each side of the gates,' replied a gangly, bearded man.

'Perhaps another half dozen along the rest of the wall,' added another, shorter one.

'That few?' said Rusticus dismissively, rubbing his hands. 'This will be easy.'

Lembit threw him an angry glance. 'It will be easy only if we get over that wall quickly.'

He dismissed the scouts and assembled his subordinates, who sat cross-legged in a circle in front of him. The light was fading fast now and their faces were difficult to make out in the dimness. The warm air was thick with the smell of pine needles and the aroma of sun-heated moss and russulas. He had brought only professional warriors with him, men whose lives were dedicated to the military arts, not farmers who played at being soldiers. He now addressed them.

'We attack at dawn. Each of you will lead your men against a section of the wall. You must cross the ditch and get over the palisade as quickly as possible. The enemy are few and cannot defend all the perimeter.'

'What about their men of iron on horseback?' enquired one.

The ironclad knights on horseback were feared throughout Estonia, and with good reason. They attacked in densely packed ranks – big men on huge warhorses whose charge was irresistible.

117

'We will be over the walls before they can sally forth and get among us,' said Lembit. 'Once we are inside the perimeter our superiority in numbers will decide things in our favour.'

The men moved out just after midnight, cloth wrapped around their boots to muffle the sound of their footsteps. They moved slowly in long files, each man trailing his spear so the warrior behind could hold the shaft and follow in his footsteps in the darkness. They sweated as they carried their weapons, the scaling ladders and the logs lashed together to be thrown across the ditch, their shields strapped to their backs. Excitement infused Lembit's body. If he took the castle at Wenden it would be a devastating, perhaps fatal, blow to the crusader kingdom and would give heart to the oppressed people of Livonia. They would rally to his side instead of the traitor Caupo's.

*****

Conrad was already awake when the bell began to ring. In his previous life he had been used to rising before dawn and so found the Sword Brothers' hour of rising easy to get used to, unlike Hans, though now even his slim friend had grown accustomed to rising at an early hour. He heard the bell and rose from his bed, only this morning the sound was different. It was not a calm sequence of sounds to signal the new day's beginning and the first set of prayers; rather, it was frantic ringing.

Rudolf burst into the room, dressed in his mail armour and white surcoat and carrying his helmet.

'Up, up!' he shouted, 'the castle is under attack.'

The guards at the gates had first spotted the groups of warriors beyond the ditch and had rung the alarm bell on the perimeter wall, the bell in the castle responding in a similar fashion. Beyond the dry moat bleary eyed mercenaries were coming from their huts putting on their clothes, while from other cabins came crying children, frightened women in their bedclothes and their artisan husbands. Henke and Otto had rushed down to the dwellings and now stood, swords in hands, shouting at the workers and their families to get to the castle as quickly as possible.

Conrad and the others hastily put on their clothes, pulled on their boots and rushed out of the dormitory into the courtyard to meet a scene of chaos. Sergeants in their gambesons and kettle helmets were shepherding the civilians running across the drawbridge towards the chapel. Master Berthold stood in the middle of the courtyard with his arms by his side calling for calm, his booming voice instructing people not to run and to trust in the protection of the Lord. Rudolf and Lucas were standing by the armoury as mercenaries came to collect quivers of bolts, weapons, shields and armour before making their way to the perimeter wall. Conrad and his companions remained outside their dormitory, unsure what to do. Lukas saw them and ordered them over to him. Conrad noticed that some of the brother knights were leading their horses from the stables, both rider and beast fully equipped for war.

Lukas pointed at them. 'Get yourselves in the chapel.'

Hans looked at Conrad and then the others.

'We want to fight,' declared Conrad before blushing intensely and staring down at the ground, mortified that he had spoken so.

He did not know why he had said the words and expected to be flogged for his insolence.

'If we could, sir,' said Anton. The others nodded their agreement at Lukas. Conrad looked at Hans who nodded at him determinedly. Lukas laughed and pointed towards the groups of men forming up beyond the perimeter wall in the post-dawn light.

'Do you know what they are?' he said. The youths looked at him blankly. 'I will tell you,' he continued. 'They are Estonians and they want to get inside these walls, butcher all the men and carry off the women and children as slaves.'

Conrad stared at the Estonians. He counted ten widely spread enemy groups moving towards the wall, which was now filling with spearmen and crossbowmen, though not along its entire length. He also saw the engineers who had arrived with the bishop's army frantically assembling what looked like wooden frames on wheels.

'What use is learning to use weapons if we are not allowed to fight with them to defend ourselves?' said Conrad, who this time looked directly at Lukas.

The instructor moved to stand before Conrad, his face inches from the boy's. 'You have a lot to say for yourself all of a sudden.'

Conrad stepped back. 'My apologies, Brother Lukas. I do not want to be a slave.'

'Time is pressing, Lukas,' said Rudolf as the last of the civilians scurried past to disappear into the now very crowded chapel. 'Let them fight if they wish then we shall see how good an instructor you are.'

Lukas turned and looked at Rudolf with concern. 'They are not ready.'

Rudolf smiled. 'No, but they can still shoot a crossbow and we need every pair of hands.'

Lukas shrugged and turned back to face Conrad. 'Very well. You all want to fight?'

He smiled and the others said they did. Lukas sighed.

'Come with me.'

Minutes later they were all eagerly following him across the drawbridge armed with crossbows. Attached to their belts were black leather quivers shaped like an hourglass with wooden backs and bottoms and that held twenty quarrels, points up. At the armoury they had been issued with gambesons that were white but carried no insignia. Conrad felt a surge of pride as he marched behind Lukas, who was carrying his helmet in the crook of his arm. The mercenaries were at the wall now and Conrad's heart raced as he heard the snapping sound of crossbows being shot at the enemy. His mouth was dry and he suddenly felt afraid. All the bravado he had displayed at the castle had disappeared by the time Lukas called a halt and arranged him and the others in a line facing the gates. He glanced behind him, at the castle that seemed a hundred miles away.

He had forgotten about the strange frames on wheels that he had spied earlier but now there was a loud bang to his left that made him jump.

'Easy,' said Lukas, 'it is only a mangonel.'

Conrad and his pale-faced companions glanced at the machine as it launched a rock that arched into the sky and disappeared on the other side of the wall. Then there was another bang, and another and another as the other mangonels launched their missiles. These one-armed throwing machines used a bundle of twisted hair or sinew called a skein that was strung across a frame. In the middle of the skein the wooden throwing arm was inserted upright. At the end of this arm was a sling.

Conrad watched as the four-man crew lowered the arm and secured it in the horizontal position, then lifted one of the stones from the two-wheeled cart pulled by a horse positioned behind it and placed it in the sling. The chief engineer released a handle and the arm flew forward to release the stone, hitting a padded buffer attached to an upright frame that acted as a stopper. The mangonels had been set up around fifty yards back from the perimeter ramparts, allowing their missiles to land some sixty yards beyond the wall.

Arrows came from the ranks of the Estonians, most being shot at the defenders on the walls but a few arching high into the sky to land a few yards in front of Conrad and his companions.

'Keep your eyes out for those arrows. Load!' shouted Lukas, putting on his helmet and drawing his sword.

Despite being frightened Conrad instinctively hooked the double-pronged metal claw that was attached to the front of his belt over the centre of the bowstring.

He raised his right foot and placed it in the metal stirrup attached to the fore-end of the crossbow's stock. He straightened his bent leg and in this way forced the crossbow downwards. The bowstring, attached to the claw, was restrained from following the movement of the weapon and was thus forcibly drawn along the stock of the crossbow until it slipped over the catch of the lock. His training was paying off.

Ahead he could see spearmen fighting furiously with Estonians at the top of ladders. He then saw more enemy soldiers coming over a section of the timber wall that was not defended. His heart pounded in his chest as he pulled a quarrel from his quiver and placed it in the groove in the stock. Lukas shoved his helmet back on his head.

'Don't shoot our own men!' he bellowed at them.

Moments later the defenders, having failed to hold the wall, suddenly abandoned their positions and ran down the sloping earth bank on which the wall stood. Conrad was appalled – they were fleeing to leave him and his companions to face the enemy alone. But he was wrong and seemingly instantaneously the spearmen and sergeants formed a line in front of him with the crossbowmen standing directly behind. Lukas waved the boys forward to take up position behind a dozen spearmen standing with their weapons levelled and their shields locked.

The Estonians flooded down the bank and formed up at the bottom, hurling insults and shouting obscenities at the Christians. Conrad saw a banner bearing a red wolf and saw warriors clustered around a man in a gilded helmet. Beside him, carrying a large round shield and armed with a vicious-looking axe, was a giant of a man. Conrad stared wide-eyed at the savage half-men who stood only a few yards away, shouting and banging their weapons on their shields.

'Ready!' shouted the commander of the mercenaries. The crossbowmen brought up their weapons.

'Shoot!' he bellowed and twenty crossbow bolts hissed through the air.

Conrad pulled his trigger and was elated as the quarrel left his weapon. Seconds later there was another volley as the crossbowmen expertly reloaded and shot their missiles. Conrad likewise reloaded and released his trigger as Estonians screamed and fell to the ground, quarrels in their flesh.

The crossbowmen got off two more volleys before the Estonians charged, yelling their war cries and raising their axes above their heads. Conrad reloaded again and shot another bolt that struck a man in the shoulder and pitched him onto the ground, two Estonians directly behind tripping over his prostrate body. But the rest smashed into the line of spearmen and began hacking at them with their axes and thrusting with their spears. Conrad saw Lukas thrust his sword forward into a man's face, step back to avoid an axe being swung at his head and then bring his blade down on the arm holding the weapon, shattering the bone.

Then the brother knights charged.

They thundered down the track that led from the castle between the huts that housed the mercenaries and the civilian dwellings to the main gates in the outer perimeter. They numbered only eleven brother knights and Walter, all in a solid line with their lances couched, but their appearance tipped the scales of the battle. They did not scream war cries or hurl abuse at their foes as they rode towards where the spearmen and crossbowmen were being forced back by the great press of Estonians wielding their weapons. The unarmed engineers had fled back up the track to the castle, leaving their machines to the enemy. But now the knights charged straight into the midst of Lembit's warriors.

The fifty mercenaries and thirty sergeants had managed to retain their formation but had been pushed back towards the three mangonels that had been positioned directly in front of the civilian huts. But while Lembit and half of his warriors hacked and slashed at these soldiers, forcing them back, Rusticus had assembled another group on his chief's left flank, ready to race up the track and storm the castle itself. It was this group that the knights struck.

Eleven men against at least a hundred. But they were big men attired in mail and full-face helmets, riding big horses whose iron-shod hoofs pounded the ground and put the fear of God into the heathens. Rusticus screamed orders at his men to hold their ground and lock their shields. He knew that not even the horses of the iron men could break a solid shield wall. But his men did not have the brute courage he possessed and so they ran. They ran back towards the ramparts over which they had flooded, hoping to put as much distance between them and the accursed horsemen who were galloping towards them as possible. Rusticus hurried right to be with Lembit as the knights rode among their fleeing foes.

They used their lances first, skewering Estonians in the back with ease, then drew their swords and slashed left and right to split helmets, skulls and shoulder blades. But as they scattered one half of the Estonians Lembit finally broke the resistance of the mercenary spearmen.

Ten lay dead or wounded on the ground and although the crossbowmen had taken a heavy toll of the Estonians, their ammunition was now spent.

'Back to the castle,' ordered Lukas, his helmet shoved back on his head as he quickly appraised the situation. He saw the knights to his right riding among the enemy and dealing death with their swords. But in front of him the Estonians were literally hacking his men to pieces.

The German crossbowmen did not need telling a second time: they turned tail and ran as fast as their legs would carry them. The sergeants and spearmen attempted a more disciplined withdrawal, for if they ran they would surely be cut down by a herd of feral Estonians. Horn calls came from the latter's ranks and their rearmost warriors turned to see the knights hacking down the remnants of those men who had fled back over the ramparts. The presence of the iron men behind them resulted in their ferocious advance faltering, which was just as well for Conrad.

He had been standing beside Hans shooting his crossbow, just behind a line of spearmen who had been forlornly attempting to stop the Estonians. Then Lukas had given the order to retreat and chaos had broken out. The spearmen and sergeants were still thrusting at the enemy with their spears as they shuffled back but the mercenary crossbowmen ran for their lives. Conrad, Hans and the others looked at each other, unsure what to do, just as the crusaders broke and Estonians came at them.

'Run!' shouted Conrad. Hans spun round and ran straight into a mangonel. He had not realised that as the spearmen in front were forced back they had got close to the machines. Hans sprawled on the ground and seconds later a great mail-clad Estonian was over him, raising his axe high in the air to split Hans' skull. Conrad shot the man with a quarrel that went straight into his armpit, causing him to cry out in pain and collapse on the ground. He rushed over to Hans and hauled his friend to his feet.

'Move, Hans,' he said, his friend pointing past him, fear etched on his face.

Conrad turned to see another Estonian running at him with an axe in his right hand. The man swung the weapon at Conrad, who ducked at the last moment and avoided the blade that embedded itself in the mangonel's frame. Hans shot the man with a quarrel as he tried to yank the axe free. The youths withdrew a few paces as a series of individual duels between spearmen and Estonians erupted around them. Conrad reached into his quiver, extracted another bolt and reloaded his crossbow. The fear that he had felt earlier had now dissipated and a strange calm had taken possession of him. He reloaded with ease and then looked around, seeking targets. He gestured to Hans to stay close to him as he walked slowly backwards, ensuring there were no more machines on his line of retreat.

They were among the civilian huts now, some of the Estonians darting inside to see if there were any women to be had to rape or loot. Then he saw Lukas to his right, surrounded by five enemy warriors who were swinging their axes at him. The brother knight was fighting with skill but would surely fall fighting such odds.

'Hans,' Conrad called, pointing at the outnumbered Lukas. Conrad brought up his crossbow and shot it, the quarrel slamming into the back of one of the Estonians. The man arched his back and pitched forward onto the ground, to be joined by a second as Hans shot his weapon and slew another Estonian. Conrad reloaded and ran over to where Lukas was fighting, the knight slicing the hamstring of an Estonian with a deft swing of his sword before retreating to face another of his attackers. Hans shot that man while the fifth, realising he was now outnumbered, backed away swiftly. The Estonian with the cut hamstring tried to hobble away but Lukas raced forward and killed him with a single thrust of his sword. He pointed the bloody weapon at Conrad and Hans.

'You two back to the castle. Now!'

Conrad nodded and raced off, Hans beside him. They rounded one of the huts and came face to face with half a dozen enemy warriors carrying shields bearing a wolf's face, one of which was wearing a gilded helmet. They all turned as Conrad and Hans stopped and stared at them. For a few seconds nothing happened. And then two of the Estonians raced at them. *Keep moving to stay alive.* Conrad heard the words of Lukas in his head as he shot his crossbow to drop one of the warriors and then leapt aside as the other man swung his sword at him but cut only air. Hans' shot hit the shield of the man with the gilded helmet, who now turned to face Conrad's friend. The others made to attack Hans but the warrior with the quarrel lodged in his shield waved them back and calmly walked towards Hans. The latter frantically tried to reload his crossbow but in his panic he dropped his quarrel and then had his weapon knocked out of his hands before being barged to the ground.

Conrad dropped his crossbow and picked up the dead warrior's sword to face the second man who had charged. The man carried a wolf shield and kept it close to his body but Conrad's training served him well and he avoided his adversary's clumsy strikes with ease, and then cut the man's sword arm with a downward stroke of his own weapon, forcing the warrior to drop his blade as he yelped in pain. Conrad saw the warrior with the gilded helmet standing over Hans, sword in hand, ready to kill his friend. He sprinted over to where his crossbow lay on the ground, bolt still in its groove, and picked it up.

'No!' he screamed, causing the man to turn his head just as Conrad released the trigger. The bolt grazed the left cheek of the man with the rich helmet, then thudded into the eye socket of the warrior standing behind him, who toppled over onto his back, dead. The man with the cut cheek glared in anger at Conrad and, ignoring Hans, calmly walked over to him just as a dozen more Estonians appeared led by a huge ugly brute. Conrad gulped. He and Hans would surely die now.

Rusticus grabbed Lembit's arm.

'We must go, lord. The iron men on their horses are behind us and word has reached me that more enemies are approaching the castle.' He saw blood oozing down his lord's cheek. 'You are hurt.'

Lembit yanked his arm free. 'It is nothing. What enemies are approaching?'

'Thalibald and his men.'

Lembit pointed his sword at Conrad, who stood with his sword held ready to defend himself. The Estonian chief was angry that victory was slipping from his grasp rather than with this tall boy with blue-grey eyes who had nearly killed him. He decided to vent his fury on him nevertheless.

'This is not over boy,' he shouted at Conrad who had no knowledge of Estonian, 'I will see you again and then we will settle things between us.'

Lukas suddenly appeared and rushed over to stand beside Conrad. Lembit sneered at them both, turned and raced away, Rusticus and his men covering his withdrawal. The Estonian chief stopped and turned to again point his sword at Conrad.

'Remember me, boy, for I will surely remember you.'

And then he was gone. Lukas took off his helmet and held it out for Conrad to take, went over to the prostrate Hans and pulled him to his feet.

'Conrad saved my life,' he stammered.

Lukas smiled. 'I am glad all that training I have lavished upon him has not gone to waste.'

Conrad felt his legs go weak under him and had to lean against the side of a hut to stop himself collapsing. Then he was violently sick.

'Don't fill my helmet,' said Lukas, coming to his side. He wiped his bloody sword blade on his surcoat and then replaced it in his scabbard. He placed an arm on Conrad's shoulder.

'After-battle nerves. Nothing to worry about.'

'Who was that man in the shiny helmet?' asked Hans who continued to look around, fearing the enemy would reappear.

125

'His name is Lembit,' said Lukas, 'and he's the imp of Satan who leads the Estonian people against the church.'

'He was going to kill me but then Conrad shot him in the face. He saved my life.'

Rudolf and Henke appeared on their panting horses, swords in hand but helmets shoved back on their heads. Both were sweating heavily.

'Lembit flees,' said Henke without emotion.

'Young Conrad here slit his face,' said Lukas, 'and saved the life of his friend at the same time.'

'God smiles on you,' Rudolf said to him. 'Master Berthold requires our attendance, Lukas.'

They raised their swords to their friend and wheeled their horses away. Lukas, Conrad and Hans walked back to the castle as the perimeter gates were opened to allow Thalibald and his men to enter the compound that was now littered with dead. Master Berthold ordered no pursuit as Lembit and his warriors disappeared into the forest to the north of Wenden. Rather, he commanded a service of thanksgiving to be held in the courtyard, which everyone attended. The women sang most heartily for they knew that if the castle had fallen they and their young daughters would have been either raped and killed or raped and taken as slaves.

Word soon spread of Conrad's exploits in saving Hans and nearly killing Lembit and after the service women kissed him on the cheek and gruff mercenaries offered him their congratulations. His nausea had disappeared and he felt ten feet tall, an emotion soon dispelled when Rudolf ordered him and the other boys to take their crossbows, quivers and gambesons back to the armoury, telling Conrad to also hand in the sword he had taken off the dead pagan.

'God has a purpose for you, Conrad, of that I am sure,' said Rudolf, 'but not with a heathen sword in your hand. When the time comes you will be given your own sword with which to smite the enemies of our Lord.'

'Not until he learns to shoot a crossbow accurately,' remarked Lukas behind them. 'You're lucky Lembit didn't cut you in half. You might not be so lucky next time so it's back to the training fields for you and your companions.'

And so it was: back to the endless hours of learning to wield a sword, spear and shoot a crossbow, intermingled with instruction on the many and varied ways to kill an enemy with a dagger. But in the aftermath of the battle Conrad and the others helped to collect the enemy dead outside and inside the perimeter. They had recoiled in horror when tasked with heaping onto the backs of carts men whose heads had been smashed in when hit by a rock from a mangonel, or a warrior whose skull had been split in two by a knight on horseback. But Lukas told them that it was good for them to get used to seeing death and horror, as the war in Livonia would go on for many years to come.

Those score of Estonians who had been wounded and left behind by their comrades were herded into a pigpen where Master Berthold visited them. They were given a stark choice: baptism or death. Conrad watched as the twelve who had refused the offer to become Christians were burned to death outside the perimeter wall. All the mercenaries, sergeants and brother knights were witnesses to their execution as the flames licked around their feet and they began screaming and calling to their gods as the fire ate away their legs and then their torsos. Walter was as usual kneeling, his hands clasped together in worship, his lips reciting a prayer and his eyes closed.

Conrad thought it a cruel death and his face must have registered disapproval, which was noticed by Rudolf standing beside him as the air was filled with the pagans' ghastly screams.

'You find the judgement of Master Berthold disagreeable, Conrad?'

'No, sir, but I think that there are quicker ways to execute people rather than roasting them to death.'

The brushwood that had been piled high around the feet of the Estonians who had been chained to wooden posts was blazing with a fury now, incinerating their bodies. Though two unfortunates still appeared to be alive judging by the way their heads were thrashing about, mercifully there were no more screams. Hans beside him was looking decidedly ashen and Anton appeared to be on the verge of throwing up.

'Burning is the punishment for heresy, Conrad. It is Church law.'

'I have little regard for the law, sir,' replied Conrad, anger in his voice. 'It was the law that failed to protect my family and unjustly condemned my father to death.'

He glanced at Rudolf and blushed, for he had spoken out of turn to his superior. Rudolf looked at the roaring fires that had finally consumed the bodies of the Estonians.

'There is the law of men, Conrad, and the law of God. You must have faith that you will see justice done, though you must learn patience to see it so. You must also have faith, Conrad, for if you do then you will be rewarded.'

Conrad thought Rudolf spoke in riddles but said nothing further on the matter. He noticed Thalibald and his warriors grouped behind him, all staring impassively at the fire. The chief was dressed in simple grey leggings fixed at the calves with gaiters, a mail tunic and a sword in a scabbard at his waist. He held an iron helmet in the crook of his right arm and wore a red cloak around his shoulders. He was of medium height with a stocky frame, brown beard and shoulder-length hair.

His men looked similar to the Estonians who had attacked the castle, most of them wearing iron helmets, round wooden shields slung on their backs and spears in their hands. The warriors grouped immediately behind the chief were clad in mail and were armed with swords, while those behind wore no armour and had axes tucked into their belts instead of swords. They looked a rough lot.

'They are allies?' asked Conrad, looking at Thalibald with distaste.

'They are,' replied Rudolf. 'Chief Thalibald is a servant of the church but, more importantly, an enemy of the Estonians, especially Lembit who frequently sent his warriors south to raid these lands before the time of the Sword Brothers. He knows that when this castle is finished his lands will be more secure and his womenfolk and children will not be murdered or taken as slaves by the heathens.'

'But *they* are heathens,' said Conrad dismissively.

'Remember our conversation on the tower? Rome was not built in a day, Conrad. Do you know what that means?'

Conrad shook his head. 'No, sir.'

'It means that it takes time for great schemes to come to fruition.'

When the fire had died down Master Berthold dismissed the assembly and walked with Thalibald back to the castle. Conrad walked behind Lukas, Henke and Rudolf in the company of the other boys as they headed towards the chapel for midday mass. He looked behind him as Thalibald's warriors filed through the open gates into the compound, which had now been cleared of dead Estonians.

'Do you think we will get our swords now?' said Anton.

'I am sure we will,' said Bruno with certainty, who walked forward and slapped Conrad on the back, 'especially after Conrad's heroics.'

'I had to give up the sword I took,' said Conrad despondently.

'That is because you will be given a better one,' announced Johann.

Ilona came to the side of Rudolf who put his hand around her waist. She giggled and tossed back her long black hair. Rudolf said something to her and she turned to look at Conrad and then walked over to him. It was the first time he had been this close to her, though he had seen her often. She parted her full lips to smile at him and then leaned forward to kiss him gently on the cheek.

128

'A reward for the hero of the hour.' Her accent was strange, her voice sultry. Conrad blushed and looked down at the ground. Ilona laughed and then went back to Rudolf's side. Hans dug a finger into Conrad's ribs and Bruno slapped him on the back again.

After mass Conrad and the others reported to the armoury to be given armour to repair. Then they would eat lunch before their afternoon training session.

'Well, young Conrad, it looks like we were right to save your skin that night outside the cathedral.'

He snapped out of his daydream to see the powerful figure of Henke beside him as he left the armoury.

'Gave that bastard Lembit a present, I hear.'

'Yes, sir,' said Conrad proudly. He made to speak but stopped himself.

'If you have something to say spit it out,' said Henke tersely.

'Brother knights and sergeants of the Sword Brothers are forbidden to marry,' said Conrad, avoiding Henke's cold eyes.

'That is true.'

'But is Ilona Brother Rudolf's wife?'

Henke grinned. 'Not exactly. As a brother knight Rudolf cannot marry. Poverty, chastity, obedience, that is what we all swore when we agreed to fight in this land of heathens, forests and lakes. But Ilona is special.'

Conrad was perplexed. 'How so?'

'You are a curious little wretch,' sad Henke, 'but seeing as you did well in the battle I will tell you instead of giving you a good beating.

'Ilona was the one who pulled Rudolf out of the burning stables at Holm when the Russians raided it. And for that she earned Rudolf's eternal gratitude. Mine too.'

Holm on the Dvina, near Riga, was one of the first stone castles in Livonia.

'Attacked by the Russians it was,' continued Henke, 'led by a bastard named Domash Tverdislavich. That's a mouthful, ain't it?'

'What happened to him?' asked Conrad.

Henke spat on the ground. 'Hopefully he died a horrible death but I suspect he crawled back to Novgorod.'

He saw Conrad's blank look. 'It's a Russian city many miles from here. Hopefully one day we will catch up with him and then Rudolf can repay him for trying to roast him to death. Now, I've wasted enough time gossiping to you. Haven't you got weapons training to attend to?'

129

Conrad scurried off, having not been fully satisfied by Henke's answer. But at least he now knew where Rudolf had got his scars.

*****

Lembit sat beside the fire as the healer applied powder derived from dried yarrow onto his cut face. He did not flinch as the powder entered the wound and pain shot through his cheek. Yarrow was well known for its healing qualities and when dried and ground into powder it would staunch the flow of blood.

The healer then placed a bandage against the wound and asked Lembit to hold it in place.

'How long for?' he snapped.

'Half an hour should suffice, lord, unless you require a more permanent dressing.'

Lembit shook his head.

'Of course,' continued the healer, a wiry man with thinning hair and bony fingers. 'There will be a scar.'

Lembit waved him away and was left alone with his thoughts. Victory had been so close he could have touched it. And then it was cruelly snatched away by that traitor Thalibald. There was a time when he had accorded his rival the title 'valiant foe' but now he was nothing more than a crusader lackey, a man who had discarded his roots to suck at the teat of Bishop Albert and his revolting religion. He was beyond contempt. Lembit growled with anger.

'Are you all right, lord?' Rusticus crouched by his side.

'I am very far from all right,' Lembit hissed.

'The wound is deeper than you thought?'

Lembit looked at him with confusion. 'What? No, no. I was referring to the affair at Wenden.'

'We could go back, lord,' smiled Rusticus, who relished nothing more than the thought of more slaughter.

After retreating from Wenden they had moved north at speed, continuing their march through the forest during the night and only halting in the pre-dawn light of the next morning. Fortunately there was no pursuit and so they had made camp, dressed their wounds and filled their bellies. He estimated they were at least fifteen miles north of the castle, having suffered seventy dead and forty-five wounded, a dozen of them seriously. He had brought four hundred warriors with him and now over a quarter was either dead or wounded.

130

'No, we go back to Lehola and await the crusaders' next move. I have a debt to settle with Thalibald, though.'

'Do you wish me to go back and kill him, lord?' said Rusticus, a glint in his eye.

Lembit was tempted but decided his deputy was too valuable to be put at risk for the sake of a personal grudge.

'No. Thalibald can wait. Send a courier to the Oeselians, though, with a message for King Olaf.'

'What message?'

Lembit smiled savagely. 'That I accept his offer of an alliance.'

Rusticus raised his hand in acknowledgement and went to organise a party to journey to Oesel. It was a curious thing. Though Thalibald had robbed him of victory Lembit's thoughts were not about him but rather the boy who had nearly killed him. He saw his determined face, his eyes full of hatred and his youthful frame. If Rusticus had not appeared when he did then he would have killed the boy and made him pay for his inaccurate shooting. He held the bandage against his wounded cheek, which was now throbbing. The boy lived and that was unforgivable. He comforted himself with the thought that he might get another opportunity to assault Wenden next year when he would have the Oeselians by his side. Perhaps there would be no need. Perhaps the Kurs had defeated the crusader army, burned Riga to the ground and thrown the bishop and his pale-skinned priests on a fire. That would be a spectacle worth witnessing. And without their crusader allies there would be no place to hide for men such as Caupo and Thalibald.

*****

A pall of gloom hung over the bishop's palace in Riga, not only in a physical sense with regard to the dozens of funeral pyres that had been lit to cremate the bodies of dead Kurs who had been killed during the battle with the returning crusader army, but also metaphorically because the attack of the Kurs had come close to capturing the town itself. Archdeacon Stefan was still visibly shaken by the whole experience and had hidden in the castle while the Kurs had been attempting to scale its walls. He may have been a man of God but he had no desire to meet his maker just yet. Only the return of the bishop and his army had saved the town and defeated the pagans, who had suffered great losses at the hands of the mounted knights.

Archdeacon Stefan poured more wine into his cup and drank it greedily. 'The garrison must be strengthened, lord bishop,' he said. 'The Kurs may return and next time they may succeed.'

Bishop Albert frowned at his nephew who was usually a model of composure. 'The danger has passed, Stefan, there is no cause for alarm.'

They were sitting on chairs covered with silk around a large oak table in the palace's withdrawing chamber; a linen cover laid over its surface.

'And the Lithuanians crossed the Dvina to attack Kokenhusen,' continued Stefan, drinking more wine. 'It is as if all the demons of hell have been unleashed against us.'

The crusader leader who had accompanied Bishop Albert to Wenden also sat at the table, as did Grand Master Volquin, Caupo and Abbot Theodoric of the fortified monastery at Dünamünde, located on the northern bank of the Dvina near the Baltic. Theodoric had been converting the pagans in Livonia for nearly twenty years and had an intimate knowledge of the area and its peoples. The bishop valued him because he was a gruff, no-nonsense individual who retained a clear head in a crisis. No more so than now. Tall, gaunt and with hardly any hair on his bony head, he had a deep, commanding voice.

'The Kurs will not return this year,' he said, 'so calm yourself archdeacon. They are pirates and scavengers who look for easy victories. They have received a bloody nose and will be licking their wounds for a long time. Of more immediate concern is the Lithuanians.'

'Fortunately their assault against Kokenhusen was beaten off,' said the bishop, 'we have Prince Vsevolod to thank for that. He at least is loyal.'

'The garrison at Kokenhusen should be reinforced, lord bishop,' said Volquin, 'to deter any further Lithuanian aggression.'

The bishop smiled at the crusader commander. 'I would ask that you send some of your knights to the castle for the next few months, Sir Frederick.'

Frederick nodded and then stroked his beard. 'What of the campaign against the Estonians?'

'We cannot march against the Estonians,' Volquin answered for the bishop, 'without first securing Riga and the outlying castles. As well as Kokenhusen we must reinforce the garrisons of Holm, Uexkull and Lennewarden. Who knows where the Lithuanians will attack next?'

'Where indeed?' said the bishop.

'And do not forget Riga, lord bishop,' said Stefan who was now quite drunk. 'It stands naked in the face of its enemies.'

'Hardly that,' replied the bishop, 'though I agree that its defences also need strengthening.' He sighed. 'I therefore have no option but to postpone the crusade against the Estonians until next year when hopefully our position will be much stronger.'

'Those who came with me from Germany will be disappointed, lord bishop,' said Frederick.

'Those who stay might yet be able to wash their swords in heathen blood,' remarked Volquin, causing Frederick to look at him with interest.

'How so?' said Frederick.

'Once the winter sets in the swamps, rivers and lakes freeze hard and our horsemen can use them as roads, our wagons too. Those who stay will be able to test their mettle against the pagans, that I promise.'

Though it was customary for crusaders and their retinues to stay for a year, individuals were under no compulsion to stay in Livonia for twelve months, the more so if there was little prospect of campaigning.

Frederick was pleased by Volquin's words and smiled at the grand master, though Stefan was far from reassured.

'Frozen rivers may mean that your soldiers can march over them, Grand Master Volquin, but it also means that the Lithuanians can flood across the Dvina.'

'The Dvina does not freeze, archdeacon,' said Theodoric dismissively. 'At least not enough to allow an army to walk across it.'

'That may be so,' continued Stefan, slurring his words, 'but...'

Bishop Albert held up a hand to still him. 'The reinforced garrisons along the Dvina will halt any Lithuanian invasion, archdeacon, or at least stay it long enough for us to organise a riposte. In the meantime I will send word to the Lithuanians via Prince Vsevolod requesting a meeting. I believe the prince's wife is a native of the peoples who inhabit the lands south of the Dvina, so hopefully he has some influence among them.'

'We should take the army across the river and teach them a lesson,' said Frederick, sipping his wine.

'Alas,' replied the bishop, 'our resources do not allow us to wage war against the Lithuanians and the Estonians at the same time.'

There was a knock at the door and one of the young monks entered carrying a silver tray, upon which was a small rolled note. The monk, a boy no more than thirteen or fourteen, went over to the bishop, bowed his head and held out the tray. Everyone's eyes were upon Albert as he took the note and unfolded it, his brow creasing as he read the words. He sighed.

'Word form Master Berthold at Wenden. Lembit has attacked the castle but was beaten off, praise God.'

'That means the Estonians are only fifty miles from Riga,' said Volquin, causing Stefan to reach for the wine jug and refill his flagon.

Caupo, who until this moment had remained silent, now spoke. 'I must return to my lands, lord bishop. Lembit is a cruel enemy who will burn farms and rape my people and your loyal subjects. My men are needed in the north.'

Bishop Albert nodded his head. 'Go, lord king, and may God go with you.'

Caupo rose, bowed his head to the bishop and then followed the young monk out of the room.

Stefan's eyes widened in horror. 'We need Caupo's warriors here, lord bishop, to protect Riga from the heathens.'

'They are all slaughtered, archdeacon,' announced Frederick with pride. 'Have you not seen the landscape decorated with their funeral pyres?'

Stefan twisted up his nose. 'I have both seen and smelled them, Sir Frederick, but that does not mean that more will not return to avenge their dead kin.'

Volquin was tiring of the archdeacon's mouse-like utterances. 'The pagans will not return. They do not have an unlimited supply of warriors, archdeacon, despite your wild imaginings. The main threat lies to the north, as it always has done.'

Stefan cast Volquin a disdainful look and went back to his wine. It would soon be autumn and the crops would be gathered in, except that the crops and most of the farms around Riga had been destroyed by the Kurs, the farmers and their families having been either roasted alive in their homes or slaughtered in the fields. The people of Riga might have escaped such a fate but they now faced a winter of food shortages.

'God is testing us,' said the bishop, 'and we must remain steadfast in our determination to spread His word. We therefore consolidate our position around Riga, strengthen our defences along the Dvina and seek to make peace with the Lithuanians. Then we will be free to campaign against Lembit next year.'

'In the meantime our priority is gathering supplies to see us through the winter. Grand Master Volquin, I will leave the matter in your capable hands.'

Volquin nodded sternly and Stefan belched. The bishop had considered replacing him as administrator of the town with Theodoric, but the latter was a visionary and brave preacher not an intriguer. And for all Stefan's faults he was an able clerk. Theodoric would have a richer reward for his services when the time came.

*****

Vetseke saw the German patrol and sank deeper behind the lichen around the base of the tree to stay concealed. Luckily for him he had a green cloak to cover his mail shirt and he had lost his helmet days ago. The soldiers were about thirty yards away: two men on horseback and four men on foot – two spearmen and two crossbowmen. Vetseke kept very still. He was well acquainted with the lethality of crusader crossbows and had no wish to follow his men into the afterlife. He had landed with the Kurs along with a hundred of his warriors, the last of the retainers from his lands around Kokenhusen, but now the Kurs were defeated and his men were dead. At first the attack against Riga had exceeded all expectations. The settlers had been taken completely by surprise and the Kurs had seized the land all round the town. But instead of establishing proper siege lines and sending out patrols they had indulged in rape, pillage and destruction, so that when the crusader army appeared they had been cut to pieces by the mail-clad crusaders on horseback. Now the Germans were scouring the countryside for survivors. To be taken back to Riga and hanged, no doubt.

He slowed his breathing as the patrol halted on the track. The forest was silent, the air still and he could hear their voices. He had knowledge of their wretched language, having received instruction in different tongues as part of his upbringing as a prince.

'I heard something, I know I did.'

'Can you see anything?' asked another.

'Only trees.' There was laughter.

'Be quiet,' snapped another, presumably the commander.

Then there was silence. Vetseke thought that the thumping of his heart in his chest would give him away. He heard the tapping of a woodpecker in the distance and hoped that the patrol would think the bird was the sound its members heard. He remained frozen then heard the sound of running.

'There!'

He heard someone shout and raised his head a couple of inches to peer over the lichen.

He saw the crossbowmen shooting their weapons in the opposite direction to where he was hiding and then the two riders spurred their horses into the trees on the other side of the track. He thought he saw a fleeting glimpse of a figure in a white tunic fleeing from the patrol. Then he heard a scream and decided to head deeper into the forest before the patrol returned. Whoever he was who had broken cover and made a run for it had saved his life, at the expense of his own.

He kept moving for the rest of the day. He had not eaten for three days and his face carried four days' growth. He was tired but he knew he had to keep moving, keep moving east and then south to the Dvina. If he could find a boatman prepared to take him upriver he might yet save himself. Night came and he stumbled over large stones, fell down steep slopes and tripped over tree roots. He rested by the side of an oak tree for a few minutes and closed his eyes.

He awoke to the calls of finches and larks. It was light and he was infuriated with himself for sleeping for so long. He grasped the hilt of his sword and looked around. No sign of any patrols. He listened intently. No sounds of men tramping through the forest. He felt grubby and his mouth was dry. Keep moving east.

Three hours later, his limbs aching and a nausea induced by lack of nourishment sweeping over him, he crouched down in the trees fifty yards from the black waters of the Dvina. He stayed hidden until he saw a small fishing vessel approaching the sand bank directly in front of his position. It was of the type that had plied the Dvina for centuries: a simple boat with a hull made from ash stakes and withies, over which a skin of animal hide had been stretched. It had a small mast that was secured into a tapering hole cut into an oak mast board that was lashed to the boat's frame. The mast was supported by a similar hole in the central oak plank that also served as a seat. These riverboats had a wattle ash panel that served as a deck for standing on when getting in and out of the boat. An elderly man sat on the spars at the stern of the boat, steering the vessel.

It ran aground on the sand and the fisherman stood, stepped into the water and then hauled the vessel onto the sand bank. He then began to furl the sail. Vetseke pondered his choices as the fisherman began to prepare a small fire with which to cook a large catfish that he hauled from the boat and tossed on the sand. He could kill him and take his boat. But he had no knowledge of steering boats or navigating the Dvina. He decided to take a more civilised approach.

He broke cover and walked towards the fisherman who was using a flint to light the kindle. He sensed Vetseke's presence immediately and jumped to his feet, spinning round with a knife in his hand. The prince spread his arms to indicate he intended no violence.

'Greetings, friend,' he said.

The fisherman, still holding out his knife, looked past him to the trees to ascertain whether the stranger was alone.

'I do not know you,' said the fisherman, 'so how can I be your friend?'

Vetseke halted and let his arms fall by his side.

'State your business,' said the fisherman.

'I wish to journey upstream,' replied Vetseke. 'I will pay you well if you take me where I want to go. I have gold.'

The fisherman's eyes lit up at the mention of gold. He was obviously poor judging by his tattered leggings, bare feet and filthy, threadbare tunic and gold could transform his life, or at least make it a lot more comfortable than it was at present. The fisherman lowered his knife. His eyes narrowed as he weighed up the prince standing before him. Despite his bedraggled appearance and dark stubble on his face Vetseke still gave the appearance of one who enjoyed rank and privilege: his green cloak edged with fur, his mail shirt and his sword in its red scabbard.

'Where do you wish to go?' enquired the fishermen in a less aggressive tone.

Vetseke smiled. He knew he was winning him over. 'East of Kokenhusen.'

The fisherman sniffed. 'That is a long way from here and will take many days, especially if the wind is against us. Show me the gold.'

Vetseke was unused to being spoken to like this and for a moment thought that perhaps he should kill the miserable wretch after all. But that would still leave him with the problem of how to steer the boat. He smiled at the fisherman and untied a leather pouch that was attached to his belt. He shook a few tiny ingots into his palm and held it out to show the fisherman, whose eyes lit up at the sight of the means to change his life but a few feet away.

'I will take you,' he grinned at Vetseke, revealing a row of discoloured teeth.

Vetseke put the ingots back in the pouch and nodded towards the catfish.

'I have not eaten for a while and would appreciate a meal.'

As a sign of good faith Vetseke gave the fisherman one of the ingots, which delighted him to such an extent that he started singing as he lit the kindle and started the fire to cook the fish. Vetseke unbuckled his sword belt and flopped down on the sand, leaning his back against the man's boat. The day was warm and bright, a slight breeze blowing from the west – a good sign. The Dvina was calm, the current slow at this spot. Even though there were rapids along the length of the river the lightweight boat could be beached and hauled around them easily enough.

After they had eaten the fisherman unfurled the sail of his boat and he and Vetseke pushed it into the water and jumped aboard. The prince sat on the bench amidships while the fisherman steered the vessel. The westerly breeze held so their progress was excellent and Vetseke began to relax. Each minute placed him further away from the accursed crusaders and closer to the Russians. Though he was not of that race and had been a vassal of the Principality of Polotsk the Russians had always treated him with respect, leaving him free to rule his own, smaller Principality of Kokenhusen. So much so that when the crusaders had attacked his lands the Russians had sent him no aid. But now his castle and lands were in the hands of Bishop Albert and his Sword Brothers and his people enslaved. He had made a mistake in throwing in his lot with the Kurs, in the process losing all his men and almost his life. Now he would throw himself on the mercy of his neighbour, Prince Vsevolod, in the hope that he would give him sanctuary. He had always maintained amiable relations with Vsevolod but knew that he had close relations with the Lithuanians through his marriage to the daughter of Grand Duke Daugerutis. He had no love for the Lithuanians who had frequently raided his lands and carried off his people into slavery. But he knew and so did Vsevolod that Gerzika was the next stronghold in the crusader advance and that alone made him and the prince allies.

When the boat passed by Kokenhusen Vetseke purposely looked away towards the southern bank of the river, so aggrieved was he that the banners of the Sword Brothers flew from the towers of his own stronghold. He heard the fisherman whistling at the stern of the boat. Perhaps he would kill him after all when they reached the end of their journey. That at least would make him happier. He turned and smiled at the foul-looking man who grinned enthusiastically back at him. The gods would surely thank him for ridding the world of such an inconsequential individual.

Chapter 6

Conrad sat dead still in the saddle as the pony he was riding walked south towards the village of Chief Thalibald. Following the defeat of Lembit and his Estonians life had returned to normal at Wenden, which for him and his comrades meant a return to the training fields to continue their education in martial skills. But today they were going to assist the locals to harvest their crops. The day was hot and he sweated as he sat on the chestnut-coloured pony, the beast occasionally flicking its tail to swat away the plague of midges that had greeted the riders as they skirted a lake two miles south of Wenden. Before they had left all the boys had been given tansy leaves to rub on their arms and necks to ward off the tiny pests. So far it had worked.

They rode at a gentle pace, as it was the first time that Conrad and the others, aside from Anton, had been in the saddle. Lukas, Rudolf and Henke accompanied them, the brother knights riding on horses and armed with swords, shields and helmets dangling from their saddles. Thalibald's village was five miles south of Wenden, one of the many small settlements that ringed the castle. Though most of the landscape was covered with trees and lakes, around the villages the land had been cleared to create fields that grew crops, some of which were sent to Wenden to feed its occupants. It was accorded a minor miracle that Lembit did not send his warriors to raid the villages and slaughter their livestock, or burn the ripened crops in the fields, and focused entirely on assaulting the castle. Thus had the food supply for the coming winter been saved and everyone had breathed a sigh of relief. The boys did not appreciate it and Bruno and Johann were complaining to each other that it was a waste of their time to be harvesting crops.

Lukas heard their moans. '*I* will decide how your time is spent. I assume you want to eat during the winter?'

Hans nodded his head enthusiastically. 'Yes, Brother Lukas, food is very important.'

The other boys laughed and even Lukas smiled. Hans always put his stomach above all other concerns.

'Well, then,' said Lukas, 'you all go to do valuable work.'

'Do not the villagers harvest their own crops?' asked Conrad, his eyes fixed on the head of his pony and his hands gripping the reins tightly.

'Of course,' said Rudolf, 'but we send help when we can spare it. It shows goodwill and helps build good relations with the villagers.'

139

'They should do as they are told,' sneered Anton, betraying his family's attitude towards society's lower orders.

'This is not Germany,' Rudolf reminded him. 'We would have the loyalty of the locals, not their hatred, if we are to build a new Jerusalem in this land.'

Henke riding beside him grunted his disapproval but said nothing. Henke had never enjoyed the privileged upbringing of his friend and commander and believed the strong ruled and the weak suffered. But even he understood that men needed to eat.

'The Sword Brothers are not Estonians,' Lukas told them all. 'We exist to protect native and pilgrim alike in this land. You should all remember that.'

Henke shook his head and smiled wryly but Conrad was impressed. He liked the idea of being a member of an organisation that protected the weak, just as Rudolf and Henke had protected him and his sister in their hour of need.

'Besides,' said Lukas, 'on a more practical level we are ensuring that our investment has been used wisely.'

Conrad was confused. 'Investment, Brother Lukas?'

'Seed, ploughs and oxen,' answered Lukas. 'All gifts from the Sword Brothers to help seal our bond with Thalibald's people.'

'A people who are our allies, Anton,' said Rudolf, 'not our slaves.'

'A farmer's life is a hard one,' said Lukas, 'so it is only right that we lend a hand when we can.'

He was certainly right about that.

The ploughing usually began in April when the soil was soft enough to turn easily by the heavy ploughs supplied by the Sword Brothers. The team of oxen that pulled the ploughs had also been a gift from the order, as were the seed for the crops: barley, oats, peas, beans and vetches. And in April the cows came back into full milk as they grazed in the meadows rather than on sparse winter fodder. Between May and the end of September each year every cow was expected to produce enough milk to make nearly a hundred pounds of cheese and fifteen pounds of butter. That Lembit and his warriors had not stolen or slaughtered the cows of Thalibald's people had been a minor miracle and was the subject of a service of thanksgiving in Wenden's chapel in the days after his attack.

In June haymaking was the main activity of the villagers. The meadows were scythed to collect hay, which was vital as it provided the main winter fodder for animals. Lambs were weaned as early as possible because sheep's milk was rich and highly prized. Shearing usually began late in the month.

In July, while Conrad and his companions had been learning to wield their swords, the villagers had been pulling up flax and hemp. The plants were laid out in the sun to dry before being retted: placed in a stream to rot away their fleshy parts. Once the fibres were clean they were then beaten to separate them and then hung up to dry. Afterwards the hemp could be wound into rope or cord. Flax was placed on a distaff to be spun into yarn.

The harvest began in August, the winter crops – wheat and rye – being harvested first followed by the spring grains: barley and oats. The wheat was harvested with a sickle, which Conrad now swung to slice right through an ear of wheat.

'Not like that,' said Lukas, 'cut it two hands breadths below the ear to leave the long stubble still standing. Not too high, not too low.'

Hans sweating beside him grinned. 'I bet you wish you were killing Estonians rather than doing this.'

'I never realised it was so hard,' Conrad replied, standing up to stretch his back. They had been bent over for an hour now and the muscles in his lower back ached like fury. As he stopped and looked around, to his consternation he saw that the local men and women were scything with aplomb, cutting through the wheat with gusto. The progress of Conrad and the other boys was dire by contrast.

'Pitiful,' said Rudolf as Conrad leaned against the wheel of a cart heaped high with harvested crops, beads of sweat on his forehead. The other boys were likewise sweating profusely.

'I hope you perform better when you face an enemy,' Rudolf teased them.

Conrad was tempted to ask when he and the other two brother knights were going to lend a hand but thought better of it. In any case he liked them, even the fierce Henke, and saw no purpose in provoking them. Nevertheless, their short stint in the fields had been a stark introduction to the hard life of a farmer. He peered into the sky to see if any clouds were forming that might offer some relief from the sun. Nothing! Hans nudged him in the ribs and pointed to a line of teenage girls approaching, each one with a wooden yoke across her shoulders, from which hung two buckets. By the girls' laboured movements Conrad judged them to be full.

'Refreshments,' announced Rudolf, looking at his exhausted charges, 'not that you deserve any.'

He grinned at Lukas who smiled and shook his head. The boys all stood as the girls approached, making their way along the track that led from Thalibald's

141

village to the field. The other villagers in the fields stopped, looked at the girls and went back to their scything.

Conrad was in awe of their stamina. 'I did not know farmers and their wives had so much strength,' he said to Rudolf.

'It is a strength born of desperation,' he replied.

Conrad looked at him in confusion.

'They have to harvest the crops as quickly as possible. If the rains come they can ruin the crops and that means starvation. We are at war with the pagans but the war these people fight against nature is constant and unyielding. That is why we help them.'

Conrad began to see the villagers in a different light and bent down to pick up his scythe. He heard a shout and saw that one of the girls had tripped and was on her knees, though she had managed to sit the buckets down on the track before she tumbled. Conrad dropped his scythe and ran over to her, helping her to her feet.

'Thank you,' she said in German, smiling at him.

Conrad smiled back, still holding her arm. 'You speak our language.'

'My father taught me,' she replied, her green eyes sparkling.

Conrad admired her as she adjusted the yoke and lifted the buckets holding water off the ground. She was a striking girl with an oval face, narrow nose with a pointed tip, high cheekbones and full lips.

'Can I carry those for you?' he asked, blushing slightly.

'No, thank you,' she replied, 'though you can let go of me now.'

He blushed some more as he realised that his hand was still on her arm. He snapped his arm back and mumbled an apology as she giggled at the other girls. He trailed after her like a puppy as she and they went to the wagons. Conrad estimated her to be about his age, perhaps two inches shorter, with shoulder-length light brown hair. She and the other four girls, who paled somewhat beside her, put down their buckets in front of the now standing boys and offered ladles of water, serving Rudolf, Henke and Lukas first.

Rudolf took the ladle off the brown-haired beauty and drank. 'Thank you, Daina,' he said. So her name was Daina.

Conrad waited eagerly behind him as the mail-clad knights took their fill before moving aside to let him drink. He smiled sheepishly as Daina handed him some water. Though her body was wrapped in a white linen shift beneath a sleeveless blue dress that was fastened at the front by laces, he could see that she had a slim frame, unlike two of her friends who were rather plump in appearance.

142

Conrad downed his drink and was about to say something to the dazzler that had stirred his boyhood feelings, but then Rudolf slapped him on the back.

'Say goodbye to Daina, Conrad. Time to get back to work.'

Conrad half-smiled at her, blushed, mumbled something under his breath and then picked up his scythe and followed the others back to the field. He glanced over his shoulder to catch a last sight of her. Daina tilted her head and smiled at him before hoisting the buckets back on her shoulders and returning with the other girls back to the village. Conrad's mind was filled with images of her for the rest of the day and he forgot entirely about his aching back and tired limbs.

He and the others spent three days helping to harvest the crops. Though it was a break from their instruction in the martial arts, Lukas and Rudolf thought it an invaluable lesson in how their fate was bound up with the locals and what they produced. At night they slept in one of the huts that Thalibald made available in his village, which was filled with a hall, huts, barns and animals pens. It stank of the latter but was located near a fast-flowing stream filled with cool water where they could wash the aroma of animals and straw from their bodies every morning. A timber wall ringed the village itself with a ditch in front of it, a wooden bridge over the ditch and a single gate giving access to the settlement. Rudolf told the boys that it had a palisade because it was where Thalibald lived but the other villages had no defences.

When the August harvest had been collected the chief gave a feast in his hall to celebrate, which was attended by the whole village. Men and boys occupied long benches while the womenfolk served the food before sitting with their families to share in the meal. Thalibald sat on the top table with his fair-haired wife Helena and flanked by his two sons, Rameke and Waribule. The latter was older and more severe looking than his younger sibling, but both had inherited their father's stocky frame. Rudolf, Henke and Lukas also sat at the top table, Conrad and the others sitting on a bench at right angles directly in front of Rudolf.

The kitchens were attached to the side of the hall, but before the women served the food everyone stood in silence while Thalibald offered a prayer of thanks to God for the good weather that had ripened the crops and allowed them to be harvested. Then the men and boys took their seats while the women ferried the food from the kitchens. Despite the tangible air of happiness and relief in the air the feast was remarkably quiet and restrained. Rudolf told Conrad afterwards that this was because before Christianity came to this land the locals had viewed sitting down to a meal to be a serious business that demanded calmness and decorum.

Notwithstanding the earnestness of the occasion the food was excellent both in terms of quality and quantity. Hans was like a fox that had got into a chicken coop as he held out his bowl to be filled with roasted boar, duck and chicken, all flavoured with caraway seeds, onions, garlic and white mustard.

There was also a plentiful supply of a drink called *kvass* that was made from rye bread and flavoured with strawberries. It was thirst quenching but non-intoxicating, thus ensuring that the feast did not descend into raucousness.

Johann sat opposite Hans watching him stuff some *piragi* – bread filled with diced, fatty bacon and onion – into his mouth.

'I have thought of a way of defeating the Estonians.'

Conrad and the others looked at him.

'It is true,' he continued. 'All we have to do is send Hans into their territory to eat up all their food supplies and they will starve to death.'

They laughed as Hans finished his *piragi* and reached for another. Conrad sensed a presence beside him and turned to see Daina standing holding a wooden plate, upon which was a loaf of bread. The room was hot and stuffy and Conrad felt sweat trickle down his neck as his heart raced at the sight of her.

She looked at him with her bright green eyes. 'My people believe that bread baked from the first harvest has special powers.'

She offered Conrad a slice of the bread. He took it eagerly, Hans and the others staring at Daina.

'They believe,' she continued, 'that if you make a wish when eating this bread the wish will be granted.'

Conrad said nothing as he stuffed the bread into his mouth and swallowed it, wishing that he could see more of this delightful girl. Daina smiled at him. 'That is what my people believe.'

Then she turned and went to another table to serve others. His companions laughed and pointed at him as they made fun of him. He picked up his cup and drank some *kvass*, then turned to see Rudolf studying him. Conrad felt embarrassed and knew that it was wrong to believe in pagan superstition. But Rudolf smiled and raised his cup to him. Conrad did not see Daina the next morning as they saddled their ponies prior to riding back to Wenden but he left Thalibald's village with a happy heart. It was now early September and the rich shades of green were slowly turning into hues of yellow and brown as the leaves changed colour before they fell to the ground. The days were still warm and sunny though the nights were now cool and the sky was filled with flocks of migratory birds heading to warmer climes, the white stork being the first to leave Livonia.

*****

He had been hunting the boar all morning, following its trail through the tunnels made by the animals among the thickets and trees that filled this part of Oesel. He had caught only fleeting glimpses of the beast but enough to know it had powerful shoulders and massive jaws, its four tusks being able to inflict terrible injuries. It was also big, perhaps weighing around three hundred pounds. Eric crept forward slowly, being careful not to step on any twigs that might snap and give him away. He looked behind him at his hunting party – men armed with spears and bows – and waved them back. He did not want them blundering forward and making a noise that would scare off his prey. Not that 'scare' was an appropriate word to use when talking about a wild boar. Every Oeselian knew them to be notoriously bad tempered and territorial, aggressive when threatened and generally preferring fight to flight when boxed into a corner.

Eric moved forward once more, skirting a thicket and stepping into the muddy water of a small stream. He knew this was ideal boar terrain: moist with dense cover and near water. Boars love water. They cannot sweat and so wallowing in a stream cools them down and also protects them from insects and parasites. And after a good wallowing came a vigorous rub, usually against a tree.

Eric moved slowly through the ankle-deep water, keeping a tight grip on his boar spear. He wore no armour on his body or head and carried only a knife as a backup, preferring to be as lightly equipped as possible to spring into the attack and move speedily out of the way of a charging boar. His spear comprised a six-foot shaft with a broad steel tip and two lugs on the spear socket, behind the blade. These lugs prevented a raging boar working its way up the spear shaft towards the hunter once impaled.

Crouching low, Eric emerged from the stream and stepped gingerly forward. He heard grunts and peered around a thicket to see his prey rubbing his great body against a tree. It was a large male with a red coat, so totally engrossed in his scratching that he was unaware of Eric's presence. He smiled. A startled boar was a very dangerous creature and not to be underestimated. He knew this as he moved beyond the thicket to stand out in the open around ten paces from the boar. He roared a challenge and then levelled his spear.

The boar turned in an instant and charged. It covered the ground between them in no time, squealing in rage as it ran at Eric's legs to slash and rip his muscles, tendons and arteries with its tusks. He knew that a spear thrust into the animal's heart from the front would kill it quickly, but the red monster had his head down as he charged so Eric shifted the weight onto his left foot as he leaped aside and plunged the spear into the boar's side, right behind its front legs. The animal squealed in pain and anger and twisted right with all its strength. Eric's legs gave way and he fell to the wet earth with three hundred pounds of enraged boar on top of him. He could smell its rancid breath, his face covered with foam coming from the animal's mouth as it tried to gouge him with its tusks, the spear sticking in its right side pumping blood on his shirt and leggings. He heard shouts as his men rushed to assist him but the enraged boar was thrashing around violently, its tusks ripping his shirt and cutting his arm. A boar's upper jaw carries stumpy tusks called 'whetters' that are razor sharp. Eric cried out in pain as these sliced the flesh on his arm. With his right arm he pulled the dagger from the sheath on his belt and rammed the long blade into the boar's side, forcing the point down. It stopped thrashing as the point of the weapon found its heart and killed it.

His men appeared, crashing through the undergrowth.

'Get this stinking thing off me,' he shouted as the boar's bladder involuntarily opened and it pissed all over him.

It took three men to haul the beast off their lord while another pulled him to his feet. He was covered in mud, blood – his own and the animal's – and urine but he threw his head back and roared with laughter and triumph at his victory. He looked at the boar.

'A fine kill, lord,' said his deputy.

Eric slapped him on the arm and then grimaced as the blood-rush of victory subsided and pain began to lance through his injured left arm. He also rubbed his ribs.

'The monster nearly crushed me to death,' he grinned.

He heard horn blasts and horses' hooves and cries of 'make way for the king' and then his father and brothers were in front of him, the men of the royal bodyguard behind them. His father brought his light brown mare to a halt a few paces from him, the hunting party bowing their heads at him as he looked at his eldest son and then at the dead boar.

'You will soon have more challenging foes to kill, Eric. The Estonians have provisionally agreed to an alliance with us.'

146

Eric signalled to one of his party to bandage his arm as he slid his knife back into its sheath.

'So we are servants of the Estonians now?'

'Allies, Eric,' said Sigurd next to Olaf, 'with whom we shall destroy the Christian settlers and take their lands.'

The man finished bandaging Eric's arm and another handed him his spear that had been lodged in the boar's side.

'The Estonians are weak,' he sneered, 'that is why they agree to our friendship.'

'Not so weak that they cannot strike at the enemy's strongholds,' said Sigurd smugly.

'Word has reached us that Lembit attacked the crusader castle at Wenden,' said Olaf, 'one of their strongest citadels.'

Eric was unconvinced. 'Did he take it?'

Sigurd shook his head. Eric laughed.

'That rather proves my point. The Estonians are a weak people.'

Olaf frowned. 'That may be, but combined we stand a better chance of defeating the crusaders than fighting alone. Next year we will act in unison with Lembit to strike a fatal blow against the Christians.'

'Why not now?' asked Eric, a glint in his eye.

Olaf shook his head. 'It is too late in the year. The rivers will soon be iced over and too dangerous for our boats.'

He nodded approvingly at the dead boar. 'Taarapita has smiled on you, my son.'

Taarapita was the god of the Oeselians, the God of Thunder and War.

'Let us hope He also blesses our alliance with the Estonians,' replied Eric as his men fastened the boar's carcass to a length of wood for transportation back to the island's capital.

*****

As the autumn drew to a close Conrad and his companions continued to receive martial instruction from Lukas. As the days became cooler they were lashed by wind and rain and the trees turned brown and yellow. At Riga some of the crusaders returned home following the defeat of the Kurs, though Bishop Albert persuaded others to stay to provide security against further raids. He also sent messages of peace to the Lithuanians but received no reply and so soldiers had to be

147

despatched to the castles along the Dvina to bolster Livonia's southern defence line. At Wenden the mercenaries accompanied the sergeants and brother knights on great hunting trips to collect meat for the winter. Hundreds of crossbow bolts were used to slaughter dozens of elk, deer and wild boar, the carcasses being taken back to the castle to be skinned and gutted to produce cured meat for the winter. Conrad and his associates went on these trips but were not issued with crossbows; rather, they had the unsavoury task of assisting the crossbowmen in digging their bolts out of the carcasses of slaughtered animals.

Conrad was kneeling beside the body of a large elk that had three quarrels lodged in its side. It was one of a dozen arranged on the ground in the camp, along with rows of dead deer and wild boars, all of which had been shot. The stench of blood was nauseating. Conrad turned up his nose as he dug a bolt out of the elk with his knife. He objected to being here when he could be sharpening his sword skills, albeit with a wooden waster. He yanked out the quarrel and handed it to a crossbowman kneeling beside another elk carcass. The man with his leathery face nodded in thanks, wiped the blood off the bolt and slipped it back into his quiver.

'Waste of time,' muttered Conrad.

'When you're shivering your balls off and your belly is aching because it's empty you will think differently, boy.'

Conrad, who had never been better fed, thought that unlikely. The man saw his sceptical expression.

He grinned maliciously. 'Winters are long and cold in this land, boy, and there are many mouths to feed at Wenden. It is good to collect as much food now rather than starve later.'

'Are we going to eat the rabbits too?' asked Conrad. For weeks traps had been laid around the castle to trap rabbits, squirrels, martens and foxes.

'No, boy. The hides of all the small animals are shipped south to Riga for sale to fur merchants to raise money.'

'Money for what?' asked Conrad, handing him another bloody quarrel.

The crossbowman laughed. 'How do you think the Sword Brothers pay for me and my comrades, the stonemasons, carpenters and the others who live at Wenden? Wars and crusades don't come cheap, boy, and so Master Berthold sells furs and timber to support his garrison and build his castle.'

He wiped his nose on his bloody cloth. 'Now, the pious knight who arrived at the same time as you.'

'Walter,' said Conrad.

'Yes, that's him. Now people like him come with a big donation to the holy crusade in Livonia, which is paid to the bishop in Riga but shared with whatever castle he ends up in. In his case Wenden. But there's never enough money. Even salt has to be imported.'

'Salt?'

'To cure the meat from these beasts,' he said. 'There's none of it here so it has to be imported.'

Conrad was glad when the hunting trips ended and he could return to his training. He and the others were taught to ride holding a shield and lance, receiving instruction in how to jump into the saddle from the ground rather than using stirrups. They practised on the garrison's ponies, not the expensive warhorses that were treated like equine kings. Lukas also took them on long-distance runs through the forest to improve their stamina.

'You are all gaining in strength but there is no point in being able to wield a sword in battle if you are too exhausted to lift it.'

Conrad tried to be clever. 'I thought you told us to finish an opponent as quickly as possible, Brother Lukas.'

'So I did, Conrad, but you may be surprised to know that in battle you will face more than one opponent. We are almost always outnumbered so we must have the stamina to stay on our feet to kill many opponents.'

Even though the hours of daylight were shortening they trained until past dusk, honing their skills until they became second nature. They all asked when they would be issued with real swords and were given extra fatigue duties for their impudence. In the end they gave up asking but all of them looked forward to the day when they had their own swords.

The regime they lived under was hard but fair and though the brother knights were a rough lot they were not cruel. Master Berthold was a wise old fox who tolerated no ill discipline among his subordinates. And he ruled with an iron fist. One day Conrad stood with his companions in a heavy rain as justice was meted out to one of the mercenaries who had attempted to rape the young daughter of a stonemason. The brother knights sat on their warhorses in their armour and helmets as Otto stood on the back of a cart saying prayers beside the ashen-faced prisoner who had a noose around his neck, his hands bound behind his back. He looked imploringly but forlornly at his fellow mercenaries who were arrayed before him in their ranks. But they had no sympathy for his plight: the Sword Brothers paid well for their services and they were unwilling to risk their livelihoods for the sake of a stupid man.

The priest stopped reciting prayers and the prisoner looked at the stony faced civilians on one side of the three-sided square who had been assembled to witness justice being administered. He licked his lips and began shaking as Master Berthold nodded his head and one of the sergeants slapped the horse that was hitched to the cart. The beast walked forward and the prisoner was left dangling from the wooden crossbeam. His legs kicked frantically for perhaps a minute and his body twisted on the rope but then he was still. Master Berthold made everyone remain in their positions for at least ten minutes before dismissing the assembly. Conrad's mind was filled with images of his father's execution and he shuddered. He detested seeing people being put to death, whatever their crimes.

As the days shortened Lukas introduced them to the quintain, a method of teaching a rider to charge carrying a lance. The device consisted of a shield fixed to the end of a swinging arm, with a sandbag attached to the arm's other end. A rider rode at the shield and struck it with his lance, whereupon the arm would rotate and the sandbag would swing round. The rider's task was therefore not only to strike the shield but also avoid being struck on the back by the sandbag and unhorsed. The quintain itself was a simple structure made from pine with a heavy base to prevent it being toppled over when it was struck.

The boys' first attempts at training with the quintain were lamentable, each of them being so intent on not being hit by the sandbag that they missed the shield altogether. Their lances had no metal points but rather blunt ends so as to minimise any chance of injury, which seemed highly unlike as Conrad and the others cantered at the targets and missed them.

'You are thinking about the bag and not the target,' Lukas shouted at them. 'Go again.'

Conrad wrapped the reins of his pony around his left hand and concentrated on the target a hundred yards in front of him. It had been rainy and the ground was already cutting up. His pony grunted as Conrad felt the stirrups beneath his feet and dug his spurs into its flanks.

'Concentrate on the target, Conrad,' Lukas bellowed as the pony trotted forward and then broke into a canter. He gripped the lance tucked under his right arm and brought up the blunt end as the shield came into view. This time he would not miss. He focused on the target as the distance between him and it shortened – fifty yards, thirty yards, ten yards – and then he struck it. He smiled as his lance hit the shield dead centre and shoved it aside. He gave out a triumphant shout and was knocked from the saddle as the wooden arm swung round and slammed the sandbag into his back. He fell heavily, his padded gambeson preventing any serious injury, but he was still winded. He gasped for air as the other boys cheered and burst into laughter. Lukas ambled over and helped him to his feet.

'Well done, Conrad. Try to remember the bag next time.'

After a month he and the others had gained a certain amount of competency against the quintain and were introduced to 'running at the rings'. For this they were given lances with steel tips and rode at a gallop against metal rings suspended on a cord from a beam, which they attempted to carry off on the tip of their lances. After several weeks they were all comfortable in the saddle and so Lukas took them out into the countryside to undertake mock patrols, armed with their wooden swords and shields. They learned to ride in column formation and deploy into line at a moment's notice. They began to feel like real knights until their fantasy was dashed one afternoon when they were 'attacked' by Rudolf and Henke armed with blunted lances with padded ends. The brother knights knocked Conrad and the others out of their saddles and then scattered their ponies, providing a salutary lesson in the art of ambush. Their spirits were deflated further when Lukas told them that it would be three or four years before they would be judged capable of taking part in real raids and patrols.

As the weeks passed the land changed as winter gripped Livonia. The pine and spruce trees retained their green foliage but as the temperature dropped the birch and oaks lost their leaves and became black shapes in a bleak landscape. The first snow fell in November, the flakes blanketing the land in a sea of white though it was not yet bitterly cold and so the rivers and streams were still ice-free. Travel via the waterways was still possible and at the end of the month Bishop Albert himself came to Wenden by riverboat, accompanied by Grand Master Volquin, Sir Frederick and a hundred knights and squires. Once more Conrad and the others were turfed out of the dormitory to accommodate the senior officers of the bishop's retinue. On the first evening of the bishop's visit Conrad and his companions were ordered to act as attendants as Master Berthold feasted his new arrivals in his hall that now had a completed vaulted roof.

The kitchens prepared a meal of stew and roasted pork. Most of the animals had already been slaughtered and their meat cured but the garrison still retained a small number of cows and pigs, the latter being able to subsist on scraps that were fed to them. A fire raged in the hall to keep the guests warm as Conrad served mulled wine from a jug to those gathered round the table: the bishop, the bishop's chaplain, Grand Master Volquin, Sir Frederick, Master Berthold and Brother Rudolf. The chaplain said prayers and then Hans, Bruno and Johann brought meat, stew and bread from the kitchens to the table. Anton and Conrad emptied their jugs as the guests drank their fill and then brought more mulled wine as the table was cleared. He and Anton remained in the hall, Conrad standing behind the bishop and Anton behind Master Berthold, while the rest were dismissed. Conrad smiled when he saw Hans picking up food from Sir Frederick's half-empty plate and stuffing it into his mouth as he went back to the kitchens.

The fire crackled and spat in the hearth as the light from the candles around the table cast the guests in an eerie pale yellow glow. The bishop ran a finger around the rim of his cup.

'These are trying times, my friends. Though we defeated the Kurs the lands around Riga were laid waste, with the result that there is a food shortage in the town. I have made appeals for food through the churches in northern Germany to be sent to Riga but this winter will be a hard one.'

Sir Frederick drained his cup and held it out for Anton to refill it.

'I have, through Prince Vsevolod, made appeals to the Lithuanians for talks so that we can reconcile our differences and halt their raids across the Dvina.'

'Do you think that is likely, lord bishop?' asked Master Berthold.

The bishop shrugged. 'I believe that the Lithuanians may have been encouraged by the audacity of the Kur attack against Riga to cross the Dvina and test our defences along the river. The defeat of the Kurs, plus their own failure at Kokenhusen, will hopefully deter the Lithuanians from attempting any more river crossings. In any case I am confident that Prince Vsevolod will be a restraining influence on his father-in-law.'

'Should this not be so,' added Grand Master Volquin, 'we have strengthened the garrison of Kokenhusen plus those of Holm, Uexkull and Lennewarden. As long as we control the river line the Lithuanians can be contained.'

'Which leaves Lembit and his Estonians as the most pressing threat,' said the bishop. He looked at Master Berthold. 'What news do you have of him?'

Berthold scratched his beard. 'That he sits in his stronghold at Lehola boasting of how he nearly took Wenden.'

The bishop wore a worried look. 'That he felt confident to venture this far south and assault this stronghold is bad enough, but his audacity gives hope to the pagan cause and is an affront to the Holy Church.'

'He will be brought to heel next year easily enough,' boasted Sir Frederick, wiping his wine-soaked beard on his sleeve.

'That may be,' replied the bishop, 'but the spectre of Lembit casts a log shadow over this land. Caupo fears that his exploits make our cause look weak, which in turn might fan the flames of rebellion in our own lands.'

The room smelt of wood smoke and Conrad's eyes smarted a little as the wind outside blew down the chimney. He saw Berthold look at Rudolf, who nodded.

'Lord bishop,' said the master, 'my deputy, Brother Rudolf, has an audacious plan that I think you should consider. One that may exorcise the spectre of Lembit.'

The mask of doom disappeared from the bishop's face. 'Let us hear this most wondrous scheme.'

Rudolf took a sip of his wine. 'It is quite simple, lord bishop, we strike at Lembit before he can strike at us, thereby illustrating that our cause is the stronger.'

Sir Frederick was unimpressed. 'Of course we are going to attack. Next spring we will be marching north with all our strength. Not much of a plan.'

Rudolf continued. 'I propose that we attack Lembit in two months' time.'

'In January?' said the bishop with surprise.

'Impossible,' barked Sir Frederick, 'the land is already covered in snow. In January there will be more.'

'Precisely,' said Rudolf triumphantly. 'The land will be frozen solid, which means that we can use the lakes and rivers as roads with ease.'

'Campaigning in winter is most unusual,' cautioned Grand Master Volquin.

'But audacious,' said Master Berthold.

'And Lembit will not be expecting an attack,' added Rudolf. 'It will be our turn to surprise him.'

The bishop began to drum his fingers on the table as he pondered Rudolf's suggestion. The latter looked at Conrad and then at the bishop to indicate that he should fill his cup. Conrad stepped forward and poured wine into the cup. The bishop stopped his drumming and half-smiled at Conrad.

'You may be interested to know that during the recent assault upon Wenden, lord bishop,' said Rudolf, 'this novice, Conrad Wolff, fought a personal duel with Lembit and wounded him in the face.'

The bishop looked up at Conrad, his square face highlighted by the glow of the fire. He nodded at Conrad.

'Well done, young lad.' The bishop studied Conrad for a few seconds, making the boy feel most uncomfortable. 'Well, it would appear that God has a plan for you, Master Conrad, one that involves smiting the infidel.'

Conrad bowed his head and Rudolf waved him back.

'What about attacking Lembit?' said Sir Frederick impatiently.

The bishop was still unsure. 'Fighting in winter carries grave risks, Brother Rudolf. If our forces were to get trapped in enemy territory we would have no way to reinforce them by river, or indeed evacuate them by water.'

Rudolf shook his head. 'The pagans will not be expecting an attack, lord bishop. As a result their warriors will be scattered among the villages of Estonia. We can raid those villages, steal their winter supplies and burn them before we assault our objective.'

'Which is?' asked the bishop.

'The fort of Fellin,' answered Rudolf, located around seventy miles due north of this castle. It is located only ten miles south of Lembit's own stronghold of Lehola.'

'Can we take and hold a place so deep in enemy territory?' queried the bishop.

'We do not hold it,' replied Master Berthold. 'By taking it we demonstrate that Lembit is unable to protect his territory and people, unlike the garrison of Wenden, and in so doing prove that our cause is righteous.'

Sir Frederick was nodding his approval and Grand Master Volquin was impressed by the idea of his subordinates. Now all their eyes turned to the bishop. He brought his hands together and rested his chin on his thumbs.

'Very well. You have my blessing.'

'More wine, Conrad,' said Rudolf, a smile creeping across his face.

Later, when the bishop and the other guests had retired to bed and the table had been cleared, Conrad lay in the hut that had been allocated to him and the other boys, unable to sleep. The others were deep in slumber wrapped in their blankets. The straw that had been laid on the earth floor was dry but cold and the door was rattling in the wind.

'Hans,' whispered Conrad.

There was no reply from his friend sleeping beside him.

'Hans,' he hissed more loudly.

The blanket next to him moved.

'Mm?'

154

Conrad propped himself up on one elbow. 'We are going to war.'

Hans was only half awake as he turned his head towards Conrad.

'What war?'

'We are going to fight the Estonians in two months, to attack a place called Fellin.'

'Where is that?' asked Hans.

'I do not know. But it is a fortress of the enemy.'

Hans had fallen back to sleep but Conrad lay on his back and thought of glory and slaying the enemy hordes. The idea that he and the others would not take part in the fighting did not cross his mind. He was going to war with Rudolf, Lukas and Walter to smite the enemies of the Lord.

The birth of Christ was celebrated at Wenden as the snow lay thick on the ground all around the castle, weighing down the branches of the spruce and pine. The Gauja began to freeze in the middle of December, together with the streams and smaller rivers that fed it, the lakes and the marshes also becoming covered in ice. The boys' training on horseback came to a temporary halt as Lukas instructed them on surviving the Livonian winter. Anton told Hans that because he was so thin he would freeze to death in the icy conditions but they were all issued with winter clothing as worn by the locals: felt capes, woollen underwear, woollen leg wraps, fur caps, mittens and socks. Hans was delighted to discover that not only did he not freeze but was actually warm in his winter clothing.

They carried on with their training but their bulky attire took some getting used to, in particular their large winter boots. The ground in the castle compound froze solid and every day received a fresh covering of snow that had to be cleared from the main track, paths and castle courtyard. Construction work slowed and then stopped, the carpenters being diverted from their usual duties to construct a siege tower that would be dismantled for the journey north and then reassembled at Fellin. The huts of the civilian families and the mercenaries were heated by burning peat blocks that had been cut and dried during the summer and extra food rations were issued to feed the women and children.

The boys had been at Wenden for nearly nine months now and each of them had become stronger, more agile and able to wield a waster with some dexterity. Two days after they had celebrated the birth of Christ in a packed chapel with the other members of the garrison, on a freezing late December afternoon under a clear blue sky, Lukas blew a whistle to call a halt to their exercises with a sword and shield. He waved them over to him.

'Next month the Sword Brothers and those crusaders who have remained in Livonia for the winter will be marching north against the Estonians and all of you will be accompanying the army.'

Conrad grinned at Hans and the others looked like foxes that had forced their way into a chicken coop.

'Will we get real swords, Brother Lukas?' asked Conrad.

'You will not. Nor will you be doing any fighting. You will help with the wagons and supplies. Brother Rudolf thinks that the experience of a winter campaign will be good for you all and I agree.'

He saw their disappointed faces. 'However, if the Estonians overwhelm the army you have my permission to pick up any weapon that comes to hand in the brief time between the army's defeat and your own deaths at the hands of Lembit's warriors. Either that or run as fast as you can.'

Lukas laughed. 'Not that it will come to that, God willing.'

Hans shook one of his boots. 'It is impossible to run in these boots. Why have we been issued with boots that are too large, Brother Rudolf?'

Lukas pointed at Anton. 'In winter what is a fighter's most important instrument?'

'His sword,' answered Anton to murmurs of agreement from the others.

Lukas smiled. 'Wrong. His feet.'

The boys stared at each other and their boots in confusion.

'It is true,' continued Lukas. 'In winter if your feet get cold and wet then you will get frostbite. If that happens you will not be able to walk and might lose your toes, even your life. What use is a sword if you cannot stand up?

'You are all wearing thick socks so your boots must be roomy enough to permit you to move your toes. Tight clothes and footwear impede the circulation which might lead to frostbite.'

At the end of the day Lukas watched over them in the dormitory as they cleaned their boots and rubbed them with grease.

'Snow is an enemy of leather and so they must be cleaned and greased daily. Use your hands not a cloth because grease rubbed vigorously with a hand will warm it and will penetrate the leather more easily.

'Do not let boots dry near a fire as they will either burn or become hard and brittle.'

When December ended so did their training as preparations were speeded up for the assault against Fellin. The boys were sent out to scour the surrounding countryside for the wood of dead fir trees because it is the best for winter fires. They loaded the branches onto horse-drawn sleds and then chopped the branches into firewood at Wenden. At night they lay in their beds and listened to the mournful howls of hungry wolves that filled the nearby forest. Parties of crossbowmen were sent out to hunt them down, partly to collect their carcasses for fresh meat and fur but also to rid the night of their dreadful sounds, a somewhat forlorn objective.

Conrad accompanied Rudolf, the leather-faced crossbowman who had taken part in the autumn hunt and four of his companions. It was four days into a cold snap and Rudolf was confident that they would be successful. His breath misted as he exhaled and looked into the savage blue sky.

'The wolves will be desperate for food now and more receptive to calling.'

They pulled small sleds behind them as they headed towards the forest, trudging through the snow which Conrad found tiring after a while. 'Leather face' kept looking into the sky and spotted Conrad looking quizzically at him.

'Ravens circling is a good indication of a fresh kill site. Mind you, the wolves have probably hunted and killed all the prey in the area.'

'That is why we brought you along,' said Rudolf, a crossbow slung over his shoulder.

'Will they move away, then?' asked Conrad.

'What, the wolves?' said leather face. 'No, they are like the Sword Brothers: very territorial.'

Rudolf shook his head. 'Just keep your eyes peeled for tracks, damn your eyes. I don't want to be out here when it gets dark and even colder.'

Leather face winked at Conrad. 'Doesn't want to be wolf bait, more like.'

They trudged through the snow for an hour, leather face at the front of the column following the tracks he had picked up when they had entered the forest. Conrad found the latter unnerving, a quiet, desolate place seemingly devoid of life. There were no wolves here.

Leather face suddenly held up a hand and the column halted. Rudolf indicated to Conrad and the others to huddle round as the crossbowman walked back to them.

'I'll stay here and start calling. You all move ahead a hundred paces in front and get into position. And keep low and silent. Wolves are intelligent creatures.' He looked at Rudolf. 'Unlike the Sword Brothers.'

'Perhaps we should kill you and save our ears from your idiotic utterances.'

They left the sleds behind as they walked forward, Conrad shadowing Rudolf.

'Even if a wolf responds to the calls,' said Rudolf, 'he will keep a safe distance. As my insolent friend said, they are intelligent creatures.'

All the party wore white cloaks, white tunics and white leggings to blend into the terrain, with white cloth covers over their boots. Conrad knelt beside a spruce, its branches covered in snow, Rudolf next to him. Suddenly he heard a wolf howl behind him, followed by a dreadful high-pitched screech.

'He is calling the wolves,' whispered Rudolf. 'The last sound was the call of a cow elk. Wolves hunt elks so hopefully they will take the bait.'

'Why the wolf call?' said Conrad.

'Wolves are territorial but if a pack thinks another wolf or wolves have entered their territory they will come to investigate.'

Leather face made his calls again and minutes later Conrad saw fleeting shapes among the trees: dark grey beasts moving stealthily through the forest. He had already loaded his crossbow and now he brought up the stock to his shoulder. He glanced at Rudolf who was staring ahead, unblinking. The wolves were about two hundred paces away now, moving cautiously in their pack. Conrad knew that wolves did not travel alone but in groups. They looked bigger up close, with great jaws and snarling visages. They walked forward a few paces and he focused on one of the animals, a large wolf with a dark grey coat. He waited for Rudolf's shot before he released his trigger. He heard a crack and then shot his bolt, the iron head slamming into the chest of his target and dropping it.

He did not know if the others had shot their crossbows but in an instant the other wolves turned and fled. Rudolf reloaded his crossbow and raced forward, Conrad doing the same, holding it ready to shoot. He saw the other four crossbowmen also advancing with levelled weapons, ready to shoot down another wolf. But the beasts were long gone.

He reached his target to see the wolf lying dead, a small bloodstain under its head. Rudolf had only wounded his beast, which was whimpering in pain until he used his dagger to slit its throat and put it out of its misery. He stood up and looked around. The other crossbowmen signalled to him that they had killed their targets.

'Six wolves,' he slapped Conrad on the shoulder. 'Well done.'

Leather face joined them as they unloaded their bows and dug their quarrels out of the dead animals.

'Nice shooting,' he said to Rudolf, grinning. 'Are you going after the rest?'

'They will be a long way away soon. We have to get back to Wenden before it gets dark.'

Leather face winked at Conrad. 'Afraid of the dark, Rudolf?'

'We could always leave you here to wait until they come back if you like,' replied Rudolf.

'And miss out on a big meal of roasted wolf?' said leather face. 'No chance.'

So they loaded the carcasses onto the sleds and pulled them back to Wenden. It was dusk when they reached the castle but they took the wolves straight to the kitchens where they were skinned and gutted, and later the meat was cooked and served. As usual the brother knights sat down to eat first, followed by the sergeants and then Conrad and his companions with those crossbowmen who had formed part of the hunting parties. Leather face sat opposite Conrad as Hans beside his friend stuffed his face with meat and bread. Leather face looked at him.

'He looks as though he hasn't had a meal in a month.'

'No talking!' shouted Henke who was stalking up and down the dining hall.

Hans grinned and continued to feed his mouth from his large, over-filled bowl. Conrad shook his head at leather face, indicating that he should say no more. It was one of the rules of the Sword Brothers that all meals were to be eaten in silence.

Henke stood over leather face with a malevolent expression. 'It is forbidden to talk at meal times.'

'Bloody stupid rule,' murmured leather face under his breath.

'What?' snapped Henke.

Leather face looked up at him. 'Nothing, Henke. Excellent meal.'

The next day, as a reward for killing a wolf, Rudolf took Conrad to Thalibald's village. They rode on a sleigh, one of many that were being assembled at Wenden. A local pony pulled it on another glorious winter day, the air freezing and still and the snow-covered land dazzlingly white under a bright sun. Rudolf was armed with his sword and Conrad carried a dagger but the latter felt strangely vulnerable as the sleigh glided over the track's frozen surface. He continually looked around and behind him as they travelled through the forest south of the castle. Rudolf noticed his apprehension and halted the pony.

'What is troubling you, Conrad?'

'Nothing, Brother Rudolf,' he replied, peering into the trees.

'You suspect that the forest might be filled with Estonians?'

Conrad felt himself blushing. Rudolf laughed.

'Tell me, what do you hear?'

There was no wind, no movement among the branches of the trees and no birds in the sky. The only sound he could hear was the breathing of the pony in front of him.

'Nothing.'

'Precisely. In this clear, frosty weather noises carry to great distances. This tells me there are no hostile forces anywhere near and so we are perfectly safe. You must learn to use the terrain and weather to your advantage, Conrad. This may appear strange to you now but in time it will become your friend.'

Rudolf flicked the reins and the pony began to move forward. Rudolf nodded at his flowing mane.

'Hardy beasts, these local ponies. They can endure extreme cold and subsist on low rations.'

'They are small compared to our warhorses,' said Conrad.

'Size is not everything, Conrad,' replied Rudolf, 'and we will not be taking the warhorses north.'

'You won't?'

Rudolf shook his head. 'They would be useless in a siege and they are worth too much to risk dying of cold standing around idle. So they will stay at Wenden.'

Guards wrapped in cloaks stood on the timber wall of Thalibald's village as the sleigh entered the settlement and halted before his hall. The sentries had alerted their chief of its approach and now he stood outside its doors with his wife, two sons and Daina to greet the arrivals. Even though the journey had been short Conrad's face was frozen and he was glad to get inside where a fire was raging in the stone hearth and drink some warm milk, and even gladder to be served by Daina. She was wrapped in fox furs, her green eyes lighting up when she handed Conrad the cup.

'The gallant knight returns,' she smiled.

Conrad's cheeks reddened slightly as Rudolf and Thalibald began discussing the coming campaign.

'We will need all the sleighs and ponies you can muster,' said Rudolf. 'The army will be arriving soon and I can guarantee that it will not bring enough supplies with it.'

'The king will be accompanying it?' asked Thalibald, referring to Caupo.

'Unlikely,' replied Rudolf, 'but Master Berthold would appreciate your own presence and that of some of your warriors.'

'You go to kill Lembit?' asked Thalibald.

160

Rudolf cast him a wry smile. 'The bishop would prefer his baptism.'

'Lembit may bend his knee to the bishop but in his heart he will never yield to Riga, I think.'

While this conversation was going on Conrad sat down on a bench near the fire and gave Daina furtive looks. She was holding her tray and talking to one of her brothers, a stocky boy about the same age as Conrad. He had big hands and thick, shoulder-length hair. He too had green eyes though his face was long like his father's. He saw Conrad admiring his sister.

'You have an admirer, sister.'

Conrad turned away quickly and stared at his cup, his cheeks starting to burn as he blushed.

'Leave our guest alone, Rameke,' said Daina. 'He is most polite and helpful. You may be interested to know that he wounded Lembit in a fight.'

Rameke rose from his bench and came over to sit opposite Conrad, offering his hand across the table.

'A shame you did not slay him but a wound is a good start.'

Conrad smiled and took his hand.

'My name is Conrad Wolff.'

'And I am Rameke, youngest son of Chief Thalibald.'

Conrad estimated his age to be the same as his own but looked with envy at the sword in its scabbard strapped to his belt, a weapon also carried by his elder brother Waribule.

'Daina,' said Rameke, 'fetch more milk for us.'

Daina came over and Conrad stood up, much to her amusement.

'Would *you* like more milk, Conrad?' she asked, ignoring her brother.

'Thank you,' Conrad stammered, reaching for his cup and knocking it over. He blushed again and Rameke laughed.

'Conrad, we are leaving,' called Rudolf, who embraced Thalibald and walked with the chief towards the hall's exit. Conrad excused himself and hurried after them, turning to catch a last glimpse of Daina.

'Thank you for the milk.'

She dazzled him with a smile and a slight curtsy as Conrad raised his hand to Rameke and Waribule. He replaced his fur cap on his head and stepped onto the front of the sleigh. Rudolf tugged on the reins and the pony walked forward, turned right and trotted from the village. Conrad looked behind him as Thalibald was joined by his sons outside the hall but not by his wife or daughter.

'Daina is a fine girl,' remarked Rudolf casually when they were half a mile from the village.

'She is,' agreed Conrad.

'Would you like to wear the surcoat of the Sword Brothers one day, Conrad?'

'Yes, Brother Rudolf.'

'Do you know what "chastity" means, Conrad?'

'No.'

'It means that you cannot enter the order of Sword Brothers if you take a wife, Conrad, for only those who are pure of mind and body can truly serve God. Do you understand?'

Conrad did not, really. All he knew was that he wanted to be like Rudolf and Henke and wear a white surcoat bearing a red cross and sword and fight the pagans. He also knew that he wanted to see more of the fairest Daina. But most of all he wanted to march north to fight the Estonians.

The days following were filled with activity as Thalibald and his sons arrived with fifty warriors, each one driving a sleigh pulled by a pony. Master Berthold had sent a plethora of messages via pigeon to Bishop Albert at Riga concerning the size of the force that would march to Fellin. He emphasised that a large force would soon eat up all the supplies he had amassed at Wenden and, unless they brought their own food, would probably have to retreat before it could achieve anything. The bishop wrote back saying that because he had had to send soldiers to reinforce the garrisons along the Dvina, and also keep troops in and around Riga to safeguard the area from further Kur attacks and also reassure the citizens, the force that would march north would be a pale imitation of the army that had assembled at Wenden in the summer. In addition, many crusaders had returned to Germany rather than spend the winter in Livonia.

In the first week of January Sir Frederick arrived at the head of his crusaders: twenty knights, forty lesser armoured knights, a score of squires, fifty of the bishop's crossbowmen, an additional fifty of his spearmen, and various support personnel – carpenters, armourers, surgeons and priests – a further forty men. Sir Frederick and his knights came attired in their war gear and accompanied by their warhorses.

'Those beasts will never return to Riga,' said Lukas to the boys as the squires pitched tents outside the castle perimeter and Sir Frederick rode through the gates at the head of his knights on his way to the castle. 'Shame.'

Along the way he had linked up with the brother knights, sergeants and mercenaries of the garrisons of Segewold and Kremon, who had been furnished with

162

sleighs and ponies provided by Caupo. Combined with the men from Wenden's garrison these totalled thirty-six brother knights, fifty sergeants, thirty crossbowmen and the same number of spearmen. Master Berthold was still concerned that there were too many mouths to feed but was persuaded by Rudolf that there were enough supplies to feed such a host, especially as most of the horses brought by Sir Frederick and his crusaders would soon expire from the freezing conditions.

Two days after their arrival the army left Wenden, the crusaders mocking the Sword Brothers riding on their little ponies. Thalibald and Rudolf rode ahead with a small party of scouts to map the trail the long column of sleighs, men on foot and horsemen were to follow to Lembit's stronghold of Fellin.

*****

'I've always hated the snow,' remarked Vetseke as he sipped at his drink. He had been morose since his arrival at Gerzika in the autumn, looking like a beggar in his tattered cloak, his face unshaven and his hair unkempt. His cloak had been repaired and he had been given fresh clothes but his mood had darkened as the days grew shorter and the temperature dropped. Vsevolod looked at his wife and rolled his eyes but said nothing.

'Even with the fires burning,' continued Vetseke, now taking great gulps of his beverage, 'Kokenhusen was always cold during the winter.'

'I trust your quarters here are warm enough,' said Vsevolod.

Vetseke drained his finely engraved silver tankard and held it out for one of the slaves standing around the wall of the hall to fill it. One came forward, bowed his head and poured more *stavlenniy myod* into the vessel. This honey based drink, similar to the mead that the Catholics drank, was strong and was best imbibed in moderation, not consumed like water as Vetseke was doing.

The former ruler of Kokenhusen managed a half smile. 'Warm, thank you.'

'Perhaps a life in a warmer clime might be beneficial to you, prince,' hissed Rasa, barely able to conceal her contempt. The daughter of Grand Duke Daugerutis had received her name after the first thing her father had seen after holding his new-born daughter. It meant 'dew' and her father thought it most appropriate as he thought the child was soft and gentle. But Rasa grew into a cunning and ruthless woman whose red hair, slim frame and piercing brown eyes gave her a savage beauty, a quality matched by her callous temperament. Vsevolod had a similar disposition, which had been the reason he had wanted to marry her, that and because she was the daughter of Lithuania's most powerful duke. But sometimes she over-reached herself.

Her mood had darkened of late when news came from her father that her brother, the grand duke's heir, had been killed in a hunting accident. He had fallen from his horse and broken his neck. Rasa and her brother had never been close but the news of his death had still been a shock.

Vetseke looked at the wife of his host, dressed as she was in a rich white robe called a *rubakha* with wide sleeves that allowed her to display the even richer blue *rubakha* underneath with gold-inlaid sleeve cuffs. Around her shoulders she was wearing a white cloak edged with fox fur that was fastened at the right shoulder by a golden brooch. Pampered bitch! 'I will never desert Kokenhusen,' slurred Vetseke. 'To be a landless prince, a vagrant condemned to wander the earth, homeless?' He slammed his tankard down on the table, causing several of the slaves to jump. 'Never!'

Vsevolod looked at his wife disapprovingly but she waved away his censure.

'Quite right, prince,' said Vsevolod, 'to which end I have had communications with Prince Vladimir of Polotsk who would welcome you at his court, so valuable an ally have you been to him.'

There was a time when the Principality of Polotsk had ruled all the lands from the city to the shores of the Baltic, but internal dynastic strife and wars with the more powerful Kingdom of Kiev to the south had weakened it considerably. Strongholds like Kokenhusen and Gerzika had originally been vassal kingdoms of Polotsk but now were actually self-governing domains, though still tied to it by trade, culture and treaties. But Polotsk could still muster large armies, which could be used against Bishop Albert if Prince Vladimir could be manipulated to do so.

Vetseke seemed pleased by this. 'He is a great ruler who appreciates those who have been loyal to him.'

'When the snow clears I will give you an escort so that you may arrive at his court as befitting yours status,' said Vsevolod.

'Not before?' added Rasa, smiling icily at Vetseke.

Vsevolod glared at her. 'I am certain that Vladimir will provide you with soldiers so that you may retake Kokenhusen.'

Vetseke's spirits rose as he drank more alcohol and contemplated his visit to Polotsk. He was carried back to his quarters in a drunken, semi-conscious state, happy in the knowledge that he would soon be back in his own stronghold.

In their private quarters Rasa sat brushing her hair as Vsevolod flopped down in a chair on the other side of their large bed with its red ornamented canopy, rich hangings and fine linen sheets.

'You should have him killed,' said Rasa.

'Who?' asked Vsevolod, rubbing his tired eyes.

'Vetseke, of course.'

Vsevolod was horrified. 'He is our guest.'

Rasa stopped brushing her hair and turned to look at him. 'He is a burden who will bring the unwelcome attention of that heathen bishop upon us. But more than that, he has no army, no land and no purpose.'

Her eyes burned with hatred for Vetseke.

Vsevolod rose and walked over to her, cupping her face in his hands.

'The bishop, my dear, has expressed his gratitude to me for taking my army to the aid of Kokenhusen. And has further asked that I perform the role of intermediary between him and your father.'

Rasa's eyes narrowed. 'Why would you do such a thing? My father will never bow his knee to the devil of Riga. My father is still angry with you for your inactivity at Kokenhusen. Prince Stecse says that you deserted him.'

Vsevolod released his hold on Rasa's face and began pacing up and down in front of her.

'Prince? He is nothing more than a dotard who thinks that banging his head against a palisade makes him a great warlord. The bishop's approach shows that he is weak at this moment and fears conflict with your father.'

'So he should,' said Rasa smugly.

Vsevolod stopped and held up a hand to her. 'The point is that if Vladimir can be persuaded to support Vetseke, or better still march west himself, then we can combine with him and your father to strike a fatal blow against my dear friend Bishop Albert. That is why Vetseke must be kept alive.'

'Vladimir will never agree to march beside my father. There is too much bad blood between them,' she said disparagingly.

Vsevolod sighed. He loved his wife but her habit of seeing everything in black and white sometimes blinded her to the obvious.

'Both your father and Vladimir are great warlords who know that there is strength in unity and who also know that our friend the bishop presents the greatest immediate danger.'

165

She placed her hairbrush on her table. 'So where does Vetseke fit in with your grand scheme?'

Vsevolod smiled cunningly at her. 'For one thing moving him to Polotsk will get him away from Gerzika, thus maintaining the illusion that I am an ally of the bishop. But, more importantly, Vetseke is a Liv not a Russian, and while he lives he can serve as a rallying figure for those of his race who live under the crusader heel and who wish to free themselves of the servants of the heretical Church of Rome.

'Just think, how long will the bishop last with rebellion in his lands and Russian and Lithuanian armies marching against him?'

Rasa looked at him affectionately. 'You have it all worked out, don't you?'

He shrugged coyly. 'One does what one can, my sweet.'

Chapter 7

The march to Fellin began in a snowstorm, a biting northerly wind making Conrad pull the hood of his cape up and bow his head as he walked with Hans and the others beside a sleigh loaded with tools. The heads of the ponies and horses were similarly down as the flecks of snow swirled around them, severely reducing visibility and making it almost impossible to convey commands. Not that the Sword Brothers needed to convey many commands during the march as they maintained strict discipline even when travelling through friendly territory. Much to the annoyance of Sir Frederick and his crusaders the Sword Brothers were placed in the rear and vanguard of the army, the most vulnerable and dangerous places when on the march. The banner of the order, a great white flag bearing a red sword and cross, was held by Henke at the very tip of the army, though as soon as it had begun to snow it had been wrapped in a waxed sleeve to preserve it from the wet.

Soon after leaving Sir Frederick had ridden to the vanguard to enquire why the rate of advance was so slow. He was informed by Master Berthold that marching in winter sapped the stamina of both horses and men and that he desired to arrive at Fellin with all the animals and men in fighting order, not half-dead or having expired along the route. The crusaders grumbled in their ranks but had little choice but to acquiesce in the master's wishes, as they had no local knowledge. Their banners and heraldic shields provided a vivid splash of colour against the brilliant white terrain until the snowstorm engulfed the column. The rate of advance decreased further when the brother knights and sergeants dismounted and proceeded on foot. The crusaders had no choice but to do so likewise.

Conrad was relieved when the column entered a forest three miles north of Wenden and the blizzard lessened in severity, though the snow still fell thickly. They marched through the forest for what seemed an age but was probably around three hours, the brothers ordering short stops of between five and ten minutes but no longer, as standing around in freezing conditions could be fatal. The army covered barely six miles the first day before Master Berthold gave the order to make camp next to the southern side of a great forest of firs that extended east and west for miles. The tents were pitched two hundred paces from the trees to create an area of open ground across which any potential attackers could not cross without being spotted. The march had been relatively easy for Conrad and his companions, notwithstanding the snow, but their real work began when the camp was erected. Not only did they have to assist in putting up the tents, hammering angular steel pegs into the frozen ground, they were also given axes and saws and sent off into the forest along with a dozen other parties to cut wood, specifically the wood of dead fir trees.

'How did you think we would make fires?' asked Lukas as he hacked at the black branches of a dead tree?'

'Surely there is enough firewood and peat at Wenden?' replied Hans, throwing another branch onto the rapidly increasing pile of sticks.

'Food and fuel are precious commodities,' said Lukas, 'especially in winter. Do you wish the garrison and the families who live there to freeze to death? To say nothing of the animals?' He saw Bruno and Anton chatting. 'Stop gossiping and start hacking unless you want to spend the night with no fire.'

The wind dropped as the light began to fade and the forest reverberated to the sounds of chopping and sawing as firewood was collected and ferried back to camp. The tents had all been pitched by now and sergeants and squires had begun to prepare evening meals. Cooking pots hung suspended over fires on metal frames as the first batches of wood were set alight. Lukas instructed Conrad and the others to stop collecting wood and return to camp as the light in the forest faded rapidly. Out of the gloom came Thalibald, Rameke and a dozen Liv warriors carrying shields and spears. Conrad felt inadequate when Rameke recognised him and strolled beside him as his father walked ahead with Lukas. He had an armful of dead wood while the son of the chief was helmeted, wore a mail shirt and carried a spear and sword. However, the chief's son was friendly rather than patronising.

'Conrad, how are you?'

'Tired of cutting wood. You were scouting?'

Rameke nodded. 'Not that there was anything to see apart from trees and snow.'

'No Estonians?'

Rameke laughed. 'They are all inside their homes out of the cold, like I wish I was.'

Conrad was surprised. 'You do not like the cold?'

'Of course not. I would rather be wrapped in furs beside a warm fire.'

'Like Daina,' said Conrad sheepishly.

'Like *all* women. Their role is to marry, feed their husbands and bear future warriors. Not that I can imagine anyone wanting to marry my sister.'

'She has no suitor?' asked Conrad evasively.

'Daina?' Rameke laughed out loud, causing his father to turn and scold him for making too much noise.

'We are in enemy territory, boy, not on a summer stroll.'

'My father will have to pay a big dowry to get rid of my sister,' whispered Rameke. 'Who would want to marry her?'

Conrad said nothing but his heart soared and the bundle of firewood he was carrying seemed as light as a feather. He also forgot about Rudolf's words concerning marriage and membership of the Sword Brothers.

The camp was a sprawling collection of round and oval tents arranged in three sections. One part comprised the great round tent of Master Berthold himself, next to which was the chapel tent, in which the services that were conducted at Wenden and all the other Sword Brother garrisons could be reciprocated while on campaign. The tent where the members of the order and their servants ate their meals was also pitched near the master's, while the individual tents of the brother knights ringed them all. Then there were the tents of the sergeants, crossbowmen, spearmen, engineers and support personnel. The crusaders and their squires and footmen pitched their tents around the great portable residence of Sir Frederick, while Thalibald and his warriors grouped their felt dwellings around their sleighs and ponies, which like those of the Sword Brothers slept in the open with blankets on their backs, all grouped together and shielded by temporary stalls of wood and canvas. Even though the wind had dropped the night sky was cloudless and filled by a thousand stars, causing the temperature to plummet.

Lukas called Conrad and the other boys together and showed them how to make a fire, clearing a patch of ground and then taking some tinder from a box he had brought along and placing it on the ground in a loose pile. He then placed a small amount of twigs and sticks over it and lit the tinder using sparks created by striking steel against flint. Soon the tinder was alight and consuming the twigs and sticks. Lukas instructed Hans to place bigger sticks on the fire.

'Not too big otherwise you'll smother it.'

After a short while the fire took hold and logs could be placed on the flames from a nearby pile.

'Just keep putting logs on at regular intervals and it gives out a constant heat all night,' said Lukas.

'Who will do that?' asked Anton.

'All of you,' replied Lukas. 'You will take it in turns to keep watch along with everyone else. Conrad will take the first watch.'

169

In fact Master Berthold liaised with Sir Frederick and Thalibald to ensure that there were sentries posted all around the camp throughout the night so there was no need for Conrad and the others to stand watch. But Lukas thought it excellent practice for when they finished their schooling in arms. That night, at evening prayers in the canvas chapel, Conrad asked God to care for Daina as well as Marie.

It took nine days to reach Fellin, nine days of walking along tracks heaped high with snow, crossing frozen rivers and streams and digging sleighs out of snow banks. And with each day that passed more and more of the crusaders' horses died from the cold. Unused to the severe Latvian winter and already weakened by their march to Wenden, they collapsed and expired despite being beaten and whipped by their owners. They were not the only ones to suffer. Conrad and the other boys were well equipped with their felt caps and hoods, spare underwear, leg wraps, tunics, mittens and socks, in addition to being issued with two pairs of boots, but the squires of the crusaders suffered terribly from the cold. On the fourth night Rudolf discovered one dead from exposure, having spent the night standing guard.

The Sword Brothers and Thalibald's warriors used their knowledge of the terrain to traverse the land with a minimum of difficulty, but the crusaders wished only to slaughter pagans and had no time for delays, pushing themselves and their horses to the limit to reach their destination. They believed that because their horses had been fitted with winter horseshoes they could ride across the frozen land with ease and could even cross frozen waterways without a thought.

'The horseshoes have little spikes that give a horse grip on snow and ice,' remarked Rameke as he and Conrad stood watching Sir Frederick and his knights canter across the frozen River Kopu, five miles southwest of Fellin, 'but the thickness of river ice can vary and it is not advisable to ride a host of horses over it thus.'

The Sword Brothers led their mounts across on foot at widely spaced intervals, the rest of the army crossing in many widely spaced columns to prevent the ice cracking. Conrad walked across with Rameke and the other boys beside the sleighs that carried their tents, tools, food, weapons and spare clothing, each of them looking left and right at the shiny surface. The sleigh drivers dismounted and led their ponies across. Each sleigh carried around five hundred pounds of cargo and thus it was wise for the driver to alight to lessen the load. To their right, around fifty paces away, half a dozen shivering squires were leading a line of pack horses loaded with weapons and armour across the river.

170

'Stop, there's a crack!' shouted Hans, pointing down at the ice.

The sleigh driver holding the reins of his pony next to him looked at the ice, then at Hans, shook his head and carried on leading his animal. Conrad and Rameke hurried to Hans' side followed by the others as the sleighs continued on to the far bank. Hans stared wide-eyes in alarm at the large crack that ran from left to right. Rameke pointed at it.

'There is nothing to fear. It is a single crack across our line of march and thus will not lessen the carrying capacity of the ice. The ones to watch out for are large cracks that appear parallel to the line of march. They indicate an exhausted carrying capacity and a new crossing must be sought away from them.'

Anton slapped Hans on the back. 'See, nothing to worry about.'

There was a loud crack and everyone's eyes turned right to see one of the squires fall through the ice. It was as if sorcery had been used to make him disappear. One moment he was there and the next he was gone. Rameke was the first to react, running over to where the hole had appeared in the ice.

'Move further to the right,' he shouted at the other squires who had halted to stare at the hole into which their companion had disappeared.

'Do not halt on the ice,' cried Rameke as he knelt down and crawled on his belly towards the hole in the ice. Conrad and Johann raced after him.

'Hold my ankles,' Rameke said to them as he inched towards the hole. From the far bank came a group of Sword Brothers as the other squires led their horses to the right and away from the weakened ice. Rameke thrust his arm into the black water and then ducked his head under in a vain attempt to see the squire. He lifted his head and gasped for air.

'He's gone.'

He inched backwards and then rose as Conrad and Johann did the same.

'Do not stand still on the ice,' he told them, heading back to the line of sleighs they had left. 'The knights on horseback have weakened the ice, that is why it collapsed.'

'That idiot Sir Frederick,' remarked Johann.

'He will have to clean his own armour now,' said Conrad.

Rameke saw Rudolf, Henke, Lukas and three sergeants from Wenden approaching. He pointed at the ice hole. 'Have a care,' he shouted, 'the ice is weak there.'

The Sword Brothers joined the three boys and walked with them to the river's northern bank.

'Brave but foolish, Rameke,' commented Rudolf. 'What would your father say if you had fallen into the water too?'

'That he has another son to carry on his line, lord.'

Henke laughed. 'Well said, but Rudolf is right, young wolf cub. You should die with a sword in your hand in battle not drowning in freezing water.'

Lukas pointed at Johann and Conrad. 'That goes for you two as well. I have not spent hundreds of hours training you to use weapons so you can go swimming under the ice.'

'Does that mean we will be getting weapons when we reach our destination, Brother Lukas?' asked Conrad hopefully.

'Certainly not.'

That night another squire and four crusader horses died of exposure.

The army's camp was established a mile north of the river and the next morning Sir Frederick, his knights and lesser armoured knights, the brother knights and sergeants of the Sword Brothers rode out of camp to raid the countryside around Fellin. The spearmen, squires and crossbowmen remained to escort the sleighs and support personnel the short distance to Fellin, there to establish siege lines around the fort and to await the return of the horsemen. Lukas was left behind to command the foot soldiers and the sleighs. It was a beautiful winter's day, the sun bright in a blue, cloudless sky. There was no wind but Conrad could see his breath misting as he walked along the track leading to the enemy fort. After an hour the column of men and sleighs began to skirt the western shore of a great frozen lake nestling in the middle of a forested valley. This was an area of rolling hills, valleys, lakes and rivers but as yet they had seen no villages or farms.

'That is because Fellin is on the southern boundary of Saccalia,' said Lukas when Conrad had questioned him about the lack of dwellings along their route. 'There are villages around Fellin but these are being cleared as we speak.'

Half an hour later columns of black smoke began to appear in the distance as the horsemen that had left earlier raided the Estonians. Conrad and the other boys nudged each other and pointed at the six smoke columns in the sky. They were still marching adjacent to the shore of the lake but the pace slowed as Lukas gave the order for the crossbowmen and spearmen to stay close to the sleighs. Thalibald and his scouts had returned. Fellin was now only a mile to the northwest and Lukas was concerned that there might be a war party of Estonians in the forest that lay on their left flank, though Thalibald had seen no signs of the enemy.

172

The Estonians may have had scouts out but they used them to shepherd those villagers living nearest the fort into its confines, for when the army finally arrived at Fellin the walls of the fort were lined with warriors. The stronghold stood on a hillock half a mile to the northwest of the lake that the army had marched alongside. It was a square-shaped timber fort of some strength, having towers with shingle roofs in each corner and more roofed shooting positions on the walls between the corner towers. The walls themselves were over twenty feet high and at least four hundred feet in length on all sides. At the base of the hillock, surrounding the fort on all four sides, was a moat, the main entrance to the stronghold being located on its eastern side.

When the crusader army had appeared the warriors on the walls and in the towers had started to whistle and jeer, though none attempted to shoot any arrows as it was well out of range. Conrad stood with Hans and the others watching the commotion as Lukas began talking with a tall, very thin elderly man with a wispy white beard and deathly pale skin. The latter was pointing at the fort and then turned to point at the collection of sleighs and packhorses that stood south of the stronghold. Lukas nodded and walked back towards the boys. Conrad had seen the elderly man before at Wenden but had given scant regard to him.

'Who is that man you were talking to, Brother Lukas?' he said.

'Master Thaddeus, chief engineer. We'll make camp a hundred paces back from this spot so he can set up his siege engines. Unload the tents.'

He strode off to converse with Thalibald and the commanders of the foot soldiers as the garrison of Fellin began cheering and then broke into some sort of war song, the words of which the boys did not understand but which nevertheless unnerved them. As the order was relayed throughout the column to establish camp, sleighs were unloaded and tents pitched. Conrad kept glancing at the Estonian warriors observing them, the sun glinting off whetted spear points and axe blades.

'Do you think they will attack us?' said Bruno.

'They fear our knights on horseback,' answered Anton.

'Except the knights are not here,' said Conrad, looking around anxiously.

'We should be issued with swords,' said Johann.

'At least we would die with weapons in our hands,' added Hans.

They all stopped working and stared apprehensively at the fort, the garrison of which was still singing its mournful war song.

'Is there a religious holiday I am not aware of?' Lukas appeared seemingly out of nowhere.

'Holiday, Brother Lukas?' enquired Anton.

Rudolf folded his arms in front of him. 'I was merely wondering why you had stopped work.'

'We were watching the enemy, brother,' said Conrad, 'for signs they might attack.'

'You saw those columns of smoke in the sky earlier?' said Lukas. 'Well that means our horsemen are burning Estonian villages, which means that the garrison in that fort knows that there are mail-clad men on horseback in this area, which means that they will stay behind their timber walls where they are safe. Now, if that is an adequate explanation perhaps you could all kindly return to your duties.'

'We think that we should be armed, Brother Lukas,' said Conrad, looking at the others who nodded optimistically. 'So as to be able to defend ourselves.'

Lukas rubbed his beard. 'Mm, I see. I will consider your impudent request. Meanwhile, get the tents erected.'

It was noon before all the tents had been pitched, the camp filling the ground between the lake and forest to the south of the fort to a distance of at least a quarter of a mile. Lukas established a line of crossbowmen and spearmen beyond the camp's northern extent as a precaution against a sally from the garrison. But the latter grew tired of watching tents being erected and singing and left the battlements. Two hours after noon the knights returned.

They returned with bloodied lances and herding a score of prisoners before them, all of them men of different ages. Some were wounded and had torn tunics. They resembled the Livs in appearance with their brown tunics, white shirts, and grey leggings with gaiters. Many of the horsemen carried sacks of grain behind them – plundered from the villages they had burnt.

The appearance of the knights signalled the reappearance of the garrison on the battlements, but this time there was no signing or jeering as the warriors watched the knights dismount and lead their horses and ponies through the camp to the corrals that were being sited in its centre. After pitching the tents Lukas took the boys over to where Thaddeus was organising the positioning of the siege engines. The engineers were unloading the constituent parts from sleighs prior to their assembly.

'These are trainees of our order,' Lukas said to Thaddeus, 'and it will help their military education if they could observe your machines being assembled.'

Thaddeus was wrapped in a great cloak of brown bear and had a fox fur hat on his head but he was still shaking from the cold. 'Yes, yes, of course. Most useful.'

174

The imposing figure of Sir Frederick came towards the chief engineer, sword still in his hand and blood spots on his surcoat bearing a unicorn.

He ignored Lukas. 'When will the machines be ready?'

Thaddeus was intimidated by his demeanour and retreated a few steps. 'Tomorrow they will be ready, my lord.'

'Tomorrow? We attack the fort today, within the hour, and I expect your machines to be able to support our assault.'

'An assault now would be inadvisable,' said Lukas.

'We have burnt their villages and now we take their pile of sticks,' he spat dismissively.

Lukas remained calm. 'If you assault the stronghold you will fail.'

Sir Frederick's eyes narrowed as he observed Lukas in his mail and surcoat, his coif resting on his shoulders and his sword in its scabbard. He wanted to provoke Lukas so he could display his prowess with a blade but he had seen the ruthlessness of the Sword Brothers earlier when they had butchered villagers with abandon. He also knew that Lukas and his few brother knights at Wenden had defended the castle against heavy odds last year.

'I do not need machines or the Sword Brothers,' he said contemptuously.

Sir Frederick may have been arrogant but he did not lack for courage, helping to carry an assault ladder and leading the attack against the fort's southern wall. Despite the efforts of Master Berthold to persuade him otherwise, he organised assault parties of his knights and spearmen, covered by the quarrels of crossbowmen. Master Berthold added the crossbowmen of the Sword Brothers to his force, who crouched down and shot at the warriors on the walls as the crusaders, shields held before them, rushed to the moat, scrambled down and up its sides, up the earth bank and placed their ladders against the timber wall.

Rudolf had walked over to speak to Lukas. He kept looking at the fort and the dozens of crusaders rushing towards the wall and shaking his head. The crossbowmen had stopped shooting because the walls were empty.

'You will not need your machines today, Thaddeus,' said Rudolf to the chief engineer.

Lukas looked at him and then Rudolf. 'What do you think, Rudolf, one attack or two?'

'Only one,' sighed Rudolf. He looked at Conrad. 'Where do you think the Estonians have gone?'

'They must have fled,' declared Conrad with confidence. The other boys nodded in agreement.

They could see Sir Frederick ascending his ladder, one of a dozen that had been placed against the wall. Like ants his men were scrambling up them in a seemingly irresistible wave. And then the ramparts erupted in a blast of noise as the Estonians leapt up and hurled stones and spears down upon the heads of the crusaders. Conrad stared in horror as men were knocked off their ladders by stones or were pierced by spear points. The deluge of missiles was overpowering and stopped the attack dead in its tracks. Sir Frederick managed to use his shield to deflect stones and spears as he inched back down his ladder, bellowing orders for those beneath him to move aside, but in a matter of minutes a score of his men were killed and a further six wounded. The crossbowmen began shooting as soon as the Estonians appeared and Conrad thought he saw warriors being hit, but the attack had been defeated. As quickly as the Estonians had appeared they vanished and the crossbowmen ceased their shooting. There were still ladders propped against the wall and limp bodies of crusaders hung from two of them. The crossbowmen covered the retreat of Sir Frederick and his men as they trudged disconsolately back to camp and then there was silence. It was as if the attack had never happened.

'Never underestimate your enemy, Conrad,' said Rudolf. He pointed at the fort. 'Those men died for nothing. A stupid waste.'

'We will be needing your machines in the next few days, Master Thaddeus,' said Lukas.

The next morning, following mass and breakfast, Lukas summoned Conrad and the other boys to his tent. He stood in the entrance as they lined up before him. The sun was a pale yellow ball hanging low in the eastern sky and once again there was no wind. It would be another very cold day. Lukas was wearing boots over his mail chausses to prevent them rusting in the snow.

'I have something for you all,' he said, grinning. 'Your weapons.'

They all smiled at him and each other as they waited to be issued with their swords.

Lukas pointed at Conrad. 'Step forward, Conrad.'

He did so, a look of triumph on his face, as Lukas reached for something behind the tent flap and handed Conrad an axe.

'I do not understand, brother,' he said, his face etched with disappointment.

'It is an axe, Conrad, with which you can cut down trees.'

Lukas ordered the others to come forward and gave axes to both Anton and Johann, while Hans and Bruno were given a large saw with a handle at each end. Lukas saw their disappointed looks.

'You all saw the abortive attack yesterday. Well now you will learn how to conduct a proper siege.'

Conrad looked dejectedly at his axe. 'With axes and a saw?'

Lukas slapped him on the arm. 'You will see.'

They followed Lukas into the forest where squires and mercenaries were busy hacking and sawing at trees. Conrad also saw Rameke and raised his hand to him, noticing that the son of Thalibald was also engaged in chopping wood. His father and half the Liv warriors had left the camp just after dawn to form a defensive screen to the north, west and east of the fort, both to ensure that nothing and no one entered Fellin but also to give the crusaders prior warning of the approach of any relief force. This was thought unlikely because Lembit's warriors would be in their winter quarters: the villages that dotted Saccalia. It would take him weeks to assemble a sizeable army. Still, his own stronghold of Lehola was relatively close and once word reached him that there was a crusader army at Fellin he would no doubt lead some sort of relief effort. If that happened it was imperative that they had prior knowledge of his whereabouts.

After they had walked two hundred paces into the forest Lukas halted and ordered the boys to gather round him.

'Sieges are not all about charging heroically at the enemy with scaling ladders. Yesterday should have taught you that at least. We are here to take the fort, not to provide easy targets for the garrison. So we establish defensive lines around it, fill in the moat to allow the siege tower to approach the wall and manufacture mantlets for the crossbowmen.'

Hans was confused. 'Mantlets?'

'Mobile defensive screens,' answered Lukas, 'behind which the crossbowmen can get close to the walls without being shot down and there to provide covering missile volleys for the attackers. Your task is to cut the wood so that they can be created.'

And so they spent the whole morning cutting down trees to provide the materials to create wooden screens for the crossbowmen. Some of the carpenters were on hand to organise the different categories of timber that were required: the lower trunks to fill in the moat, the thicker branches and tops of the trunks for the mantlets. Fir boughs were also collected so that the horses and ponies could be bedded down during the siege.

Conrad and the others stood beside a pine as Lukas pointed to the other teams cutting down trees at widely spaced intervals.

'You may think that felling a tree is easy but as with all things there is a right way and a wrong way to go about it. Hans and Bruno step forward.'

Conrad had to admit, notwithstanding his disappointment at not having been issued with a sword, he found the tree cutting interesting as Lukas explained to them how it should be done.

'First of all you must know the height of the tree to discern the spot where the top will fall when it is felled. Now this pine is about fifty feet so we'll say seventeen footsteps. Anton, mark it out. Walk from the trunk that distance into the forest.'

Anton did as he was told and then stood and turned when he had walked seventeen paces.

'So,' said Lukas, 'that is where the top of the tree will fall. We want the tree to fall in the direction that Anton walked, which is the safest direction for it to fall so it won't kill anyone working to the left or right of us.'

'What about Anton?' asked a concerned Hans.

'Oh, he will stand where he is and be killed when the tree falls,' replied Lukas.

Johann was appalled. 'Really?'

'No, not really,' said Lukas. 'Hans and Bruno, stand either side of the tree and with your saw notch the tree on the side facing the direction in which you want it to fall. That is, towards Anton.'

They did as they were told and began to make a straight cut into the tree at waist height with the saw. Lukas recalled Anton as the two cut into the tree, beads of sweat forming on their foreheads from the exertion. When they had sawed halfway through Lukas instructed them to make a downward cut at a forty-five degree angle that went to the centre of the tree and hit the first cut. This created a large wedge that Johann knocked out with Lukas' hammer.

'Note how the space you have created is open in the direction you want the tree to fall,' he said. 'Now, take the saw out and begin to saw on the other side of the tree, level with your first cut.'

Hans and Bruno took the saw and began moving it back and forth until the teeth were inches from the first horizontal cut on the other side.

'Stop!' said Lukas. 'Have a care!' he shouted and then looked at the tree. There was a creaking sound and then a splintering noise and the trunk began to tilt in the direction where Anton had been standing. There was a loud crack and then the tree crashed to the ground. Lukas told Conrad, Johann and Anton to use their axes to cut it into manageable pieces while Hans and Bruno rested.

They spent the whole morning felling trees while Thaddeus and his engineers assembled their machines covered by a screen of spearmen. The small number of Estonians manning the walls watched in silence as three mangonels were sited against the fort's western wall and the other three were placed to face the southern wall. After a midday meal Lukas took his young charges back to see Thaddeus who was setting up his trebuchet.

The camp behind them was filled with feverish activity as the crossbowmen completed their mantlets and positioned them in front of the siege engines. The trebuchet was a wondrous thing: a long beam that pivoted around an axle positioned on a wooden structure. The axle divided the beam into a long and short arm. At the end of the short arm hung a hinged counterweight; at the end of the long arm a sling. Conrad and the others stood admiring this machine, not really understanding how it worked. Some two hundred paces behind the trebuchet stood the assembled siege tower: three storeys high and open at the rear where there was a climbing frame to allow access to the top platform. A drawbridge mounted at the top of the tower gave access to enemy battlements when lowered. The other three sides were protected by wooden planks covered with animal hides as a precaution against the threat of fire.

'We will soon be ready, Brother Lukas,' said Thaddeus, his face framed by his fox-fur hat with earflaps that he had tied under his chin. 'Will there be an assault today?'

Lukas looked at the sun that was now descending in the west. 'Not today, Master Thaddeus.'

There were now more Estonian warriors on the battlements, some of them wearing the helmets they had taken from the corpses of the dead crusaders hanging from the assault ladders that still leaned against the walls.

'Why does the enemy not attack to destroy the siege engines?' asked Conrad.

'Because they have never seen them before,' remarked Thaddeus, 'and though they may guess at their purpose they cannot be sure.'

He pointed at the siege tower. 'Now they have probably guessed that the tower is designed to be placed against their wall, what with its wheels and top platform. But they believe that their moat will keep it away from their ramparts.'

'Which it will,' said Anton, thinking out loud.

Thaddeus tapped his beak-like nose and smiled. 'Not if we fill it in.'

'How can it be filled in?' said Bruno.

'Some of those logs you cut this morning,' said Lukas, 'will be used to fill in the moat and create a bridge, over which the tower will be pushed.'

'Won't the pagans launch their missiles at it when it gets near?' asked Conrad.

Thaddeus brought his hands together. 'What inquiring minds they have, Brother Lukas.'

'Indeed, if a little over-active at times.'

After assisting the mucking out and feeding of the horses and ponies and cleaning the brother knights' weapons and armour, that night the boys stood outside their tent warming their hands at the fire. They were all tired from their exertions but the prospect of the next day's assault against the fort filled them with excitement and blocked out all thoughts of sleep.

'How long do you think it will take to storm the fort?' said Anton.

'With all the machines we have it will fall in less than a day,' offered Johann.

'Perhaps the defenders will surrender tomorrow,' said Bruno.

'No they won't,' said Conrad, 'they will fight.'

'Of course they will,' Henke appeared from between the tents, wrapped in a great white cloak sporting a red cross and sword, a hood pulled over his head. He walked up to the fire and warmed his hands on the flames. Hans placed more logs on it.

Henke pulled the hood off his head, his eyes black and cold in the glow of the fire. 'The Estonians are good fighters and the ones in Fellin are Lembit's men. It will be a hard fight.'

'Is this Lembit a king?' asked Hans.

Henke rubbed his hands. 'He is a chief who leads a tribe called the Saccalians. We are standing on part of his land. He has managed to unite all the other Estonian tribes against us by swearing to kill all the Christians in Livonia and destroy their towns and castles.'

'Is he in the fort?' asked Conrad.

Henke shook his head. 'No. He would have showed his face on the battlements yesterday if he was. Pity you didn't kill him at Wenden, Conrad, because that is the only way this war is going to end – with his death.'

'Won't the Estonians find another leader after his death?' said Anton.

180

'Not if we defeat his army at the same time we kill him,' replied Henke. 'That will break the fighting spirit of the Estonians and will leave us as masters of their lands.'

'If he is not in the fort why then are we here?' asked Johann.

Henke smiled mischievously. 'To goad him and to show his people that we can enter his land and burn his villages at will. He will have no choice but to retaliate and lead his army south, and then we can engage him in battle and destroy him.'

He slapped Conrad on the arm. 'Who knows, perhaps young Conrad here will put a bolt into his brain next time. Now you should all get some sleep. It will be a long day tomorrow.'

But though they retired to their tent Conrad could not sleep. He lay awake thinking about Lembit and the day he had faced him at Wenden. Perhaps he would be given a crossbow tomorrow with which to shoot at the enemy. His last thoughts before dozing off were of his family and the sweet smiling face of Daina.

The new day dawned icy and misty. A great fog hung over the frozen lake and crept over the crusader camp to make everyone feel cold and miserable. Conrad shivered as he pulled on his cool boots then put on his padded gambeson over his shirt and tunic. Everything felt cold and damp and in the half-light of the tent and no one spoke as they dressed and then stumbled out into the freezing early morning gloom. Mist hung all around, visibility was less than fifty feet and the only sounds were men coughing, spitting and complaining.

The boys hurried to the centre of the camp to attend mass at the chapel tent, which was full of brother knights plus Sir Frederick and his knights, and so Conrad and the others knelt on the cold, damp ground as the priests recited prayers and asked God to bless the forthcoming attack on the fort. They then reported to Lukas who informed them of their duties to be performed before breakfast: help muck out, groom and feed the horses and ponies and cut down fresh fir boughs for the beasts to sleep on. The ponies were doing well but another warhorse and three packhorses had died during the night. It looked as though Rudolf's prediction would come true. They also heard that another squire had been found dead that morning, curled up in a ball by the side of a sleigh, his body frozen solid.

Conrad felt sorry for the squires. They shivered in inadequate clothing and ran around after their masters all day long. Lukas said each one served a master for seven years in the hope that they too would become knights. But they were treated more like slaves than apprentices and some did not even become knights, accepting the life of a squire into their adult years. Not to say that the daily routine in the

Sword Brothers was not onerous; it was. But the boys had ample clothing and the food was filling and plentiful. Lukas had informed Conrad that the Sword Brothers had been founded by Bishop Albert to resemble another religious order called the Templars that fought the infidels in the Holy Land. Hans had been appalled when Lukas had also told them that the brother knights in the Templars often fasted to purify their bodies and bring them closer to God.

'Do not worry, Hans,' Lukas had told him, 'the Templars fight in a land that is always hot and so they do not need as much food as you. In the cold of Livonia Grand Master Volquin is of the opinion that his fighters need ample food so they can battle the pagans to maximum effect, thereby spreading the word of God more quickly among the unbelievers.'

Hans loved his life in the Sword Brothers, even on this chilly, misty morning in the depths of an Estonian winter. He sat opposite Conrad at breakfast shovelling heaped spoonfuls of hot porridge into his mouth into the cavernous hole that was his stomach. For someone whose only friend had been starvation the regular meals of the order were worth the minor discomfort of sleeping in a freezing tent, shovelling horse dung and cleaning the weapons and armour of the brother knights.

Lukas collected them after they had filled their bellies and took them to where Thaddeus was overseeing the operation of his trebuchet.

'You are all under the command of Master Thaddeus today,' he told them, 'I have more important matters to attend to.'

'You will take part in the assault, Brother Lukas?' Conrad asked him.

Lukas nodded. 'After Master Thaddeus' machines have softened up the enemy first.'

'May God go with you, brother,' said Thaddeus.

'And you,' replied Lukas. 'And don't cause any trouble,' he told the boys, raising his hand and then walking forward to where the army was assembling before the fort.

The crusaders and Sword Brother knights and sergeants formed up in groups behind the lines of spearmen that faced the southern and western ramparts of the fort. The crossbowmen inched forward under cover of their mantlets, two men taking position behind each sloping wood shelter, until they were within one hundred paces of the moat. But the freezing fog was refusing to dissipate and was covering everything with a thin coating of ice. Visibility was poor and Conrad could barely see the fort's southern side, but he could hear it. The warriors were shouting, whistling and jeering at the crusaders, taunting them to launch another attack. But their noise abated as the prisoners that had been taken in the raids on the villages were shoved forward towards the moat. They were cold and filthy, several of them glancing left and right at the soldiers arrayed before the fort.

Conrad saw Rudolf, Henke and a score of sergeants from Wenden herding the prisoners forward, using the points of their swords to keep them moving as they stood behind them. Eventually they formed the prisoners into a line in front of the moat and Rudolf began shouting up at the now silent warriors lining the battlements. He was speaking a coarse language that Conrad did not understand.

'He is requesting the garrison's surrender,' said Thaddeus.

Rudolf finished shouting and waited for an answer. It came when at least a dozen warriors pulled down their leggings and showed their bare arses to him, followed by jeers and catcalls as others pissed over the battlements. Rudolf smiled, raised his sword to them and barked an order. Seconds later the brother knights and sergeants standing behind the prisoners thrust their swords into the captives' backs and threw their corpses into the moat. They then raced back to the safety of the Christian lines as the garrison shot arrows at them.

'Negotiations have failed, it seems,' remarked Thaddeus dryly.

The Estonians began singing another of their awful songs, which sounded to Conrad like a constipated elk. It served only to add to the overall misery of the morning. After ten minutes he heard a succession of thwacks and thought he discerned one or two screams coming from the fort.

'The crossbowmen have begun to pick off the Estonians,' said Thaddeus, turning to one of his men at the trebuchet and nodding to him.

'Stand back, please,' he said to the boys.

They watched as a stone was placed in the trebuchet's leather sling. Conrad felt a tingle of excitement as the machine was readied for use.

'The trebuchet is a simple machine,' Thaddeus said to them, 'but the key is in the correct use of materials for its construction. For example, the base and framework must be heavy enough to support the throwing arm and counterweight. For this reason a heavier wood such as oak is preferred for the framing whereas the throwing arm is made of a lighter wood, fir in this case.'

The singing from the fort had ceased abruptly when crossbow bolts had begun to strike faces and shoulders and sent the Estonians scurrying for cover. Thaddeus nodded to the man next to the machine who pulled back the release pin to drop the hinged counterweight and throw the stone in the sling towards the fort. Conrad was captivated as he saw it fly through the air and strike the roof of one of the end towers, sending tiles in all directions as it tore it off. Then the mangonels commenced shooting, sending stones crashing against the walls and towers, splintering wood and crushing the skulls of those in the path of the missiles.

'When does the assault begin?' asked Anton excitedly.

'Not until the ditch is filled in,' said Thaddeus, 'so that the siege tower can approach the walls.'

The mangonels and trebuchet maintained a steady rate of operation as the crossbowmen on the fort's southern side directed their shooting at any enemy bowmen who showed themselves on the walls. Sir Frederick and his knights grew restless when Master Berthold informed them that there would be no assault this day, which would be given over to filling the ditch with the tree trunks that had been felled the day before. Mantlets were pushed closer to the moat as the spearmen left their ranks to haul the logs that had been stacked to the rear of the mangonels. The Estonians had few archers so the risk of being shot by an arrow was small, even more so with the crossbowmen and stones keeping their heads down.

They worked at a frantic pace, bringing the logs forward and hurling them into the moat. Conrad saw their efforts and felt helpless. A hundred spearmen were using ropes to pull the logs to the moat. Occasionally one would fall after being hit by an arrow, to be either helped back to the surgeons' tent or, if dead, placed on the ground to be later buried.

'Come on,' he shouted at the others, 'we cut down some of those trees so we should help to fill the moat.'

Hans looked at him. 'I'm with you.'

'Me too,' said Anton. Bruno and Johann nodded their agreement and so all five of them ran over to the piles of logs. Sweating soldiers working in teams of four picked up a log, two on each side, and then ran the short distance to the moat, stones and crossbow bolts flying above them against the fort's timber wall.

Conrad and the others stood over a trunk, bent down and lifted it up. They were surprised by its weight and their legs almost buckled as they lifted it to waist height.

'Hold it!' hissed Anton.

They tried to run but could only manage a brisk walk as they took the trunk towards the moat. Conrad's heart began to pound in his chest as he passed crossbowmen crouching behind mantlets and saw an arrow slam into the turf a few feet from him. He also saw leather face who grinned and gave him the thumbs up.

His breathing became heavier as they neared the moat. They had to turn the log to roll it into the depression on top of the others.

Conrad stopped and called behind him as a rock deflected off the top of the battlements and crushed the face of an Estonian. The corpse was flipped over the wall and thudded into the ground at the base of the wall.

'Turn the log!' shouted Conrad, who felt as though every member of the garrison was looking at him.

They tossed the log on top of the others and then sprinted back out of range of enemy arrows as more logs were carried forward in an unending relay. They transported four more logs before an angry Lukas stopped their activities and ordered them back to their tent. By the time night had fallen a bridge of logs had been created in the moat on the fort's southern side. The cost had been five spearmen killed and a further ten injured. Conrad and the others spent the night holding torches and cutting down trees in the forest as a punishment for disobeying orders. They were also denied an evening meal and breakfast the next day. Hans was close to despair.

One bright spot amidst their misery was that Walter the Penitent joined them in the forest during the evening to share their punishment. He too denied himself an evening meal and breakfast but appeared to be remarkably fresh as the others stood shivering in the pre-dawn gloom, their eyes red and puffy and their teeth chattering. Lukas came to collect them for morning mass, inspecting their pile of logs before they departed. Walter shook his hand and then marched off to don his armour and weapons to partake in the coming day's siege.

Lukas watched him go. 'Piety and discipline. A powerful combination. You could all learn a lot by studying Walter's behaviour. He has turned his back on a life of luxury and high living to fight in this wasteland against the pagans. To be a warrior of Christ and live a life of poverty, chastity and obedience.'

He turned to face them, their young faces pale; their fingers cold and chapped. 'Obedience. You need to learn the meaning of that word. All of you have the makings of fine soldiers, and in time one or two of you may even enter the ranks of the brother knights of the Sword Brothers. But you will come to nothing if you do not learn to obey orders. You disobey me again and you will be flogged. Now go and report to the farrier. You can spend the day shovelling dung.'

They trooped off with heads bowed to the stabling area as Thalibald and his warriors once more headed north to form a defensive screen around the army and keep watch for any relief force. As the Livs marched in a long file armed with spears and swords and carrying large round shields, Conrad looked at their painted shields bearing ancient Latvian symbols. Most sported the Sign of the Moon, the symbol of warriors that resembled the letter 'c'. Other shields were decorated with the Cross of Crosses, a combination of four pagan crosses, the Sign of the Thunder God, the symbol of fire, thunder, health and prosperity, or the Sign of Mara – a zigzag line. Rameke came over to him as the boys trudged the other way, Conrad looking enviously at the spear he clutched and the sword that hung at his left hip.

'You will take part in the assault today?' said Rameke, his long hair under his helmet.

'We are to spend the day heaping dung into wheelbarrows,' replied Conrad bitterly.

Rameke looked at him with sympathy. 'Almost as bad as patrolling empty forests.'

'You have seen no Estonians?'

Rameke shook his head. 'We spend our time walking among trees, hoping to see the enemy, but the only activity is the odd elk. Perhaps today will be different.' He looked at the line of spearmen heading out of camp. 'I have to go.'

Conrad extended his hand. 'God go with you.'

Rameke smiled and clasped his forearm. 'You too, my friend.'

That morning the besiegers moved a 'cat' – a protective shed on wheels with a V-shaped roof – across the log bridge spanning the moat so that a team of engineers equipped with picks and shovels could remove part of the fort's sloping rampart. In this way the siege tower could be pushed up against the wall. Once more the crossbowmen behind their mantlets shot at any Estonians who showed themselves on the battlements and tried to throw spears or rocks down on the cat.

Thaddeus kept his machines throwing stones against the towers and walls at a desultory rate in order to conserve their ammunition. Sir Frederick grew bored at waiting around for a second day and took out his frustration on a squire, beating the poor lad senseless before Master Berthold interceded. The lord's humour was not improved when he and his knights retired to his tent to eat a midday meal and was informed that his own warhorse had died of exposure. By the end of the day sufficient earth had been removed from the hillock to allow the siege tower to be moved forward the next morning. Thalibald and his men returned after dusk to report they had seen no Estonians.

The new day dawned bright and frosty, the siege tower finally moving forward towards the fort. The defenders swelled the ramparts and placed all their few

186

archers on the southern wall to shoot at the great wooden monster as it inched its way towards them. Lukas ordered the boys to stay with Master Thaddeus at the trebuchet as Sir Frederick and his knights stood on the top platform of the tower. Conrad saw Master Berthold and the brother knights standing to his left, together with the order's sergeants, the latter holding scaling ladders at the ready. He felt a tingle of excitement ripple through him. If only he could be allowed to join them.

The crossbowmen behind their mantlets were once again directing their bolts against the defenders, who had nailed planks to the top of the battlements in an effort to provide additional cover for their warriors. The defenders now knew that the main assault would be directed against the southern wall and so had lined the western wall with only a few men. But it was from that direction that the mangonels began shooting new projectiles – barrels of burning tar. Conrad saw pillars of black smoke billowing up into the ice-blue sky from within the fort. He looked at Thaddeus in confusion.

'Barrels of burning tar shot into the fort to set fire to the buildings,' said Thaddeus. 'The defenders will have to take men from the walls to extinguish them. Either that or let them burn.'

The mangonels facing the fort's south side were still shooting rocks at what was left of the towers, which had all lost their roofs and had their timber supports smashed and splintered. The trebuchet had stopped shooting as the siege tower was now between it and the fort. The closed drawbridge at the front of its top platform meant that Sir Frederick and his men were safe from enemy missiles as the tower was pushed forward by fifty spearmen in and behind its base. Conrad watched admiringly as the tower creaked and groaned as it approached the moat at an agonisingly slow pace. More knights stood on the climbing frame at the rear of the tower, shields strapped on their backs and armed with a variety of swords, short axes and maces.

The black smoke coming from within the fort increased as more flaming barrels found their targets. But the number of defenders on the southern wall showed no signs of lessening. The tower was now across the log bridge and against the wall, and suddenly the drawbridge crashed down onto the timber palisade and Sir Frederick led the charge on to the ramparts. Cries and screams carried across the battlefield as a bloody mêlée took place on the battlements. Then there was a cry of 'God with us!' and the Sword Brothers raced forward.

Conrad thought that the Estonians would be crushed with ease as a white tide of brother knights and sergeants flooded forward, swept down into the ditch and then placed their assault ladders against the timber walls. He and the other boys

187

began cheering as the order's soldiers scaled the ladders and began hacking at the warriors above with their swords. Crossbow bolts picked off defenders and Conrad saw knights ascending the rungs at the back of the tower as those ahead of them reached the platform and reinforced Sir Frederick fighting on the walls. The fort was falling!

The quartermaster appeared by the side of Thaddeus, a huge fat man with an ill-fitting gambeson, bushy white beard and a ruddy complexion.

'I need these boys to carry spare quivers to the crossbowmen,' he said unceremoniously.

'Brother Lukas left me in charge of them,' said Thaddeus, somewhat flustered. 'I don't think he wants them placed in danger.'

The quartermaster spat on the ground. 'If the fort doesn't fall soon we will all be in danger.' He pointed at the boys. 'You all follow me.'

Conrad did nothing. He looked at Thaddeus, who merely shrugged.

'Now!' bellowed the quartermaster. 'I will take full responsibility,' he said to Thaddeus.

For such a large man he moved remarkably sprightly as he led the boys to a sleigh fifty paces to the rear of the trebuchet. He pulled back the canvas cover behind the driver's seat to reveal neatly packed rows of quivers holding quarrels. He pointed at the crossbowmen behind the mantlets, most of whom were no longer shooting but were looking expectantly at where the boys were standing.

'They have run out of ammunition, see?' said the quartermaster. 'Here, take these and give them to the crossbowmen.'

He held out four quivers to Conrad, who took them in his arms. 'And don't drop them. Off you go.'

Conrad clutched the quivers close to his chest and ran towards two crossbowmen crouched behind their mantlet. Fierce fighting was still raging on the walls and occasionally the body of an Estonian or crusader would fall to the ground to add to the piles of bodies that were collecting at the foot of the wall. Thick black smoke was now billowing into the sky from burning buildings inside the fort.

Conrad threw himself behind the mantlet, between the two crossbowmen, who looked at him with amusement.

'A wasted trip, lad.' Conrad recognised the distinctive features of leather face who cocked his head towards the fort. 'Too many of each side mixed up to get a clear shot.' He took two of the quivers. 'Still, these might come in useful if our soldiers have to retreat.'

Conrad handed the other two quivers to leather face's companion. 'You think that is likely?'

'Not now we are on the walls,' said leather face, 'just a matter of time now.'

But he was wrong, and after two hours of battling on the walls, in which dozens of Estonians were killed along with thirty spearmen, four knights and three brother knights and eight sergeants of the Sword Brothers, the fort had still not fallen. The defenders eventually abandoned the southern wall and retreated to another inner wall that was set back twenty paces from the outer wall. It was shorter and had no towers but the defenders gathered behind it and prepared to repel the crusaders. But the latter consolidated their hold on the outer wall and did not launch any more attacks. Night fell and Fellin still defied the crusaders.

Sir Frederick had suffered numerous wounds during the fighting, though none appeared to be serious. Nevertheless, an axe blow had cut through his mail hauberk and inflicted a nasty arm wound and a spear thrust had pierced his mail chausses. He would not be taking part in the next day's fighting. Rudolf, Henke and Lukas were still capable of fighting, though Henke was most upset that an axe had dented the face mask of his helmet, a blow that had broken his nose. Conrad and the other boys had been ordered to attend the surgeons in the medical tent after the battle where Henke sat on a bench holding a bloody cloth over his nose. Conrad and Hans carried in a charcoal brazier using long metal handles.

'Over here and quick about it,' snapped one of the surgeons who was extracting pieces of chain mail from Sir Frederick's arm wound. The knight sat in a chair near Henke and winced as the surgeon yanked a shard of metal out of his flesh with pliers.

'Apologies, my lord.'

Conrad and Hans set down the brazier. Sir Frederick looked at Conrad.

'What is your name, boy?'

'Conrad Wolff, sir.'

The surgeon placed one of his cauterising irons, which had a wedge-shaped end like a ship's prow designed for treating wounds inflicted by spear thrusts, in the coals of the brazier.

'Are you a squire?'

'No, sir, a novice of the Sword Brothers.'

Henke removed his bloody bandage. 'In his short time with us Conrad has saved the life of one of our brother knights and wounded Lembit himself, my lord.'

Sir Frederick was most impressed. 'Excellent! Give him a sword and he can stand beside me tomorrow when we finish off the enemy. Would you like that, young Conrad?'

'Yes, lord,' beamed Conrad as the surgeon took the red-hot iron out of the fire and used the head to burn the raw edges of the wound. Beads of sweat formed on Sir Frederick's forehead and he shook to contain his emotions as intense pain shot through him. He waved Conrad away as the surgeon looked with satisfaction at his handiwork.

The next morning the Estonians surrendered.

The deluge of quarrels, stones and barrels of pitch, in addition to the heavy fighting on the walls, had thinned the numbers of the garrison to such an extent that the fort's commander thought it futile to continue. He sent an emissary to Master Berthold as the crusader army once more deployed to assault the fort. A sizeable number of soldiers had been left in the siege tower during the night to prevent it from being burnt by Fellin's occupants but also to shoot at any Estonians that showed themselves. This meant that the fires inside the fort could not be extinguished and so half of its shelters and stores went up in flames.

The morning dawned cold and grey, the sky heaped with leaden clouds that blocked out the sun and promised snow. After a brief meeting to discuss the situation Master Berthold sent the emissary back to the fort with his terms. They were generous: the garrison was to accept baptism and promise not to take up arms against Christians in the future. The survivors would be allowed to remain at Fellin rather than being taken south as captives; they would also keep what was left of their food supplies. Sir Frederick thought this over-charitable but his wound was still painful and so he and the other crusaders grumbled but did not protest.

Priests were sent into the fort to sprinkle the buildings and occupants with holy water by way of baptism, after which the bodies of those killed were collected. The Estonians cremated their dead but Master Berthold ordered that the Christian slain be taken south. Thus Conrad was one of those detailed to collect frozen corpses, wrap them in winding sheets and place them on the backs of sleighs.

'I do not understand,' he said to Lukas as he and Hans hauled another dead spearman onto a sleigh. They had already stripped the corpse and taken the man's armour and weapons to the quartermaster.

'What don't you understand?' said Lukas.

'Why can't the dead be buried here, where they fell?'

Lukas wrapped his cloak around him as the first flecks of snow began to fall. 'Because Master Berthold wants the dead to be buried in consecrated ground, not left here to be dug up and burnt by the Estonians.'

Hans was appalled. 'Dug up?'

Lukas nodded. 'Yes, Hans. The Estonians consign their own dead to the fires and would not think twice about exhuming our dead once we have left and throwing them onto a fire. An act of desecration that we are not prepared to allow to happen.'

The flecks of snow had now turned to large flakes that were falling at a steady rate. Lukas looked up into the sky.

'If this carries on it will be a hard journey back to Wenden.'

And so it was.

The trebuchet and mangonels were dismantled and their constituent parts stowed on sleighs, the siege tower was set on fire, and by midday the camp had been dismantled and the journey south commenced. The army only managed three hours of travel the first day and covered only five miles, but Master Berthold, having achieved what he set out to accomplish, was eager to be away before a relief army appeared. The crusaders had eaten half their food supplies, half their horses had died and their numbers had been depleted by deaths in battle, frostbite and injuries inflicted by the enemy. This meant that of the three hundred and fifty fighting men who had set out from Wenden only two hundred were fit for duty. The men of the Sword Brothers were well provided with warm clothing but those crusaders who had come from Germany suffered terribly in the cold, their fingers turning black as the column made slow progress south.

The snow fall got heavier by the hour so that the rate of advance barely exceeded five miles a day, Conrad and the other boys assisting in digging through high snow drifts that had to be cleared before the column could move forward. Thalibald still sent out patrols, his men fashioning snowshoes from branches interwoven with cords to allow them to walk across the thick snow. After three days he ordered that his men cease their patrols and help with clearing paths for the sleighs. And still it snowed.

On the fourth day from Fellin Lukas ordered Conrad to attend Sir Frederick, whose wound had worsened and who now sat on a sleigh wrapped in furs shivering. His eyes were black-ringed and sunken and he had developed a hacking cough that shook his whole body. His squire was dead, he had lost his horse and, it seemed to Conrad, all hope. That night Conrad took hot porridge to his tent after ensuring the noble was wrapped in dry furs. His shaking had abated somewhat and there was a semblance of colour in his cheeks but he now had difficulty moving his wounded arm. After he had finished eating the surgeon came and examined and dressed his wound. Sir Frederick asked him how it was healing and was informed as well as inspected. After the man had left Sir Frederick told Conrad to fetch him some wine.

'He's lying, of course,' he said, draining his cup and holding it out for Conrad to fill. 'I could see it in his eyes. Bloody butchers. All they can do is cut and saw in the hope that they can cure you. Useless idiots.'

Conrad stood holding the flask of wine, ready to fill the knight's cup again.

'Where are you from, Conrad?' said Sir Frederick, squirming uncomfortably in his chair.

'Lübeck, lord.'

'A most prosperous city. Why would you leave it to come to this bleak land of ice and pagans?'

Conrad felt reluctant to speak of his misfortune. 'It is a long story, lord.'

Sir Frederick held out his cup. 'Fill it up and get another flask. As I am in pain and cannot sleep your tale can make me forget about my miserable condition, unless you want me to inform Brother Lukas that you have been insubordinate.'

So Conrad stood and told the knight about the death of his family, how fate had brought him into contact with Rudolf and Henke and how he had travelled back with them to Livonia. Sir Frederick sat in his chair, drank and nodded his head as Conrad relayed his tale. When he had finished the knight did not speak but sat with his head down, running a finger around the rim of his cup. At last he spoke.

'I have done the things that were committed against your family. I have raped, killed and robbed with impunity because I am a lord and those I wronged were poor and uneducated.'

He looked at Conrad. 'How many sons who have lost their parents and siblings now curse the name Sir Frederick of Tangermünde?'

He now looked deathly pale in the ghostly glow cast by the thin candles on the small table beside him.

'Do you know why I took the cross and came on crusade in Livonia?'

'No, lord.'

He winced as pain shot through his arm. 'To cleanse my soul. To atone for my sins. To kill pagans is a great deed in God's eyes and to fall while on crusade is to guarantee a place in heaven. Or so the priests tell me.'

He looked at Conrad. 'What do you think?'

'The Sword Brothers teach that it is so, lord.'

Sir Frederick emitted a low laugh. 'Let me tell you about the Sword Brothers, young Conrad. They may wear the mantle of Christian knights but for the most part they are ruthless killers who learned their trade as mercenaries in Germany. Rudolf Kassel was known in northern Germany for being the brutal leader of a mercenary band before he became deputy commander at Wenden. Did you know that?'

Conrad shook his head. Sir Frederick waved a hand at him.

'It matters not now. But he will have to slay many pagans before God looks favourably on him, that much is certain.'

The next day, after he had packed away Sir Frederick's tent and belongings and assisted him into the sleigh next to the driver, Conrad once more joined his young companions as they shovelled snow aside to clear a path for the column. Even though they were now travelling through a large forest it was still snowing and the drifts were long and deep. It was exhausting work and reduced the rate of advance to a snail's pace. Horses were collapsing from exhaustion and could not rise, so had their throats cut for a merciful end. Even a few of the ponies expired and some of the sleighs had to be abandoned. Conrad and the others resembled snowmen as they toiled in their white capes and hoods. He was delighted to have the company of Rameke one morning, both of them heaping snow from the track onto the verges. His friend was in a sombre mood.

'This has been a wasted trip,' he complained.

'We captured the fort,' said Conrad.

'I did not dip my sword in the blood of my enemies. The son of a chief should have battle scars otherwise his warriors will not respect him.'

'The brothers teach us that impatience is a vice,' said Conrad, 'and that patience is a virtue.'

Rameke was unconvinced. 'My brother killed his first enemy when he was thirteen, Conrad, so you will appreciate my haste.'

Conrad wondered how long he would have to wait before he was trusted to carry a sword and fight beside the order's brother knights and sergeants. At least Rameke had a sword.

He looked around. 'It's stopped snowing.'

Sixteen days after leaving Fellin the tired and hungry crusaders at last saw the welcome sight of Wenden Castle, its partially built towers framed against a clear blue sky.

Chapter 8

Lembit stood next to the charred and battered southern wall of Fellin, studying the blackened remains of the siege tower that the crusaders had used to assault the stronghold. Word had reached him that Fellin was under siege but he had been helpless to intervene, being on a visit to the elders of Wierland at the time. Though his wolf shields were at Lehola, a mere ten miles to the north, he had sent an urgent despatch forbidding them from making a relief attempt. Rusticus had been left in command at Lehola and the last thing he wanted was his best soldiers being killed in vain. It was now February and the crusaders were long gone. What had not disappeared was the damage to his reputation, which would have to be rebuilt in the coming year. The damage to the fort could be repaired easily enough; his prestige would take longer to restore.

He heard footsteps in the snow and turned to see his deputy approaching.

'Where are the dead?'

Rusticus looked confused. 'Dead, lord?'

'The crusader dead. Where have they been interred? Unless they suffered no losses, that is.'

'They took them back south,' said Rusticus.

Lembit laughed grimly. 'So we are denied the pleasure of digging them up and burning them. It appears I am to be denied any solace from this sorry episode.'

Rusticus shovelled snow with his boot. 'We could pursue them, lord.'

Lembit rolled his eyes in despair. 'And add to our losses? I think not. No, we will have to wait until the spring to exact payment for this outrage.'

Rusticus mumbled something under his breath.

'You have something to say?' Lembit said to him.

'Apologies, lord, but we could have attempted to relieve the fort. I was but a short distance away.'

Lembit did not want to reveal to his subordinate that he did not trust him with command of an army. 'It would not have been appropriate for you to lead the army and not I. What would the other tribal chiefs have said if you had relieved Fellin while I was away in Wierland?'

'We will attack in the spring?' asked Rusticus.

Lembit smiled savagely. 'Yes, and this time we will not be alone. Time to see if our new-found allies are prepared to back up their words with warriors.'

Rusticus scraped at the snow with his boot some more. 'You trust the Oeselians, lord?'

'Trust has nothing to do with it. The Oeselians want to use us and we want to use them, but even the most simple-minded idiot knows that it is better to stand together than fight the Christians separately.' He glanced at Rusticus. 'Well, perhaps not all idiots.'

'What do want to do with the garrison?' asked his deputy.

Now it was Lembit's turn to be confused. 'The garrison?'

'Do you want me to organise their execution?'

'Why should I desire their execution?'

'They surrendered rather than fighting to the death,' shrugged Rusticus. 'And they accepted Christian baptism.' Rusticus spat to avert evil.

Lembit laughed. 'You want me to kill my own soldiers because some man in a woman's attire sprinkled them with water? No. Besides, if you kill them who will rebuild the fort?'

Rusticus thought for a moment. 'We could execute them after they have rebuilt the fort, lord.'

'Do you ever think about anything else other than killing?'

'Lord?'

Lembit waved a hand at him. 'It doesn't matter. We go back to Lehola to organise the spring campaign with our Oeselian allies. Leave some men here to assist with the fort's repairs. And no killing anyone.'

*****

Conrad and the others went back to their training upon their return to Wenden. It was now February and the snow fell almost every day, blanketing the land and making travel almost impossible. Inside the castle compound people cleared paths and the track of snow and in the citadel itself the courtyard was kept free of ice. But construction on the towers and walls had come to a halt until the spring. The workers and their families shivered in their huts, the peat blocks being strictly rationed now that all the firewood had been used up. Parties were sent into the forests to collect dead wood but that was only enough to provide fuel for cooking, not heating. The more so since the crusaders who had assaulted Fellin were also being accommodated within the castle grounds.

Sir Frederick was housed in Master Berthold's quarters but his conditioned worsened. Prayers were said for him daily in the chapel but it became apparent that the hand of death was upon him. He insisted that Conrad attended him on a daily basis, which the youth found irksome at first. He would have preferred to be on the training field instead of in the room of a dying man. But the knight insisted and so did Lukas and so Conrad found himself feeding the lord hot porridge and wiping his forehead when his body was wracked by intense pain. The fire was heaped high and burned brightly but Sir Frederick was still cold and so Conrad wrapped him in furs after the surgeons had washed and dressed his stinking wound in fresh bandages and Otto recited his prayers.

When he was conscious the knight spent most of his time talking to Conrad, though not in a manner that required the youth to answer him. Otto offered to be his confessor but Sir Frederick gave him short shrift.

'Get out, you shaven-headed crow. Go and administer to someone who is prepared to listen.'

It was the first time Conrad had seen the fierce Otto lost for words as the priest stormed from the room and slammed the door.

'Halfwit,' spat Sir Frederick. 'Don't become like him, Conrad.'

'I hope to be a sergeant, lord, not a priest.'

'I have butchered men, women and children and was told afterwards by priests that I was doing God's work. Thrown innocents onto great pyres and heard their screams as the flames consumed them. Is that God's work? I sometimes wonder. Do you think I should leave my lands and gold to the church, Conrad?'

'I do not know, lord.'

Sir Frederick looked at him with his sunken eyes. 'Give me an answer, boy. I command you.'

'I think so, lord, yes,' he answered falteringly.

'So I can be assured of my place in heaven?'

Conrad nodded.

Sir Frederick laughed sardonically. 'So be it, then. At the very least I will be able to go before God and ask Him why he sent a plague that killed my wife and children.'

Conrad was alarmed by the knight's blasphemy. Sir Frederick saw his expression.

'You think my words are impious?'

'It is not for me to say, lord.'

Sir Frederick cackled, then shook as the pain gripped him once more. Conrad held him until the spasm had passed and then the knight slipped into unconsciousness.

The next day, as he and the other youths, together with all the sergeants, were sweeping the courtyard in a vain attempt to keep it clear of the snow that was falling heavily, Otto stood at the entrance to the master's quarters and bellowed at Conrad to attend him. He turned and ran over to the tall priest.

'Sir Frederick wants to see you before he dies.'

Conrad went inside the hall and walked to Master Berthold's bedroom. The smell of decaying flesh met his nostrils before he entered the chamber where he found crusaders and Sword Brothers gathered around Sir Frederick. Another priest was reciting prayers and a scribe was recording the will of the dying man, observed by Master Berthold and two crusaders. Rudolf stood at the foot of the bed and he beckoned Conrad over.

'Sir Frederick wishes to speak to you. Be quick, his time on earth is nearly over.'

Though he had been attending Sir Frederick for many days Conrad suddenly felt nervous around him. The atmosphere in the room had changed now that the knight was close to death. He felt as though God himself was now watching the scene. Would He punish the knight for all the sacrilegious things he had said?

The knight saw Conrad and weakly lifted his hand to wave him over. The priest was administering the last rights and those around the bed had their heads bowed in reverence to a servant of the church. Conrad leaned over to hear Sir Frederick's words.

'I have something for you,' his voice was weak and faltering.

One of his knights held out a sword in a scabbard to Conrad, who looked at it in surprise.

'It is my sword,' said Sir Frederick, 'and I bequeath it to you, young Conrad. Learn to use it well and then hopefully God will let you kill that bastard who murdered your family. Take it.'

Conrad stepped back and took the sword offered to him. Sir Frederick smiled weakly and then closed his eyes. He cradled the sword in his arms as the knight breathed his last and everyone brought their hands together to join the priest in prayer. Rudolf moved to Conrad's side and told him he was excused. He left the room and walked through the hall back into the courtyard. The snow had stopped and the sweepers were winning their battle to clear the courtyard.

Hans and the others saw Conrad reappear with the sword and gathered around him.

'Where did you get that?' enquired Anton enviously.

'Sir Frederick gave it to me. It was his sword,' answered Conrad.

'Let us see it,' said Hans.

It was in a simple scabbard of wood covered with black leather but when Conrad pulled the sword from it they all could see that it was a magnificent weapon, a lord's weapon. The birch grip was wrapped with black leather, topped by a disc-shaped pommel in which a unicorn's head had been etched on each side. Each of the steel arms of the cross-guard was 'waisted', flaring back to their original width at the ends. It had a broad and evenly tapering blade, the point curving gradually to a sharp point. The blade itself was just over thirty inches long with fullers along three-quarters of its length. It was surprisingly light and had excellent handling characteristics.

The boys stood in silence, admiring the sword, and did not see Lukas approaching.

'I will take that.'

Conrad looked at the sword, then at the Sword Brother and his heart sank.

'It was a gift from Sir Frederick,' he said quietly, sliding the sword back into the scabbard.

Lukas held out his hand. 'I know that. A noble gesture from a true knight and servant of the church. When you learn how to use it properly you can have it back. Until then it will be stored in the armoury.'

Conrad handed the sword to Lukas.

'No one will use it but you,' said the brother knight, 'that I promise.'

And so Conrad went back to using a waster, training every day with the others as the snow lay thick on the ground. He and they helped to hack at the cold earth to dig Sir Frederick's grave, the first in the area to the south of the moat designated to be Wenden's cemetery. As February ended snow still blanketed the ground but the temperature rose slightly and the hours of daylight increased. In the middle of the month it stopped freezing and the ice on the Gauja began to break up, great floes floating downstream to make any sort of travel on the river treacherous. By the end of March the ice had gone and so had the crusaders and the bishop's soldiers from Riga, marching south across a sodden land. The surviving siege engines were left at Wenden.

It had been nearly a year since Conrad and the others had arrived at the castle and in that time their bodies had grown stronger and fitter. They knew how to ride, wield a sword, shield and spear, had survived being under siege and had taken part in their first campaign. As Conrad reached his fifteenth birthday he wondered how his sister was faring in the convent in Lübeck. He also wondered when he would be given his sword.

*****

Vetseke stood in the cavernous interior of Polotsk's St Sophia's Cathedral, one of only three stone cathedrals in all Russia, the other two being at Novgorod and Kiev. He had endured a thoroughly miserable journey to reach the city, travelling in an open sleigh wrapped in furs and being lashed by biting winds. Prince Vsevolod had provided him with a small escort of a dozen soldiers, who had spent the entire journey complaining and cursing about their lot and he was glad to see the back of them. Now he stood alone, a landless prince seeking aid from the very principality he had treated with contempt not so long ago. But that had been when Kokenhusen had been a principality in its own right, an independent kingdom that answered to no one. But now Kokenhusen was under the control of the Sword Brothers and he was a vagrant in all but name.

He looked around the imposing structure. The cathedral had magnificent apses and its eastern façade contained a multitude of vaults where the former rulers of Polotsk were interred. Located on the Dvina where the small River Palata flows into it, over a hundred miles southeast of Gerzika, the city had formerly received tribute from smaller principalities along the Dvina all the way to the Baltic coast. Polotsk had first been a settlement seven hundred years ago. Originally under the control of the larger city of Kiev to the south, it broke free of Kiev's rule over a hundred years ago under its greatest leader, Prince Vseslav the Sorcerer, so-called because he had the ability to supposedly turn himself into a wolf. It was he who ordered the construction of this cathedral in which Vetseke stood, a lasting symbol of Polotsk's independence and grandeur. But since then even the mighty power of the principality had waned.

He heard footsteps approaching. A mail-clad guard saluted him.

'The council will see you now, highness.'

He followed the soldier through the aisle to a door leading to a room that received foreign ambassadors. Indeed, the interior of the cathedral also contained a library, archive, treasury and a magistrate's office. The guard opened the door, bowed his head and then closed it when Vetseke entered the room.

Inside the members of the town council sat at a long table, a row of severe-looking middle-aged men with black beards dressed in rich, light-coloured dalmaticas. In the centre sat Prince Vladimir, the man elected by the council to rule over the principality. Now in his sixties, he rose and extended an arm to a chair positioned in front of the table.

'Prince Vetseke, welcome. Please be seated.'

He bowed his head to Vladimir and took his seat.

Vladimir smiled at him. 'How can we be of assistance to you?'

Vetseke looked at the six other faces in the room. These men were the real power in the town: individuals who were elected by a vote of free adult males to decide who should be Polotsk's ruler and decree on matters of war and peace. Their hard faces told him that it would be useless to try flattery.

'I come here a prince without a principality, a general without an army and a man seeking friends. A new power is rising in the west that threatens to engulf all the principalities along the Dvina and enslave them to the Church of Rome. I have sworn to fight this power and ask only for assistance in my fight.'

The faces looking at him remained silent, studying him with their eyes. The room was airless and filled with the sweet aroma of cassia incense, a mixture of cinnamon and cloves that was used in the cathedral's religious services. At length Vladimir spoke.

'What assistance do you require, Prince Vetseke?'

'Soldiers with which I can retake Kokenhusen and once more make that domain a servant of Polotsk.'

'Kokenhusen's problems are not ours,' said one of the council, a dour-looking man with a thin face.

Vetseke smiled politely at him. 'With respect, they are very much your problem. Twenty years ago there was no crusader kingdom in this land. But now a new town – Riga – has arisen at the mouth of the Dvina and Catholic castles take root along that river and along the Gauja to the north. How long, my lords, before the Bishop of Riga and his hordes are knocking at the gates of this very city?'

There were frowns of consternation from the council at his words but Vladimir was stroking his beard thoughtfully.

'You expect Polotsk to fight on your behalf to restore you to your throne?' asked another member of the council.

201

'No, lord,' replied Vetseke, 'I ask only for your assistance. I will be doing the fighting.'

'With our soldiers,' said another man with deep-set eyes. 'And if we give you aid then the crusaders will turn their attention to us and Polotsk will be drawn into a needless war.'

Vetseke's temper was beginning to rise. 'With respect, lord, Polotsk has already been drawn into a war, whether it knows it or not.'

'In what way?' asked Vladimir.

'How long will it be,' asked Vetseke, 'before Riga demands tolls from the boats that transport Polotsk's goods down the Dvina? How long will it be before the Bishop of Riga demands that Polotsk pays him tribute in return for peace?'

The man with deep-set eyes leaned back in his chair and wagged a finger at him.

'The Catholics would not dare to do such a thing.'

Vetseke sighed loudly. 'Their arrogance knows no bounds, my lord, and with every year that passes their strength increases. They wage war against the Estonians, against the Oeselians and against the Lithuanians. Soon they will turn their spears towards you.'

'Polotsk is a great power,' declared Vladimir. 'The Bishop of Riga does not have the strength to challenge us.'

Vetseke clenched his fists. 'The Catholics wage crusade against heretics, my lord, and they view the Holy Church of Russia as a heresy. Each year a new army lands at Riga to wage the bishop's crusade against paganism.'

'We are not pagans,' said Vladimir.

'No, lord,' replied Vetseke, 'but to the crusaders we are the same as the Livs, Estonians, Oeselians and Lithuanians. Peoples to be subjugated or destroyed.'

Murmurs of anger greeted these words but Vladimir said nothing, placing his elbows on the table and resting his chin on his hands.

'Would you give us a few minutes, Prince Vetseke?'

Vetseke rose, bowed his head and left the room, a guard closing the door behind him.

Vladimir played with a gold ring on his finger. 'He is right.'

The others sighed and grunted their disagreement.

'He has lost his crown and now he comes here thinking that we will give him an army to reclaim it,' said a man at the end of the table. 'It is out of the question.'

202

'But he is right about the rising power and threat of the Catholic crusaders,' replied Vladimir. 'As Vetseke stated, twenty years ago Riga did not exist. But now the crusaders advance east along the Dvina. How long before they are knocking at our gates?'

'Prince Vsevolod at Gerzika has reported no threat to his domain,' said one of the council.

'That is because he has the support of the Lithuanians,' replied Vladimir. 'But the Lithuanians were repulsed recently from Kokenhusen. Vetseke is correct in declaring that the power of the crusaders increases.'

'Do you propose declaring war upon the Bishop of Riga?' asked the thin-faced man.

Vladimir shook his head. 'That would not serve our interests.'

'Then what would?' asked the man with the deep-set eyes.

'Why are we wasting our time considering aiding a Liv?' said the thin-faced man in exasperation. 'He is not Russian.'

Vladimir smiled at him. 'That is precisely why we should help him.'

The others stared at him in confusion.

'There are no doubt others of his people who chafe at the yoke of Catholic rule,' explained Vladimir. 'That being the case it would make sense to send Vetseke back to his people to foment trouble. If the crusaders are fighting an internal revolt they will have no resources to devote to their eastward expansion.'

The others nodded in agreement. Vladimir raised a finger to the guard.

'Show Prince Vetseke in.'

Moments later the former ruler of Kokenhusen entered and Vladimir explained to him that Polotsk would provide aid to enable him to win back his kingdom, though it would not involve the principality sending its own soldiers west to battle the crusaders.

'Then how can I reclaim my kingdom?' asked Vetseke.

'The people of your race,' said Vladimir, 'who live under the tyranny of Catholicism may prove fiercer warriors than Russian soldiers. Word will be sent up the Dvina that those Livs who wish to regain their freedom can find sanctuary at Polotsk. Those who seek refuge here may be sympathetic to your cause, Prince Vetseke. We will furnish them with weapons so that you can take them west to lead them against their oppressors.'

The other council members nodded solemnly at Vladimir's words. It was less than Vetseke had hoped for but perhaps more than he could have expected. He rose from his chair and bowed his head to Vladimir.

'Your offer is most generous, lord prince, and I thank you. Once more you have proved that the nobility and hospitality of Polotsk has no equal among the Slav lands.'

The council was touched by these words and broke into polite applause. Vladimir smiled at Vetseke. This landless prince might yet prove useful to his kingdom.

*****

They had sailed across the black, wind-flecked Baltic with a biting wind stinging their faces. When they reached the Estonian coast they headed south. No longer could they run their boats up on the shore and disembark to attack undefended villages before returning to Oesel laden with slaves and booty, their savagery having been sated by rape, torture and murder. Now they had an alliance with the Estonians and so they sailed close to the shore but left the inhabitants alone. The warriors grumbled as they sat on the chests and pulled at the oars to increase their speed.

'Silence!' bellowed Eric, a great bearskin cloak wrapped around him. It might have been April but the air was still icy and the sea freezing to the touch.

'Seems strange to be so near the coast and not dip our swords in Rotalian blood,' said Magnus, Eric's deputy on this voyage.

Eric stood at the prow of the fleet's leading boat, the nineteen others grouped behind it. He turned and looked at Magnus. He was clearly unhappy.

'Row, you worthless dogs,' he shouted, 'otherwise I will drop you off here and you can go and live with the worthless Estonians.'

'You have not changed your opinion of our new allies, then?' smirked Magnus as the boat cut through the saltwater.

Eric spat over the side. 'Allies? They are lambs who were created so our swords could cut their throats. But my father in his dotage believes there is merit in forming an alliance with this Lembit and his people. I do not.'

The spring had brought an end to the ice and snow and had also brought Lembit to Oesel, who was accorded a reception more fitting to a king than a bandit. Eric had sat at his father's table fuming as Olaf had indulged and flattered Lembit, aided by his brother Sigurd. Lembit and his father had agreed upon a plan to ravage the crusader kingdom with a two-pronged attack: the Estonians would advance from the north and the Oeselians would sail up the River Gauja. Both forces would unite at the hill fort of the traitorous King Caupo, which would be taken by assault. Thereafter the land would be laid waste and emptied of people before a new crusader army arrived at Riga. Eric had had no enthusiasm for the plan, much less cooperating with the Estonians, but his father was insistent and so he found himself leading a raiding expedition up the Gauja.

He would have preferred to have been leading a flotilla of longships, whose appearance was often enough to strike fear into enemies. But though the Gauja would be swollen by spring melt water longships were too large to navigate the waterway easily. So Eric commanded twenty riverboats, each one having a clinker-built hull of oak strakes. Nearly eighty feet long and seventeen feet wide, a single sail plus sixteen pairs of oars powered each vessel. Fifty warriors were carried in each boat – a thousand men to inflict death and destruction upon Caupo's people. Eric comforted himself with the thought that even if the Estonians failed to appear his men would still be able to return home with slaves and plunder after their raid.

The voyage to the mouth of the Gauja was uneventful. The Oeselians ruled the eastern Baltic and their ships roamed the seas unmolested. Though the ships of the crusaders were tall and difficult to capture, they were slow and unwieldy and never instigated an attack. When the boats had entered the Gauja estuary Eric had seen a few small fishing vessels whose owners had frantically tried to avoid them. The Oeselians ignored them as they furled their sails to rely solely on the oarsmen for propulsion. The boats were slim and fast and even against the current achieved an average speed of two miles an hour. By the end of the first day of their journey along the river the Oeselians were ten miles upstream and two days' journey away from their objective: Caupo's stronghold at Treiden.

Eric's guide was an old man who had once fought under his father when Olaf had been a young prince. They had raided up the Gauja many times before the crusaders had arrived to build their stone castles. Looking at his wizened face and frail body Eric found it hard to believe that he had once been a member of his father's bodyguard. The man had told him that they should make camp on a long sandbank beside a high sandstone rock face.

'We are near the crusader castle at Kremon,' said the old man, 'so no fires tonight, my lord.'

The boats had run aground on the sand and their sails had been used to make tents over the hulls, in which the men could spend an uncomfortable night.

Guards had been posted inland from the riverbank and Magnus had wanted to send raiding parties to sack any nearby villages but the old warrior urged against such a venture.

'There are plenty of villages around Treiden to raid. The quieter we approach the more likely the inhabitants will be taken by surprise. Their king too.'

They sat shivering under the sail in the boat, Eric wrapped in his bearskin with his knees drawn up to his chin. He was not in a good mood. Skulking around like a thief in the night did not suit the heir of King Olaf.

'You will have to watch for the crusaders, though,' said the old man.

Eric looked up at him. 'What crusaders?'

'Caupo's stronghold lies close to the crusader castle at Segewold, but on the other side of the river.'

'We should leave some boats on the river to deter a river crossing,' said Magnus, chewing on a piece of cured meat.

'Caupo's stronghold lies to the north of the river?' asked Eric.

The old man nodded. 'There is another crusader castle, at Kremon, and that is also north of the river, a short distance from Treiden.'

'What is the size of its garrison?' asked Eric.

The old man shrugged. 'I have no idea but as far as I know it is still a small wooden hill fort. Around fifty men, maybe more.'

'And what is the size of Caupo's garrison?' said Magnus.

The old man gave him a toothless grin. 'No more than a hundred men, perhaps less. Most of the warriors will be scattered among his villages.'

'We will attack Treiden tomorrow,' declared Eric.

'What about the Estonians?' said Magnus.

Eric smiled. 'What about them? We can accomplish our task without them. If they appear then so much the better. If not, then all the more plunder for us.'

*****

Lembit's army contained warriors from all the Estonian tribes. Its core was the hundred wolf shields that acted as his bodyguard and best troops, but the force also contained Harrien, Wierlanders, Jerwen, Rotalians and Ungannians – two thousand men in all. They had gathered at Lehola when the snow had cleared and the spring mud had disappeared, or at least had dried enough to allow horsemen to travel along tracks and across meadows. He had left a sizeable number of his wolf shields behind at Lehola in case the crusaders attempted another assault against Fellin, also

206

reinforcing the garrison at the latter fort. He thought another attack against it was unlikely, especially as he had planned a diversion to keep the garrison at Wenden occupied.

The men travelled light, the land was now blooming and green shoots were appearing on plants and trees. The ponies on which they rode could graze on the abundance of grass and the men could hunt the wildlife that was now appearing, or alternatively catch fish in Estonia's hundreds of lakes and dozens of rivers. Now the land was no longer frozen the column had to use guides to plot a course around reed-filled marshlands and flooded meadows occupied by corncrakes and great snipes. A fourth of Estonia was covered by peatlands that were crisscrossed by tracks and paths, and it took the army many days to thread its way south across them. Even in the bog forests of pine men had to be wary, dismounting and leading their ponies along tracks flanked by bog mosses, cotton grasses and bog whortleberry. Occasionally they would disturb a black grouse or hear a flying squirrel in the trees above them, but mostly the only sounds were the jangling of pony bits and the curses of men who had strayed off the track and stepped into marsh, sinking up to their waists before they were hauled out.

Lembit rode at the head of the column, his standard of a red wolf on a black background held behind him. Beside him was Rusticus and ahead rode his Saccalian guides. These paths were hundreds of years old, used by tribes to raid the Livs to the south. Raids were designed to strike quickly to seize tools, weapons, jewellery, precious metals and women and children who could then be sold or kept as slaves. Men were invariably killed because they were too troublesome and likely to try to escape. But Lembit did not go to plunder; he went to kill Caupo and destroy his lands.

After ten days the army reached the southern shore of Lake Burtnieks, the great inland stretch of water a mere thirty miles directly north of Wenden. The Estonians were also north of the River Gauja and could march unimpeded towards Caupo's stronghold at Treiden. Once they had left the wetlands of Estonia Lembit had sent out scouts to ensure no crusader patrols would intercept them, but he knew that last year's German knights would have returned to their homeland and this year's crop had yet to arrive.

As the warriors and their mounts rested along the lake's southern shore and some of them waded into the shallow water to fish for salmon, chub and pike, Lembit summoned Rusticus to his tent. His wolf shields were camped around their chief, the felt tents organised in a haphazard fashion among tethered ponies and campfires. The warriors from the other tribes grouped their two-man tents around the dwelling of their warlords – men selected by their tribal elders to lead the various contingents that had been sent south with Lembit. Their shields sported the designs of Estonian mythology and identity – the lynx, oak leaf, spear, eight-heeled star, wolf and bear – and around their necks men wore the wheel cross and eight-pointed star for luck and protection. Others had necklaces bearing pendants engraved with the cornflower, the ancient symbol of vitality.

Lembit saw that his large deputy wore an unhappy expression.

'As we agreed, then, Rusticus. You will take fifty men and a guide will take you to a shallow spot on the Gauja.'

'I should be at your side,' grumbled his subordinate.

'We've talked about that and decided that you will be of more use gaining the attention of Wenden's garrison.'

'I do not trust the Oeselians,' said Rusticus.

Lembit rolled his eyes. 'It has nothing to do with trust, as I have told you.'

Rusticus was still far from convinced. 'They might not even appear, then you will be isolated deep in enemy territory.'

'If that is the case then I will withdraw. And if it is so you and fifty warriors will not make much of a difference. What *will* make a difference is if Wenden's garrison is occupied rather than hunting for me if I am forced to beat a hasty retreat.' He looked at Rusticus. 'I am relying on you to do what you do best.'

Rusticus looked at him blankly.

'To plunder and kill,' continued Lembit.

Rusticus cheered up at this prospect. 'Of course.'

'And remember that you are to keep Wenden's soldiers occupied. Do not assault the castle or get yourself caught. I need you.'

The next morning Lembit led his army south towards Treiden and Rusticus and fifty other warriors rode southeast towards the Gauja. Lembit hoped that Rusticus' savage tendencies would not get the better of him and that he would remember his mission and not indulge in wanton rape and slaughter against the first village he came across. Thus far the guides had steered them away from settlements, but it was only a matter of time before the presence of such a large party of warriors was spotted and reported to Treiden. Lembit sent instructions ahead to increase the rate of march. Caupo's stronghold was only forty miles away – two days' ride.

*****

Conrad and the others were most excited. It had been a year since their arrival at Wenden and they now gathered in the castle's round chapel to witness the induction of Walter the Penitent into the Sword Brothers. Their attendance at the ceremony was deemed most unusual but Walter had specifically requested it as he and they had travelled on board the same ship that had brought them all to Livonia and then to Wenden. All the chapels of the order were round in imitation of the rotunda of the Church of the Holy Sepulchre in Jerusalem. Also present were Master Berthold, who would conduct the admission ceremony, Otto and the official witnesses: Rudolf and Henke.

Walter, dressed in a simple white shirt and brown leggings, was kneeling before Master Berthold. He had been alone in the chapel all through the night, praying to God, and looked tired and a little apprehensive, this knight who was fearless on the battlefield yet as gentle as a lamb off it. The first rays of the sun were shining through the chapel's windows for admission ceremonies were always conducted just after dawn. The master, Henke and Rudolf were attired in white woollen coats with hoods, over which they wore their white mantles bearing the insignia of the Sword Brothers on the left shoulder. Rudolf held a spare mantle in his arms, which would be placed around the shoulders of Walter after the ceremony had ended.

Conrad felt immensely proud of Walter as Master Berthold asked the young knight the questions that all applicants had to answer. Are you married? *No.* Do you owe anyone money? *No.* Are you anyone's slave? *No.* Master Berthold then explained to Walter that the only reason for joining the order was to escape the sinful world, do God's work and do penance for his sins.

'You will become a slave of the Order, never to leave it without the permission of the Grand Master,' Master Berthold announced. 'You should always be prepared to shed your blood for Christ and to lay down your life for God with desire and the sword. What say you, Walter? Do you promise to live chastely and without personal property, and to keep the traditions and customs of the order? Do you promise to do all these things?'

Walter looked up at the master. 'I promise the chastity of my body, and poverty and obedience to God, Holy Mary and to the Grand Master of the Sword Brothers, and his successors, according to the rules and practices of the order, obedience unto death.'

Otto said a prayer and then Master Berthold ordered Walter to rise, turning to Rudolf to receive the white mantle he held. He then placed the garment around

209

Walter's shoulders and welcomed him into the order, fastening the laces that secured it. Berthold also gave Walter a woollen cord to tie around his waist as a symbol of chastity and a soft cap usually worn by religious men. The master then embraced Walter, as did Rudolf and Henke, while the dour Otto offered him his hand. A beaming Walter then turned to Conrad and the other boys, who walked forward and embraced him. At that moment each of them was imagining their own admission ceremony into the order, when they too would be inducted into the Sword Brothers.

Conrad knew that among them only Anton, who came from a wealthy noble family, would be a brother knight. Like the other Catholic religious orders the Sword Brothers preferred their knights to have noble blood flowing in their veins. There were exceptions. Henke, for example, was low born but he had been part of Rudolf's mercenary band and so had been allowed to become a brother knight, as had Lukas. But the majority of town inhabitants and countrymen who joined the order became sergeants: individuals of a lower social level. Sergeants wore mail without sleeves or gloves and a kettle hat instead of a full-face helmet. But apart from these minor differences they fought on horseback or on foot beside the brother knights and were regarded as valued members of the Sword Brothers. Conrad would be proud to be such a man.

The relaxed, happy atmosphere was shattered by the sound of the alarm bell being rung. Master Berthold, Rudolf and Henke ran outside as Walter bowed to the altar and crossed himself before following. Conrad looked at Hans, unsure what to do.

'All of you outside, now!' shouted Rudolf as the garrison began to form up in the courtyard.

Conrad sprinted from the chapel and saw one of Thalibald's warriors speaking to Master Berthold, frequently turning to point south.

Most of the sergeants were already in formation: three ranks of eight men on the west side of the courtyard, the others manning the perimeter wall. The brother knights, including Walter, assembled behind Master Berthold on the north side of the courtyard. The mercenaries arrayed themselves opposite the sergeants. Once the alarm was sounded the perimeter gates were automatically closed and the civilian workers and their families would take refuge within the castle itself. They did so now: men, children and women with infants in their arms hurrying across the bridge over the moat to fill the southern side of the courtyard. Lukas called the boys over to stand beside him behind the master.

The bell stopped ringing and Master Berthold raised his arms.

'I have just received word that the stronghold of King Caupo at Treiden is under attack.'

There was a collective groan from among the civilians. None knew where Treiden was but any mention of war and violence was enough to unnerve them, especially the women. Master Berthold called for calm.

'The pagans are on the other side of the river and there are no crossing places nearby so you are quite safe. However, most of the garrison will be leaving to march to the king's relief. For your own safety and that of Wenden the gates will be closed while we are away and no one will be permitted to leave the compound. Now return to your homes.'

The civilians grumbled and complained among themselves as they filed back across the bridge to their huts, while the soldiers were dismissed and ordered to make preparations to march to the relief of Treiden. Master Berthold told Thalibald's lieutenant that he would leave Wenden as soon as he had orders from Grand Master Volquin at Riga, but was alarmed to discover that Thalibald had already mustered his men and was preparing to lead them towards Treiden before the day was out. He was persuaded to ride back to Thalibald with a plea from Master Berthold that he do nothing until a strategy had been formulated, which meant waiting for news from Riga.

A pigeon arrived from Segewold Castle that afternoon, carrying a message that the bishop had arrived back from Germany with a fresh batch of crusaders and urgent preparations were under way to assemble an army for the relief of Treiden. The garrison of Wenden was ordered to march to Segewold but wait for the bishop to arrive before crossing the Gauja. The missive stated that the bishop had every confidence that Caupo would hold out in the face of the Oeselian assault.

'Oeselians? Weren't they the ones that attacked our ship last year?' said Hans, resting on his shovel after heaping another load of horse dung into the wheelbarrow. The brother knights and twenty-five of the sergeants had ridden south to Thalibald's village the following morning, forty of the mercenaries accompanying them on foot and escorting ten wagons loaded with food and supplies. They would reach the village by the afternoon and link up with the chief, the combined force then heading for Segewold, ten miles to the south.

The warhorses and palfreys had gone south with the men but the ponies remained and required mucking out.

'Yes,' replied Conrad, 'but I thought they were pirates.'

'So they are,' said Lukas who had appeared as if by magic. The other boys stopped their resting and continued to clear out the dirty stalls. 'But they are not averse to sailing up rivers in their boats if there is plunder to be had. But in this case they appear to want to kill Caupo.'

'Why, Brother Lukas?' asked Bruno.

'I do not know,' replied Lukas, 'it is most strange.'

The work continued on the castle, the towers slowly increasing in height as the stonemasons laboured each day and the carpenters manufactured floorboards, doors and ceiling supports. Lukas had been left in charge of the castle in the absence of Master Berthold, and in between dealing with the civilian workforce and organising the tiny remaining garrison he insisted that the boy's training continue as normal. It was on the third morning following Master Berthold's departure that a Liv warrior appeared at the perimeter gates, an elderly man riding a ragged pony who demanded entry to see the garrison commander, identifying himself as the man whom Thalibald had left in charge of his village in the chief's absence. As chance would have it Lukas was near the entrance, overseeing the boys' morning practise. They stopped when a sergeant on the fighting platform above the gates called to him, asking if the Liv should be admitted, saying his name was Fricis. Lukas knew him and ordered the gates to be opened.

Fricis rode into the compound and halted when he saw Lukas. Conrad could see that he had been riding his pony hard by its heavy breathing. Its head was low as Fricis dismounted and clasped Lukas' forearm. Conrad and the others gathered behind Lukas as an agitated and sweating Fricis spoke to him in impeccable German.

'I request your urgent assistance, Brother Lukas. A great disaster has occurred.'

'Would you like to retire to the castle, Fricis, to refresh yourself?'

Fricis shook his head. 'There is no time. An Estonian raiding party has attacked us. They have killed many men and taken the women and girls captive. Even as we speak they are heading north back to their homeland. They have captured Thalibald's wife and daughter.'

Conrad felt a knot tighten in his stomach. He thought of the beautiful Daina in peril and a rage rose within him.

Lukas was horrified. 'Estonians? Did they capture the chief's village?'

'No,' said Fricis, 'the women were working in the fields sowing the spring crops when the Estonians appeared on their ponies. They killed the guards and those like me who were too old to march north and took away the women and girls, slitting the throats of those women who were too old to be of any use to them.'

'Bastards,' hissed Conrad to murmurs of agreement from the others.

Lukas spun round. 'Silence!'

'I ride back to the village,' continued Fricis, 'where a score of old men with rusty swords wait to ride after them. I ask you for aid in our moment of need.'

Lukas scratched his head. He wanted to help but he had a castle full of civilian workers and their families and a tiny garrison. And he was loath to weaken it further with Estonian raiders in the area. He looked at Fricis with sympathy.

'I cannot spare any men. I am sorry.'

'Please, Brother Lukas,' implored Fricis. 'A handful of your men could mean the difference between success and failure.'

Conrad could tell that Lukas was distraught in letting Fricis down. 'I really can spare no one.'

Fricis' features hardened. 'What about them?' He pointed at the boys behind Lukas. The latter turned in confusion.

'They are mere boys, Fricis.'

'We will go, brother,' said Conrad.

'Let us go, please,' implored Anton. The others nodded and voiced their eagerness to accompany Fricis.

'I said silence!' snapped Lukas.

He looked back at Fricis and then at the boys who were like hunting dogs straining at the leash. He shook his head. 'I must be out of my mind.'

Conrad could barely contain his excitement as he and the others ran to the stables to saddle ponies. Fricis embraced Lukas and told him that Thalibald would make him a blood brother for getting back his wife and daughter.

'We haven't got them back yet,' he mumbled as he strode with him into the stables where the boys were leading their ponies from the stalls.

'All of you in the courtyard. Tie your ponies up near the water trough.'

Conrad was surprised to see leather face and three of his fellow crossbowmen being issued with quivers from the armoury and then pass him as they went to the stables.

'You are going with us?' said Conrad.

Leather face winked at him. 'Just because we do most of our fighting on foot doesn't mean we can't ride. I can teach you a thing or two.'

'Conrad,' shouted Lukas, 'move your arse.'

Lukas was now at the new stone armoury, a large squat building with a solid oak door and tiny windows covered with iron grilles. Inside were racks of spears, lances, swords and axes, shelves holding crossbows and quivers, chests full of crossbow bolts, walls covered with shields hanging on hooks and a corner containing mail armour, helmets and leather belts. The armourers, all of them stocky individuals with huge hands and rugged features, handed the boys lances, swords in scabbards, sword belts and daggers in sheaths. Hans whooped with joy and Anton beamed with delight. Johann could hardly believe that he was strapping on a real sword while Bruno pulled his sword from its scabbard and stared at it in disbelief. Lukas handed Conrad Sir Frederick's sword and then shouted at them all to assemble outside. Fricis sat on his pony in front of the mounted crossbowmen.

'I have decided, against my better judgement,' Lukas said to the boys, 'to let you take part in this rescue attempt. I cannot in all conscience stand idly by in Fricis' hour of need, but I also cannot leave this castle without first telling you that you may reconsider and stay at Wenden. It is no disgrace.'

His words were met by a row of resolute stares. He smiled. 'Very well. Let us pray that we are not too late.'

Conrad felt like a warrior king as he cantered out of the courtyard, across the bridge and down the track to the gates. He glanced at Sir Frederick's sword – now his sword – at his hip and tightened the grip on his reins. Only Lukas wore full mail armour, he and the others being equipped in gambesons, the boys wearing kettle helmets and the crossbowmen mail coifs. He touched the leather guige – strap – of the shield strapped slung on his back and smiled. He was going to fight at long last.

*****

Rusticus was very happy. He had wanted to accompany his lord south to take part in the assault against Treiden and had been most annoyed that he had been given the task of being a mere decoy. But things had turned out to his advantage. His scouts had led him on a circuitous route through the thick pine forests to the east of Wenden, before heading west to arrive at a spot where he could observe the castle unseen. He had been most surprised to see the garrison leave one morning: a line of horsemen, wagons and soldiers on foot, and even more surprised when his scouts reported warriors leaving the nearby villages, also heading south. He knew they were going to Treiden and that he had failed Lembit, arriving too late to gain the attention of the garrison. But to his delight he discovered that only youths and old men had been left behind to guard the Liv villages, only one of which was defended by a moat and timber wall.

So he had led his men on a wide sweep of the countryside, riding into fields where women were sowing crops. The Estonians butchered the few old guards, raped and then slit the throats of the old women and enslaved the women and girls. They would either make good slaves or could be traded for gold and weapons with the Russians. Now he led his warriors north back to their homeland, with over forty Liv women trailing behind them.

They were riding in column along a dirt track through a forest near the Gauja. It was late afternoon and the sun was lancing through the gaps in the canopy above, the warm air thick with the aroma of pine. The ponies were walking slowly, the men's shields hanging from their saddles and their spears resting on their shoulders. All of them wore steel helmets but only Rusticus had mail armour. The best-equipped men had gone south with Lembit. The atmosphere was sleep inducing, interrupted only by the flight of a black stork when the column passed by a lake or the distant tapping of a white-backed woodpecker. Rusticus heard a pony approaching and halted his mount, his lieutenant riding up beside him. Behind them the column had ground to a halt.

'A problem with the women, lord.'

Rusticus snapped out of his daydream. 'What problem?'

'One of them is heavily pregnant and has collapsed. The others are refusing to move without her. Do you want me to kill her?'

'Of course not,' replied Rusticus before grinning wickedly. 'Not until we have raped her.'

His subordinate nodded approvingly. 'I did not think of that.'

Rusticus rubbed his hands together. 'That is why I am a warlord and you are not.'

He was going to organise the rape of the prisoners once they had made camp but a pleasant diversion in the meantime would not do any harm.

'Heavily pregnant, you say?'

'Will calf any day now,' leered his deputy.

Rusticus' eyes lit up. 'Lovely.'

Thud.

The grin on the subordinate's face disappeared as he looked down in disbelief at the crossbow bolt stuck in his belly, then slumped forward in the saddle. Rusticus may have been fat and ugly but his warrior instincts never deserted him and he leapt from his pony and grabbed his shield to cover him, drawing his sword as three more of his men were toppled from their saddles by quarrels.

'Ambush!' he screamed.

The Livs had been tracking the Estonians for three hours, catching up with the column that was slowed down by women prisoners on foot. They and the soldiers from Wenden then swung east deeper into the forest before cantering north to put them ahead of Rusticus and his band of raiders. Leather face and his crossbowmen were placed on the track where they could shoot at the head of the column. Once they commenced their shooting to halt the column the Livs, Lukas and the five boys would charge the eastern flank of the Estonians. Lukas hoped that the element of surprise would tip the scales in their favour but it was still long odds: himself, twenty old Livs and five boys against twice that number of Estonians.

'God with us!' shouted Lukas, digging his spurs into his horse.

Conrad couched his lance and stared ahead, his pony racing through the trees towards the enemy. They were in a long line, big men on ponies wearing helmets and carrying spears. He saw his target and dug his spurs into his mount. He had been taught to charge knee to knee with other riders to present a wall of men and horseflesh but the trees made that impossible. He glanced right and saw Hans a few yards away and right to glimpse Anton. His target had tugged on his reins to wheel his beast to the right. He had seen him. Conrad screamed as his pony strained to increase its speed. The Estonian lowered his spear as Conrad's lance struck his shield and the steel point went through leather and wood to pierce flesh. He released the shaft, pulled his sword from its scabbard and swung the blade right as he passed the stricken Estonian, the edge biting into the man's lower neck.

Hans was by his side having likewise speared his man. Their initial charge had unhorsed at least a dozen Estonians but now the rest were fighting back, thrusting their spears at the Livs as they passed through their line, felling at least four. An Estonian directed his pony at Conrad, spear held tight to his right side.

Keep moving, don't become a stationary target.

He heard the words of Lukas as he spurred his mount forward, shield tucked tight into his left side. He pulled hard on his reins to wheel his pony left and the Estonian's spear missed him. He swung his sword up and down to shatter the bone in the enemy's arm. The man screamed in pain, dropping his spear, allowing Conrad to thrust the point of his sword into the man's guts. The man coughed as his dirty tunic suddenly showed a large bloodstain.

Keep moving.

Conrad yanked on his reins to take his mount away from the wounded warrior.

A wounded man may have strength to kill you before he dies. Do not take any chances.

The sword felt as light as a feather in his hand, his senses were heightened and strength infused his limbs. But he did not forget his training. He saw Lukas surrounded by four enemy warriors and watched as he killed each one in turn, sword, shield and man in perfect harmony as he parried sword blows, used his shield to knock a man from the saddle, split Estonian helmets and killed with single thrusts of his sword.

Conrad's pony suddenly collapsed beneath him and then he was on the ground, his foot trapped under the dead beast. He saw a big brute in mail armour leering at him, an ugly man carrying a large round shield and an axe in his right hand. He had seen this warrior before, at Wenden when Lembit had attacked the castle.

Conrad desperately tried to free himself but it was too late. The warrior moved with a deftness that defied his bulk and stood over him, axe raised ready to strike. He heard a scream and then saw Anton riding hard at the fat Estonian, who also heard him and swung round to avoid the boy's sword that swung at his head. Conrad yanked his leg out from under the dead pony and leapt up as Anton rode past and the fat brute once again focused upon Conrad.

Conrad was younger, half his weight and inexperienced, but he was quick and agile and avoided the Estonian's axe blows, catching one on his shield that almost knocked him over. The warrior was screaming at Conrad in a language he did not understand, though he caught the gist of the stream of invective that was being spat in his direction. The sounds of battle were echoing through the forest as steel struck shields, shattered shields and cut flesh.

The brute came at Conrad with a succession of axe strikes that forced him back, slicing open the leather covering of his shield and chipping the wood underneath. He screamed as he swung the axe at Conrad's head, the youth ducking and jabbing the point of his sword forward to cut into the Estonian's upper arm. He growled with malice that this boy had dared to wound him but as far as Conrad could tell it had no effect on him. Was he a man or a devil?

Two other Estonians came to the big man's side and for the first time Conrad felt afraid. They closed on him but then one pitched forward and collapsed on the ground, a quarrel lodged in his back. The other two looked round and another

217

was hit in the belly by a quarrel as leather face and another crossbowman advanced towards them. The big man pointed his axe at Conrad.

'This is not over, boy.'

Then he sprinted away to a standing pony and leaped into the saddle. Conrad saw him screaming some words, heard a horn being sounded and then the Estonians began to disengage and ride north behind their leader. Lukas, still on his horse, his sword and mantle splattered with blood, began riding up and down. He took off his helmet.

'Let them go, let them go.'

Conrad raised his sword in the air and gave a roar of triumph, then remembered why they had come. Daina!

He saw Fricis riding towards the rear of what had been the Estonian column and ran after him, past dead and wounded ponies groaning in pain, jumped over corpses and saw Lukas sheathing his sword. He was suddenly filled with fear that she and the other women had been wounded or even killed. But then he saw her and his heart leapt.

'Daina,' he shouted. She turned and her green eyes lit up when she saw him. She cried and laughed as Conrad replaced his sword in its scabbard and ran up her.

'My gallant knight,' she cried, throwing her arms around him and hugging him. He held her close, smelling her hair and feeling her arms around him. So this was how it felt to be a hero.

'Put her down, Conrad.' The words of Lukas broke his dream.

He could barely contain his joy and he reluctantly stepped back and looked into the eyes of the most beautiful creature he had ever met.

'I take it from your demeanour that you are unhurt,' queried the brother knight.

'Yes, Brother Lukas,' said Conrad, not taking his eyes off Daina's. Her face was a little pale but she seemed none the worse for her ordeal.

'And you, young princess,' Lukas asked her, 'are you hurt?'

She smiled at him. 'I am very well, Lukas, thank you.'

Lukas frowned as she reached out to take Conrad's hands and gave her champion a dazzling smile.

'Brother Lukas.'

Conrad heard Hans' voice and knew something was wrong. 'I must go,' he told Daina and followed Lukas to where a group was gathered round something. Lukas dismounted as the men parted to allow him access. Conrad followed and saw with horror the body of Bruno lying on the ground. Lukas knelt beside it as Hans, Anton and Johann looked on with anguished faces.

'He is dead,' said Lukas. 'He is in God's keeping now.'

Conrad could not believe it and stood in stunned silence. Their comrade had been killed by a stab to the stomach that had gone through his gambeson, which was now stained with blood. Lukas began to pray over the body of Bruno and Conrad and the other boys went down on their knees and joined him in worship, tears coming to their eyes.

They wrapped Bruno in a sheet and took him back to Wenden strapped on the back of a pony. The women captives were given ponies to ride back to their villages, Conrad walking beside the ones carrying Daina and her mother. The Liv dead – seven men – were likewise taken back to their villages. The score of dead Estonians was left to the wolves. Conrad walked in silence, thinking of his dead friend. He would never see him again and though he had not known him for long, the year they had spent at Wenden had created a special bond between them. He had done well in his first real battle, had helped to rescue his beautiful Daina and should have felt the happiest young man in Christendom. But he was utterly miserable.

*****

Treiden hill fort was a great sprawling timber structure built upon a great earth mound a third of a mile inland from the River Gauja. The stronghold of Caupo, King of the Livs, it was surrounded by dozens of wooden huts of varying size interspersed with animals pens containing pigs and goats, with fenced-off fields further out holding cattle and oxen. In these dwellings lived Caupo's subjects: men, women and children who farmed the land, hunted in the forests and caught fish on the river. For the past twenty years they had, like their lord, worshipped the Christian God and counted the Bishop of Riga as their friend. It was to this god that they now prayed as the Oeselians flooded ashore from their riverboats, butchering all in their path.

Eric heard the horns of the enemy and the screams of their women as he ran across the sandy strip his boat had run aground on to head inland. The forest had been cleared from this area long ago to provide the building materials for Caupo's stronghold and the huts of his people. He could see the hill fort on the hill ahead and below it the settlement. He ran past small fishing boats that littered the sandy beach and earth riverbank, slashing at fleeing men and boys who had watched in stunned silence as the Oeselian fleet had appeared on the river. Then they ran for their lives when the boats disgorged hundreds of heavily armed warriors.

A fisherman attempted to skewer Eric with a spear but a shield brushed his clumsy thrust aside and then the Oeselian chief swung his sword that chopped into the side of the man's skull, knocking him unconscious. Eric sprinted forward, ducking an axe swing from a Liv warrior before thrusting his sword into the man's belly. He was at the settlement now, running along dirt paths between huts to reach the stronghold.

His men were under strict orders not to indulge in rape and plunder until they had taken the stronghold. A man ran from a hut with a spear levelled at his belly. Eric saw him, moved his shield around to deflect the blow and then swung his sword down on top of the man's bare head. A woman came from the same hut, screaming in despair at seeing her man on the ground with his head split open. Magnus stabbed her with his sword and ran after his chief, who seemed determined to capture Treiden single-handedly.

'On, on!' screamed Eric as his men smashed down fences and cut down women and children as they advanced towards the fort. Dozens of women and wailing children were running up the hill to the fort's entrance: twin wooden gates that led to the compound that held the king's warehouses, armoury, barracks and stables, while in front of the fort a ragged line of warriors was forming up to meet the invaders. Some of the people headed towards a wooden church that had been built by Caupo when he had returned from Rome eight years previously. So impressed had Pope Innocent III been by this former pagan's piety that he had given him a bible to take back to his homeland. Caupo had laid a hand on this book moments before rushing from his hall to lead the fight against the pagan invaders.

His bodyguard – a hundred men in mail armour, helmets and armed with spears and swords – grouped round him as he raced from the compound, through the gates, across the bridge spanning the moat and joined the warriors forming up a hundred yards down the hill. His people were still desperately attempting to reach refuge in the fort but now a great swarm of Oeselians was emerging from the settlement.

Eric halted and looked right and left. He had failed to take the fort by surprise, the defenders now forming a line to bar his entry. He raised his hand to signal a stop. He saw men, women and children running into the trees or attempting to scale the hill around the fort.

'Send men to bring those wretches to me,' he ordered Magnus.

From behind he heard the sound of some sort of dreadful singing, mournful and imploring. His men were now forming a great shield wall behind him, around two hundred paces from the Liv warriors further up the hill. He called forward one of his men.

'What is that noise?'

The bearded warrior looked behind at the church with its slanted roof and single bell hanging over the entrance, a cross mounted above it.

'Some sort of church, lord. Christian, I think.'

'Take ten men and burn it and all inside. I do not want to hear Christian singing. It offends my ears.'

The warrior grinned and paced away.

The Oeselian shield wall was now formed – a great phalanx of mail-clad warriors in five ranks, their large round shields overlapping in a defensive posture to await their lord's orders. Magnus returned with two score of men dragging sobbing and frightened women and children, striking them across the face when they tried to resist their captors. The terrified Livs were shoved in front of the Oeselian ranks.

Magnus stood beside Eric. 'Boar's head?'

Eric nodded. Magnus turned and screamed his order. 'Boar's head!'

A boar's head was a wedge-shaped formation that concentrated the shock impact of an assault on a small frontage aimed at smashing through an enemy line. The Oeselians began hurling abuse and jeering at the three hundred or so Livs standing in their own shield wall, archers lining the walls of the fort behind them.

Eric and Magnus would fight at the tip of the wedge, their best men immediately behind them gripping axes with which they would hack their way through the Livs. Eric walked forward directly towards the figure of Caupo in his gilded helmet standing in the middle of the enemy line. The hostages were herded forward as the archers began shooting at the Oeselians, their arrows striking raised shields but also the women and children. The Livs groaned and cried in anguish as the last of hostages were felled and trampled upon by the Oeselian warriors. Then Eric and his men charged.

Even though the Oeselians were charging uphill the force of their assault buckled and then shattered the outnumbered Liv line. Eric failed to reach Caupo, who was bundled to the rear by his bodyguard as Oeselian axes and swords hacked and slashed at them. Eric barged his shield into a warrior directly in front of him, the force of the impact knocking him off balance and leaving him helpless as Eric drove the sword into his belly. There was a plethora of sickening thuds as Oeselian axes and swords hacked into the Liv line, which had now been splintered into dozens of individual mêlées, men yelping and groaning as blades inflicted horrendous injuries on their bodies. Eric was consumed by bloodlust as he cut down anyone in his path, but screamed in rage when he saw the gates of the fort being slammed shut.

He began hacking with his sword at a dead Liv at his feet, reducing the head to a bloody pulp as he vented his frustration. Magnus grasped his arm.

'We must withdraw immediately, lord.'

Eric snarled at him but then regained his senses as the fighting platforms on the walls above began to fill with Liv soldiers.

'Back, back!' screamed Magnus, retaining the grip on his lord's sleeve as he hauled him back, as a deluge of spears and arrows fell among the Oeselians.

Eric was unharmed as he and Magnus withdrew down the hill, their warriors forming a shield wall once more, holding their shields above their heads as they shuffled back. A tideline of over two hundred dead marked the spot where the battle had taken place. The screams of those being incinerated inside the church had stopped by the time Magnus had organised patrols to scour the countryside for Livs, the rounding up of livestock to feed the raiders and the allocation of huts to house warriors. Siege lines were also established around the base of the hill upon which the fort was built, not that they had any siege engines. Two days later Lembit and his Estonians arrived at Treiden. But unknown to either him or Eric a crusader army was already approaching their position.

Chapter 9

The Oeselian boats had been spotted as soon as they had entered the Gauja estuary, the news being conveyed immediately to the bishop's palace in Riga and the office of Grand Master Volquin in the town's castle. With the bishop still away in Germany the threat to the crusader kingdom was severe, especially as the garrisons along the Dvina could not be stripped out of fear that the uneasy peace with the Lithuanians might not hold. Nevertheless, Volquin decided that the brother knights and sergeants from the castle of Holm must be sent north to join the relief force being assembled at Segewold that would attempt to save Treiden. If the stronghold fell and Caupo was killed such a calamity might spark a general revolt of the whole Liv people, with catastrophic consequences for Livonia.

Volquin tried to impress the gravity of the situation upon Archdeacon Stefan, to no avail. He stubbornly refused to release any soldiers for the relief of Treiden, declaring that Riga itself was in peril. He kept babbling on about the Kurs returning and said that the knights, sergeants, spearmen and crossbowmen must remain to defend the town. But he was also most insistent that the native warriors who lived in and around the town should go with Volquin as he suspected their loyalty, the more so if Caupo was killed. Volquin despised the archdeacon but as long as he held the favour of the bishop there was nothing to be done. So Volquin called for a muster at Segewold of the brother knights and sergeants from Wenden, Segewold itself and Holm, together with their respective foot soldiers. In this way he hoped to raise thirty brother knights, over a hundred mounted sergeants and two hundred foot soldiers. He hoped this would be enough to raise the siege of Treiden.

Two things raised the grand master's spirits as he prepared to ride to Segewold, which came as a welcome relief following the news that the small castle of Kremon was also under siege. The first was a visit from the stern Theodoric, who declared that he was coming with Volquin to Segewold rather than sitting in his monastery waiting for news. The second was the arrival at Riga of two ships carrying a contingent of crusaders.

Sir Helmold was a quarrelsome, fearsome lord from Saxony, a man who had devoted his life to war and fathering sons. Now in his fifties, he had managed to sire four strapping sons who had followed their father into the martial life, sallying forth from Sir Helmold's great castle at Plesse to raid neighbouring towns and districts. He loved nothing more than engaging in battle with anyone who dared to cross him, taking particular delight in hanging priests who berated him for his bloodthirsty ways. Feared and loathed in equal measure, Sir Helmold of Plesse was totally unrepentant of his ways. Until his wife was taken ill.

In descending order Sir Helmold loved his wife, Agnes, his pack of hunting dogs, his falcon and his sons. So when the pestilence visited Saxony and his wife was stricken he was distraught. He railed against God and offered his own life in exchange for that of his true love. But God did not listen and Agnes became more sick and frail by the day. Physicians and old hags who supposedly had healing talents came to the castle and failed in their attempts to cure her and Sir Helmold, bereft of hope, resigned himself to his wife's death, vowing to kill himself the moment she closed her eyes for the last time, though this was a sin in the church's eyes.

It so happened that a young Cistercian monk came to Plesse soon after, from where no one knew. He said he had heard of the plight of Lady Agnes and asked that he be allowed to pray at the foot of her bed. Such was the despair of Sir Helmold that he agreed to the request of this pale, white-attired young man who walked in sandals and had no belongings, even though it was the depth of winter. And then a miracle happened, for Lady Agnes recovered. Sir Helmold was joyous and promised the young monk that he would build a Cistercian monastery at the foot of the hill on which his castle stood, but the young brother told him that if he really wanted to thank God he should take the cross and fight the pagans. And so the lord took his sons, fifteen other knights and twenty squires and set off for Lübeck. Eager to get to grips with the heathens Sir Helmold had demurred to wait for other crusaders and had taken ship almost immediately, arriving at Riga three days before Grand Master Volquin was to march to Segewold.

Sir Helmold's men carried Saxon heraldic banners – Plesse's golden lion on a red background, a boar's head on a black background over green and yellow – but their lord wore no insignia on his shield or on his horse's caparison save a red cross on a white background. He placed himself and his men under the absolute command of Grand Master Volquin when informed that Livonia was under threat. When the soldiers from Holm arrived at Riga the Sword Brothers marched to the relief of Treiden.

It was May now and fortunately the spring mud had gone. The tracks were still rutted, which slowed the rate of advance and halted it altogether when some of the wagons lost their wheels, but at least the army could march overland directly to Segewold. Not that it was much of an army. Volquin had called for volunteers from among the German settlers in and around Riga, which had mustered seventy men, mostly spearmen who had to be issued with shields and helmets from the town's castle, but also twenty-five crossbowmen. Added to the foot soldiers from the office of the grand master in Riga and Holm this gave a total of seventy-five crossbowmen and eighty-five spearmen. The number of Liv warriors who had been mustered from around Riga and Holm numbered two hundred, with an equal number of men to attend to the ponies and wagons that carried weapons, ammunition, food and tents for the army. They pushed their beasts hard to reach Segewold – thirty miles to the northeast – in three days.

Segewold had formerly been a pagan hill fort a short distance south of the Gauja. Unlike at Wenden the garrison had not commenced replacing the timber walls and towers with stone, and so the only indication that it was no longer a pagan citadel was the banner of the Sword Brothers hanging above the main entrance. The relief army camped around the ramparts as Sir Helmold and the brother knights were lodged in the fort's main hall. To the south of the castle were camped the Livs from the areas around Wenden and Segewold, all under the leadership of Thalibald – two hundred men – giving a total of five hundred Liv warriors to support the crusaders. Already at Segewold were the dozen brother knights, twenty sergeants and thirty mercenaries of the garrison, plus the twelve brother knights, twenty sergeants and forty mercenaries from Wenden. Thus did the army mustered to relief Treiden number just over eight hundred and fifty men.

'Do we know how many the Oeselians number?' asked Volquin.

He and the order's masters and their deputies were gathered in the fort's main hall, an austere rectangular room with a stone fireplace positioned in the centre and a wooden platform that formerly held a chief's throne. Now an oak table sat upon it, around which were gathered the Sword Brothers, Thalibald, Theodoric and Sir Helmold.

'The scouts I sent across the river estimate Oeselian numbers at over a thousand.'

Sir Helmold studied the wild features of Thalibald, his strange dress and even stranger accent but said nothing. He wondered how loyal this former pagan and his warriors were to the Holy Church. But then, until a short while ago he took great delight in hanging Catholic priests. How strange fate was.

'Numbers do not concern me,' stated Volquin. 'Of more immediate concern is how we are going to cross the river.'

'That will be easy enough, grand master,' said Master Bertram, the commander at Segewold. 'Half a mile west of here the Gauja is less than two hundred feet wide. We can lash together the local fishing vessels to create a bridge that will make a crossing possible.'

'Do we know if Treiden still stands?' Theodoric asked Thalibald.

'It still stands, lord,' answered the Liv chief.

The door opened and a guard asked for permission to admit a visitor: a soaking Rameke who had hurried to the castle as a thunderstorm broke. Volquin beckoned him in when Thalibald explained who he was. Water dripped off the boy's cloak as he made his way to his father, nodding at Rudolf when he saw the brother knight at the table. He also bowed to Volquin before bending down and whispering into his father's ear.

'Are you certain?' asked Thalibald.

Rameke nodded and was waved away by his father. He brushed a strand of soaking hair from his forehead as he left and the door was closed.

Thalibald slumped in his chair.

'A scouting party has just returned from across the river. Lembit is at Treiden.'

Shock greeted this news. 'Lembit?' said Volquin. 'Are your scouts certain?'

Thalibald nodded. 'They saw his wolf banner. He has brought hundreds of men south.'

'Who is this Lembit?' asked Sir Helmold.

'Our greatest enemy,' answered Volquin solemnly. 'A man who has united all the pagans in Estonia, the land to the north, against the Holy Church.'

'A servant of the devil himself,' added Theodoric.

Master Berthold was frowning and looking at Rudolf, who was shaking his head. Volquin noticed their discomfort.

'Is there something you wish to say, Master Berthold?'

'Though the presence of Lembit is unwelcome news, grand master,' said Berthold, 'of greater importance is that he has formed some sort of alliance with the Oeselians. If they are cooperating rather than fighting each other then our task becomes much harder.'

Volquin nodded. 'It is as you say, Berthold.'

'Do we then not attempt to relieve King Caupo?' asked Thalibald with concern.

Volquin smiled at him. 'We must still cross the river and battle the heathens. To do otherwise will make us look weak and helpless.'

Though no one said so, to attempt a river crossing and engage an enemy with a numerical advantage of at least two to one was a risky venture. But to remain inactive would mean the fall of Treiden, to say nothing of Kremon that was also surrounded. If that happened the whole of the land north of the Gauja would be in pagan hands. The thought was too horrible to contemplate.

'We cross the river tomorrow,' said Volquin.

Theodoric brought his hands together. 'Let us ask God for his guidance.'

Sir Helmold did the same and caught sight of the Liv chief closing his eyes to pray. How odd was this land and its people.

*****

'We must leave this place,' said Lembit, pacing up and down in front of Eric, who was lounging in a chair, one leg dangling over one of its arms, cup of beer in hand. Eric looked at Magnus leaning against the wall of the hut and laughed.

'Leave? We have just got here. Why should we leave?'

Lembit stopped pacing and pointed to one of his men standing near the door.

'Why? I will tell you why.'

The hut was larger than most in the settlement, with rooms leading off its central space. It was obviously the dwelling of a chief. Eric and Magnus had taken it over after the battle while Lembit had taken up residence in a nearby village, his men and their ponies occupying a wide area around the besieged fort. He had also sent men to reinforce the small force Eric had sent to encircle Kremon. The Oeselian leader had taken to siege warfare like a duck to water, his time divided between conducting tours of the siege lines and raping local women who had been captured and confined in nearby huts.

Two of Lembit's men brought in a man with his hands pinioned behind his back. He had a black eye, gashed cheek and blood was seeping through the arm of his shirt, which was ripped.

Lembit pointed at him as he was violently forced onto his knees. 'This is a Liv whom we caught trying to swim across the river.'

Eric finished his cup and held it out to Magnus so it could be refilled. 'So?'

'He was one of a patrol that was scouting our positions. We caught three of them. The rest escaped.'

Eric sighed with boredom. 'Is there any point to this?'

Lembit reached down and grabbed the Liv's long hair, twisting it hard. 'Tell him.'

The Liv's face was contorted in pain. 'A great army is forming on the other side of the river, crusaders and Livs, who will soon cross and deliver our king.'

Lembit let go of his hair and struck his head with the back of his hand. He looked at a bemused Eric. 'That is why we must withdraw.'

Eric changed from bemusement to being annoyed. 'We stay until the fort has fallen and all inside have been enslaved or slaughtered. I did not travel all the way here in an uncomfortable boat to turn tail and run without achieving victory.'

Lembit was shaking his head. 'If we are to stay then at least get your boats on the river to prevent the crusaders crossing.'

'Why are you so frightened of these Christians?' asked Magnus.

'I was wondering that,' said Eric.

'It is not a case of fear but prudence,' said Lembit firmly. 'If the crusaders get their horsemen across the river then we will not be able to withstand their charge.'

'A few men on horses cannot break an Oeselian shield wall,' boasted Magnus.

'You are wrong,' said the Liv prisoner, eyeing him defiantly. 'The men of iron will sweep you away.'

In one movement Lembit drew his sword and thrust it into the Liv's back. He screamed and arched his back in a spasm of pain before collapsing in a heap on the floor. Blood began to ooze from his body.

Eric was mortified. 'I have to live in this hut. Guards!'

Two spearmen rushed in. 'Get this piece of carrion out of here before there is blood all over.'

They hauled the body away as Eric stared at the bloodstain on the earth floor. 'We need some mats in here to cover it.'

'What about the crusaders?' said Lembit impatiently.

'What about them?' shrugged Eric. 'Let them come. Caupo can watch while we destroy them before his own death.'

'You will not get your boats onto the river?'

'I would have thought that you would welcome an opportunity to engage and defeat the crusaders,' said Eric, suddenly showing a remarkable degree of perception. 'Is that not the only way to prevent their conquest of your homeland: to defeat them in battle? Why else did you agree to an alliance with my father if not to destroy the crusaders?'

228

Lembit said nothing.

'I will take your silence as confirmation,' said Eric smugly. 'We destroy the crusaders, kill Caupo and then cross the river ourselves and lay waste to the crusader kingdom as agreed.'

He walked over to Lembit and placed a hand on his shoulder. 'Why should we turn away from a golden opportunity that presents itself?'

Lembit thought Eric was a boorish brute but he had to accept that his words had merit. He was right that if the Estonian tribes were to remain free the crusaders had to be defeated and their kingdom destroyed. And yet he had seen the irresistible charge of the mail-clad knights on horseback, witnessed the devastating power of their crossbows and siege engines and was rightly wary of offering battle. And they were far from home. The Oeselians were confident but they could escape in their boats if need be. But to flee in the face of the enemy would risk losing the support of the other tribes when news reached Estonia that he had ordered a retreat. If that happened his people would be divided and the crusaders' task would be made easier. In addition, this alliance with the Oeselians had not been greeted with universal approval by all the tribes, especially the Rotalians. If he fled his credibility would receive a crushing blow. He may have been a brute but Eric, son of Olaf, had left him with no choice.

'Very well,' he said to the Oeselian chief, 'we will give battle to the crusaders.'

*****

The crusaders left Segewold before dawn, the vanguard being fifty crossbowmen and the hundred Liv warriors from Wenden led by Thalibald, who crossed the Gauja in boats to establish a defensive position on the northern bank of the river while a bridge of boats was constructed to allow the rest of the army to cross. It took three hours to assemble the boats, lash them together and overlay them with planks to facilitate the crossing of the horsemen. Once the pontoon bridge had been constructed the rest of the Livs, who were on foot, the crossbowmen and spearmen marched over the river. The horsemen followed, the planks having been covered with dirt to fool the horses into thinking that it was a dirt track so as not to alarm them.

Leading the knights was Grand Master Volquin and Sir Helmold, behind them the Sword Brother masters and Sir Helmold's sons. Then came the crusader knights from Saxony wearing their colours, followed by the brother knights of the order, all of them on great warhorses covered in caparisons matching the surcoats worn by their masters, the latter's faces covered by their helmets. The squires of the crusaders came after, also attired in mail armour, and then the Sword Brother sergeants in their kettle helmets.

It had rained during the night and although the temperature was warm the ground was still soft underfoot. Thalibald sent his scouts forward as soon as the horsemen were safely across the river as they were only two miles south of Treiden. It was clearly visible ahead, a great timber stronghold atop a high hill. There was a single track that ran parallel to the river leading to Caupo's fortress and that is what the horsemen followed as they walked their mounts slowly forward. The spearmen and crossbowmen took up position on the flanks of the horsemen, moving through the trees and keeping watch for signs of the enemy. The air was fresh with the aroma of pine but the crusaders sweated in their armour and helmets. At first there was no noise save for the jangling of the horses' bits, no birds, no wind in the trees and only occasionally the snapping of a branch as a soldier stepped on it. After a while the silence became oppressive.

Rudolf shoved his helmet up on his head. 'The enemy are close. I can sense them.'

Henke beside him took off his helmet. 'They made a mistake not trying to stop us at the river.'

Sir Helmold in front turned in his saddle. 'Perhaps the pagans have fled.'

Rudolf detected the note of disappointment in his voice. 'Have no fear, my lord, you will get your chance to smite the heathen yet.'

Grand Master Volquin also removed his helmet. 'We go to spread the word of God, Brother Rudolf. We fight only if compelled. We kill for necessity, not for pleasure.'

'I kill for pleasure,' remarked Henke. Sir Helmold smiled.

The forest to their left suddenly erupted with screams and shouts, and then there were the telltale thwacks of crossbow bolts being shot. The crossbowmen marching alongside the horsemen shouldered their weapons as Volquin called a halt. Half a minute later Thalibald came running from the forest with four of his warriors to report to the grand master.

'The trees end just ahead from where we have ejected enemy scouts. The enemy army is deployed half a mile from the treeline.'

'How many?' inquired Volquin.

'Many foot drawn in one body, perhaps a thousand. On their right stands the Estonians.'

Volquin nodded. 'Thank you, Thalibald, we will deploy into battle positions once we have exited the trees.'

The knights continued to ride along the track for another quarter of a mile until the trees on their left ended and they came into what appeared to be a large meadow, but which was actually an area of cleared forest. The trees that had grown where the hill fort now stood had been felled decades before and used to construct the stronghold, and then the surrounding forest had been cut down to provide materials for huts, fences, fishing boats and firewood. This meant that the land to the west and north of Caupo's fort was mostly flat – ideal for horsemen.

A hundred paces beyond the end of the forest was a small stream that Thalibald's warriors flooded across as they chased after the Oeselian scouts, halting when they were met with a volley of arrows shot by the handful of archers standing in the rear of Eric's shield wall. The knights and sergeants trotted over the small wooden bridge that spanned the stream before wheeling left to halt behind the Livs and the mercenary spearmen and crossbowmen. Theodoric slid off his horse and called for all the horsemen to take off their helmets and bow their heads as he said a prayer to ask God for victory in the coming battle.

*****

'Is that all they've got?' sneered Eric, chewing on a piece of cooked pork as he stood in front of his men's shield wall.

On his left was Magnus, like him wearing helmet and mail armour and holding the grip of his shield with his left hand. Lembit stood on Eric's right. His men were also deployed in a shield wall – nearly a thousand warriors standing shoulder to shoulder on the right flank of the Oeselians. Behind them a hundred warriors stood in reserve and also guarded the ponies that the Estonians had ridden to get here.

Eric saw the Livs shuffling into line directly opposite his men, around four hundred paces away. Despite being a king's son Eric wore a simple helmet comprising a single iron band that circled his head around the brow and riveted to two iron bands that crossed at the top of the head. The four openings were filled by riveted iron plates that created the bowl shape, with a nose guard riveted to the brow band itself. The large, hinged cheek guards were tied under his chin by leather straps, with a sheepskin lining to absorb both impacts from enemy blows and sweat.

231

All the Oeselians wore helmets and mail armour but only the front two ranks of the Estonians were similarly equipped. The rest had no armour or head protection, such was the poverty of Lembit's people. He also had only a paltry number or archers, though at least all his men carried light throwing spears in addition to the heavier models designed for thrusting. He saw the well-equipped Christian spearmen deploying opposite his own men, small parties of crossbowmen standing a few paces in front of them.

'We must outnumber them at least two to one, perhaps more,' said Magnus.

'This won't take long,' boasted Eric, tossing the leg of pork to the ground. He looked at Lembit. 'As soon as we attack the Livs direct your men against the Christian foot soldiers.'

Lembit saw the lances and banners of the knights to the rear of the Christian army. 'What about their horsemen?'

'Once we break their foot they will flee. I count only a few dozen lances. Too few to withstand our charge.'

Lembit was unsure but was bolstered by Eric's certainty that he would defeat the enemy. He nodded at his ally and ran back to his wolf shields that stood in the centre of the Estonian line. Each shield wall occupied a frontage of around a hundred and sixty paces, the shields of the front rank overlapping so there were no gaps in the line. But there was an inviting gap between the Oeselians who stood to the west of the huts of the settlement and the Estonians who were grouped to the north. This was not a conscious decision taken by their respective commanders; rather, a desire by the Oeselians to be near their boats that were beached on the banks of the Gauja and a wish by the Estonians to be close to their ponies. It would prove to be their undoing.

The Oeselians began chanting war cries and hurling abuse at the Livs opposite, horns sounding above the din to signal the advance. The sea raiders began banging their spear shafts and axe hafts against the inside of their shields as they walked forward, arrows hissing over their heads from the archers in the rear rank. The Livs brought up their shields to deflect the missiles and then Thalibald signalled the advance. Hearing the dreadful din on his left flank Lembit turned, raised his sword in the air and then walked forward towards the Christian foot soldiers facing his Estonians. His wolf shields closed around him for the crusaders had positioned crossbowmen in front of their spearmen and these now began shooting at the packed ranks of the Estonians.

Volquin had placed only forty crossbowmen with his spearmen, which themselves numbered only one hundred and thirty-five men in two ranks – a paper-thin defence against a thousand Estonians. But numbers are only one part of a battle.

Shooting four bolts a minute each, the crossbowmen managed to discharge six volleys before they retired through the ranks of the spearmen. This not only killed and wounded around a hundred a fifty Estonians, it also slowed the momentum of Lembit's men as they saw their comrades struck down by the iron-tipped bolts, their shields offering little protection as the range between the two lines closed and the missiles pierced leather and wood with ease. This gave the spearmen time to withdraw in the face of the enemy shield wall, just as Grand Master Volquin and Sir Helmold led their knights forward.

As planned the Livs were also giving ground, albeit grudgingly, as Eric's men hacked and slashed with their swords and axes at Thalibald's warriors. Outnumbered two to one, the Livs maintained their cohesion as they pulled back. Then the earth shook as fifty-nine knights galloped forward, Sir Helmold with his score of crusaders, Grand Master Volquin in the front rank of the Sword Brothers riding knee to knee, lances couched, shields across chests, legs locked in stirrups and bodies braced against saddle bows. They rode forward and then veered left to take them behind the Estonians, led by Volquin holding the great banner of the Sword Brothers – a white standard edged with gold bearing a red silk cross and sword. And behind the knights rode ninety-five sergeants of the order and twenty Saxon squires, each one attired in mail armour and carrying a lance.

The horsemen swung left again as Volquin led them in a charge against the rear ranks of the Estonians, which had now become separated from those in front as terrified men turned around to face the iron men on their big horses who were bearing down on them. Men who had little or no armour and few weapons were traditionally placed in the rear of the shield wall whilst the most heavily armed and armoured fought in the front ranks. So now those Estonians who wore only leather coverings on their heads and carried only a spear and a knife, plus a shield, faced the full might of the crusaders' heavy horsemen. The result was a foregone conclusion.

The knights slowed their horses as they closed with the enemy, thrusting their lances through shields and into flesh as they skewered the rearmost ranks of the enemy. Then they went to work with their swords, axes and maces, standing up in their stirrups to hack left and right to rain blows down on heads and shoulders. The sergeants and squires behind them rode right to bring them alongside their masters in the mêlée, likewise thrusting first with their lances and then going to work with

233

their close-quarter weapons. Within minutes the horsemen were cutting into the Estonian formation and bringing it to a halt.

The frantic horn blasts brought the front ranks of Lembit's men to a halt before they could get to grips with the Christian spearmen, who had continued to fall back methodically in the face of the pagan advance. Now the crossbowmen reappeared to begin shooting more volleys at the shield wall. Lembit turned and saw the helmets and slashing weapons of the knights behind him and knew that he faced defeat. The thuds and groans in front of him and screams and yelps behind foretold the destruction of his men so he made the only decision that made sense: he and his men would cut their way through the enemy to reach their ponies and then flee north, back to Estonia. Prince Eric was on his own.

*****

Eric thrust his sword forward into the belly of a Liv, who groaned and slumped to the ground. He stood on the man as another enemy directed a downward strike with an axe against his helmet. He stopped the blow with his shield, the weapon's edge cutting through the leather covering and biting deep into the wood. Before the Liv could free his weapon Eric crouched low and drove his sword upwards into the man's groin. He gave an ear-splitting scream and then toppled backwards.

Eric lived for this. Lived for the close-quarter mêlée where a man's courage and skill were tested to the full. He loved war and battle. Loved the intoxicating smell of piss, dung and blood that flooded the nostrils and bloodlust that infused the senses. He felt alive in the white heat of combat, his senses heightened to such an extent that the blows and strikes of the enemy seemed slow and cumbersome. He anticipated them with ease, ducking and parrying flailing weapons whilst striking himself with deadly accuracy. He saw the Liv spears and axes coming at him: slow, predictable and half-hearted, defeating them with ease. On the Oeselians pushed, cutting down the Livs as the latter gave ground, withdrawing as though they had already given up and were thinking of flight.

Then fighting erupted on the right flank and behind the Oeselian line.

Unknown to Eric and his men the Estonian shield wall had disintegrated as the horsemen cut deep into their ranks and Lembit simultaneously led a charge to the northeast to reach the ponies. The Christian spearmen and crossbowmen, now reinforced by an additional forty-five of the latter – a small reserve created by

234

Volquin – left the fleeing Estonians to the horsemen and wheeled right towards the exposed right flank of the Oeselian warriors.

And then the gates of Treiden hill fort swung open and Caupo led his warriors from the stronghold. They flooded down the hill and swung right when they reached the settlement, running between the huts to exit the village and bring them into the meadow where the battle was being fought, directly behind the Oeselians.

Eric heard the horns and saw his men disengage from the battered line of Livs to withdraw a few paces as his warriors obeyed the signal. They closed up and locked shields as a succession of thwacks was heard to the north. Magnus pushed through the ranks, his sword smeared with blood, his helmet dented and his mail shirt missing links.

'There are crusader foot soldiers on our right flank and Caupo has stopped hiding in his fort and forms up behind us.'

Eric took off his helmet and wiped his sweaty brow with the back of his hand. 'Where are the Estonians?'

Magnus' expression told him they had fled.

'We should leave this place, Eric,' said his subordinate.

The crossbowmen fired another volley at the locked shields of the Oeselians, splintering shields and piercing mail armour.

Eric shoved his helmet back on his head. 'No! We stay and we fight.'

He ordered his men to goad the Livs who faced their front and rear. They dropped their leggings to reveal their genitals and bent over to show the enemy their arses, calling them women and cowards who were unfit to carry weapons. Thalibald took the bait and ordered his men to break the enemy shield wall. He had seen his king issuing forth from the fort and knew that he was on the other side of the Oeselian formation. And so he raised his sword and ran at the shield wall flanked by his two sons. On the other side of the Oeselian shield wall Caupo also led his men forward. There was a horrible grinding sound as the Livs smashed into Eric's men and a huge mêlée ensued.

Sir Helmold and his sons had wanted to pursue the fleeing Estonians as they mounted their ponies and rode north through the forests that surrounded Treiden. But Grand Master Volquin asked him to remain on the field of battle, stating that the victory was only half won. He did, however, dispatch half his mounted sergeants to harry Lembit's men, around four hundred of whom already lay dead among the long grass. He told them to kill as many as they could catch but to retreat if the enemy launched any counterattacks.

'Lembit escapes our clutches,' said Sir Helmold bitterly, his helmet in his hand and his sword sheathed. None of his sons had been hurt in the fight with the Estonians and now they wanted to go after the rest of the fleeing enemy.

'It would be shameful to abandon our friend and ally who needs our help,' Grand Master Volquin admonished them. 'God will ensure that Lembit is smitten by our swords, though perhaps not today.'

Sir Helmold gestured with his hand for his sons to hold their tongues as Theodoric, Master Berthold and Rudolf rode to the grand master's side.

'Losses?' inquired Volquin.

'Five dead, seven wounded, grand master,' answered Berthold.

Volquin crossed himself.

'Thus do they become martyrs and enter the house of the Lord,' said Theodoric.

The others likewise crossed themselves.

'Time to rid the land of the Oeselian pestilence,' said Rudolf savagely, placing his helmet back on his head.

'As you say brother,' said Volquin.

He still carried the order's banner that now formed a rallying point as once more the knights formed into line with the squires and sergeants behind them. They trotted forward towards the slaughter that was taking place immediately west of the settlement.

*****

Eric's men were tiring now. They had been standing in their ranks for over two hours in the spring heat, hacking at their enemies and forcing them back. Because his men were all well armed and armoured those in the front ranks could be replaced by fresher men standing behind them, but now they were fighting on two sides of the shield wall this was not possible. And on their right flank the Christian crossbows were exacting a steady toll on the Oeselians. Thalibald's Livs were also tired and so the fighting on that side of the shield wall degenerated into a desultory, haphazard series of duels between small groups of warriors, who dashed forward, exchanged a few blows and then retreated back to their lines. On the other side of the formation, however, Caupo and his men were fighting with frenzy to exact revenge for their fallen wives and comrades.

'We must leave,' said a panting Magnus to Eric, his mail shirt now ripped at the right shoulder and left breast. 'The crusader horsemen are approaching.'

236

Eric looked north to see the white surcoats and shields of the Sword Brothers, the sun flashing off helmets. He was loath to flee like the coward Lembit but what Magnus said made sense.

'Back to the boats, then,' he said through gritted teeth.

Magnus shouted the order and the signallers blew their horns and as one the Oeselians began moving towards the river. Those who still held javelins threw them at the Livs before withdrawing. Thalibald's battered and bleeding warriors did not give chase so exhausted were they. Instead they rested their shields on the ground and leaned on them. They were all possessed of a raging thirst but were glad to be alive.

Caupo's men followed the Oeselians as they fell back to the riverbank where their boats sat on the sand. They had suffered many casualties during the fighting, though, and so stood off as the invaders retained their formation and shuffled backwards. Volquin forbade his foot soldiers from pursuing the Oeselians, instead ordering them and his horseman back to the pontoon bridge they had used earlier.

'I do not understand,' said Sir Helmold.

'If you will indulge me in this matter, my lord,' said Volquin, his words muffled by his helmet, 'we may yet reap a rich harvest.'

His spearmen, having taken no part in the fighting, were relatively fresh and so they were able to trot back to the track that led to the river, the crossbowmen following. The latter, having begun the fighting with four full quivers per man, were each down to their last twenty quarrels.

Grand Master Volquin rode with Sir Helmold, Berthold, Bertram, Rudolf and Henke to pay his compliments to Thalibald who had played a pivotal role in the battle.

'Your king and I owe you a debt of gratitude, lord,' said Volquin, who had now taken off his helmet and offered his hand to the Liv chief.

Thalibald took his hand. 'It has been an honour, grand master.'

Rudolf nodded at a weary Rameke standing at his father's side. 'You are a great warrior, Rameke. You too, Waribule.'

Rameke beamed with pride and Waribule raised his sword as Thalibald gave the order to his men to form ranks once more.

'My king has need of me,' he said to Volquin, raising his arm in salute and walking off to where Caupo was shepherding the Oeselians to the river.

*****

Only thirteen boats pushed off into the Gauja, though many were crammed full of warriors. The fact was, though, that the Oeselians had suffered a substantial number of casualties, especially at the hands of the crossbowmen as well as during the fighting with the Livs. The most savage combat had taken place just off the beach where the boats had been berthed. It was there that the rearguard had bought time for the vessels to be loaded and cast off, at a cost of their lives. Eric stood on the prow of the leading boat with a bleeding Magnus beside him as the oarsmen began powering the vessel downriver.

'I am going to kill that bastard Lembit,' he vowed, 'and slaughter his people.'

The boats were in midstream now, their tired crews pulling slowly on their oars to take them away from the Liv warriors who now lined the riverbank. Eric's boat rounded a bend in the river to leave Treiden behind and the chief heard his deputy curse under his breath. He looked ahead and saw a bridge of boats barring his escape, and on that bridge stood dozens of enemy soldiers.

*****

Grand Master Volquin had ordered all the horses be taken across the river, to be tethered on the southern bank, while his brother knights and sergeants took up position on the bridge. Sir Helmold stood beside him with his sword drawn, waiting for the Oeselian boats. His sons, fellow Saxon knights and squires stood beside him, shouting insults at the approaching pagans and urging them to row faster so that they might meet their deaths quicker. The Sword Brothers stood in stoic silence as they awaited the enemy.

'Will they attack?' asked Sir Helmold.

'They have no choice,' said Volquin, 'they have nowhere to go.'

The crossbowmen ran from the northern end of the pontoon bridge and formed a line in front of the knights, loading their weapons as the boats got nearer. The Oeselians had slowed their speed when they had spotted the impediment that barred their way, forming into line as crossbow bolts hissed across the water to hit the boats and their crews. The latter frantically pulled in their oars so that more boats could be brought into the Oeselian battle line, for the river was narrow at this point and only nine boats could be accommodated side by side in the water at this spot.

'Ready!' shouted Volquin as the boats drifted on the current towards the bridge.

238

The knights stopped their shouting and closed ranks, the spearmen on their flanks levelling their lances and the crossbowmen loosing one final volley as the riverboats nudged the pontoon bridge and the Oeselians leaped from their vessels.

Rudolf hamstrung the first warrior who lunged at him with a downward cut of his sword, then used his shield to force him backwards into his companions following. Henke fought on the left side of his friend, thrusting his sword forward in lightning-fast movements aimed at enemy faces and necks. His strikes were controlled, carefully aimed and designed to kill immediately. Rudolf was a master with a sword whereas to Henke a sword was just another tool to kill opponents quickly.

The crusaders stood firm on the bridge, killing or wounding the Oeselians as they tried to force their way onto the planks. The initial attack of the river raiders was fierce and desperate but its energy was soon spent as its force broke against an unyielding crusader wall of iron and steel. Magnus, already wounded, fell in the first rush when Sir Helmold drove the point of his sword through his neck. Eric killed two Sword Brothers with his sword and stood triumphant on the bridge, only to be struck in the back by two crossbow bolts shot from the riverbank. He fell on the planks and his body was unceremoniously thrown into the water, the mail armour dragging him down to the riverbed. The death of their leader extinguished the last vestiges of fight within the Oeselians and those still alive threw down their weapons and submitted to the mercy of the Sword Brothers.

Afterwards Theodoric gathered the knights and Sword Brothers at Segewold and gave a service of thanksgiving for the great victory over the pagans. Caupo came to the castle the next day in the company of Thalibald and his sons. He had made Rameke's father his chief warlord, a great honour that elevated Thalibald to the second-most important Liv in the kingdom. His new position had been bought at high cost, though, with two hundred Livs being killed in the battle and a further fifty injured. Both Rameke and Waribule were unhurt, for which their father gave thanks to God.

He was kneeling in silence before the altar in the small chapel at Segewold – thus far the only stone building in the stronghold – when Sir Helmold entered. The knight was dressed in his mail armour and white surcoat emblazoned with a red cross but wore nothing on his head. Thalibald stood up when he heard footsteps. Sir Helmold looked at the great beard and long hair of the chief, so different from his own neatly cropped beard and short hair. A few days ago he looked down on these former heathens and their strange dress and language. But he had seen how Grand

Master Volquin and the other Sword Brothers treated this Thalibald and his king as equals and trusted allies. He had also seen them fight side by side in the recent battle. It was most odd, though perhaps no stranger than the course that his own life had taken.

'I did not mean to disturb you,' he said to Thalibald. 'I will leave if you wish.'

'There is no need for that, lord. But you are welcome to join me in prayer.'

Sir Helmold hesitated. He was used to praying in his own castle chapel when he could be bothered, alone and certainly not in the company of a foreigner. And yet...

Thalibald saw the reluctance in his eyes and smiled. He knew that many of the crusaders who came from Germany looked down on his people and secretly despised them. A few made it plain that they came to rid Livonia of all natives, regardless of whether they followed Christ or not. Others came just to kill and plunder and were not averse to slaughtering Livs if the opportunity arose.

'I will leave, lord,' Thalibald said, 'so that you may pray in peace.'

At that moment Sir Helmold thought of his wife, a poor Cistercian monk in sandals and his former life. 'No. No, not at all. It is I who have disturbed you and will leave so that you may finish your prayers.'

'Perhaps we might pray together,' suggested Thalibald, 'just as we fought together.'

Sir Helmold smiled. 'That would be most agreeable.'

In the days afterwards the sergeants who had been detailed to pursue the Estonians returned with news that Lembit had escaped their clutches. The garrisons of Wenden and Holm returned to their castles, the men of the latter taking the German vassals who had been recruited from Riga back with them. Caupo ordered the rebuilding of his settlement and while the master of Kremon, whose besiegers had also fled north, rode to Segewold to pay his respects to Grand Master Volquin. The dead Sword Brothers were buried in the cemetery at Segewold and the enemy slain were cremated on great pyres that burned fiercely in the meadow where the battle had been fought. Another pyre was built below the ramparts of Segewold where the prisoners were assembled to hear their fate.

Sir Helmold stood beside Thalibald as Grand Master Volquin informed the Oeselians, their hands tied behind their backs, bare footed, bare chested and their heads bowed, that they had a simple choice: receive baptism into the Holy Church or be consigned to the fires. It was a beautiful sunny day and the brother knights and crusader knights sweated in their mail armour as they stood in a long line in front of the prisoners, the sergeants forming two lines either side of the captives and the pyre, the Livs from Treiden standing behind the sergeants. Their king stood between Volquin and Theodoric, Caupo impassive as priests went among the Oeselians, calling for those who wished to serve God to step forward so they could be taken to the river to be baptised. About fifty did so, being spat on by their comrades and jeered at for their cowardice. These men were led away under armed guard, the priests singing hymns as they walked at the head of the column of half-naked men.

The pyre was lit and within minutes had become a raging inferno, the sergeants standing near it sweating in their armour as the heat blasted them. The flames snaked high into the air and the wood hissed and crackled and the pyre became a huge red and yellow monster demanding to be fed.

Grand Master Volquin crossed himself and then nodded to the commander of the two score of sergeants who had been detailed to carry out the grisly business. Theodoric brought his hands together and began praying as groups of sergeants, attired in mail but carrying no shields, seized individual Oeselians and began throwing them into the flames. The Livs erupted in wild cheering as the men who had raped and murdered their friends and families were cremated alive, the screams of Eric's men being drowned out by the tumult of exaltation celebrating their deaths.

The death throes of some of the Oeselians was a hideous spectacle as they thrashed around in the flames for a short period before their flesh melted and they expired. Some tried to run away before they were hurled onto the pyre, but the sergeants with swords drawn slashed their hamstrings or stabbed them in the belly. They fell to the ground, groaning in pain. Then they were hauled to their feet, dragged to the edge of the flames and thrown into the inferno.

In twenty minutes it was all over and the crowd quickly dispersed as the sickly smell of roasting human flesh permeated the air. Grand Master Volquin dismissed the assembly and walked briskly back to the castle holding a cloth over his nose. Sir Helmold's sons were retching and complaining about the stench but their father had seen and smelt roasting flesh before.

'Will those who have been baptised stay loyal?' he asked Thalibald walking beside him.

'As long as no weapons get into their hands.'

'What will happen to them?'

'They will be given to the king's chief warriors as slaves,' said Thalibald, 'though some might yet be killed if their new masters give them to the families of those who have lost loved ones at their hands.'

'The bishop allows slavery?' said Sir Helmold with surprise.

Thalibald shrugged. 'He frowns upon it but turns a blind eye, hoping it will wither and die as the new religion becomes more firmly rooted in this land.'

'And you, Thalibald, do you keep slaves?'

'I was a slave, or near enough one.'

Sir Helmold was shocked.

'It is true,' continued Thalibald. 'The chief who ruled what is now the Sword Brother stronghold at Wenden was a tyrant who treated his people as slaves. He tortured, raped and stole from his people. He was feared and despised in equal measure and demanded unquestioning obedience. But when the bishop and his Sword Brothers arrived his people turned against him.'

'What happened to him?'

'I killed him,' replied Thalibald with satisfaction. 'The bishop delivered us from an oppressor and for that he has my eternal gratitude.'

Sir Helmold nodded and thought of the excesses he had committed during his days as a tyrant. How many women had lost their chastity to his lust and how many innocent lives had he taken? He had revelled in death and destruction and now the aroma of decay hung over him.

'The smell of death,' he said aloud.

'It will soon wash off when the flames have died down,' said Thalibald, hearing him.

Sir Helmold smiled. 'It will take more than water, my friend.'

Thalibald looked at him quizzically.

Sir Helmold gave him a rueful smile. 'It does not matter.'

A week later Bishop Albert arrived from Germany with twenty ships filled with crusaders. Upon hearing of the great victory at Treiden he created Theodoric Bishop of Estonia and promised that he would be able to assume control of his new bishopric within two years.

*****

Bruno was laid to rest in Wenden's cemetery, the other boys having dug his grave, washed his body and buried him after Otto had said prayers over him. Conrad and the others were ashen faced as they laid their comrade and friend to rest. He had not known Bruno for long but his passing affected him deeply. For days afterwards, when he and the others had finished their early morning prayers and duties and were walking to the training ground, he found himself looking at the plot of ground that had been earmarked for the cemetery. Two things prevented him becoming too morose: training and the presence of Daina within the castle.

It had been viewed as too dangerous for the women to return to their villages while Thalibald and his warriors were away, the more so because Lukas did not have any soldiers to spare for guarding the villages and no one knew if there were any more Estonian raiding parties in the area. It was unlikely but he was not prepared to take the risk. And so all the women were accommodated in the mercenaries' huts until they and the others returned. The weather was getting warmer now and the days longer, the air fresh and sweet with the aroma of flowers. The forests were teeming with wild boar, bears, elk and deer, the tributaries of the Gauja filled with hunting otters. The forest floor was thick with soft, spring lichens, reindeer moss forming carpets of white in innumerable pine groves.

Following a particularly hard morning training session with their wasters and shields, in which the four boys had paired off and fought each other to a standstill, Lukas informed them that Grand Master Volquin had won a great victory over the pagans. Lembit's army had been destroyed, as had an Oeselian force that had rowed up the Gauja in boats.

'In a few days Master Berthold will return with the soldiers of the garrison,' Lukas told them. 'Two of Wenden's brother knights fell in the battle, along with three sergeants. Thalibald will also be returning. He has been elevated to become Caupo's chief warlord and adviser and I am sure he will be delighted to learn that you all helped to save the lives of his womenfolk. God has truly smiled on us.'

Conrad cast Hans a sideways glance and smiled with pride, Anton puffed out his chest and Johann wore a stupid grin that made Lukas shake his head.

'In the short space of time that you have been here all of you have done well and have applied yourself to learning swordsmanship and the uses of other weapons. Well done.'

Though she was in the compound Conrad saw little of Daina. Lukas ensured that they were kept apart for though he liked the chief's daughter, he knew how tempting an attractive young woman could be to boys approaching manhood. In any case hard training was an excellent cure for lewd thoughts. He was partly thwarted in his plan when Berthold and Thalibald returned and Daina informed her father about being captured and rescued by Conrad and his friends. She specifically mentioned him and requested that he accompany her back to their village. It was a joyous day when the garrison returned and even more delightful when Conrad walked beside the pony carrying Daina the next day. The other Liv women were also riding ponies,

243

Hans, Anton and Johann walking ahead leading more ponies. For the journey they had been issued with their swords. Rudolf and Henke rode behind Daina, having been promised a barrel of *kvass* each by the chief. They were both in a mischievous mood.

'So, Conrad,' said Rudolf, 'while we were away saving the kingdom from collapse you were amusing yourself running around the forest chasing Estonians.'

'Fat, useless Estonians, I have heard,' added Henke.

Daina turned in her saddle. 'Conrad was very brave and rescued my mother and me, which I have told my father about. He will surely reward him.'

'Reward him?' Did you hear that, Henke? And to think when I first brought him here he was a poor wretched creature who could not even hold a sword. Now he is a hero.'

'Daina,' said Henke, 'did you know that the sword Conrad wears once belonged to a great knight from Germany who gave it to him on his deathbed.'

'Of course,' replied Daina, 'a knight's sword for a knight.'

Rudolf laughed out loud. 'A knight, is he? Conrad, would you like to ride and I will walk, for surely it is not fitting that such a great warrior should wear out his shoe leather?'

'And I will carry your sword, lord knight,' said Henke, 'if it is too heavy for you.'

Conrad felt his cheeks blushing as he stared directly ahead. 'No, thank you.'

'What reward do you think your father will bestow upon young Conrad?' Rudolf asked Daina.

'A few goats, perhaps,' suggested Henke.

Daina pulled up her pony and looked around at Henke. 'A few goats? Is that all you think I am worth, Brother Henke?'

Henke winked at her. 'All right, a cow then.'

She stuck her tongue out at him and resumed her journey. 'He might bestow a most precious gift, one that is dear to his heart,' she said casually.

Rudolf knew where this was leading. 'You do know that Conrad is training to be a Sword Brother, Daina. To be a servant of God who forswears pleasures of the flesh. Is that not so, Conrad?'

Daina looked down at him but Conrad continued to look ahead. 'It is as you say, Brother Rudolf.'

'What if my father asks that Conrad be released from your service?' she teased Rudolf.

'Then we will have to give him up,' replied Rudolf. Conrad desperately wanted to be a Sword Brother but at this moment, with the delectable Daina beside him showering him with compliments, his heart was ruling his head and he wanted nothing more than to be with her always.

'Poor Conrad,' remarked Henke, 'thus does he consider entering a life of slavery willingly.'

'A veritable martyr,' said Rudolf before they both began laughing.

Sadly for Conrad Thalibald did not ask that Master Berthold release Conrad from his service so that he could marry his daughter. He did personally thank him and the other boys who had rescued his womenfolk and gave Henke and Rudolf their barrels to take back to Wenden.

There was a great celebratory feast that night in Thalibald's hall, at which Hans devoured a seemingly never-ending flow of roasted deer, wild boar, duck and goose. Spits turned over great fires, cauldrons hung over hearths and ovens baked bread. As was traditional the food was eaten in silence to show respect for those who had gathered the food – the farmers – and those who cooked and served it: the women. But as the evening wore on the level of chatter increased as drink loosened tongues.

The radiant Daina served Conrad and the other boys *piragi* and filled their wooden cups with a delightful beer called *medalus* – honey beer – brewed from barley and hops and flavoured with honey. Thalibald sat at the top table flanked by his two sons, Rudolf and Henke, the chief in good heart notwithstanding that thirty men from the hundred he had taken to Treiden had not returned.

'The bishop will take his army north into Estonia now that Lembit's army has been crushed?' he asked Rudolf.

'Yes, lord,' answered Wenden's deputy commander.

Thalibald took a gulp from his cup. 'And will he cross the sea to assault the Oeselians?'

'That may have to wait, lord,' said Rudolf. 'I fear it will take more than one campaign to subdue the Estonian tribes.'

Thalibald sat back in his chair as he observed Daina flirting with Conrad. 'Lembit's defeat will have weakened his position among the other tribes. This will make the bishop's task easier.' He pointed at Conrad.

'I remember that boy. He seems to be making a name for himself. What do you know of him?'

Henke shook his head ruefully. He knew that Thalibald was expecting to hear that the boy was the son of a knight.

'He was the son of a baker from Lübeck, lord,' said Rudolf.

'His parents are wealthy?' enquired Thalibald.

Henke emitted a low laugh. Rudolf cleared his throat. 'His parents are dead, lord. He came to Livonia a pauper to begin a new life.'

Thalibald's face wore a deep frown. 'My daughter shows too much of an interest in him, I think. He could not support a wife who is the daughter of a king.'

'Have no fear on that front, lord,' said Rudolf. 'His destiny is to wear the white mantle of the Sword Brothers.'

Thalibald seemed comforted by this. 'Good. Better that he uses his sword to protect my daughter and her people rather than his body warming her bed.'

'Have you informed her of that, lord?' enquired Henke as Daina giggled girlishly sitting herself down next to Conrad.

'Daughters obey their fathers, have no fear,' said Thalibald sternly.

*****

Vsevolod picked at his black rye bread. Not even its heavy fragrance could restore his appetite. The fare he had been served was excellent: tender strips of wild boar, chicken legs, cooked eggs, wheat flour pies and white curd cheese. The hall was packed with Grand Duke Daugerutis' warlords, all of whom were casting hateful stares in his direction. He felt as welcome as a fox in a chicken coop. He looked across at the fair faces of the *Vaidilutes* – virgins dressed all in white who guarded the sacred groves and forests of the Lithuanians and maintained the sacred fires – and was met with steely expressions and eyes filled with disdain. Even the *Krivu Krivaitis*, the chief priest, was barely concealing his contempt for the ruler of Gerzika.

'I admire your courage, Vsevolod,' said Daugerutis. 'There are many among my people who say that you should be banned from my court for your actions, or rather inaction, at Kokenhusen.'

It was the first time that Vsevolod had crossed the Dvina since the abortive attack on the castle. He had hoped that time would calm Lithuanian wrath, which clearly it had not. However, his wife had begged him to go to her father's stronghold of Panemunis to dispel any doubts concerning his allegiance. He loved his wife but did not tell her that his primary loyalty was to himself, not her father and certainly not to the Lithuanians. Nevertheless, he recognised that he had to keep the goodwill

246

of the latter if he was to retain his kingdom. That said, the sea of unwelcoming faces made him think that he should have delayed his visit for a while longer.

'The difficulties of coordinating an assault are many and varied, father,' replied Vsevolod.

The grand duke looked at the table where Prince Stecse sat with his lieutenants. 'Not according to Stecse.'

Vsevolod hated the upstart prince, not because he was a simple-minded fool, though he was that, but more because he had wormed himself into the affections of the grand duke and thus became a direct nuisance.

'Prince Stecse is a brave warrior,' said Vsevolod, 'but perhaps does not appreciate matters of strategy. For example, the Bishop of Riga finds himself embroiled in a long war in the north against the Estonians. This being the case, out of strategic necessity he desires peace along the Dvina.'

The grand duke began chewing on a piece of black bread dipped in *juka*. 'Why should I give him peace?'

Vsevolod smiled. 'Because, my lord, he offers something that you desire.'

The grand duke pushed the bread into his mouth. 'What?'

'To cross the Dvina to attack the Principality of Novgorod and thus avenge the many wrongs the Russians have committed against you.'

The grand duke stopped eating and turned to face his son-in-law. 'He will allow me to cross the river and march through his territory with an army?'

Vsevolod mustered his most earnest expression. 'He will, my lord.'

'Why?'

'Out of strategic necessity, lord, as I said. He desires peace with all the Lithuanian tribes and will accommodate your wishes to achieve that peace.'

'He has forgotten the assault on Kokenhusen?'

Vsevolod spread his hands. 'He recognises that you are a great warlord and he is just a priest who can muster few troops in comparison to the mighty army you can assemble. He fears you, my lord, and wishes to appease you.'

The grand duke toyed with one of the silver rings on his fingers. 'You will arrange it, Vsevolod, and then perhaps I may forget your error at Kokenhusen.'

Vsevolod bowed his head. 'Your servant, lord.'

Lembit stood in his hall at Lehola, his lieutenants assembled before him. He had managed to evade his pursuers to get back to his homeland, most of the men of the other tribes having deserted him during the journey back to Estonia. The campaign had been a disaster, the only bright spot being the return of Rusticus from the diversion at Wenden. It was now summer and he knew that soon a vengeful crusader army led by the newly returned Bishop Albert would be marching north into Saccalia. He also feared that the Oeselians would revert to being enemies instead of allies following the debacle at Treiden. But at least most of his wolf shields were still alive and he retained the loyalty of his Saccalians. There was absolute silence in the hall as his men awaited his words.

'I will not lie to you. We suffered a reverse at Treiden and were forced to retreat. Soon the crusaders will be marching north into our homeland, intent on enslaving us and forcing us to kneel to their god. This I will not allow.'

His men murmured their defiance. He raised his hands. 'The crusaders will gather their forces and march as one army, but we will counter them by dividing our forces.'

His men looked at each other in confusion.

Lembit smirked. 'The crusaders cannot be everywhere at once. Just as Rusticus led a party south, so will you lead small groups to raid the enemy's territory. In this way the crusaders will be unable to keep their army together. They will be forced to send parties to hunt you down.'

'Make sure they don't catch you,' said Rusticus. 'Kill, burn, destroy and then melt back into the forests.'

'How long are we to remain in Livonia, lord?' asked one of the warriors.

'Until the autumn,' answered Lembit. 'By then the rains will have come and the crusaders will be unable to transport their siege engines through the mud. You will leave in the morning. Rusticus will supply you with details.'

His men were in good spirits as they filed out of the hall and the guards closed the doors behind them.

'Excellent idea,' said Rusticus approvingly, 'should keep the barbarians away.'

Lembit flopped into his chair. 'It will buy us time, nothing more. The chiefs of the other tribes will no doubt be demanding a gathering where they can air their grievances concerning the failure at Treiden.'

'They whine like old women,' sneered Rusticus.

'That may be. But I need their continued allegiance if we are to prevail in this war.'

'What of the Oeselians?'

Lembit leaned back and closed his eyes. 'It seems unlikely that they will wish to continue with our alliance following the failure at Treiden. I have no doubt that Eric will be bending his father's ear and blaming me for the failure to take Caupo's stronghold.'

'No great loss,' sniffed Rusticus.

Lembit opened his eyes and looked at him. 'On the contrary. If the Oeselians become our enemies it means their longships will be raiding the lands of the Rotalians once more. And if that happens then we will lose their warriors in the war against the crusaders. I will send an envoy to Olaf requesting a meeting.'

Rusticus looked alarmed. 'He will kill you.'

'He might, but remember that it was he who made the first approach not the other way round. Hopefully he still sees the merit of an alliance between our two peoples.'

'I do not trust him,' said Rusticus.

'You are obsessed by the notion of trust. As I told you, trust has nothing to do with it. Olaf knows that if Estonia becomes the domain of the Christians then his island will be next. Self interest, pure and simple.'

'Do you wish me to lead one of the raiding parties?' inquired Rusticus.

Lembit shook his head. 'I need you at Fellin to stiffen the hearts of the garrison. I will remain here and invite my fellow chiefs to a gathering to allay their fears. You may go.'

Rusticus strolled towards the doors, stopped and turned.

'I forgot something. You remember that boy who gave you the scar on your cheek?'

'How could I forget him?' said Lembit. 'I carry a permanent reminder of his existence. What of him?'

'I saw him when the crusaders and Livs rescued the women we had taken near Wenden,' replied Rusticus.

Lembit was disinterested. 'So?'

'So that is the second time we have encountered him. And directly afterwards I heard wolves howling.'

Lembit rolled his eyes. 'Wolves?'

'An ill omen, it means war.'

249

Lembit sighed. He knew many of his people were superstitious, seeing omens and divine signs in the forests, lakes and rivers. But he had little time for such nonsense and was surprised that his deputy did.

'Wolves howl, Rusticus, and we are already at war so I think you can calm your fears.'

But Rusticus would not let the matter pass. 'Twice we have encountered that boy and twice he has lived. It is a sign from the gods. The boy represents ill luck. He needs to be killed to avert disaster.'

Lembit was growing tired of this nonsense. 'You speak of things that are inconsequential. Concentrate on the matter to hand.'

Rusticus was mumbling to himself as he took leave of his lord, leaving the chief alone with his thoughts. It was nearly mid-summer now and the tracks and roads that led north would be dry enough to bear the wagons of the crusaders carrying their infernal siege machines. They had proved at Fellin that they could batter down the timber walls of his hill forts with ease. The only way to protect his strongholds was to keep them away from Estonian soil. And so the next morning a dozen groups left Lehola to lay waste Livonia. They rode on ponies and scattered to take different routes into the bishop's kingdom, each one numbering no more that twenty warriors. Lembit stood on the battlements and watched them go. Later Rusticus also rode south to assume command of the garrison at Fellin. Lembit stayed on the wall until his deputy was but a small speck on the horizon and then disappeared altogether. Then he returned to his hall to dictate a letter to Olaf.

*****

Conrad had never seen such a great collection of soldiers that gathered at Wenden that summer, led by Bishop Albert himself in his mail armour, his great banner of Riga being pitched in the middle of the camp that surrounded the castle like a huge besieging army. This was to be the final campaign that was to subdue Lembit and the Estonians: to create a Christian kingdom from the River Dvina all the way to the Gulf of Finland. The pagans had been defeated at Treiden and now Estonia lay prostrate before the crusaders. Caupo came with five hundred of his Livs, supplemented by Thalibald and a hundred of his warriors. There were knights and squires from Saxony, Thuringia, Franconia and even Swabia and Bavaria. The banners of these lords were planted around the standard of the bishop so that it seemed that a new forest of silk and linen had arisen. There were dozens of gonfalons – standards with streamers flown from a horizontal bar, supported by a

250

vertical pole. Gold-fringed pennons fluttered from lances and banners hung from the trumpets of musicians in the service of the wealthiest lords. The sun shone, the knights feasted and boasted of the coming conquest of the pagans and Theodoric dreamed of his new bishopric.

And it was all an illusion.

The first indication that the army would not be marching north was when Caupo led a large party of his warriors east, and then a sizeable number of crusader knights and their squires left Wenden and headed back to Riga. As the days passed the number of knights at Wenden gradually decreased as parties left the castle, including Bishop Albert himself.

'Estonian raiding parties are destroying our farms and villages,' said Rameke as he helped Conrad place a stone into the back of a cart.

Now that summer was here Conrad and the other boys were detailed to assist the transportation of stone that was being used in the construction of the castle from the quarry located five miles to the east.

The stone being quarried was dolostone, a hard limestone that blunted the chisels of the masons and the metal wedges used by the quarrymen to separate the stone blocks from the rock face.

'Estonians?' Conrad was surprised. 'I thought they had been defeated at Treiden.'

'They were,' said Rameke, exhaling loudly as he let go of the stone block. 'But Lembit has sent others south to raid our lands. My father has been forced to send men back to their villages to protect the women and the old.'

'Including your father's own village I hope,' said Conrad with concern.

Rameke smiled. 'Do not worry, my friend, my sister is quite safe.'

Conrad blushed and looked away. 'I do not know what you mean.'

'She talks of you often,' Rameke continued. 'You have a made a great impression on her.'

'And you two talk too much,' said Lukas, appearing beside the cart as if by magic. 'There are more stones to load before we head back to the castle. As your father placed you under my command, Rameke, it would be remiss of me to allow you to loiter in idle gossip.'

Rameke wiped his sweaty brow on his shirtsleeve. 'No chance of that, Brother Lukas.'

The brother knight was fully armed and accompanied by a dozen sergeants and a score of Thalibald's warriors, in addition to the five spearmen and five

251

crossbowmen who guarded the quarrymen during the day. The latter were local Livs who also brought their weapons to work – the quarry would be a very tempting target for an Estonian raiding party.

The sweating Anton heaved another stone slab into the wagon. 'Will they attack Wenden again?'

Lukas shook his head. 'It is too strong, but an undefended quarry is easy pickings.'

Anton looked over at his sword and shield stacked with the weapons of the other boys nearby.

Lukas laughed. 'They won't show their faces while there are so many soldiers here. They prefer to attack weak, undefended targets.'

'Like a village full of children and women,' said Rameke.

Lukas nodded his head. 'Precisely.'

A line of wagons stood waiting to be loaded with stone, the quarrymen ferrying the varyingly sized stones to them. The quarry had been in operation for three years now, the top layer of stone, called 'rag' and being of inferior quality, was used for rubble, for infill to walls or to make lime. It would be functioning for many years yet to provide the materials to complete Wenden, earmarked to be an impregnable stronghold of the Sword Brothers. But it was a laborious, time-consuming business. Every stone had to be first prised from the cliff face and then split into a slab before being broken into usable stone, after which it was transported to the castle and then hauled or dragged to the top of the wall for the masons to move into place. Slowly but inexorably the walls and towers of Wenden were rising from the escarpment upon which the castle was positioned.

Two days later a large force of crusader horse and foot marched past the quarry to ensure that there were no Estonians in the immediate vicinity. Other parties were sent north into Ungannia and Saccalia to retaliate against Lembit's audacity, but the Estonian leader had succeeded in nullifying the bishop's efforts to conquer the pagan kingdom.

As the crusader force gathered at Wenden slowly dissipated and then disappeared altogether, Conrad continued to hone his weapon skills. His gangly frame had begun to fill out now, though Hans, notwithstanding his attempt to empty the castle's food stores single handed, still looked skinny. But he was no longer pale and gaunt but rosy cheeked and hale and his sinewy frame possessed a strength that belied his appearance. Johann and Anton likewise grew in strength and stature as they practised day in, day out.

Conrad enjoyed that summer, though he and the others saw no fighting. The days were long and warm, the forests were full of game and the rivers and lakes teeming with fish. After the cold and misery of the winter everyone ate well from the abundance that was all around them. The fields were planted and the crops grew, watered by frequent summer storms and warmed by the sun. More workers and their families came to Wenden, along with farmers who had been promised plots of land, though when they arrived they were surprised to discover that their new farms had to be carved from the forest first. But Master Berthold provided assistance in the form of Conrad and his companions and sergeants, who helped to fell the trees and extract the stumps from the ground. The farmers used the timber to build their homes and the fences that held their pigs and goats, and slowly the area directly north of Wenden filled with settlers' homes.

Patrols were still mounted to the north and east as mid-summer passed but there were no signs of Estonians. Several raiding parties had been intercepted and destroyed by crusader forces but Lembit's warriors had caused considerable damage to the south and southeast of Wenden, and had also alarmed the citizens of Riga. Thus did the bishop spend the summer at Riga providing protection for his flock instead of smiting the heathen.

At Wenden Conrad and his companions were taught to use the mace, a three-foot-long piece of iron with protruding edges of sharpened iron on one end. These flanges were fixed all round the mace so that the weapon was radially symmetric, so that a blow could be delivered equally effectively with any side of the head. Lukas had invited Henke to explain to them the subtleties of the mace as he was reckoned to be the most proficient in its use. He stood before them in shirt, leggings and boots, sweat running down his powerful neck for it was a blisteringly hot day.

'The mace is a very simple weapon. It is quick, effective and brutal.'

'A bit like Henke,' said Rudolf standing nearby.

Henke ignored him, swinging the mace upwards. 'It can be used on foot or in the saddle. A forceful blow with a mace will crush bones and armour. If you strike an opponent's helmet hard enough the force of the blow will break his neck, even if the helmet is undamaged. If you strike an enemy on the arm or leg you will break the bone even if you do not penetrate his armour, such is the power of a mace blow.'

He pointed the end of his mace at the boys. 'When you are defending yourselves against a mace you have to keep it away from your body. You cannot rely on your helmet or armour to protect you.'

He told Conrad to attack him with his waster and shield. 'Remember,' he told him, 'keep it away from your body.'

Henke swung at Conrad with a downward strike of the mace that Conrad caught on his shield. The force of the blow amazed him. It was like a giant hammer had hit it. Henke jumped aside and aimed a sideways strike at him, which Conrad parried with his shield at the cost of the bottom of the leather and wood being cut and fractured. Henke was amazingly quick for his size, nimbly changing the weight on each foot as he avoided Conrad's sword blows and then delivering a succession of strikes against him. He could tell that Henke was not trying to kill or hurt him, but after less than two minutes half his shield had been destroyed.

Henke, his shirt now soaked in sweat, stepped back and nodded at Conrad.

'Well done.' He turned to the others. 'You see how effective a mace can be. Powerful blows, that is the key. Anything you hit will either be dented or broken. Don't waste your energy, though. Like you have been taught: kill quickly and move on.'

So they learned to use a mace and then in combination with other weapons: the sword and mace, dagger and mace and axe and mace. They were allowed to wear their swords now, both during the day and while on guard duty. But they were not allowed to use them in training.

'Your swords are far too valuable to be blunted or damaged during training sessions,' Lukas told them. 'That is why you have your wasters.'

The days went by in a blur, filled with prayers, training and assisting in the construction of the castle. The walls and towers were draped in wooden scaffolding as they inched ever upwards, workers scurrying around like ants ferrying stone and mortar to the top platforms. And then treadmill cranes were erected to hoist stone onto the walls. These great wooden machines used a treadmill powered by men to drive round the windlass for winding up the lifting ropes attached to loads. And the daylight hours were filled with the sound of men chiselling, hammering, sawing and cursing as Wenden began to take shape.

In the sparse amount of free time allowed him Conrad sought out the company of Ilona, the raven-haired mysterious beauty who lived in the compound but was free to move around the castle at will. Treated with a degree of respect and awe, she spent her days taking care of the children of the castle workers or collecting herbs in the meadows and forests to enable her to practice her healing arts, always accompanied by guards whenever she ventured out of the castle compound. Conrad wondered if this was because she was a slave of the order, which caused Lukas to smile.

'Slave? More like a queen, boy. Rudolf always makes sure she is well guarded and has everything she wants.'

'Why?' asked Conrad.

'You know why. She was the one who pulled him out of the fire when the Russians attacked Holm. She was the one who tended his wounds and brought him back to life and she is the one who shares his soul with God. That's why. She has my gratitude for that, the others as well.'

'Thalibald is her lord?' said Conrad.

'She is from Holm,' replied Lukas, 'on the River Dvina.'

This lithe beauty who outwardly appeared to be Rudolf's wife, though he knew that was impossible, intrigued Conrad.

'I would like to learn to speak the language of the Livs,' he said to Lukas, 'and was wondering if she might teach me.'

Lukas shrugged. 'You will have to ask her yourself. Make sure it does not interfere with your duties, mind.'

'No, brother, of course.'

'And behave yourself around her,' Lukas teased him. 'No improper thoughts.'

Conrad was mortified. 'I would never…'

Lukas waved a hand at him. 'I jest with you, Conrad. Now I believe you have an armour-cleaning session before prayers.'

The next afternoon Conrad searched out Ilona and found her waiting for him, along with four sergeants, outside her hut. She was dressed in a simple brown woollen skirt and a brown tunic with a V-shaped neck, a green sash around her waist and her long black hair hanging freely about her shoulders. She was holding an empty wicker basket in front of her and smiled at Conrad as he approached.

The sergeants were dressed in short-sleeved mail shirts and kettle helmets and were armed with short axes, swords and daggers, their shields strapped to their backs. Conrad also wore a kettle helmet though only his padded gambeson for armour. He gripped the hilt of his sword as he got nearer to the group, his shield likewise slung on his back. It was a measure of the trust placed in him and the other boys that they were now allowed to carry weapons inside and outside the castle complex. He too carried a dagger in a sheath on his right hip.

'Welcome, Conrad Wolff,' she smiled, nodding at one of the sergeants before turning on her heels and striding towards the gates. Conrad hurried to catch up, walking a couple of paces behind her. He felt slightly uncomfortable.

'So,' she said, waving to a group of children who were following their mothers towards their huts, 'you wish to learn the tongue of my people.'

'Yes, madam.'

She giggled. 'You make me sound like an old maid. Call me Ilona. Why do you want to learn the language of the Livs?'

The question puzzled him. 'To understand the native people more.'

She turned and smiled at him. 'The people or just one in particular?'

He felt his cheeks flush. 'I do not understand.'

'Oh, I think you do. The young man who saved the life of Brother Rudolf, wounded Lembit and saved the life of Thalibald's daughter has become famous in these parts, Conrad. How could I resist the request of such a hero?'

Conrad was embarrassed and delighted in equal measure and the sergeants smiled at his discomfiture.

'Daina will be enchanted that you take an interest in her ways.'

Conrad tried to be clever. 'Daina?'

Ilona stopped and faced him. 'If we are to get along then I think we should be honest with each other. You know Daina, do you not?'

Conrad, crestfallen, nodded.

'And you like her?'

He nodded again.

'And you thought it would be courteous to learn her language so that you may converse with her in her native tongue?'

He nodded a third time.

She resumed her walk. 'There, that wasn't so difficult, was it?'

They went only a short distance from the castle, to the edge of the trees that filled the area from the banks of the Gauja extending east.

'Wild raspberries,' said Ilona, 'that is what we are here to pick.'

Two of the sergeants stood guard while Conrad and the other two helped her fill her basket with the black berries.

'I shall be delighted to teach you,' she said to Conrad. 'Rudolf holds you in high regard.'

She told him that the berries were used to make a drink that could cure colds, headaches and high fevers, telling him that the Liv word for raspberry was

256

skaidrojumi. Thereafter Ilona taught Conrad the words for the things he saw every day: horse, wagon, hill, forest, meadow and so on. He found it difficult at first. He had never learned to read or write and so did not know how his own language was constructed. But as the weeks passed the constant repetition of words gradually implanted themselves in his mind and he found that he could repeat them with ease. The next phase was learning basic sentences, which again he first found difficult but with great patience and tenacity on the part of Ilona he began to master.

The summer waned, the raiding parties that Lembit had sent south were either hunted down and destroyed or pursued back into their own lands where the crusaders laid waste a great number of villages. The knights who had journeyed from Germany prepared to spend a winter in Livonia. The bishop, encouraged by the earlier attack on Fellin, was determined to mount another winter campaign against the pagans. The walls of Wenden continued to slowly increase in height as stone was ferried from the quarry on a daily basis. The Sword Brothers were determined that the castle would be the strongest in all Livonia, a lasting testament to the power of the Holy Church and the might of the military order based there.

'We are running short of funds,' said Master Berthold, his swarthy features illuminated in the half-light of his hall's candles.

He sat opposite Rudolf in the dimness, a sheaf of parchments on the table between them. Berthold picked up one of the papers.

'We are fortunate that this land is rich in wildlife and fish that we can eat, not to mention the fertile soil that allows us to grow our crops. Nevertheless, the costs of constructing the castle and maintaining the garrison are proving exorbitant.'

'I did not realise things were that bad,' said Rudolf.

Berthold held up the parchment. 'This is the list of costs pertaining to just one month of work carried out on the castle.'

He handed it to Rudolf who perused it. There was a long list of artisans in the left-hand column and their respective wages in the right-hand column. There were carters – men who brought wood and stone to the castle from the quarry – carpenters who built flooring, roofing, furniture, panelling and scaffolding, masons who worked the stone and woodworkers who worked in the forest to cut the wood for joists and beams.

Berthold picked up another parchment. 'Wages for cooks, blacksmiths and clerks. The list is almost endless.'

Rudolf also knew that mail armour, helmets, swords, maces, axes, daggers and horse furniture, as well as the horses themselves, had to be imported from

257

Germany, adding a further drain on Wenden's expenses. Then there were the armourers who maintained the weapons and armour, in addition to the atilliators – the skilled workers who made and maintained crossbows.

Master Berthold picked up another parchment and shook his head, the weight of the world seemingly on his shoulders. 'And lest we forget, the not inconsiderable sums paid to our resident mercenaries. Ruinous.'

Rudolf studied the figures again, vainly thinking that if he stared at them hard enough they would seem less daunting.

'By the end of the year the treasury will be empty and all work will grind to a halt,' lamented Berthold.

'Winter brings a halt to all construction anyway,' said Rudolf.

'Though not, alas, the need to pay those engaged in it,' added Berthold.

Rudolf put the parchment back on the table. 'What is to be done?'

Berthold ran a hand over his crown. 'We will have to go to the bishop and beg for more money.'

Rudolf toyed with the parchments in front of him. He knew that among the brother knights and sergeants only he and Master Berthold could read and write. And Brother Walter, of course.

'Walter, yes,' said Rudolf.

'Walter?' Berthold was perplexed.

'Walter gave all his fortune to the Sword Brothers,' said Rudolf, 'as did Sir Frederick. Have we exhausted all those funds already?'

Berthold looked at him with heavy eyes. 'Alas, my friend, they left their money to the Holy Church and not Wenden. All donations are received by the bishop's palace in Riga.'

'Then we must go and collect what is rightfully ours,' said Rudolf.

They set off the next day, taking boat down the Gauja and then riding south the short distance to Riga. The river was filled with boats taking supplies and men to the garrisons at Wenden, Segewold and Kremon, other, smaller vessels on the water containing fishermen casting their nets to trap the large sturgeon that swam under the surface. War and destruction seemed far away, the land was well tended and the people well fed and seemingly prosperous. When they got nearer to Riga, however, they passed burnt-out farmsteads and smashed fences – evidence of the destruction the Kurs had visited on the area.

Riga itself was bustling, its dirt streets heaving with carts, donkeys and people, the shops full of wares and the markets teeming with livestock. The harbour area had been rebuilt after the Kur incursion, great warehouses set back from its extensive quay and jetties extending out into the Dvina where a variety of different-sized vessels were moored: cogs, hulks, keels, knarrs and river boats.

They made their way through the thriving, disorganised streets to the castle to report to Grand Master Volquin. They found him inspecting a line of potential novices to the Sword Brothers who had just arrived from Germany, most of them scrawny, half-starved teenagers who had no doubt been saved from the gallows by the bishop's court in Lübeck. They looked relieved at having survived the journey to Riga, though whether they would live through their fist Livonian winter remained to be seen. Grand Master Volquin welcomed them to Riga and told them that they would leave for Holm Castle in the morning, not that any of them knew where that was. Volquin dismissed them and instructed a sergeant to take them to the dining hall to get some food into their malnourished bodies.

He stood in the castle courtyard shaking his head as they trudged disconsolately into the citadel. The rectangular courtyard stood in front of this structure, with four rectangular towers in each corner of the compound. He saw Berthold and Rudolf dismount from their horses and walk over to him. They bowed their heads to him.

'Welcome,' said Volquin. 'I received the message that you would be arriving. All is well, I hope.'

'At the moment, grand master,' replied Berthold sternly, 'though if matters are not addressed then they will not remain so.'

Volquin tilted his head towards the last of the boys entering the castle. 'The bishop believes it to be an act of charity to bring them here. Waifs and strays, mostly. Most will not live to see next summer.'

'A fate that might befall Wenden as well,' said Berthold dryly.

Volquin looked at him with alarm. 'Wenden is in danger?'

'Not from the pagans, grand master,' replied Berthold. 'Other threats present themselves.'

After they had been shown to their quarters in the north wing and had eaten a meal of cooked herring Berthold and Rudolf sat in the grand master's office. The shutters on the windows were open and the rich aroma of the town was drifting in on a northerly wind. They explained the financial difficulties that would soon engulf Wenden.

Volquin nodded solemnly. 'I have received similar reports from the other masters of our order, imploring me to send them more funds. The power to distribute largess is, unfortunately, not mine to grant. Each request must be laid before the bishop himself. You are fortunate in that he is in situ at the moment, for otherwise the decision would be left to the discretion of Archdeacon Stefan.'

'The bishop's puppy?' sneered Berthold.

Volquin raised his eyebrows at his subordinate. 'You would do well to temper your opinions when we see the bishop, Master Berthold. Our friend Stefan has been created governor of Riga with all the responsibilities and power that comes with that office. He also retains his clerical powers.'

'He rises in the world,' commented Rudolf.

'His ambition has no limits,' remarked Volquin. 'It is rumoured that he urged the bishop to create Theodoric Bishop of Estonia.'

'They are allies?' said Rudolf.

'On the contrary, brother,' replied Volquin. 'They detest each other, so Stefan agitated for Theodoric's appointment to rule over the Estonians and thus remove him from Riga. He is not to be underestimated.'

Berthold and Rudolf discovered this for themselves when they met him and the bishop in the latter's palace the next morning. Half the building was covered in wooden scaffolding, the archdeacon having authorised the construction of more bedrooms and a second audience chamber. The meeting was held in the original audience chamber, which had been refurbished with silk-covered chairs and a beautifully carved oak table, behind which the bishop and his nephew sat.

Bishop Albert and Stefan rose when the three Sword Brothers entered and Stefan ordered wine to be served. The monks who poured it into silver flagons were even younger than the ones who had attended him last time, Rudolf thought. The day was warm but the atmosphere in the room soon turned cool.

'Grand Master Volquin has alerted me to your financial difficulties,' the bishop said to Master Berthold, 'and we are most sympathetic to your plight. However, I have to tell you that the flow of funds from Germany is not as generous as I would like. Though there are many knights who are willing to take the cross to support our crusade, the German kings and princes are less willing to support our cause financially.'

Rudolf looked at the rich white dalmatic being worn by Stefan and his gold pectoral cross hanging around his neck. Clearly Riga did not suffer from financial difficulties.

Master Berthold nodded and smiled. 'Of course, bishop, we understand. But there is the matter of the donations promised to Wenden by our newest brother knight, Walter, and Sir Frederick who was martyred and now lies in the castle's cemetery.'

'A brave servant of God,' said the bishop.

'Indeed,' added Stefan. 'But the fact is that all donations are sent to Riga where they are distributed according to need. I am sorry to report that the recent assault on this town has necessitated the strengthening of its defences and an increase in the size of the garrison. I am afraid that just as your treasury is empty, Master Berthold, so our exchequer is poorly stocked.'

Stefan smiled slyly and brought his hands together in front of his chest. What a contrast he presented to the bishop, the latter with his stern, chiselled features and determined personality, the archdeacon with his flabby, effeminate features and delicate fingers. Every year the bishop led a crusader army to war. Rudolf doubted if Stefan had ever stepped foot beyond the comfortable confines of this palace.

But Berthold was not so easily deflected. 'If you cannot spare any funds, lord bishop, then perhaps Riga could release some of the troops of its garrison to me. In that way I could dismiss some of my mercenaries and thus save expenditure.'

Stefan blanched. 'The garrison of Riga? Out of the question! Have you forgotten so soon the attack of the Kurs, the assault on Kokenhusen by the Lithuanians and Estonian raiders who recently invaded the kingdom? Lord bishop, it is out of the question that the garrison of Riga should be weakened.'

'I have to concur with my governor,' said the bishop. 'That said, I am willing to cede control of all the territory around Wenden to the Sword Brothers if this would help. You would not have to send any yearly tribute to Riga.'

This was a hollow victory because Wenden had never sent any tribute to Riga, as the bishop well knew. In theory Livonia was a crusader kingdom in which those who owned land, including the Sword Brothers, paid dues to the bishop's palace in Riga. The reality was that each castle was barely able to support itself and had no spare monies to lavish on the clothing of the town governor.

'Perhaps Wenden could make more use of the local population,' offered Stefan.

'The local population?' said Berthold.

Stefan smiled at him, turning the gold ring on his finger as he did so. 'The Livs who populate Wenden's lands. Surely they can be recruited to your cause.'

Berthold shook his head. 'They already pay rents to the order and work in the quarry.'

'You pay those who work wages?' asked Stefan.

Berthold frowned. 'Of course.'

Rudolf knew where this was leading. 'Thalibald and his people are valuable allies. It would be unwise to make them enemies by making unreasonable demands upon them.'

Stefan spread his hands. 'Is God's work unreasonable, brother? We build a new Jerusalem here and just as our Lord suffered hardship and hostility so should we expect to be subjected to trials in our mission.'

Stefan took a sip of his wine. Rudolf sniffed contemptuously. 'We need money, lord bishop, otherwise the work on Wenden will cease.'

'It is as Brother Rudolf says, lord bishop,' confirmed Berthold.

'Wenden is your most northerly stronghold, lord bishop,' continued Rudolf. 'It is also the most exposed and will be the first target should Lembit once again bring his warriors south. Perhaps we might have a temporary share of the profits from the Dvina trade.'

Stefan was appalled. 'The Dvina trade?'

It was common knowledge that the trade in fur, flax, timber, tar, corns and hides along the Dvina was very lucrative. Many of the goods were sold in the markets of Riga, which were taxed by the bishop.

'Out of the question,' snapped Stefan. 'All taxes raised from trade are directed to the upkeep of the castle and walls, the bishop's palace and the cathedral.'

Berthold leaned back in his chair. 'Cathedral, Archdeacon Stefan?'

'The design is still being finalised but we expect to begin this most worthy project in two or three years.'

'Let us hope that there is still a Riga left in which to build it,' said Rudolf.

Stefan was about to rise to the bait when the bishop raised a hand to still him. 'I sympathise with your position, Master Berthold, but at the moment I cannot release any funds to you. However, you may be fortified by the knowledge that, following the capture of Fellin earlier this year, I have decided to launch another winter campaign against the Estonians. Once Lembit has been destroyed the whole of Estonia will become a Christian land and Wenden will share in its riches.'

Rudolf was about to say what riches but thought better of it. Thus did the meeting come to an end and the Sword Brothers walked back to the castle.

'The bishop exaggerates the wealth of Estonia, I fear,' remarked Berthold.

'Even if it can be conquered in one campaign, which I doubt,' added Rudolf.

'The bishop returns to Lübeck soon,' said Volquin. 'I will go with him to endeavour to raise funds from the merchants of the city. I will prevail upon him to earmark these funds for Wenden. I should be away no longer than three months.'

Berthold and Rudolf went back to Wenden in a boat containing helmets and mail armour for the garrison, which had arrived from Germany on a cog four days earlier. They were a gift from the richest citizens of Magdeburg.

'At least we don't have to pay for them,' sniffed Rudolf.

'Perhaps the grand master's trip will reap a rich harvest,' remarked Berthold.

They were both sitting on chests as the rowers pulled on their oars and the boat glided across the smooth surface of the Gauja.

'Perhaps,' said Rudolf. 'There is another way of raising money.'

Berthold stared at the water in the bottom of the boat. 'That is our last recourse, Rudolf. The bishop would not approve.'

Rudolf laughed. 'No, I don't suppose he would.'

*****

Not all those Oeselians who accompanied Eric to Treiden died. A riverboat full of wounded warriors, the last one to push off from the shore, followed the others downstream. When the crusader pontoon bridge was spotted an order was transmitted to them from Eric to turn around and row upriver to Estonia. He probably realised that the battle at the bridge would be futile and so wanted to save those whose bodies were already wounded and bleeding. Thirty men were in that boat. They rowed up the Gauja and then walked north once they believed they were out of enemy territory. They walked for days, drinking from lakes and streams, stumbling through peat bogs and forests, eating wild berries and occasionally the odd hare they trapped. They lost ten of their number in the first week and another six in the week following. The rest, emaciated and half-dead, eventually stumbled upon an Estonian village where they were disarmed and thrown into a hut. They explained to the village elder that they had fought beside an Estonian leader named Lembit at a place called Treiden. They were lucky: they had wandered into Saccalia – Lembit's own kingdom – and so their wounds were tended. After a few days they were escorted west to the coast where they took boat back to Oesel. But not before another five had succumbed to their wounds.

The surviving nine stood before Olaf in his great oak hall, the king seated on his wooden throne flanked by his remaining sons, his ashen-faced queen beside him. The heavy doors had been closed and guards stood on either side of them and behind the thrones, more guards lining the walls, light provided by small stone lamps hanging from the ceiling, filled with fish liver oil with a lighted wick of cottonweed. The oppressive silence in the hall was broken by the sound of scurrying mice.

Olaf held the pommel of his sword between his legs and turned the great weapon on its point. He stopped and raised his eyes to the line of unshaven, filthy men standing before him.

'So, Eric is dead.'

They nodded. He had been told how they had been ordered to leave by his son and their subsequent travails in Estonia.

'What of Lembit?' asked Olaf.

'He came with his soldiers, majesty,' answered one of them, his eyes cast down. 'And he fought beside us against the crusaders.'

'Is he dead as well?'

The man looked at the others. 'I, we, do not know, majesty. We heard that...'

Olaf stood. 'What did you hear? Answer!'

'It was only a rumour, majesty. But we heard that Lembit wanted to withdraw as soon as we got wind that the crusader relief force had arrived. But the prince...'

Olaf could see that the man was sweating, out of fear of speaking the truth, no doubt. He sat back down and saved the poor wretch the effort.

'But the prince wanted to fight.'

The man swallowed and shook his head. The others murmured their agreement. Olaf waved a hand at them.

'Get out. I will decide what to do with you later.'

They trudged out and the doors were closed. Dalla jumped up and began pacing in front of her husband and sons. Her fists were clenched in anger as she looked at Olaf, though her eyes were moist with tears.

'You should have them executed to show what happens to deserters. And you should send longships against the Estonians to exact vengeance for Eric's death.'

Stark and Kalf were nodding enthusiastically though Sigurd was staring down at the floor and keeping his counsel.

'It is obvious that this Lembit deserted Eric in his hour of need,' spat Dalla, becoming more hysterical by the minute. She stopped and faced Olaf. 'I demand justice for my dead son.'

Olaf stepped forward and embraced his wife as she buried her head in his chest and began weeping. It had all been too much for her and the desire to lash out in her grief was understandable. Olaf called for his wife's women servants, who entered the hall minutes afterwards.

'Take her to our longhouse,' he commanded. He held his wife's face in his hands and kissed her forehead. 'I will be along shortly, after I have discussed with our sons our next course of action.'

'I miss him,' she said softly.

He smiled at her. 'So do I.' He waved the women forward and they led his wife from the hall. Aside from the scratching of the mice silence returned to the hall.

'When do we sail against the Estonians, father?' asked Stark, his eyes burning with the fire of vengeance.

'We will kill all of the Rotalians,' boasted Kalf.

Olaf sighed and caught Sigurd's eye. He walked back to his throne and retook it.

'Sigurd is now my heir,' he announced, 'and you two will speak only when asked to do so,' he rebuked Stark and Kalf. 'Eric died in battle, which I would have thought you would all approve of. Your mother is upset because that is what women do. They weep and wail when their sons are killed. But you are not women. You are princes and should act accordingly. Sigurd, what say you on this?'

'We all grieve Eric's death, father, none more so than me,' said Sigurd. 'But our enemies are the crusaders, not the Estonians.'

Stark laughed derisively.

Sigurd remained calm. 'You may wish to wage war against the Estonians, Stark, but to what end? We know that Lembit honoured his pledge to bring his army to Treiden and now we know that Eric gave battle when it would have been more prudent to withdraw. We should preserve the alliance with the Estonians.'

Stark and Kalf were outraged but Olaf ordered them to be silent.

'We have always raided the Estonian coast,' said Olaf, 'and also sent our longships into the Baltic to plunder shipping. We have never sought allies in the past but now circumstances are different. If the crusaders conquer Estonia then they will turn their eyes towards Oesel. Eric's death has not changed this. We will continue our alliance with Lembit. That is my decision.'

Sigurd nodded his approval as Stark and Kalf fumed in silence.

'What about the deserters?' said Stark, hoping to have vengeance upon them if he was to be denied Estonian blood.

Olaf scratched his beard. 'They will be fed and given time to heal their wounds. We will need all the warriors who can wield a sword in the coming months.' He rose from his throne, a weary look on his face. 'And now I must comfort your mother for the loss of her son.'

They stood as he walked from the hall, the guards opening the doors to allow him to pass. He envied Dalla. His anger at his son's idiocy prevented him from grieving the death of Eric. He could not find it in his heart to forgive him for the loss of nearly a thousand Oeselian warriors.

*****

Lembit looked into the sky and saw a great flock of cranes above, all heading for warmer climes now it was autumn and the icy grip of winter would soon be upon the land.

'Lucky devils,' he muttered, drawing his cloak tighter around him.

He and his men had just been subjected to a heavy rainfall that had drenched them and their ponies. Now he was cold as the grey sky continued to wet them, this time with a tedious drizzle that added to the general gloom. The tops of the trees on the higher ground were wreathed in mist and the ground was sodden. Behind him fifty of his wolf shields rode in silence, the heads of both men and animals bowed in the face of the precipitation.

His strategy of sending raiding parties south had had the desired effect of dispersing the crusader army and thus saving Estonia from an invasion, for this year at least. Unfortunately, rather than congratulating him the leaders of the other tribes had spent the summer sulking over the loss of their men at Treiden. This seething resentment had now manifested itself in a meeting of the tribal chiefs at the great hill fort of Varbola, the stronghold of the Harrien people. Lembit had no option but to attend this 'voluntary' gathering, for not to do so would threaten his position as Grand Warlord, a rank accorded him by the other tribal chiefs. Though only if he gave them an endless string of victories, it appeared.

The track took them through trees stripped of their bark by elk and scratched by wild boar and bears, the forests increasing in size as they travelled further north. Lembit looked at Rusticus riding beside him, who seemed remarkably cheerful considering the adverse weather conditions. Having no feelings was obviously a great advantage in such dreariness.

266

'Tell me, Rusticus,' said Lembit, 'do you think that because the land of the Harrien is so dismal the crusaders will not invade it, preferring regions with more agreeable climes to subjugate?'

Rusticus looked perplexed, his ugly face made more unsightly as a frown creased it. 'I think the crusaders wish to conquer the whole world, lord.'

Lembit was taken aback by his unexpected insight. 'I think you are right. Though the men of iron would undoubtedly rust in such a climate.'

'They will not come in the autumn,' said Rusticus, water dripping off his helmet. 'The land is flooded and too muddy.'

'But it becomes more solid in the winter,' remarked Lembit, 'and I am sure that they will return when the rivers and lakes are frozen.'

'We will be ready for them next time,' said Rusticus defiantly.

'Let us hope that the other tribes will be standing by us,' said Lembit glumly. He looked around at the gloomy forest through which they had been travelling for hours. The land of the Harrien was over a hundred miles from the most northerly crusader fortress and its people no doubt thought that they were safe. His own people, the Saccalians, had once thought that and now the crusaders were on their borders.

'Fools,' spat Lembit.

Rusticus looked at him. 'Lord?'

Lembit shook his head. 'Nothing.'

It took them two more days to reach the great circular hill fort of Varbola, the stronghold of the leader of the Harrien: Alva, which meant 'elf warrior'. Lembit found this most peculiar as he was tall and thin rather than short but he seemed to revel in the name, encouraging his people to believe that he had mythical ancestors. Whether he did was debatable. What was not was the strength of his fortress. Varbola was built on the northern side of a knoll that had the shape of an eagle's beak, beside a huge, brooding forest. Its timber palisade had been erected on an earth rampart fronted with limestone rocks, in front of which was a dry moat that was at least thirty feet wide. The perimeter of the fort was reportedly two thousand feet in extent, wooden towers at regular intervals along its entire length. Alva boasted that Varbola was the biggest, strongest hill fort among all the Estonian tribes, a brag that Lembit believed.

Varbola had two entrances, in the south and east, Lembit and his men entering via the former. They rode through two sets of gates before entering the fort's expansive interior, comprising dozens of huts, a great hall in the centre and stables, storerooms, armouries and smiths around the edge. Above the gates hung great banners bearing Alva's symbol: the lynx.

Lembit walked his pony forward to where Alva and the other chiefs awaited him. He was the last to arrive. Good, it was fitting that they should stand before their supreme leader. The drizzle had finally stopped and the sun was attempting to peak from behind the grey clouds that filled the sky. The fort was filled with the smell of pony dung, cooking fires and charcoal forges.

Lembit slid off his pony as Rusticus did the same to stand beside him, his standard bearer hurrying to take his position behind them. Alva stood with a stupid grin on his face in the middle of the other chiefs. Behind them were the banner men with their standards, though the flags hung limply on their staffs in the windless fort. But Lembit knew them well enough. The boar of the Wierlanders, the Lynx of the Harrien, the bear of the Jerwen, the golden eagle of the Ungannians and the stag of the Rotalians.

Lembit spreads his arms. 'Greetings, brothers. It has been too long since we have all been together.'

Alva stepped forward. 'Hail Lembit, lion of Estonia.' He embraced his ally as the other chiefs walked forward to likewise offer their respects.

The feast that night in Alva's great hall was a magnificent affair, the benches filled with warriors of all the tribes. Lembit was placed next to his host at the top table, flanked by the other leaders as their men gorged themselves on great quantities of bean soup, pig's head broth, roasted pork, cheese and rye bread. They drank huge amounts of beer and honey mead and as the evening wore on arguments and fights broke out among the assembled host. No weapons were drawn as only the chiefs were allowed to wear their swords in Alva's hall, but plenty of noses were broken as men slugged it out in drunken bouts before their cheering comrades. Afterwards the antagonists invariably swore eternal friendship and embraced each other before either staggering back to their seats or passing out and being dragged outside and doused with cold water.

Lembit indulged in polite conversation with the other chiefs, finding the evening agreeable enough but knowing that the real business would begin the next morning. And so it was, as slaves cleared away the vomit, beer and food encrusted reeds from the floors and replaced them with fresh ones, that the chiefs gathered once more in the hall to discuss matters of strategy. It was a curious thing that among the drunken brawls and raucous behaviour bread was never thrown or stepped on at feasts, being considered sacred by Estonians.

268

Rusticus belched loudly and sat his great bulk on a bench, head in his hands at the table. He looked pale and about to vomit, his shirt drenched after he had emptied a bucket of water over his head in the courtyard in an attempt to freshen himself up.

The tall 'elf warrior' was already in his hall, accompanied by his stocky, barrel-chested champion who also looked the worse for wear. The other chiefs began to arrive: Edvin, leader of the Wierlanders, round faced with a mop of curly blonde hair; Jaak of the Jerwen, a man with a narrow face and untrusting eyes; and the hard, uncompromising Kalju of the Ungannians. It meant 'rock' and was most apt. Finally there was Nigul, chief of the Rotalians, a thoughtful individual who looked more like a holy man with his thinning white hair and wild blue eyes.

The doors of the hall had been open but the room still stank of sweat, vomit and beer from the previous evening. Slaves cleared away the tables and benches, stacking them against the walls and then bringing high-backed chairs that Alva ordered be arranged in a circle near the fire burning in the central stone hearth, smoke drifting up to the vent in the roof.

The chiefs sat facing each other with their subordinates behind them. Slaves finished scattering fresh reeds on the floor and then disappeared to the kitchens to fetch refreshments. In the morning it was customary for the leftovers from the night before to be heated up, supplemented by fresh bread and Baltic herring on the side. Lembit refused anything to eat but did take a cup of warm milk offered him. He glanced behind him and saw Rusticus heartily tucking in to a platter heaped with food. The man had the constitution of an ox.

Lembit decided to cut to the chase. 'My friends, I assume you requested this gathering because you have something to say concerning our war with the crusaders.'

Alva smiled politely. 'Some of us believe that, following the reverse at Treiden, it might be better to seek an accommodation with the crusaders rather than continuing hostilities.'

It was amazing how a single reverse could lead to an outbreak of defeatism. Were these the great warlords of Estonia? Lembit nodded gravely. 'It is, of course, the prerogative of each tribe to look after its own interests, and no chief would put the interests of the Estonian race above those of his own people. However, if we do not stand together then we shall surely fall one by one.'

'Not if we have peace with the crusaders,' said Edvin.

Lembit smiled at him. 'The crusaders wish to subjugate the whole of Estonia, to turn it into another Livonia where their religion spreads over the land like a plague. They have been ordered to do this by their great leader.'

'You mean the Bishop of Riga?' said Jaak.

'No,' answered Lembit. 'Their supreme leader is called a pope and he lives in another land. It is he who sends ships filled with crusaders to our land who burn our villages and kill and enslave our people. He views us as heathens to be either wiped out or enslaved.'

'You do not offer much hope,' remarked Jaak, his dark eyes narrowing on Lembit.

'There is hope in unity,' said Lembit.

'Under your leadership,' scowled Kalju.

Lembit feigned a hurt expression. 'If you all wish to elect another grand warlord then I will readily accept your decision.'

'We wish for peace, Lembit,' said Nigul.

'Of course you do, we all do,' replied Lembit. 'But I believe that we can achieve peace through strength not negotiation. If we make the crusaders fight for every inch of ground they wish to take, if we raid their lands just as they raid ours, and if we enlist allies just as they bring foreigners to our lands, then I believe that eventually they will have no choice but to accept that they will never master us.'

'By allies you mean the Oeselians,' said Alva.

Lembit nodded. 'I do.'

'Many among my people are unhappy that we fight beside Olaf,' said Alva.

Lembit sighed. Each Estonian village had an elder who sat on a council of elders formed when villages banded together into districts, who elected one of their number to sit on a provincial council made up of several districts. When a chief wanted to raise an army all he had to do was to alert his provincial councils, which would muster the men of their districts. However, this chain of councils could also be a never-ending source of complaints and grumbling, especially if a chief was prepared to listen to them.

'What of your people, Nigul?' asked Lembit. 'Are they unhappy that their villages are no longer raided by the Oeselians, or that the spectre of longships along their shores no longer presages death and destruction?'

'They are pleased that the sea no longer brings death,' agreed Nigul.

'We cannot have endless war,' pleaded Edvin.

270

'My people are first to feel the wrath of the crusaders,' added Kalju. 'Ungannia is on their frontier.'

Lembit stood and spread his arms. 'As is Saccalia. It is my people who are the first to experience the fire and sword of the crusaders. And yet we do not flinch from the struggle. If my kingdom falls then your people will be next, Jaak.' He pointed at Kalju. 'If Saccalia falls then you will have the crusaders on your southern and western borders. Do you want that, Kalju?'

The Ungannian chief frowned. 'What do *you* want, Lembit?'

Lembit regained his chair. 'Another year. Give me another year and if the crusaders have not been halted then I will stand aside and another can become grand warlord.'

The fire crackled and spat as the chiefs pondered his offer. They all desired peace but knew that Lembit was right. The Saccalians were the largest and most warlike among the Estonian people. If they were conquered then the crusaders would undoubtedly be emboldened to continue their expansion north. But if they could be stopped…

'Another year, I agree,' said Alva.

'As do I,' added Edvin.

Jaak was unhappy but nodded his assent.

'You have your year,' said Kalju.

'And the peace with the Oeselians will hold?' asked Nigul.

Lembit smiled triumphantly. 'Of course, brother,' he said, not knowing what Olaf would do following the defeat at Treiden.

'Then I too grant you another year,' replied Nigul.

The journey back to Lehola was made through intermittent rain and drizzle but Lembit was more cheerful than he had been during the trip to Varbola. He had the continued support of the other tribes, albeit grudgingly, and his raiding parties had kept the crusaders occupied in their own kingdom, which had kept them away from Estonian lands. When he arrived at his stronghold he found a letter from Sigurd, Olaf's son, waiting for him. In answer to his own missive the Oeselians pledged their continuing support in the war against the Bishop of Riga.

The autumn was nearing its end and the first frosts were whitening the land. Lembit sat in his hall and contemplated the future. The beginning of the year had witnessed the fall of his fort at Fellin, and his venture against Caupo had come to naught. But the year was ending with the Estonian tribes still united under his leadership and the alliance with the Oeselians intact. He doubted whether the crusaders would attempt another winter assault upon Fellin, which he had anyway strengthened. For the first time in a while he was optimistic about the future.

Chapter 11

'You hair is like a goat.'

Daina looked at Conrad and suppressed a laugh. When he had arrived at her father's village following a hunting trip in the company of Thalibald and Rameke he had insisted on conversing in her native tongue. He had spent hours with Ilona learning words, sentences and phrases and now he was determined to put his learning into practice. The hunting trip had been a great success, Thalibald's men laying out the game they had killed earlier in front of his hall for his villagers to admire. Ever since Conrad had assisted in the rescue of the women when the menfolk were away, he and the other boys had been held in high regard by the chief, his sons and their warriors. Thalibald had invited them to hunt and stay as his guests for the night, though to ensure they did not over-indulge in revelry Lukas and Rudolf had accompanied them.

Now they stood with the Sword Brothers and admired their handiwork with the crossbow. Rameke had killed the most with his bow but Conrad reckoned his total of two roe deer was more than adequate to satisfy expectations. The Liv warriors arranged the day's kills in a long line: boars, elk, deer, bears and lynx. It had been a wonderful day and now he conversed with his beloved Daina in her own language.

'You have the eyes of a rat.'

Daina scowled, Lukas looked at Conrad as though he was possessed by madness and Rudolf shook his head.

Hans nudged Anton in the ribs. 'Conrad has learnt to speak the language of the Livs.'

Conrad grasped the hilt of his sword. 'My sword is always at your lake.'

'Perhaps it would be better if we spoke in your language,' Daina said to him in flawless German.

But Conrad was adamant. 'No, no. I have learnt your forest especially.'

Hans, Anton and Johann, not knowing what their companion was saying but being impressed nevertheless, stood in awed silence as Conrad spoke the strange words.

Daina smiled at him. 'I really think we should speak in your language, Conrad.'

'Ilona has taught me many baskets,' said Conrad with pride.

'Which he has mostly forgotten,' said Rudolf in excellent Liv. Daina put a finger to her mouth to hush him.

'Speak German, Conrad,' said Lukas. 'You make a fool of yourself.'

Conrad frowned but did as he was told as the dead animals were taken away to the kitchens where they would be prepared for the evening feast. As he said a temporary farewell to Daina and followed Hans and the others to the hut that had been set aside for them, he reflected on the strange turn his life had taken. Not so long ago he had been a poor orphan but now he had learnt to use a sword and was on his way to becoming a fully trained soldier. He had also learnt another language and had won the heart of a local beauty. Every day he prayed for his parents and his sister Marie and God had answered his prayers. He felt genuinely happy and looked forward to what the future held for him.

*****

The banks of the Dvina were now turning brown and red as the trees began to show their autumn colours. The days were shortening but it was still relatively warm, the harsh winter some time off yet. The surface of the river was like a black mirror, the current mild and the wind weak. Prince Vsevolod was glad for that at least as the rowers of his boat pulled on their oars to propel it through the smooth water. Behind were another two boats, one containing fifty of his bodyguard, his boat containing an additional score of warriors, the other a gift for the bishop. He might profess to be a friend of the bishop but he did not trust the Sword Brothers' garrisons in the castles he had to pass on his way to Riga: Kokenhusen, Lennewarden, Uexkull and Holm. He also had men looking towards the southern shore where Prince Stecse and his Lithuanians might be tempted to attack his small flotilla. His nerves were frayed to say the least for the river was packed with other vessels carrying goods to the markets in Riga, and others returning to Gerzika and Polotsk with wares they had purchased in the crusader town: iron, salt, woollen cloth and wine. He thought every vessel was full of potential assassins but they turned out to contain nothing but goods and ugly, stinking sailors and traders. It was a most curious thing. Of all the things that roamed the Russian lands the Catholics coveted the fur of the grey squirrel most. Squirrel fur was inexpensive when compared to sable and marten and so was in great demand. Thus the princes of northern Russia became rich from harvesting the fur of the grey squirrel. They exported other commodities of course, such as fox fur, honey and wax, but squirrel fur was the jewel in their crown.

It was the first time he had visited Riga and was surprised by the size of the harbour area with its great warehouses and long jetties and the height of the town's walls. The crusaders liked to use stone to build their strongholds whereas the Livs, Estonians and Russians used timber for their fortresses. He had never seen Archdeacon Stefan, though the two had conversed with each other by letter on many occasions, but now the Catholic priest stood on a jetty as Vsevolod's boat glided towards him, the prince shielding his eyes as the sun dipped in the west. Soldiers in mail and helmets flanked the priest, each one armed with a spear and sword and carrying long shields emblazoned with a cross keys symbol.

Vsevolod's rowers pulled in their oars as one of his bodyguard threw a rope to a soldier on the jetty who tied it around a wooden post. Another rope secured the stern of the boat as it was pulled alongside and Stefan stepped forward, a flattering smile on his face.

'Greetings, Prince Vsevolod. Welcome to Riga.'

The Russian smiled back and then two of his bodyguard assisted him onto the jetty. The other two boats had pulled in behind the jetty as Stefan and Vsevolod walked towards the town. When they reached one of the boats Vsevolod stopped and indicated to one of the crew to loosen the ropes that secured a canvas covering.

'A gift for the bishop,' said Vsevolod as the sailor removed the canvas to reveal two pallets heaped high with fox fur.

Stefan's eyes lit up. 'A most lavish gift, prince. The bishop will be most pleased by your generosity.' He had a feeling that he would get on with this richly attired Russian prince.

Vsevolod was accommodated in the bishop's palace, his men being allocated quarters in the castle where Grand Master Volquin raised an eyebrow at the sudden appearance of a host of bearded brutes clad in mail and all heavily armed. Stefan had not informed him of the invitation he had extended to Vsevolod. He found the Order of Sword Brothers irksome and coarse. The bishop had created them to butcher pagans not to indulge in matters of diplomacy. For this reason he did not invite Volquin to the meal that he shared with Vsevolod later that evening. He was rather perturbed that the prince insisted that four of his brutish soldiers stand behind him for the whole meal, but after a while forgot that they were there as the wine and conversation flowed.

'The bishop has returned to Germany for the winter,' said Stefan, 'leaving me in charge of his affairs.'

Vsevolod raised his wine flagon. 'He leaves his kingdom in most capable hands.'

Stefan was warming to the Russian by the minute. 'How can I be of assistance to you, lord prince?'

'As you know I am married to the daughter of Grand Duke Daugerutis,' said Vsevolod.

'A mating of eagles,' gushed Stefan.

Vsevolod suddenly looked very serious. 'I have to tell you that the grand duke is most unhappy concerning events north of the River Dvina.'

Stefan gulped some wine. 'Oh?'

'Before the bishop came the grand duke waged war against the prince of Novgorod, the man who frequently raided Lithuanian lands. But now the crusaders bar his way and prevent him seeking rightful retribution against this plunderer. I have tried to temper his wrath and thirst for revenge, but have found it increasingly difficult of late. In addition, many of the grand duke's more warlike and less intelligent chiefs strain at the leash to prove themselves against the crusaders. The assault upon Kokenhusen is but a foretaste of things to come, I fear.'

Stefan looked alarmed. 'Is there nothing to be done?'

Vsevolod held up his hands. 'Fear not. The grand duke is prepared to enter into a formal truce with the bishop.'

Relief swept through Stefan. 'Excellent.'

Vsevolod held up one hand. '*If* he is allowed to cross the Dvina to make war upon Novgorod.'

'The bishop would not tolerate a Lithuanian army marching through his territory,' said Stefan glumly.

'He has nothing to fear on that matter, archdeacon. The grand duke would cross at Gerzika and march through my own territory. His concern is that if he did so then the crusaders would ambush him during his return journey.'

Stefan toyed with the gold cross hanging around his neck. 'And the grand duke has no designs on the bishop's lands?'

'None at all. The assault against Kokenhusen was carried out by a troublesome chief name Stecse and was done so without the grand duke's knowledge. As soon as I heard I marched my army to its relief so outraged was I.'

Stefan toasted him. 'The bishop is most grateful that he has such a brave and loyal ally.'

Vsevolod leaned forward. 'If I can have an official document stating that the bishop has no objection to my father-in-law crossing the Dvina to make war against Novgorod, then I can guarantee that your southern border will be peaceful and secure.'

Vsevolod knew that he had cornered his prey. Now it was time to snare it.

'As a sign of his goodwill, the grand duke is also prepared to send an expedition against the Kurs. He knows that they have proved troublesome to the bishop.'

Stefan brought his hands together. 'I think I can say that the bishop will find these terms acceptable.'

'And I can tell the grand duke that when he returns he will draw up a document that will give his assent?'

Stefan leaned back in his well-appointed chair. 'You will be able to take said document with you tomorrow if you wish. I am the bishop's deputy and have been entrusted with his seal.'

This was better than Vsevolod could have hoped for. 'Then I can say with certainty, my lord archdeacon, that you have achieved not only peace along the Dvina but also gained a new ally in Grand Duke Daugerutis.'

Vsevolod left the next afternoon, in his hand a vellum document bearing the seal of Riga giving his father-in-law permission to cross the Dvina to attack Novgorod. It stipulated that the Lithuanians were to agree to a two-year peace with the bishop, in return for which the Kurs were to be punished by Grand Duke Daugerutis.

It had been a most profitable journey. His new found friendship with Archdeacon Stefan meant he had influence with the Bishop of Riga, which also meant that he had leverage over his father-in-law. More importantly, if the Lithuanians attacked Novgorod then his powerful Russian northern neighbour might be weakened, allowing him to seize some of their territory. If God really looked on him favourably then the grand duke might even be killed fighting the Novgorodians, resulting in him gaining substantial territory to the south of the Dvina when his wife gained her inheritance. A most profitable journey indeed.

*****

Christmas at Wenden was a joyous affair. Thalibald and his family were invited to celebrate the birth of Christ at the castle. The beautiful Daina wrapped in furs arrived in a horse-drawn sledge. After a moving service in a packed chapel, the

Sword Brothers gave a great feast in the dining hall at which the brother knights, sergeants and Conrad and the other boys served the civilian families their Christmas meal of cooked goose. The mercenaries manned the ramparts, Master Berthold having promised them double pay for doing so.

Thalibald and his family sat on the top table in the dining hall, Master Berthold and Rudolf serving them their food. Conrad had begged Rudolf to be allowed to help him serve at the top table and he had assented. He thus became Daina's personal servant, hovering over her like a mother hen as she ate her meal, giggled with her mother and smiled at Conrad. He brought a jug of hot wassail, a strong drink that was a mixture of ale, honey and spices, her cheeks becoming flushed as the alcohol took effect.

Usually the dining hall was quiet when the brother knights and sergeants ate their meals but today it was turmoil as families chatted loudly and children squealed in delight as they were served with hot mince pies filled with shredded meat.

Conrad placed one before Daina, who looked up at him with sparkling green eyes.

'What is this?'

'It is a mince pie,' said Conrad. 'They are filled with meat and cooked in oblong trays to represent Christ's crib. The meat is spiced with cinnamon, cloves and nutmeg to represent the three gifts given to Christ by the Magi. The Magi are…'

'The three kings from the East who came to pay homage to Christ after his birth. Yes, I know,' replied Daina.

She turned up her nose at the boar's head that was served to her father by Master Berthold but otherwise had a delightful time and was enchanted by Conrad's attentiveness.

In the kitchens the boys took sips from the cauldrons where the cooks were preparing the wassail, and after a while all of them were quite merry. Conrad stood in the door that led to the kitchens, admiring Daina from afar.

'Are you glad you came to Livonia, Conrad?' asked Rudolf behind him.

'Yes, Brother Rudolf,' beamed Conrad.

'I believe that God brought you here for a purpose, Conrad, though it might not be the one you currently believe it to be.'

'Yes, Brother Rudolf,' the boy replied.

Rudolf shook his head and took the tray of cups he was holding into the hall. Conrad was not listening. He was dreaming of the life he would have with Daina, the chief's daughter whom he was falling in love with. He imagined them living together in between his time when he was fighting the foes of the Sword Brothers. In his boyish innocence he imagined that he could have both Daina and wear the white mantle of the order. He did not realise that wanting and having were too entirely different things. But for the moment he stared and dreamed of things that might be.

'Conrad Wolff, get your lazy arse here,' shouted one of the cooks, a man who looked like an ogre and had a temper to match. Conrad smiled, turned and went back into the kitchens to continue his duties as a serving boy.

Three weeks later he was sitting on a pony in the company of the other boys, ten brother knights, thirty sergeants and a dozen mounted crossbowmen, including leather face. Conrad and his companions wore their gambesons, kettle helmets and were fully armed with lances, swords and daggers, their shields slung over their backs. The latter were painted white but did not bear the insignia of the Sword Brothers, as they were not yet members of the order. They also wore white cloaks around their shoulders and mittens on their hands for it was bitterly cold. There was no wind and the sun in the cloudless sky made the snow-covered terrain around the castle dazzlingly white, forcing Conrad to squint in the brightness when he peered between the gaps in the still-low-lying walls at the landscape beyond.

They stood in the courtyard waiting for Rudolf to emerge from the master's hall to lead them on their expedition, though no one knew precisely what is was. The week before a large force of crusaders had passed through Wenden on its way north into Estonia. They took with them no siege engines and carried supplies on packhorses. Master Thaddeus had told the boys that they were going solely to pillage and burn in retaliation for the previous year's raids by Lembit's forces, as well as his attack against Caupo. The latter had also appeared at Wenden, stopping only a day before similarly marching north with a horde of his warriors, including Thalibald and his men. Conrad was relieved to learn that Rameke had stayed behind with a contingent of warriors to guard the villages and womenfolk. Thus would Daina be out of harm's way. But he was confused as to why the garrison of Wenden had not gone north with the crusaders and Sword Brothers from other castles.

'Perhaps we are not going north,' opined Hans sitting on the pony beside him.

'Then where are we going?' said Conrad.

'Across the river,' said Anton with conviction, not really knowing what lay in that direction.

Henke turned in his saddle. 'Quiet. Your incessant gossiping is getting on my nerves.'

'We were just wondering where we are going, Brother Henke?' said Johann.

'You will know when we arrive,' snapped Henke. 'Now be silent.'

'Definitely over the river,' said Anton in a hushed voice.

Each of them held the reins of a pony loaded with supplies for the journey, as did the sergeants – tents, food, spare clothing, medical supplies, crossbow bolts, spare lances and shields. Conrad began to feel his nose get cold as he sat in the saddle, his breath misting and his pony snorting in boredom. Eventually Master Berthold walked from his hall into the courtyard in the company of Rudolf and a man Conrad had never seen before. He was dressed in furs with a felt hat pulled down over his face to obscure his features. All three walked to their ponies and took to their saddles, then trotted over the cobbles to where the gatehouse would eventually stand, across the bridge and down into the compound. The brother knights followed them, after which came the sergeants, crossbowmen and Conrad and his companions.

The column rode out the gates in the perimeter wall and swung left to ride east towards the snow-covered quarry that was now dormant until the spring came. They trotted along the track until they had ridden halfway through a forest of pine and spruce, then left the trail to head into the trees, all the while being led by the mysterious stranger swathed in furs. No one spoke, the only sound being the breathing of the ponies, the crunching of their hooves in the snow and the jangling of their bits. Of the brother knights, Lukas had stayed behind at Wenden to assume command of the garrison. Walter also remained at the castle, Conrad hearing a rumour that he would not approve of the expedition, though he did not know what this meant.

For two days they travelled through forests, by the side of frozen lakes and across snow-covered meadows between gently rolling hills, the guide leading the column through a land empty of people. Wolves snarled at them from the treeline and occasionally a lynx or fox would be seen scurrying through the deep snow. At night Master Berthold and Rudolf could be seen huddling round a fire in the company of the guide, who had shoulder-length fair hair and wore a gold torc around his neck. Conrad asked about him but Henke gave him short shrift, telling him to attend to his duties and keep his nose out of the order's business. So he and the other boys sat outside their tent guessing who the man was and what they were doing in this bleak land.

'Perhaps we are going to kill Lembit,' offered Anton.

'We are too few to fight the leader of the Estonians,' said Conrad.

'What did Henke say when you asked him?' queried Hans.

'He's like a bear with a sore head. You won't get anything out of him.'

'This must be a raid of some sort,' suggested Johann, though when questioned about the precise nature of such an enterprise he had no answers.

They found out the next day when they were ordered to leave the tents where they were and assemble in the middle of the camp. The brother knights, sergeants and crossbowmen also gathered around Master Berthold, Rudolf and the mysterious stranger standing behind him.

'I will make this short,' said the castellan of Wenden. 'Today we assault an Estonian village. Our intention is to take prisoners: women, girls and young boys. Kill all those capable of bearing arms but do not harm the rest.' He pointed at the crossbowmen, some of whom were rubbing their hands in anticipation of loot. 'Any plunder of value will be surrendered to me after the assault. Anyone who indulges in rape will be hanged.'

Leather face wore a hurt expression. 'No rape?'

Berthold looked at him contemptuously. 'The women, young girls, infants and young boys are to be captured unharmed and unsullied. I will personally behead anyone I see acting in a depraved manner.'

'What about the old women?' asked leather face.

Master Berthold looked at him as though he was attempting levity. 'The old women?'

'Yes,' replied leather face, deadly serious, 'can we rape them as you don't want them?'

There was a ripple of laughter among his comrades.

'Silence!' shouted Berthold. 'There will be no raping. Obey your orders and pray to God that He may forgive you for your depravity.'

'Pray that He keeps my aim true, more like,' sneered leather face.

Master Berthold glowered at him but thereafter ignored him as he gave the orders for the raid. The mounted brother knights were to attack the village, which was an hour's walk away, to create a diversion while the sergeants and crossbowmen would assault on foot.

'Brother Henke will take charge of the novices,' said Master Berthold in conclusion.

Though they knew how to shoot a crossbow Conrad and his companions were armed with their swords and shields for the raid. They left their cloaks in camp as they walked with Henke in the rear of the column of sergeants and crossbowmen.

The packhorses and ponies in camp were tethered to branches with several fires having been lit around its perimeter to keep predators away, two crossbowmen being left behind just to make sure.

Henke was in a foul mood as he walked through the snow, not only because he was not mounted like the rest of the brother knights but because he also objected to being a nursemaid to the novices. The riders took a wide detour to the village, which was located in the middle of a broad valley between two great woods. A frozen lake lay south of the settlement and to the north lay another large expanse of evergreen trees.

After less than an hour the party on foot was approaching the lake and Henke gave the order to deploy into line and to stay silent. Conrad took the shield off his back and slid his left arm through the leather straps and gripped the last one. He drew his sword, crouched low and began to walk forward. He glanced left at Hans who nodded, then right at Anton and Johann, both of them staring ahead. The crossbowmen formed a thin vanguard in front of the sergeants, the boys being on the left flank of the line, nearest to the lake.

Their approach was silent as they stepped through the snow. Ahead Conrad could see no movement in the snow-covered village. It was two hours after dawn. Perhaps the villagers were still asleep. They were around five hundred paces away when dogs suddenly started barking.

'Move,' shouted Henke.

Shouts were heard coming from the village and then, further away, the sound of drums. Conrad looked at a perplexed Hans. He felt his heart pounding in his chest as he broke into a brisk walk. It was impossible to run in the snow that came up to his ankles, and he noticed the sergeants and crossbowmen were still walking but were talking longer and higher steps to avoid toppling over. They had closed to within three hundred paces of the village now and it appeared to comprise many huts of varying size. The biggest was a tall longhouse with an arched roof that seemed to be in the centre of the settlement.

The mounted brother knights had made a wide diversion through the trees so they could assault the village from the north. Two of their number carried drums of stretched skinheads that had a brass hook so they could be hung from their belts. They began banging the drums as they approached the village, the riders extending into a line with pennants fluttering from their lances. The noise had the desired effect: the menfolk of the village poured from their huts and deployed into a small shield wall in front of the village. And all the while the foot soldiers approached silently and unseen from the south.

The crossbowmen had been members of the garrison for a long time and they knew the tactics of the Sword Brothers. Henke gave the signal and the sergeants divided into small groups, each one accompanied by two crossbowmen as they entered the village.

'You stay close to me,' Henke hissed to the boys as they reached the first hut. Ahead Conrad could hear the shouts of the village's warriors as they rallied around their chief in the shield wall. The drums were still sounding as the horses of brother knights continued to approach the village at a slow walk.

The foot soldiers moved stealthily through the huts that had their doors fastened shut. They reached the chief's great hut and swept around it to head for the northern end of the village. Conrad estimated that the settlement must have numbered fifty huts at least. He hoped they had enough soldiers to fight the villagers. He followed Henke along frozen muddy paths, past squat sheds and empty animal pens, the occupants having long since been slaughtered to proved food for the inhabitants. Then they were at the northern extend of the settlement, beyond which stood a group of warriors standing with their backs to the village, shields locked as they waited to receive the charge of the brother knights, who had now halted some three hundred paces from them. The drummers continued to hit the skins of their instruments to keep the Estonians focused on them as the crossbowmen reformed into a line with the sergeants behind them. Henke fell in at the extreme left of the line of sergeants, Conrad and the other boys behind him.

In the rear of the Estonian shield wall, which must have numbered at least sixty men, were dogs held on leashes that would be released at the riders when they made their charge. But now the beasts began barking at the foot soldiers that had appeared behind them, causing their masters to turn round and spot Henke's party. Then the crossbowmen began shooting.

In thirty seconds they shot twenty quarrels before the Estonians had a chance to respond. In the next thirty seconds they shot a further twenty bolts that killed the dogs and also their owners. Some of the warriors broke ranks and ran at the crossbowmen, tripping in the snow and falling over. When they jumped up they were hit by quarrels and collapsed again. Conrad watched leather face load, shoot his crossbow and then reload it again, untroubled by the enraged warriors who had now turned around and locked shields. Bolts slammed into wooden shields. The crossbowmen stopped shooting and retired behind the sergeants, who now walked forward with swords drawn, shields held in front of them.

The Estonians, armed with a variety of axes, spears, clubs and only a few swords, had forgotten about the mounted knights as they shuffled forward to give battle to the footmen who had appeared behind them. But now Master Berthold and his men dug their spurs into the ponies and charged forward. They never achieved more than a quick trot in the snow but within no time they were at the rear of the shield wall, plunging their lances into Estonian backs and then drawing their swords to hack at the enemy.

'Now!' screamed Henke as he and sergeants charged at the shield wall. The Estonians, their shields overlapping as they inched forward, had not expected the outnumbered men in mail and white surcoats to attack but that is what they now did.

Conrad screamed and ran after Henke as cries came from the rear of the shield wall as the brother knights began cutting down Estonians. The latter might have included a few men who had battle experience but most were poor farmers who spent their lives toiling on the land. Attacked from the front and rear, what little discipline and order they might have possessed evaporated in the face of the Sword Brother assault.

The Estonian shield wall fell apart as Henke and the sergeants ran at it, held their shields in front of them to block axe blows and spear thrusts and then plunged their swords into faces and necks. Only a few villagers wore helmets, the rest either fighting bare headed or wearing leather skullcaps for protection. But they offered little defence, particularly from the downward strikes of the brother knights.

A warrior ran at Conrad, a man in a shirt and leggings with no headgear and armed with only a spear. He jumped to the right, brushed away the spear with his shield and then cut down with his sword to slice open the man's left calf. The Estonian howled in pain and collapsed on the ground. He was silenced as Hans thrust his sword down to sever his spinal cord.

The fight had now degenerated into a series of single combats, Henke being surrounded by three men wielding axes determined to hack him to pieces. He killed the man facing him when he chopped the shaft of his adversary's axe with his sword and then rammed the end of his cross guard into the man's eye. Spinning round, the other two ran at him, axes raised above their heads. He jumped to the right and swung his sword as they passed, cutting into the skull of one. He ignored him and ran at the last villager, barging into him with his shield and driving the point of his sword forward with such force that it went through the man's shield and into his

284

guts. He released the hilt and the Estonian collapsed to the ground, blood oozing from his belly. Henke placed a foot on the pierced shield on top of his body and yanked his sword free, then walked over to the man with the gashed head. He sheathed his sword, drew his dagger and slit his throat.

The fighting was over now. The last to fall was the village chief with a few loyal men around him, cut down by the crossbowmen. Sergeants went among the dead and wounded and dispatched the latter with their daggers. The riders did not enter the village but rather hunted down those men who tried to reach the safety of the trees, circling the settlement and heading off the fleeing warriors.

Henke pointed at Conrad and the other boys.

'You are with me.'

He walked back into the village and began banging on doors, ordering the occupants to show themselves. Or at least that is what Conrad thought as he was speaking in Estonian. He pointed at Conrad and Hans.

'You two make yourself useful and turf out those inside the huts. And keep alert. Just because their menfolk are dead doesn't mean that the women are not dangerous.'

He then pointed at Anton and Johann. 'You two as well. Get moving.'

Obviously his bout of slaughter had not improved Henke's humour as he went inside a hut and hauled out the occupants – a young woman and an old hag – and threw them to the ground. Anton kicked in a door and fell back as he was hit in the face by a wooden stool. A plumpish woman stood in the doorway with the seat in her hand.

'Stupid bitch.' Anton ran his sword through her body and kicked her back inside the hut.

Henke saw what had happened as Johann went to the side of his friend with his shield raised and sword at the ready.

'What did I tell you?' Henke said to Anton.

'She hit me, brother.'

Henke sheathed his sword and struck Anton across the face with the back of his hand. 'I want them all alive.'

He grabbed Anton by the scruff of the neck and threw him into the hut. He turned to Johann. 'Move, idiot.'

Conrad went into the hut and saw a terrified young woman huddled in the corner holding two infants. Tears were streaming down her face and she was shaking with fear. He looked at Hans.

285

'This is wrong.'

'We have our orders, Conrad.' His fear of Henke was overriding any doubts he may have had regarding the right or wrong of his actions. Conrad sighed and pointed at the woman, sheathing his sword and gesturing her to come forward.

'Please.'

She did not understand what he was saying but did understand what was required of her when Henke walked in, grabbed her by the hair and pulled her outside. She was still clutching the babies who began to wail as their mother was taken to the open space in front of the chief's hut where the other villagers were being gathered. There were about seventy of them, all in various stages of distress. Young, terrified children clinging to their mothers and elderly couples seeking solace in each other's arms. They huddled together as crossbowmen and sergeants stood guard over them.

Conrad stood by the young mother and her two screeching babies, his shield over his back, his sword in its scabbard.

Henke pointed at her. 'Shut her up.'

Conrad knew that something very wrong was occurring and resented having to be a part of it. He was just a novice but the sermons he had listened to in the chapel every week had made a deep impression upon him, particularly the notion of Christian charity.

'Do it yourself,' he heard himself say.

Hans, Anton and Johann looked aghast at him as Henke stomped over.

'What did you say?'

Conrad, though nervous, stood his ground. 'Threatening babies will have no effect.'

Henke moved closer, his sneering face inches from Conrad's. 'Are you disobeying me, *boy*?'

'No, brother,' replied Conrad, 'it is just that...'

Henke slapped Conrad's face hard with the back of his hand, nearly knocking him over. Rage flowed through Conrad and without thinking he stepped back and drew his sword. Henke laughed and drew his blade and Conrad prepared to die.

'Henke!

Rudolf jumped from his saddle and walked over to place himself between Henke and Conrad, facing the former.

'Put away your swords. Both of you.'

Conrad did so instantly but for a few seconds Henke hesitated before sniffing and sheathing his blade.

Master Berthold frowned and then announced to the Estonians in their own tongue that they would not be harmed but that they had to leave with him. There were wails and more outbreaks of crying but Berthold shouted at them to be quiet and ordered them to leave the village immediately. The women and children did not have their hands bound as it was unlikely that they would attempt to escape, especially the ones carrying infants, though the five boys aged ten and over were tethered. Then the captives were herded away to the south, towards the Sword Brother camp. The brother knights gave up their ponies for the youngest children to save them having to trek through the snow. Henke was the last to leave, keeping Conrad and the other boys behind to guard the score of elderly Estonians who had been captured in the village.

'What shall we do with them?' he asked Rudolf brusquely

'What do you suggest?'

Henke looked at Conrad with an evil grin. 'Lock them in a hut and burn them.'

'I think not,' said Rudolf. 'We will leave them here.'

Henke curled his lip. 'You are getting soft. The Rudolf of old would not have batted an eyelid at killing them.'

Rudolf sighed. 'We are warriors of Christ now, Henke, so do as you are told.'

Henke turned to the boys. 'Move!'

Two hours later Conrad was cooking porridge to feed the captives, who had been placed in the spare tents that the raiding party had brought. The temperature was dropping rapidly and Master Berthold was most insistent that the prisoners be fed and issued with blankets. Conrad went among the morose Estonians, offering them bowls of hot porridge. The women took the food but avoided his eyes as they fed their children and wrapped the blankets around them. He felt utterly miserable.

Later, when he was standing guard duty, his cloak wrapped around him and his breath misting in the icy night air, he encountered Rudolf making his rounds. In the distance wolves were howling, their mournful cries causing the infants in camp to cry. But there was no movement among the trees, though Conrad knew the beasts were studying the camp from afar.

'All is well?' enquired Rudolf. Conrad nodded.

Rudolf stood beside the young novice.

'You disagree with the actions taken in the village?'

Conrad stared into the blackness of the forest. 'It is not my place to question the decision of Master Berthold.'

'Answer the question, Conrad. Your attempt at cleverness makes you look foolish.'

'Last summer,' said Conrad, 'Brother Lukas led a party that rescued Liv womenfolk who had been captured by the Estonians. Bruno died in that operation. That was a good day. But now we take women and children ourselves and in doing so become as base as the pagans. That cannot be right.'

'You are correct, Conrad. It is not right,' said Rudolf. 'And yet circumstances force us to experience the bitter taste of expediency. All you need to know is that our actions are to safeguard the future of Wenden and therefore the whole of Livonia.'

'I do not understand.'

Rudolf sighed. 'You will one day.'

'What would God say?'

'Pagans are unbelievers,' replied Rudolf, 'and can be treated accordingly. Or so says the Church. Suffice to say that I take no pleasure in what we have done but I have a duty to my order. I hope God understands.'

Conrad nodded but thought that it was wrong to take women and children from their homes. What would be done with them? He was just a novice and thus his opinion did not matter. But he thought of his mother and sister and was uneasy. Then he thought of how he had annoyed Henke and felt even more uncomfortable.

It took three days to get back to Wenden. Three days of listening to wailing women, crying babies and enduring the freezing cold. On the second day it began to snow and Master Berthold ordered that all the captives were to be issued with cloaks, which meant that Conrad and his companions had to give up theirs, as did the brother knights.

Hans, who did not have an ounce of fat on his body to insulate him from the cold, was most unhappy. 'Why are the prisoners being treated so well, what is so special about them?'

'I have no idea,' answered a shivering Conrad.

The sergeants also surrendered their cloaks, though this did not stop the women crying or their infants screeching. When they finally saw the welcoming ramparts of Wenden the whole party was mightily relieved, none more so than Berthold because not one of the captives had been lost to the cold. They were housed in the huts used to quarter the mercenaries, the latter being instructed that they would have to live in tents until the matter was resolved.

'I heard that you and Henke had an altercation,' remarked Lukas as he stood before the boys in the snow during their first training session after returning from the raid. It was still snowing but the flakes were small and were being blown around by an icy eastern wind.

Conrad did not understand what 'altercation' meant so just stared at Lukas with a vacant look on his face.

Lukas raised his eyes to the sky. 'It means argument.'

'I would not say that, Brother Lukas.'

'I would,' replied the brother knight. He pointed his sword at all the boys before him. 'What have I told you all? The cornerstones of our order are obedience, poverty and chastity, in that order. As soldiers you must obey orders.'

He pointed at Conrad. 'Lucky for you that Henke was in a good mood, otherwise he would have given you a good hiding for your insubordination.'

'Is it right to make war upon women and children, Brother Lukas?' asked Conrad, who hoped he had not spoken out of turn.

Lukas looked at the tall, gangly youth who had come to Wenden a poor orphan but who was turning into a fine soldier, if he could keep his mouth in check. He could also see from the expressions on their faces that the other boys were thinking the same as Conrad.

'I do not have to explain anything to you, Conrad, or any of you,' said Lukas, who sheathed his sword and folded his arms across his chest. 'You want to know what was the purpose of the raid? I will tell you. It was to capture women and children to sell as slaves.'

Conrad was appalled. 'Slaves?'

'That is right, young Conrad. Slaves. We will sell them to the Russians who will transport them south to the slave markets of Byzantium where there is a thriving market for white-skinned women and infants.'

'Why?' said Hans.

'For money, of course,' replied Lukas. 'Money to pay the mercenaries who defend this castle and the wages of the workers who are building it. Unless you think that everyone at Wenden is working for nothing.'

In truth Conrad had paid no thought to who paid for the mercenaries, the civilian workers or for the materials that arrived by riverboat having been shipped from Germany. He just thought. Just thought what?

Lukas unfolded his arms. 'The uniforms you wear, the weapons you wield and the horses you ride all have to be paid for.' He looked at Conrad. 'Remember that, Conrad Wolff, the next time you wish to give a sermon to a knight of the Sword Brothers.'

The prisoners remained at Wenden for a week, and then a group of bearded men wrapped in overcoats, fur-lined cloaks and high boots arrived and clapped them in irons. After inspecting the captives and stripping some of the women naked they paid Master Berthold gold and took them away, packed onto sleds pulled by ponies. Even though they were brutes they took great care to ensure that the Estonians were covered from head to foot in furs to prevent them freezing to death on their journey. Conrad stopped practising with Hans and turned to watch the long column of sleds depart Wenden, catching site of the young woman he had first seen in her hut in the Estonian village they had raided. She was clutching her two young children to her chest and wore a look of utter misery. In that moment he could have wept for her and for the life that she would be condemned to. Her face stayed in his minds for days afterwards.

*****

Domash Tverdislavich dismissed the soldier in the lamellar armour and pointed helmet. The ruler of Novgorod, Prince Mstislav, had sent him to inform Domash that the prince himself would be arriving at his palace that very afternoon. Novgorod had been founded nearly four hundreds years ago as an outpost of the great kingdom of Kiev Rus, but was now a powerful, self-ruling city in northern Russia. Located on the River Volkhov, it was surrounded mostly by swamps, which largely prohibited agriculture. But Novgorod was rich, its fur trade the most lucrative among all the Russian principalities. Its goods were shipped to the Gulf of Finland, overland to the Dvina and thence to the Baltic, and even south as far as Kiev and Byzantium. Its kremlin – castle – was built of stone and its magnificent Cathedral of St Sophia was one of the wonders of the world.

Domash's family had always been members of Novgorod's *veche* – parliament – comprised of the city's boyar families who appointed a *knez*, or prince, to rule them. For twenty years that man had been Prince Mstislav. Now nearly sixty years old, he usually stayed in Novgorod surrounded by his aristocrats, bishops and scholars, for Novgorod was a centre of literacy and printing as well as a place of iron processing, woodworking, tanning and jewellery production. But now he was about to arrive at Pskov.

Domash tapped the arm of his chair. Gleb chuckled.

'Why would the prince travel a hundred and twenty miles through the snow to see you? You must have committed a major transgression.'

Domash frowned at the white-haired man leaning against the wall beside his throne. Technically he was the *posadnik* – mayor – of Pskov, sent by the prince to rule the city that was the 'younger brother' of Novgorod. However, Domash ruled Pskov like a prince, rarely deferring to the city on the Volkhov.

'Be quiet,' he snapped.

'Still, you have had a reasonably long reign,' continued Gleb, 'it is no shame to be taken back to Novgorod in chains for your crimes.'

Domash glowered at him. 'Crimes?'

Gleb left the wall and began pacing up and down in front of the mayor, counting with his fingers as he listed Domash's wrongdoings.

'Let's see. Seducing most of the daughters of Pskov's boyars. Raiding adjacent territories without permission. Ignoring the proclamations of the church, though I will grant you that is only a minor offence. Stealing from church lands. Dealing in slaves. Need I go on?'

Domash waved a hand at him. 'No, you need not. I don't know why I tolerate you.'

Gleb walked back to the wall and picked up his *gusli*, his multi-stringed instrument. 'Oh, I think you do.'

Domash sneered as the white-haired oaf began plucking at the strings of his instrument. But the truth was that Gleb was worth his weight in gold. He was a *Skomorokh*, one of the ancient strolling performers who entertained people with songs, comic plays, tricks and dances. No one knew the precise details of their origins but the people believed them to be the last custodians of Russia's pagan past, a link to a bygone age of gods, forest fairies and river monsters. The Orthodox Church hated them, giving them the disparaging name 'devil servants', but the truth was that the *Skomorokhs* had enormous influence among a populace that still clung to hundreds of years of superstition and mysticism.

'No one is indispensible,' said Domash, menace in his voice.

The truth was, though, that his rule in Pskov was made much smoother by having Gleb at his side. Most *Skomorokhs* travelled from town to town, but some rich boyars asked them to live in their households, as Domash had done with Gleb. He remembered the day of his arrival: a stormy, rain-swept evening when a drenched Gleb turned up at the gates of his palace, requesting entrance. The guards had let him in without asking any questions for they believed him to be a servant of Perun, chief of the ancient pagan gods who ruled the world from his citadel atop the World Tree. They saw his rich blue tunic, his *gusli* and his white hair and were convinced that Perun had sent him. Everyone knew that the god had silver hair and a golden moustache. What's more, the name Gleb means 'heir of god'. Perun was also the God of Thunder, Lightning and War and Gleb's arrival on such a stormy night was an omen that could not be ignored. For his part Domash saw his arrival as a golden opportunity to strengthen his authority.

Gleb began singing as he played his instrument. 'The prince is going to take you away, take you away, take you away.'

'I should have your head for your insolence.'

Gleb stopped playing. 'Talking of which, don't forget you have an execution to witness today.'

Domash looked confused then waved forward one of his advisers, a middle-aged man with a thick beard and fur hat.

'There is an execution this afternoon?' he asked.

'Yes, highness.'

'What crime has the condemned committed?'

The adviser looked embarrassed. 'Sodomy, highness.'

Domash screwed up his face. 'Disgusting.'

A cluster of priests standing near the throne began nodding in agreement, which was noticed by Gleb.

'They should execute all the sodomites in the clergy. I have been told that it is rife among the priests and monks.'

There were loud gasps from the clergymen as Gleb began playing his *gusli* once more, singing very loudly as he did so.

'The priests are all sodomites, the priests are all sodomites.'

The guards standing around the walls were trying hard not to laugh but Domash saw nothing amusing in his disrespect. He rose from his throne.

'Silence! Gleb, you are dismissed.'

Gleb smiled mockingly at the priests, bowed to Domash and skipped from the room. How the clergy would have loved to consign him to the fire but they knew that he had the protection of the mayor and was loved by the people. This made his blasphemy even harder to bear. The fertile agricultural land that surrounded Pskov was dotted with tiny churches spreading the word of God, but sometimes they appeared as Christian islands in a pagan sea.

Domash dismissed the clergymen and advisers and then went to collect Gleb before making his way with an armed guard to the city square where executions took place. He always liked to be seen in public with Gleb so the people would be reminded that he had an adviser sent to him by the gods. It was all nonsense, of course, but the people were simple minded and easily fooled. Though they could take to violence with alarming rapidity if roused.

The roofs of the wooden buildings were covered in snow and the day was freezing as they made their way from the palace to the city square. The main thoroughfares in the city had wood-paved streets to prevent them turning into seas of mud and slush during the winter months, and Domash and his retinue now walked on them as people began to gather around and follow him. He had a score of spearmen with him but he always became nervous when the lower orders of the city, with their pockmarked faces, filthy clothes and obnoxious body odour, got too close.

Gleb was in his element, shaking hands, smiling at women and kissing babies held up to him by their mothers. Some tried to touch the cloak of Domash, which sent a shiver down his spine.

'Filthy scum.'

'Good crowd today,' said Gleb loudly.

They reached the square that was heaving with people, a priest standing on the scaffold in the company of four executioners who stood around a wooden frame that occupied the centre of the scaffold. The crowd were babbling excitedly but the executioners looked bored. A viewing platform had been erected directly opposite the scaffold, a row of seats arranged on the wooden planks. Domash ascended the steps and took his place in the middle seat, the other chairs being occupied by the city's richest boyars and their wives. They rose when he appeared, smiling and bowing their heads to Pskov's ruler. He acknowledged them but was still thinking about the purpose of the prince's visit when the ashen-faced prisoner was manhandled onto the scaffold.

A ripple of anticipation went through the crowd as he was stripped naked and ropes fastened around each of his ankles, which were then thrown over the wooden frame. The chattering and excitement among the crowd grew louder as the priest began reciting prayers and two of the executioners pulled on the ropes to hoist the condemned up by his ankles. Now upside down, ropes were tied around his wrists that were then secured to hooks on the bottom of the frame's uprights. The ropes around his ankles were wrapped around the crossbeam of the frame so the prisoner was held firmly in place, upside down with his legs apart.

The chief executioner turned to look at Domash who nodded his assent. This was the signal for one of his assistants to pick up a two-handed wood saw that had been lying on the straw that had been scattered over the scaffold. He lifted it up and passed it to a second assistant standing on the other side of the prisoner. They each took a firm grip on the handles and then began sawing through the condemned, the iron teeth cutting through his genitals and groin with ease.

The prisoner screamed loudly and thrashed around as the ghastly sentence was carried out, blood gushing onto the executioners and priest, the shrieking drowned out as the crowd erupted in wild cheering and applause. The wooden frame shook as the prisoner was gripped by superhuman strength as he tried to escape the awful punishment being visited upon him. The executioners used measured strokes as they forced the saw's teeth through his belly and chest, each stroke ripping out guts, bits of bone and vital organs as they cut down. Domash never ceased to be amazed by how much blood a human body contained, most of which now seemed to be on the fronts of the executioners and the straw that had been sprayed crimson. The priest had retreated to a safe distance down the steps that led from the scaffold, the crowd pelting him with vegetables and snowballs for his cowardice. Then the prisoner stopped moving as the saw's teeth cut through his spinal cord and his torment was over. The guests on the viewing platform clapped politely as the executioners cut down the cadaver and threw it on a waiting cart, which would take it to the city rubbish dump beyond the walls.

A guard appeared behind Domash and whispered in his ear.

'He's here?'

The guard nodded. Domash rose from his chair and pointed at Gleb, who was flirting with one of the boyar's wives.

'You are with me.'

The ruler of Pskov left the platform just as a young woman on the scaffold was stripped to the waist and had her wrists secured to the bloody frame prior to being flogged, her eyes bulging in fear at her debasement and the prospect of her back being cut open. Domash walked briskly back to the palace, annoyed that his entertainment had been so rudely interrupted. When he arrived at the throne room he found Prince Mstislav sitting in his place, lamellar armour of steel scales encompassing his great bulk. With his thick black hair and bushy beard Mstislav looked like a bear, as befitting Novgorod's coat of arms of two black bears either side of a throne. He may have been almost sixty but the prince looked every inch the fierce warrior who had fought the Cumans, Bulgars and Polovtsians.

294

Domash halted in front of the throne and bowed his head. 'Hail Mstislav, Prince of Novgorod.'

Mstislav nodded. 'I trust my city of Pskov thrives,' he growled.

Domash smiled. 'Indeed, highness, and its people will be delighted to see their prince within their walls.'

'Though their mayor is not delighted that someone else is sitting in his chair,' added Gleb mischievously from behind Domash.

The latter spun round and glared at him but Gleb just smiled and Mstislav chuckled. He knew all about the *Skomorokhs* and although his bishops did not approve of them he knew they had enormous influence among the common people. The prince raised himself up.

'Then let us withdraw and leave the throne to your jester,' said the prince, smiling at Gleb.

He and Domash retired to a small dining hall adjacent to the throne room where slaves brought hot broth and large cups filled with *kvass*. Mstislav ate heartily, tearing great chunks from the loaves placed before him and dipping the pieces in the broth.

'Your reports concerning the Estonian tribes have been most illuminating,' he said to Domash.

'They have united under a single leader to fight the crusaders, highness.'

Mstislav emptied his bowl of broth and held it out for a slave to take and refill. 'My army is but a short distance away.'

Domash was surprised. 'Your army, highness?'

'When it arrives you and your garrison will join me. We go to make war on this Lembit and his tribes.'

This was most unexpected. As long as the river routes to the Baltic and Gulf of Finland remained open most Russian princes showed little interest in what was happening among the pagan tribes living on their western borders. The prince saw the look of surprise on Domash's face.

'The world is changing. The Catholic crusaders carve out a kingdom on my western borders and threaten my interests.

'The Bishop of Riga has threatened you, highness?'

Mstislav took a great gulp of his *kvass*. 'No. But soon he will have conquered the Estonians just as he crushed the Livs. After that he and his crusaders will turn their gaze towards the lands on their eastern borders. This Lembit is already finished, though he may not know it. Therefore I will strike west into Ungannia to demonstrate the strength of Novgorod and send a signal to the Bishop of Riga that a great power lies to the east of his kingdom.'

The prince's army arrived at Pskov the next day. It numbered thirteen thousand foot and horse and was accompanied by a huge number of large wagons filled with supplies. It had taken twenty days to cover the one hundred and twenty miles between Novgorod and Pskov, a large vanguard of men with shovels clearing the route of snow and ice ahead of the army. The élite of the prince's host was the *Druzhina*, his standing army of mounted boyars and their relatives and bodyguards. They wore short-sleeved mail hauberks beneath lamellar armour, open-faced helmets with aventail and shields similar in shape to the ones carried by the Sword Brothers. Their weapons included lance, sword, dagger and axe and they almost always fought on horseback, never engaging in siege warfare. Their shields carried the images of religious icons, bears, lynxes, eagles and Orthodox crosses, the banner of Novgorod being carried at the head of their column. It was a sign of the city's wealth that Mstislav was able to muster fifteen hundred of these well-equipped and trained horsemen.

Next came Novgorod's urban militia, men who had been equipped by the city authorities and included archers as well as spearmen. Most of the latter had helmets and mail armour and they numbered two thousand men. Last in terms of quality and equipment were the *Voi*, the levies recruited from the villages around Novgorod. Almost entirely devoid of any body or head armour, they were armed with an assortment of spears and axes and numbered nine thousand in total.

It took three days to organise the troops from Pskov who would accompany the prince on his expedition. Domash had five hundred soldiers of his own *Druzhina*, a mixture of men he had brought with him from Novgorod and boyars from Pskov. The latter all sported the emblem of the city on their shields: a golden snow leopard on a blue background, the same design on the banner that fluttered at the head of the fifteen hundred men of the city militia, a hundred crossbowmen within their ranks as well as fifty horsemen.

Domash marched at the head of Pskov's troops from the city square to the gates in the southern wall. Pskov was a strong fortress sited on a promontory of two rivers – the Pskova and Velikaya – and was surrounded by an earthen rampart topped with a wooden palisade. On the vulnerable, southern side was a moat that connected the two rivers and thus surrounded all four sides of the city with water, making it virtually impregnable.

But as he trotted across the wide wooden bridge spanning the moat Domash wondered what an army of fifteen thousand men would achieve if not to conquer territory. He himself had taken part in raids designed to capture slaves, cattle and supplies many times, but the raiding parties were invariably small and mounted. Estonian villagers would be able to avoid a slow-moving army easily enough.

They skirted the southern shore of the frozen Lake Pskov, the great inland waterway that was covered in ice for six months of the year, and then struck northwest into Ungannia. The army managed to march a paltry six miles a day, the prince and his bodyguard riding out each morning wrapped in fur hats, wolfskin cloaks and high, padded boots to frighten the local populace and plunder their villages. But as Domash had feared the locals were alerted to the army's presence long before it reached them and fled north into the Estonian heartland.

When the sun dipped on the snow-blanketed western horizon the prince rode into camp boasting of how he had fired villages but the lack of any captives indicated that the settlements had been abandoned long before his arrival. The scouts located a number of hill forts where villagers had taken refuge but the lack of siege equipment meant they could not be assaulted. The large size of the prince's army made starving them into submission impossible for it would starve first. After two weeks of fruitless campaigning, in which a thousand *Voi* had died of exposure, Mstislav gave the order to return to Pskov. After a week he got bored and departed with his *Druzhina*, leaving Domash in command of the remaining horsemen, the city militias and the rapidly diminishing *Voi*.

'I will be waiting for you at Pskov,' said Mstislav. 'I grow tired of Estonia.'

It was a crystal clear day when the prince and his fifteen hundred horsemen departed, but as the days passed the sky became heaped with dark grey clouds that threatened snowfall. The threat turned into a reality on the third day after the prince had left the army as snow flakes began to fall, a few at first but as the day wore on visibility dropped as the fall became heavier. That night camp was made near the western shore of Lake Pskov. Domash called together the senior officers to his tent and announced that to save time and lives, rather than skirting the lake the army would march across its frozen surface.

It snowed all through the night and showed no signs of letting up as the men trudged along with heads bowed after striking camp, the horsemen leading their animals on foot. The archers had unstrung their bows and placed the bowstrings under their fur hats to keep them dry, the crossbowmen carrying their weapons slung on their backs, but stashed them under covers on the wagons when it snowed. The ice was thick enough to allow fully loaded wagons to be pulled across its surface, many of them now filled with *Voi* suffering from exposure and frostbite.

By mid-morning a northerly wind had begun to blow, blasting snowflakes into men's faces. Soldiers who had them pulled hoods over their heads to shield them from the ice particles. Domash halted and looked behind at the bedraggled column of men and horses fading in the blizzard. If the snow let up he and the army would be back in Pskov in three days, longer if they were forced to make camp and wait until the storm blew itself out. If that happened he wondered how many Russian corpses would be littering the frozen surface of Lake Pskov.

*****

Kalju's hard features were even more rock-like as he stared into the snow, dozens of his warriors gathered around him. He and they were wrapped in furs and wore skis on their feet: strips of pine six and a half feet long and secured to the wearer's feet by means of a leather strap attached to the top of the ski. When he had heard about the Russian invasion he had given orders that his people must leave their villages and take refuge in the nearest hill fort. The settlements had been laid to waste by the Russians but at least his Ungannians had escaped being enslaved. He had mustered five hundred warriors and they had shadowed the invaders as they advanced and then suddenly turned around and retreated. His scouts had reported that the banner of the Prince of Novgorod had been seen fluttering at the head of a great number of horsemen who had left the main Russian force some days ago, thus reducing the strength of the invaders.

'Mstislav flees back to his city,' remarked Lembit who had come to Kalju's side.

Though crusader raiding parties had assaulted his own territory, Lembit judged it prudent to march to aid the Ungannians to demonstrate solidarity with his fellow Estonian chief. In this way he hoped Kalju would support him when it came to his re-election as Estonia's grand warlord. He had brought two hundred of his wolf shields to fight alongside the Ungannians, all of them wearing skis on their feet and armed with one-handed axes and swords. They all wore helmets and mail shirts beneath their fur-lined cloaks.

Kalju looked at the snow flurries around him. 'They will not see us approaching. We will strike the rear of the column where the mostly poorly armed men are gathered.'

Lembit nodded his approval. 'Let us cover this lake with Russian corpses.'

The Ungannians cheered and banged their axe hafts on the insides of their shields and an evil grin creased Kalju's face. He raised his axe and pushed himself forward, his skis coursing over the snow-covered ice with ease. His warriors followed as Lembit made his way back to the Saccalians. Rusticus was standing ahead of the line of wolf shields, his cloak covered in snow.

'I hope you are in the mood for slaughter,' Lembit said to him.

Rusticus smiled. 'Always.'

Lembit raised his axe and looked behind. 'Saccalians. Your orders are to kill the invaders. Show no mercy. I will kill the first man I see with pity in his eyes. Forward!'

The wolf shields gave a mighty cheer and followed their chief into the whiteout, the wind at their backs as they skied south across Lake Pskov. Two hundred warriors moved silently through the snowstorm, the natural pine resin lubricating the underside of their skis to make their journey easier, aided by the northerly wind. Rusticus pushed ahead eagerly, gripping the shaft of his axe. He loved the moments just before battle when the anticipation of carnage filled his mind. He liked rape and pillage well enough but he loved war; loved the feeling that came with slicing open a man's guts in battle and the sensation of crushing an opponent's skull with an axe. It was in such moments that life truly became worth living. He screamed his war cry and sped ahead.

The Estonian warriors were widely spaced at they made their way across the ice, becoming even more separated in the swirling snowflakes that blotted out the horizon. But at least they knew approximately where the Russian army was; unlike Domash's men who were blissfully unaware of their attackers until they were upon them like a pack of starving wolves.

Rusticus saw the stooped figure appear suddenly in front of him, a soldier wrapped in a cape clutching a spear. He glided towards him, raised his axe and then smashed it into the back of his skull as he passed behind him. The next Russian saw him, transfixed as Rusticus brought his weapon up and swung it sharply to his right to hit the man square in the face, obliterating his nose. The man screamed and fell in the snow, to be killed by an axe blow to the back of the head delivered by a following wolf shield. Within moments the roar of the wind was intermingled with the screams and cries of men being struck by axes and swords as the Estonians smashed into the Russians.

Horses and ponies bolted as the raiders went straight through the ragged Russian column, halted, turned and then went back to the slaughter. The *Voi* suffered the most. Already cold, hungry and demoralised, hundreds of them were cut down in the initial Estonian assault. Trumpets blew from among the Russian ranks as the city militias gathered round their standards and locked shields to fight off the attackers.

Lembit stopped hacking at the bloody pulp that had been an archer at his feet and looked around. It was chaos. Snow flurries reduced visibility to less than fifty feet, making any sort of control all but impossible. He had a score of wolf shields with him but where were the rest? And where was Rusticus?

'Sound horn,' he ordered.

The signaller blew his horn but it was barely audible above the wind and the dreadful sounds of battle raging all around. The snow was littered with Russian dead, making it difficult to ski around the corpses. Rusticus then suddenly appeared, the head and shaft of his axe covered with blood and gore.

'Good sport,' he beamed. Behind him came many wolf shields, their weapons similarly adorned with Russian blood. Their assault had been spectacularly successful.

'We must find the Ungannians,' said Lembit, ordering his signaller to blow his horn once more. 'To finish these Russian barbarians.'

The initial assault by Kalju's men was similarly successful, nearly a thousand Russians being cut down when the Ungannians appeared out of the snowstorm. Thereafter, though, the fighting became harder as the more professional city militias rallied and fought back. And then the *Druzhina* launched a counterattack.

Domash heard the din suddenly erupt behind him and knew that the column was under attack. Most of the horsemen were positioned at the front of the army, though he had deployed his five hundred riders from Pskov behind the *Voi* to provide a rearguard. Unfortunately these took the full force of the Saccalian assault and were almost immediately scattered. To their credit their commanders managed to rally some but they got lost in the snow and actually rode away from the army.

*****

Domash gave the order for his men to mount their horses and led them towards the rear. But his progress was slowed almost immediately as figures on skis came out of the hail of snowflakes to hack at horses and riders alike. Beasts cried out in pain and then collapsed in the snow, trapping their riders beneath them. He ran one skier through with his lance but more and more appeared among his horsemen, and suddenly there were dozens of individual mêlées being fought around him.

More of his *Druzhina* came trotting from the army's vanguard, spearing skiers and slashing left and right with their swords. After nearly half an hour the warriors on skis were either dead and or had been forced to flee back into the white maelstrom, leaving Domash free to rally his men and lead them towards the rear where the sounds of battle could still be heard. But their progress was agonisingly slow, made worse by the swirling snow that blinded the horses and confused their riders. Skiers would suddenly appear in front and behind them, the latter slashing at the hindquarters of the horses with their swords, inflicting fearful wounds. The animals would either collapse or cry out in pain and bolt into the whiteout.

The thousand men of the Pskov militia had been immediately behind the horsemen in the line of march, their wagons deployed in the centre of their formation. The spearmen formed the outer files of the militiamen, the archers and crossbowmen walking beside the wagons as the latter's weapons were stored under canvas sheets in the carts to keep them dry and the bowmen were carrying their bowstrings under their hats. The spearmen on the left flank of the march formation were the ones who took the full force of the Ungannian attack, most being unable to react as the skiers appeared out of the snow and hacked them down with their axes. Kalju's men began killing the archers and crossbowmen before the Pskovian spearmen on the other side of the wagons mounted a counterattack then forced the Estonians back.

It was the same story with the Novgorod militia, which suffered fewer casualties because its numbers were greater and the Ungannians found it more difficult to cut through their denser files. When the *Druzhina* appeared the Estonians retreated before them rather than stand and be cut down, falling back towards the rear of the Russian column where the hapless *Voi* lay dead in heaps in the snow. And as the Ungannians retreated so the Saccalians advanced until the two literally bumped into each other. Kalju saw the black banner of Lembit and skied over to it.

'The Russian horsemen will soon be arriving in our midst.'

'Time to disappear into the snow, I think,' said Lembit.

'They are almost finished. We cannot flee with victory within reach,' implored Rusticus, his light grey wolfskin cloak splattered with blood, none of it his own.

'We cannot defeat horsemen,' said Lembit firmly. He turned to his signaller. 'Sound retreat.'

The high-pitched wail of the horn prompted the Saccalians to move away from the scene of carnage and back towards the northwest. Kalju gave a similar order and his men also made their escape. They would ski as fast as they could away from the Russians, hoping that the snowfall and lack of visibility would deter any mounted pursuit. When the storm had blown itself out they would regroup to the northwest, beyond the shores of the lake, to tend to their wounds and boast of their kills.

Before he left Kalju extended a hand to Lembit. 'You have my gratitude and my loyalty.'

Lembit clasped his forearm. 'My enemies are your enemies, my friend.'

They heard a horse's snort.

'We must go,' said Rusticus.

Lembit nodded to Kalju and began to ski away into the snow flurries.

There was no pursuit. The snow continued to fall and the wind showed no signs of abating as Domash and his men continued their ride along what remained of the prince's army. The Pskov and Novgorod militias managed to regroup around their wagons but the *Voi* had all but ceased to exist. Not only had they suffered heavy casualties at the hands of the Estonians, many had fled in terror at the appearance of the axe-wielding skiers, running away from the column towards the south. Whether they would be able to find their way back to shelter and food before darkness fell no one knew.

It was now two hours after midday and the light was fading fast. The wind continued to blow in the faces of tense and cold Russian soldiers as they awaited another assault that never came. By the time night had fallen it had stopped snowing, the bodies of the dead being covered in a blanket of white. Domash ordered that the men stand to arms all through the night on the ice. The wind dropped and clouds parted to allow moonlight to flood Lake Pskov. There was no sound aside from the soft moaning of the wounded; then total quiet as the cold quickly claimed them.

Domash stayed awake all night, in the morning standing beside a wagon holding a spear, his beard frosted and his eyes red. There was no wind or falling snow and all around there was nothing but deep snow and ice. He gave the order for food to be distributed and a roll call to be taken. He also sent out parties of scouts to make sure they would not be attacked again. It was two hours before what was left of the army recommenced its journey to Pskov, which was only two days' march away. The return of three hundred of the mounted men of the Pskov militia raised morale a little but men's spirits soon slipped back into despair as the enormity of the calamity that had befallen them became clear.

His own *Druzhina* had suffered ten killed and thirty wounded during the fighting, the Pskov militia suffering a hundred losses and the Novgorodians twice that number. But the heaviest losses had occurred among the *Voi*: two thousand dead and a further thousand missing. He did not know why his commanders had reported the latter as missing. He knew they were dead from exposure, having spent the previous night wandering around on the ice before they succumbed to the cold. Their frozen corpses provided a fitting epitaph to Prince Mstislav's abortive expedition into Estonia.

Chapter 12

Bishop Albert finished prayers, took his seat at the table and invited the others to do the same. He had arrived back from Germany three weeks before in the company of a thousand crusaders. Together with those knights who had remained in Livonia and who had taken part in the winter raids against the Estonians, he could now muster four thousand foot and horse to crusade against the pagans. In addition, he had the troops of the Rigan garrison plus the Sword Brothers and their mercenary forces. To which would be added the hundreds of warriors that Caupo could raise.

It was now summer and Livonia was bathed in glorious sunlight. The roads were dry and would soon be filled by a great army marching north to do battle with Lembit. Albert had gathered the masters of the Sword Brothers to inform them of his plans. They now sat at his table in their mail armour and white surcoats with their deputies: Grand Master Volquin, Master Berthold of Wenden, Master Bertram of Segewold, Master Mathias of Kremon, Master Gerhard of Holm, Master Friedhelm of Uexkull, Master Aldous of Lennewarden and Master Griswold of Kokenhusen. He looked with satisfaction at their hard features, these religious warriors whose garrisons held back the heathen hordes.

Bishop Albert brought his hands together. 'I will soon march against Lembit in what will be the final campaign against the Estonian pagans. A great army musters outside the walls of Riga to bring the word of God to the heathens.'

The Sword Brothers smiled at the bishop and each other.

'A fitting reward for your industry and conviction, lord bishop,' said Volquin. The others murmured their approval of his words.

The bishop held up a hand. 'I am merely a poor servant of God who has been chosen to undertake His work.

'But now, finally, we are on the eve of the subjugation of the whole of Estonia. Master Berthold, perhaps you would be so kind as to provide us with details concerning the state of the Estonian tribes.'

Berthold cleared his throat. 'Thank you, lord bishop. At Wenden we have received reports that in addition to our own incursions, Prince Mstislav of Novgorod led a great army into Ungannia to plunder that land. So I would estimate that Lembit has lost a sizeable number of men during the recent winter, as well as many of his villages destroyed.'

'Does Novgorod covet Estonia?' asked Master Bertram.

'He may,' answered Berthold, 'though we also heard that the Russian army was worsted on the ice of Lake Pskov as it headed for home.'

Master Mathias laughed gruffly. 'They underestimated that bastard Lembit. They are not the only ones.'

Archdeacon Stefan sitting next to the bishop frowned at his language but the bishop himself was more interested in Mathias' meaning.

'You think *we* underestimate Lembit, Master Mathias?'

'I think the sooner we kill him the better,' replied Mathias. The others nodded their agreement.

'We do not go to kill but to convert,' emphasised the bishop. 'Our numbers alone should be enough to cower the Estonians into submission.'

'And what of the Oeselians?' asked Master Friedhelm.

'The Oeselians?' said the bishop.

'Yes, lord bishop,' continued Friedhelm. 'They are allies of the Estonians and will have to be dealt with if we are to have peace in Livonia and the sea that surrounds it.'

'Their vessels still prey on our shipping,' said Master Gerhard.

The bishop considered for a moment. 'The matter of the Oeselians will have to wait until Estonia is conquered. In the meantime you will all muster your garrisons and join the army that I will be taking north.'

Griswold of Kokenhusen and Aldous of Lennewarden looked at each other in alarm.

'You would strip Kokenhusen of its garrison?' said Griswold with disbelief.

'And that of Lennewarden?' added Aldous.

'Because of the diligence of Archdeacon Stefan,' said the bishop, 'we have peace with the Lithuanians. I therefore see little reason to keep garrisons sitting idle when their soldiers could be aiding the conversion of the Estonians.'

'Do we trust the Lithuanians, lord bishop?' enquired Master Gerhard. 'They are, after all, also pagans.'

The bishop looked at Stefan, who wore a smarmy smile.

'Prince Vsevolod has brokered a treaty between Riga and the Lithuanians that guarantees peace along the Dvina,' said Stefan.

'I do not trust the Lithuanians or Vsevolod,' said Griswold.

'Nor do I,' added Aldous.

Stefan sighed loudly. 'I would have thought, Master Griswold, that the fact Prince Vsevolod came to your relief when Kokenhusen was assaulted by the

Lithuanians proves that not only can he be trusted but also that he should be thought of as a valuable ally.'

Griswold gave a grim chuckle. 'How little you know of the ambitions of princes, archdeacon. He may have told you that he brought his army to the walls of my castle in order to offer help, but I am also mindful that he is related to Grand Duke Daugerutis, lord of all the Lithuanian tribes.'

Stefan wagged a finger at the castellan of Kokenhusen.

'Prince Vsevolod is a man of honour.'

Griswold looked surprised. 'Do Russians have any honour?'

The other Sword Brothers laughed as Stefan blushed but the bishop was not amused.

'Quiet. This is not a gathering in a back-alley tavern. I have every confidence in the peace secured by the efforts of Archdeacon Stefan and Prince Vsevolod with the Lithuanians. If any of you have information pertaining to Lithuanian aggression then state it now.'

Aldous and Griswold shrugged with indifference and the others looked disinterested.

'Very well, then,' continued the bishop. 'You will all assemble at Riga with your men in a month's time, except the garrisons of Kremon, Segewold and Wenden. The soldiers from those places will join us as we march north to Estonia.'

He nodded to Volquin who announced that the meeting was over. The Sword Brothers rose, bowed their heads to the bishop and then made to leave the audience chamber of the bishop's palace.

'Master Berthold and Brother Rudolf from Wenden will remain for a few moments.'

The others left and the doors were closed behind them. The bishop smiled at Stefan.

'If you would give us a few minutes, nephew.'

Stefan sighed, rose, bowed his head and then scurried from the room as Berthold and Rudolf flopped back down in their beautifully appointed chairs. The bishop leaned back in his similarly appointed chair and regarded the master of Wenden and his deputy.

'Word has reached me that the garrison of Wenden has been engaged in nefarious activities.'

Berthold raised an eyebrow. 'Oh?'

306

The bishop's eyes narrowed. 'Specifically, selling Estonians to Russian slave traders.'

'A most lucrative enterprise that will pay for the continuing construction of your castle at Wenden, lord bishop,' said Berthold.

Albert was taken aback. 'You do not deny the charge?'

Berthold looked at Rudolf. 'Deny? Deny what, lord bishop? You were aware of the financial problems concerning paying the civilian workers and mercenaries at my castle. The lack of funds from Riga gave me little choice but to think of more inventive ways to raise funds.'

'You will be pleased to know that we now have enough money to continue building the defences for another year,' added Rudolf.

The bishop pointed at them both. 'We are not here to engage in the slave trade. It is an offence in the eyes of God and I therefore forbid it.'

'Would you have preferred us to have killed the women and children instead of selling them, lord bishop?' asked Rudolf.

'If Riga provides the funds I can perhaps buy them back,' said Berthold irreverently.

Bishop Albert gave them an icy stare. 'You forget to whom you are talking. I am the pope's representative in Livonia and have the power of excommunication over all its subjects.'

'Perhaps if Riga made more funds available, lord bishop,' suggested Berthold, 'then Wenden would not be forced to take drastic measures to secure its future.'

The bishop twisted up his mouth in annoyance. 'We discussed that on an earlier occasion. Riga has no funds to spare.'

'Riga has soldiers who do nothing but stand around in their nice new uniforms looking pretty,' said Rudolf.

'The defence of Riga relies on a strong garrison,' snapped the bishop in irritation.

'With respect, lord bishop,' said Berthold firmly, 'the defence of Riga rests upon the castles of the Sword Brothers. If they fall so will Riga.'

Bishop Albert held up his hands to them. 'We stand on the verge of victory against Lembit. Let us not bicker on the eve of such an auspicious event. I know that the garrison of Wenden stands as an example to the rest of Livonia in terms of courage and faithfulness. It is because of this that I was saddened to hear of the trading of slaves. The Sword Brothers must maintain the highest standards of behaviour as befitting the warriors of Christ.'

He spread his hands and smiled at them both. 'I will say no more on the subject. But know that I hold you both in the highest esteem and affection.'

Afterwards Rudolf and Berthold walked back to their quarters in Riga's castle. It, the city and the surrounding countryside were full to the brim with knights, squires, crossbowmen, spearmen, labourers, armourers, fletchers, surgeons and priests, the latter almost an army in themselves, having been brought from Germany as the personal ministers of the richest noblemen. Riga itself was also crammed with citizens, cogs bringing new arrivals every summer to plant Livonia with Christians.

'The bishop makes a new Jerusalem here,' remarked Berthold as they walked through the castle gates into a courtyard filled with wagons and carts for the forthcoming campaign.

Rudolf sniffed the air. 'A new pigpen, more like. The sun warms the filth of Riga's streets well enough. It will be good to smell the sweet air of Wenden once more, especially after our rebuke at the hands of the bishop.'

'Bishop Albert is a good man with a crusading fire in his belly,' said Berthold, 'but he knows nothing about building a castle and maintaining its garrison. Until he does we must continue to look to our own resources to keep Wenden strong.'

'Even if it means excommunication?' remarked Rudolf casually.

'I would not have thought that would bother you, brother,' replied Berthold, 'having been excommunicated for your depredations in Germany when you were a mercenary.'

Rudolf laid a hand on his white mantle. 'Surely these clothes and my oath to the Sword Brothers have washed away my sins?'

'I'm not sure there is enough holy water in the whole world to wash away your sins, Rudolf.'

They left for Wenden the next day, riding through the tents and wagons of the great army that Bishop Albert had assembled to crush Lembit and bring the Estonian tribes under the control of the Holy Church.

Two days later pestilence broke out among the assembled host.

The thousands of men camped outside its walls and the thousands of citizens herded into its densely packed streets resulted in Riga becoming a vast breeding ground for disease. Much time and money had been devoted to strengthening its defences but no thought had been given to sanitation. Raw sewage was dumped in the streets alongside butchers' waste, and outside the walls the crusader army filled the ground with dung and urine with little thought to the consequences. The warm, humid conditions combined with the press of people in a small area resulted in an outbreak of the 'bloody flux'.

The first outbreak was among the soldiery in the tent city outside the walls but it soon spread through Riga itself. A raw stench had hung over the town anyway but within days of the outbreak it had turned into a nauseating reek as hundreds began to manifest symptoms of the illness: bloody stools, cramps, fever and weakness. Hardened mercenaries wept and clutched the hands of priests as they lay in their tents with blood pouring from their rectums.

The first to die were the infants, whose small bodies could not cope with the sudden sapping of their strength. Their weeping parents took their bodies to the burial pits dug outside the town walls where priests wearing face masks conducted mass funerals. Then the soldiers began dying and the lords made plans to take ship back to Germany rather than wait for the flux to strike them down. The bishop implored them to stay but even his own governor fled Riga, Archdeacon Stefan hurrying to the monastery at Dünamünde, and so it was almost impossible to persuade the lords to stay. In any case, they pointed out, there would be no campaign when half the army would be laid low for weeks. And so a steady procession of cogs left Riga's harbour carrying knights and their squires, abandoning the common soldiery to their fate.

When Caupo heard of the outbreak of pestilence at Riga he sent his tribal healers to the bishop with supplies of blackberry syrup, hollyhock and a drink made from the bark of trees that could stop the voiding of guts. The result was that fewer than one in ten of the bishop's army succumbed to the flux. But the rest had been grievously weakened and would be in no fit state to make war on the Estonians. A bitterly disappointed Bishop Albert wrote to each of his castellans informing them that there would be no campaign against Lembit for at least another year.

He ordered Stefan to return to Riga, the sheepish archdeacon slipping back into the town two weeks later. Men were still dying of the flux but at a greatly reduced rate, the dead having been interred in great pits to the north of the town. The bishop ordered him to attend a meeting held in Grand Master Volquin's office in the castle, which was no longer thronged with crusaders. Stefan sat next to the bishop and opposite the grand master on the other side of the great oak desk.

'There is no need for the mask now, archdeacon,' said Volquin.

Stefan shook his head. 'It is common knowledge that the flux is caused by bad air, grand master.'

'It is the will of God,' snapped the bishop, 'that is the reason that Riga has been punished.'

'He may punish us more, yet, lord bishop,' added Volquin glumly.

Stefan looked at him. 'Oh?'

'Word of the pestilence will have spread,' continued Volquin. 'Our foes may seek to take advantage of our weakness.'

'You are certain that the peace with the Lithuanians will hold,' the bishop asked Stefan.

'I have no reason to doubt the sincerity of Prince Vsevolod, or the word of his father-in-law, lord bishop,' replied Stefan.

The bishop leaned forward and placed his head in his hands. When he looked up he seemed to have visibly aged.

'Just as you have brokered peace with the Lithuanians, Archdeacon Stefan, so must I taste the bitter bread of humility and seek a truce with Lembit, though I would rather cut off my hand than offer it to such a heathen.'

Stefan pulled down his mask. 'You will make peace with the Estonians?'

'A temporary truce, that is all,' said the bishop softly. 'To buy time.'

'A wise decision, lord bishop,' said Volquin. 'We should not seek a war we cannot win.'

*****

Prince Vetseke stood in the centre of the village as his men hauled the priest into his presence and threw him at his feet. He was an elderly man with a tonsure and a simple undyed habit, a poor monk of the Cistercian order who had come to Livonia to spread the word of God. He was one of a tiny number of German monks who lived among the natives, the priests preferring to live in the castles of the Sword Brothers and travel around their 'parishes' under armed protection. In any case few of them could speak the local language and so it made more sense for them to travel in the company of men appointed by local chiefs who could act as interpreters. This monk was different: he could converse with the locals and believed that living among them, sharing their hardships and helping them in the fields would bring them and him closer together, and would also bring the Livs closer to God.

'Get up, priest,' ordered Vetseke.

Two of his men hauled the monk to his feet. The Cistercian, though bruised and bloodied, stood defiantly before the Liv prince.

'You speak our language, priest?' spat Vetseke.

'I do.'

The villagers had now gathered in the small square before the headman's hut. It was a large village around twenty miles north of Kokenhusen, one of many that had formerly owed allegiance to the prince when he resided in his stronghold. The original plan had been for Vetseke to raise an army of Liv exiles at Polotsk. Then word reached the Russian city that a great plague had ravaged the crusaders and the town of Riga. Traffic on the Dvina had dwindled to almost nothing as Russian merchants stayed away for fear of catching the terrible plague and Vetseke saw his chance. He persuaded Vladimir that a golden opportunity presented itself to strike a blow against the Bishop of Riga. So the prince had given Vetseke a hundred Russian soldiers to assist him raise the standard of rebellion in Livonia. He took his Russian soldiers by riverboat as far as Kokenhusen, disembarking them ten miles downstream of his former home, and then set about travelling around his kingdom to raise an army.

Vetseke, dressed in a new green cloak, his sword in a red scabbard, looked at the monk.

'Do you know who I am?'

'I am afraid that I do not,' said the monk, blood trickling from his nose down his chin.

Vetseke looked at the people, *his* people, clustered behind the priest. He cast a disdainful glance at the village headman who had been roused from his bed and brought to him, for it was early and there was still dew on the grass beyond the village perimeter. The headman's family – two sons and a wife – shifted on their feet nervously behind him. The Russians formed a cordon around the villagers.

'Has no one told this foreign priest about the lord of this land?' said Vetseke. 'Have you all forgotten so quickly the family who ruled over you, your fathers and forefathers?'

There was silence among the villagers, many of whom had their heads cast down.

Vetseke left the bleeding monk and began to walk among them.

'Have you forgotten the gods who bless you and this land? Mara, the Great Mother; Saule, the Sky God, and Jumis who blesses the land that gives you the food that fills the bellies of your children? Have you been so corrupted by the false god of the crusaders that you tolerate this barbarian priest among you?'

They averted their eyes as he walked back to stand before the monk once more.

311

'They have all accepted baptism into the Holy Church,' said the monk. 'They are no longer lost lambs.'

'They are my people!' bellowed Vetseke. He waved forward two of his men. 'You have a hut in this village, priest?'

'It is a church, heathen,' replied the monk, 'a house of the Lord though it be a simple affair.'

Vetseke smiled maliciously. 'Excellent. Nail him to its door.'

'You may kill me, heathen,' said the monk as he was bundled away, 'but you cannot extinguish the flame of the Lord.'

The villagers started to groan and mutter among themselves.

'Silence!' barked Vetseke. 'I have been away too long and can see that the fever of treachery has spread among you.'

The headman, alarmed, shuffled forward. 'Highness, he is a gentle man who meant no harm.'

With lightning speed Vetseke pulled his sword from his scabbard and swung it right to slash the headman's neck. He clutched at the gaping wound as blood sheeted over his hands and he collapsed to the ground, groaning faintly before he died.

'I am not,' said Vetseke.

The headman's wife screamed in anguish and rushed to her husband's body while his sons drew their swords and advanced on Vetseke. They were both hacked to pieces by the prince's Russian guards. The villagers, horrified and terrified in equal measure, stood in silence as more screams came to their ears as nails were driven through the monk's palms to pin him to the door of his tiny wooden church.

'If the god of the crusaders is so powerful,' said Vetseke, 'then why does he allow his priests to be so easily humiliated?'

One of his men brought him a lighted torch. Vetseke walked to where the monk, slumped with his head down, was reciting a prayer, his voice weak. The villagers followed the prince, 'encouraged' by the spears of the Russians. Vetseke looked at the small wooden cross fixed to the thatched roof of the hut. Vetseke tossed the torch on to the roof, which was soon ablaze. The women among the crowd began to groan and sob as the flames consumed the thatch, spread to the wooden walls and began to roast the friar's flesh. He screamed and tried to wrench his pinioned hands free, to no avail. There was a great roar and then the hut became a huge fireball as the flames consumed it and the priest.

Vetseke turned to face the villagers. 'I go to reclaim my kingdom and call on those with courage still in their veins to march with me to rid this land of the crusaders. Those who wish to remain living on their knees can stay behind with the women.'

The villagers had been fond of the kind-hearted monk who had dipped their heads under the water to baptise them into the faith followed by Caupo, their king, but many remembered their oaths of allegiance that had been sworn to their prince. Many had thought him long dead and though they did not agree with his killing of the monk and the headman and his family, his appearance had shamed them. Those young men with no families therefore collected their axes and shields and marched after the prince, who after a week had collected five hundred impressionable young men around him and had made his base in the great forest ten miles north of Kokenhusen.

Not all the Livs in his former principality were loyal. It was soon reported to Master Griswold at the castle that Prince Vetseke had returned and was gathering an army. Those Livs still loyal to the Christian faith brought their weapons and families into the castle while Griswold sat with his deputy and the leader of the loyal Liv warriors, plus the commander of a crusader detachment, Rudolf von Jerichow, who had been sent to the castle to strengthen the garrison. Kokenhusen was the most easterly of the Sword Brother castles along the Dvina and as such was, like Wenden on the Gauja, the most vulnerable. It had been taken from Vetseke only three years before but was already assuming the features of a mighty fortress. Masons laboured on scaffolding to replace the timber walls and towers with stone bastions. Inside the great enclosure on the wedge-shaped hill were kitchens, a brewery, bakery, mill, dining hall, chapel, barracks, forge, granary, stables and hall of the master. The meeting took place in the latter, Griswold sitting at a large table where once Prince Vetseke had taken his meals.

'I thought he was dead,' remarked the master.

'He is very much alive,' said the Liv chief, a middle-aged man with wild blonde hair.

'Who is this Vetseke?' asked Sir Rudolf.

'This was once his castle,' answered Griswold. 'And now he wants it back, it seems.'

'His camp is but half a day's ride from here,' said the chief.

'Then tomorrow we will ride out and bring this pagan pretender to heel,' smiled Griswold. 'I will send him to Riga in chains. The bishop can deal with him.'

'It will be good to fight,' said Sir Rudolf, 'I and my knights grow tired of sitting by this river.'

'Better than dying of the flux in Riga, my lord,' said Griswold's deputy.

Master Griswold smiled at Sir Rudolf. 'Well, my lord, tomorrow we will give battle to Prince Vetseke and his rabble.'

There was a knock on the door and one of the garrison's sergeants entered, walking up to Griswold and saluting.

'The duty officer requests your presence on the walls, master.'

'I am in the middle of a meeting,' Griswold rebuked him.

'Apologies, master,' said the sergeant, 'but he said that you would want to see it.'

Griswold folded his arms in irritation. 'See what?'

'The Lithuanians, master. They are crossing the river.'

Master Griswold rushed from the hall followed by Sir Rudolf, his deputy and the Liv chief. The alarm bell was being rung in the courtyard, sending brother knights, sergeants, crossbowmen and spearmen racing to the armoury to collect their weapons before manning the walls. The latter were still mostly timber palisades though the foundations of five stone towers had already been laid, the two largest of which would face the Dvina.

Master Griswold stood on the battlements watching boats leaving the opposite bank of the river being rowed across the wide expanse of water. Five were already in mid-stream with another half dozen leaving the far shore. They were all filled with warriors whose shields hung on the sides of the boats. From the first boat flew the banner of a black bear on all fours on a red background – the emblem of Grand Duke Daugerutis.

'Daugerutis himself comes?' said Griswold's deputy.

'Not with just ten boats,' answered Griswold, who looked behind him at the mangonels being loaded with rocks to shoot at the boats.

Sir Rudolf's knights and squires – a hundred men – were also lining the walls now, together with the Livs who had fled from Vetseke. Men gripped their weapons and shield straps as they waited for the enemy attack.

'They do not appear to be in any hurry,' remarked Sir Rudolf.

'No, indeed,' agreed Griswold.

In fact the approach of the boats could only be called leisurely, the oars dipping into the water in short strokes. And as the lead boat came closer those on

314

the walls saw that a man in mail armour at the prow held not a spear or sword but a sprig of oak. He held it aloft for those on the walls to see.

'What pagan trick is this?' said Sir Rudolf.

'No trick, my lord,' said Griswold, 'it is a signal that they want to talk not fight.'

Half an hour later Master Griswold and Sir Rudolf led a party of Sword Brothers and crusaders from the castle to the sandy riverbank at the foot of the castle. The Lithuanian boats had all crossed the river but their crews had shipped their oars and now sat in their vessels while their leader and the crew of his boat left their vessel and stood on the sand. One man remained on board holding the banner of Grand Duke Daugerutis that fluttered in the stiff breeze. The two groups halted a few paces from each other.

'Prince Stecse,' said Griswold. 'Have you come to attempt once more to take my castle?'

Stecse flashed an impudent smile. 'Not this time, Master Griswold. Today I am here to attend to the grand duke's business.'

Sir Rudolf did not understand the language of the Lithuanians and so stood frowning at the pagan lord who strutted before him.

'My apologies, lord,' Griswold said to him, 'this is Prince Stecse, a vassal of Grand Duke Daugerutis.'

'Vassal?' said Stecse in German. 'Chief warlord is more correct, Master Griswold.'

Griswold rubbed his beard. 'Your star rises, prince.'

Stecse looked at the stern, mail-clad knight clad in a red surcoat sporting a yellow unicorn.

'This is Sir Rudolf von Jerichow, a noble knight from Germany,' said Griswold, who had noticed that Stecse was holding a rolled parchment.

Stecse bowed his head at Sir Rudolf who looked with disdain on the long-haired barbarian in his midst.

'What business brings you to the walls of my castle, prince,' enquired Griswold, 'and with so many men?'

Stecse looked hurt. 'You would not expect me to present myself naked surely, Master Griswold?'

'Apparently not,' sighed Griswold.

'The grand duke wishes to cross the river with his army to make war upon Novgorod,' announced Stecse, which was greeted by laughter from the brother knights behind Griswold.

The master held up a hand to silence them. 'Your humour has improved since our last meeting, prince.'

Stecse shook his head and held out the document. 'I am deadly serious, and so is the grand duke.'

Griswold took the parchment and unrolled it.

'You recognise the seal, I think,' said Stecse as Griswold's eyes widened with surprise and horror as he read the words.

'This cannot be,' said the Sword Brother.

'A two-year truce in exchange for the right to cross the Dvina and march through Livonia, as agreed by the bishop himself,' said Stecse triumphantly.

Sir Rudolf was horrified when Griswold told him about the document's contents. 'This must be a trick.'

Griswold rolled up the parchment and handed it back to Stecse. 'When?'

'In two weeks. The grand duke wishes to make Novgorod bleed and be back in his castle before the autumn comes. He had thought to cross at Gerzika but Kokenhusen is much closer to his objective.'

'My soldiers will act as guides to ensure there are no depredations against the local populace.'

Stecse wore a hurt look again. 'Depredations, master? Grand Duke Daugerutis is a great warrior not a brigand.'

'Nevertheless, I have been charged by the bishop to protect this region so my men will ensure there are no regrettable incidents.'

'Surely you are not going to allow this outrage?' said Sir Rudolf.

'I have no choice, lord,' answered Griswold. 'The bishop himself has authorised it.'

Stecse tapped the document in his palm. 'Excellent! I shall convey your accommodating demeanour to the grand duke.'

He bowed his head to Griswold and Sir Frederick, turned on his heels and walked towards his boat, his men following. He stopped suddenly and returned to the master, leaning forward to whisper into his ear.

'You think Prince Vsevolod is a friend but you are mistaken. You may look south but you have enemies on this side of the river. This I say as one warrior to another.'

When he returned to the castle Griswold sent a letter by pigeon to Riga requesting verification of the document he had seen earlier. But he knew the bishop's seal and had no reason to doubt its authenticity. Why had the bishop agreed to such a compact? He wrestled with this question as he waited for a reply.

The next day he called a council of war to announce that he would still be leading an expedition against Prince Vetseke. But at midday, as he sat on his horse in the courtyard with Sir Rudolf at the head of their soldiers, a scout arrived with news that Vetseke had stolen a march on them and had left his camp at dawn. He was leading his army west towards Riga itself. With the imminent prospect of a Lithuanian army crossing the Dvina Master Griswold had no choice but to stand down his men and write another despatch to Riga alerting the bishop that Vetseke was approaching the town.

*****

'Do we know how many they number?'

Bishop Albert sat with his elbows on the table as he looked at Grand Master Volquin, the Sword Brother stroking his beard thoughtfully.

'Master Griswold's most recent report was that Vetseke had gathered around a thousand men to his banner.'

When Griswold's message had reached the bishop he had summoned Volquin and Stefan to his audience chamber. He had decided to keep the matter of Prince Vetseke's uprising to himself for the moment, not least because it might spark panic in Riga, whose citizens were already in a state of terror over the recent outbreak of the bloody flux.

'How many soldiers are fit for duty among the crusaders?' he asked Volquin.

The grand master sighed deeply. 'Before the pestilence nearly four thousand men were camped outside Riga's walls ready to march against Lembit.' He spread his arms. 'Now barely half of that number remain, and of those hardly two-thirds are fit for duty, if that.'

'That few?' Stefan was horrified. 'We must send an urgent summons to Germany for more soldiers to defend this holy place against Vetseke with what resources we can muster.'

'You must order your castellans to gather here, at Riga,' Stefan said to Volquin, his agitation clearly visible.

'Calm yourself, Stefan,' said the bishop. 'It is unseemly to panic in the face of adversity. What would you advise, grand master?'

317

Volquin rose from his chair and walked over to the large vellum map of Livonia and the surrounding kingdoms mounted on the wall of the bishop's chamber. He pulled his dagger from its sheath and used it as a pointer.

'If we do not march against Lembit then he will be tempted to send his warriors south, if only in retaliation for our raids against him during the winter. This means that the garrisons at Segewold, Kremon and Wenden cannot be weakened.'

He looked at the bishop. 'You still intend to offer him the hand of peace, lord bishop?'

Albert nodded. 'I do, though not until we have defeated Vetseke. Lembit will respond more positively if we bargain from a position of strength, I think.'

Volquin nodded approvingly. He turned back to the map. 'Along the Dvina only the garrisons of Holm and Uexkull can be called upon. The forces at Lennewarden and Kokenhusen must be left where they are to stand watch over the forces of Grand Duke Daugerutis that are to be allowed to cross over the river.'

He frowned disapprovingly at Stefan but the archdeacon dismissed his fears.

'The duke is an ally. If he wishes to make war upon the Russians instead of us then he should be encouraged to do so.'

Volquin replaced his dagger in its sheath and returned to the table. 'Whether the grand duke is our ally remains to be seen. But your agreement with him, archdeacon, forces our hand and loses us the garrisons of two castles in our fight against Vetseke.'

Stefan, growing in confidence, waved a hand in the air. 'Vetseke. What is he but a landless pagan who wanders the earth like a beggar?'

'That may be,' said Volquin, 'but he comes knocking on Riga's gates with an army at his back.'

Stefan raised an eyebrow but said no more. Bishop Albert looked at the map and then at Volquin.

'Very well. Summon masters Gerhard and Friedhelm to Riga. Instruct them to empty their castles and bring the garrisons here. Let us hope they arrive before Vetseke.'

The troops from Holm and Uexkull did arrive before Vetseke, as did Bishop Theodoric and the prior, dean and monks from the monastery at Dünamünde. Theodoric was eager to bring his clergy to fortify the soldiery against the pagans, though for the first few days after their arrival they treated those still suffering from the bloody flux. Bishop Albert himself went among the crusader army, imploring the soldiers to rise from their state of lethargy and march forth to fight the heathen.

Some eight hundred did so, donning their mail armour and helmets, picking up their shields, spears and crossbows to muster on the fields east of their camp and about a mile from Riga's eastern gates.

From the town itself marched all that remained of the garrison of Riga – fifty spearmen and the same number of crossbowmen – plus fifty well-armed men of Riga's militia and a hundred Liv warriors raised from the surrounding villages. The garrisons of Holm and Uexkull numbered seventy-seven men and seventy-two men respectively, reinforced by a hundred Liv warriors supplied to each of the two castellans.

The largest contingent of the bishop's army was the crusader element: two hundred knights, the same number of squires, two hundred lesser knights and eight hundred foot soldiers. This gave a total of just over two thousand men, including the two brother knights, five sergeants and ten mercenaries employed by the office of Grand Master Volquin, who assumed joint second-in-command of the army under the bishop's supreme leadership. The other deputy commander was a knight from the Ruhr valley: Count Walram of Jülich, who had lost a third of his body weight to the flux but was still determined to lead the crusaders. A huge man with great hands and a round face, his cheeks were now sunken and his eyes hollow. Clearly still gravely ill, he could barely strap on his sword belt let alone pull it from his scabbard. Nevertheless, men were heartened when they saw him on his horse with his great banner of a rampant black lion on a yellow background fluttering behind him. The bishop entrusted him to lead the six hundred horsemen of the crusaders, the mounted brother knights and the sergeants of the Sword Brothers. However, the masters of Holm and Uexkull would ensure that they were employed with care when battle was joined.

Grand Master Volquin commanded the foot soldiers: eight hundred brought by the crusaders, three hundred Livs, Riga's militia, the Bishop's guards and the order's mercenaries.

Before the expected arrival of Vetseke the bishop, Count Walram and Grand Master Volquin finalised their battle plan. The rebels had no siege engines, no horsemen, or at least no heavily armoured knights, and comprised in the main farmers armed with spears and axes. The Christian army would march out of Riga and do battle with Vetseke on the flat ground east of the town where the trees had long since been cleared and replaced by fields and villages. The foot would be drawn up in the centre with the horsemen on the flanks. Crossbowmen would be arrayed in front of the spearmen and would shoot the Livs to pieces before the horsemen charged to finish them off.

It was the middle of August when scouts rode to Riga's castle to report that Vetseke and his army were two days' march from the town. Volquin alerted the bishop and Count Walram, the latter giving orders to his knights to prepare for the coming battle. The days were warm now and though the pestilence had abated the stench of human dung still hung over the crusader camp and the town. The burial pits north of Riga had been covered with earth and the death rate had dropped precipitously, though infants were still succumbing to the flux. On the day that Vetseke and his rebels finally appeared the Sword Brothers and crusaders, notwithstanding their depleted numbers, were supremely confident that the Livs would be crushed with ease.

*****

Vetseke knew that to offer battle to the crusaders was madness, yet to avoid doing so would mean his insurrection would come to nothing. He had no machines with which to batter the walls of the Christian castles and so the only way to demonstrate the validity of his cause was to defeat the crusaders in battle. As soon as he had heard that a great pestilence had broken our among the crusader army at Riga he knew he had to seize his chance. The river gossip along the Dvina had told of death and demoralisation at Riga, of ships taking crusaders back across the water and great pits being dug outside the town to accommodate the dead. When he saw the walls of Riga on a bright, windless summer morning he had over four thousand men. He had raised nearly a thousand from among the villages of his former kingdom and had collected many more recruits as he neared Riga. They were mostly young men eager for vengeance and battle. They were disaffected and resentful at their treatment at the hands of the arrogant and haughty Christian crusaders, who destroyed the sacred forest groves where their people had worshipped for generations. They resented having to grow crops then having to give a portion to the Sword Brothers who sat in their castles and demanded allegiance. When Prince Vetseke appeared among them they interpreted it as a sign from the gods that they should take up arms to banish the crusaders and return to the old ways.

Vetseke knew that ordinarily he could not defeat the crusaders in open battle. But these were not ordinary circumstances. As his men walked from the trees into the fields filled with ripening crops he peered at the gaudy flags and banners of the crusader army. He could see men on horseback, both riders and horses wearing red, purple, blue, yellow, green, orange and combinations of these colours. If there had been any wind he would also have seen Count Walram's huge lion banner, the flag of Grand Master Volquin and the cross keys insignia of the Bishop of Riga. But there was no wind and even though it was still early morning he could feel sweat running down his neck. It would be a long, hot day. He smiled. Long may the sun shine down from a cloudless sky.

*****

The trumpets sounded assembly just as the first rays of dawn were lancing the eastern sky, hundreds of spearmen putting on their quilted aketons, then their mail hauberks, helmets and sword belts. They hoisted up their shields, grabbed their spears and filed out of camp to form up in their companies. Crossbowmen in gambesons waited at wagons to be issued with quivers of quarrels and squires rushed around saddling their masters' horses before their own. Many of the men were pale and gaunt after suffering the effects of the bloody flux, while dozens wore nothing below their waists save a loincloth and boots as they still had little control over their bowels. It was already stiflingly hot and men in full armour were beginning to feel drained.

The bishop rode from Riga in the company of Grand Master Volquin and Count Walram, who had black bags under his sunken eyes and was sweating profusely. He looked very ill but his companions were too polite to say anything. But the bishop was not so reticent when it came to Vetseke's army.

'There are very many of them,' he sighed. 'It saddens me to think that so many Livs hate us so much.'

'I would not take it personally, lord bishop,' said Volquin, trying to reassure him, 'young heads are easily turned. We beat Vetseke today and any rebelliousness within Liv hearts will quickly wither and die.'

Count Walram pointed at the block of Liv warriors forming up beside his own crusader foot soldiers. 'What about them?'

'They can be trusted, my lord,' said Volquin. 'Have no fear.'

'I have no fear in the face of godless pagans,' sniffed the count, before a fit of coughing gripped him. He was really not well at all.

Already Bishop Theodoric and the monks from his monastery were standing in front of the foot soldiers administering prayers, while other priests from Riga and those from Germany were similarly going among the crusaders to strengthen their resolve with prayers. Soldiers went down on their knees before the priests, reciting prayers and asking God to preserve them in the coming fight. Some did not rise, pitching forward as they passed out from exhaustion. Their comrades took them to the rear where they were ferried back to camp on the backs of carts. Weeks of extreme diarrhoea and vomiting had weakened bodies to such an extent that they were unfit for duty, even more so under a hot sun in full equipment. Spearmen used their shafts for support as the time passed slowly and the armies did not move.

It was now mid-morning and the sun was roasting hundreds of men encased in mail armour and helmets.

The two armies presented a contrasting sight as they stared at each other across the quarter-mile space that constituted no-man's land. On the left flank of the bishop's army were Count Walram's mounted crusaders with their profusion of differently coloured surcoats, pennants and caparisons. The sun glinted off whetted lance points and full-face helmets, horses scraping at the ground and swatting away the hordes of flies with their tails. This was a great block of six hundred horsemen, an irresistible hammer of mail and horseflesh that could batter its way through pagan foot soldiers with ease.

Next to the crusader horsemen stood the one hundred men of the bishop's garrison of Riga, men fully equipped in helmets, mail hauberks, shields and armed with spears, swords and daggers. In front of them stood the twenty-five crossbowmen of the Rigan militia, the spearmen of the latter providing a reserve behind the bishop's guards. Moving south towards the River Dvina, and deployed on the right flank of the Rigan forces, was grouped the crusader foot: eight hundred men in four groups and including a screen of crossbowmen. Many of the latter were lying on the ground resting until the fighting began.

The last group of foot soldiers in the crusader battle line comprised the Liv warriors – three hundred men – and the Sword Brother mercenaries on the end of the line: ninety battle-hardened soldiers. The right flank of the crusader army was made up of the horsemen from the castles at Uexkull and Holm: twenty-four brother knights with forty-five sergeants mounted behind them. The crusader line was thin in order to match the frontage of the four thousand Liv warriors opposite. The latter stood silently in their ranks, as did the crusaders, an eerie stillness hanging over the two armies.

*****

'Send forward a delegation requesting a parley,' said Vetseke to the commander of his Russians, a man wearing a mail hauberk, leggings, aventail and gilded helmet with a brass nasal guard.

'A parley, highness? I do not understand.'

'Anything to waste time,' replied the prince. He looked into the cloudless sky. 'This heat is insufferable. Ask the bishop if he would be so kind as to surrender.'

The Russian's eyes widened with surprise but he did as he was ordered, walking forward with two of his men and holding aloft a sprig of fir to show he came in peace.

Vetseke smiled as he saw a party of horsemen leave the crusader ranks and trot into no-man's land. There was then a short meeting out of earshot, the outcome of which he already knew. His commander returned with confirmation.

'The bishop refused your offer, highness. One of the crusader lords became very angry and...'

'And?' said Vetseke.

'He insulted you, highness, his words are not fit for your ears.'

Vetseke laughed. 'Give the order to begin. Your men have fully briefed the Livs?'

'Yes, highness.'

Vetseke drew his sword. 'Then let us shake up these haughty crusaders.'

*****

Count Walram drank from his water bottle, replaced the cork and tossed it to his squire mounted behind him.

'Arrogant bastards. Time to ride them down.'

The bishop blanched at his intemperate words as the count signalled his trumpeters to sound the advance, just at the moment when a great cheer came from the Liv army opposite and the green- and brown-clad warriors began walking forward.

'It would appear that they too are eager to get to grips with you, count,' said the bishop.

'God be with you, bishop,' said Walram before putting on his helmet.

'And with you, my son,' replied Albert.

'With your permission, lord bishop,' said Volquin, as he nodded and wheeled his horse away to take command of the foot soldiers, his small bodyguard of two brother knights and five sergeants cantering after him.

The Livs were banging their spear shafts against the insides of their large round shields, the thumping sound echoing across the battlefield. The Christian crossbowmen rose to their feet and loaded their weapons, while behind them a spearman collapsed from exhaustion every thirty seconds. Dozens had already been transported to the rear and not a few had died of their exertions, leaving the crusader line even thinner. The Livs were hurling insults as they closed to within four hundred paces of the bishop's army, the crossbowmen loosing bolts as they got closer. Livs were hit and disappeared among the crops as trumpet blasts on the Christian right wing signalled the advance of Count Walram and his crusader horsemen.

A succession of horn blasts from within the Liv ranks brought their advance to a halt and then they began to fall back. Count Walram saw the pagans beginning to retreat from behind the vision slits in his helmet and grinned. Slaughtering heathens would make him feel much better. He raised his lance and dug his spurs into his warhorse, which broke into a gallop and the ground shook as the hooves of six hundred horses pounded the earth. Following the lead of the horsemen, Grand Master Volquin gave the order for the spearmen to advance. They did so through the screen of crossbowmen in front of them, the latter reloading their weapons and following behind the spearmen. And on the right flank the small number of mounted Sword Brothers likewise trotted forward to follow the Liv rebels who were falling back.

Count Walram felt alive for the first time in weeks, the dreadful effects of the bloody flux finally being exorcised by the exhilaration of battle. He lowered his lance and then his horse reared up and groaned in pain before crashing to the ground and throwing him from the saddle. Other riders were likewise thrown as their mounts stumbled and collapsed on the ground, breaking legs and thrashing around in pain to crush their riders underneath their great bulks. Where moments before there had been an irresistible torrent of men of iron on horseback there was now bloody chaos. For among the crops had been spread a deadly crop.

They had originally been called 'star thistles' but most people knew them as caltrops. They were simple enough – two double-pointed strips of iron cold hammered together to resemble a ground thistle – but when they were scattered on the ground the four spikes were twisted in such a way that one always pointed upwards. And when stepped on by a man or horse they inflicted grave, sometimes, fatal wounds. Polotsk's smiths had spent many weeks producing hundreds of caltrops that the retreating Livs had scattered on the ground as they fell back.

The charge of the crusader horsemen was halted as the front ranks stepped on the deadly iron spikes, those behind careering into them and adding to the chaos. Horses reared up on their hind legs and threw their riders, some bolted away from the confusion, many with empty saddles. And then there was a great blast of horns and the Livs stopped retreating. Just as they had been instructed and just as they had practised on their march, they rushed forward a few paces and hurled their javelins at the now stationary crusader horsemen. Dozens of javelins were hurled at the Christians, volley after volley as nearly a thousand men threw their missiles over the carpet of caltrops at the mass of disorganised horsemen. After bringing the men of iron to an ignominious stop the Livs raised their shields in the air and cheered loudly. Never a thing had happened before and they revelled in their triumph.

On the other wing it was a similar story, though as soon as the first riders had fallen Gerhard and Friedhelm had recalled their men and sent an urgent summons to the Sword Brother mercenary foot deployed on their left flank to assist them. Seeing the Sword Brother horsemen retreat, the thousand Liv warriors on Vetseke's left wing halted their withdrawal and then advanced to hurl their javelins. But the Sword Brothers had also retreated and the Livs could not pursue them over the strip of caltrops they had sown. They therefore stood and began to whistle and jeer at the crusaders, until the crossbowmen from Holm and Uexkull began shooting at them. They numbered only thirty but they each shot four quarrels a minute and after five minutes had killed or wounded nearly three hundred Livs. The latter began to edge back and the right flank of the bishop's army had been saved. But in the centre a catastrophe was unfolding.

As soon as his wings had halted the crusader horsemen Vetseke gave the order for the two blocks of warriors that had been withdrawing before the Christian foot – each numbering a thousand men – to halt and then launch a counterattack. It took several minutes for the signallers to relay the command among the warriors. They may have been farmers but they were they were young, eager and strong and now they gripped their axes and spears and followed their prince as he charged at the head of his Russians.

Vetseke had no horsemen, no archers and only a hundred professional soldiers, but he had two thousand Liv warriors at his back as he ran at the crusader foot. He had studied the tactics and weapons of the crusaders closely and knew that to achieve any success he had to defeat their horsemen. He had done that and now he led a charge against their weakened centre. He knew it was weakened because the mail-clad men who formed it had been ravaged by a terrible pestilence that had killed many of their comrades. They had been standing in the sun for hours now and instead of an easy victory they were about to be engulfed by a pagan tide.

He ran ahead of that tide, shield grasped tightly to his body, his sword held high, and launched himself at a spearman with his spear levelled. The spear point glanced off his shield as he emitted a feral scream and plunged his sword into the man's neck, his death groan drowned out by a loud scraping sound as the two lines collided. The Russians behind the prince began to cut their way through the Christian foot easily enough, forming a compact wedge with Vetseke at its apex, thrusting their spears forward like a giant steel-hedgehog. The first rank of Livs mostly died when they smashed into the Christian line, their spear and axe thrusts being defeated by seasoned professionals who used their shields to ward off blows and then plunged their own spears into unarmoured torsos. But they then faced a deluge of attackers as more and more Livs hurled themselves at the crusader line, hacking with their axes and jabbing with their spears. The crusader line momentarily held, buckled and then gave way under the sheer weight of the attack.

Hundreds of Livs died in that mêlée and hundreds more were wounded, but they killed dozens of crusader spearmen and pushed the survivors back. And from the wings came dozens more Livs who were eager to share in the victory that was unfolding in the centre.

*****

Grand Master Volquin watched as the mass of green- and brown-clad warriors in front of him charged the lines of advancing Christian spearmen and then forced them back. The foot had been spread thinly enough but now they risked being literally swamped by the pagan mass. On the right the Sword Brothers appeared to have stabilised the situation, while on the left flank Count Walram's riders resembled a herd of spooked horses. There were frantic trumpet calls as some knights tried to establish a semblance of order, but the crusader horsemen fought as individuals not as a disciplined body under a single commander, so Volquin doubted that the horsemen would be able to intervene in the battle quickly. The crossbowmen that had been deployed in front of the spearmen had been rendered useless when the latter had advanced through them to pursue the Livs. Volquin also noticed that a battle within a battle was taking place on the right flank of his centre where the three hundred loyal Livs were engaged in a particularly vicious fight with Vetseke's men. It was apparent that the centre was about to break and there was nothing he could do to prevent it.

Bishop Albert had also seen the confusion within Count Walram's horsemen and the misfortune that had beset his foot soldiers. The commander of his guards had urged him to leave the field and retreat back to Riga. He waved the man away. Now he sat on his horse in front of his standard bearer as his guards left the crusader foot to their fate and closed around him, the men of Riga's militia also forming up around their bishop. Noble as this might have been it robbed Grand Master Volquin of what few reserves he could call on to reverse the disaster that was unfolding in the centre. He rode over to the bishop, bringing his attendant brother knights, sergeants and foot soldiers with him.

'I would advise withdrawing back to Riga, my lord bishop,' urged Volquin.

Bishop Albert had removed his helmet with its steel mitre, his face streaked with sweat. 'I will not abandon the Lord's work, grand master.'

Volquin pointed at the bishop's guards and militia grouped round him. 'I need these men, lord bishop, if the day is to be saved.'

The bishop nodded. 'Then let us lead them together.'

There was an almighty cheer and Volquin looked behind him to see the Christian centre give way as dozens of spearmen abandoned their weapons and attempted to flee back to Riga, a mile distant. The crossbowmen behind them managed to loose a volley or two before they were caught up in the rout and also ran for their lives. The centre of the bishop's army had ceased to exist.

The bishop dug his spurs into the sides of his horse and moved forward, scattering those of his guards standing to his right. Without any regard for his personal danger he charged towards the Livs who were now chasing after the retreating spearmen and crossbowmen. If they continued unchecked they would not only run down the fleeing Christian foot soldiers but would also reach the crusader camp, and perhaps gain entry into Riga itself.

Volquin galloped after the bishop, followed by the brother knights and sergeants of the Sword Brothers, together with around fifty knights who had left Count Walram's disorganised wing and rallied to the bishop. The foot soldiers followed the horsemen who were soon among the Livs, trying to stem the pagan flood.

*****

'God with us!' shouted Master Berthold, replacing his helmet on his head and then spurring his horse forward.

'God with us!' answered the men of Segewold, Kremon and Wenden, who joined the castellan of the latter as they lowered their lances and galloped towards the rear of the Liv army.

Behind the thirty-six brother knights came sixty sergeants dressed exactly the same as the former aside from their kettle helmets. And behind the sergeants rode Conrad, Hans, Anton and Johann. Just over a hundred horsemen charging into a mass of pagan warriors.

Grand Master Volquin had ordered that the garrisons along the Gauja remain where they were. But Thalibald's scouts had reported that Vetseke had gathered a great army and Master Berthold knew that the flux had greatly weakened the bishop's forces at Riga. He therefore disobeyed orders and rode south with his men. He asked Thalibald to reinforce the garrison at Wenden and made the same request of Caupo regarding the castles of Segewold and Kremon. Now he had arrived on the battlefield, his men exiting the trees that had sheltered Vetseke's army the night before. He could see the banners of the crusader horsemen on the right, heard the sound of fighting to his front and could not discern any activity on the left. He had no time to formulate a plan so ordered a charge into the heart of the enemy army.

Conrad looked over at Hans and grinned as he couched his lance and urged his horse on. Hans was on his left while Anton and Johann rode on his right. Lukas had ordered them to remain in the rear of the formation but as the Sword Brothers thundered across the beaten-down crops the sergeants divided into two groups and galloped to the right and left flanks of the brother knights. Fearful of disobeying Lukas' orders Conrad and the others remained behind the front line, and then there was no time to think about formations as the Sword Brothers hit the Livs like a mailed fist punching soft flesh.

The collapse of the Christian centre had increased the numbers of Liv warriors leaving the flanks to join their victorious comrades in the centre, resulting in a great press of men eagerly waiting to join the slaughter being enjoyed by those men in front. If they even saw the Sword Brothers who had charged out of the forest it was only fleetingly, before they were speared and cut down by Christian weapons. Those Livs Master Berthold's men killed first had been widely spaced with their backs to the Sword Brothers. When their comrades turned around to see the source of the tumult that had suddenly erupted behind them the mailed horsemen were already among them.

Conrad rammed his lance through the back of a Liv warrior, let go of the shaft and drew his sword, bringing it down on the bare head of another warrior who turned and froze in horror as Sir Frederick's sword split his skull. On Conrad rode, through the scattering Livs, hacking left and right at any targets within reach. Hans and the others clung to him as he forgot about Master Berthold, Rudolf, Henke and the others and just thought of killing the enemy. Around him hundreds of men were fighting for their lives as Sword Brothers charged headlong into the seething mass of pagans, the momentum of their charge stuttering and then dying as the enemy swarmed around them.

*****

'To me. Rally to me!'

Vetseke held up his gore-covered sword and waited for his Russians to close around him. He had seen the crusader wings being halted, had led the charge that had shattered their centre and now spied the man who was the cause of all his misfortune: Bishop Albert. The prelate was on his horse amidst his warriors, desperately trying to stem the pagan victory that was unfolding. He forgot about storming the crusader camp and butchering all inside, ignored the flood of warriors heading towards Riga and thought of only one thing: kill Bishop Albert.

His men were breathing heavily, their hauberks ripped and torn, their shields splintered and their helmets dented. But they once more formed into a wedge formation and followed Vetseke as he walked purposely towards the man who had polluted his beloved land with foreigners. The bishop's guards had valiantly charged into the Livs but had been simply overwhelmed and now most of their corpses lay trampled underfoot. Around a dozen still stood, desperately trying to fend off a ring of predators.

And then the Russians closed as one on the bishop, cutting down his guards and then killing his horse, causing the prelate to fall to the ground. Grand Master Volquin jumped from his saddle to stand beside him. He fought well but there were too many of the enemy and as he fended them off he became separated from the bishop and looked on, helplessly, as a burly Russian barged him to the ground. The bishop lay prostrate as the Russian raised his sword above the bishop's head to kill him.

Conrad thrust his sword into the Russian's shoulder blade as he passed, then slashed at another mail-clad giant on his left side, his blade glancing off the man's shield. He tugged on his reins to halt his horse but then the beast collapsed beneath him and he was lying on his side, his right leg under the animal. He heard Lukas' words in his mind – *keep moving* – as he yanked himself free and sprang to his feet. A warrior, a brute in a pointed helmet and mail armour, had killed his horse with a spear thrust and now he was determined to kill him.

Conrad glanced behind him and saw the bishop struggling to his feet. He turned and spat at the Russian and then ran to the side of Bishop Albert. He grabbed his arm and hauled him to his feet.

'Have no fear, lord bishop,' he said grandly.

Hans leaped from his horse and came to Conrad's side as half a dozen Russians approached them like ravenous wolves. Then Anton and Johann appeared behind them and split the helmets of two with their swords. Conrad shouted with joy and sprang at the four survivors, crouching low at the last moment to catch the enemy sword on his shield before thrusting his sword beneath the Russian's shield and into his belly. The man groaned as Conrad attacked the soldier next to him, Hans fighting beside him. They were fresh and strong and forced their opponents back with a series of lightning-fast sword strikes.

Anton and Johann, having both dismounted, rushed to their friends' sides and now it was four against four. Conrad's opponent was bigger than him but he was faster and cut the man's thigh with the point of his sword, the metal biting deep into his leg. The Russian hobbled and tried to chop Conrad's neck with his sword but the youth caught the blow on his shield and then thrust his sword into the enemy's armpit. The man yelped and collapsed, then died as Conrad rammed his blade through the man's throat.

'Defend the bishop,' shouted Conrad as Hans killed his opponent with a single strike to the groin.

Conrad and the others retreated to stand in front of Bishop Albert, who had now been joined by Grand Master Volquin, a score of mounted crusaders, Master Berthold and Rudolf.

Volquin looked in alarm at the bishop. 'Are you hurt, lord bishop?'

Albert, helmetless and sweating, laid a hand on his shoulder. 'No, thanks to these boys who appeared as if sent by the Lord himself. Master Berthold, never have I been so glad to see you and your brother knights.'

'Your servant, lord bishop,' said Berthold, raising his sword to him.

The pagan tide had ebbed now as more and more crusader horsemen from Count Walram's wing had joined the battle in the centre, riders heading towards the crusader camp to cut down Livs moving towards the town. And from the Christian right wing the Sword Brothers from Holm and Uexkull had launched a charge against the Livs, cutting down dozens and forcing hundreds more to retreat back to the forest.

The bishop walked forward and pointed at Conrad. 'This young man saved my life. What is your name?'

'Conrad Wolff, lord bishop.'

Albert looked thoughtful. 'I have heard that name before.'

'You saw me when you last came to Wenden, lord bishop.'

The prelate nodded. 'Ah. Yes, of course. The boy who wounded Lembit.'

He turned to look at Berthold sitting on his horse. 'You must be most proud to have such young lions among your garrison.'

Berthold nodded approvingly. 'Yes, lord bishop.'

'Even if they have lost their horses,' remarked Rudolf.

Conrad looked at Hans and the others and felt his cheeks flush. The bishop laughed.

'As have I. So you are all in good company. Now, someone fetch me a horse so we may bring this drama to a rightful end.'

*****

Vetseke saw the four riders collide into his Russians and growled in frustration. He had been on the verge of a great victory but triumph had been cruelly snatched from him with the arrival of Christian reinforcements. He watched in despair as the Sword Brothers came from nowhere and began scything down his warriors. The fifty or so Russians still alive forgot about killing the bishop and closed ranks around him, forming a small shield fort to ward off any horsemen. But the Livs were not so fortunate. They had no protection as the knights rode among them, first spearing them with their lances and then using their swords to wreak havoc.

'We must leave, highness,' urged his Russian commander. 'Their crossbowmen will finish what the horsemen have started.'

He was right. After the knights had finished their butchery the crossbowmen would reap a grim harvest with their weapons.

'We must retreat back to the trees, highness,' his subordinate insisted.

'I will remain,' said Vetseke. 'I release you from your obligations.'

'We cannot leave you, highness.'

'I order you to go!' Vetseke snapped. He attempted a half-smile. 'Go. Save yourselves.'

The man saluted, barked an order to his men who began to shuffle in the direction of the trees, making their way across the flattened crops and lacerated bodies.

Groups of Livs were now throwing down their weapons and raising their hands in surrender as mounted knights surrounded them to prevent their escape. The bishop, now back on a horse, was riding among them ordering them to give themselves up and promising them their lives if they did so. Leaderless, surrounded and faced by crossbowmen with weapons loaded, they were only too glad to consent. Where there had been the clatter of battle there was suddenly a dire quiet, interlaced with the groans and cries of the wounded.

Vetseke stood alone among the carnage, observing without emotion the approach of Bishop Albert with a group of Sword Brothers and crusaders. The bishop halted twenty paces from him as Grand Master Volquin, Master Berthold and the other brother knights circled him. Vetseke sheathed his sword and took off his helmet, placing it in the crook of his arm. He looked directly at the bishop and ignored the others. He did notice, however, a youth standing beside the bishop's horse, a tall individual dressed in a gambeson with a kettle helmet on his head. A servant, no doubt. And immediately behind him were three other young servants, except that they were mounted.

The bishop rested his hands on the saddle's high and broad pommel. 'Prince Vetseke. It has been a while since we last met, an event that took place under more agreeable circumstances, I seem to remember.'

Vetseke tilted his head ever so slightly at the bishop. 'It would appear that you have the advantage once more, bishop.'

Albert looked around, a pained expression on his face. 'It saddens me to see so much blood spilt in so fruitless a cause.'

'Fighting for one's homeland against foreign invaders is not fruitless, bishop,' Vetseke sneered.

'Foreign invaders, prince? Surely you must place yourself in that category. You were, after all, the ruler of Kokenhusen and not Riga if my memory serves me well.'

Vetseke folded his arms. 'You will never plant your foreign faith in this land.'

The bishop sighed. 'That remains to be seen but for the moment I must address more immediate matters. I must ask you to surrender your sword.'

Vetseke smiled and drew it, prompting the Sword Brothers to nudge their horses towards him. 'If I am to die I would prefer it to be here, with a sword in my hand.'

The bishop was appalled. 'You will be my guest in my palace, prince. There has been too much killing today. But I must ask you to give up your sword temporarily. You have my word that no harm will befall you.'

'I must request that the same courtesy is extended to those you have captured,' said Vetseke.

'Of course,' replied the bishop.

Volquin turned in his saddle. 'My lord bishop, the penalty for rebellion is death.'

'Do the Sword Brothers presume to instruct their bishop on the laws of Livonia, grand master?' snapped the bishop.

Volquin looked most discomfited. 'No, lord bishop, of course not.'

Bishop Albert looked sternly at Vetseke. 'I would have your sword, prince. Now. And then we may leave this place of dead flesh to carry on our discussion in more pleasant surroundings.'

Vetseke curled his lip at Volquin and unbuckled his sword belt.

'Conrad,' said the bishop, 'go and bring me the prince's sword.'

Conrad looked at the prince and then at Rudolf sitting next to Volquin, who nodded at him. He swallowed and walked forward, feeling most uncomfortable as a score of pairs of eyes watched him. Vetseke regarded him for a few seconds, his stare met by steely blue-grey eyes. He seemed to have a very expensive sword for a servant. Most odd. He shrugged and handed Conrad his belt and sword. The bishop smiled.

'Bring a horse for the prince.'

Conrad stood in front of Hans' horse as the bishop rode back to Riga in the company of the man who had plotted to kill him. Behind rode the Sword Brothers and the crusader knights. Rudolf halted his horse.

'You boys report to the castle. Where is your horse, Conrad?'

'Dead, Brother Rudolf.'

'I am sure that the bishop will be able to find you a new one. Hans, give Conrad a ride.' Rudolf smiled at them. 'You all fought well. I am glad to see that you all remembered Lukas' instruction.'

Conrad decided to walk to Riga so the others dismounted and led their horses among the battlefield dead. By now they had grown accustomed to the sight of slaughter and hardly raised an eyebrow as they passed bodies with crushed skulls and severed limbs. They did notice the swarms of flies that were gorging on flesh and the odour of death that was permeating the summer afternoon.

The battle had been fought and won but at a heavy cost. Just over two thousand men had marched out to face Prince Vetseke's army and now over a quarter of them lay dead in the fields to the east of Riga, among them Count Walram. When his body was retrieved and conveyed back to camp it was discovered there was not a mark on it, the physicians concluding that he had died of exhaustion brought about by the bout of flux he had suffered. Among the crusader foot casualties totalled three hundred dead spearmen, most killed by the enemy but a portion dying of the exertions inflicted upon their weakened bodies after the flux. A hundred loyal Livs had died, together with fifty of the bishop's guards, a hundred mounted crusaders and twenty fatalities among the Sword Brothers. And that night the tents of the crusader camp were filled with hundreds more who had been wounded in the battle. The bishop may have won the fight but his army had been sorely depleted. For this reason alone he was inclined to leniency and mercy when he gathered his commanders in his palace two days afterwards.

The day was stifling and though the windows were open the heat in the room was oppressive, despite no one wearing armour. The Sword Brothers were attired in the white mantles of their order. Bishop Albert was poring over the casualty lists that had been drawn up, both for his own forces and the enemy.

'It is most important that all the bodies are interred as quickly as possible,' he commented. 'How many enemy dead?'

'Over a thousand, lord bishop,' answered Volquin, 'and another four hundred will most likely die of their wounds before the week is out.'

The bishop shook his head. 'Captives?'

'Two thousand held in the castle courtyard,' said Volquin.

'Release them so they can make their way home in time for the harvest.'

Berthold looked at Gerhard and Friedhelm. 'You would release them, lord bishop?'

'What choice do I have?'

Berthold smiled. 'I have often found that making an example of individuals has a deterring effect.'

Albert froze him with a glare. 'There will be none of that. I would have the loyalty of these people.'

334

'There is the more pressing matter of what to do with Vetseke, lord bishop,' said Volquin.

'He must die,' remarked Berthold.

'And quickly,' added Friedhelm.

The bishop turned and handed the sheets of parchment to a clerk. 'I will banish him, never to return to Livonia.'

Volquin sighed in exasperation. 'You cannot let him go, lord bishop. He has openly rebelled against your rule and to let him go free will make you look weak. When you go to make peace with Lembit it would be better if the body of Vetseke was hanging from Riga's walls.'

'Lembit will be impressed by such a gesture,' agreed Gerhard.

Bishop Albert held up his hands. 'Brothers, Vetseke will be banished. That is my decision. You all seem to forget that we are but servants of God who has a plan for this land. It was He who gave us victory over the pagans and it will be He who protects Livonia in the face of their godlessness. I do not need to act cruelly in order to impress heathens, not when God himself watches over us.'

And so Vetseke was spared and the bishop prepared to meet Lembit to discuss a temporary truce.

Chapter 13

It took two days for the army of Grand Duke Daugerutis to cross over the Dvina to enter Livonia. First came the élite horsemen: men wearing mail or lamellar armour, helmets, aventails and mail on their legs and arms. These were the personal guards and men of substance of the princes who had come to march beside their duke. They wore leather boots, carried pavise-like shields and wore rich, brightly coloured cloaks around their shoulders. Prince Stecse was among them, wearing a shining helmet and armed with a sword given to him by the grand duke himself. All the élite Lithuanian horsemen wore swords but also carried axes and maces dangling from their saddles. They and the other horsemen were ferried over the river continuously until there were eight thousand horsemen and double that number of horses on the northern bank of the Dvina.

The grand duke brought only horsemen into the land of the crusaders, his army's supplies being carried on a spare horse that followed each rider. The boats were rowed across the river by the farmers that populated the area immediately south of the Dvina: free men who were tied to their local lord by oaths of loyalty, the lord in turn owing allegiance to his prince, the latter paying homage to Grand Duke Daugerutis. It was an ancient system that had kept the Lithuanian people strong and free, able to defeat the aggression of the Russians, Kurs, crusaders and, finally, pagan Prussian tribes that lived on their southern borders.

The warlord of all the Lithuanians sat on a stool outside his tent as his men cooked a roe deer they had caught earlier, the rich aroma of roasting meat filling the late afternoon air. Stecse sat next to his lord as his son, a gangly youth of twelve summers with a long face, sat on the ground nearby cleaning his father's sword.

The ground was covered with small two-man tents, groups of horses tethered in long lines between them. Stacks of light spears called *spisas* stood throughout the camp along with a multitude of campfires that produced a pall of wispy smoke that hung still in the windless air. In front of the grand duke four guards suddenly drew their swords and stood in a line. Ahead of them a group of riders wearing white surcoats was approaching, flanked by twice as many Lithuanian horsemen. The grand duke stood and a hand went to his sword hilt but as Stecse rose he reassured his lord.

'It is Master Griswold from Kokenhusen, my lord. Coming to pay his compliments, no doubt.'

Griswold had thought it prudent to let Daugerutis know that he and his army were being observed as he made his way through Livonia to attack the Novgorodians. He had disagreed with the treaty made between Riga and the grand duke but had no option but to accept it. It was true that there had been no hostilities along the river since the agreement but he was still uneasy about letting thousands of pagans traverse Livonia freely. Griswold had brought a brother knight and two sergeants as an escort, more for company than security amid such a host.

The Sword Brothers dismounted as their mounted escort did likewise and walked alongside the Christians as they ambled towards the grand duke. The four guards barred their way and requested their weapons. Prince Stecse, all smiles, pushed his way through the guards.

'Greetings, Master Griswold. The grand duke is most eager to meet you. Please surrender your swords. A precaution, you understand.'

Griswold nodded at him and instructed his men to stay where they were. He unbuckled his belt, handed his sword to the guard in front of him and was allowed to pass. The other Lithuanians observed the Sword Brothers warily but the latter merely stood holding the reins of their horses while their master conducted his business.

Stecse introduced the grand duke and then addressed the boy cleaning his sword.

'Mindaugas, a stool for our guest.'

The boy jumped up and disappeared into the tent to retrieve another stool. Daugerutis held out his hand to it.

'I am sorry my hospitality is so austere, Master Griswold.'

Griswold smiled politely and sat down on the stool. 'The order of Sword Brothers prefers austerity over extravagance, grand duke.'

Daugerutis sat beside him. 'So I have heard.'

Griswold decided to get straight to the point. 'You go to attack the Russians?'

'I do.'

'And how long will you be this side of the river?'

Daugerutis smiled. 'Abrupt and to the point. I like that.'

'I am a soldier, grand duke, not a diplomat.'

The boy offered Griswold a full cup. He took it and was surprised that it was water. The grand duke noticed his shock.

'I am a soldier too, master. I come to fight not to give banquets.'

The boy went back to cleaning the sword.

'You bring boys to fight the Russians?' he asked.

'My son Mindaugas,' said Stecse. 'This is his first campaign.'

'Let us hope that it is not his last,' remarked Griswold. He addressed the grand duke. 'I must insist that your men do not molest the Livs as you pass through their territory. It would be unfortunate if you were to breach the terms of the agreement.'

Daugerutis noticed the mild threat but did not rise to it. 'My men are under strict orders not to pillage the land, Master Griswold. But surely the Livs are in open rebellion against the bishop?'

'A number of misguided individuals was seduced by Prince Vetseke, former ruler of Kokenhusen, but they have been destroyed and the prince currently languishes in chains to await the bishop's judgement on him.'

'Vetseke,' said Stecse. 'I thought he was long dead.'

Griswold smiled. 'He soon will be. The bishop's wrath, though slow to rise, can be swift and terrible.'

Daugerutis nodded approvingly. He liked this Christian warrior who did not mince his words.

'I will have a care not to inflame the bishop's passions, Master Griswold.'

The Sword Brother took a sip of his water. 'I have heard, grand duke, that the Russians frequently raided your lands.'

Daugerutis stared into the fire. 'The Novgorodians, master, often raided as far as the Dvina and sometimes even into Lithuania itself. They are of your religion, I believe.'

'They follow the Orthodox religion,' Griswold corrected him, 'not the Holy Church of Rome.'

The names meant nothing to Daugerutis. 'They are your enemies?'

'At the moment the Russians are content to trade with us. They covet Estonia.'

'As does the bishop,' said Stecse.

'It is our duty to bring the Estonians into the Christian faith,' said Griswold, 'just as we have done with the Livs.'

Daugerutis continued to stare at the deer roasting over the fire. 'And after you have subdued the Estonians, who will be next on the bishop's list of people to be enslaved?'

'I am not privy to the bishop's decisions, grand duke,' said Griswold. 'As I said, I am merely a soldier.'

338

Of course both he and the grand duke knew that the pope had commanded that all the pagan peoples in the Baltic should be brought under the rule of God, which included the Lithuanians. But the grand duke also knew that if he attacked Novgorod then the Russians would be enraged that the Bishop of Riga had allowed him free passage through his territory. This in turn might lead to the Russians waging war on Livonia, which in turn would keep conflict away from his own lands. Vsevolod had done him a great service to broker the treaty with the bishop. He would ensure that his soldiers kept well away from Gerzika's lands so as not to embroil his son-in-law in the conflicts that might arise in the near future.

*****

Conrad rode back to Wenden in the company of the others of the garrison. Word of his saving of the bishop, aided by his three companions, had spread and he felt immensely happy. The bishop himself had given him a new horse and had promised to mention him when he wrote to the pope concerning the late battle against Prince Vetseke. The latter was still confined in Riga's castle, though in a well-appointed room rather than a dungeon, and the Livs who had been captured during the battle had all been released to make their way back to their homes to take part in the harvest.

'It was a bad decision,' complained Henke.

'No doubt you would have been more satisfied if he had been summarily executed,' said Master Berthold.

They were riding back to Wenden along tracks that were bone dry, the air filled with the scent of pine as they made their way through the forests adjacent to the Gauja.

'I would, master,' replied Henke.

As a reward for their conduct during the battle Conrad and the other boys had been allowed to ride in the company of the master, his deputy, Henke and Lukas on their return journey to Wenden. Everyone's spirits were high, not least because not one of the garrison had been killed during the battle against Vetseke.

'Henke believes that there are only two types of people in the world,' said Rudolf. 'Those who are friends and those who are enemies, and the latter should always be killed as quickly as possible.'

Lukas laughed as Henke looked unconcerned.

'Releasing Vetseke will be a mistake,' said Henke. 'It merely postpones the inevitable.'

'Which is?' enquired Master Berthold.

'That we will have to kill him,' replied Henke. 'Better to kill him now before he can cause any more trouble.'

'What do you think, Conrad?' said Rudolf, turning in his saddle to look at him. 'After all, you currently have the ear of the bishop.'

'I do not know, brother,' replied Conrad, embarrassed by the attention being given him.

'Speak your mind,' said Berthold, 'never be afraid to speak your mind.'

Hans looked at Conrad and nodded, urging him to say something.

'I think the bishop is a very wise man,' said Conrad.

Henke guffawed loudly. 'That is no answer at all. It's a good job you are more forthright with a sword in your hand. You should have stuck Vetseke with your blade.'

'I did not see him at the time, brother,' said Conrad.

'But if you had encountered him on the battlefield,' said Rudolf, 'you would have killed him?'

'Oh, yes,' said Conrad without hesitation.

'I must congratulate you, Brother Lukas,' remarked Berthold, 'you have crafted a group of fine young soldiers.'

'They still require some polishing, master,' said Lukas, 'but it is pleasing to discover that they have been paying attention during their training.'

'Where will we be campaigning next, Master Berthold?' asked Anton.

'Nowhere, young man,' said Berthold. 'We are to have peace with the Estonians.'

'Peace? Peace is only the short interval between wars,' spat Henke, causing everyone to smile.

The bishop arrived at Wenden two weeks later, accompanied by fifty knights and their squires, a hundred spearmen, the same number of crossbowmen, Caupo and a hundred of his warriors. Once more the area around the castle was covered with tents as the bishop took up residence in the master's hall and couriers were despatched to Lembit requesting his presence at a conference where a two-year peace would be agreed between him and the bishop. Though the pestilence had finally passed Albert believed that a two-year suspension of hostilities was essential for the continued growth of Riga, suppression of any latent rebelliousness among the Livs and the collection of funds from Germany for the ongoing construction of the Sword Brother castles.

340

While he waited for Lembit's answer the bishop attended to more pleasant tasks, such as inspecting Wenden's growing fortifications, being introduced to Thalibald's sons and daughter and taking a service in the castle's chapel. He also rewarded those who had saved his life during the Battle of Riga.

Conrad stood with Hans, Johann and Anton outside the reception room of the master's hall following a summons from the bishop. Rudolf himself had walked down to the training area and informed Lukas that their presence was required in the master's hall. Henke had seen the boys walking across the courtyard and followed them into the hall where they waited anxiously outside the thick oak door with Lukas. Rudolf went back inside the reception room where he had spent the morning dealing with business in the company of Berthold and the bishop.

Henke had an evil grin on his face. 'Nervous?' he asked Conrad.

'No, brother.'

'You are all to be rewarded by the bishop,' continued Henke, 'my congratulations.'

He placed an arm around Conrad's shoulders, who thought that most unusual as they had barely exchanged words since the affair of the Estonian female captives.

'I should not really say anything but I have it on good authority that the bishop has decided that you shall all be castratos in his new cathedral in Riga.'

Lukas turned away and stifled a laugh as the boys looked at each other in confusion.

'Castratos?' said Hans.

Henke smiled. 'Yes, indeed. The word comes from castration and is used to describe those boys who have their balls cut off so they can sing with voices that resemble the song of the nightingale. You should all consider yourselves very honoured.'

Anton was ashen faced. 'Surely you are mistaken?'

Henke looked deadly serious. 'Mistaken? Being a castrato is accorded one of the highest honours of the church. I both envy and admire you for this most special privilege that is about to be bestowed on you all.'

'But, but we are to be sergeants,' implored Johann.

Henke shook his head as Lukas bit his lip to stop himself laughing.

'Master Berthold commented on how sweet your voices sounded in the chapel and that was that. But fear not, we will carry out the procedure here, at Wenden, to ensure that you all survive.'

341

He pulled his dagger from its sheath and pointed it at Conrad.

'Daina will be here to see it.'

Conrad, now thoroughly alarmed, was actually shaking. 'Daina?'

Henke brushed the dagger's blade with a finger to test the sharpness. 'Of course, plus Thalibald and his sons. To witness the ceremony of the castrato is accorded a great honour.'

Rudolf came from the reception room. 'The bishop will see you all now.'

He noticed the pale expressions on the boys' faces, Henke grinning like an idiot and Lukas' face twisted as he tried to hide his mirth.

'Is there a problem?'

Henke replaced his dagger in its sheath. 'No problem, Rudolf.' He smiled and walked back into the courtyard.

Rudolf frowned and instructed the boys to follow him immediately. When he took his position by the side of Berthold, who was seated beside the bishop at the end of the room under the banner of the Sword Brothers that hung on the wall behind, the boys looked as though they were about to pass out.

The bishop smiled at them as they stood before him.

'It is one of the more pleasurable duties of my office to reward those who have excelled in their service,' he began, then stopping as he noticed that beads of sweat were forming on Conrad's forehead. He also noticed that Hans seemed to be in a state of abject terror.

'Are you ill?' he asked him.

'No, lord bishop,' replied Hans.

The bishop looked at Master Berthold who was perplexed, before continuing.

'Well, in view of your heroism at Riga I have decided...'

Hans fell on his knees and clasped his hands together in prayer. 'Please do not castrate us, lord bishop, I beg you,' he implored.

The others boys began nodding frantically, resembling a row of performing dogs. The bishop looked at Master Berthold in utter confusion.

'Castration? What nonsense is this?'

Hans was too distraught to speak so Conrad took over. 'So we can sing in your cathedral, lord bishop. But we wish to fight not sing.'

'Fight,' agreed Johann.

'No singing,' pleaded Anton.

'Singing, cathedral, castration? Have you been drinking?' said the bishop accusingly.

'I think I might be able to unravel this mystery, lord bishop,' said Rudolf. 'I believe the boys have been victims of a cruel joke that has led to their state of agitation. They believe that they are to be castratos in your cathedral.'

The bishop was not amused. He looked at Hans rocking to and fro before him. 'Get up. First of all, there is no cathedral as yet in Riga so even if I wanted castratos, which I do not, they would have to wait until it was built. A long wait, I might add.'

Conrad helped Hans, who was weeping tears of relief, to his feet.

'Perhaps you might take some time to root out the practice of innuendo and falsehoods that appears to have taken root in your castle, Master Berthold,' said the bishop, clearly irritated.

'I will, lord bishop,' replied Berthold.

'To continue,' said the bishop. 'I have instructed Master Berthold that when your training period ends all of you are to be given the opportunity to enter the Brothers of the Knighthood of Christ in Livonia, more commonly known as the Sword Brothers, as brother knights and not sergeants.'

The expressions on the faces of the boys changed from anxiety to pure joy in an instant. Among them only Anton, due to his noble birth, was guaranteed the mantle of brother knight. Conrad and the others were destined to be sergeants but now that had all changed. The performing dogs returned as all of them began nodding enthusiastically at the bishop, who found their behaviour even odder.

'Very well, you are dismissed. And congratulations.' He waved them away and Rudolf escorted them from the room and then went to find Henke.

Three days later a message arrived from Lembit saying that he would meet with the bishop to discuss peace. The Estonian leader said that he would not come to Wenden but suggested a meeting on the southern shore of Lake Aster, the waterway that marked the ancient border between the Livs and the Saccalians. This great lake, some eight miles long and nearly four miles wide, was located thirty miles north of Wenden. The bishop agreed and gave orders for the knights and their squires to accompany him on his journey, together with the brother knights and sergeants from Wenden, Segewold and Kremon. He also instructed that Conrad and his companions join the expedition as a further reward for their heroism at Riga.

Caupo also accompanied the bishop, his warriors walking behind their king who rode beside the bishop. The show of strength was designed to awe Lembit and

343

make him more amenable to choose peace rather than war, which Caupo believed would be the case.

'He has been weakened by his failure at Treiden and the recent assault on his people by the Russians.'

'As we have been weakened by the pestilence and our losses at Riga, lord king' said the bishop. 'We thus appear evenly matched in our vulnerability.'

'Many of my elders are unhappy that the Lithuanians have been allowed to cross the Dvina,' said Caupo.

'I accept that the agreement with Grand Duke Daugerutis was a little unusual,' said the bishop solemnly, 'and perhaps if I had been in Riga at the time I would not have consented to it. On the other hand, it has led to peace along the Dvina, which we must thank God for.'

'When the peace with the Lithuanians ends they will cross the river to attack your castles, lord bishop.'

'You do not believe that grand Duke Daugerutis desires peace?'

Caupo looked ahead. 'I do not. The ties that unite the Lithuanian tribes are soaked in blood. They will think that you are weak for letting them cross your territory, lord bishop. They only respect strength.'

Bishop Albert smiled. 'We *are* weak, my friend, at the moment. But what is today may not be tomorrow. God has set us a great task in bringing His word to the godless, one that will not be achieved in a day, a week or a year. But it will be achieved, have no fear of that.'

'What if Lembit rejects your offer of peace?'

The bishop shrugged. 'Then we will fortify our strongholds and pray for next summer when a new army of crusaders will arrive from Germany.'

But Lembit did not reject the bishop's offer. In fact he was only too pleased to accept a cessation of hostilities. Though the raid by the Novgorodians had been repelled the other tribal chiefs had been unnerved by Mstislav's aggression. Kalju in particular had complained bitterly to Lembit that he should be safeguarding Estonian territory rather than making alliances with the Oeselians and launching attacks into Livonia. It had been his kingdom that the Russians had invaded and he wanted revenge. Lembit had wanted to bring all the tribal chiefs to the meeting with Bishop Albert but thought that Kalju might refuse to come. In the end the Ungannian did consent to attend the meeting, bringing a hundred of his warriors with him.

The sky was overcast when the Estonians made their camp on the eastern shore of Lake Aster, its grey waters rippled by an easterly wind that swayed the reeds surrounding its edges. The lake not only marked the border between Estonia and Livonia, it also marked the boundary between the Ungannians and Lembit's Saccalians, the largest of the Estonian tribes. South of the lake there was nothing but forests, marshes and meadows: no villages or hill forts. This strip of territory had for centuries been used by raiders to strike north or south in search of pillage, plunder and slaves. It was far too dangerous to live there, except if you were a bandit, mad or an outcast.

But now it was filled by a great expanse of tents of different shapes and sizes as the bishop and his entourage filled the meadows to the south of the lake, the banners of the knights of northern Germany fluttering in the stiff breeze. Conrad, Hans, Johann and Anton were given the task of erecting a tent two miles from the Christian camp that would be the venue for the meeting between the bishop and Lembit. A delegation of the latter's wolf shields had arrived bearing small branches as a sign of peace and had been escorted to the bishop's tent where he sat with Caupo, Thalibald, Grand Master Volquin and Sir Rudolf von Jerichow from Kokenhusen. The latter was now the most senior crusader lord and had been requested to attend by the bishop.

The Estonians were led by a large, coarse man with a thick beard whose bulk made his shield look like a child's toy. He walked with an arrogant swagger and in addition to the sword that hung from his hip he had an axe tucked into his belt. He told the bishop that his name was Rusticus and that he was Lembit's deputy. He ignored Caupo and Thalibald and drank greedily from a cup of wine that was offered him. He told the bishop that all the Estonian tribal leaders would be attending the meeting. When the bishop enquired if any Oeselians would be attending Rusticus feigned puzzlement as to why he would ask such a question. The large Estonian brute drank two more cups of wine before taking his leave, unconcerned that he was in the midst of a crusader army with but a handful of warriors. The bishop hoped that his rudeness did not presage a fruitless meeting with Lembit.

Conrad was leading the pony hitched to the cart that had carried the tent to the pre-arranged venue for the conference, Hans walking beside him and Anton and Johann on the other side of the draught animal. Rudolf, Henke and Lukas had accompanied the boys to ensure that nothing went awry and also to safeguard against the Estonians taking them as slaves.

'I thought we were here to discuss peace,' said Anton, swatting away a midge from his face.

'The bishop is here to talk of peace,' said Rudolf, 'the Estonians might have other ideas.'

'You think they will attack us?' said Hans, looking around the flat landscape for any sign of the enemy.

'I hope so,' remarked Henke casually, holding the reins of his horse, 'then we can finally kill Lembit and have an end to the whole sorry business.'

'It must be agonising for you, Henke,' said Lukas, who also held his horse's reins as he walked behind Conrad, 'to be so near to Lembit and not be able to run him through.'

Henke smiled grimly. 'I live in hope that the talks will fail.'

Rudolf was walking a few paces ahead of the pony and saw the group of Estonians ambling towards them.

'Look sharp,' he called, placing his foot in a stirrup and hauling himself into the saddle. Henke and Lukas did likewise.

'What's this?' said Henke, wrapping the reins round his left wrist.

'Some sort of Estonian delegation, I assume,' said Lukas, 'judging by the shields.'

'I have seen those shields before,' said Conrad with alarm.

'So have I,' snarled Henke.

Conrad saw the leering wolf insignia on the shields as the dozen warriors came closer, each of them clutching a small branch to show they came in peace.

'No trouble,' ordered Rudolf. 'Keep your swords in their scabbards.'

He urged his horse ahead as the Estonians slowed and then halted, instinctively clutching their shields closer to their bodies. Conrad halted the pony as the two sides eyed each other warily. Rudolf raised his right arm as he brought his horse to a halt in front of Rusticus. They exchanged a few terse words and then the Estonians continued on their journey.

Conrad led the pony and Henke and Lukas spurred their horses forward. The two groups were about five paces apart when they passed each other, Hans, Johann and Anton gawping at the mail-clad warriors armed with swords and axes and wearing gaiters around their lower legs. Henke and Lukas ignored them but Conrad fixed his eyes on the big leader of the Estonians, who likewise stared at the youth. They both knew they had encountered each other before but for a moment neither could place the other. Then Rusticus realised where he had last seen the tall, imposing youth with the expensive sword at his hip. He sneered and spat on the ground before looking away from Conrad.

'You were the one who tried to take Daina,' Conrad said aloud.

'What?' queried Hans.

Conrad let go of the pony and turned around, without thinking drawing his sword. 'Coward!' he called out.

Hans also drew his sword and stood beside his friend, Henke and Lukas turning in their saddles as Rusticus nodded, grinned and spun round. The other warriors stopped as their leader walked back towards the boy.

Conrad had not only been learning Daina's language but also some Estonian under the expert tutelage of Ilona, and though his pronunciation may have been poor Rusticus would have understood what had been thrown at him well enough.

The brute now drew his own sword as the weapons of Anton and Johann also came out of their scabbards. The pony grunted nervously as Rusticus halted a few feet from Conrad.

'You have something to say to me, *boy*?'

Rudolf had wheeled his horse around and now manoeuvred it between Conrad and Rusticus.

'What is going on here?' he demanded in perfect Estonian.

Rusticus tilted his head at Conrad. 'This *brat* insulted me.'

'Is it possible to insult an Estonian?' asked Henke, walking his horse to stand opposite Rudolf's. By now the other Estonians had drawn their weapons to stand behind their leader, who was staring unblinking at Conrad.

'Put your sword away, Conrad,' ordered Rudolf.

Conrad pointed it at Rusticus. 'But he was the one who attacked Wenden and kidnapped Daina.'

'Now!' bellowed Rudolf, causing his horse to lift its head in alarm.

Rusticus leered at Conrad. 'That's right, put it away before you cut yourself with it, boy.'

Lukas had drawn his own sword and now rested the blade on his right shoulder as he walked his horse forward to face the Estonian warriors, some of whom repositioned themselves to meet any charge he might make.

'Be gone, Estonian,' snapped Rudolf, 'and take your heathens with you.'

Rusticus still fixed Conrad with his stare, while the latter for his part met the bigger man's black eyes. He carefully and slowly slid his sword back in its scabbard and looked up at Rudolf and then Henke.

'I will buy this boy from you. How much? I will give you a good price.'

Conrad looked at Hans, his mouth open in shock.

347

'He's not for sale,' said Rudolf.

'Course he is,' said Rusticus. 'I've heard that the Sword Brothers are proficient slave traders.'

'You heard wrongly,' snapped Rudolf. 'You have out-stayed your welcome.'

Rusticus waved a hand at his men, indicating they were to resume their march north. He looked at Conrad.

'Maybe I will visit Wenden again and take him myself.'

'You know where it is,' said Henke. 'We will be waiting.'

'You understand our language,' Rusticus said to Conrad, 'that is good. Slaves should know the language of their masters.'

Conrad's hand went to the hilt of his sword. How he wanted to kill this foul brute who insulted him.

'Attend to your duties, Conrad,' ordered Rudolf. 'And you other boys put away your weapons. You don't want to risk ruining the blades with Estonian blood.'

Rusticus grinned. 'I look forward to meeting you all again tomorrow. Think on my offer of selling me the slave.'

Conrad was fuming as he led the pony back to camp. All he could think about was the oaf who had nearly taken Daina away from him. He wished that the bishop had not come to make peace with the Estonians; then he could kill that ugly brute and take his hideous head back to her as a trophy.

Henke thought the whole business hilarious. 'You should have lopped his head off, Conrad. You made a mistake back there.'

'Conrad nearly killed him when we rescued the women from Thalibald's village,' said Hans with pride.

'Nearly killing someone isn't good enough,' remarked Henke. 'What have you been teaching these lads, Lukas?'

'To obey orders,' replied Lukas flatly.

'Yes, orders,' said Rudolf. He halted his horse to face the boys. 'You are brave enough but you must curb your rashness, especially you, Conrad.'

That night Lukas ordered Conrad to groom his own, Rudolf and Henke's horse and wax the saddles as a punishment for drawing his sword.

'I was provoked,' pleaded Conrad.

'You must learn to follow the example of our Lord and turn the other cheek until you are ordered otherwise. You are being punished for your indiscipline, Conrad. No one doubts your courage but you are like a sword blade that has yet to be tempered. You understand?'

348

He didn't at all. 'Yes, brother.'

The next day the meeting took place against a backdrop of a sky heaped with grey clouds and a continuing easterly wind that whipped the banners of the Estonians and crusaders alike. As the bishop wanted the meeting to be short and to the point there were no tables or chairs inside the oblong tent that Conrad and his comrades had erected the day before, though at least it provided shelter from the rain that began to fall after the dignitaries had arrived. The banner men of Lembit, Alva, Edvin, Jaak, Kalju and Nigul stood outside one entrance getting progressively wetter while their chiefs discussed matters of import inside. Outside the opposite entrance a group of Sword Brothers and crusaders were also getting soaked. Happily for Conrad he was ordered to attend the bishop personally inside the tent, Albert considering his presence a lucky mascot for the meeting.

The air inside the tent stank of stale ale and sweat emanating from the Estonians who had feasted and drank to excess the night before. The bishop recoiled from the powerful odour but maintained a dignified air as the tribal chiefs belched and scratched their groins in a boorish display of masculine prowess. In contrast Lembit stood rock-like, alert and calculating, studying the Christian delegation opposite. They were Bishop Albert, Caupo, Thalibald, Grand Master Volquin, Sir Rudolf and a youth. His eyes narrowed as they settled on Conrad, then opened wide as he recognised him as the one who had given him the scar that now decorated his left cheek. He wondered if his presence was just coincidence or a carefully designed insult on the part of the bishop.

'You requested this meeting, bishop,' he said. 'State your terms so that we, the free peoples of Estonia, may consider them.'

Lembit's German was excellent, though his condescending tone made Volquin and Sir Rudolf bristle.

'A two-year cessation of hostilities, to begin immediately' answered the bishop curtly.

'Why?' probed Lembit. 'Why would you wish to halt your crusade against us?'

'I am not here to answer to you,' snapped the bishop.

Lembit smiled. 'Then I will tell you. Your kingdom of the false god lies broken and weakened by the plague and an internal rebellion. You offer peace like a slave whines for mercy.'

'Enough Lembit,' said Volquin. 'We are not here to be lectured.'

Lembit spread his arms. 'I do not lecture but state the truth, Grand Master Volquin. What if I and my brothers decide to reject your overtures, to raise a great army of Estonians and march south to finish the war that you have started?'

'That is your prerogative,' the bishop answered. 'But would you leave your lands undefended while an army of Lithuanians is on your border.'

Lembit's calculating demeanour slipped, albeit momentarily. 'Lithuanians?'

The bishop nodded knowingly. 'Even as we stand here Grand Duke Daugerutis leads his army against the Principality of Novgorod. I do not believe that he wishes to make war upon the Estonians, but who knows what will happen if he discovers that your people are defenceless when their warriors are away?'

Lembit turned and spoke quietly to his fellow chiefs. None had knowledge of German and so did not understand the bishop's words, but they became agitated when Lembit informed them of what he had said. Kalju in particular was most disturbed and for good reason. Having experienced a Russian invasion in the winter the last thing he desired was a Lithuanian incursion. Conrad, who was holding the bishop's cloak, stood behind the prelate and saw Lembit arguing with the chief of the Ungannians. He saw the scar on the former's cheek and basked in pride that he had inflicted the wound on the greatest enemy of the Sword Brothers. Eventually Lembit cajoled Kalju into silence and retuned to his conversation with the bishop.

'Why should we believe you?'

The bishop sighed. 'It does not matter if you believe me or not, Lembit. My words will not alter the fact that the Lithuanians are marching to attack the Russians.'

Lembit looked behind him to see a fuming Kalju, the veins in his neck bulging.

'Do we have peace or not?' demanded Volquin.

Lembit looked at the grand master, then back at his chiefs. Alva and Edvin nodded while Jaak and Nigul looked bored and disinterested.

'You have your peace,' said Lembit tersely. 'I pledge not to lead my warriors into Livonia for the duration of the peace.'

'And no Christian soldiers will set foot on Estonian territory,' said the bishop, smiling and bringing his hands together. 'Praise God.'

'Our business here is done,' said Volquin, pointing at the cloak held by Conrad. The latter stepped forward and draped it around the bishop's shoulders.

'Thank you, Conrad.'

Lembit's ears pricked up as behind him his chiefs filed out of the tent.

'Conrad?'

350

The bishop looked at him in surprise, then at Conrad. 'You know this young man?'

Lembit rubbed a thumb along his scar. 'We have met before, I think, but have not been formally introduced.'

'This is Conrad Wolff, a most promising novice of the Sword Brothers.'

'From the garrison of Wenden, I believe,' said Lembit casually.

'How well informed you are,' replied the bishop. 'Well, I wish you good fortune on your journey back to Lehola.'

The bishop turned and left the tent in the company of Volquin and Sir Rudolf. Conrad made to follow when Lembit called him back.

'Conrad Wolff.'

Conrad turned to face him. They were now alone in the tent.

'I heard about the incident yesterday on the road,' remarked Lembit in German. 'It would appear that our destinies are linked in some strange way.'

'I do not know of such things,' said Conrad.

'And yet,' continued Lembit, 'every time I make war upon Livonia you appear as if by magic.'

'Perhaps you should not make war upon Livonia, then.'

Lembit moved closer until their faces were only inches apart. 'I owe you a scar, young pup. A man should always pay his debts, don't you think?'

'I do,' replied Conrad.

'The next time I come south I will exact payment from you.'

Conrad smiled. 'To our next meeting, then.'

The bishop called his name. 'Your master calls,' said Lembit. 'Go to him, little dog.'

'I will mark you well for those words, pagan.' Conrad turned and walked from the tent to follow the bishop and his party back to camp.

The other chiefs were waiting for Lembit as he came from the tent. He beckoned over Kalju whose hard features showed concern.

'Get your people to their hill forts as quickly as possible.'

'You think that what that priest said, about the Lithuanians, was true?' said Kalju.

Lembit hunched his shoulders. 'I have no idea. But it is best to take no chances.

'Have the crusaders and Lithuanians made an alliance?' asked Edvin.

'I doubt it,' Lembit replied. 'They are not of the same faith and Daugerutis has often crossed the Dvina to raid the crusaders' lands.'

Lembit's guards closed around him as he and the other chiefs walked back to their camp.

'Will the peace with the crusaders hold?' said Alva.

Lembit smiled. 'The one thing about these Christian priests is that they put great store in their promises. The peace will hold until I decide to break it. They also dislike lying, which leads me to conclude that there is indeed a Lithuanian army marching towards Novgorod.'

*****

But the Lithuanians did not attack Novgorod, the dour city amid swamps and forests that lay two hundred miles north of the Dvina. Instead Grand Duke Daugerutis led his horsemen north towards the rich lands around Pskov, the prosperous city set amid gently rolling hills where ancient villages nestled on hilltops and white-painted churches and monasteries littered the many hay meadows and pasture lands. Though a third of the land south of the city was covered with trees, the great tracts of forest lay to the north where huge expanses of pine, birch and fir blanketed the terrain. The more temperate climate around Pskov and to the south resulted in deciduous trees predominating, among them oak, linden, maple and elm.

This was a peaceful land bordering the Principality of Gerzika, a kingdom of fellow Russians, ensuring its southern frontier was untroubled by raiders. To the west lay Estonian Ungannia but the rulers of Pskov had always endeavoured to maintain amicable relations with its pagan neighbours, backed up by a large force of *Druzhina* and a well-trained city militia.

Domash Tverdislavich sat on his horse and cursed his luck. Pskov had lost a sizeable number of men during the prince's ill-judged invasion of Ungannia and now he faced a Lithuanian invasion alone. He had sent urgent messages to Novgorod requesting reinforcements but knew that they would never arrive in time. Now he waited with the men of his *Druzhina* – four hundred horsemen – as villagers flooded past him towards the safety of Pskov.

Normally a Russian army would deploy for battle in five sections – van, centre, rear and two wings – with the urban militias in the centre of the line with low-grade *Voi* either side of them. Ahead of the foot soldiers would stand the archers and crossbowmen, while on the wings would be arrayed the horsemen with a reserve in the rear. But Domash had allocated the city militia to the defence of

Pskov, its missile troops lining the walls, especially the southern ramparts where the refugees were flooding through the two gates.

The land immediately around the city was mostly arable and had been largely cleared of trees. As such it was ideal country for horsemen, which was unfortunate, as he had learned that the Lithuanian invaders were all mounted. Once they arrived in Novgorodian territory they had systematically set about burning and destroying everything they came across: villages, churches and monasteries. Scouts had brought messages to Pskov telling of all the inhabitants of villages being rounded up, herded into buildings that were then set alight. Nuns were raped and then murdered and monks and priests were hanged from their places of worship. It was apparent that the Lithuanians had come only to kill and destroy.

Some villagers had fled with their possessions into the woods but had been hunted down and slaughtered. The only safe place of refuge was behind the strong walls of Pskov. The inhabitants of the villages around the city had been evacuated days before and the groups of people now hurrying towards Domash's stronghold were from those settlements located twenty or thirty miles away. They flooded the great plain south of the city, women clutching infants and holding the hands of wailing children. Men pulled two-wheeled carts on which were loaded food, their few belongings and the elderly, while others armed with spears and axes formed a ragged, nervous rearguard.

Domash gave the order to advance as civilians rushed passed his men in terror, some bare footed and others wearing *bast* shoes made from birch bark. His men were the cream of the city's boyar class: each one encased in steel lamellar armour, helmet, aventail, and armed with sword, shield and lance. But as they trotted forward the far end of the valley suddenly filled with Lithuanian riders. The civilians, hearing the screams of those nearest the pagan invaders, abandoned their carts and belongings and fled towards the city.

The Lithuanians fought under the chiefs of the princes, their banners showing the ancient symbols of his tribes – Selonian and Nalsen – Daugerutis had brought across the Dvina: the white stork, auroch, wolf and elk. They ran down the fleeing Russians and killed them with their swords, axes and maces, while those who stood and attempted to form a shield wall were showered with *spisas* and then cut to pieces by horsemen who rode among their disorganised ranks. As they had done during the previous days the Lithuanians set about killing as many as they could.

Behind him his boyars seethed with anger and despair at the horrible spectacle unfolding before them but Domash did not give the order to charge.

353

Instead he halted his men and ordered them to deploy into two ranks. There were now upwards of a thousand Lithuanians at least on the plain and more were appearing all the time. His charge would have to be well timed for it would probably be the only one before the *Druzhina* were overwhelmed by sheer weight of numbers.

Then he spied a great column of horsemen that dwarfed the other groups galloping around and slaying civilians. This force was advancing at speed directly at the city and straight for his men. As it got closer it expanded in width as its riders deployed from column into line, in the middle of which flew a huge red banner showing a black bear on all fours. He turned and ordered his trumpeter to signal the advance. A mighty cheer answered the shrill blast as his horsemen broke into a trot and lowered their lances to move forward to engage the Lithuanians.

There was no disciplined advance, no effort to maintain order, just a mad rush to get to grips with the Lithuanians. The golden snow leopard of Pskov billowed in the wind behind Domash as he griped his lance and headed for the huge man on a big horse in the middle of the Lithuanian line. He could feel the strain of his horse as the beast hurtled across the grass, its iron shoes kicking up great sods of earth as it pounded the ground. The distance between the two sets of horsemen seemed to vanish in the blink of an eye and then there was a sickening crunch as they collided.

The big Lithuanian had been shielded by a horde of his men as Domash brought his shield up to deflect a *spisa*, one of many that were thrown at the Russians, before thrusting his lance through a rider's mail armour and into his belly. He let go of the haft and drew his sword to hack at the neck of an opponent who passed him on his left side. His horse slowed as he and the other boyars fought desperately to stem the Lithuanian tide. Suddenly hundreds of men were engaged in a desperate mêlée, the clash of weapons resembling the sound of a load of metal cutlery being thrown down stone steps.

The boyars of Pskov wore blue feathers in their helmets as a means of identification but as the fighting intensified it appeared to Domash that he was an island in a Lithuanian sea. He could see no other Russian as he slashed the arm of a rider wielding a mace before turning to his left to see a Lithuanian raising an axe, about to spit open his helmet. The man screamed and brought the axe down at the instant when Domash's horse collapsed to the ground.

The Lithuanian's animal tripped over it and threw its rider as Domash lay on his back, surprised and mildly stunned. His horse was dead, a *spisa* sticking out of its chest. He breathed a sigh of relief and got to his feet, retrieving his sword from the ground, and realised that he was surrounded by half a dozen enemy riders, in addition to the one who had been thrown, three of whom were armed with lances. He held his sword at the ready, prepared to take as many as possible with him before he too died.

The non-stop clashing of blades and squeals and cries of wounded men and horses continued unabated as one Lithuanian charged at him, his lance levelled at his chest. Domash threw himself aside to avoid the metal point and then thrust his sword into the rider's leg, who yelped and released his lance. He swung around just in time to catch a mace blow on his shield, the metal flanges splitting the leather and wood. Another rider thrust the point of his *spisa* into his right hamstring. Domash grimaced with pain and went down on one knee. He was finished.

The Lithuanians were in no hurry now. They knew they had him and grinned at each other at the prospect of giving this Russian a slow death. Domash winced with pained as he hauled himself up. At least he would sell his life dearly.

'Come on, then!' he shouted at them as behind him he heard a new sound: the banging of drums and the blast of trumpets.

He heard several thuds and saw two of the Lithuanians pitch forward and fall from their saddles. Another thud and an enemy rider trotted from behind him slumped in the saddle, a crossbow bolt in his back. And then there were cries and suddenly he was surrounded by spearmen with blue plumes in their helmets, thrusting their spears upwards at Lithuanians while behind them crossbowmen shot them down.

'On, on, save the mayor.'

Domash hobbled backwards as men of the Pskov militia methodically advanced and forced back the Lithuanians, many of the latter's saddles being emptied by well-aimed quarrels. Domash recognised that voice.

'A ride back to the city, my lord?'

Domash looked round to see a grinning Gleb sitting beside the driver of a cart.

'What are you doing here?' he asked.

'Saving your arse,' Gleb replied.

'I thought I gave orders for the militia to man the walls.'

Glad waved a hand at him. 'There are plenty of men to stand around doing nothing except hold a spear. The militia were needed here.'

Domash hobbled over the cart, Gleb hauling him onto the bench next to the driver. Behind the cart were a dozen drummers and trumpeters. Ahead the spearmen had halted in a line to allow the fifty crossbowmen to shoot accurately at the rapidly retreating Lithuanians.

'Don't hit any of our own men,' called Domash, wincing as pain shot through his wounded leg.

'Don't worry about them,' said Gleb standing on the cart behind him. 'They know what they are doing, unlike you.'

'Just get me back to the city, damn you,' said Domash.

Gleb turned and gave the order to the trumpeters to signal withdrawal as the crossbowmen shot another volley at the Lithuanians.

The appearance of the city militia had saved what was left of the *Druzhina*, though two hundred of them had been slain in the engagement. As the crossbowmen kept the seething mass of Lithuanians at bay with their accurate shooting, the boyars and their commander limped back to Pskov. Honour and not a few civilians had been saved, but at a price.

Domash ripped off a length of his shirt and bound his leg as the cart rumbled across the moat and through one of the city's two southern gates.

'How many managed to get into the city?' asked Domash.

'More than the city's food supplies can feed,' replied Gleb, raising his hand to the soldiers lining the walls above.

Behind the spearmen and crossbowmen were conducting an expert withdrawal, groups of boyar horsemen trotting over the bridge across the moat as the foot soldiers kept the Lithuanians at bay. Domash looked behind at the riders with damaged shields, dented armour and ripped flesh, their horses sweating and some also wounded.

'Many fines ladies will be weeping tonight.'

'Very poetic,' remarked Gleb. 'Perhaps you could write a long poem during the coming siege while you wait for the prince. Where is he, by the way?'

'On his way, God willing.'

'Ah, yes,' mused Gleb as the cart wound its way through a throng of refugees to the mayor's palace. 'You will be pleased to know that the priests are wailing and burning incense in their churches, calling upon God to save them. So far he appears to have ignored their appeals.'

'You should watch your words, Gleb,' warned Domash. 'The church has great power in the city.'

'Though not among the citizenry, I think,' smiled Gleb. 'It is amazing how crises bring out the old ways in people. If food runs low we could always eat some priests, though they are so scrawny that they would not make much of a meal.'

Domash tightened the ligature on his leg. 'It might come to that if the Lithuanians besiege us and prevent the prince from relieving the city.'

*****

Grand Duke Daugerutis established his headquarters in an abandoned white-walled church ten miles south of Pskov. His own and the horses of his senior commanders were tethered in the nave while he and they sat at a small table where the altar had been situated. The walls were covered in religious paintings and there was a domed roof just before the sanctuary. His army filled the surrounding countryside, using wood from the village huts that had surrounded the church to make fires. All the cows, pigs and goats had been abandoned by the villagers when they fled to Pskov and now the Lithuanians feasted on their meat as they availed themselves of Russian hospitality.

'We leave in the morning,' announced the grand duke, the juices from a piece of roasted pork dripping onto his beard.

'We will not assault Pskov?' said Stecse in surprise, a soldier offering him more meat from a platter.

Daugerutis shook his head. 'It's surrounded on three sides by water and on its landward side there are strong walls and a deep moat. It would be madness to attempt an assault.'

'A siege then?' asked another of his commanders.

'Sieges take a long time,' answered the grand duke. 'Autumn will soon be here and I have no doubt that Mstislav is on his way.'

He beckoned over the soldier with the platter. 'Besides, I have no desire to occupy Pskov. What would I do with a Russian city over a hundred miles from my own kingdom?'

'Burn it to the ground' suggested Stecse. The others laughed.

'We have done enough burning,' said the grand duke. He looked at the son of Stecse sitting beside his father. The boy sat in silence, occasionally looking at the fearsome warrior chiefs around the table.

'Well, young Mindaugas,' said the grand duke, throwing a bone to the floor, 'how do you like your first campaign.'

'It is very loud, lord.'

357

Daugerutis gave a great belly laugh. 'Ha! A good answer. Your ears will get accustomed to the screams of men having their guts ripped out, have no fear.'

But Mindaugas was not thinking about the battle. He and his father had arrived on the field late in that day, when the Pskov militia was covering the retreat of the boyars back to the city. He was referring to the roaring of the flames when the Lithuanians had fired villages and incinerated people inside churches. He had found it fascinating, particularly watching people's death throes when they changed from terrified, writhing individuals who begged for life to still corpses with glazed, unblinking eyes and frozen expressions. Fascinating.

'To burn our way to the gates of Pskov is triumph enough,' said the grand duke contentedly. He looked at the hardened faces around him. 'You have all fought well and obeyed my orders to kill and burn. As a reward I give you permission to take as many slaves and livestock as you wish on the return journey.'

They looked at each other in confusion. Stecse articulated their thoughts.

'Those Russians who did not fall under our swords are either in Pskov or hiding in the neighbouring forests, lord.'

'And we killed all their livestock on the way here,' said another.

The serving soldier brought another platter heaped with sizzling meat, the grand duke taking a large slice and shoving it into his mouth.

'I came here to lay waste a large part of Novgorodian territory, which I have done. Now I authorise you to plunder Livonia to fill your halls with slaves to serve you at your tables and keep your beds warm.'

'Livonia, lord?' queried Stecse.

The grand duke smiled slyly. 'The crusaders were weak to allow me to cross the Dvina. Now they will learn the price of their weakness as I empty Caupo's villages of their children and womenfolk. Next year I will cross the Dvina and make war upon the bishop. This I pledge.'

They all cheered and thanked the grand duke for his generosity. To return from campaign with a great haul of booty was to win prestige among the Lithuanian people, and slaves were the greatest prizes of all.

The grand duke led his horsemen south the next morning, the Lithuanians breaking camp in the pre-dawn light and heading south to retrace the route they had taken to reach Pskov. They moved fast, covering twenty miles the first day and a similar distance the day after to keep any pursuers at a safe distance. It was only when the horses of his warriors were drinking from the cool waters of Lake Lubans, forty miles north of the Dvina, did the pace slacken. The surface of the lake was covered in migratory waterfowl.

The grand duke established his camp on the southern shore of the lake while his warlords led a dozen raiding parties west into Livonia. Whereas before they were intent on murder and destruction, this time they were resolved to capture slaves. They did this by creating diversions: half of a party would make themselves very visible on the outskirts of a village and make a lot of noise. The menfolk would arm themselves and march out to do battle with the raiders, the latter retreating in the face of the village elder and his men, leading them ever further away from their homes. The other half of the raiders, having hidden themselves among trees on the other side of the settlement, would ride into the village and capture as many women and children as time allowed before fleeing. So speedy was their assault and retreat that there was no time for rape or killing the elderly. Though the villages were filled with goats and pigs and cows and sheep grazed in the fields, the raiders did not bother with livestock. But they reaped a rich harvest of slaves.

Grand Duke Daugerutis had taken eight thousand horsemen across the Dvina to raid Novgorodian territory. When he recrossed the river he had with him five thousand, four hundred warriors. Six hundred had died during the expedition, most during the battle before Pskov, but the other two thousand were with Prince Stecse as they headed directly south into the Principality of Gerzika. The prince had sent prior warning to Vsevolod that he was entering his territory with a large party of his father-in-law's soldiers. But the ruler of Gerzika was far from amused when he met the Lithuanians at a spot on the Dvina five miles north of his city.

The Lithuanian tents filled the riverbank for hundreds of yards, extending inland for a quarter of a mile. As Vsevolod rode among them with his escort he also noticed groups of women and children, tied together with guards watching over them. The sullen and apprehensive mood among these captives contrasted sharply with the relaxed atmosphere in the camp.

Vsevolod was escorted to the tent of Prince Stecse located in the centre of the camp. Warriors were grooming their horses, others cleaning their armour, sharpening their swords or engaging in wrestling matches. The ruler of Gerzika sneered at their love for the base things in life but was fuming that they had wandered into his territory uninvited.

'The grand duke thought it better to cross the river here, away from the prying eyes of the garrison of Kokenhusen,' explained Stecse who ordered Mindaugas to bring a stool for Vsevolod to sit on.

'Taking Livs as slaves will place me in a very difficult position with the bishop,' complained Vsevolod.

'Livs?' said Stecse incredulously.

'Do you take me for a fool?' snapped Vsevolod.

Stecse did, and more. 'Of course not, my lord.'

'Your captives are Livs. You have violated the terms of the agreement I brokered with the bishop.'

Fifty paces away a great cheer erupted as a wrestling match between two fat monsters stripped to the waist ended when one slammed the other on his back and then fell on top of him to pin him to the ground. Vsevolod was disgusted as the rank smell of warriors who had not bathed in weeks reached his nostrils.

'The agreement allowed the grand duke to cross the river and make war upon the Novgorodians,' said Stecse casually. 'Slaves are taken in war. The crusaders should know that.'

'When Riga learns of what you have done....'

'What the *grand duke* has done,' Stecse corrected him.

'The bishop will be very angry and will most likely send his soldiers against the grand duke.'

Stecse nodded. 'Most likely.'

'You seemed unconcerned by such a prospect,' said Vsevolod.

'Perhaps the grand duke will cross the river and make war against the crusaders himself.'

Vsevolod knew that Stecse did not have the brains to think of such a thing himself.

'The grand duke has told you this?'

'Perhaps you should speak to your father-in-law yourself,' answered Stecse evasively.

'That would violate the peace treaty,' said Vsevolod.

'And interrupt your profitable trade with Riga, no doubt' said Stecse casually.

'You dare to suggest that I place profit above my loyalty to the grand duke?'

'I suggest nothing, lord,' replied Stecse, 'only observe that the grand duke regards the bishop and his followers as weak. And that next time he will not ask their permission to cross the river.'

'And when will that be?'

Stecse shrugged. 'I am not party to the grand duke's decisions, lord.'

Vsevolod realised that this upstart knew when the grand duke would cross the Dvina and Stecse knew that Vsevolod knew that he did. Vsevolod stood.

'You and your captives will be gone from my territory tomorrow.'

Stecse remained seated. 'As you wish, my lord.'

Vsevolod waved over the soldier who was holding his horse. He hoisted himself into the saddle.

'You underestimate both the bishop and the crusaders, prince. You think that because they are currently in a weakened state that they will always be so, but you are wrong.'

'Then tell the grand duke, my lord.'

Vsevolod tugged on his reins. 'I shall, you can be certain of that. Remember, Prince Stecse, you have one day to leave my kingdom.'

The Lithuanians crossed the Dvina the next morning, taking their thousand Liv slaves with them.

*****

Caupo paced up and down in the withdrawing chamber of the bishop's palace as Thalibald looked on. The bishop was seated in a plush chair next to Archdeacon Stefan, who looked most uncomfortable. After his return to Riga the bishop had been informed of Grand Duke Daugerutis' raid into Novgorodian territory and subsequent assault upon Livonia. The elders of the villages that had lost their children and womenfolk had pleaded with their king to be allowed to cross over the Dvina to get their people back.

'I cannot allow that, my friend,' said the bishop. 'We must have peace in order to rebuild our strength. There is little merit in creating peace in the north to then make war in the south.'

'My elders cry out for revenge,' snapped Caupo.

'Revenge is a most unattractive trait,' remarked Stefan haughtily.

The bishop held up a hand to his subordinate as Caupo stopped pacing and glared at the archdeacon. 'If you had not signed a treaty with the Lithuanians, archdeacon, then my warriors would not now be without their wives and children. They and I must have justice, lord bishop.'

Bishop Albert looked with sad eyes at his friend. 'What Grand Duke Daugerutis has done is inexcusable and has imperilled his soul, of that I have no doubt. But I cannot sanction the opening of hostilities against the Lithuanians. Our forces are depleted and weakened and require rest and recuperation.'

'Perhaps it is the will of God,' remarked Stefan.

The bishop and Caupo looked at him in confusion. Stefan smiled at Caupo.

'Forgive me, lord king, but am I correct in thinking that the villages that were raided by the Lithuanians recently are the same ones that supplied warriors to aid Prince Vetseke in his rebellion against the bishop.'

Caupo looked at Thalibald and then Stefan. 'I fail to see that has any bearing on anything.'

Stefan brought his hands together. 'I am a poor shepherd of the Lord, majesty, but even I can discern divine retribution at work. Perhaps if the villagers had not raised their hands against the bishop the Lord would not have sent the Lithuanians to punish them.'

Caupo was outraged. 'Lord bishop, I must protest.'

Albert held up his hands to placate the king. 'We cannot presume to know the mind of God, archdeacon, so it is the height of frivolity to engage in such discussions.'

'My men are clamouring to cross the river,' said Caupo tersely.

'That I cannot allow,' said the bishop firmly.

Caupo's face reddened with anger. 'Lord bishop, I cannot stand idly by while my people are abused and I am mocked.'

There was an awkward silence as the bishop rested his chin on his thumbs, deep in thought as Stefan stared out of the window.

'We could buy them back,' suggested Thalibald.

The bishop looked at him. 'Buy them back?'

'Riga is rich, lord bishop,' said Thalibald. 'Its treasury fills with silver and gold from the donations of noble crusaders and the trade on the Dvina.'

Stefan stopped looking out of the window. 'Impossible!'

But the bishop was intrigued. 'You think Daugerutis would be receptive to such an offer?'

'A Lithuanian would sell his own mother if the price was right,' sneered Caupo.

'Lord bishop,' said Stefan with alarm, 'I really must protest.'

But Albert stopped his words a second time. 'I desire peace above all at this time. But I agree with King Caupo that the atrocity committed against his people cannot be allowed to pass without action.'

'But, lord bishop,' pleaded Stefan, 'your cathedral.'

'Can wait,' said the bishop. 'I will authorise the release of the necessary funds with which to purchase the lives of the innocents so cruelly snatched from their homes.'

The colour drained from Stefan's cheeks as Caupo's returned to its normal complexion. The king laid a hand on his chest and bowed his head to the bishop.

'You are most just and pious, lord.'

'Soon I travel to Germany,' announced the bishop, 'and would go with a clear conscience.' He looked at Stefan. 'As it was my subordinate who made the treaty with the Lithuanians and thus encouraged Grand Duke Daugerutis to cross the Dvina, it is my responsibility to right the wrongs that have been committed by the Lithuanians. Go and tell your people, lord king, that their women and children will be returned to them soon.'

Caupo bowed deeply to him, ignored Stefan and then retreated from the room in the company of Thalibald. The door was closed behind them.

The bishop rose and poured wine into a silver cup, handing it to Stefan.

'I know you do not hold with what has been agreed, Stefan, but in this instance I must override you.'

Stefan sipped at the wine. 'As you wish, lord bishop.'

Albert walked over to the window and gazed at Riga outside.

'Time is on our side, Stefan. When I return from Germany I shall bring with me not only crusaders but also men and women who will make their lives in Livonia. With the passing of every year the castles of the Sword Brothers grow stronger and the population of Riga increases. We may suffer reverses but God's ultimate victory is assured.'

Stefan took another sip of his wine.

'It is twenty-five years since Jerusalem fell to the infidels, Stefan. I do not intend Riga to suffer the same fate and if that means making unpalatable decisions in the name of expediency, so be it.'

'What if Grand Duke Daugerutis interprets your generosity as weakness, lord bishop?' said Stefan.

'Then more fool him.'

That afternoon Prince Vetseke was brought from the castle to meet with the bishop. Volquin and the rest of the Sword Brother commanders had wanted his public execution as a warning to others but the bishop would have none of it. He ensured that the prince was treated with civility and dignity as befitting his status. He met with the prince in his palace, though Volquin insisted that he be present and also that the number of guards inside the palace's reception hall was doubled.

The prince stood before the bishop who sat in a high-backed chair, a banner bearing the cross keys of Riga hanging on the wall behind him. Despite his confinement the prince looked remarkably hale and was allowed to wear his sword for the meeting, though Volquin stood near him, resting his hand on the hilt of his own sword, in case any mischief was attempted. The hall was quiet as the bishop cleared his throat. To one side scribes at desks held their quills ready to record his words.

'Prince Vetseke, having been confined in Riga's castle these past few weeks for fomenting and leading a rebellion against God's own city, I have summoned you here so that you may hear the sentence that will be passed on you.'

Vetseke stood, rock like, staring at the bishop. He already knew the punishment for failed rebellions.

'You are hereby banished from Livonia for the rest of your life upon pain of death. You shall never see Kokenhusen again nor know the fealty of your people. I cast you out, Prince Vetseke, just as our Lord cast out the devils in Galilee. Go where you will. But know that if you set foot in Livonia again you will suffer the sentence of death. And may God have mercy on your soul.'

The scribes scribbled on their parchment as Volquin beckoned four guards forward to escort Vetseke from the hall. His expression remained impassive as he was ushered from the room and the door was closed behind him.

'I sincerely hope that is the last we see of him, lord bishop,' said Volquin without conviction.

'If the plan to purchase the Livs from Grand Duke Daugerutis comes to fruition then we have nothing to worry about concerning the machinations of Prince Vetseke, grand master,' said the bishop. 'For a vine cannot grow in stony ground and if the Livs get back their women and children then their allegiance to the Holy Church will be guaranteed and there will be no more rebellions.'

*****

As Vetseke trudged alone out of Riga's gates Master Griswold sent a message to Vsevolod requesting his presence at Kokenhusen. When the Russian prince arrived he was informed that the bishop was most displeased with the actions of Grand Duke Daugerutis. However, in order to preserve the peace between the

Lithuanians and Livonia the bishop was prepared to buy back the Livonians who had been captured by the grand duke in Livonia.

'The grand duke can name his price,' Griswold informed Vsevolod.

The latter's eyes lit up. Griswold knew that the prince would add his own commission to any sum agreed.

'You can leave the matter with me, Master Griswold,' Vsevolod assured him. 'I am most desirous that this matter is brought to a speedy conclusion.'

Griswold looked at him contemptuously. 'Of that I have no doubt.'

Chapter 14

The harvest in Livonia that year was excellent. The crusader army at Riga may have been devastated by the bloody flux, the Lithuanians may have stolen the women and children from the villages in the path of Grand Duke Daugerutis' army and some of those villages had a deficiency in menfolk after the crushing of Prince Vetseke's rebellion, but the rains had watered the earth and the sun had ripened the crops. The bishop and his priests believed that God had smiled upon the land and blessed his peace with the Estonians and the ransom he had paid the Lithuanians for the return of the slaves they had taken.

The negotiations were conducted through Vsevolod, on account of his ties to Daugerutis, and though Archdeacon Stefan believed that the sum demanded by the grand duke was exorbitant, the bishop was adamant that it should be paid. Grand Master Volquin also grumbled, not least because Master Griswold had informed him that Vsevolod could not be trusted, but mainly because he knew that funds paid to the Lithuanians would result in the slowing of construction work on the order's castles. But the bishop was no fool and when the Lithuanians sent back the slaves there was great rejoicing among the Livs. And their joy also extinguished any remaining flames of rebelliousness among the natives. With peace secured along the Dvina and a truce agreed with the Estonians Bishop Albert returned to Germany, taking with him those crusaders who had survived the flux and the battle against Vetseke. A few stayed behind to make their lives in Livonia, adding to the steadily growing population of non-native Christians there.

At Wenden the sale of the Estonian slaves to the Russians, the absence of any hostilities and destruction on account of the peace with Lembit, plus the release of modest funds from the treasury at Riga, had allowed the work on the fortifications to continue. The first floor of the north tower was now complete, though the great wooden dormitory that provided the quarters for the brother knights and sergeants was still extant. That would be the last to be converted to stone, the order believing that hardship was good for the souls of its fighting men and that luxury was to be avoided at all cost.

As far as Conrad was concerned that autumn was the happiest since his arrival in Livonia. He and the other novices were now accorded a modicum of respect among the brother knights and sergeants on account of their actions at Riga, not least because the bishop himself had singled them out for praise. A few eyebrows had been raised in the town that he had promised to make them all brother knights but at Wenden this passed without comment. Master Berthold was delighted that his four novices had distinguished themselves in battle and commended Brother Lukas for his diligence in training them. For his part Lukas increased the length and intensity of their daily training sessions lest they became boastful or apt to rest on their laurels. Conrad did not mind and embraced the extra work. He knew that it was harvest time and that meant he and the others would soon be sent to Thalibald's village to assist with the gathering of the crops. Which meant that he would see Daina.

He was sixteen and she was seventeen and just as his body was turning from a gangly, awkward youth into an athletic young man so was her girlish frame becoming more womanly. Her breasts were getting larger, her hips were widening and her green eyes were filled not only with warmth but also temptation. She and the other girls and young women brought water to the men working in the fields as before. But this time when she passed a cup of cool liquid to Conrad her fingers brushed his and her eyes lit up as he looked at her.

Master Berthold decreed that all the brother knights and half the sergeants from the castle should assist in the collection of the harvest, not only because the back-breaking work would be good for their souls but also because it was good politics. Because the Sword Brothers was an order of the Holy Church it collected one sheaf out of every ten in tithes and Berthold considered it only proper that the garrison assist in the collection of the crops that would help to feed it during the winter months. Individuals such as Vetseke tried to portray the bishop and the Sword Brothers as masters who treated the Livs as slaves but that was a lie. Thalibald doubted whether a ruler such as Vetseke would have bothered to get his daughter back if he had been lord at Wenden.

The first crops to be harvested were the wheat and rye, which ripened first, followed by the barley and oats. The wheat was harvested by men working in groups of five – four reapers and a binder – who could harvest around two acres of crops a day. Lukas oversaw Conrad, Hans, Johann and Anton as they went to work with their sickles, the wheat extending before them like a golden ocean. It was hot, dry and windless and soon they were stripped to the waist and sweating profusely.

To one side was another team composed of Rudolf, Henke, Walter and two other brother knights, who were swinging their sickles with gusto. The powerful, broad-shouldered Henke stood beside the slimmer Rudolf, the burn scars showing clearly on his neck and chest.

367

'That must have been painful,' remarked Hans as he nodded at Rudolf's wounds.

'I'm surprised he doesn't hate the Russians for doing that to him,' said Conrad, arching his back to relieve the ache at the base of his spine.

Johann was surprised. 'The Russians?'

Lukas looked behind to see Daina and a dozen other young women with yokes over their shoulders hauling water buckets.

'Hold your sickles. Yes, Johann, the Russians. Before the bishop came the Russians viewed Livonia as a large hunting ground to pillage and burn. Easy target, you see. They burnt Holm when it was just a timber fortress and Rudolf got caught inside. It was Ilona who dragged him out of the fire and tended his wounds. She's been with us ever since, God bless her.'

'Did the Russians escape?' asked Anton, putting down his sickle and wiping his sweat-covered brow with a cloth.

'Unfortunately,' said Lukas, his voice laced with bitterness. 'We gave chase but they slipped through our hands. They were led by a man named Domash Tverdislavich.'

'What a ridiculous name,' said Hans.

Conrad remembered the name from a conversation with Henke.

'Do you think he will return to Livonia?' enquired Anton.

Lukas shook his head. 'Not now. The Sword Brothers are too well established in Livonia. There are no easy pickings for the Russians.'

'What are they like?' asked Johann.

'The Russians? Like wolves. You don't want to turn your back on them.'

'And yet we trade with them,' remarked Conrad casually.

'Needs must, Conrad,' replied Lukas. 'Henke told me that you disagreed with the whole sorry business of the slaves. Is that not so?'

Conrad did not say anything but avoided Lukas' eyes.

'Speak freely,' the instructor barked.

'I did not hold with stealing defenceless women and children from their homes and selling them into slavery, no.'

The other boys looked at him wide eyed but Lukas merely nodded.

'Neither did I or most of those who took part in the raid,' he said softly. 'Circumstances forced us to take a hateful decision. It will be for God to judge us.'

The melancholy air that suddenly enveloped them was swept aside by the appearance of the glowing Daina, who rested the buckets on the ground.

'Water for the beasts of burden,' she teased, grinning at Conrad.

She handed him and the others a cup and they dipped them in the water, gulping it down.

'Slow down,' ordered Lukas. 'You drink too much too fast you will want to throw up and might even pass out.'

'I hate the Russians,' Conrad said suddenly. 'And the Estonians.'

'So do I,' agreed Hans.

'And I,' added Johann.

'Me too,' said Anton.

'You should never hate your enemies,' Lukas admonished them. 'Hate clouds a soldier's judgement. What have I told you all?'

They looked at him with blank expressions. He raised his eyes to the heavens. 'I despair. Control. Control at all times. Even in the fiercest fight when all are losing their minds to frenzy. The man who stays in control at all times has the edge. You start to hate your enemies then they have the edge over you. That is why Rudolf and Henke are so proficient in battle. And Thalibald. Is that not right, Daina?'

She flashed a smile at him. 'I do not know of such things, Brother Lukas. Only that I am glad that you are here to help us gather the harvest.'

Lukas looked at her and then Conrad. 'All of us or just one?'

She feigned innocence. 'I do not know what you mean.'

He smiled at her. 'Of course not.'

As they stood quenching their thirsts Daina sidled up to Conrad.

'I heard that you saved the bishop.'

He shrugged. 'It was nothing.'

'My father says that you are already a great warrior and are destined for even greater things.'

He felt his cheeks flush with embarrassment. 'I got lucky.'

She sighed. 'Perhaps I might get lucky when my father chooses a husband for me.'

It felt as though his legs had been pulled from under him. 'Your father is choosing you a husband?' He wanted his life to end.

She toyed with the ends of her long hair. 'I told him that my heart belongs to only one man.'

'Oh?'

369

She smiled that most beautiful of smiles. 'He asked me who it was and I told him and he was happy.'

He felt deflated. 'He must be a worthy man to have your father's approval.'

'Very worthy,' she agreed.

'A chief's daughter should have a chief's son for a husband,' he said.

'He is not the son of a chief.'

Conrad felt his heart stir. 'Not a chief's son?'

She smiled at him knowingly. 'He is not even of my people.'

His heart felt as though it would burst from his chest. 'And your father will allow this?'

She moved closer so no one else would hear. 'For the one who saved his daughter he would deny nothing.'

'Right. Back to work,' barked Lukas as a wave of exhilaration surged through Conrad like floodwater after a thunderstorm. Hans looked at him.

'Are you all right, Conrad?'

He slapped Hans on the back and picked up his sickle. 'Never better, my friend, never better.'

Daina picked up the yoke and said goodbye to them all, then skipped away to join the other girls from the village who had brought water to those toiling in the fields.

'Who do you think is the best?' said Anton, pointing his sickle at Rudolf and Henke swinging their tools.

'Rudolf,' answered Hans.

'Henke,' said Conrad. 'He's a cold killer.'

'It has to be Rudolf,' suggested Johann. 'He's quicker.'

'What about Walter?' said Lukas as he listened to the conversation.

Hans laughed.

'Walter?' said Conrad dismissively.

'A good knight, Walter,' said Lukas. 'Remorse, if channelled correctly, can be the making of an excellent soldier.'

The weather remained fine as the sheaves were collected and taken back to Thalibald's village, the tithe portion being loaded onto carts to be ferried back to Wenden. Once safely under cover the grain was processed by being threshed with a flail to separate the individual grains from the ear. On average one man could thresh up to seven bushels of wheat a day. After threshing the grain was winnowed to remove the chaff and straw, which was collected for use as animal fodder.

The men from Wenden returned to the castle with their share of the crops following a great feast in Thalibald's hall at which Daina promised Conrad that she would marry no man aside from him. This made him deliriously happy and led to him drinking too much *medalus* and passing out. Hans and Anton carried him back to their hut and in the morning he was forced to walk beside the cart as the others sat in it as it travelled back to Wenden.

*****

Lembit stood on the sand and watched as the longships ran aground and men jumped from their decks. It was cold and he drew his fur-lined cloak around him. A dozen of his wolf shields rested on their spears and pulled the hoods of their cloaks over their helmets. Only Rusticus appeared not to be feeling the cold as he stood beside his master and eyed warily the four great ships that silently slid onto the brown sand. Parnu Bay was an inlet of the Gulf of Riga that was shallow and sheltered from the Baltic. As such it was a haven for shipping with its calm waters and mild climate, though today the wind was brisk and the sea grey and forbidding. Lembit hoped that the conditions were not an omen for his meeting with the king of the Oeselians.

He watched as the boats furled their great sails and the rowers shipped their oars, the crews expertly going about their business just as their fathers and forefathers had done. He smiled. These men were the last remnants of the once all-conquering Vikings who had spread terror throughout the Baltic and beyond. And now the Oeselians, formerly known as the Eastern Vikings, were the only ones left. He looked at the great carved dragon heads at the prow of each longship. Once they had raided along the length of the coast of the Estonians and the Livs, sailing up the Gauja and Dvina with impunity, to raid and burn but also to trade. Now the crusaders had closed these two great waterways to them. How long would it be before the Bishop of Riga besieged Oesel itself, and the days of the longships and tall men came to an end?

'We should have brought more men,' growled Rusticus, looking with alarm at the warriors jumping from each vessel and wading through the wind-flecked water.

Lembit snapped out of his melancholy thoughts. 'We are here to talk, not fight.'

There were now at least fifty warriors grouped around a squat figure in full mail armour heading towards them. Olaf was bare headed, his white hair and beard standing out against the grey of his surroundings. Lembit felt a spit of rain on his face and looked up at the grey clouds that filled the sky. He hoped the meeting would not last for long otherwise they would get soaked.

'Talk is for women,' mumbled Rusticus. 'Men fight.'

'But not today, Rusticus, not today.'

Lembit walked towards Olaf, the cold seawater lapping round his boots. He extended his arm.

'Greetings Olaf, King of the Oeselians. Welcome to Estonia.'

Olaf grasped his forearm and held it in an iron embrace for a few seconds.

'Hail Lembit, King of the Estonians.'

Lembit laughed, the first time he had done so in a while.

'There is no King of all the Estonians, just a collection of chiefs.'

Olaf screwed up his face at the cool wind. 'Walk with me.'

He waved his men away and they ambled onto the sand while Lembit indicated to Rusticus that he should stay with the wolf shields.

'A cold winter is coming,' said Olaf whose forearms were bare, though Lembit did not see any sign of goose bumps.

He had requested this meeting alone with Olaf and had not informed the other chiefs. He had learned long ago that the smaller the gathering the more could be achieved. Large meetings resulted in a lot of noise and little result. He wanted to see Olaf to explain the peace he had agreed with the bishop.

'You think it will hold?' said Olaf.

'Until each side has rebuilt its strength. It is a truce only but at least it gives me time to organise.'

He glanced at Olaf. 'I am sorry for your son.'

'He died a warrior's death,' replied Olaf without emotion. 'It is all we can hope for. He wished to lead the expedition. I have other sons.'

He stopped and peered at the long, flat beach.

'The world changes. When my father was king these shores were his playground and your people his prey. Now we are allies and face a greater enemy that threatens our very way of life.'

'There is more than one danger,' said Lembit glumly.

Olaf looked at him, his blue eyes widening in surprise.

'The Russians stir in the east,' continued Lembit, twisting the sole of his boot in the sand. 'They seek to expand their territory at my expense while I fight the crusaders.'

'Men are like wolves,' said Olaf. 'They circle their prey waiting for him to weaken.'

Lembit nodded. 'I dealt with the Russians on Lake Pskov, and we heard that the bishop allowed the Lithuanians to pass through his territory to attack them.'

'The bishop and the Lithuanians are allies?' said Olaf in alarm.

Lembit shook his head. 'I do not know why the crusaders allowed the Lithuanians into their territory but it was not for friendship. The Lithuanians do not worship the god of the crusaders.'

'Then the game is still finely poised,' said Olaf.

More spits of rain began hitting Lembit's face and the sky grew darker.

'A game with high stakes, I fear,' offered Lembit. 'And yet I feel that one great battle will decide all our fates, lord king.'

He looked at the squat Oeselian. 'I hope I can stand beside you when that day comes.'

'Our alliance still holds, Lembit, as long as I remain king. But my warriors crave revenge against the crusaders for the death of my son.'

Lembit squinted into the bitter, rain-filled wind. 'And you, lord king, do you seek vengeance against your son's killers?'

Olaf rubbed his forearms. So he was human after all.

'His mother bickers me incessantly to lead my ships against Riga and my lords thirst for Christian blood. But a king must know when to strike. Having lost a good many men at Treiden I have no desire to repeat the experience. I agree with you that one battle will decide things. The question is, my Estonian friend, can the crusaders be engaged at a time and place that is advantageous to us and the opposite for them?'

They walked on for a few yards in silence, the wind blowing in from the sea and the spits of rain slowly turning into drops.

'The crusaders seemingly have everything in their advantage,' said Lembit. 'Their stone castles grow from the ground as impregnable citadels and every year more and more iron-clad horsemen arrive at Riga to make war against us. And yet there is a chink in their armour, one thing that may undo all their work and yet give us victory.'

Olaf stopped and looked up at him, wracking his brains to think what it could be. He shrugged his shoulders to signal his ignorance.

'Their arrogance,' said Lembit. 'Their unshakable belief that the world belongs to their Christian god and that all other peoples are destined to kneel before it.'

Olaf was unimpressed. 'Every king and chief is arrogant, Lembit. How else can he lead his people if not possessed of the conviction that he alone has the courage and skills to do so?'

Lembit began wagging his finger at the king. 'Quite right, lord king. But the crusaders who arrive every year at Riga thirst for battle and conquest and their bishop encourages their desires. Eventually they will over-extend themselves and find themselves deep in enemy territory surrounded by enemies. Then, my lord, then we will offer battle and defeat them.'

'You think they will just walk into a trap?' asked Olaf.

'They view us as savages, lord, fit only to serve them as slaves. To them we are incapable of formulating tactics and strategy. We do not have to deceive them; they deceive themselves.

'Did you know that the Bishop of Riga has a brother bishop, my lord?'

'I did not,' said Olaf.

'His name is Theodoric and he has already been made Bishop of Estonia, as if the crusaders have already conquered my people. So you see, my lord, they give us scarcely a thought. We are just chaff to be swept away.'

Olaf twisted his face against the rain that now filled the air.

'Then I will keep my longships ready until I hear word from you, Lembit. Time to get out of this wretched weather, I think. It will be a harsh winter.'

They walked back to where their men waited with hunched shoulders and backs to the wind and rain. For Olaf the journey back to Oesel would be a short one, the island lying only sixty miles to the west of Parnu Bay. He and his men would lie up under canvas covers until the wind and rain abated, rowing out to sea once the conditions were more favourable. Lembit would retire to the nearest village to partake of its hospitality and assure the inhabitants that there was nothing to fear from the four longships that were moored just a short distance away. How right Olaf was: the world was changing.

*****

Olaf was right about the winter: its icy grip extended over the land in early December and did not let up until March. And yet for Conrad the snow, never-ending religious services, duties, weapons training and numbing cold were hardly

374

noticeable as his thoughts were filled with Daina. After the crops were gathered in there had been a great festival of thanksgiving in Thalibald's village to which he and the other novices were invited. His knowledge of the Liv language had expanded apace thanks to the diligent efforts of Ilona and he was now able to have simple conversations with Daina in her own language. She laughed and tossed her long hair back when he became confused and said something ridiculous, her green eyes sparkling with mischief as she trapped him with words.

When the birth of Christ was celebrated she came to Wenden in the company of her father, mother and brothers, wrapped in furs, her cheeks rosy in the cold air. As before he and the others served them during the Christmas feast and gave up their quarters so they could stay at the castle for a few days. Master Berthold and Rudolf entertained Thalibald and his sons in the days following by organising hunts in the surrounding forests. They returned each afternoon with sleighs stacked with dead wolves, elk and wild boar, the cooks skinning the corpses so the hides could be presented to the chief as gifts. The meat was cooked and eaten in the dining hall in the evening, Daina and her parents and siblings sitting at the top table with the master and Rudolf.

As the new year began the ice was thick on the Gauja and the many lakes that dotted the landscape around Wenden. Though the stores were well stocked with food and fuel, parties were sent out every day to hunt game and fish in the lakes through holes cut in the ice. Winters were long in Livonia and Wenden was now like a village complete with women and children that had to be clothed, fed and kept warm. As Master Berthold was always reminding the garrison during his long sermons, the Lord had stocked the land and waterways with an abundance of living things that could be caught and eaten. It was therefore a sin to ignore this bounty that God had provided.

Sometimes Rameke came from his father's village and he, Conrad and the other novices donned skis and travelled to one of the lakes for an ice fishing expedition. They each pulled sleds loaded with ice augers for drilling holes, skimmers to scrape out slush from the holes in the ice made by the augers, and gaff hooks that were used to hoist fish from the holes. They also hauled ice shanties: easily assembled wooden structures measuring six foot by six foot that were erected on the ice for shelter. Each one had a bench for two and was tall enough to stand up in.

They left before dawn to reach the lake that Rameke recommended for their expedition, reaching it after an hour.

'It is not very big,' said a disappointed Anton.

'Better for fishing,' replied Rameke. 'This lake is shallow and that means the fish are not far from the surface. It will be a good haul.'

The first two hours were frantic as they each bored holes in the ice and set up the baited hooks. The ice was eight inches thick and it took over two hours for the five of them to create forty holes in the ice. Then they had to cut branches from the firs around the lake with their axes to fashion small sticks, to which the fishing lines were tied. Small pieces of cloth were tied to the other end of the sticks and then other sticks were cut that were longer than the diameter of the holes in the ice.

Rameke kept looking into the sky and urged them to speed up their work.

'What is the rush?' asked Conrad, his breath misting in the cold.

'We have to get the lines set up before midday,' answered Rameke.

'Why?' said Hans.

'You ask too many questions,' replied Rameke. 'Just trust me.'

So they tied the small flagpoles at right angles to the longer sticks and rested them beside each hole in the ice, the fishing line and hooks dangling in the water. Each piece of cloth was flat on the ice beside a hole, and when they had set up all forty lines they erected the two ice shanties on the ice and waited.

'What if the fish don't bite?' said Johann.

Rameke smiled. 'They will bite. Just be patient.'

Hans began chewing on some cured meat that they had brought along. Even though he had been fed like a fighting cock since his arrival at Wenden and had grown considerably in height, he was still stick-thin, though his wiry frame was surprisingly strong. He also still ate every meal as though it was the first he had had in a month, devouring great quantities of food at every sitting. It was just as well that the rivers, lakes and forests of Livonia were teeming with fish and game else Hans would surely starve.

It was perfectly still, the trees standing as if frozen in time, their branches weighed down with snow. The whiteness extended in all directions and the sky was a piercing, pure blue. As they sat there, waiting for the fish to bite, it seemed like they were the only living things in the land.

'It is peaceful,' mused Hans, biting off another piece of meat.

'No winter campaign this year,' said Johann.

'Perhaps no winter campaigns ever again,' suggested Anton.

Rameke scoffed at the notion. 'There will be war soon enough, and much of it. My father says that the Estonians sought peace in order to rebuild their strength after their losses at King Caupo's stronghold.'

376

'More crusaders will be arriving in the spring,' said Conrad. 'Then the bishop will renew his war against Lembit.'

Rameke shook his head. 'He agreed a two-year peace with Lembit and he will not break it. He is a man of his word.'

'And what about Lembit?' queried Conrad.

'He has no honour,' sneered Rameke. 'It is my wish to kill him in battle.'

'I think Conrad will beat you to it,' said Johann. 'After all, he nearly killed him at Wenden with his crossbow.'

'A pity you didn't,' sighed Rameke. 'You would have done my people a great service.'

'If there is to be no war against Lembit for two years,' said Hans, 'then what is the point of the bishop bringing fresh crusaders with him from Germany when he returns in the spring?'

None of them had an answer to this so they sat in silence, staring at the holes in the ice. Conrad was beginning to think that their journey had been a waste of time when, suddenly, one of the small flags jerked and tipped up into the vertical position. Then another and another flag flipped up.

'What did I tell you?' said Rameke with pride. 'This lake is full of perch and pike and during the winter they feed most intensively in the middle of the day. Come on!'

He jumped up, grabbed his gaff hook and walked quickly over to where the first flag had tipped up. The others also grabbed their hooks and followed him as flag after flag stood up to indicate a fish had been snared. The first fished hauled onto the ice and into wicker baskets were perch: around a foot long and weighing no more than three pounds. But some lines yielded the much larger pike. Hans shouted with delight as he hooked a great dark green monster with razor-sharp teeth. The others whooped with joy as it thrashed around on the ice before he pulled the axe from his belt and battered it with the side of the iron head. Then he lifted it above his head in triumph. It must have been over four feet in length and weighing fifty pounds or more.

They spent two more hours on the ice, pulling up fish and filling baskets, then rebating the hooks and casting the lines back in the water. And then, suddenly, the fish stopped biting as they stopped feeding and returned to the bottom of the lake where the temperature was less cold than nearer the surface. They cooked some of the perch using dry firewood they had brought with them but did not touch any of the two-dozen pike they had caught. These fish contained numerous small bones and required expert filleting before they could be eaten. They would be left to Wenden's cooks to deal with.

The temperature was dropping rapidly by the time they had finished eating, stacked the baskets of fish on two of the sleds and tied the fishing equipment and shelters to the others. The only sound was their exertions as they dragged the sleds along the path they had used to reach the lake, their marks still visible in the deep snow. The snow-cleared ramparts of Wenden came into view just as the sun was sinking behind its walls and towers. Sentries stood warming their hands over braziers and the banner of the Sword Brothers hung limply from the northern tower and above the gatehouse in the perimeter wall. The new year heralded a time of peace and an opportunity to continue the building of the bishop's most northerly stronghold.

*****

Grand Duke Daugerutis sent two hundred men to the Dvina to clear a path from the river to his stronghold of Panemunis so that the journey of his daughter, son-in-law and their children would be as speedy as possible. When the snow had been cleared and the sleighs and guards assembled at the river the Prince of Gerzika and his retinue rode from their seat of power before alighting from the sleighs and walking across the iron-hard ice. Vsevolod was worried that the ice might crack and they might all fall into the icy water and freeze to death, so great was the number of servants and soldiers on the river. But it did not and soon the prince and his wife were riding behind a vanguard of fifty horsemen sent by the duke, his own hundred and fifty guards interspersed between the sleighs carrying tents, servants, food and clothes and a rearguard. It would take two days to reach his father-in-law's castle and he resented being dragged from his well-appointed, warm home to undertake a journey through the frozen forests of Lithuania. But the grand duke was most insistent that he should come, his wife wanted to see her father and his children thought it a great adventure.

Rasa snapped at them to be quiet as they moved through a snow-covered meadow between two great swathes of forests, the spruce and birch blanketed with snow. Fortunately there was no wind or snowfall but it was still bitterly cold so they were all wrapped in furs, the children seated behind the prince and his wife, who in turn were behind the driver directing the two horses pulling the sleigh.

'Two days staring at horses' arses,' complained Vsevolod, 'just what I desired.'

'Stop complaining,' Rasa rebuked him. 'It will be good to see father again.'

'I have no objection seeing your father, light of my life, it is the brutes he gathers round him that I object to. If I never see Prince Stecse again, it will be too soon.'

'Perhaps my father wishes to thank you in person for the gold he received in exchange for the Liv slaves he captured last year.'

Perhaps he had heard of the tidy sum that Vsevolod had made as a result of acting as mediator, more like. Perhaps he wanted his own share of the gold. He suddenly felt miserable and sank into silence. The grand duke had never struck him as a greedy man but perhaps the acquisition of so much gold had turned his head. He never realised that there was so much wealth within the walls of Riga. The bishop and his followers were rich, that much was certain. But to waste gold on worthless Livs – senseless.

Panemunis was worse than he could have imagined. Not only had the grand duke summoned all his princes and chiefs, Vsevolod learned that he had also invited the other Lithuanian dukes. Grand Duke Daugerutis controlled all the lands of the Selonians and Nalsen, extending far into the Lithuanian hinterland. Those lands to the south and west were the domains of dukes who occasionally warred among themselves and paid homage to Grand Duke Daugerutis. But here they were, together with their personal bodyguards, the dukes having been given quarters in the castle, their men living in tents pitched in the courtyard. The latter was a sea of mud, despite the boards that had been laid for ease of traversing it, and by the time Vsevolod and his family had been settled in their rooms his boots and cloak were splattered with dirt. This did nothing to improve his humour.

His mood lightened later when he sat beside the grand duke in his hall as he gave a great feast for his guests. The forests around the castle must have been emptied of all of its wild boar such was the quantity of roasted pork that was brought into the hall from the kitchens on huge wooden platters. The tables could barely accommodate the vast amounts of black rye bread, blood soup, eggs and pies loaded onto them. The grand duke also made sure their drinking horns were always full of the reddish-brown rye beer that even Vsevolod had to admit was delicious.

Not that anyone drank to excess. The great red banner bearing a black bear on all fours hung behind the top table, a reminder to everyone present that this was the citadel of Grand Duke Daugerutis, the man who ruled the greatest extent of Lithuania, and around the hall were posted guards whose shields were painted with the black bear. The other tables were arranged in a circle so as not to offend his guests and make them feel they were equal to their host, which everyone knew was not the case. The table to the immediate right of the top table was where Stecse and the grand duke's other important warlords were seated, the prince having kissed Rasa's hand when she had entered the hall with her father and nodded curtly to Vsevolod.

The other four tables held the other dukes who had been invited to Panemunis. Each sat with their most trusted warriors and warlords, though none was allowed to carry weapons save the dukes themselves. Vsevolod chuckled when he saw that all of them had also brought tasters to ensure they were not poisoned. How little they knew of Daugerutis. He was a man who preferred to kill his enemies on the battlefield, preferably with his own hand, rather than leave the business to lowly cooks. He could be the most intractable of enemies but also the most generous of hosts. He had invited them to his hall and all that interested him was that they relax and partake of his hospitality.

They were a curious collection of individuals, all long hair and thick beards with warrior rings on their fingers and thick torcs round their necks. There was Ykintas, Duke of the Semgallians, who had thick black hair and an even thicker black beard. His banner carried the symbol of the Iron Wolf, a mythical beast that supposedly prowled the great forests of Lithuania. On the next table sat the aloof Butantas, whose slight frame belied his cunning and ruthlessness. The Duke of the Samogitians, he had fought a very long and bloody war against Daugerutis, one that he had lost, along with a sizeable portion of his territory. Then there was the Duke of the Aukstaitija tribe – Kitenis – a bear of a man who wore leather armour painted with his symbol of the black axe. Finally there was Gedvilas, a red-haired jovial fellow who was the Duke of the Southern Kurs. The Kurs were a people who relished raiding on sea and land and viewed the lands of other peoples as their personal hunting grounds. The only duke who had not answered the invitation of Daugerutis had been Arturus, the leader of the Northern Kurs who had tried to capture Riga. He thought himself a king who did not answer to anyone, not least to the man whose warriors had attacked his eastern borders and who led the Selonians and Nalsen, tribes who were the traditional enemies of the Kurs. For that reason Daugerutis was particularly pleased that one of the Kur leaders had accepted his invitation.

The evening passed without incident and the next morning the grand duke invited his fellow leaders to a more formal meeting in his hall. Vsevolod attended but Rasa did not, women being banned from the important affairs of men. So she donned leggings, tied her hair behind her neck and accepted an invitation from Stecse to go hunting wolves. The prince also took his son, Mindaugas, along though Vsevolod forbade his two daughters attending. He loved Rasa but thought that she should make more of an effort to shrug off her pagan heritage and adopt more civilised, womanly hobbies rather than hunting. He certainly did not want his daughters being brought up as Lithuanians.

A great fire was raging in the stone hearth when he arrived in the hall to find Daugerutis pacing up and down, slaves spreading fresh straw on the earth floor. The kitchens had been working since before dawn, baking fresh bread and making hot porridge to fill cold bellies. Like Vsevolod the other dukes had eaten in their quarters with their warlords before making their way to the hall, each of them wrapped in fur-lined cloaks for it was still mercilessly cold, icicles hanging from roof beams and the beards of sentries turned white. When they came into the hall they all warmed their hands on the fire before accepting warmed beer offered to them by slaves.

'A man could freeze to death just taking a piss,' said Ykintas, throwing his cloak on a bench.

Kitenis drained his cup of beer and belched. 'I hope we have been dragged here for a good reason. I would rather be in my bed with a young slave girl than talking words of peace.'

'Not peace, my friend,' said Daugerutis, 'but war.'

He snapped his fingers and ordered the slave to bring more beer.

'I know your journeys here have been long and arduous and for that I thank you. Please, be seated.'

More slaves arranged high-backed chairs around the fire as Daugerutis waved away some of the guards that lined the walls. As the dukes took their places facing the fire a tall, white-robed man entered the hall and then closed the twin doors behind him. He walked purposefully over to the side of Daugerutis, who bowed his head to him. The white-haired man with a long white beard said nothing but the others knew who he was: *Kriviu Krivaitis*, the high priest of the Lithuanian religion, a man who lived in the sacred oak grove where the Eternal Flame burned. Daugerutis may have conquered by the sword but he ruled because the *Kriviu Krivaitis* lived on his land and every Lithuanian, high- or low-born, knew that Dievas himself spoke through him. The priesthood, the *Kriviai*, could travel freely throughout Lithuania without let or hindrance, for to interfere with them was to incur the wrath of the gods. And now the high priest himself stood before them in the hall of the grand duke.

381

Vsevolod took a seat, the others frowning at the presence of this foreigner among them, but Daugerutis remained standing. The presence of the *Kriviu Krivaitis* had impressed them all, even the fierce Kitenis, and they all waited to hear what the grand duke had to say. All except Vsevolod who was abruptly asked to leave.

'Unless you wish to embrace our faith, my son,' said Daugerutis, 'you cannot be present when *Kriviu Krivaitis* calls upon the gods.'

The others murmured in agreement and cast the Prince of Gerzika hostile glances. They only tolerated his presence because he was related to the grand duke. Vsevolod rose and bowed to his father-in-law. He had no wish to attend a heathen ceremony anyway.

'Of course, my lord.'

He ignored the others as he made his way to the doors, which were opened by the guards and then shut behind him.

Kriviu Krivaitis used his hands to order the dukes to rise from their chairs. As they and the grand duke bowed their heads he faced the fire and spread his arms, closing his eyes as he prayed to Dievas. To many people fire was a source of light and warmth but to Lithuanians it was much more. Fire symbolised the unbroken lifeline of a family and its ancestry. The Eternal Flame over which the chief priest and virgins stood guard over was the unifying link with ancestors who had long since died and were now with the gods. And every Lithuanian believed that numerous generations of his family's dead continued to live on at the hearth of his fire.

For this reason fire was not to be harmed, insulted or polluted. Fire was treated with reverence and awe. No one spat into a fire or kicked at it, and no live coals or smouldering ashes were extinguished for this was considered a sin. Rather, everyone waited until the fire burned out of its own accord before the hearth was cleared.

As the fire crackled and spat in the hall the priest at last spoke, his voice deep and severe.

'Great Dievas who created the world and all that is in it, look upon these, your most devout servants and bless them.

'The fire is burning.

'Shine as light.

'We are your children.

'Shine as light.

'Smoulder as covered.

'Give us strength.

'Unite us.

'Help us prosper.

'Bless us.'

The others murmured 'bless us' as the priest let his arms fall to his side and sat down in a chair next to the grand duke's. Daugerutis remained standing. Vsevolod was readmitted as the others retook their seats. After they had done so a detachment of guards entered carrying four wooden chests, which were placed on the floor in front of the dukes. Daugerutis dismissed the guards and went to each chest, lifting the lid to reveal a hoard of gold and silver plate.

'A chest for each of you. I appreciate you dragging yourselves here through snow and ice. You have my gratitude.'

Butantas' eyes opened wide as he stood and began rifling through his chest, picking up gold coins and biting them to ensure they were the real things. Ykintas laughed at him but he too perused the contents of his chest to make certain his was as well stocked as that of the Duke of the Samogitians.

'Most generous, lord,' beamed Gedvilas, grinning to reveal a row of white teeth.

Vsevolod looked most surprised and wondered why his father-in-law was giving away the ransom that the Bishop of Riga had given him for the release of the Liv slaves. For his part Kitenis merely regarded his chest with indifference before looking at Daugerutis.

'What do you want?'

The grand duke laughed. 'Honest and to the point. I like that.'

Daugerutis sat in his chair next to the high priest. 'Last year, as you all know, I crossed the Dvina to lead an expedition against my enemy the Prince of Novgorod. On the return journey I helped myself to a few slaves.'

The others laughed. The grand duke held up his hands to still them.

'You can imagine my surprise when the Bishop of Riga sent a request via my son-in-law to purchase the slaves back. The treasure you see before you is the sum the Christians paid to get back their worthless Liv subjects.

'You asked me what I wanted, Duke Kitenis. I will tell you. Last year I led a raid across the Dvina; this year I will lead a campaign of conquest. I intend to seize all the Christian lands north of the river, and after that all of Estonia and the Principality of Novgorod. And I want your help to do it.'

Kitenis nodded approvingly and Gedvilas smiled once more. Butantas rubbed his beard thoughtfully and Ykintas gestured to a slave for his cup to be refilled.

Only Vsevolod was alarmed. He had thought that his role as a mediator between Daugerutis and the Bishop of Riga would strengthen his position at Gerzika by being the ally of both the Lithuanians and the crusaders. But now he could be crushed between two mighty powers.

'Two thousand men,' said Daugerutis. 'That is what I require of each of you. I intend to take twenty thousand men across the river. More than enough to sweep the Christians from Livonia.'

'Ever since they arrived north of the Dvina the Christians have expanded their power,' remarked Butantas. 'Why are you so certain that they can be so easily defeated?'

Daugerutis smiled. 'Because they are weak.' He pointed at the chests. 'Why else would they allow me to march through their territory with armed men, to bleat like women when I took their subjects and pay me this great sum instead of sending an army to punish me?'

The grand duke continued. 'My son-in-law informed me that the Christians begged the leader of the Estonians for peace and that their much-vaunted army was ravaged by plague and was barely able to crush a Liv rebellion. Livonia stands like ripe fruit for picking.'

He stood. 'Just as Perkunas, the Heavenly Smith, created the sun and moon and hammered them into existence, so shall I forge the lands north and south of the Dvina into one kingdom and that realm will be Lithuanian.'

'The gods approve of such a venture,' announced *Kriviu Krivaitis* solemnly.

The others looked at each other for a few seconds and then shouted their approval. Vsevolod's heart sank as he cursed his own tongue for divulging to the grand duke what Archdeacon Stefan had told him in his letters. He smiled at his father-in-law politely as his mind began frantically searching for a way out of the calamity that was about to envelop him and his kingdom.

Things darkened the next day when a gloating Prince Stecse stood beside the grand duke in his hall while the latter explained to Vsevolod what his role would be in the forthcoming war.

'While I roast the Christians in Livonia,' said the grand duke, chewing on a great piece of wild boar and sitting in his chair, 'I grant you the privilege of taking your army, my son, to ravage the land of the Novgorodians.'

384

Vsevolod's heart sank. 'Novgorod, lord?'

Daugerutis spat a chunk of gristle on the floor. 'Yes! The Christians will fall to us as stubble to our swords but do not think that I have forgotten the Prince of Novgorod.'

'The enemy of our people,' said Stecse, fixing his eyes upon Vsevolod, who had to think fast.

'The army of Gerzika, small and ill equipped though it is,' said Vsevolod, 'will of course be at your disposal, father. Though I shall have to retain some soldiers in my city to safeguard against an attack from the east.'

Daugerutis looked at him in confusion and then at Stecse. 'From the east?'

'The Principality of Polotsk, lord,' answered Vsevolod.

Stecse was unimpressed. 'Polotsk lies over a hundred miles from Gerzika and you are of the same blood as its rulers.'

Vsevolod glared at Stecse. 'I am fully aware of the geography of my kingdom, prince. If I am seen aiding the enemies of Mother Russia I may incur the wrath of both Novgorod and Polotsk.'

'Mother Russia?' sneered Daugerutis. 'Who is this whore you speak of?'

'The rallying cry of all Russians, lord,' replied Vsevolod. 'You must understand, lord, that my position is most invidious. Many lords north of the Dvina mistrust me.'

'Not just north of the river,' remarked Stecse.

Vsevolod had had enough of this upstart who whispered poison into his father-in-law's ear. A task, after all, that he was far more suited to.

'How dare you!'

Daugerutis held up a hand to Stecse.

'You exceed yourself.'

Stecse bowed his head. 'My apologies, lord, I meant no offence.'

Daugerutis looked at Vsevolod. 'Now is the time to stand by your family, Vsevolod. You may be a Russian but you are united to the Lithuanian people through your marriage to my daughter, my only heir. It may fortify your courage to know that I have informed my lords that you will rule them should anything befall me during the coming war.'

Vsevolod was taken aback by this and was momentarily speechless. He had always assumed that because Rasa was a woman she would not inherit her father's kingdom, and as a Russian he had always believed that Daugerutis would never contemplate him becoming a Lithuanian ruler. He regained his composure and looked at Stecse in triumph. If anything happened to the grand duke one of his first acts as Lithuanian leader would be to have the upstart executed.

Daugerutis saw Vsevolod's look of triumph. 'There is more. I know that many among my people will not agree with my decision, the more so because my daughter is married to a foreigner who has sired no sons.'

Vsevolod bristled at this. 'Only God determines what children a man may or may not have, lord.'

Daugerutis held up a hand to still him. 'I attach no blame to you, my son, even if your god turned a deaf ear to your pleas. But the fact is that if you and my daughter are to rule from this hall then your reign will need legitimacy. That is why the son of Prince Stecse will be *your* heir, Vsevolod.

'I do not understand,' said the latter.

'It is quite simple,' said the grand duke irritably. 'Stecse is the most valiant and able among my lords and is accepted by all of them as such. He is in the fortunate position of having enemies that are either dead or banished. That being the case his son, Mindaugas, will be acceptable as your heir, my son. It will also consolidate your rule after my death.'

'Which I hope is many years away,' said Vsevolod. Daugerutis waved away his flattery.

'You honour me greatly, lord,' said a dumfounded Stecse.

'Honour has nothing to do with it,' replied the grand duke. 'I wish to see my daughter be accorded her position as my only surviving child but I am also mindful that my successors must have the loyalty of my princes. I like your son, Stecse, he will make a fine ruler one day.'

Stecse bowed his head and Vsevolod smiled perfunctorily at the grand duke. He did not like the idea that a son of Stecse would be his heir. Still, that he might be made the heir of Daugerutis had not even crossed his mind. How strange was fate. Then again it did not solve the immediate problem of how he was going to extricate himself from the forthcoming war with the Bishop of Riga. Ideally he would have liked to sit it out but this was not an option, not least because it would jeopardise his new role as the grand duke's heir. With these thoughts swirling in his mind he left his father-in-law to inform his wife of this new development.

*****

The air was still cool and there was frost in the mornings when Grand Duke Daugerutis invaded Livonia. He knew that in the spring the bishop would arrive back from Germany accompanied by hundreds, perhaps thousands, of crusaders with their warhorses and crossbowmen. But he would return to a blackened wasteland where there were no crusaders or pliant Livs, just a mighty Lithuania that straddled the Dvina like a colossus. His army – twenty thousand men – crossed the river just below the Castle of Kokenhusen, his men building a bridge of boats on the icy water so that the Christians could see his warriors cross. At dawn he and Stecse had boarded a small riverboat that had been rowed near to the opposite bank where the Sword Brother castle stood. He had brandished a spear and shouted up at the battlements that the hour of their doom had come, before hurling the spear into the black waters to signal that he was at war with the Christians.

It took all morning to build the bridge of boats, the grand duke sending over a thousand men in boats to secure the northern riverbank and ensure the crusaders at Kokenhusen did not interfere with his arrangements. The southern bank of the river was filled with men and horses that quickly turned the ground to mud as they waited to cross. Everyone was wrapped in cloaks for the morning was overcast and the air dank, an easterly wind pinching flesh and watering eyes.

When the bridge had been completed and planks nailed in place to allow men and beasts to cross, the austere and severe *Kriviu Krivaitis* walked across followed by the *Vaidilutes*, the virgins who guarded the sacred Eternal Flame. The high priest's face was white from the cold and his eyes red from the wind as he strode across the bridge, but the young women who followed him must have been numb with cold in their flimsy long white dresses, bare arms and light shoes. The grand duke had arranged for them to be wrapped in furs and given hot mead when they reached the northern riverbank, but the symbolism of their presence was immense as they carried lighted torches that had been lit by the Sacred Flame over the river to plant in Christian territory. The thousands of men watched in silence as the tall, white-clothed priest and his virgins walked across the river, a scene also observed by the Sword Brothers and crusaders on Kokenhusen's battlements, before cheering wildly as the torches were taken from the frozen virgins and used to light great bonfires on the far bank. Then the army crossed.

The other dukes, seduced by the lure of more gold and easy conquest, had brought their men and they now rode across the Dvina in the company of Daugerutis. In the biting wind their colourful banners fluttered behind the huge red banner sporting a black bear. There was the iron wolf of Duke Ykintas, the elk antlers of Duke Butantas, the black axe of Duke Kitenis and the golden eagle of Duke Gedvilas. And behind them came rank upon rank of horsemen in armour, cloaks wrapped around them and helmeted heads covered in hoods. Each rider carried two *spisas* in addition to his pavise-like shield, sword and axe, occasionally a mace.

The largest contingent was the grand duke's: four thousand horsemen and eight thousand foot. Of the other dukes, Ykintas brought five hundred horsemen and fifteen hundred warriors on foot. Butantas mustered a thousand horsemen and the same number of foot soldiers, while six hundred horsemen and fourteen hundred foot accompanied Kitenis. Duke Gedvilas, being the ruler of the poorest kingdom, brought only two hundred horsemen along with eighteen hundred foot.

Daugerutis could have mustered twenty thousand warriors on his own but he wanted the other dukes to be a part of his war, not least because if they were creating havoc in Livonia it meant that his own borders were secure. As he and they stood watching the unending line of horsemen file across the river he looked behind him at the white walls of Kokenhusen in the distance. How accommodating of their bishop to give him the funds that had allowed him to bribe them. Perkunas was surely smiling on him and his venture.

He looked at the young man with a long face sitting beside Stecse.

'You are a lucky boy, Mindaugas,' he said to him. 'To be alive at this auspicious time.'

'Yes, lord. Thank you,' replied Mindaugas nervously. He was overawed at being in the company of Lithuania's great warlords. For their part they were bored and cold.

'I need one of those virgins to warm me up,' remarked Kitenis irreverently.

Gedvilas laughed. 'They are sacred, you old goat. You will have to settle for a Liv slave to keep the cold away from your old bones.'

'Perhaps the Bishop of Riga will buy them back a second time,' remarked Butantas.

'There will be no Livonia,' stated Daugerutis. 'We are here to stay.'

To bring his plan to fruition he had prepared the campaign carefully and had stationed an additional three thousand men to the south of the river, in his own territory, to safeguard the crossing point over the Dvina. He knew that he and the other dukes had no siege equipment with which to take the castles of the crusaders. But he gambled that he could besiege those along the Dvina with foot soldiers while his horsemen ravaged the countryside. With the bishop in Germany and with no hope of relief, they would have no alternative but to surrender.

388

When the six thousand, three hundred horsemen had passed over and were led by the grand duke towards Kokenhusen to begin the investment of that place, the other dukes in attendance, Stecse remained at the river to oversee the crossing of over thirteen and half thousand foot soldiers. They wore fur-lined leather caps for both warmth and protection and kaftans over long tunics. The bottoms of their leggings were secured by leather thongs, their feet already soaked due to hours of trudging through mud. The lucky ones, those who could afford them, wore leather boots and mail armour and might even have a sword. But the vast majority of these warrior farmers were armed only with a spear and an axe tucked in their belts. A small number, professional huntsmen, carried bows and quivers full of arrows and others shouldered clubs and maces, including a variety of the latter named *kistien*: a ball-and-chain weapon that without training could be just as lethal to its owner as well as an opponent.

The army camped around Kokenhusen the first night, Daugerutis and the other dukes taking shelter in the village nearest the castle, the inhabitants having fled to the fortress upon hearing of the approach of the Lithuanians. The grand duke was pleased. The more Livs who flocked to the castles of the Sword Brother the quicker their food supplies would be exhausted.

The next day, after leaving five hundred of his own men to besiege Kokenhusen, under strict orders not to launch an assault, the grand duke rode west with the other dukes to besiege the other Christian castles long the Dvina: Lennewarden, Uexkull and Holm. Seven days after crossing the river he had those places and Kokenhusen besieged and led the other dukes and his horsemen for an attack north against Caupo.

*****

The Lithuanian invasion had produced a flurry of messages between the castles of the Sword Brothers and Riga. Archdeacon Stefan ordered the immediate closing of the town gates, much to the alarm of those German settlers and Livs who lived beyond Riga's walls.

Soon there was a great crowd clamouring to be let into the town, mothers holding up weeping infants, imploring the bishop's guards on the walls to at least save their children. It was a pitiful spectacle that moved even the hardest hearts but Stefan would not relent and so the crowd increased in size and the wailing below them moved the guards to tears. In the end Grand Master Volquin stormed from his office in the castle and gave the order to open the gates, an action that earned him an immediate summons to the bishop's palace.

Stefan was in an agitated state as he paced up and down in front of the grand master in the audience chamber of the bishop's residence, fidgeting nervously with his pectoral cross. Volquin stood before him with his arms folded. He noticed that the archdeacon's pectoral cross was now solid gold, as was the chain. Stefan had no time for the virtue of poverty, it seemed.

'You should not have opened the gates, grand master, not at all.'

Volquin raised an eyebrow. 'The Lithuanians are not upon us yet, archdeacon, so there was no danger.'

Stefan's eyes opened wide. 'No danger? May I remind you that the town's food supplies are low after the winter and can hardly support the influx of a great number of civilians.'

'They have brought what food they had with them,' stated Volquin.

Stefan walked back to his chair and began fidgeting with the silk-covered arms. 'Food that will be consumed soon enough.'

Volquin moved closer to him. 'Archdeacon, it would be bad for morale if, when, the Lithuanians arrive the garrison was forced to watch civilians being butchered by them. You have to remember that people who live in Riga have relatives beyond the walls. We cannot abandon them.'

'And where are the heathen Lithuanians?'

'They encircled Kokenhusen a week ago, Lennewarden three days later and arrived before Uexkull yesterday. They will be here in four or five days.'

Stefan crossed himself. 'The Lord save us.'

Volquin sighed. 'The walls of Riga are thick enough to deter an assault, archdeacon. In any case the last despatch I had from Kokenhusen indicated that the Lithuanian strategy is to sit outside the walls and starve the occupants into surrender.

Stefan went pale. 'The last despatch from Kokenhusen? Has the castle fallen?'

Volquin wanted to laugh at this absurd little man whom the bishop had made governor.

'No, archdeacon, it has not fallen. Nor will it. And that is the same for all the other castles of my order that are surrounded by the Lithuanians. My castellans are men of iron, not rotten wood. But the Lithuanians will ensure that no messages leave the garrisons or enter. They use hawks to kill the courier pigeons.'

Stefan tightened his lips. 'Barbarians. They must be made to pay for their treachery.'

He looked at Volquin. 'You will be organising a relief force, I assume?'

'Relief force?'

Stefan frowned at him. 'To save our castles along the Dvina.'

Volquin shook his head. 'I have too few men, archdeacon, even counting those knights who remained here during the winter. Master Griswold at Kokenhusen reported that thousands of Lithuanians crossed the river. That is why they can lay siege to each castle.'

'Then what is your plan, grand master?'

'I have sent letters to King Caupo to bring his warriors to Riga. Combined with our own forces we will have enough to defeat the Lithuanians. After that those enemy soldiers besieging our castles will disappear as quickly as snow in spring.'

Stefan was not convinced. 'Caupo? We leave the safety of the whole of Livonia in the hands of a pagan?'

'*King* Caupo,' said Volquin firmly, 'is a friend and ally of the bishop. I have fought by his side and he is a good man. I trust him implicitly.'

Stefan rose from his chair once more to recommence his pacing. 'You would be well advised not to trust anyone in this land, grand master. I trusted Prince Vsevolod and look where that has got me. The bishop has made a peace with the heathen Lembit but will he honour it? I think not. The only thing we can trust in this land is our own kind and God's mercy.'

'Our own kind?' queried Volquin.

Stefan waved a hand in the air. 'Christians from Germany and other godly lands, of course. They will supplant the natives and then we will have a truly god-fearing kingdom, free from Livs, Estonians and Lithuanians and all the other dross that we currently have to endure.'

Volquin raised an eyebrow. 'That is the bishop's view?'

'The bishop's time is devoted to enlisting knights and funds for his holy crusade in Livonia. He leaves the day-to-day running of the kingdom to me.'

'How fortunate he is,' remarked Volquin dryly.

Stefan, who stopped pacing, noted his tone. 'That being the case, I would prefer that it was a Christian army that defeated the Lithuanians, not one filled with Livs.'

'King Caupo and his men are Christians, archdeacon.'

'That is a matter open to debate,' sneered Stefan.

But whatever Stefan may have thought of Caupo and his Livs he and they did not want for courage. Upon hearing of the Lithuanian invasion the king gathered his chiefs and marched south to do battle with Grand Duke Daugerutis. The castellans of Segewold, Kremon and Wenden were ordered to fortify their strongholds and await reinforcements. Ideally Volquin would have liked to have ordered Caupo to do likewise but he had no authority over the Liv king, and in any case he understood that Caupo could not stand by idly while the Lithuanians were overrunning his people. And so he marched from Treiden at the head of three thousand men, including Thalibald and his eldest son Waribule, and met Daugerutis in battle by the shore of Lake Inesis, some sixty miles east of Riga. The king and his men fought well but at the end of the day the lake and its western shore were filled with Liv dead. Daugerutis brought four thousand horse and eight thousand foot soldiers to the battlefield and Caupo and his men were simply overwhelmed by a Lithuanian tide. The king was resigned to die fighting among the remnants of his army but Thalibald physically put him on a horse and ordered what remained of Caupo's bodyguard to take their king back to Treiden. Caupo was in tears as he looked back to see the banner of Thalibald fall beneath a mass of Lithuanians.

Grand Duke Daugerutis did not halt to celebrate his victory at Inesis. He consigned his own dead to the fires, left the Liv slain to rot and then marched his men north, towards the Gauja and Wenden.

Chapter 15

Master Berthold had assembled the garrison of Wenden and those Livs who had sought sanctuary in the castle in the courtyard to inform them that the Lithuanians had defeated King Caupo and his army and were now on the way to the castle. Conrad felt a knot in his stomach as he wondered what had happened to Thalibald and Waribule. Rameke and a score of warriors had escorted the women and children from his and other villages to the castle where they had been accommodated in the castle quarters. He and the other novices had been unceremoniously consigned to tents inside the perimeter, among the huts of the civilian workers. He did not mind because it meant that Daina was safe.

But the daughter of Thalibald was distraught when she learned about Caupo's defeat, as were most of the Liv women, because it meant that her father, brother and their menfolk were probably dead. Conrad held her in his arms as she sobbed her heart out after learning of the king's defeat, while Rameke swore revenge on the Lithuanians.

'I will ride south with what few men I can muster,' he hissed. 'I am chief now.'

Conrad was shocked, not by his desire to exact vengeance but by the fact that he was now the chief of his people.

'I will come with you,' he said, holding Daina tight.

'Me too,' said Hans.

Anton nodded in agreement and Johann slapped Rameke on the back.

'None of you are going anywhere,' hissed Lukas, 'not even you, Rameke.'

'I lead my people now, Lukas,' snapped Rameke, looking at his sister sobbing.

Lukas smiled and laid a hand on his shoulder. 'Listen. Cool heads are needed in a crisis. Your first responsibility as the leader of your people is to ensure their safety and not to ride away on some stupid revenge mission that will only get you killed. Who will lead your people then?'

'But...' Rameke protested.

Lukas held up a hand. 'Have all your people been gathered in?'

Rameke looked around at the dozens of women, young children and infants that filled the courtyard. He nodded.

'Very well,' said Lukas. 'Help me and the master get them settled into their quarters and then you and Master Berthold can discuss what needs to be done.'

393

Rameke nodded his head sullenly and slapped Johann on the shoulder.

Lukas walked over to Daina and gently laid his hands on her shoulders.

'Perhaps it would be better if your brother consoled you, Daina. Conrad has duties to attend to.'

'I do?' said Conrad.

Lukas glared at him. 'Yes, you do.'

Conrad kissed Daina on the head.

'I love you,' he whispered.

She pulled away from him and looked at him with tear-filled eyes.

'And I you.'

Lukas gestured for Rameke to take his sister to her quarters and waved Conrad and the others away. Somewhat crestfallen, Rameke put an arm around his sister and they walked towards the dormitory.

'And Rameke,' Lukas called after him.

Rameke stopped and looked at the brother knight.

'Your father was a good man and like a brother to me and the other brother knights here. We will avenge his death.'

Lukas watched them disappear into the dormitory as sergeants, who had also been ejected from their quarters, began herding the Liv women and children into the building that their new chief would also occupy. And because there were so many new civilians the dining hall was also given over to housing them.

'Where will we eat?' asked Hans with alarm. The others laughed.

'You won't have time to eat,' replied Lukas.

Hans smiled. 'I always have time to eat, Brother Lukas.'

At that moment the alarm bell began ringing at the gatehouse in the perimeter wall, to be reciprocated by the bell in the courtyard.

Lukas pointed at Hans. 'You think so?'

The sergeants hurried everyone inside as brother knights and mercenaries rushed to the armoury to collect their weapons. There were guards at the perimeter gatehouse and on the timber ramparts at all times but they would need reinforcing if the castle's outer wall was to hold. Lukas told Conrad and others to collect crossbows from the armoury. They were all allowed to wear their swords now, but their helmets and shields were deposited in the armoury and so they had to retrieve them.

'And don't forget to collect at least three quivers of bolts each,' he said to them.

394

As they waited in line Conrad saw leather face exit the squat stone building with his crossbow on his shoulder and holding four quivers. The grizzled old mercenary smiled at him.

'Never fought the Lithuanians before. Should be interesting.'

'You have enough quivers there,' said Conrad.

'Now don't you boys worry,' said leather face, 'there will be plenty of Lithuanians to go round.'

He grinned to show his rotting teeth before sauntering off as though he had not a care in the world.

When he at last got to the armoury the armourers were already flustered and irritable, slamming down full quivers on the bench that served as a makeshift counter between them and the outside world. They guarded the armoury like an eagle watches over its nest. But they knew their business and soon furnished Conrad with everything he needed: crossbow, two sets of bowstrings, kettle helmet, shield, three full quivers and a one-handed axe, which he tucked in his belt. Then he and the others went outside and ran from the courtyard to man the outer wall.

As he raced across the bridge over the moat he saw horsemen riding up and down beyond the perimeter wall, dozens of them. They were obviously acting as a screen for the hundreds of foot soldiers that were being marshalled into position behind them.

'Do you think three quivers each will be enough?' said Anton with alarm.

As they descended the slope to where the civilian huts stood they passed their occupants rushing the other way to the safety of the castle, clutching their children and a few pathetic belongings. The gates in the perimeter wall had been closed and braced with logs but as Conrad looked to the left and right to see members of the garrison loading crossbows on the ramparts, he realised that the defenders of Wenden were vastly outnumbered.

He was comforted by the fact that the outer perimeter defences had been considerably strengthened since Lembit's men had managed to breach them quite easily. Under the supervision of Master Thaddeus the ditch that ran along the entire length of the outer perimeter had been deepened, the earth that had been dug from it being used to raise the rampart. Thus the height of the ditch equalled the height of the adjoining rampart, with a narrow, horizontal strip of ground called a berm left between the ditch and the rampart to prevent the latter sliding into the former. The bottom of the ditch, which was dry, was filled with sharpened stakes to impale anyone unfortunate enough to fall in it.

But it was the timber walls themselves that had been entirely rebuilt. Now the defences on top of the rampart comprised a series of log cells placed side by side along the whole perimeter. Each 'cell' had three walls: one facing the outer side of the rampart and two at right angles to the outer wall. These defences were built around the superiority of the crossbow, which could be shot through loopholes in the parapet. In addition, the upper part of the wall had been built slightly forward, overhanging the lower part, to create a gap between the two parts. Through this gap could be shot crossbow bolts at any enemy soldiers who had reached the berm at the foot of the wall. Finally, the log cells were covered with gable roofs to protect against the weather and enemy missiles.

Conrad placed his quivers on the floor beside him, leaned the crossbow against the wall and peered through a loophole. Each 'cell' could accommodate up to four men but because the perimeter wall was extensive and the garrison meagre, two were usually allocated to each one. So he and Hans checked their weapons and were left alone with their own thoughts, Anton and Johann occupying the adjacent 'cell'.

The Lithuanians had made no attempt to move closer to the walls but seemed to be content to stand in blocks of spearmen as the horsemen continued to ride up and down in front of them. After a while the enemy began banging drums, the irksome din reverberating around the perimeter. After the initial excitement following the appearance of the enemy and frayed nerves as the garrison rushed to man the walls, a sense of anti-climax descended on the defenders. Lukas climbed the ladder to reach Conrad and Hans and articulated everyone's thoughts.

'They are not going to attack.'

'Perhaps they are waiting for reinforcements,' suggested Conrad.

Lukas walked to a loophole and looked through it. 'Perhaps. But there must be over a thousand of them out there so I suspect their strategy is to sit outside the walls.'

'To what end?' said Hans.

Lukas smiled sadistically. 'To starve us out, of course. No point in wasting men when hunger can do their work for them.'

Conrad laughed. 'The other garrisons will send a relief force long before that happens.'

Lukas looked away from the Lithuanians. 'The other garrisons are also besieged, or so we've heard.'

'Then who will save us?' asked an alarmed Hans.

Lukas shrugged. 'Who indeed?'

As the hours passed and the Lithuanians began to make camp around Wenden, Master Berthold stood down the men on the perimeter wall, leaving a small number to keep watch on the enemy. It was obvious that there would be no assault and so he wrote a short note and ordered it to be sent to Riga. He would take no action until he heard from Grand Master Volquin.

*****

Stecse took the message that had been attached to the dead pigeon and handed it to Daugerutis. Like at the other Sword Brother castles that had been encircled hawkers had been placed around the walls, ready to bring down any courier pigeons that flew from the garrison.

'The commander awaits the orders of Riga, lord.'

Daugerutis smiled. He sat on his horse several hundred paces from the gatehouse in Wenden's outer perimeter wall, the other dukes clustered behind him. His strategy had thus far worked perfectly. He had the castles of Kokenhusen, Lennewarden, Uexkull and Holm besieged along the Dvina. He had defeated and destroyed the Liv army of King Caupo and afterwards pushed on to the Gauja to surround Segewold Castle. Now he had arrived at Wenden, the strongest crusader castle second only to Riga, and watched as his soldiers had surrounded it with ease. It was true that he had six thousand men tied down in sieges but there was no crusader army in Livonia that could mount a relief operation. Soon he would march against Riga itself and adopt the same strategy, and then the crusader castles would fall one by one, and after them Riga itself. And then he would be the master of all Livonia.

'He will be waiting for a long time,' remarked the grand duke.

'We should launch an attack,' growled Ykintas, 'instead of sitting here like old women.'

Thus far the leader of the Semgallians had retained his full complement of men rather than seeing them allocated to siege operations. He had fought well at Inesis, as had the other dukes, though the truth was that Caupo had been so outnumbered that it had been more of a rout than a battle. Lithuanian losses had been light whereas the Livs had lost hundreds. Now the Iron Wolf wanted to batter his way into Wenden. Daugerutis knew that the crusader castles were not to be underestimated, despite the small size of their garrisons.

Daugerutis turned in his saddle. 'What do you think, Thalibald? Do you think Wenden's walls can be breached?'

397

Thalibald and his eldest son sat in sullen silence on their horses. At the end of the Battle of Inesis they had decided to make a final stand and kill as many of the enemy before they died. However, though their men had indeed been slaughtered, he and Waribule had been overpowered and captured. Daugerutis had treated them with courtesy but they were continually accompanied by a score of guards to prevent their escape. Their swords had also been taken from them. The grand duke knew that Thalibald was second in importance only to Caupo among the Livs. He therefore might prove useful, and if not then he would have him and his son killed. For the present, though, it amused him to entertain them.

'The Sword Brothers are no fools,' said Thalibald.

'They are cowardly women who hide behind their walls,' boomed Ykintas.

Daugerutis held Thalibald's hateful gaze. 'Perhaps you are right, Ykintas. Perhaps my tactics are too cautious. Perhaps it is time for the banner of the Iron Wolf to fly from those walls.'

Ykintas gave a cheer of triumph and wheeled his horse away to lead his men. Stecse brought his horse alongside the grand duke's.

'Lord, it is folly to assault those walls.'

Daugerutis looked at him. 'I know. But it will be a useful lesson for Ykintas to learn and I grow tired of his bluster.'

Duke Ykintas still had fourteen hundred foot with him and now he ordered them to fashion scaling ladders by felling trees in the surrounding forests while the rest of the army also collected wood, though for cooking fires not ladders. It was now two hours past noon and there were at least four hours of daylight left – plenty of time to take the castle, so Ykintas thought, and roast any prisoners alive before sitting down to an evening feast with the other dukes. Thalibald and Waribule were escorted back to their village, which was now the headquarters of Grand Duke Daugerutis and his fellow dukes. They feasted in Thalibald's hall while the Liv chief and his son were kept locked up in a small hut.

*****

'I thought I saw Thalibald,' said Conrad, straining his eyes as he looked through the loophole.

After prayers and a meal he and Hans had returned to the walls to undertake two hours of guard duty.

'Thalibald is dead,' said Hans glumly.

Conrad peered through the loophole again. He saw a group of riders disappearing into the distance and a group of horsemen standing several hundred feet in front of the gatehouse.

'It was him, I swear.'

'It is your mind playing tricks on you,' said Hans.

Conrad stopped looking at the multitude of campfires that were being lit around the castle and sat down with his back against the parapet.

'Perhaps you are right.'

Hans looked through a peephole and shook his head. 'Their numbers increase by the hour. Do you think anyone will come to save us?'

Conrad took a quarrel from a quiver and examined the metal head. 'I do not know, but if I am to die then I can think of no better place to leave this life.'

'Are you afraid to die?' asked Hans.

'I've never really thought about it. If the enemy storms the castle then I won't have time to think about it before I am cut down. I think of all the deaths, to die in battle is the best.'

Hans nodded. 'Master Berthold says that all those who die fighting the pagans are guaranteed to get to heaven. I would like to see my mother. I never knew her. Do you think she is waiting for me?'

'I am certain of it, my friend, just as I know that my parents are waiting to greet me.'

Their conversation was interrupted by a sudden increase in the volume of drumming from beyond the walls, which had mercifully greatly lessened during the previous two hours, to be followed by the ringing of the alarm bell at the gatehouse in the perimeter wall. Then the bell in the castle also began to ring and men began to pour from its half-built walls, running across the bridge over the moat and down the hill to the perimeter. Conrad rose and looked through a peephole to see hundreds of Lithuanians approaching the walls.

Conrad and Hans loaded their crossbows and rested the foot stirrups on the loopholes. They shook each other's hands.

'Just in case we are too busy to say goodbye,' said Conrad.

He felt a tingle of excitement ripple through him. It was not fear, for he was now almost a veteran when it came to battle, more like a feeling of relish and expectation that gripped him. He glanced down at his sword and said a silent prayer to God that his conduct would be worthy of its former owner. Then he went down on one knee, closed his eyes and said another prayer, asking that God take his life instead of Daina's. He rose to his feet just as Lukas appeared behind them.

'Remember your training,' he told them. 'And no heroics. If you hear the signal to withdraw obey it. We are thinly spread and the master wants his garrison to fight well and fall back to the castle if this wall is breached. Remember you are servants of God and your lives are His, not yours. So obey commands. Are you listening, Conrad?'

Conrad smiled. 'Yes, Brother Lukas.'

Lukas looked kindly at them. 'God be with you both.'

He turned to descend the ladder but then stopped.

'And no wasting ammunition. Pick your targets before you shoot, and make every bolt count.'

They nodded and then he was gone. The Lithuanians were now three hundred paces from the ditch, shields held before them as they inched forward. Every other warrior seemed to be carrying a scaling ladder, which not only slowed their progress but also left inviting gaps between their shields. The mercenary crossbowmen of the garrison were the best shots at Wenden and they began loosing bolts when the Lithuanians were four hundred paces away, figures falling among the dark groups of enemy warriors. The drummers behind each block drowned out any other sounds and as they got closer to the ditch their banging became more frantic as they tried to fortify their comrades' resolve.

*****

Ykintas had dismounted his best warriors, his horsemen, leaving every tenth man behind to look after the beasts. Numbering nearly four hundred men, these well-equipped warriors were members of his guard and his most loyal men. Attired in helmets sporting wolf tails and with wolf-head motifs on their shields, mail shirts and all armed with swords, they grouped around him as he led them on foot towards the enemy gatehouse. The other chieftains organised their men into formations a hundred strong: fourteen of them deployed all around Wenden's perimeter wall. Though all the chiefs and the small number of their bodyguards had helmets and mail or lamellar armour, their men were deficient in both weapons and armour. Most had a shield and helmet but almost none wore armour over their tunics and none had swords. They carried spears but a great number also had to shoulder scaling ladders to climb the log walls, though no one had given any thought to the ditch lined with stakes. The horsemen who had been screening the army might have reported its presence but would also have told the dukes that it was dry and could thus be traversed with ease.

The great Iron Wolf banner hardly stirred in the gentle breeze as Ykintas stood in the front rank of his men and marched towards the gatehouse, the standards of the Sword Brothers hanging limply from the flagpole on each tower either side of the gates. The ground was level and open all around the castle, which made an approach very easy. It also gave crossbowmen on the walls an excellent field of view, which became very apparent when the first of the duke's Semgallians began to fall after being hit by bolts. He ignored the high-pitched screams and headed nonchalantly towards the thick oak gates, his men carrying a battering ram fashioned from a tree trunk. Thus far the campaign had served only to cover the name of Grand Duke Daugerutis in glory; now it was time for the Iron Wolf to show his fangs.

The Semgallians closed to within two hundred paces of the walls before breaking into a charge, the warriors splitting ranks and racing towards the ramparts – nearly eighteen hundred men set to sweep over the timber walls like a great pagan wave – to fall headlong into the ditch. The front ranks pulled up when they reached the top of the ditch and saw the forest of sharpened stakes below them, only to be shoved forward as those behind continued their charge. There was a cacophony of high-pitched screams as dozens of men were heaved into the ditch, to be pierced and impaled on the stakes. And as the ditch filled with writhing Lithuanians, above them Wenden's crossbowmen continued to shoot their weapons.

*****

Conrad pointed his crossbow and released the trigger, then watched as the bolt struck a warrior attempting to haul himself out of the ditch. He jerked as the bolt hit him in the back and became limp as life left him. He and Hans worked calmly; they were well accustomed to the sights and sounds of battle by now and felt very safe behind the wall of logs and under the gable roof. Though there were a great many Lithuanians below they appeared to have no archers among their ranks, which meant he and Hans could shoot with impunity. As long as the walls were not breached.

They did not talk as they went about their work. The garrison of Wenden was small in comparison to the army beyond the walls, but it was made up of men who knew their trade, and that trade was war. A dozen brother knights, thirty sergeants, four novices and thirty mercenary crossbowmen manned the perimeter wall. Each was armed with a crossbow, shooting bolts at a rate of two per minute – a hundred and fifty missiles every sixty seconds. Within two minutes of reaching the ditch two hundred Lithuanians had been slain by crossbow bolts; a further hundred and fifty were either dead or wounded from being pierced by wooden stakes. Unknown to him, Duke Ykintas had lost nearly a quarter of his men as he charged the gates.

Conrad placed his right foot in the metal stirrup of his crossbow before hooking the double-pronged claw attached to the front of his belt over the centre of the bowstring. He straightened his bent right leg to force the crossbow down, which had the effect of drawing the bowstring back along the stock of the weapon until it slipped over the catch of the lock. He unhooked the claw, pulled a quarrel from a quiver and placed it in the groove in the stock, then rested the stirrup on the bottom of a loophole.

'Hans, shoot at those carrying ladders.'

Below them most of the Lithuanians were endeavouring to extricate themselves from the horrors of the ditch, those unharmed casting aside ladders to scramble up the slope and get as far away from the stakes and enemy missiles as fast as they could. They were, after all, mostly farmers who had been ordered to accompany their chiefs across the Dvina. Now, seeing their friends and kin slaughtered, their resolve dissolved and they fled for their lives. A few, however, pressed on, using axes to clear a path through the stakes before scrambling up the ditch to reach the berm next to the timber wall. They screamed for ladders to be brought to them so they could scale the walls, only to be killed as crossbowmen aimed their weapons through the gap between the overhanging top half of the wall and the bottom timbers.

Conrad pointed his crossbow down to where a man was struggling with a ladder, trying to pull it up from the corpse-strewn ditch, cursing as he did so. He gave a groan as he heaved it up and rested one end on the berm. Thus far he had made it to the ditch, crossed over the stake-filled obstacle and now stood at the foot of the timber palisade. Now he braced the ladder against the wall and shouted at his comrades to scale it to storm the Christian fortress. But then he stopped, his sixth sense telling him that something was wrong. He looked up and saw Conrad pointing a crossbow at him. For a few seconds they stared at each other, both oblivious to the battle raging around them. Time slowed as Conrad released the trigger and watched the bolt slam into the Lithuanian just below the neck. His eyes glazed over and his mouth opened in shock as he slumped to the ground, dead. Hans killed a second man who tried to climb the ladder and seconds later Conrad felled another enemy who climbed over the corpse and attempted to ascend the ladder. And then there were only dead bodies on the berm and in the ditch. The Lithuanians were falling back in disarray.

*****

Duke Ykintas did not see dozens of his warriors fleeing back to the safety of Lithuanian lines, did not see the dozens of their corpses littering the ground or observe the wounded dragging themselves away from the fortress to get out of range of the accursed Christian crossbows. All he was interested in was smashing in the gates and leading his men into the castle so he could butcher the defenders and fly his banner from the highest tower. He did not even hear the screams of the men around him whose flesh was pierced by crossbow bolts, the iron heads going through wooden shields and mail armour. Or if he did he did not care. It was not the task of a duke to worry about the deaths of his soldiers, only ensure that they were led heroically. He also did not see the large stones that suddenly landed among his men.

Master Thaddeus knew that the main focus of an enemy assault would always be against the gatehouse, not least because there was a bridge over the ditch that gave access to the gates. Notwithstanding that the gates were thick and flanked by two towers, an enemy would always be tempted to attack them. After all, all that was required was for the gates to be smashed in. And so Ykintas led four hundred and fifty of his finest warriors straight at them, and straight into a missile storm.

The best crossbowmen – leather face and a dozen of his mercenary comrades – were deployed in the two-story towers at the gatehouse. But behind the gates themselves and to the side of each tower, were Thaddeus' mangonels – three to the right rear of one tower and three more to the left rear of the other tower. Thaddeus and his engineers had worked out the optimum position for their machines and had practised shooting projectiles over the ramparts into a pre-arranged killing zone in front of the gatehouse. They had hammered stakes into the ground to indicate where the mangonels should be sited and beyond the walls had placed white-painted stones at regular intervals to indicate different ranges. The Lithuanians who marched towards them did not notice these stones but Thaddeus in one of the towers did as he looked through a peephole. He hoisted a red flag and waved it to his mangonel crews behind the towers, their cue to let loose their projectiles.

Several of the Lithuanians halted and watched the six stones arch into the sky and then descend towards them, the ten-pound projectiles hitting the densely packed ranks with a sickening crump. Even Ykintas stopped as the face of the man beside him disappeared when a stone smashed into his skull. The man made no sound as his head was crushed and he crumbled to the ground. The whole formation ground to a halt as stones careered through the warriors, inflicting far more psychological than physical damage as they did so.

'Move!' screamed Ykintas, his exhortation followed by a succession of thuds that signalled half-a-dozen men being killed by crossbow bolts.

His men shouted their defiance and continued their advance. Half a minute later a fresh volley of mangonel missiles appeared in the sky and reaped another grim harvest of smashed bones and pulped flesh. The path of the duke's men to the gates was marked by their bodies, over a hundred of whom had now been killed or wounded. Master Thaddeus managed to loose a third volley of stones before the duke led a charge against the gates and his men began smashing their battering ram into them.

Unfortunately the loopholes in the towers and above the gates, plus the clearance between the overhanging top half of the walls and the lower half, meant that the crossbowmen had an excellent view of the packed ranks of the Lithuanians. And they commenced a murderous volume of missiles against them. Shooting up to four bolts a minute, leather face and his companions found gaps in the roof of Lithuanian shields to cut down the enemy.

Ykintas helped to ram the tree trunk into the gates, which were not budging. He screamed his frustration as his men were hit by bolts and collapsed, others screaming in pain as quarrels went through shields into their arms. Even he realised that they were being slaughtered to no effect but his stubbornness meant he refused to acknowledge that he was beaten. A man slumped over the battering ram behind him, a bolt lodged in his shoulder. He turned to lift him off the ram so that it could be hauled back and then thrust forward again, to be struck in the back of the neck by a bolt. The iron head severed his spinal cord and killed him instantly. The Iron Wolf collapsed face down on the ground as a fresh volley of crossbow bolts cut down ten men around him.

Seeing their duke killed before their eyes and suffering heavy casualties for no result, the Lithuanians dumped the battering ram and fled from the gates, holding their shields above their heads as they did so. Many tripped and fell and others threw aside their spears and shields to speed their flight. As Daugerutis knew it would, the attack had failed miserably. What happened next took him totally by surprise, though. The other dukes, appalled at the defeat of Ykintas and then learning of his death, railed at the Christians and swore revenge, and then led their men in another attack against the walls of Wenden.

They were led by Kitenis, a man prone to act first and think later, and who now dug his spurs into his horse and raced across the ground to where Ykintas had fallen. A thousand of his men had been detached to conduct the siege of Holm and so he had only six hundred horsemen and four hundred foot with him, but now his riders followed their lord and, seeing the banner of the black axe being carried towards the enemy castle, the chiefs standing ahead of his warriors on foot likewise signalled the advance.

'Stop, you idiot,' shouted Daugerutis as Kitenis and his horsemen thundered towards the castle.

It was too late, and then Daugerutis looked on in horror as Butantas and Gedvilas also led their horsemen forward. The former had a thousand riders with him but no foot soldiers as they had been detailed to lay siege to Lennewarden. A mere two hundred horsemen accompanied Gedvilas, but he had brought eight hundred warriors on foot to Wenden, having agreed that another thousand should surround Uexkull. Now he rode over to where his warriors were standing, pulled his sword from its scabbard and ordered them to follow him as he joined the two other dukes in their assault on the castle.

'This is madness,' shouted Daugerutis.

'Do you wish me to support them, lord?' asked Stecse beside him.

'Why?' snapped the grand duke, 'so you can have a glorious and futile death like them?'

His officers behind him murmured their disappointment at not being allowed to join the great assault that was unfolding but Daugerutis would have none of it.

'Silence!' he shouted. They wanted glory but he knew that it was folly and would result in more lives wasted for no result.

Ahead he saw the great Lithuanian wave approach the perimeter ramparts of the castle. In the centre were Kitenis and his Aukstaitijans, the black axe standard flying before the mail-clad horsemen and the spearmen following them. On the right flew the golden eagle banner of Gedvilas and his Kurs – the horsemen riding hard to reach the walls and the foot trying desperately to keep up. There was no discipline or order, just a thousand men following their red-haired lord to glory. And on the left

405

were Butantas and his thousand horsemen, the riders veering away from the gatehouse and following the perimeter wall so they could assault the castle from the north. Perhaps they thought that the defences were weaker in that sector and that the Christians had neglected to build an earth rampart and wooden palisade in that part of the perimeter. They were soon disabused of that notion.

The horsemen reached the ditch first and some rode or fell down its sloping side, their animals impaled on stakes and issuing dreadful screams that echoed across the battlefield. Others pulled up sharply when they saw the obstacle and were thrown from their horses, to fall headlong into the ditch to be skewered on the stakes. There was no way across the ditch and even if they had managed to get over it they had no ladders with which to scale the wall that rose up in front of them. In frustration they hurled their *spisas* at the timber, drew their swords and hurled abuse at the defenders. Kitenis called them whores and cowards and bellowed for them to fight him like men, his face reddening with rage as the first crossbow bolts were shot from loopholes to kill those around him.

In the northern sector of the wall Rameke and his Liv warriors held the defences. Armed with bows instead of crossbows, they found it easy enough to shoot down the Samogitian horsemen, the wiry Butantas quickly realising that he had been foolish to attempt an assault against the walls. He gave the order to withdraw out of range of the defenders but not before two hundred of his men had been killed or wounded by Liv arrows.

Unfortunately neither Kitenis nor Gedvilas retained a cool head when their horsemen began falling to enemy missiles. Kitenis in particular was gripped by a mighty rage and he jumped from his horse, took an axe, ran into the ditch and stepped on the bodies of dead Semgallians to cross it, bellowing at his men to follow him. He gave no thought to his own safety or how he would scale the wall as he hastened up the slope and reached the berm below it. He then began hacking at the timbers with his axe, the weapon looking puny in his paw-like hands as he chopped at the defences. He used so much force swinging the axe that its handle splintered after a dozen blows. He howled in frustration and cast it aside, screaming for another to be brought to him, oblivious to the hisses of crossbow bolts flying through the air before hitting his men. Nearly two and half thousand men took part in this second attack against Wenden's perimeter and had Daugerutis committed more men to it he might just have succeeded in taking the castle. For unknown to him a crisis was unfolding behind its stout defences.

*****

'I'm running out of ammunition,' shouted Hans, loading another quarrel in the groove of the crossbow's stock.

Conrad released his trigger and hit a horseman in the belly, causing him to slump in the saddle and then fall to the ground. He and his friend had been alarmed when the Lithuanians had launched a second attack, but relieved when they saw that it was led by men on horses. What were the Lithuanians thinking? To throw horsemen against defences? Madness. They waited until the riders were at the ditch and then began shooting at them as those who had not fallen into the ditch milled around just beyond it. They made easy targets and he and Hans emptied many saddles. They were euphoric, until they realised that empty quivers lay at their feet.

'That was my last bolt,' said Conrad with alarm.

He put down his weapon and ran to the edge of the rampart.

'More ammunition, we need more ammunition,' he shouted, a call that was soon being repeated by others as the defenders began to run out of crossbow bolts.

Anton peered round the wall of his 'cell'. 'Conrad, we have no bolts either.'

They looked at each other as the Lithuanians began hacking at the logs that made up the walls. They looked up at the castle and saw figures running across the bridge over the moat. Then they saw Rudolf below them.

'Keep calm,' he shouted up at them. 'Fresh ammunition is on its way.'

Conrad heard a succession of loud cracks and saw the mangonel crews lowering the throwing arms of their machines after they had launched another volley of stones. Rudolf pointed at Conrad.

'Get down here.'

He climbed down the ladder and ran down the sloping earth rampart to reach Wenden's deputy commander.

'If they keep this pressure up,' said Rudolf, 'we will abandon the perimeter and withdraw to the castle.'

Conrad was shocked. 'Abandon the walls?'

Panting spearmen arrived with quivers slung over their shoulders, their comrades running towards various parts of the walls where men waited to be re-supplied. One gave Rudolf two quivers and then ran over to where a brother knight stood waiting. Rudolf handed them to Conrad.

'Two quivers?'

'Listen for the signal, Conrad. And when you do get your arse to the castle as quickly as you can.'

Rudolf slapped him on the arm and then was gone. Conrad walked up the slope and climbed the ladder to where Hans was waiting. He reached the wall walk and handed one quiver to Anton in the next compartment.

'Is that all you have?'

Conrad shrugged. 'That's all there is. Rudolf says we may have to abandon the wall and to listen for the signal.'

By now some of the Lithuanians had picked up the ladders that had been carried to the walls by the Semgallians and were climbing them to scale the walls. The horsemen beyond the ditch shouted their encouragement as the shooting from the defenders suddenly ceased and it appeared that the walls had been abandoned. Then the horsemen looked on in horror as bolts suddenly spat from loopholes to knock men off the ladders. In half a minute a hundred and forty men were shot off the ladders; a minute later a further hundred Lithuanians had been killed and the morale of the attackers collapsed. Like the warriors of Duke Ykintas they began fleeing back towards their own lines, despite the threats and implorings of their chiefs. Kitenis had to be physically pulled back by four of his chiefs, spitting obscenities at them and the defenders as he was dragged back over the ditch and placed on a horse.

Conrad released his trigger and hit a warrior wearing a fur-trimmed leather cap in the chest. The man staggered for a few seconds and then his legs buckled from under him. He looked down at the quiver. Empty! He looked through a peephole and saw the Lithuanians falling back and heaved a huge sigh of relief. He smiled at Hans and they embraced. They had fought off the enemy by the skin of their teeth. Suddenly exhausted and thirsty, they slumped down against the wall and thanked God for their deliverance.

*****

Kitenis' anger did not diminish; rather, it swelled in direct proportion to the amount of beer that he drank in the aftermath of his attack. As his men, those who still lived, licked their wounds in camp he was joined by an equally irate Gedvilas and Butantas, who also consumed a monumental amount of alcohol in a very short space of time. They all witnessed the body of Ykintas being carried through the sprawling multitude of two-man tents that had been pitched to the west of the castle and their patience, such as it was, snapped.

Kitenis, still in his helmet and armour, his beard soaked with beer, paced over to the tent of the grand duke where Daugerutis and Stecse were deep in conversation.

'I am returning back to my homeland,' shouted Kitenis loudly enough for everyone around to hear. 'I have seen my men slaughtered for no result and now I will take what remains of them back to Aukstaitija. You can have your gold back. The purchase price is too high.'

Stecse moved to place himself between the grand duke and the drunken Kitenis. The latter pulled his sword from its scabbard.

'Stand aside, puppy, unless you wish to feel the bite of my sword.'

'Stecse,' said Daugerutis as his guards closed around the grand duke, 'let him through.'

Kitenis strode forward before stopping as the guards lowered their spears.

'Would you fight all my men alone, Duke Kitenis?' remarked Daugerutis casually.

'Not alone,' said Butantas appearing behind Kitenis, 'the Duke of Samogitia and his warriors stand beside their brothers from Aukstaitija.'

'As do the Kurs,' said Gedvilas, standing beside Butantas.

Daugerutis assessed the situation carefully before replying.

'Let us discuss things in my tent rather than out in the open.'

He ordered his men to lower their spears and held open the flap of the tent to invite the others inside. He momentarily thought of ordering their deaths but dismissed it from his mind. He did not wish the Christians to be spectators to a bloody fight between the various Lithuanian tribes before their walls.

'Duke Ykintas insisted on leading an attack,' said Daugerutis calmly, 'despite my protestations.'

'We nearly broke them,' lamented Kitenis, not really listening to the grand duke's words. 'All it would have taken is for you to have committed your men.'

Daugerutis sighed. 'Before we began this campaign I explained what our strategy would be: surround the crusader castles and starve them into submission.'

'It was a misguided strategy,' said Butantas, 'all we have done is to disperse our forces and scatter them throughout Livonia.'

Daugerutis' patience was being sorely tested. 'How short is your memory, Butantas? Did we not surround the crusader castles with ease? Did we not destroy Caupo and his army? And now you wish to return home with victory within our grasp?'

'What victory?' bellowed Kitenis, spittle shooting from his mouth. 'You call butchering a few Livs victory?'

'Have a care, my lord,' Daugerutis warned him, 'your tongue may yet talk your head off its shoulders.'

Kitenis drew his sword once more and before Stecse could draw his had turned it in his hand to hold out the hilt to Daugerutis.

'Then do it. And if not do not stand in my way when I lead my men south in the morning.'

Daugerutis could have killed him with ease at that moment, but to do so would be futile. He had three thousand men across the river that could be brought into Livonia to replace those soldiers of the other dukes who now sat before Lennewarden, Holm and Uexkull. And he still had nearly ten thousand of his own men here, at Wenden, the majority of whom could be used for an attack against Riga. He did not need them.

He waved his hand at Kitenis. 'Go then. I do not need you.'

He looked beyond him to Butantas and Gedvilas. 'Any of you.'

Kitenis sneered at him, turned and pushed past the other two dukes and stormed from the tent. Butantas and Gedvilas looked awkward for a few seconds before nodding half-heartedly and leaving.

'My lord,' said Stecse with concern, 'can we afford to lose so many warriors?'

'We do not need them,' replied Daugerutis.

'But…'

The grand duke held up a hand to silence him. 'Send riders immediately to the besiegers of Lennewarden, Holm and Uexkull. Inform the commanders that the castle of Wenden has fallen and they are to launch their own assaults immediately.'

'I do not understand,' said Stecse.

The duke smiled. 'It is quite simple. By the time our former allies have slept off their night of drinking and organised what is left of their soldiers, your couriers will be well on their way to their destinations. By the time the dukes link up with their men conducting siege operations they will find their numbers sorely depleted.'

'To what end?' queried Stecse.

'To emphasise to my fellow dukes that insolence incurs a heavy price and to weaken them so they will not be tempted to attack my strongholds when they cross over the Dvina.'

'They might do that anyway, lord.'

'Not with you at Panemunis, they won't. Take five hundred horsemen and get yourself back to my capital as quickly as possible. Take Thalibald and his son with you. They might prove useful in the future. And if not I can always kill them.'

410

'I would rather stay here with you, lord.'

Daugerutis frowned at him. 'And I would rather you obeyed orders. Before you despatch the couriers, speak to the chiefs of the Semgallians. They might be tempted to follow the other dukes. Offer them and their men gold to stay.'

The next morning Kitenis, Butantas and Gedvilas left the army without paying their respects to the grand duke. Despite his protestations Stecse also left that morning, taking Thalibald and Waribule with him. Happily the Semgallians had accepted the offer of gold and now mustered in their ranks as the grand duke's army arrayed itself before Wenden, at a safe distance from the walls.

The bodies of those slain the previous day littered the ground in front of the ditch, the latter also filled with the corpses of men and horses. The weather was warm now as spring at last came to Livonia and already flies were buzzing around dead flesh. Soon the foul stench of rotting gore would become unbearable for those manning the perimeter wall. In life the soldiers of the other dukes had failed to take Wenden; in death they would add to the general misery of a garrison under siege.

Daugerutis arrayed his army partly to awe the defenders but also to mask the departure of just over two thousand men. It would have been three thousand but over nine hundred warriors of the departing three dukes lay rotting on the ground in front of the castle. An additional three hundred had been slain during Duke Ykintas' abortive attack. Fortunately a pleasant breeze was currently blowing from the west so the odour of death was not in the faces of the army as it stood in silence facing the castle. The standard of the black bear flew proudly among the ranks of the six thousand foot soldiers the grand duke had brought to this place.

*****

'When they launch another assault how do we stop them?' queried Conrad as he rested his shield against the timber wall and observed the Lithuanian army through a peephole.

'We don't,' answered Rudolf. 'The perimeter will be abandoned and we will make our stand in the castle itself.'

The deputy commander of the garrison had been visiting his soldiers on the walls, giving instructions on what to do in the event of an assault. Throughout the night Master Thaddeus had overseen the dismantling of the mangonels and their relocation to the castle courtyard. No one wanted them to fall into the hands of the enemy when the inevitable assault and breach of the perimeter occurred. As a result

411

no one had had more than two hours of sleep. Conrad had black rings round his eyes and his mouth tasted dry.

'How is Rameke?' he asked.

'As well as can be expected in the circumstances,' answered Rudolf. 'He and his men are out of arrows just as we are out of crossbow bolts.'

'And Daina?' said Conrad casually.

'She grieves for her father,' replied Rudolf, 'as do we all. Thalibald was a good man.'

Conrad was sure he had seen him among the ranks of the enemy but said nothing. Perhaps it was in his imagination.

Rudolf went to a peephole and looked down. 'These bodies will soon start rotting. The stench will be awful.'

'Will not the Lithuanians collect their dead for burial?' enquired Hans who looked pale and tired.

Rudolf shook his head. 'Not without a parley and Master Berthold is not mindful to grant such a courtesy to pagans. Besides, if the enemy attacks and takes these walls then the dead will be their problem.'

But the Lithuanians did not attack and after an hour they dispersed back to camp, which now extended all round the castle. As the breeze slackened and the sun peeped out from behind huge white puffy clouds the exhausted garrison took the opportunity to snatch some well-earned sleep. Those Lithuanians who did not have tents cut down trees to fashion makeshift shelters and soon the air echoed with the sound of hundreds of men chopping wood.

Master Berthold called a council of war at which Rudolf conveyed the happy news that the garrison had suffered only one casualty during the previous day's fighting: one of the crossbowmen had broken an ankle after falling from a ladder. It had been a remarkably one-sided battle and the master personally thanked Master Thaddeus for his skill in strengthening the perimeter wall. Rudolf then dampened spirits by reporting that the armoury had been emptied of crossbow bolts and Rameke stated that he and his warriors were similarly out of arrows. Nevertheless, Berthold was optimistic that the castle could hold out in the face of the Lithuanians, notwithstanding that it was crammed with dozens of women and children in addition to the soldiers of the garrison, horses and ponies and half a dozen cows that had been brought in from the fields before the enemy had arrived, plus the livestock the Livs had brought with them. Food supplies were adequate for the time being and fortunately the well in the courtyard was a reliable source of fresh water. Once the animal fodder was exhausted the cows, ponies and then the horses would be slaughtered for meat. For the moment the garrison would sleep in the civilian huts in front of the castle, but once the perimeter was breached the huts would be fired and everyone would retreat up the hill and into the castle itself. Everyone prayed that the bishop would arrive from Germany before that happened.

As the days passed the Lithuanians made no attempt to storm the perimeter, being content to ring the fortress and starve the occupants into surrender. The stench of rotting flesh became unbearable but Master Berthold would not relent on his determination not to ask the pagans for a parley. And so those on guard duty wore face masks as rats and flies feasted on bloated corpses in and around the ditch.

The only thing of note was the stench that permeated the air around the perimeter, those in the castle higher up fortunately being saved from the worst of the nauseous aroma. It was May now and the days were getting longer and warmer but no messages reached the garrison, and Lithuanian hawks brought down every pigeon sent out. After the enemy assault Conrad had managed to see Daina and Rameke, who had been given the master's hall for their quarters. Their mother, overcome with grief, had locked herself away in the master's bedroom and would see no one. Berthold had been a friend of Thalibald and said that he was not too grand to sleep in a wooden hut, and in any case he thought it more fitting that a Liv chief should have lodgings appropriate to his rank.

'I do not feel like a chief,' said Rameke morosely, 'my village and lands are occupied by the enemy.'

'It is only temporary,' said Conrad, trying to cheer him up, though he had no idea whether Wenden would be relieved or whether they would all be killed that very day. He had spent the night on guard duty and, following early morning mass, had eaten a sparse breakfast of biscuit and water before having two hours of sleep. He felt dirty and tired but Lukas had given him permission to visit the Liv chief and his sister.

Daina smiled wanly at him. Even in mourning she looked perfect, her pale face only accentuating her green eyes and full lips.

'You are very kind, Conrad.'

'The enemy will never take this castle,' he said grandly.

'As long as I die fighting with a sword in my hand I do not care,' said Rameke.

'You are a chief now, Rameke,' Daina reprehended him, 'and should think of your people rather than yourself.'

Rameke laughed bitterly. 'My people? A score of warriors and a few dozen women and children?'

'They are still your people and you have a responsibility to them,' she responded firmly. 'Where there is life there is hope.'

Conrad looked at her with admiration. In adversity she was lovelier than ever, even with her hair tied back and attired in a simple white dress. At that moment he vowed to himself that should the castle walls be breached, he would leave his post to be beside her, fighting to his last breath to save her. After all, they would all be dead anyway so deserting his post would be irrelevant. He hoped God would forgive him, though. He gazed at her lovingly and forgot about Rameke.

'Are you all right, Conrad?' asked the chief.

'Mm. What? Yes, of course. Just a little tired,' blurted Conrad.

'You are both very brave,' said Daina.

Rameke rolled his eyes but Conrad smiled shyly and felt his cheeks flush.

'I must return to my duties,' he said.

'As must I,' added Rameke, rising from the grand master's chair.

Conrad nodded at it. 'It suits you.'

Rameke buckled on his sword. 'What, the chair?'

'No, command and authority.'

Daina, who had been sitting beside him, jumped up and held Conrad's hands, then leaned forward and kissed him on the cheek.

'For my brave warrior.'

All three left the master's hall, Conrad back to the perimeter wall, Rameke to a council of war in the north tower's newly completed ground floor and Daina to assist in the kitchens that were struggling to feed the dozens of new arrivals. A semblance of order had been restored to the castle following the arrival of the Livs, though the courtyard was full of pens that contained the animals that they had managed to bring, including the oxen that the Sword Brothers had originally given to Thalibald to plough his fields. Conrad looked at them as he passed their pen. How he would like a meal of roast beef.

'Tempted to slaughter one?'

He turned to see Henke approaching, shield slung over his back and holding a short spear in his right hand and a mace in the other. His own shield was also slung on his back.

'The women and children come first.'

Henke smiled evilly. 'Very noble. You'll think different after a few weeks of being on half then quarter rations.'

Conrad began walking towards the bridge over the moat. The original timber walls still stood in this part of the castle wall, along with the two towers that flanked the gated entrance. Though the stonemasons and carpenters worked hard, the towers and walls grew but slowly. Rudolf had told him that it might take twenty years to complete the castle – if it survived this summer, that is.

'Been to see the fair Daina?' grinned Henke, who appeared to be unusually chatty today. Normally he was like an ill-tempered bear and best left alone. The perilous situation he found himself in obviously brought out his talkative side.

'Yes,' replied Conrad guardedly.

'She will make someone a fine wife, if she lives.'

'She will live,' said Conrad forcefully.

They walked over the bridge spanning the moat.

'You fancy yourself as her husband, do you not?' teased Henke.

'I did not say that.'

He grinned. 'You don't have to. It's written all over your face. You aim high, boy, I'll give you that. But you seem to have forgotten one thing.'

'Oh?'

'You are to become a brother knight, which means you cannot marry anyone. The oath of chastity, though rape and plunder on campaign does not count. So if you want to bed her you'd better be quick about it.'

Conrad shot him a hateful glance. He respected Henke for his skill with weapons and his loyalty to Rudolf but he did not like him particularly. But he also knew that he did not have the skill with a sword to better him in a fight. Not yet, anyhow. Henke saw the look.

'I offend you? I state the truth, young Conrad.'

Conrad also disliked being called 'young'. He was seventeen now and reckoned himself a man.

'I said nothing about marriage to Daina,' snapped Conrad.

Henke stopped and rested the end of his spear on the ground.

'Listen, Lukas has said that you have the makings of a fine knight and I accord his word great import. And your actions to date have confirmed this to me.' He pointed at his white surcoat emblazoned with the arms of the Sword Brothers.

'You wish to wear one of these?'

'Of course,' said Conrad without hesitation.

415

'Then you can't have Daina. You should put her out of your mind rather than torture yourself with things that are beyond your reach.'

He looked up at the clear blue sky. 'Wife, child, hearth and home.'

Then he looked at Conrad. 'It's not for you, Conrad. You remember that time when I rescued you and your sister outside the cathedral in Lübeck?'

'When you *and* Brother Rudolf rescued us. Yes, I remember.'

Henke smiled. 'As you will. Well, do you think it was a coincidence that we were there to assist you and thereafter you came to Livonia?'

'I do not know.'

Henke lifted his spear and strode away. 'I do. God has a plan for you whether you like it or not.'

'If we all survive,' Conrad called after him.

'You'll survive, Conrad. Just put your faith in God and keep your eyes peeled and your sword sharp.'

The day passed without incident, the Lithuanian horde around the castle being content to cut down more trees for shelter and firewood and keep at a safe distance from the wall. The bodies in and around the ditch continued to bloat and rot, occasionally exploding as the gases built up inside them tearing the putrefying flesh. The incessant buzzing of the flies feeding on their flesh was even worse than the smell and so those on guard duty stood, suffered and waited.

That night Conrad and Hans resumed their position in their 'cell' and peered through loopholes to keep watch on the myriad of campfires that illuminated the darkness.

'There seems more of them than last night,' said Hans, his face mask muffling his voice.

'I wish they would attack and get it over with. This waiting is driving me insane.'

'Soldiers of Wenden, I bring you a message.'

Conrad turned to Hans. 'What?'

'I said nothing.'

'Soldiers of Wenden, I bring you a message.'

The voice was coming from beneath them, from the berm at the base of the outside of the wall. The both drew their swords and lifted their shields from the floor.

'Soldiers of Wenden, do you hear me?' hissed the voice in the darkness.

Conrad pulled down his face mask and knelt by the clearance in the floor.

'Careful, Conrad,' warned Hans, 'it might be a trap.'

'State your business,' ordered Conrad.

'I am from King Caupo and I bring a message for Master Berthold,' came the reply.

Conrad felt a sense of relief sweep through, though he was still cautious. Words were cheap and there might be hundreds of Lithuanian warriors waiting to attack.

'Go and fetch Lukas,' he said to Hans.

His friend scrambled down the ladder and scurried away to search for Lukas.

'You must let me in,' pleaded the voice, 'it is a matter of utmost urgency.'

'Be patient,' replied Conrad. 'My commander is coming.'

For what seemed like an eternity Conrad alternated between crouching by the gap and looking through the peepholes to search for any signs of movement in front of the ditch. He saw none, though there was no moon and it was pitch black between the ditch and the enemy campfires.

Lukas arrived in the company of Hans and crouched by the gap. He spoke first to Conrad in a whisper.

'Is he alone?'

'As far as I can tell, brother.'

'Who are you and what do you want?' asked Lukas.

'I am Valdis,' came the hushed reply from below, 'I have a message from my king for Master Berthold.'

Lukas slapped Conrad on the arm. 'Welcome Valdis it is I, Brother Lukas. We have met before, at Treiden.'

'Brother Lukas, yes, I remember,' replied Valdis.

'Listen, my friend,' said Lukas hurriedly, 'get yourself to the gates, which are but a short distance to the left of where you are. There is a door in one of the gates that will be opened. Now hurry.'

'Thank you, brother,' said Valdis.

Lukas stood and pointed at Conrad and Hans. 'You two with me.'

They climbed down the ladder on to the earth rampart and walked to the gates that gave access into the castle grounds. Two sergeants stood guard behind the gates and a further four in the wooden towers that flanked them. Torches secured in wall brackets illuminated the inside of the gates where the sergeants warmed their hands on a brazier, for the spring nights were still cool. Lukas walked over to them with Conrad and Hans in tow.

417

'Open the door in the gates,' he ordered.

The sergeants looked at each other and then at Lukas. 'Open the gates, Brother Lukas?' said one.

'That is what I said. A friend of the master wishes to enter.'

'From outside?' queried the other sergeant.

'Time is of the essence,' snapped Lukas.

The sergeants saluted and then walked over to the right-hand gate that had a small door in its left-hand side. The gates themselves were secured by a great oak beam that had been placed in heavy iron brackets so it hung horizontally along the length of the inside of the gates. The latter were also made of oak and had iron reinforcing strips attached to both sides. They were thick and weighty and would make heavy work for a battering ram as Ykintas had discovered to his cost. Lukas drew his sword and held his shield before him.

'Draw your weapons,' he said to Conrad and Hans, 'just in case.'

The sergeants had the same idea because as one unlocked the door that was only four feet in height, the other held his spear pointed at it. When the door swung inwards the other sergeant jumped back and drew his sword as a figure in a black tunic and leggings and black boots stepped through it. He stood and held up both hands in an act of submission.

'It is quite safe,' said Lukas. 'Close it.'

He beckoned the dark-clothed figure over as the door was closed and locked. He held out his hand.

'Welcome Valdis, you are indeed a sight for sore eyes.'

Valdis took Lukas' hand. 'Greetings Brother Lukas, it is good to see you.'

The Liv was slight of build with a thick black beard and long black hair. It was impossible to estimate his age, though he was certainly not young. He carried only a knife for a weapon, tucked in a sheath that was attached to his belt.

'I have an urgent message for Master Berthold,' said Valdis.

'Then you must give it to him,' replied Lukas. 'Follow me.'

They strode off on the track, Lukas calling after Hans and Conrad.

'Hans, back to your guard duty. Conrad, go and find Rameke and bring him to the north tower.'

Conrad slid his sword back in its scabbard and ran past Lukas and Valdis towards the castle. He arrived panting in the courtyard and went to the master's hall where two Liv guards stood outside the entrance. They barred his way with their spears.

'I have an urgent message for Rameke, that is Chief Rameke,' said Conrad.

'It is late, the chief sleeps,' said one of the guards.

'The message is from his king,' continued Conrad. 'One of his men just came into the castle with a message from Caupo.'

The two guards looked at each other and one nodded.

'Wait here.'

He went inside the hall as Conrad began pacing up and down outside. A few minute later Rameke appeared, buckling on his sword and rubbing his eyes.

'Conrad, what nonsense is this?'

Conrad smiled at him. 'No nonsense, my friend. A man named Valdis came over the wall with a message from King Caupo for Master Berthold. I was told to request your presence in the north tower.'

Rameke looked surprised. 'Valdis, here?' He straightened his mail shirt and readjusted his sword belt. 'Well, let us go and see what news he brings.'

Daina appeared from the hall, wrapped in a red cloak, her hair wild around her shoulders.

'I'm coming too.'

'I'm not sure that women are allowed at a council of war.'

She tossed her hair behind her. 'I am a princess. Of course I am allowed,' and stepped into the courtyard to walk towards the north tower. Conrad sprinted over to be by her side, followed by Rameke.

'Hello Conrad,' she said, 'you bring good news I hope.'

'I am sure of it,' he replied. 'You look...'

He stopped himself from saying that she looked beautiful.

'I look what?' she queried.

'Warm in your cloak,' he said quickly.

She and Rameke looked at him in confusion, then she smiled knowingly, sensing his attraction towards her.

'Do you think I look like a princess?' she asked coyly.

'Oh, yes,' purred Conrad. He was clearly soft clay in her hands.

'We are here now,' said Rameke irritably. 'You had better wait outside, Daina.'

She opened the door to the tower and went in. 'Nonsense.'

The ground floor of what would be a three-storey tower would eventually be a storeroom but at present was a large empty space with a rectangular table placed in its centre, around which were stools. A stone stairway adjacent to the wall opposite the door led to a trapdoor in the wooden roof and gave access to what would be the second storey, when it was built. There were no windows in the walls at this level and thick wax candles on the table, filling the room with a ghostly glow, provided the only lighting.

Master Berthold had been roused from his slumbers and now sat at the head of the table, Valdis on his right and Rudolf on his left. Lukas was seated next to the Liv and Henke sat beside the deputy commander. Stoneware jugs sat on the table, from which people helped themselves to wine. It was all very different from the wealth and finery of the bishop's palace in Riga.

Berthold saw Daina and smiled. 'I fear the discourse of men might bore you, princess.'

'I would hear what my king has to say, Master Berthold.'

He held out his hand for her to sit at the table, Valdis rising and bowing his head to her and to Rameke who took his seat opposite Berthold. Henke poured wine into cups and passed them to Daina and Rameke while Conrad stood back from the table, feeling awkward. Rudolf noticed him and nodded. Henke shook his head and smiled. Lukas turned to him.

'You can serve wine, Conrad, if you would.'

He went to the table and picked up one of the jugs, refilling Berthold's cup as Valdis relayed his message.

'After the battle at Lake Inesis and the death of Chief Thalibald,' he said, casting his eyes down, 'the king retreated north to Treiden, there to rebuild what remained of his army. His scouts have been observing the Lithuanians since that unhappy day and have been reporting back to him the events that have taken place south of the Gauja.'

'And what are those events?' asked Berthold.

'The Lithuanians have encircled the castle of Segewold and send raiding parties towards Riga but as yet Daugerutis makes no move to take his army west. It remains at Wenden but has been weakened by the departure of the other dukes since the assault against these walls.'

'Why did they leave?' asked Rudolf.

'I do not know,' replied Valdis. 'But my king judges that the inertia of the Lithuanians is a sign from God that they should be attacked here, at Wenden. To this end he has gathered every man and boy that can carry a weapon and intends to strike the heathens at dawn the day after tomorrow.'

420

'Yes,' hissed Conrad without thinking, which earned him stares of rebuke from the Sword Brothers, though not from Daina who flashed him a smile. Henke saw it and laughed.

Berthold frowned. 'Is something amusing you, Brother Henke?'

Henke held up his cup for Conrad to fill. 'No, Master Berthold. I was thinking that we should send out young Conrad against the enemy. With his luck he could probably kill Daugerutis on his own and save the rest of us the effort.'

Berthold was not amused. 'This is not the time for levity, Brother Henke. Livonia is in peril and the Sword Brothers are stretched thinly.'

'Daugerutis may have brought many men to Wenden, master,' snarled Henke, 'but how many of them are soldiers? How many can fight?'

'Enough,' said Valdis. 'I know, I was at Lake Inesis.'

'The king wishes us to strike the enemy when he attacks?' said Rudolf.

Valdis nodded. 'Master Mathias and the horsemen of Kremon will be accompanying the king when he crosses the river and strikes at the enemy camp. He feels that the addition of the garrison of Wenden will decide the outcome in his favour.'

'I and my men will be joining the garrison,' stated Rameke.

'The king greatly laments the loss of your father, Chief Rameke,' said Valdis, 'and hopes to convey his commiserations to you in person following the battle.'

'If he and us are still alive,' remarked Henke dryly.

'Do not the Lithuanians have scouts of their own to warn of such an attack?' Lukas asked Valdis, holding up his cup for Conrad to fill.

'They grow lax in their discipline, Brother Lukas,' replied Valdis, 'so confident are they that Livonia is already theirs.'

'Did you see my father fall?' said Daina suddenly.

'I did not, princess,' said Valdis softly. 'He and your brother gave their lives so that the king could live. It was a brave and selfless act.'

Daina looked very sad and Conrad had to restrain himself from putting his arms around her.

'I am glad that the king still lives,' she sighed. 'I hope my father and brother are in Heaven.'

'They reside with the angels along with all those who have martyred themselves in God's service,' said Berthold with conviction. 'And they will be avenged.'

'Yes, they will,' added Rameke.

'Wenden will join the king's attack,' said Berthold. 'You can tell him that. I grow tired of looking at enemy campfires encircling my castle.'

Valdis smiled and drained his cup. He rose. 'Then by your leave, I must be away before the dawn breaks.'

'Do you wish for an escort?' enquired Berthold.

'No, master, I can move quicker and unseen on my own.'

'Conrad,' said Lukas, 'take Chief Valdis to the kitchens and wake the cooks. You will find your wits are sharper with some food in your belly, my friend.'

Valdis smiled and thanked those present as Conrad waited at the door to escort the Liv to the kitchens. He caught Daina's eye one last time, who tilted her head and smiled at him before Valdis walked past him into the courtyard and he followed.

The next day, after he had slept, attended mass and eaten, Conrad stood with Hans, Anton and Johann at the grave of Bruno in Wenden's cemetery. Their friend had a gravestone now and although it was not as grand as the one for Sir Frederick in the adjacent plot, it was a fine dolostone piece that had been carved with care and affection. A gardener from Lübeck maintained the cemetery and he kept the graves in an immaculate condition.

It was a beautiful spring day with a gentle breeze that blew from the east and brought air that was not tainted with the odour of rotting bodies.

'It seems so long ago when Bruno died,' said Hans sadly.

Conrad looked at the grave of Sir Frederick and then touched the hilt of his sword. 'He is in good company here.'

Anton looked up at the castle. 'I would like to be buried here.'

'That is a morbid thought,' remarked Johann.

Anton looked at him. 'We might all die tomorrow.'

'You should not say such things,' Hans rebuked him. 'Sometimes saying them can make them happen.'

'It is all in God's hands,' said Conrad. 'But at least we will die fighting rather than being starved to death.'

Hans shuddered. 'No, indeed. Infinitely preferable.'

'Do you think we will all meet again, when we are dead, I mean?' said Anton.

'Of course,' replied Johann, 'for are we not brothers?'

He held out an arm over Bruno's grave. 'Brothers.'

Anton extended his right arm and placed his palm over Johann's hand. 'Brothers.'

Conrad and Hans did the same and uttered the same pledge as the breeze blew and the Sword Brother banner flying over Wenden stirred.

*****

Grand Duke Daugerutis had addressed the Semgallians earlier and had told them that though their duke was dead, he would lead them to victory, glory and riches. They had cheered when he stated that he was now the ruler of Livonia and that the Christians were finished, cowering as they did behind their walls while the flower of Lithuanian manhood was free to plunder the land and enslave the local population. He had elicited more cheering when he informed them that their victory over Caupo was just a foretaste of things to come. He had retired to his tent most satisfied that he had won them over, notwithstanding the bribe he had paid them.

He knew that the other dukes would withdraw their men who were laying siege to Lennewarden, Holm and Uexkull, but he comforted himself with the fact that their garrisons were small and even if they combined would be unable to halt his advance to Riga. He had a thousand of his own men besieging Segewold and would leave five hundred to starve Wenden into surrender. But he would still march with nearly twelve thousand men, more than enough to take Riga. The town was only fifty miles away and even moving along dirt tracks and through dense forests he would be before its walls in around ten days. He had given orders that the army would march tomorrow, breaking camp just after dawn to begin the part of the campaign that would see him made grand duke of Lithuania and Livonia. Afterwards he would crush the other dukes, conquer Estonia and take the city of Novgorod. The screams of its citizens being roasted to death would be a fitting end to his campaign.

And yet, unknown to him, it was all an illusion.

Chapter 16

Conrad was in the saddle before the eastern sky was filled with the first rays of the sun. He and sixty-six other horsemen – twelve brother knights, thirty sergeants, three novices, Rameke and his score of warriors – waited at the gates, ready to ride out against the Lithuanians. Otto went along the line of horsemen, administering the blessing given to those on the eve of battle. He looked even more severe in the pale pre-dawn light, his battle-scarred bald scalp and glaring eyes giving him the appearance of an avenging angel. He halted beside Conrad and fixed him with his deranged, black eyes.

'Bow your heads, sinners,' he hissed to Conrad and Hans beside him.

They took off their helmets and lowered their heads as Otto made the sign of the cross with his hand and administered the blessing.

'God of power and mercy, maker and lover of peace, to know you is to live, and to serve you is to reign. Through the intercession of St Michael, the archangel, be our protection in battle against all evil. Help us to overcome war and violence and to establish your law of love and justice. Grant this through Christ our Lord.'

Conrad and Hans said 'amen' as Otto glared at them both and then moved on to Anton and Johann sitting in front of them.

'He frightens me more than the enemy,' Hans whispered to his friend.

'I know,' agreed Conrad, 'it is a pity that priests cannot shed blood because then we could send him against the Lithuanians.'

Fortunately there had been no need to slaughter the horses and so everyone was suitably mounted, the brother knights sitting on the great warhorses that were bred for battle. All the warhorses wore mail over a padded cover, the white cloth completing the caparison that was emblazoned with the insignia of the Sword Brothers. The horses of the sergeants, the coursers, did not have chainmail protection but did wear thick padding that could deflect arrow strikes at least. Conrad and the other novices rode palfreys, which in theory were inferior to the other two classes of horses but suited the youths well enough. They too were protected by thick padding and white caparisons that bore the red sword and cross insignia. Conrad and the other three novices wore mail over their gambesons and white surcoats, though the latter bore no insignia as they were not yet brother knights. And like the sergeants they wore kettle helmets rather than the full-face helms worn by Rudolf, Henke and the others.

It was cool as the first glimmers of red and orange light began to appear on the horizon. Conrad shivered, though he was unsure whether it was because of the cold or through fear. He comforted himself by thinking it was the former. Aside from the stern blessings being issued by Otto there was little sound. Horses grunted and scraped at the ground and men sneezed and coughed, but Master Berthold had ordered that there would be no war cries or trumpet calls. The column would ride from the castle grounds, deploy into line and then assault their objective: the tent of Grand Duke Daugerutis where his great bear banner was pitched. The mercenaries were left to guard the perimeter wall and the castle, though if Caupo's attack failed then the chances of the horsemen returning to Wenden were slim and the castle would undoubtedly fall. Conrad closed his eyes and prayed to God that He spare Daina if He saw fit.

Spearmen lifted the oak beam from its brackets and then opened the gates to allow Master Berthold to lead the horsemen out from the castle grounds. As the banner of the Sword Brothers carried behind the master exited the gates the sound of thousands of men cheering and horn blasts came from the west – Caupo's attack.

The horses trotted a hundred paces from the gates and then the brother knights deployed into line, closing up and couching their lances as they moved forward. As though they were on the training field the two files of sergeants behind them divided into two: the left-hand column peeling off to deploy into a single line on the left flank of the brother knights; the right-hand column to form line on the brother knights' right flank. Conrad and the other three novices had been ordered to deploy on the extreme left of the battle line. Rameke and his men, though not trained to fight in the style of the Sword Brothers, were allocated the extreme right of the line – accorded the place of honour in battle.

Once everyone was in line the formation broke into a canter, the riders moving forward knee to knee against a mass of brown shapes ahead who appeared to be running around in confusion as the Lithuanians rose from their slumber and grabbed weapons in response to the alarms being sounded. There was no wind and the banner of Daugerutis hung limply on its flagpole but it and the tent were still visible as the rays of the sun lit up the new morning.

The sounds of battle were coming from the west as Caupo's men attacked from the river, Lithuanians running in that direction to meet the threat. Conrad glanced right and saw, in the distance, other brown shapes moving south, parallel to the riders – Lithuanians who had been camped to the west of Wenden and who were now being recalled to the main camp that was being assaulted. He smiled. Thus far the line of three score of horsemen had been unnoticed by the enemy.

Then, ahead, he saw enemy horsemen carrying long spears and strange square-like shields, dozens of them. They were riding in an east-west direction, no doubt to reinforce the foot soldiers battling Caupo's Livs. Master Berthold's horse broke into a slow gallop and everyone followed his lead. The enemy horsemen, seemingly oblivious to the white-clad threat bearing down on them, continued to ride towards the river, only halting when horns were blown among them to signal danger on their right flank, just at the moment the Sword Brothers struck them.

There was a succession of loud thuds as the Christian lances struck their targets, the points driving through mail and lamellar armour to skewer their owners. Conrad thrust his lance into the belly of a warrior wearing mail on his body, arms and legs, the Lithuanian turning his head and opening his mouth in alarm just as his belly was ripped open. Conrad released the shaft and slid his right hand through the leather strap of the axe that hung on the right side of saddle, in its specially designed leather scabbard, and gripped the handle.

After their heroics at Riga the previous summer Lukas had cautioned them on using swords when in the saddle.

'Cutting down ill-armed villagers with swords is fine, but in a mêlée with other armoured horsemen the last thing you want to be doing is blunting expensive swords. Weapons that can deliver heavy blows are more preferable.'

And so they had trained using axes and maces when in the saddle. Conrad preferred his axe: a short-hafted weapon just under two feet in length that had a steel blade just over six inches long. It had a metal spike on the opposite side of the blade to enable it to pierce armour and another spike on top of the haft. Along the latter were riveted metal strips called langlets to protect against cuts to the wood. Weighing only two and half pounds, it could be wielded easily from the saddle.

He passed the rider he had just lanced to hack at another horseman behind, standing up in his stirrups to deliver a blow that split the man's helmet open. He caught a lance blow on his shield and swung his axe left to shatter the arm that had been holding the *spisa*. The Lithuanian screamed and let go of the weapon, his right arm hanging limply. He tried to manoeuvre his horse away from Conrad's but in vain as his nose was split open by the novice's axe, toppling him from the saddle.

Surprise and shock action resulted in the Sword Brothers driving deep into the Lithuanians and killing the enemy at a rate of sixty a minute before the momentum of their assault was halted and a general mêlée ensued. But the pagans

426

were leaderless and demoralised and suddenly began fleeing in all directions, some rallying to the grand duke's side. Daugerutis had managed to gain his saddle and lead a countercharge against the Sword Brothers, but he led no more than a dozen men and soon found himself alone and surrounded.

His skills as a warrior were formidable though, and he killed two of Rameke's warriors and wounded two brother knights before Henke caved in his skull with his mace, reducing the grand duke's head to a bloody pulp atop his torso as he stood in his stirrups and delivered a torrent of blows with his weapon. He had to be ordered to stop by Berthold himself, Henke's surcoat being painted red with the grand duke's blood. Thus died Daugerutis and his dream of ruling all the lands north of the River Dvina.

Master Berthold rallied his men around his banner, Rameke also answering his call. The Liv had lost five of his men but he had killed more of the enemy himself, his sword greasy with their blood. Conrad, sweat pouring down his face and neck, nodded to him as they formed into line behind the master. He grinned at Hans, Anton and Johann who all appeared to be unhurt.

Berthold raised his sword and pointed it to the west where a great battle was still raging between Caupo's Livs and the Lithuanians. The latter had the numerical superiority but they had been surprised, their soldiers were scattered over a wide area and their leader was now dead. Conrad could see groups of men battling other formations but he had no idea who was winning or losing.

'See ahead,' shouted Berthold, his helmet in the crook of his left arm, 'the banner of the brethren of Kremon. We must link up with Master Mathias and his men. God with us!'

Everyone responded by shouting 'God with us!' The master replaced his helmet on his head and spurred his horse forward, the brother knights, sergeants, novices and Livs once again forming into line alongside him. The pace was slower now, riders saving the strength of their horses as the sun climbed into the sky and the temperature rose. Conrad did not know how many of the garrison had been killed in the first fight but as he cantered forward, axe in hand and battered shield clutched to his left side, he saw a mass of enemy foot soldiers ahead. And beyond them the white-attired garrison of Kremon was hacking at their ranks. He could see brother knights standing tall in their saddles scything at the enemy with maces and axes like farmers cutting corn, the sun catching the steel edges of the weapons as they chopped left and right.

The Lithuanians appeared to have lost all semblance of order and discipline, their ranks widely spaced and some men already fleeing from the fight. Conrad was now around two hundred paces from the rear ranks of the enemy mass and could see the banners of the Livs who were fighting beside Master Mathias' men – the symbols of Jumis, Mara and Laima – and above them all a great standard bearing the Christian cross – the flag of Caupo himself.

As Berthold and his men broke into a slow gallop the rear ranks of the Lithuanians turned and saw in horror the riders bearing down on them. Some rammed the butts of their spears in the ground, the points towards the horsemen, but they were too few and did not form a continuous, unbroken line. And so the Sword Brothers guided their horses around them as they smashed into the enemy. The better-armed and armoured Lithuanians were battling the Livs and horsemen of Kremon at the front of the formation. Those with few weapons and no armour were in the rear ranks and felt the full force of Master Berthold's attack.

Once more Conrad swung left and right with his axe, but this time he was aiming at bare heads and men wearing only tunics as his blade easily found flesh and bone. The horsemen drove deep into the Lithuanians, cutting down dozens for no loss as they slowed their horses and methodically cut down men who appeared to their left and right. A few Lithuanians endeavoured to fight back but most, already disheartened and disorientated by Caupo's assault, ran for their lives, fleeing in any direction to get away from the dreadful armoured horsemen in their midst. And then the entire Lithuanian formation dissolved into chaos as Caupo's men pressed forward and the shield wall of their enemy broke.

Several brother knights and sergeants were unhorsed as frightened men barged into their horses in their eagerness to flee, causing the animals to rear up in panic and throw their riders. Master Berthold gave the order for the signaller to sound assembly in an effort to rally his men. Conrad swung his axe at a man running by his right side, who skidded on a piece of churned-up earth and avoided having his head cleaved in two. He was moving so fast that Conrad had no chance to aim another blow at him. He then had to grab his reins and attempt to steady his mount as a flood of unarmed men ran past him. He saw Wenden's standard and spurred his horse towards it, Hans following.

'Are you hurt?' Conrad called to him.

'No. I still have all my limbs,' came the reply.

At the banner Henke had thrown off his helmet and was shouting in frustration at the fleeing enemy.

'Come back and fight, you cowards! We are few and you are many. Come back and fight!'

His mace, arm and surcoat were covered in blood. It was as if he had been dipped in a vat of red paint.

'Calm yourself, Brother Henke,' ordered Berthold. 'And pick your helmet up.'

Henke glared at him but Rudolf at his side gestured with his hand that he should lower his weapon. Henke spat towards the south, the direction in which the bulk of the Lithuanians were fleeing, dismounted and retrieved his helmet.

'Still alive, then.'

Conrad turned and saw Anton and Johann ride up to him. All four shook hands and congratulated each other, boyish grins on their faces. They were glad to have won a great victory but even gladder to be still breathing. And then a strange silence descended on the battlefield as the killing stopped and the sounds of clashing steel, screams and cries were replaced by the sobs and moans of the wounded.

Master Mathias and what was left of the garrison of Kremon arrived, the caparisons of their horses cut and splattered with blood. Conrad counted only six men with full-face helmets, meaning half the brother knights had been killed or wounded. Mathias and Berthold dismounted and embraced each other, then ordered that everyone dismount and kneel to give thanks to God for their victory and deliverance. Rudolf wanted to organise a pursuit of the Lithuanians but Berthold would have none of it. And so the brother knights, sergeants, novices, Rameke and his warriors knelt on the ground around the banners of Wenden and Kremon and gave thanks to God.

There was no pursuit of the enemy. Caupo himself arrived ten minutes later accompanied by his bodyguard, his face gaunt and his eyes black ringed. He had obviously had little sleep since his defeat at the hands of Daugerutis and even the great triumph he had just won could not banish the anguish that obviously haunted him. Conrad stood holding the reins of his horse as the king made his way through the now standing horsemen to reach Master Berthold. The latter bowed his head.

'Greetings, majesty. God has blessed this day with a great victory over the heathen Lithuanians.'

Caupo half smiled at him. 'It was dearly bought, my friend. I pray that we do not see its like again.'

The king saw Rameke and walked over to him, Conrad's friend going down on one knee before him.

Caupo lifted him to his feet. 'Valiant chief. I grieve with you for the loss of your father and brother. Thalibald was my right arm and I miss him greatly.'

'I hope to be as great a servant to your majesty as he was, lord,' replied Rameke.

Caupo placed a hand on his shoulder. 'I have no doubt you will be.'

Berthold invited the king and Master Mathias to Wenden where they could rest their weary bodies. It was now nearly midday and very warm, the horses in their armour and coverings hanging their heads and their riders drenched in sweat. As the euphoria of victory quickly evaporated a raging thirst gripped Conrad and his limbs felt as though they were made of lead. Like the others he took off his helmet and led his horse on foot back to Wenden.

They passed men lying on the ground, their guts sliced open and their limbs shattered and bloody. They ignored their pitiful cries for help, though Henke did leave the column once to slit the throat of a man whose body was so mangled and twisted that it looked barely human. Conrad was taken back to that dreadful day in Lübeck when his father had been broken on the wheel and shuddered. He hoped that he would never be wounded in battle but would rather have a quick death. He knew that healers such as Ilona could work miracles with their herbs and treatments, but wounds inflicted by swords, lances and axes could rarely be treated. Amputation was often the only solution and then the patient might die from shock and loss of blood. And what sort of life could a man live with only one arm or leg? No, a quick death was infinitely preferable.

As he trudged along Walter came to his side, looking remarkably fresh after the exertions of battle.

'It gladden me to see you unhurt, Conrad.' He looked behind at Hans, Anton and Johann. 'To see you all unhurt. Praise God.'

'You too, Walter,' said Conrad. 'That is Brother Walter.'

'You do not need to stand on ceremony with me, Conrad. We came to this land together and have fought side by side ever since. That makes us all brothers, I think.'

'Do you like being here?' said Conrad.

Walter's handsome face wore a smile. 'Of course. I have found a peace here I thought I would never have. A serenity that calms my soul.'

Conrad looked at the blood on his surcoat and the arms of his hauberk. In battle he was a remorseless killing machine but was softly spoken and thoughtful when not fighting.

430

'Do you miss it?' asked Conrad.

'Miss what?'

'Your former life. You were a Saxon knight from a rich and powerful family. You had everything.'

Walter sighed. 'You are correct. I did have everything. Everything that wealth could buy: horses, women, banquets, tournaments and hunting without end. It was a life of selfish indulgence and a life that was devoid of purpose. What profit a man, Conrad, if he gains the world yet loses his soul? No, I do not miss it.

'And what of you, who is earning himself a reputation as a fine soldier? Have you found contentment?'

They were nearing Wenden's perimeter wall now and Conrad looked up and saw Daina at the top of one of the towers, the wind that had suddenly appeared ruffling her long locks. She saw Caupo nearing the gates and bowed her head to him. She then saw Conrad and waved at him, causing the others ahead, including the king, to turn their heads to see who she was waving to. Conrad waved back, saw everyone looking at him and blushed.

'I see that you perhaps have found what you are looking for,' smiled Walter as Berthold frowned at the young novice before walking through the gates beside Caupo. Rudolf smiled and shook his head and Lukas rolled his eyes.

'Daina is a fine young woman,' continued Walter.

'She is a princess and I am just a penniless novice,' said Conrad, suddenly struck by the reality of their respective positions.

Walter dismissed his negative thoughts. 'I doubt that concerns her so it should not concern you.'

'I know how the world works,' said Conrad.

'We build a new world here, Conrad, a better world,' replied Walter. 'A kingdom of heaven where all things are possible.'

Walter's better world presented an awful sight the day after the battle. The civilian families were moved back to their huts but the Liv women and children were not allowed to return to their homes for fear they would be attacked by the thousands of Lithuanians who had fled the battle but who were still at large. Far from home and leaderless, Caupo assumed they would head south to cross over the Dvina to reach their homelands, but some might remain in Livonia to become bandits living in the forests. He therefore dispatched a thousand men to give chase, reinforced by the surviving brother knights and sergeants from Kremon and Wenden. Conrad had hoped that he would be allowed to partake in the expedition but Lukas informed him and the other novices that they had more onerous duties to attend to.

'Burying the dead,' he grinned, 'or rather throwing them on pyres. Godly work, boys, godly work.'

It may have been godly work but it was also stomach churning, the face masks they wore proving no deterrent to the disgusting stench that invaded their nostrils as they loaded decaying Lithuanians onto carts to be consigned to great pyres that had sprung up on the land to the south of the castle. Leather face and his crossbowmen had been detailed to assist the burial parties.

Hans grabbed the feet of a Lithuanian who had been killed by a crossbow bolt a hundred paces from the gates, the quarrel having pierced the man's mail armour and gone into his heart. The blood from the wound had long since turned black and the body was bloated with noxious gases.

'Careful Hans,' said Conrad, grabbing the corpse's wrists, 'we don't want to drop it and release the gases.'

'It already stinks foul,' said Hans, climbing from the side of the ditch where the body had rested for several days.

'Yes,' agreed Conrad, 'but if you get any of his insides on you it could be fatal.'

They had gingerly moved the corpses a few feet from the ditch, the two-wheeled cart hitched to a pony twenty paces away, when leather face came bounding over.

'Hold on boys, not so fast.'

He gestured for them to put the corpse down.

'It has to go on the cart,' said Conrad irritably.

'And it will, just need a little look first.'

'For what?' queried Hans.

Leather face knelt bedside the corpse and whipped out a set of pliers from a pocket in his leggings. He picked up one of the hands.

'You remember that first attack against the walls and the enemy horsemen around that great banner they had?'

He jammed a finger that had a ring on it between the pliers' side cutters and squeezed them. There was a loud crunch as he severed the finger.

'Well,' continued leather face, 'you might not have noticed, being godly and sworn to a life of poverty and all that, but those horsemen were lords and chiefs and men of some wealth.'

He pulled the ring off the severed finger and placed it in a small leather pouch that hung from his belt, casting the limb aside.

'And men of wealth like to wear things of value,' said leather face, lifting the dead man's mail shirt to see if there was a pouch underneath.

Conrad shook his head and pulled down his mask.

'You rob the dead?'

Leather face stood up. 'Now don't you get so high and mighty. I have been a mercenary for more years than I care to remember and all I've got to show for it is a bent back and a few scars. They ain't going to buy me that little ale house back in Germany so I can live out my dotage in peace.'

He walked over to another corpse, this one wearing a red cloak in addition to mail armour and leather boots. He pulled off the boots and then rummaged through the blood-crusted clothes, whooping with joy when he yanked a pouch from the leather belt. He opened it and examined the contents before emptying them into his own pouch.

'Rewards of the job,' he beamed. 'And Lord knows there aren't many of those in my line of work. You can get back to burning them, now.'

He moved on to the other corpses they had been ordered to haul away to the pyres, and Conrad noticed that the other mercenaries were also examining the dead and stripping them of anything of value.

It took two days to dispose of the dead, the funeral pyres burning day and night as fuel and corpses were thrown on them. The dreadful smell of roasting flesh permeated the air over the castle and the surrounding area. Caupo had brought nearly five thousand men to Wenden and a thousand had fallen during the relief assault. They had to be buried too and so a thousand of their comrades dug a great burial pit half a mile north of the castle where the bodies were interred according to the Christian faith. Otto told Conrad that it was appropriate that the bodies of dead pagans should be burned as they were going to hell anyway where they would burn for all eternity.

Leather face and his fellow mercenaries deposited their ill-gotten gains in the armoury and Caupo departed with his warriors. Word arrived from Master Bertram at Segewold that the Lithuanians besieging his castle had mysteriously vanished, the patrols he had despatched to discover their whereabouts having returned with news that they were marching south at speed, no doubt having heard of Caupo's defeat of Daugerutis at Wenden. No one knew if they would encounter the Livs and Sword Brothers that had been sent after the Lithuanians who had fled from Wenden.

Conrad cursed his luck that he would miss the great slaughter that Rudolf, Henke and Lukas would take part in when they finally caught up with the enemy. He was even glummer when Rameke took his people, including Daina, back to his village south of Wenden to begin his new life as their chief. The castle suddenly seemed vast and empty as he and the other novices went back to their duties and the workers went back to their building work.

*****

It had been four days since Stecse had left his lord at Wenden to take the Liv chief and his son across the Dvina. He had tried to be civil to Thalibald and Waribule but they made it plain that they had no time for politeness or conversation, grunting one-word replies to his questions and avoiding his eyes. After two days of their insolence he had grown tired of their company and rode at the head of his column of men, alongside his son whose company he found infinitely more agreeable. Even though he had only seen thirteen summers Mindaugas was growing into a fine young man. He had brought him on campaign because he had wanted him to witness the great Lithuanian invasion of Livonia. He also wanted him to see the sights and sounds of war as part of the preparation to become a warlord. He had taken no part in the fighting at Lake Inesis, Stecse having assigned a bodyguard to ensure he stayed out of danger, but his son had shown no fear in the face of the enemy. Soon he would be ready to kill with his own sword.

The frosts had disappeared now and the days were pleasant, though the nights still cool. The vast forests of birch, spruce and pine were alive with red foxes, elk, lynx, deer, wild boar and marten. The few settlements they had come across had been deserted, the inhabitants having fled into the forest with their food and belongings to wait until the invaders had passed.

They would take refuge in their sacred groves deep in the forest where oaks believed to be possessed by the spirits of the gods would protect them. Stecse smiled to himself; the crusaders believed that they had eradicated the old religion but they were wrong. Beliefs over a thousand years old would not disappear overnight.

'Is this land now Lithuanian, father?' enquired Mindaugas beside him.

'To all intents and purposes, yes.'

'And will we live here when the war has ended?'

'It will be for the grand duke to decide, my son.'

'What will the Livs do?' said Mindaugas.

'They will obey, like all beaten peoples. That is the way of the world.'

'What of the crusaders?'

'What of them? They are few and we are many. The grand duke has planned this war well. By the time they arrive their castles will have fallen and Riga itself will be besieged. They will lose heart when they see that the kingdom they have created has crumbled.'

'I have heard that the god they worship was executed by his enemies,' said Mindaugas. 'If that is true, why do they follow such a weak god?'

'The one who was executed was the son of their god and was called the Christ,' Stecse corrected him. 'I do not have knowledge of their religion but I believe that they fight to avenge his death.'

'What is the father of this Christ called?'

Stecse shrugged. 'He has no name, he is just their god.'

Mindaugas was silent for a few seconds. 'It is a strange religion.'

Stecse nodded. 'They are a strange people. They seek to convert all peoples to their religion, either peacefully or by the sword. That is why they send armies to this land every year. That is why they are called crusaders.'

'The Lithuanian people would never abandon their gods,' said Mindaugas defiantly. 'How did the son of their god, this Christ, die?'

'He was crucified, I believe,' answered Stecse.

'A criminal's death,' sneered Mindaugas. He looked behind to where Thalibald and Waribule rode on their horses. 'No wonder Caupo and his men were beaten so easily following such a weak god. Only the strong deserve to triumph.'

The quiet of the afternoon was interrupted by the appearance of four riders from the rear who galloped up to the head of the column, their horses sweating and breathing heavily, their riders agitated and fretful. They wore no armour save helmets and round shields, *spisas* and axes their weapons. The scouts brought their horses to a halt beside Stecse who gave the order to stop.

The commander raised his hand. 'Crusaders approaching, lord.'

'Crusaders?' said Stecse. 'From where?'

'I do not know, lord. They approach from the west,' replied the sweating leader. 'Many horse and foot.'

'How many?' asked Stecse.

'Five, six hundred, lord.'

'How far are they away?'

'Two miles at most, lord.'

435

Stecse looked back at his men. He had five hundred well-armed and equipped riders. They were in open ground on an old track that meandered its way between two great forests, with a hundred paces of meadow each side of the track before the trees began. If he made a stand here his men could not be outflanked. On the other hand the crusaders probably had crossbowmen among their ranks and he had seen what these weapons could do at Kokenhusen. He also had his orders, which were to get his captives across the Dvina.

'We will continue on to the Dvina,' he ordered.

'We will not fight the crusaders?' said a surprised Mindaugas.

'We do not know how many they number,' replied Stecse. 'And my priority is to get the prisoners back across the river.'

'But father...' protested Mindaugas.

Stecse held up a hand to quieten him, then looked around with concern. It was suddenly eerily still and he sensed something was wrong. During their journey they had seen many birds and had surprised deer among the trees and in the meadows, occasionally disturbing a black stork by a stretch of water. But now there was nothing.

A twig snapped and Stecse instinctively grabbed his son's arm and pulled him from the saddle. A succession of thwacks came from the trees and two of the scouts were struck in the back by crossbow bolts, pitching them forward onto the necks of their horses before they fell from the saddle.

'Ambush!' screamed Stecse as the other two scouts brought up their shields to protect themselves from the lethal hail that was being shot from the trees. Stecse's horse screamed in pain as it was hit by bolts and collapsed, writhing in agony. He grabbed his shield lying on the ground and forced his son behind it.

'Stay here,' he ordered.

Mindaugas went to protest but a bolt struck the rim of the shield and stopped only inches from his face.

Stecse grabbed the reins of his son's horse before it bolted and used it as a shield as he called to his men.

'Clear them from the trees.'

Horns were already sounding as the first score of riders galloped forward and charged the treeline, *spisas* held above their heads ready to throw. Crossbow bolts cut half down before they got to within fifty paces of the forest but the others managed to reach the trees and launch their missiles. Then came another fifty riders that charged into the trees, throwing their long spears before attempting to kill the crossbowmen with their swords. But it was costly work and another fifteen Lithuanians fell before the ambushers were silenced.

Stecse hauled himself into the saddle of a dead scout's horse and rode to the trees on the right side of the meadow from where the ambush had been sprung. Mindaugas regained his saddle and followed his father. The commander who had led the charge saluted. Shouts and screams were coming from within the forest.

'Recall your men,' ordered Stecse. 'There might be more of them approaching. No point in losing soldiers for no reason.'

The commander saluted and pointed at his signaller who raised the horn to his lips and blew it twice. Stecse looked at the body of a dead crossbowman a few paces away, his conical helmet with nasal guard his only protection, his simple green tunic ripped where a *spisa* had pierced his chest.

'We should send men into the forest to hunt them down,' spat Mindaugas, still discomfited by his close shave with death.

'That is what they want,' replied Stecse, 'to slow us down so their knights can toy with us. But we will not play their game.'

Mindaugas was mortified. 'We cannot run from these Christians. It is shameful. We should stand and fight.'

Before Stecse could answer there was a succession of horn calls from the meadow, and in the distance the sound of trumpets being blasted.

'You may get your wish,' said Stecse flatly before tugging on his horse's reins to retrace his steps. Mindaugas and the others followed.

In the meadow the Lithuanian horsemen were deploying into line, arrayed in their companies approximately a hundred strong, arranged in two lines.

Stecse looked at the two surviving scouts that accompanied him.

'Two miles away? Perhaps I should have scouts that can judge distances.'

'We did not lie, lord,' protested one but Stecse waved away his protest.

He galloped to the centre of the line and halted his horse in front of the first rank of Lithuanians. To the north, less than a quarter of a mile away, the land either side of the track was filling with brightly coloured horsemen, their beasts swathed in red, yellow and black coverings, their riders similarly brightly adorned. They contrasted sharply with the drab brown and green of the Lithuanians. Flags and pennants flew from the Christian lances and in the centre of the line was a huge banner that stirred only slightly in the light breeze. The mounted drummers among the Christians banged their instruments continuously as Stecse's men sat in silence and watched as more and more horsemen flooded the ground in front of them. Mindaugas drew his sword.

'You can put that away,' said Stecse. 'We are not standing here entertaining the Christians.'

His son and those within earshot looked at him in surprise.

'All you see is what is ahead of you. But I have to think of matters of more import. If the Christians are here then they might also be at the Dvina, and if they are that means that the grand duke and all the other dukes are cut off from Lithuania. Our first duty now is to reach the river and secure the bridge across it.'

The Christians were still deploying when the Lithuanians began to withdraw, a hundred men forming the rearguard as the rest trotted south towards the Dvina. The prisoners were escorted to the front of the column as Stecse took command of the rearguard. The crusaders, realising that their opponents were not going to fight, began following in one great mass of horsemen, some breaking ranks to gallop in front to charge the Lithuanians. Stecse led forward a group of half a dozen horsemen against these lone riders, killing one himself with a *spisa* thrust before withdrawing back to the rearguard. But this merely served to inspire the Christians to more acts of bravado as more and more began to gallop forward to offer single combat. But Stecse gave the order to increase the speed of the retreat and thus the rearguard managed to stay out of their reach.

After half an hour the Christians were content to follow the Lithuanians as they fell back towards the Dvina, now less than ten miles to the south. With the ground either side of the track narrowing as the tress closed in there was no scope to outflank Stecse's men and he began to relax, just as a commotion erupted behind him. He turned to see two riders burst through the ranks, spooking one of the horses directly behind him that bolted forward into his own horse, herding it to one side. He looked on helplessly as Thalibald and Waribule galloped past and headed towards the Christians. Two of his men dug their spurs into their horses to give pursuit.

'Let them go,' shouted Stecse. He had more important things to worry about now than two Liv prisoners.

Thalibald and his son, having taken advantage of the appearance of the crusaders to strike their guards and grab the reins of their horses, galloped back up the track they had ridden down, constantly looking behind to see if they were being pursued. They shouted in unison when they realised they were not, then looked in horror to see a dozen horsemen leaving the Christian ranks with lances levelled, cantering towards them. Their wrists were still bound together in front of them so they pulled on their reins to halt their horses and then raised their arms.

'We are friends,' shouted Thalibald in German as the knights approached them in an unbroken line, lances gripped under their right armpits, their heads encased in full-face helmets. The two Livs had escaped from the Lithuanians only to die at the hands of their allies.

As the faceless knights bore down on them Thalibald and Waribule continued to shout that they were friends, allies and fellow Christians. The crusaders, however, their faces enclosed by their helmets, saw only a pair of reckless, hairy barbarians in front of them and paid no heed to their shouting, which sounded strangely German. But they did take notice of the blast of trumpets behind and the appearance of their lord beside them who was surprising bare headed. He was also gesticulating frantically with his arms. Less than a hundred paces from their targets they slowed their charge to a trot and then a walk as his voiced boomed at them.

'Halt! Stand down! Stay your weapons.'

They pulled up their horses and looked at each other in confusion as he walked his horse in front of them to ensure they obeyed his commands. Then he wheeled his mount around and walked it towards the two heathens. Was he mad? Had he been seized by witchcraft? He was followed by his banner man, the great red flag he carried sporting a golden lion, a design replicated on the shield that was slung on his back and the splendid caparison that covered his huge warhorse. He brought the great steed to a halt in front of Thalibald and smiled, extending his hand to him.

'Greetings, my friend. I did not think we would meet in such strange circumstances.'

Thalibald held up his bound wrists. 'Alas, Sir Helmold, you see before you a chief reduced to the status of a slave.'

Sir Helmold pulled his dagger from its sheath and cut the chief's bonds, doing the same for his son.

'Slave no longer, my friend.'

Thalibald looked behind at the disappearing Lithuanians. 'They retreat to the Dvina.'

'We form but one of the two armies that are now approaching the river. The bishop leads the other from the west. I was sent north to aid the garrisons of Segewold and Wenden that were besieged by the enemy, but happily your king delivered their salvation.'

Thalibald thought of his youngest son and daughter. 'Wenden is safe?'

439

Sir Helmold nodded. 'Safe, my friend, and much more. Daugerutis is dead and his army scattered. It is a miracle.'

Thalibald slapped his son on the shoulder and closed his eyes. 'Praise God.'

Stecse stayed with the rearguard until he was a mile from the Dvina where the grand duke's troops had erected a rough semi-circular earth rampart surmounted by sharpened stakes that flanked the ground either side of the track, the latter being barred by great logs with iron spikes that could be laid across it. Inside the rampart that protected the bridgehead were crude log shelters and tents.

That night a tired Stecse held a council of war in one of the large tents used by one of the chiefs. Daugerutis had left his own men to secure the pontoon bridge over the Dvina as well as a thousand more to lay siege to Kokenhusen but a short distance from the bridge of boats. Stecse was already concerned about the appearance of crusaders to the north but now he received news that made him fear for the safety of Daugerutis himself.

The tent stank of human sweat as the chiefs stood around the oak table, their bearded faces haggard from too little sleep. Candles were placed on the four corners of the table and a cloth map was unfurled on its rough surface. Stecse ordered them to submit their reports. A chief with a heavily bandaged arm pointed at the map, which was a representation of the River Dvina from the Gulf of Riga to the city of Polotsk. He pointed at Riga.

'The Bishop of Riga landed with a great army of crusaders two weeks ago. The soldiers of Duke Kitenis made an abortive assault against the castle of Holm and then withdrew east to link up with those soldiers besieging Uexkull. When they arrived they found that Duke Gedvilas, Duke Kitenis and Duke Butantas were present. They…'

He fell silent and stared at the map.

'Continue,' ordered Stecse.

'Duke Butantas sent a boat across the river to the Semgallians informing them that their duke was dead and requesting boats to be sent over so his men and those of the other dukes could be evacuated. They have fled, lord, across the river, as have those men of Duke Butantas who were besieging the castle of Lennewarden.'

Stecse looked at their weary faces. 'It is true that Duke Ykintas is dead. He led an attack against the castle of Wenden and was killed. His men are still with the grand duke. The other dukes quarrelled with our lord and deserted him, may Perkunas torment them. We are on our own.'

'The Bishop of Riga will link up with the crusader garrisons as he marches east along the river,' said a chief with fair hair and beard, lamellar armour covering his broad chest. He pointed at the castles of Holm, Uexkull and Lennewarden.

Stecse nodded. 'Our priority is to protect the bridge over the river. Therefore we will withdraw eight hundred men from around Kokenhusen to reinforce the position here. The crusaders I clashed with earlier may attempt to capture the bridge in the next few days.

'I will also bring the three thousand men that the grand duke left in his lands as a reserve. If this bridgehead is destroyed then the grand duke will be trapped in Livonia.'

'Where is the grand duke?' asked the chief with a bandaged arm.

'I hope that he is marching south to the Dvina,' said Stecse, 'though at this moment in time I know as much about his whereabouts as you do.

'Organise the movement of troops from Kokenhusen tonight, and send couriers south to order the reserve to move across the river. I do not want the crusaders stealing a march on us.'

They saluted and filed out of the tent in silence. Stecse was not unduly concerned about them: they were all either Selonians or Nalsen, men who owed allegiance to Daugerutis himself. Unlike the other dukes they would not desert him. He flopped down in one of the chairs next to the table and looked at the map. His eyes settled on Gerzika, some fifty miles east of Kokenhusen. He toyed with the idea of sending a plea for help to Vsevolod, the son-in-law of Daugerutis and the grand duke's appointed heir, but dismissed the idea. He remembered Vsevolod's treachery at Kokenhusen. He would not put it past the prince to side with the bishop if events favoured him. Still, a message sent to the grand duke's wife might be more productive. He rose and walked to a smaller table by the tent's wall, upon which was a jug of beer. He poured himself a cup and returned to his seat, stretching out his legs as one of the flaps opened and a guard appeared. He saluted the prince.

'Apologies, lord, there is a man outside who wishes to see you. He says he is a prince.'

'A prince? Does he bring an army to aid me in my hour of need?'

The guard looked confused. 'No, lord. He is alone.'

'Does he have a name, this prince?' asked Stecse.

'Vetseke, lord, formerly the ruler of Kokenhusen.'

Stecse's ears pricked up at this. He had thought Vetseke long dead, for he knew that he had been captured after his revolt against the bishop had been crushed.

'Show him in,' said Stecse, 'and bring more drink.'

The guard saluted and disappeared. Moments later he reappeared with a tall man beside him dressed in mail armour and a green cloak around his shoulders. He had long black hair but, unusually, a clean-shaven face. He had a world-weary appearance but his brown eyes were still sharp. He nodded his head ever so slightly at Stecse.

'Hail Prince Stecse, commander of the armies of Grand Duke Daugerutis, lord of all Lithuania.'

Stecse extended his arm to a chair a few paces from his own. 'Please, avail yourself of my hospitality, Prince Vetseke, such as it is.'

Vetseke walked to the chair but then stopped at the table and peered at the map upon it.

'The playground of princes, dukes and bishops.' He looked at Stecse. 'Your guards relieved me of my sword. I trust I will get it back.'

Another guard brought in a full jug of beer and placed it on the smaller table, along with another cup. Stecse rose and walked over to it, filling the cup.

'Merely a precaution, I assure you. What brings you to my tent at such a late hour?'

He walked over to Vetseke and handed him the cup. The former ruler of Kokenhusen tasted the liquid and found it bitter.

'Farmhouse ale, I'm afraid,' said Stecse, 'fine dining is not high on my list of priorities at the moment.'

'Though it has been taken from me,' said Vetseke, 'I wish to offer you the service of my sword, if you will have it.'

'How many warriors do you have?' asked Stecse.

'A hundred.'

Stecse drained his cup. 'Hardly an army.'

'Hardly anything,' agreed Vetseke, 'but numbers are only one part of the equation. The ground we sit on used to be mine before the bishop and his knights came. You will know, of course, that around four hundred of the latter are currently camped but five miles to the north of this tent.'

Stecse nodded. 'The grand duke is campaigning to the north with over ten thousand men.'

Vetseke sighed and ran a finger around the rim of his cup.

'Daugerutis is dead, lord prince.'

Stecse, taken by surprise, dropped his cup. He kicked it away in anger but then quickly regained his composure.

'How can you know this?'

'You forget that this was once my kingdom. My men are camped deep in the forest but ten miles north of here, but in all the time your men have been on this side of the river they have not discovered them.'

Vetseke got up and walked to the jug of beer to refill his cup. 'When you kindly besieged my former home you removed the influence of the Sword Brothers from the land, meaning I and my men, formally forced to hide among the trees like bandits, were free to go where we wanted. I still have loyal subjects among the villages who inform me of news.'

He walked back to his chair. 'They told me of a great battle between the crusaders and Caupo at Wenden in which Daugerutis was killed and his army scattered.'

'Why should I believe village gossip?' said Stecse angrily.

'Because I know my own land and my own people,' replied Vetseke. 'I do not relay this news to you out of spite or with relish. I have more reasons to hate and despise the bishop than you, I think.

'You have to disperse the crusaders to the north, who are poised like a dagger at your bridge of boats. If you wish to remain on this side of the river, that is.'

'Why wouldn't we?' snapped Stecse.

Vetseke turned the cup in his hand. 'With Daugerutis dead I believe that you are now commander of what remains of his army. That being so, will you underestimate the crusaders as he did?'

Stecse jumped up and placed a hand on the hilt of his sword. 'You forget yourself, prince.'

Vetseke remained unconcerned. 'You may kill, Prince Stecse, and by doing so you would release me from the travails of this world. Death would free me from the torment of being a stranger in my own land, a vagrant who has been reduced to living like an animal within the forest. But that would not alter the truth that I have just told you. The decision is yours.'

He finished his drink, stood and placed the cup on the table. He bowed his head to Stecse. 'You need to strengthen your position here, lord prince, for I fear the crusaders to the north will strike at your camp within days. And within the week the bishop and his army will be here and your problems will multiply.'

'And you, Vetseke, where do you go?' said Stecse.

443

'Back to my men, there to await your decision whether you wish to enlist my aid. If you do, light a signal bonfire. I will see it.'

He stopped at the tent flap.

'You look tired, lord prince. You should get some rest for upon your shoulders rests the fate of the Lithuanian people.'

Then he was gone like a wraith in the night. Stecse refilled his cup and sank back into his chair. He dismissed the idea that Daugerutis was dead, and yet Vetseke knew this land better than he so why would he lie? He was also a mortal enemy of the bishop and the crusaders and for that reason alone made him an ally of sorts. After two more cups of beer he fell asleep in his chair, his mind a whirl of confusion and dread.

*****

After mopping up the remnants of Daugerutis' army the brother knights went back to a Wenden that had returned to normality. Rameke had taken his people back to his father's village, which was now his, and in the spring sunshine the castle grounds once more reverberated to the sounds of chisels, picks and spades as the construction work continued apace. The quarry was reopened and the armourers got to work mending mail armour, helmets and shields and making crossbow bolts. So many had been used during the siege that replacements had to be sent from Segewold and Kremon.

The garrison had rejoiced at the news that the bishop had landed with an army at Riga and Master Berthold gave a special service of thanksgiving in the chapel, at which he informed the brother knights that they would be marching south to aid the bishop to destroy the Lithuanians at Kokenhusen. By God's grace the enemy had vanished from before the walls of Holm, Uexkull and Lennewarden without a fight, and now only a few Lithuanians remained at Kokenhusen. They were currently being watched by the knights under the command of Sir Helmold of Plesse, newly arrived from Germany, until the bishop arrived to launch the decisive attack. Grand Master Volquin had ordered that the Sword Brothers present themselves at Kokenhusen to take part in the battle with the Lithuanian pagans.

It was now summer and the meadows were filled with edible mushrooms and flowering plants – bilberries, wild strawberries, cloudberries, cornflowers and blueberries – and the forests echoed to the distinctive 'creck, creck' cry of the corncrake. It was a lush land teeming with life and difficult to imagine that only a few weeks previously had been drenched with blood. And now the Sword Brothers of Kremon, Segewold and Wenden gathered at the latter to march south to the Dvina.

The fighting in the spring had depleted the garrisons of the respective castles and so Wenden mustered only nine brother knights, twenty-eight sergeants and four novices for the journey to the Dvina. Master Bertram brought ten brother knights and fifteen sergeants from Segewold, while the men of Kremon numbered only six brother knights and ten sergeants. Due to the need for haste it had been decided that only horsemen would make the journey south, the mercenaries remaining at Wenden under the command of Master Thaddeus to ensure the castle and its civilian occupants were safe. The brother knights rode palfreys and led their warhorses and the sergeants and novices led ponies loaded with spare weapons, armour, fodder and food.

Caupo came with a hundred of his mounted warriors and Rameke brought a score of his own men plus half a dozen scouts who would lead the way to the Dvina. He told Conrad that it would take five or six days to reach the river. The castle courtyard was crammed with men and horses as the three masters conferred and brother knights and sergeants sweated in their armour under a clear blue sky.

'I hope the Lithuanians do not flee across the river,' he said to his friend on the morning they left Wenden. 'I have a score to settle with those who killed my father and brother.'

'Perhaps we will invade Lithuania,' said Conrad hopefully, not really knowing where Lithuania was.

'The king has said that the bishop wishes to complete the conquest of Estonia before he converts the Lithuanians,' replied Rameke.

'How is Daina?' enquired Conrad casually.

Rameke was unimpressed by his friend's interest in his sister. He shrugged. 'Like all women, fussing around and getting in the way.'

'Any suitors?'

'I will tell you now what I told you before,' said Rameke dismissively. 'Who would want to marry my sister? She will no doubt be a tiresome burden on my household. Just one more problem that I have to deal with now I am chief.'

Conrad was seized by joy and began whistling as Master Berthold gave the order to mount up and the Sword Brothers trotted from the courtyard and filed across the bridge over the moat to descend the track to the perimeter gatehouse. Conrad was still whistling cheerily as Rameke left him to ride beside Caupo and the three masters at the head of the column. The sun was shining and the Lithuanian threat had been dealt with. All that now remained was to destroy those pagans still besieging Kokenhusen, after which the bishop would lead a retributive raid into Lithuania itself to deal the unbelievers a heavy blow.

But the Lithuanians were about to spring a nasty surprise.

Chapter 17

Five miles north of the Dvina the Sword Brothers encountered a patrol of crusaders riding towards them. They were led by a knight in a full-face helmet whose horse was covered by a magnificent red caparison and whose shield bore the emblem of a silver unicorn. Behind him were a dozen other knights wearing yellow, blue and green surcoats over their mail armour. They instantly rode up to the head of the column where the castellans of Wenden, Segewold and Kremon were located. Rameke, having found their conversation boring, had taken his leave of the masters to ride beside Conrad and the other novices, finding their company much more agreeable.

'Those are crusaders from Germany,' remarked Anton, 'we must be near the river.'

'And nearer the Lithuanians,' said Rameke. 'I pray that they have not fled back to their homeland.'

'It does not matter,' said Johann. 'I have heard the brother knights talking of the bishop leading a crusade against Lithuania to make it Christian.'

In front of them the brother knights sat on their horses and chatted to each other as the crusaders exchanged information with the masters. Conrad saw Master Berthold gesticulating with his arms before wheeling his horse around and riding back down the column. He was surprised when he halted his horse in front of Rameke.

'Joyous news, Rameke. I have just been informed that your father and brother are alive and are but a mile away, in the camp of Sir Helmold of Plesse who leads the crusaders.'

Rameke said nothing but closed his eyes and gave thanks to God, while Conrad slapped him on the back and Anton, Hans and Johann cheered, earning them a glare from Master Berthold.

'Come,' he said, 'we shall ride to the camp together so you can see the father and brother you thought dead and I can greet an old friend.'

News quickly spread among the Sword Brothers that Thalibald and Waribule were alive and when the march recommenced everyone was in high spirits. Walter said that it was truly a miracle and that God had protected the two Livs just as surely as he had watched over Daniel in the lion's den. Conrad was ecstatic, not least because when she heard that her father and brother were alive Daina would be beside herself with joy, and if she was happy then he was happy.

447

It took but a short ride to reach the crusader camp, a sprawling collection of tents of varying sizes, a few pavilions and a myriad of carts. Squires as young as ten sat by tents cleaning helmets and armour, while others came carrying firewood from the forest next to which the camp had been sited. Horses stood flicking their tails as farriers examined their hooves and knights practised with their swords. The camp had been pitched in a large meadow between the forest and a lake that was used for watering the horses of the knights and their squires and the oxen and mules that hauled the wagons and carts. Though the camp was relatively small and contained none of the usual whores, women and children who followed armies like a plague of rats, the air already stank of horse dung, leather and sweat and a permanent pall of smoke hung in the air from the multitude of campfires that burned day and night.

The track that the Sword Brothers had ridden along continued to wend its way south through the trees and by the sides of lakes until it eventually reached the Dvina. It was an ancient route, perhaps hundreds of years old, that had linked the settlement of Kokenhusen with those in the north near the Gauja, but was now used to link the crusader castles in the north and south of Livonia. Master Berthold, following discussions with Bertram and Mathias, decided to pitch their tents directly south of the crusader camp, on the eastern side of the track where the trees were less dense and where there was access to the fresh water of a stream. The order was given – 'Make camp, lord brothers, on God's behalf' – and then the novices and sergeants went to work erecting the tents while the masters and Rameke rode away to the pavilion of Sir Helmold to pay their respects to the commander of the army and embrace Thalibald and Waribule. Conrad would have liked to have accompanied them but he and the other novices had much to do: erecting the chapel tent in the middle of the camp, together with the tents of the masters and the tent where the meals would be served. The tents of the brother knights were pitched around these, with those of the sergeants and novices forming a third, outer circle. Then the horses had to be unsaddled, fed and watered, after which they were groomed and examined for any wounds. To be fair the brother knights assisted the sergeants in their tasks and soon the camp was assembled and the banner of the Sword Brothers was flying from a flagpole erected outside the chapel tent.

It was late afternoon by the time they had finished. Conrad lay on the ground outside the small tent he would share with Hans, Anton and Johann, the other three also resting on the ground and staring up at the puffy white clouds in the sky.

'What's this? Don't you know that the devil makes work for idle hands?'

Conrad groaned when he heard Henke's voice, and his heart sank when he saw the grinning brother knight carrying shovels.

'On your feet,' he smirked, throwing the shovels on the ground, 'there are latrine pits that need digging. Shouldn't take you more than two hours.'

Conrad jumped to his feet and picked up one of the tools.

'Have you heard anything about Thalibald, Brother Henke?' he enquired.

'Your future father-in-law, you mean?' replied Henke with an evil glint in his eye. 'He is well, which is a minor miracle considering he was a guest of the Lithuanians. He was lucky they didn't slice his balls off.'

'Why would they do that?' said Hans, horrified.

Henke threw him a spade as Anton and Johann picked up their shovels.

'Why?' replied Henke, 'because that is what pagans do, though to be fair the armies in Germany I fought in did much the same and worse.'

'Surely Christian armies would not do such things?' said Johann.

Henke laughed. 'Christian, pagan or Saracen, it doesn't matter once the killing starts. When we get back to Wenden ask Master Thaddeus to tell you about the antics of King Richard of England in the Holy Land. Now there was a godly monarch, had over two thousand Saracen women and children executed at a place called Acre.'

Conrad was shocked. 'Surely not?'

'King Richard wasn't like you, Conrad,' said Henke, 'he didn't object to killing women and children or selling them as slaves for the greater good.'

'Which was what?' asked Conrad.

'To take Jerusalem back from the Saracens, of course,' said Henke.

'But Jerusalem is still held by the Saracens,' replied Conrad, 'Master Thaddeus told me.'

A wicked smile crept over Henke's face. 'King Richard obviously didn't kill enough Saracens otherwise God would have given him victory.'

'Where is King Richard now?' asked Hans.

'Dead,' answered Henke, 'stupid bastard got himself killed in a siege in France, or so I heard.'

'God rest his soul,' said Anton.

'Had the Sword Brothers been in the Holy Land with Richard,' said Henke, 'then he would have taken Jerusalem because God loves the Sword Brothers. And do you know why that is?'

They looked at him with blank expressions. Henke shook his head and tutted.

'Because the Sword Brothers fill hell with the souls of dead pagans. Now get digging those latrine pits, and not too close to the stream. We don't want half the brethren falling ill with bad guts before the rout of the Lithuanians.'

He sauntered away to leave the novices to their burdensome task. Conrad began walking towards where they would dig the latrines. They had dug so many in their short time with the order that they knew the rules off by heart: latrines should be dug downhill of the camp, away from the water supply to avoid drinking filthy water and downwind if possible.

'Henke is in an unusually good mood,' commented Hans.

'The prospect of imminent slaughter always seems to cheer him,' remarked Conrad dryly.

'Next year we will be brother knights,' said Anton.

'And then no more digging latrine pits,' opined Johann.

They all laughed but Conrad did not believe that he would ever wear the white surcoat of the Sword Brothers. He believed more than ever that his destiny was to be with Daina and he began to whistle as he waded through the stream with the others to dig the pits a safe distance from it.

Later, after they had finished their back-breaking work and lay, exhausted on the ground, Rameke visited them. He looked as if a great weight had been lifted from his shoulders and he kept grinning like a small child so happy was he.

'My father and brother are well,' he told them. 'They were unharmed by the Lithuanians though nearly killed by Sir Helmold's men.'

'Where is the bishop?' said Conrad.

Rameke crouched down beside him. 'He marches east along the Dvina with the bulk of the crusader army, relieving the besieged castles as he does so. When he has relieved Kokenhusen he will send word to Sir Helmold and then we will strike south at the same time as the bishop attacks from the west. The Lithuanians will be crushed.'

'When will the bishop arrive?' queried Hans.

Rameke shrugged. 'I do not know, but Sir Helmold says that a great number of knights and foot accompanies him.' He looked sheepishly at them. 'He is giving a great feast in his pavilion tonight in celebration of my father's deliverance. I wish you could all attend.'

'We are but lowly novices,' said Johann.

'Fit only to dig latrine pits,' added Conrad, stretching his back.

Rameke stood. 'It will not always be so. Soon you too will be knights and then we shall have great feasts together where we shall boast of our victories over the pagans.'

Conrad hauled himself up and offered his hand to Rameke. 'Enjoy the feast.'

They all shook his hand before he regained his saddle and rode back to the crusader camp.

'What are we eating tonight?' asked Hans, the talk of food arousing his ever-present hunger.

'Deer if Brother Lukas allows me to take a crossbow into the woods,' said Anton.

'Well, then,' said Conrad, 'let us go and find him so we can fill the great space that is Hans' belly.'

Lukas gave his permission for the boys to mount a hunting party and that night they ate well after killing a roe deer that they skinned and butchered, roasting its flesh over a fire as darkness descended over the land. Their meal was not as grand as the feast given by Sir Helmold where squires in his livery served guests game that the crusader knights had hunted – wild boar, deer, elk and black grouse – washed down by copious quantities of wine that the lord had brought from his estates in Germany. It was a most enjoyable banquet and went on long into the night, becoming noisier as the guests became more inebriated.

*****

In Livonia in spring darkness came four hours before midnight. Sir Helmold's feast had begun just as the sun was sinking in the west and two hours later the noise coming from his pavilion could be heard hundreds of paces away. Stecse knelt beside Vetseke among the trees and observed the flicker of campfires between the trunks. He had decided to trust the Liv prince who had agreed to lead him into the forest that stretched from the Dvina for miles inland, the green canopy only being interrupted by lakes, meadows, settlements and smaller rivers that dotted the landscape.

He had brought a hundred of his most trusted men with him, which, together with the equal number of Vetseke's soldiers, made for a raiding party that was both manageable but also strong enough to inflict damage on the crusaders. Vetseke had reported that the crusaders had made camp and shown no indication that they would move until the bishop arrived. Stecse had decided that if they would not visit him then he would call upon them.

The hands and faces of the raiders were blackened with soot, they wore no mail or metal armour or helmets, being equipped with leather breastplates, caps and boots. They carried blackened shields and spears and axes in their hands so there were no jangling belts or scabbards. Not that it mattered: the noise coming from the pavilion in the centre of the camp was enough to wake the dead.

'The crusaders are celebrating their victory already,' hissed Vetseke.

'Then we should avail ourselves of their hospitality,' whispered Stecse. 'The gods be with you.'

'And you,' replied Vetseke.

Stecse tapped his subordinate next to him on the arm and got to his feet. He and Vetseke then began moving slowly towards the fires and noise ahead, carefully feeling their way in the blackness of the forest. Their men had been ordered to remain silent until they reached the enemy camp, after which they were to kill and burn quickly before withdrawing back into the forest. They had also been told that the wounded would be left behind and the same went for those who were foolish enough to be captured. As the volume of noise coming from Sir Helmold's pavilion increased, two hundred men silently crept towards the crusader camp.

*****

The riotous laughter coming from the pavilion seemed louder as night fell and quiet descended over the land. Guards had been posted around the Sword Brother camp and sergeants and brother knights gathered round campfires to talk in muted conversations. Conrad, tired from the exertions of pitching the tents, tending to the horses and digging the latrine trenches, tried to get some sleep but the noise of the celebrations kept him awake.

'Are you awake, Conrad?' said Hans.

'Yes.'

'Sounds as though the feast is going well.'

'Indeed.'

There was a great cheer from the pavilion.

Anton sat up. 'This is no good. I'm on guard duty in an hour anyway.'

He reached over to his boots, a single candle burning in a lantern hanging on the tent pole providing illumination. He looked at Johann beside him who was snoring soundly.

452

'I sometimes think that a herd of elk could stampede through camp and Johann would sleep through it all.'

Conrad and Hans laughed as another bout of riotous laughter came from Sir Helmold's tent. Then Conrad heard a different sound, a high-pitched scream that he had heard many times on the battlefield. The hairs on the back of his neck pricked up and a shiver went down his spine.

'Did you hear that?' he said.

Anton pulled on his boots. 'Hear what?'

There was another scream, fainter but still discernible.

Hans jumped up. 'I heard that.'

Conrad did likewise and kicked Johann.

'Get up, Johann, we are under attack.'

They pulled on their boots, grabbed their swords, shields and helmets and rushed outside. Henke stood beside the campfire outside their tent, along with Rudolf and Lukas. Henke saw them.

'We heard it too.'

He and the others had drawn their swords and were looking towards the crusader camp. Suddenly the alarm bell outside the chapel tent began ringing and men began running from their tents or racing to their shelters to gather their weapons. And in the crusader camp there was a plethora of shouts and screams. Instead of racing wildly towards the source of the tumult the brethren and sergeants were trained to rally at the chapel tent to receive their orders. They did so now where Rudolf, in the absence of the castellans of Wenden, Segewold and Kremon, who were at the feast and perhaps already dead, bellowed orders.

'We march to save the masters of our order. Secure Sir Helmold's pavilion. God with us!'

Eighty voices shouted 'God with us' and followed Rudolf as he ran through the Sword Brother camp and then stood at its northern end as shouts and war cries came from the crusader tents immediately to the north. Some of the tents were on fire, illuminating figures running and fighting and horses and mules bolting. It was chaos.

Just as they did when mounted on the battlefield the brethren formed into line, the brother knights in the first rank, the sergeants behind and in the rear the novices, much to their consternation. Only half the brother knights wore their mail armour and less than that had helmets, so great had been the rush to the chapel tent. But all had their shields and swords, though most preferred maces or axes for close-quarter work on foot. The sergeants were in a similar state, some being bare footed but all having one or more weapons. Conrad and the other novices had strapped on their sword belts but like the others preferred bludgeoning weapons for the fight with the night raiders.

Rudolf raised his mace and the whole formation moved forward at speed, crossing the hundred paces of open ground between the two camps in less than a minute. Small groups of crusaders and their squires were attempting to fend off black-clad warriors armed with axes and spears and carrying square-like shields. The raiders did not stop to fight but threw their spears and then moved past the Christian knights, cutting down individuals they came across and throwing burning firewood into tents and on carts.

The Sword Brothers moved as one through the camp, parting to sweep around any tents in their way, reforming their line and then continuing the advance into the heart of the camp. Men screamed as they ran from burning tents with their clothes on fire and others, severely wounded by axe blows and spear thrusts, crawled on the ground as their lifeblood seeped from their bodies. On either flank of the Sword Brothers men had to fend off darting attacks by raiders who ran at them screaming their war cries and attempting to cave in their skulls with axes. The pace slowed as these irritant attacks came from all directions.

'Look to the sides and rear!' screamed Rudolf.

Conrad and the other novices turned and began walking backwards, as did sergeants in the second line, who pulled the boys back into their ranks. A spear came from nowhere to land in the chest of the sergeant next to Conrad. He groaned and fell forward on the ground. Conrad knelt down to tend to him but then heard Hans' voice.

'Conrad!'

He leapt up to see a black-faced demon coming at him with a spear levelled at his belly. He could not duck out of the way for that would mean the brother knight in the front rank behind him would be skewered in the back, so he jumped forward and caught the spear point on his shield, the iron head going through the wood and leather and stopping a few inches from his body. In a split-second he turned the axe in his hand and swung down on the helmet of the enemy warrior. He thought the man was wearing a helmet but it turned out he wore only leather on his head and so the spike easily went through the covering and deep into his skull. In fact it went so deep that when he crumpled in a heap on the ground Conrad could

454

not pull the spike out of the man's head. And to make matters worse the warrior's spear was still embedded in his shield.

'Hans,' he called, 'hack his head off.'

Hans next to him looked at his predicament and began chopping at the dead man's neck with his own axe. After half a dozen blows he had severed the head to allow Conrad to retrieve his axe.

'And the spear shaft,' Conrad requested.

Hans cut through the haft with a single blow and they continued their advance to the Sir Helmold's pavilion, Conrad having a spear point lodged in his shield and an enemy head impaled on his axe.

They stepped over dead knights and squires, avoiding maddened, wounded horses that galloped past them as they finally closed upon the great pavilion. They gave a great cheer as they discovered that Sir Helmold was still alive, fighting sword in hand beside Thalibald, the latter's two sons also standing beside their father outside the tent. At least fifty other knights were also standing with their lord, dead enemy warriors at their feet along with a score of crusaders who had also been slain. And also there were masters Berthold, Bertram and Mathias, bloodied but unbowed as they stood with eyes full of fire and swords dipped in the blood of the enemy. They smiled when they saw the phalanx of Sword Brothers arrive.

Horns were sounding to signal the withdrawal of the raiders, who melted back into the forest.

Sir Helmold, still roaring drunk, was enraged at their cowardice. 'Rally to me, warriors of Christ! We will chase these devils back to hell where they belong.'

With that he bent down, picked up a large silver goblet, drained it and threw it aside. He then rested his sword on his shoulder and began walking from the tent's entrance in a westerly direction towards the forest. The crusaders, equally drunk with both drink and bloodlust, cheered and followed him. Berthold looked alarmed and chased after Sir Helmold, followed by Bertram, Mathias and Thalibald. A great argument ensued in which Thalibald prevailed upon his friend not to lead an expedition into the forest at night, the result of which would be more crusader casualties. He was advised by the castellans to secure the camp first and wait for the dawn when a more sober assessment of the situation could be made.

While this was going on Rameke joined Conrad and the other novices and told them what had happened.

'The raiders tried to kill us all but Sir Helmold's knights rallied to their lord and fought them off. The rest of the camp was not so lucky, it seems.

He saw Conrad holding down the severed head with one foot while he tugged at his axe to remove the spike from its bloody holder.

'A souvenir, Conrad?'

'He's going to take it back to Wenden to give it as a present to Daina,' said Hans, grinning.

'A betrothal gift,' added Anton.

'Meet your new brother,' said Johann.

Conrad blushed. 'Shut up.'

Rameke shook his head. 'I don't think my sister would appreciate such a gift, Conrad.'

Conrad gave one great tug and freed his axe spike. 'Just ignore them, Rameke.'

'Everyone knows that Conrad loves your sister, Rameke,' said Hans, 'though Conrad thinks that it is a great secret.'

Rameke looked at Conrad. 'Really? You love my sister? Most odd. My father will be delighted.'

'You must not say anything to him,' said Conrad in alarm, forgetting that Daina had already informed her father of her love for the novice. 'It will lead to much trouble.'

'Much merriment, more like,' quipped Anton.

Conrad kicked away the bloody head, which landed at Henke's feet.

'A gift, for me, you are too kind?' He pointed at Conrad and the others. 'No sleep for you four. Scour the camp to see if there are any wounded. Take the Christians to the surgeon's tent and bring any pagans here.'

Parties of sergeants and crusaders were already conducting a search of the ransacked camp, while the squires attended to the burning tents and carts and tried to round up the horses and mules. In the dark it was a hopeless task but the coming of the dawn made their work easier. It also revealed the extent of the damage and loss of life.

Sir Helmold's face was purple with fury as his commanders reported the casualties: ten knights, twenty-three of their men-at-arms and fifty squires slain and sixty others wounded. Fifty tents, a score of carts and twelve wagons wrecked and thirty mules killed. It was a miracle that the main stabling area had been positioned to the west of the camp and had thus escaped any loss. Nevertheless, the raiders had inflicted much damage, not least to Sir Helmold's reputation. He bristled with rage and he and his fellow knights thirsted for revenge.

456

The first to feel their wrath were the ten wounded pagans who were found in the camp. Over forty of their companions had been killed, most around Sir Helmold's pavilion, and now their bodies were collected and hurled onto a funeral pyre that the squires built south of the camp. Prisoners were usually given the opportunity to recant their pagan faith and accept baptism into the Holy Church before being incinerated if they refused, but Sir Helmold was adamant that they should die. So he ate a breakfast of fruit and meat broth washed down by wine as the prisoners, chained to stakes sunk into the ground in front of his pavilion with piles of burning brushwood up to their chests, writhed and screamed in agony as their flesh melted from their bones.

Conrad was one of the onlookers who were assembled around the execution site to witness the deaths but he turned away from the horror. When he witnessed executions all he saw was his pale-faced father being led to his death. Afterwards, when the charred, blackened corpses hung from the stakes and the air was heavy with the aroma of roasted human flesh, he made his way back to the Sword Brother camp alone, his still bloody axe tucked in his belt. Later that day he assisted in washing the bodies of three sergeants from Wenden who had been killed during the night. They would be transported back to the castle where they would be buried in the cemetery. The garrisons of Segewold and Kremon had also suffered a small number of slain and so a column of two-wheeled carts borrowed from the crusaders left the camp just after midday, a score of sergeants detailed to escort the bodies back to their last resting places. They would return to camp after they had completed their mission.

Security was increased in the days afterwards as everyone waited for news of the bishop's army. At night they all stood to arms in expectation of another pagan assault but none came. Ten days after the raid a party of Liv horsemen arrived with news that Caupo had ridden south to join the bishop whose army had relieved Kokenhusen. Sir Helmold was 'invited' to join him and the other lords at the river directly south of his position in order to cross the Dvina and launch the campaign in Lithuania. The riders also brought a message from Grand Master Volquin ordering the Sword Brothers to march with all haste to the Dvina. The crusaders and brethren struck camp and marched south on the track towards the Lithuanian bridgehead in high spirits.

But unknown to them and the bishop three thousand warriors had crossed over the river the day before to reinforce those soldiers under Prince Stecse who held the northern end of the pontoon bridge.

There was great rejoicing at Kokenhusen where Thalibald was united with his king. The bishop and Grand Master Volquin also warmly embraced the Liv chief and his eldest son. A service of thanksgiving was held in the castle chapel for their safe deliverance and the relief of all the Sword Brother castles along the Dvina. All that remained was the destruction of the Lithuanian bridgehead on the northern riverbank of the Dvina, which was the main topic of conversation at a council of war held the next day.

The crusader army was camped to the north of the castle, the views from which provided an excellent observation point over the river to the east and the Lithuanian bridgehead in particular. The bishop, grand master, his castellans, Caupo, Thalibald and the crusader commanders stood on the castle's eastern wall and looked towards the enemy position. It was a beautiful summer's day and the lush green of the land contrasted sharply with the deep blue waters of the Dvina as it disappeared towards the east.

Master Griswold pointed at the pontoon bridge that spanned the river. 'The Lithuanians brought over a great many soldiers a week ago and have strengthened their defences this side of the river.'

'They mean to stay, then,' remarked Sir Helmold, whose humour had improved since the arrival of the bishop, though he still thirsted for revenge over those who had had the impertinence to raid his camp.

'What defences?' queried Volquin.

'My scouts report that they have dug a ditch around the whole of their camp next to the river,' said Griswold, 'the earth dug from which they have used to form a rampart behind it. They have also placed sharpened stakes on the slope of the rampart that faces outwards, though as yet have not erected a timber wall upon the rampart.'

'A few sticks will avail them not,' sneered Sir Helmold to murmurs of agreement from the other three German lords present.

Volquin was not so sure. He pointed to the northern riverbank. 'You see how the land is flat and largely devoid of trees around the bridgehead, lord bishop. This would make a frontal assault against the enemy defences costly, I fear. And we will not be able to make use of our horsemen against the Lithuanians, thus negating our greatest asset. A frontal assault may lead to high casualties.'

The bishop toyed with the plain silver pectoral cross hanging around his neck. 'What would you suggest, grand master?'

'The Lithuanians must know by now that Daugerutis is dead and his army destroyed. I believe they can be persuaded to leave Livonia and return to Lithuania.'

'I must protest, lord bishop,' said Sir Helmold. 'We cannot allow these pagans, who have despoiled this land and your own reputation, to escape.'

The other lords nodded in agreement.

'I would agree with Sir Helmold,' said Caupo. 'Many of my people and members of your flock, lord bishop, have died at the hands of the Lithuanians these past few weeks. To let them go will make us and you look weak.'

'And let us not forget, lord bishop,' said Thalibald, 'that events in Livonia will be known to Lembit and his chiefs in Estonia, to say nothing of the Russians further to the east. If we show any weakness we may unwittingly invite them all to attack us.'

The bishop continued to rub his cross as he stared at the bridge of boats across the Dvina.

'Good faith,' he said at last.

'Bishop?' said a confused Volquin next to him.

'In good faith,' continued the bishop, 'we entered into a treaty with the Lithuanians and our reward was to see Livonia ravaged by their treachery. In good faith we paid Grand Duke Daugerutis a king's ransom to get back those who had been stolen from their families and homes, and our reward was to witness the slaughter of a great many of King Caupo's people. In good faith the Governor of Riga trusted Prince Vsevolod to be sincere and truthful in his relations with us, and our reward has been Vsevolod's silence while a hostile army has crossed over the Dvina to strike at our hearts.

'Grand Master Volquin, there is no man I esteem more in this kingdom than you, but in this matter I must agree with the opinion of Sir Helmold. The Lithuanians must be expelled from Livonia and their bridge of boats destroyed. It is like a dagger pointed at the heart of Christ's kingdom and cannot be tolerated.'

'Might not the preservation of the bridge be to our advantage, lord bishop?' said Sir Helmold casually.

The bishop looked at him quizzically. 'To our advantage in what way?'

'For our campaign in Lithuania,' answered Sir Helmold.

Volquin looked at him in alarm, as did his castellans. They knew as well as he that Livonia did not have the resources to fight a war in Lithuania in addition to the inevitable conflict with the Estonians that would break out sooner or later.

'There will be no campaign in Lithuania,' said the bishop firmly. He pointed at the pontoon bridge. 'That bridge has prevented trade along the Dvina and must be destroyed as quickly as possible, otherwise the merchants in Riga will starve and my treasury will empty.

'I give my blessing for the destruction of the abominable pagan bridgehead you see before you, but I forbid any crossing of the river. The Lithuanians will have to wait.'

'I must protest, lord bishop,' said Sir Helmold. The bishop froze him with a stare.

'You will have your revenge against the pagans, Sir Helmold, but be wary of allowing personal vanity to cloud your judgement. I would rather see you unsheathe your sword against the Estonians than the Lithuanians.'

Sir Helmold guffawed. 'Have no fear, lord bishop, after we have butchered the Lithuanians we can deal with the Estonians.'

The other crusaders grunted their approval but the bishop shook his head.

'One of the obligations of being a servant of Christ, Sir Helmold, is that once you have given your word you are forced to keep it. We have an agreement with the Estonians and cannot break it.'

'Does breaking an oath to pagans count, lord bishop?' queried one of the crusader lords, a barrel-chested individual who obviously disliked being shorter than either Caupo or Thalibald by the scornful looks he gave them.

'It is an interesting theoretical question, Count Horton,' replied the bishop, 'though one for a gathering of cardinals, I think, rather than to be debated on the eve of battle. My decision is final. We destroy the pagans on this side of the river and burn their accursed bridge. May God be with you all.'

*****

Stecse stood on the earth bank and looked west towards the rising ramparts of Kokenhusen Castle, the banners of the Sword Brothers flying from its towers. He had left two hundred men at the castle to continue the semblance of a siege but had withdrawn them when his scouts had reported the approach of the bishop's army. Now they and the eight hundred men who had also been committed to the siege were in the great camp that guarded the northern end of the bridge of boats that spanned the Dvina. Together with the three thousand he had ordered to cross the river he had more than four thousand men to defend the bridgehead against the crusaders. The great semi-circular earth rampart that surrounded the camp, together with the ditch in front of it, was enough to negate the crusaders using their mailed horsemen in an assault, and that gave him hope that he could beat off a Christian attack.

Vetseke standing beside must have been reading his thoughts.

'The Christians will be attacking this camp soon, prince. I would advise getting your men back across the river before then.'

'I cannot do that before I give the crusaders a bloody nose,' replied Stecse, still observing Kokenhusen. He noticed that Vetseke did not look at his former home once. Perhaps the memory of its loss was still too raw.

'The grand duke is dead and his army destroyed. If I retreat across the river with my tail between my legs then the campaign will have been a complete waste. I can at least save some honour by defeating the Christians.'

'You will fail,' said Vetseke flatly. 'Even if you beat off one attack the bishop will summon his engines of war to hurl fire and stone against you. And all the while you stand here the other dukes will make war on your lands in Lithuania.'

'The forts of the grand duke are strong and well sited,' replied Stecse defensively, 'and they are well manned. But I cannot withdraw without inflicting a defeat upon the Christians. I owe that to the grand duke at least.'

Vetseke smiled faintly. It all came down to honour and vengeance. Stecse would fight a battle to salve his conscience and redeem Lithuanian honour for a dead grand duke. It was all so ridiculous, but then perhaps he was no better. He was, after all, standing on this bank of earth instead of accepting reality and availing himself of the hospitality of Vladimir of Polotsk. What made him keep returning to Livonia? The vain hope that he would once again sit in the great hall of Kokenhusen? But this was his home and he was loath to leave it.

'And you?' said Stecse.

'I will take my men out of camp tonight, to seek the sanctuary of the forest.'

'A precarious existence,' remarked Stecse, 'you would be welcome to join me in Lithuania.'

'I thank you for your kind offer, prince,' said Vetseke, 'but I prefer to stay in my homeland.'

'Even though it is occupied by the enemy?'

'I hope it will not always be so.'

The sound of horses' hooves made them turn around as thirty or more mail-clad riders halted at the foot of the rampart. One of them dismounted and made his way up the bank and removed his helmet. Vetseke was surprised: he was no more than a boy. Is this what the Lithuanians were reduced to?

'I thought I asked you to stay on the other side of the river,' snapped Stecse irritably.

'I could not remain idle while you fought the heathens, father.'

Stecse shook his head and looked at Vetseke. 'This is my son Mindaugas, lord prince. And this is Prince Vetseke, Mindaugas, an ally who fights by our side.'

The boy with the long face bowed his head to Vetseke. 'An honour, sir.'

Vetseke smiled. Honour. There was that word again.

Mindaugas looked beyond the camp to the area of flat land that had been cleared of trees for hundreds of yards to provide building material for shelters, firewood and stakes that had been hammered into the outward-facing side of the rampart where they had been sharpened.

'Any sign of the enemy, father?' he asked excitedly.

'Not yet.'

'Perhaps they will not show their faces, these Christians. I have heard that they are frightened to fight.'

'Oh, they will fight,' said Stecse.

Mindaugas grinned. 'Good.'

'What of Prince Vsevolod?' asked Vetseke.

'What of him?' sneered Stecse.

'Will he not come to assist you in your hour of need?' pressed Vetseke.

'Vsevolod looks to his own interests,' spat Stecse, 'we do not need him.'

He placed a hand on his son's shoulders. 'Mindaugas wishes to fight in his first battle, is that not so?'

'Yes, sir,' beamed Mindaugas.

'You are to be granted your wish,' said Vetseke, 'for surely as day follows night the Christians will be here soon enough.'

Mindaugas looked at the ditch. 'This ditch can be used to bury them after the battle.'

Vetseke smiled politely but said nothing. More likely the ditch, and the camp for that matter, would be full of Lithuanian dead after the fighting was over. He had seen what damage the crossbowmen of the crusaders could cause, to say nothing of their machines that had battered down the defences of his own stronghold. And yet he liked Stecse and thought him an intelligent individual who did not underestimate his enemy. That was good, for he would need all his wits to battle the bishop's army when it arrived.

When darkness came he took his leave of Stecse and slipped out of camp with his men, striking towards the northeast to avoid any crusader outposts that might have been established around the bridgehead. He had become accustomed to travelling at night, like a spirit condemned to wander the earth for all eternity. His men were the remnants of those who had taken part in the rebellion the previous year, individuals who, like him, had no homes or families, or any future. He told them that one day they would return to their villages when the Christians had been defeated and the old ways had been restored. But he no longer believed his own words. Probably neither did they. But they stayed with him because they had nowhere else to go.

*****

The bishop's army left camp at dawn, long files of knights on horseback carrying maces, short spears and axes, riding with their bodyguards, retainers and personal companions. Normally these soldiers, the flower of north German chivalry, fought on horseback but today would battle on foot to take the pagan camp and plant the banner of the Bishop of Riga among their corpses. Then came the squires of the knights armed with maces and axes and wearing the surcoats of their masters. Finally there were the foot soldiers, a mixture of professional crossbowmen and spearmen plus the retainers of the knights. Three thousand crusaders in total, all intent on wiping out the Lithuanian bridgehead.

The bishop once again had his own mounted bodyguard, a score of mail-clad soldiers wearing Riga's coat of arms on their shields and surcoats and carrying a great banner bearing the cross keys of the city. He also had his own foot guards, of course, but they had been left behind in the city along with the militia after Archdeacon Stefan had protested that if they left Riga it would be as naked and defenceless as a newborn lamb.

King Caupo, Thalibald, Waribule and Rameke rode with the bishop and Bishop Theodoric, a hundred mounted Livs accompanying their king while the other eight hundred of his warriors tramped behind on foot.

In the vanguard of the army were the Sword Brothers: seventy-three brother knights and one hundred and eighty sergeants. Tiny in comparison to the number of crusaders, they were the most disciplined soldiers in all Livonia. The Sword Brothers had never been defeated in battle, the enemy had captured none of their castles and men spoke in hushed tones of reverence whenever they passed by. They were God's holy warriors, men pure of heart and spirit, and wherever they went victory surely followed.

'It's going to piss down with rain,' said Henke, looking up at the sky heaped with grey clouds. 'I hate fighting in the rain.'

'I thought you loved fighting, whatever the weather conditions,' commented Rudolf.

The masters rode at the head of the order with Volquin but the brother knights and sergeants of the garrisons stayed together. Though they had almost completed their training Lukas insisted that Conrad, Anton, Johann and Hans kept close to him on the march. They did so today, which had dawned overcast and cool, with a slight southerly breeze ruffling the dozens of standards that flew among the army behind them. Lukas and the novices rode behind Rudolf and Henke, the latter being in an irritable mood.

'Not when it means wading through mud to get to grips with the enemy,' complained Henke. 'We should leave it to those who have come for the summer from Germany.'

'That would not be charitable,' said Lukas.

'Nor very commendable,' added Rudolf.

'You can forget taking any prisoners,' moaned Henke. 'Any that try to give themselves up will have their throats slit.'

'I'm sure that will alleviate your reluctance to fight in the rain,' said Rudolf.

'Killing prisoners is a sin,' said Walter from behind Johann and Anton.

Henke rolled his eyes. 'Killing pagans is not a sin, *brother.*'

'Prisoners,' replied Walter, 'whatever their religion, must be given the opportunity to be baptised into the Holy Church before their fate is decided.'

'I leave that decision to God,' said Henke. 'I kill them and He decides what to do with their souls. Saves a lot of time and effort.'

Walter was not amused but Rudolf and Lukas laughed. Conrad felt the first spots of rain on his face and so did Henke.

'And so it begins,' he complained. 'By midday we will all be soaked and covered in mud.' He pulled his cloak around him.

'Not if the Lithuanians retreat or surrender,' said Lukas.

A pained expression crept over Henke's face. 'That would be the final straw: marching out to get soaked and covered in filth and we don't even get to fight.'

Rudolf shook his head. 'Sometimes life can be so very cruel, Henke.'

464

But the Lithuanians did not retreat or surrender and after they had marched the short distance from Kokenhusen to the enemy bridgehead the crusaders began deploying for battle. The horses were gathered and taken to the rear, the younger squires being responsible for their safekeeping. Conrad had noticed that there were other novices among the Sword Brothers now, boys younger than himself who accompanied the garrisons of the order's other castles. They led the horses to the rear while he and Wenden's other three novices took their place in the battle line.

'Keep your eyes peeled and your shields tight to your bodies,' Lukas instructed them as they walked across the flat, open ground towards the Lithuanian defences. 'The enemy will have archers behind that rampart.'

Conrad could not see anyone on the enemy rampart. 'Perhaps they have all fled, Brother Lukas.'

'They are there,' replied Lukas, 'they just aren't showing their faces.'

'They are not stupid,' said Rudolf, 'they don't want to get a crossbow bolt in their face.'

'Pity we left all our crossbowmen behind,' remarked Henke.

The Sword Brothers had brought only their brother knights, sergeants and novices into the field, leaving their mercenaries to guard the castles, which still might be attacked by Lithuanians attempting to recross the Dvina. And as no one trusted the Estonians the castles along the Gauja had to be manned at all times.

'Caupo will lend us a few archers,' said Rudolf.

The mood was relaxed and confident as the army deployed into its assault positions. It assumed a concave shape as it formed up around four hundred paces from the earth rampart that surrounded the enemy camp. There was an entrance cut in the centre of the rampart that was blocked by a pile of tree trunks festooned with iron spikes. The only way to get into the camp was over the rampart.

It took an hour for the army to get into its assault positions, eventually forming five separate 'battles.' The bishop bestowed the place of honour – the right wing – to Count Horton and a thousand crusaders, and to their left was a similar-sized division of crusaders under Sir Helmold. In the centre of the line stood the bishop with his bodyguard and a thousand crusaders. On the left flank of these men was the small 'battle' of Sword Brothers, while Caupo and his nine hundred Livs formed the army's left wing that extended almost to the river.

The king sent a number of scouts to reconnoitre the enemy's position while the army arranged itself, the men riding their ponies to within a few yards of the rampart. As they neared the Lithuanian defences a number of warriors appeared on top of the rampart to launch spears at the riders, two being struck and killed before the others retired.

'You see, I told you they were there,' said Lukas.

The Sword Brothers deployed on foot just as they would on horseback, with the brother knights in the front rank and the sergeants behind in two ranks. Thus within their division the white-clad soldiers of the various garrisons of the order formed seven separate groups, each one of three lines, standing side by side. The wind had increased now and the drizzle had turned into a light rain that blew into the crusaders' faces.

Caupo sent riders to the other divisions to inform them that there was a wide, deep ditch in front of the rampart, the latter also being decorated with sharpened stakes. It was Rameke who rode to report to the Sword Brothers. He nodded to Conrad as he spoke to Rudolf.

'My father is sending archers to support your attack, Brother Rudolf.'

'Thank him from me,' said Rudolf, 'they will be most useful.'

'When do we attack?'

Rudolf looked up at the dark grey clouds. 'Soon, otherwise we will sink into the mud and won't be able to move. Isn't that right, Henke?'

Henke said nothing but merely stared defiantly at the enemy rampart as the raindrops hit him.

'God be with you, Rameke,' said Rudolf.

Rameke smiled. 'And with you.'

He raised his hand to Conrad and then rode back to the left where his father stood in front of hundreds of Liv warriors. On the way he passed fifty archers that Thalibald had sent to support the order's assault. They were armed with bows made from yew that could shoot an arrow up to a range of two hundred and fifty paces. The archers wore no armour or helmets and so were placed behind the Sword Brothers, from where they could shoot their missiles over their heads towards the enemy. The archers with Thalibald adopted a similar tactic. In contrast, the crossbowmen accompanying the crusader 'battles' deployed in front of their divisions, a line of spearmen walking a few paces ahead of them to provide protection.

Conrad gripped the handle of his axe as the rain became heavier. There was a blast of trumpets from where the bishop sat on his horse beside Caupo in front of his and the king's mounted bodyguards. Trumpets coming from the divisions of Sir

Helmold and Count Horton answered the call, and on the left the Livs began banging the shafts of their spears on the insides of their shields.

Rudolf turned and raised his mace. 'God with us!'

The Sword Brothers answered 'God with us!' and began walking forward, the brother knights putting on their full-face helmets. Conrad felt a tingle of excitement course through him and momentarily forgot the rain that was striking his face. The visibility was beginning to diminish as the rain got heavier but he could still see no enemy troops on the rampart.

*****

The earth rampart was slippery now as Stecse scrambled up it with his son by his side. He had been observing the crusader army all morning, watching them as they formed into five divisions to surround his encampment. And now they were attacking at last. At the foot of the whole length of the rampart stood his warriors, the majority equipped with shields, helmets or leather caps, spears and leather armour, a few wearing mail but only the chiefs armed with swords. The majority had axes and knives tucked in their belts or carried the fearsome *kistien*. His few archers stood fifty paces back from the rampart, ready to shoot their arrows in a high trajectory onto the heads of the crusaders. He pointed to the left.

'Those are the soldiers that the Bishop of Riga brings with him every year from the lands over the sea, my son.'

They both heard the symphony of trumpets and saw the divisions begin to move forward.

'You see those men in front, Mindaugas?' said Stecse, pointing at the vanguard of the crusader divisions. His son nodded.

'They are the crossbowmen whose bolts can go through shields and armour. But their weapons cannot shoot through banks of earth.'

Mindaugas looked to the right, at the white-clad soldiers moving steadily towards them and the much larger brown block of warriors to their left.

'There are few Sword Brothers, father.'

'Quantity does not always equate to quality, my son.'

'Can we hold them?' asked Mindaugas, his father noting concern in his voice.

Stecse smiled at him. 'They do not outnumber us and we have the advantage of fighting behind a ditch and rampart, which also prevents them from using their crossbows. We can hold them.'

But even if they could not he had given orders that a party of horsemen was to get Mindaugas back to the other side of the river in the event of a disaster.

'To your position,' Stecse ordered.

Mindaugas' position was with the reserve – five hundred men deployed near the bridge of boats, well to the rear.

'I would prefer to stay with you, father.'

'Do as you are told!' barked Stecse. 'I have no time to babysit you and fight a battle at the same time.'

Mindaugas slunk away, humbled, while his father continued to observe the oncoming enemy.

*****

It was raining heavily now, the sturdy leather soles on the feet of Conrad's mail chausses sinking into the sodden ground and slowing his pace. Everyone else was having the same difficulty and in front of him he could hear Henke's voice coming from within his helmet.

'Bastard rain. I hate the rain.'

And still he could see no enemy on the rampart. They were around two hundred paces from the earth bank now and behind him came a series of twangs as the Liv archers stood and released their bowstrings, sending a volley or arrows arching into the rain-filled sky to drop behind the Lithuanian fortification.

'Keep your shields up,' bellowed Lukas as they continued to walk forward. Seconds later a volley of Lithuanian arrows came hurtling towards them. They immediately halted and crouched under their shields, the arrows either thumping into them or slamming into the wet earth. The Livs shot another volley and the Sword Brothers continued their advance. They were now less than a hundred paces from the ditch. To their left the Livs gave a great cheer and charged forward as another volley of enemy arrows was shot into the sky. Once more the order's soldiers stopped and sheltered under their shields, as Thalibald's warriors were hit and felled by missiles.

The Livs swarmed into the ditch and hacked their way through the wooden stakes as the top of the rampart was suddenly filled with Lithuanians, who hurled a torrent of spears at them before charging at the attackers.

There was a loud clap of thunder and the heavens opened.

The raindrops battered the two sides as the Lithuanians ascended the inside of the rampart to meet the Christian soldiers who were now swarming into the ditch on the other side. They reached the muddy top of the bank and hurled their spears at the enemy below, dozens being cut down as the crossbowmen in the front ranks of the crusader divisions were at last presented with targets.

The heavy rain loosened the stakes that were meant to stop any attack and soon Livs and crusaders were knocking them aside and scrambling up the rampart, before being swept back by a Lithuanian tide as Stecse's men hurled themselves at their opponents. The ditch was soon filled with men fighting with weapons and fists as the rain pelted them from above and liquid mud sloshed around their feet and ankles.

More and more Lithuanians poured over the top of the rampart and added to the mud-splattered press of men battling on the obverse side of the rampart and in the ditch. There were more claps of thunder and the rain became torrential, greatly reducing visibility and negating any command and control that may have existed. In the front ranks Count Horton and Sir Helmold battled with sword and shield against the leather-clad pagans, their bodyguards fighting and dying beside them. Men killed those who were in front of them and then pressed on, or were cut down and fell into the mud, some face down and drowning as their bodies were trampled on and their faces pressed down into the ooze. It was horror and chaos as the storm vented its fury on the thousands of men below. But amid the carnage one Christian division maintained its discipline and cohesion.

When they had been peppered with enemy arrows the Sword Brothers had halted and taken cover under their shields. To their left Thalibald's Livs had not halted their advance in the face of Lithuanian archers and neither had the bishop's division on their right flank. This meant that they reached the ditch and rampart later than the other 'battles', which were already battling for their lives against a well-planned Lithuanian counterattack that threatened to stop the Christian assault in its tracks. Despite the bravery of the knights they could not break the Lithuanian resistance and the ditch was slowly filling up with German dead. It was the same with Thalibald's Livs, who were literally hacking Lithuanians to pieces with their axes but were unable to make any progress. It was left to a small group of white-clad soldiers to affect a breakthrough.

Conrad had reached the ditch unharmed, two arrows lodged in his shield, and now he and the others clambered down its side and then up the other side to wrestle free the stakes. Fierce fighting was raging either side of the phalanx of Sword Brothers, which had subconsciously closed ranks to make a more compact formation.

In front of Conrad the brother knights pushed aside stakes and clawed their way up the muddy bank. He followed, looking left and right to ensure Hans, Johann and Anton were still with him. Behind the sergeants likewise clambered up the slope that was fast turning into a mudslide. His heart was beating as he used the spike on his axe to pull himself up. And then he was on top of the rampart and could see the hundreds of enemy tents and huts in the camp below. Then he heard horns and saw a mass of enemy soldiers forming up at the foot of the rampart. They had been spotted. But now they could attack downhill and scatter the heathens at the base of the rampart. Except that the rampart was now a muddy morass and keeping one's feet was difficult enough – a charge was all but impossible.

The brother knights dressed their ranks as the sergeants pressed in on them from behind and then the whole formation moved downhill. Immediately Conrad lost his footing and fell on his backside, Hans hauling him to his feet before Anton's right foot skidded and he fell onto Henke in the front rank. The latter turned and pushed up his helmet.

'Idiot! Have a care or I'll butcher you myself.'

He shoved Anton back and pulled down his helmet but all along the line brother knights and sergeants were slipping and sliding as they descended the rampart in a haphazard manner. And still the rain lashed them mercilessly. The front rank managed to lurch forward the final few steps between them and the Lithuanians to begin a mêlée that quickly degenerated into a mud-wrestling match.

The fighting soon spread over a wide area as the Sword Brothers cut their way into the enemy ranks but then found themselves surrounded as they advanced deeper into the camp. There was no reserve to back them up; the Livs and crusaders were still battling on the other side of the rampart. Soon the Sword Brothers halted as they fought enemies to their front, on their flanks and in their rear. Their formation also widened as they launched attacks from the flanks against the ever-increasing numbers of Lithuanians who appeared seemingly out of nowhere. In no time Conrad and the other novices were in the front rank fighting beside Henke, Rudolf and Lukas.

Normally Conrad would have been in constant movement in response to his training but in the mud it was a major effort not to fall over. So he planted his left foot forward and his right back and fended off a series of Lithuanian attacks. It wasn't difficult to do because these enemy soldiers were for the most part unarmoured and ill equipped. He killed a spearman who tried to stick the point in his belly but skidded forward and presented the back of his bare head to Conrad, who obligingly brought down his axe to sever the man's spinal cord. Another Lithuanian, armed with an axe similar to his, made a clumsy two-handed swing at Conrad's head that missed when he ducked. The momentum of the swing caused the man to fall over, whereupon Conrad pressed his shield onto the man's chest and chopped at his face half a dozen times with his own axe, reducing it to an unrecognisable pulp.

He removed his left arm from his shield's padded leather squab and used its leather strap to sling it on his back, then transferred the axe to his left hand and drew his sword. With this combination he beat off a succession of half-hearted enemy attacks, all the time ensuring that Hans and Anton were either side of him. But after a few minutes he noticed that the Lithuanians were falling back, shuffling towards the right. The rain was still heavy as Rudolf removed his helmet and bellowed for everyone to form lines once more.

Conrad suddenly felt cold and became aware that every part of his body was wet, the only dry bit being the crown of his head under his helmet.

'Are you unhurt?' he said to Hans.

His friend nodded and grinned. Conrad looked at Anton.

'Are you in one piece?'

'Aside from being half-drowned,' replied his friend. Johann beside him leaned forward and raised his sword to Conrad.

'What are we waiting for?' said Anton in frustration.

Conrad shrugged as Rudolf consulted with the other deputy commanders and everyone stood and sank up to their ankles in mud. In the distance Conrad saw other Lithuanians moving from left to right and wondered why the Sword Brothers were not killing them. But Rudolf was unwilling to move further forward until the other divisions had entered the camp and so he grouped his men together and waited. What he did not know was that Thalibald's Livs on the left had finally stormed the rampart and were flooding into the camp.

*****

Stecse had been standing on the reverse slope of the rampart near the blocked entrance when a subordinate brought him the news that it had been breached on the right.

'The Sword Brothers and Livs, lord, they have broken through.'

He now had a choice: commit the reserve to eject them from the camp, or use it to shield a general retreat across the river. He chose the latter and ordered the officers grouped round him to give the command to withdraw. The crusaders were still being held on the left and in the centre but the crossbowmen were taking a steady toll of his men, shooting at close range those on top of the rampart, the bolts going through their wooden shields with ease. What was the point of holding the north of the river now that the grand duke was dead and his dreams of a greater Lithuania in tatters? The pounding rain was surely a sign from the gods that they should leave this land polluted by the Christian faith and return to the green and pure domains of the Lithuanian tribes.

A tumult above made Stecse look up to see one, two, half a dozen enemy soldiers sliding down the greasy rampart, their heads encased in full-face helmets and their bodies protected by mail armour.

He drew his sword. 'Rally to me!'

He thrust his sword into the belly of the first knight who came at him, who did not have time to rise to his feet before he was killed. A score of his warriors came to his side and hacked and slashed at the invaders, overpowering them by weight of numbers rather than skill with weapons. Stecse duelled with a knight taller than him, desperately trying to keep his feet while his opponent's mace splintered the edge of his shield and then split it in half. But this blow resulted in one of the flanges getting stuck in the wood and, before the crusader could yank it free, Stecse drove the point of his sword into the knight's groin, causing him to collapse in agony. He was finished off when a warrior thrust the point of his dagger into his neck. Stecse raised his sword and his men cheered, and a crossbowman on the top of the rampart released his trigger to send a bolt into the prince's belly. A spear thrown by the man standing next to Stecse killed the crossbowman. The prince was dragged away as his chiefs began withdrawing their men from the camp's defences.

The process was slow, made worse by the rain sheeting down, but gradually the chiefs succeeded in pulling their men back from the rampart and down the reverse slope, to reform them in shield walls that edged back slowly. They may have been pagans but it was an ordered withdrawal towards the pontoon bridge. Stecse, meanwhile, his face pale as the blood gushed from his belly, was dragged to a hut where a healer examined the wound. In the excitement everyone forgot about the enemy breakthrough on the right and the necessity of committing the reserve.

The five hundred warriors stood shivering in the rain, water coursing off their helmets as their commander, a thin, balding chief of the Selonians, waited for his orders. In front of him, equally sodden, Mindaugas sat on his horse with the men his father had assigned to look after him.

'I cannot sit here doing nothing,' he uttered in frustration.

'Your father's orders were quite clear,' remarked the commander of the horsemen.

'I will reward you richly if look the other way,' said Mindaugas.

The commander was unimpressed. 'Can you give me a new head?'

Mindaugas looked at him. 'A new head?'

'That's right, young lord, for when your father discovers that I let you go and play hero he will have my head.'

Mindaugas, out-foxed, pulled his cloak around him and looked sullenly ahead, to see a rider on a pony approaching. He halted in front of him and raised his hand.

'You father has been wounded, lord, he orders you to lead the retreat across the river.'

Mindaugas spurred his horse forward and rode back up the track to find his father. The commander cursed and ordered his men to follow him as he rode after Stecse's son. And just in front of the bridge the reserve stood like statues in the rain.

*****

Also standing in the rain were the Sword Brothers who had suddenly found themselves ignored by both sides. To their left Thalibald's Livs were still battling the Lithuanians, with the latter now separated from the rest of their army and being pushed back towards the river. On the order's right flank the bishop's division had captured the rampart and was now advancing directly south towards the bridge of boats. Thus the Sword Brothers had no one to fight.

Rudolf raised his sword and took off his helmet. 'Move forward through the camp,' he shouted, 'but stay alert.'

He and the other commanders reorganised their men, deploying them into two lines to extend their frontage so they could more easily clear the camp of any Lithuanian stragglers. The rain seemed to be abating slightly though was still falling steadily. As they moved forward it became apparent that two hundred and fifty men would not be able to clear a camp covering several hectares and so they were split into small groups to search the encampment.

Lukas formed Conrad, Hans, Anton and Johann into one such group as the rain stopped and sent them on their way.

'Make sure you can see other groups and fall back if you come across any large bodies of the enemy,' he warned them.

Most of the shelters were small two-man affairs made from wicker panels but there were also wooden huts and larger tents, with temporary stables fashioned from branches and sheets. Conrad and his companions walked between shelters, stooping down to see if any were occupied. None were. They walked past rain-filled cooking pots hanging over extinguished campfires and hastily vacated tents. They could hear fighting all around them but in the immediate vicinity there was no one. Occasionally they caught a glimpse of enemy soldiers fleeing towards the river but this part of the spacious camp seemed to be deserted. They kept glancing left and right to see brother knights and sergeants examining empty tents and shelters.

There was a rumble of thunder and then it began raining again, a light downfall at first that became increasingly heavy as the sky darkened once more. Conrad's mail feet sank in the mud as he stepped forward. He looked at the others.

'I'm tempted to shelter in one of the huts until this passes.'

'Good idea,' said Anton, 'before we all drown.'

'I wonder if the enemy has left any food in the huts,' remarked Hans. The others laughed.

They continued on, stepping over pools of water that were forming all around as the rain teemed down. But of the enemy they saw nothing. The visibility had reduced to such an extent that they could see barely fifty paces in front of them. On they tramped, coming across four huts, outside which a number of horses were tethered.

'Stay alert,' called Conrad, his sixth sense telling him that they were no longer alone.

The others came alongside to form a line as they approached the first hut, a crude structure with log walls and a wicker roof. It had no windows, a hole in the roof to allow the escape of smoke and a doorway covered by a large patch of hide. The volume of rain and claps of thunder made any attempt at stealth unnecessary but the mud was becoming deeper. Conrad's right foot sank in it up to his ankle as the hide door was swept aside and a dozen Lithuanians exited the hut. Wearing helmets, mail armour and carrying shields, they at first did not see the four novices standing a few feet away.

'Get the horses,' barked the leading Lithuanian.

The enemy soldiers began wading through the mud towards the horses that had their heads down before one spotted Conrad and his companions and screamed the alarm.

'Keep your feet,' Conrad shouted to his friends. 'God with us!'

The others cried 'God with us!' in unison and then walked towards the enemy, who were also advancing towards them with swords drawn. Conrad saw that some of them wore lamellar armour as well as mail and their commander had an aventail beneath his helmet.

Conrad turned the axe handle in his left hand before swinging it up and then down so the spike went into the shield of its Lithuanian owner who raised it to defend himself from the blow. Using the axe he pulled the shield down and thrust his sword over its rim, driving the point through the man's mouth. Blood frothed at the wound and he shook violently for a few seconds before collapsing into the mud, dead.

Hans, Anton and Johann were involved in their own duels, the fights appearing to be in slow motion, as they had to make allowances for the mud and rain, their opponents similarly hamstrung by the conditions. Brother Lukas had taught them to keep moving in combat, to dart and weave around their opponents, but today they were more like old washerwomen swinging sacks of laundry.

Conrad left his axe embedded in the dead man's shield, took his own shield off his back and slid his left arm through the leather straps, then attacked a Lithuanian who was making his way towards Hans. The latter was fighting off two opponents, one of them having stepped into a pool of water and sank up to his knees. If it had not been so deadly the scene would have been comical.

The Lithuanian saw Conrad and faced him, swinging his sword over his head to bring it down on Conrad's shield. He kept swinging his sword, Conrad easily deflecting the blows but being forced back by his assailant. As they fought and the rain continued to fall he did not notice that he was being herded away from the others towards another hut. The Lithuanian continued to hack with his sword and Conrad let him. His blows were clumsy and predictable and Conrad could see that he was panting and becoming tired. But he continued to press his attack, probably convinced that the youth in front of him was inexperienced and frightened. It was a fatal assumption to make as he dragged his boots from the cloying mud to deliver a fresh succession of blows at Conrad, the latter stepping back and either parrying the swipes with his shield or ducking to the side to avoid them altogether.

'A fight is not a dance,' Lukas had told them more than once. 'Get it over as quickly as possible to conserve your energy. Tired men make mistakes.'

Tired men make mistakes. One did so now as the Lithuanian, having failed to even scratch Conrad with his blur of sword strikes, lunged forward in an attempt to drive the point into his belly. Conrad brushed aside the blade with his shield,

475

sweeping it from right to left, away from his body, to expose the Lithuanian's torso for an instant. And an instant was all that he needed. Conrad screamed and drove the sword into the man's guts, straight through the mail armour, tunic and into soft flesh and intestines. The Lithuanian, a look of horror on his face, moaned softly and went limp on the sword. Conrad tugged back his sword and the dead enemy slumped to the ground.

He saw his other companions holding their own against the Lithuanians, who seemed to be fighting a defensive battle as he saw two others going back to collect the horses. He began walking back to the fight when he heard a noise behind and turned to see the hide flap over the doorway of the nearest hut open and two men exit. Both were in war gear but one was badly wounded and was being helped to walk by a smaller individual, a boy, who had his arm round the shoulders of the older man. The latter was pale faced and had a crossbow bolt in his belly. He groaned in pain as the boy helped him out of the hut. They were going to the horses.

There was a large clap of thunder and Conrad stepped forward to bar their way. He looked behind them to ensure that there were no soldiers following but saw only an old man in tunic and leggings, a bag slung over his shoulders. The young boy froze as Conrad held his shield in front of him and brought his sword up to chest height, drawing it back so he could plunge it into the youth, and then afterwards into the wounded man. The old man gasped in alarm and froze, the boy, who had a long face, showing no fear as he matched Conrad's stare. His eyes showed hate and defiance but no fear, not even alarm. Perhaps that was why Conrad decided to let him go, or perhaps he thought it dishonourable to slay a boy who was assisting a wounded comrade. Whatever the reason he lowered his sword and backed away, the boy taking a long, hard look at him before helping the man with the bolt in his belly towards the horses.

The soldier with the aventail suddenly appeared and Conrad stepped away a few more paces. He looked left and right to ensure there were no more Lithuanians approaching and prepared to fight the well-armoured man before him. But the Lithuanian merely raised his sword and stood still, the boy and the old man helping the wounded man to the horses. When they reached them and gained their saddles the Lithuanian backed away and joined them. Conrad watched as rain coursed off his helmet and the Lithuanians rode away, their horses threading their way through the mud and filth.

He heard Hans' voice. 'Conrad.'

He saw his friend and the others making their way towards him as the Lithuanians disappeared in the rain.

'Are you all right, Conrad?'

He slammed his sword back into its scabbard. 'Fine, thank you. I saw a boy helping a badly wounded man to his horse. I could have killed them easily but I didn't. I let them go.'

'I would have done the same,' said Anton.

'Me too,' agreed Johann. He slapped Hans on the arm. 'Whereas Hans would have killed them and searched their bodies for food.'

'Better not tell Henke,' warned Anton.

'Tell Henke what?' sounded a voice from behind.

They turned to see Henke, Rudolf, Lukas and Walter a few feet away, helmets shoved on top of their heads.

'Nothing,' said Conrad, 'it was nothing, Brother Henke.'

Henke spat on the ground. 'And nothing is what we've found. I'm going to die of the chills and I haven't killed anyone for at least an hour. Complete waste of time. Where is the enemy?'

Conrad and Hans shook their heads.

'After we've cleared the camp we'll burn some of these huts, Henke,' said Rudolf. 'That should improve your humour.'

'Come on,' said Lukas, 'let's try and find him someone to kill to cheer him up.'

Henke was not amused but Rudolf and Lukas thought it hilarious while Walter frowned. He disapproved of frivolity on the battlefield. Killing in God's name was a serious business where mirth had no place.

'You boys keep checking the camp,' said Lukas. 'And watch yourselves. The enemy might have fled but there still might be a few stragglers lurking.'

He slapped Henke and on the arm and both of them pulled down their helmets and together with Walter went in search of the enemy. The boys did the same, though Conrad stopped and turned around.

'I need to retrieve my axe,' he shouted. 'I will catch you up.'

He trudged through the mud to where the dead Lithuanian he had killed lay face up, lifeless eyes staring up to the heavens, the puddle around him stained with his blood. He placed a foot on the shield and worked the axe up and down before extracting it from the wood. He slung his shield on his back and tucked the axe in his belt, turned and saw Rudolf, arms folded, looking at him.

'Brother Rudolf.'

'I knew from the beginning that you would be a good soldier, perhaps even a great one. And you keep proving me right.'

The rain was now abating once more though the wind was still blowing and the southern sky was filled with dark, threatening clouds.

'You are too kind,' said Conrad, smiling in self-satisfaction.

'Walk with me,' said Rudolf.

They waded through the mud; the only sounds the squelching made by their feet. The Lithuanians were now pouring back across the pontoon bridge and the Christian army was reluctant to pursue them. It had been a hard, bloody fight to win possession of the rampart and the crusaders had suffered many losses, as had the Livs who were stalking the Lithuanians towards the river. Thalibald thought to trap them against the riverbank and either slaughter them there or force them into the water where they would drown. But the Lithuanians on the other side of the river had despatched boats to evacuate their comrades, and in the boats were archers to keep the Livs at bay while they did so.

'Why did you let those Lithuanians go?' asked Rudolf suddenly.

'Lithuanians?'

Rudolf sighed. 'I saw with my own eyes so do not insult me by pretending otherwise.'

Conrad felt his cheeks flush. 'It was a boy helping a wounded man who looked close to death. There was an old man too. There was no honour in murdering them.'

'Let us hope that your noble decision will not have serious repercussions in the future.'

'I doubt it,' said Conrad casually, 'the wounded man had a crossbow bolt in his belly. I doubt he will live.'

'There is an old saying, Conrad. Better to kill an enemy today than let him live so that he may kill you tomorrow. Or worse, he may kill one of your comrades. Compassion on the battlefield is often purchased at a very high price, Conrad. Remember that.'

*****

Three thousand Lithuanians made it across the river to their homeland, five hundred taken off by boats while archers kept the pursuing Livs at bay. The latter had suffered nearly three hundred casualties in the battle and the crusaders had suffered a further seven hundred killed and wounded. The bishop's soldiers were wet, tired and many were wounded and for these reasons there was no pursuit over the pontoon bridge. The Sword Brothers had lost only fifteen men.

When the rain finally stopped and the wind dropped the bishop, Caupo and Sir Helmold stood at one end of the pontoon bridge and peered across the river at the locked shields of Lithuanian warriors who held the other end. The Christian end soon became wreathed in smoke as soldiers began using the two-man shelters as firewood, the soaking fuel producing copious amounts of thick white smoke.

The healer knelt beside the bed Stecse had been placed on in the first village they had come across, located two miles inland of the river. He examined the wound as the village headman, a Selonian, looked on, waving his wife and daughters away who had been standing in the doorway. Stecse's breathing was shallow and laboured. He looked up and shook his head at Mindaugas. The boy pushed past the headman and went outside where the commander of his bodyguard was standing next to his horse. He saw Mindaugas.

'The prince needs to make a decision about the bridge, young sir.'

'He is unconscious,' said Mindaugas softly.

'Sorry to hear that. But a decision has to be made nevertheless,' pressed the commander, 'otherwise the Christians will be flooding across it after they have rested.'

'Burn it,' said Mindaugas.

The commander smiled. 'Good decision.'

He called over one of his men and gave him the order to ride back to the bridge and torch it.

'Why did he let us go?' said Mindaugas.

'Sir?'

'That crusader with a red cross and sword on his shield. He could have cut me and my father down easily but he just stood there and let us go.'

The commander was uninterested. 'He was a Sword Brother, sir, and they usually like to kill first and ask questions later.'

'I am going to destroy the Sword Brothers one day,' vowed Mindaugas.

The commander started eating an apple and pointed it at the hut. 'Looks like your father has woken up.'

Mindaugas turned and saw the healer in the doorway. He went to enter the longhouse but the healer grabbed his arm.

'The wound is too deep and your father has lost too much blood. I am sorry.'

Mindaugas pulled his arm away and went back to the bedroom, ordering the headman to leave. He knelt by his father and held his hand. Stecse looked at him.

'I go to Perkunas, my son. Pray that he welcomes me into his great hall.'

Mindaugas tried not to cry but tears came to his eyes.

'You will sit beside him, father.'

Stecse's lips curled into a thin smile. 'You will rule the Lithuanian tribes, Mindaugas, but you must tread carefully. Trust no one, least of all Vsevolod. He shifts only for himself.'

His voice was very faint now. 'The daughter of the grand duke is your ally, though. Lithuanian blood flows in her veins. Serve your people and they will serve you, my son.'

Mindaugas felt his father's grip weaken and then his eyes closed. He wiped away his tears and kissed him on the forehead. Then he held his head in his hands and wept.

Chapter 18

The harvest at Wenden was bountiful that year. The peace with the Estonians held and so the crops were undisturbed by raiders and gathered in. As usual members of the garrison assisted in their collection and Conrad took the opportunity to be as near to Daina as was allowable. There was great rejoicing at the return of Thalibald and Waribule to their village, which meant that Rameke's brief reign as chief was at an end. Trade along the Dvina returned to normal and the merchants of Riga continued to prosper. Ships took furs and wax to Germany and others returned with people who wished to settle in Livonia. More mercenaries arrived at Wenden to strengthen the garrison but also farmers who had been promised virgin land and crops to plant on it. Thus did a small number of huts and animal pens appear to the north of the castle – the beginnings of the first settler village at Wenden.

Master Berthold was very enthusiastic about their presence, as a portion of the crops they produced would be given to the castle as rent. And more food meant more soldiers and civilian families could be fed.

'The problem is not food, master,' said Rudolf at the weekly gathering of the brother knights in the master's hall. 'The problem is, as ever, money. This land is rich in everything apart from gold. Without money we will not be able to pay the mercenaries or workers, or purchase weapons, armour and horses from Germany.'

'It is as Brother Rudolf says,' added Lukas. 'This castle is to be one of the strongest of the order in Livonia and yet we are starved of funds by Riga.'

'We were promised the funds bequeathed to us by Sir Frederick but they never materialised,' complained Rudolf. 'If the bishop wishes his garrisons to be strong then he needs to release funds from his treasury.'

Berthold frowned. 'Alas, Archdeacon Stefan has control over the treasury and Grand Master Volquin has informed me that he is most reluctant to release any monies until Riga's security is assured. He uses the Lithuanian threat as an excuse to strengthen the city's garrison at the expense of the order.'

'Without the order's castles there would be no Riga,' growled Henke. 'We should look to the north to satisfy our needs, there are plenty of Estonian women and girls who would fetch a handsome price in gold.'

'The Sword Brothers are not slave traders,' protested Walter. 'It is a sin and against God's law.'

Henke sniffed in disapproval but Berthold was in agreement. 'I was severely reprimanded by the bishop and the grand master for trading slaves to the Russians and will not authorise another similar mission.'

Henke shook his head in disgust but Walter was delighted. Holy warriors did not sully their hands by dealing in slaves, even if it meant starving.

'Henke is right about one thing,' said Rudolf, 'we should look to the north.'

Berthold looked at him with a bewildered expression. 'Please enlighten us, Rudolf.'

'We all know,' continued Rudolf, 'that war with Lembit is inevitable. When it comes the Sword Brothers must seize all the land it takes from the Estonians. If the bishop will not pay us from his treasury then we must have our own lands to service our needs. What we conquer we keep.'

'Makes sense,' said Henke.

'The bishop will never agree to that,' said Berthold.

'He will,' remarked Rudolf, 'when we withhold sending food supplies to Riga. Let's see how our friend Stefan likes having a starving population hammering at his door. Riga's population grows every year but Livonia's hinterland provides the food for its teeming masses. I'm sure that the other masters, and Volquin himself, will agree that the city treasury should make the strengthening of the order and its castles a priority over cushions for the bishop's palace.'

The other brother knights were nodding in agreement, even Walter, but Berthold was frowning. He held up a hand. 'I will write to the grand master requesting money to pay for our immediate needs. Brother Rudolf, you will draw up an inventory of our wants. As for the matter of Estonian lands, that can be put aside for the moment as Lembit has kept the peace and shows no sign of breaking it.'

But little did they know that the arrival at Wenden of a small group of missionaries would be the spark that would set the north aflame.

It was an overcast autumn afternoon when they arrived, three Cistercian monks led by a very tall abbot with a lean, severe face and white hair. Lukas had been tutoring the novices in swordsmanship, though by now most of the training classes became opportunities for the young men to show off their skills. All four were battle hardened and proficient in the use of weapons on foot and on horseback. Lukas was proud of them but frowned upon their increasing cockiness. They were training as matched pairs with swords, moving agilely around each other just as he had taught them. But his satisfaction turned to anger when he saw Conrad throw his sword from his right hand to his left, laughing at Hans, his opponent, as he did so.

'Stop!' shouted Lukas, marching over to Conrad.

'What are you doing?' he snapped.

'Practising with my left hand, Brother Lukas.'

Anton and Johann stopped and grinned at each other.

'Are you left handed?' asked Lukas.

Conrad shook his head. 'No, Brother Lukas.'

'Then don't let your sword out of your right hand,' said Lukas, 'and don't throw it around like it is a toy. That sort of idiotic trick will get you killed on the battlefield.'

Conrad slashed the air with his sword. 'You have trained us well, Brother Lukas.'

'Next year we will be brother knights like you,' said Johann.

'If you live that long,' said Lukas, raising an eyebrow at them. 'Now get back to your training. And anyone who tries any tricks will be spending the evening mucking out the stables.'

They laughed and went back to their training, only to stop when the white-haired abbot and his threadbare companions walked from the gatehouse along the track and diverted off it when they saw Brother Lukas. Conrad and the others stopped and stared as the tall man leading cleared his throat behind Lukas.

'Excuse me, brother, I am looking for Master Berthold.'

Lukas turned and looked up at the thin man who like his companions wore a habit of undyed wool. A smile creased his gaunt face.

'I am Abbot Hylas from the monastery at Zinna and these are some of my monks.'

'I am Brother Lukas of the Order of Sword Brothers, abbot.'

'I am pleased to meet one of our brave warriors of Christ,' said Hylas, 'perhaps you would be so kind as to direct me to Master Berthold.'

Lukas beckoned one of the spearmen at the gates to come over.

Hylas looked beyond him to the strapping novices in their leggings and gambesons. 'Are these some of your fellow knights?'

Lukas laughed. 'No, abbot, these are novices. Insolent novices at that who stop their work on the flimsiest pretext.'

Conrad and the others recommenced their training as the spearman arrived and Lukas told him to take the abbot and his monks to the master's hall. Hylas thanked him.

'What brings you to Wenden, abbot?'

Hylas followed the spearman, his tonsured monks following. 'We go to bring the word of God to the Estonians.'

Lukas scratched his head as they walked up the track that led to the castle.

'What did he mean, Brother Lukas?' enquired Conrad as the others stopped when they heard these words and gathered round.

'The White Monks they call the members of the order of Cistercians, on account of them wearing habits of undyed wool,' said Lukas. 'They only wear trousers when travelling, leading many to ridicule them for their bare-bottomed piety. Poverty and simplicity, that's what they live for. And a desire for a slow death, it seems.'

'I do not understand,' said Hans.

Lukas shook his head. 'Let me put this to you, Hans. Would you like to go into Estonia unarmed and few in number?'

'No, Brother Lukas,' replied Hans.

'Why not?' asked Lukas.

'Because the Estonians would kill me.'

'Exactly,' mused Lukas, 'exactly.'

He looked at Hans. 'You wouldn't like being a White Monk, Hans. Most of the time they eat only coarse bread, vegetables, herbs and beans. Not like at Wenden where you get lots of eggs, fish and meat to keep you fit and strong.'

'They aren't really going to Estonia are they, Brother Lukas?' asked Jchann.

'I have a dreadful fear that they might be,' said Lukas.

And so it was. Despite the remonstrations of Berthold, Rudolf and even Walter, Abbot Hylas and his monks left Wenden the next day. Henke was on the top of the completed second story of the north tower as he watched them go, four ragged individuals leading a mule loaded with a few meagre rations and a small tent that Berthold had insisted they take with them, Conrad having shown them how to erect it that morning.

'That's the last we will see of them,' said Henke dismissively.

'I fear you may be right,' agreed Rudolf.

'They must be mad.'

'Apparently,' said Rudolf, 'the abbot told Berthold that he had a vision that he was converting the Estonians who were falling to their knees at his beckoning. He walked all the way across Germany, took ship from Lübeck and found his way here, with no money or food. Imagine that. He and his monks relied on charity to get here, nothing more. Now that, my friend, is faith.'

'They will find Lembit less charitable,' sneered Henke.

*****

After the death of Daugerutis and Stecse Prince Vsevolod sent his wife and daughters to Panemunis. He did so because he wished Rasa to be at her father's capital to ensure her and their daughters' safety, since now the Lithuanian invasion had been crushed he feared that the bishop would turn his attention to Gerzika. And though he was now the heir to the Lithuanian throne, or at least those territories still controlled by what was left of the grand duke's army, the other dukes would no doubt try to increase their own territory at the expense of the Selonians and Nalsen. And if civil war broke out in Lithuania then there would be no soldiers to spare to send across the river to support Gerzika.

He was musing over these thoughts when there was a knock at the door to his study.

'Enter.'

The chief steward of the palace entered and bowed. 'Chief Aras awaits you in your hall, highness.'

Vsevolod looked up from his chair. 'Who?'

'Prince Stecse's deputy, highness.'

Vsevolod sighed. Was there no end to these tiresome, dull-witted Lithuanian lords?

'Very well, tell him I will be along shortly.'

When Vsevolod entered his hall a few minutes later he found a tall man of medium build waiting for him. Unusually, he had a smartly trimmed black beard and his hair was cut short. Most Lithuanians wore their hair and beards long and wild. In fact his overall appearance was neat and tidy, with a thigh-length mail hauberk, short leather boots, brown leggings and green tunic, his helmet held in the crook of his arm. He bowed his head when he saw the prince.

'Chief Aras?' Vsevolod sat on his high-backed wooden throne. 'What brings you to Gerzika?'

'To advise you on affairs south of the river, lord.'

Vsevolod called over his steward and ordered him to fetch wine for him and his guest.

'I have advisers, chief, and they keep me informed of affairs on both sides of the river.'

Aras nodded. 'Then you will know of the meeting between the other dukes a week ago in Semgallia.'

Vsevolod's face registered alarm.

Aras continued. 'I see that you do not. They first seek to divide the territory of Duke Ykintas between them and afterwards they will look east, to the territories of the late grand duke, your father-in-law.'

The steward returned with a silver tray holding two silver flagons. He offered one to Vsevolod and the other to Aras.

'I know who Daugerutis was,' said Vsevolod. 'What is your point?'

'I was appointed by Prince Stecse to keep an eye on his son, Mindaugas, lord. As such, I have a responsibility to ensure that he has a kingdom to inherit when he becomes a man.'

'That is my task,' said Vsevolod irritably.

Aras, unconcerned, sipped at his wine. 'Well, my lord, then I would suggest that you and your army get to Panemunis as quickly as possible to prepare for the assault of the other dukes. The death of the grand duke has whetted their appetite for power and they see an opportunity to crush the Selonians and Nalsen, especially now that Prince Stecse is dead.'

'If I abandon Gerzika,' said Vsevolod firmly, 'then I have no doubt that the crusaders will launch an attack against it.'

'They will attack it anyway, my lord. The fact that you did not aid their cause against the grand duke's invasion of Livonia will have condemned you in their eyes.'

Vsevolod waved a hand at him. 'I am a friend of the bishop. I brokered a peace treaty between him and the grand duke.'

'That the grand duke broke. I know that these Christians place great store in forgiveness and charity, but they will not forget that you did not come to their aid in the recent war.'

Vsevolod glared at Aras. 'The war was not of my making. I cannot be held responsible for events beyond my control.'

'The point is, lord,' said Aras, 'can you fight the crusaders as well as the other dukes south of the river?'

Vsevolod said nothing but began tapping his fingers on the arm of his chair. This well-dressed Lithuanian was impertinent but he was also right: the bishop was probably no longer his friend and the other Lithuanian dukes obviously sensed an opportunity to strengthen themselves at the expense of the grand duke's people. Gerzika's army, such as it was, would not be able to withstand a battle against the crusaders, and once the bishop's men were at his walls the only allies he had would be the Lithuanians across the Dvina. But if civil strife raged south of the river then he would get no help and Gerzika would surely fall. Perhaps it might fall anyway.

'You command the army of the grand duke?' queried Vsevolod.

'What is left of it, my lord,' answered Aras.

'And what is left of it?'

'The grand duke took twelve thousand of his own men across the Dvina. I mustered just over four thousand at Panemunis two weeks ago. They are in no state to fight against the other dukes, lord. I need time to rebuild the army.'

'That is not within my power to grant,' said Vsevolod.

'No, my lord, but the transfer of a few hundred of your own soldiers across the river would allow me to transfer some of my own men from garrison duties to offensive operations. To keep the wolf from the door, so to speak.'

'To do so would weaken Gerzika,' said Vsevolod.

'The land will be covered in snow in three months, lord, and the rivers and lakes will be frozen. The crusaders will not march against you until next year.'

Vsevolod could not decide whether he disliked or admired this Aras. He was certainly perceptive and what he was suggesting made sense, which was in itself irksome. But he was right about one thing: the other Lithuanian dukes presented the most immediate threat.

'Your name means "eagle", does it not?' enquired Vsevolod.

'It does, lord.'

'How apt for someone who keeps a watch on Stecse's son. I trust he prospers.'

'He thirsts for revenge, lord.'

'Ah, I see. Entirely understandable, I suppose,' remarked Vsevolod, 'to seek vengeance against those who killed his father.'

'It is my task to temper his anger with judgement,' said Aras. 'One day Mindaugas will lead the Lithuanian people.'

'I will send five hundred men to Panemunis,' announced Vsevolod, 'where they will guard my wife and daughters. Now, Chief Aras, tell me about Arturus.'

Aras was surprised. 'Arturus? He is the leader of the Northern Kurs who fights Gedvilas of the Southern Kurs, or he did the last time I heard anything about him. He was the one who attacked Riga a few years back.'

Vsevolod rose. 'Excellent. Now if you will excuse me I have business to attend to.'

Aras replaced his flagon back on the tray held by the steward and bowed his head. 'My lord.'

Vsevolod raised his hand in acknowledgement and went back to his study. An hour later he summoned his steward and presented him with a sealed letter that he had written. He found the Lithuanian language coarse but it was easy enough to write and so he did not need a translator to write down his words. He gave the steward the letter and ordered him to deliver it himself. The man had served him diligently for many years and he hoped that he would not lose his head during his mission. Still, hard times demanded great sacrifice. Vsevolod frowned when he noticed that his white silk shirt was stained with a spot of ink.

Three weeks later, after having overseen the transfer of the five hundred men from Gerzika to Panemunis, Vsevolod was seated in the dining hall of his former father-in-law's stronghold. The days were getting cooler now and a fire constantly burned in the great stone hearth in the centre of the hall. In a month's time ice would begin to form on the Dvina and the land would be covered with snow. Then he would finally feel confident that the bishop would not march against him, at least for this year.

Rasa had taken the death of her father particularly badly and had wanted him to unite his army with Aras' forces and recross the Dvina to continue the war against the bishop. She only calmed down when Aras informed her that the bridge of boats that had enabled the grand duke to cross the river had been destroyed. She cursed the Christians for burning it and he agreed that they were indeed heathens.

Today she and Vsevolod ate alone in the dining hall, both seated at the end of the top table. Aras had taken Mindaugas and their two daughters, Morta and Elze, on a hunting trip in the forest, the prince having assigned two score of his Russian warriors as bodyguards.

'You need have no fear for their safety,' Rasa censored him, 'Aras is quite loyal. He is like me, a Selonian.'

'I know, but it will take me a while to grow accustomed to Lithuanian ways.'

She picked at a slice of mutton. 'We need to think about Mindaugas.'

Vsevolod cast aside his lukewarm meat. 'Do we?'

'The death of my father has led to uncertainty within the kingdom. We must act to secure the succession.'

Vsevolod tore off a piece of black bread and dipped it in the bowl of *juka*. It tasted exquisite.

'Your father named me as his successor.'

Rasa shook her head. 'You are the guardian of the throne, nothing more.'

Vsevolod frowned. 'You are so reassuring, my sweet.'

'My people will never accept a Russian ruling over them. They tolerate you because of your marriage to me but they look to us to give them a Lithuanian duke.'

Vsevolod dropped his bread into his soup in alarm. 'You wish to bear another child?'

'I wish for Mindaugas to marry Morta.'

'He is thirteen and she is fourteen,' said Vsevolod. 'They are too young.'

'They like each other and can be married next year,' replied Rasa. 'I have spoken to the *Kriviu Krivaitis* and he will give his blessing to the union.'

'Have you ever wondered why he lives in a grove, my sweet?' enquired her husband innocently. 'You know he is completely mad, though not that insane if he has managed to surround himself with a host of virgins willing to do his every bidding.'

Rasa looked around the room in alarm. She cared nothing for the serving slaves but didn't want the guards to spread rumours of her husband's blasphemy.

'Choose your words carefully,' she hissed, 'you are not in Gerzika now.'

The doors of the hall opened and a muddy courier entered. Around his neck was a leather tubular carrying case. Two guards crossed their spears to bar his entry but Vsevolod waved him through. The man was wearing the silver griffin symbol of Gerzika on the front of his blue tunic.

Vsevolod rubbed his hands together. 'If this is what I think it is, my sweet, we may be back in Gerzika sooner rather than later.'

The courier took a letter from his carrying case and bowed his head as he handed it to the prince. Vsevolod's smile started to disappear when he saw the cross keys symbol of Riga on the seal. He broke it and read the contents, his mood darkening as he read the fawning words of Archdeacon Stefan. When he finished he tossed the parchment on the table and came to two immediate conclusions: the archdeacon was no longer his friend and he would be staying in Lithuania longer than he had hoped.

'The news is not good, I gather,' said Rasa, looking at her husband's face.

'The bishop wants his gold back.'

Rasa was confused. 'What gold?'

'The gold that was paid to your father, my sweet, for the return of the Liv slaves he took during his raid against the Novgorodians. The gold that he used to entice the other dukes to join his campaign earlier this year. The bishop views said campaign as a breach of the terms of the peace treaty that was signed between him and your father.'

'Ignore them,' said Rasa contemptuously.

Vsevolod smiled. 'The crusaders are nothing if not diligent when it comes to negotiations. They have thought of that.'

He picked up the letter and read aloud some of its contents.

'Failure to deliver the aforementioned quantity of gold to Riga before the Dvina freezes over will result in the bishop seeking alternative reparations from the Principality of Gerzika, equivalent to the amount in gold that is currently owed to the Holy Kingdom of Livonia.'

'Meaning what?' said Rasa.

'Meaning, my sweet, that if I do not pay the bishop his gold he will attack my city.'

*****

The missionaries were sweating heavily, though due to the raging fire that burned behind them or the prospect of being harmed was uncertain. They had trekked through the empty land north of Wenden that marked the frontier between Christian Livonia and pagan Estonia before coming to one of the villages near the hill fort of Fellin. There they had begun to preach to the villagers, showing them the wooden crosses that hung around their necks and calling on them to accept the Christian faith and be baptised. They were met by a variety of blank and hostile stares as none of the villagers understood German, though they recognised the crosses that they had previously seen on the shields and banners of the crusaders that had ravaged their land two years before. As Abbot Hylas and his monks prayed and preached word was sent to Fellin and a party of wolf shields arrived on ponies to seize them.

Their wrists were bound and they were dragged off to Lehola to face the judgement of Lembit. They now stood before him in his hall, their habits having been taken from them and thrown into the fire. Wolf shields stood around the walls and Rusticus stood beside his lord in his war gear, though Lembit himself wore only a plain shirt and leggings, his sword hanging at his hip. The only sound in the hall was the crackling of the huge fire.

'Do you know who I am?' he asked them in German.

'A pagan who must hear the word of the one true god,' said Hylas, looking down defiantly at Lembit.

'And you are?' said Lembit.

'Abbot Hylas of the Cistercian Order.'

'What are Cistercians?'

'A religious order that spreads the word of God.'

'I am Lembit, leader of the Estonian tribes,' he spread his arms, 'and this is my hall. It stands on my land, as does the village you invaded. The last time Christians came to my land they kidnapped women and children. Was that your intention, Abbot Hylas?'

Beads of sweat formed on Hylas' forehead as the fire roasted his and the others' backs, but he still stood defiant.

'I am here with my brothers to lead them to God.'

'So you are a kidnapper,' said Lembit, 'for you seek to steal their souls and sell them to your god. We have our own gods. We do not need your god; we do not want your god.'

Hylas sneered at Lembit. 'Your gods are false. There is only one god.'

Lembit sighed. 'I see.'

'What are you going to do with them?' said Rusticus, bored by the whole thing.

'Send them back to the bishop, of course,' answered Lembit.

The next day he sent riders to the other chiefs informing them that the truce with the Christians was over and that they should strengthen their strongholds and prepare for war next spring. Judgement was passed on Abbot Hylas and his monks that afternoon.

The first monk, the youngest, had tears streaming down his face as two wolf shields dragged him from the fort's gates to stand before Lembit, the leering Rusticus slashing the air with his sword behind him. The ramparts of the stronghold were filled with soldiers and their families, all of them curious to see the fate of these madmen who had come unarmed into their lord's lands, and who were now marched out of Lehola's gates. The monk, his skin white and pale, looked imploringly at the abbot, his teeth chattering with fear. The abbot, like his monks stripped to the waist, tried to maintain his air of authority but was distraught at the prospect of what was about to happen.

'Have courage, my son,' he called to the monk.

Lembit looked at Hylas. 'You can save him, you can save all of them as well as yourself.'

Hylas looked at him, relief mixed with suspicion at this calculating, long-haired barbarian who spoke so softly.

Lembit smiled. 'It is true. All you have to do is kneel before me, place your hand on your heart and swear allegiance to Uku.'

Hylas was perplexed and began looking round. 'Uku? Who is Uku?'

Lembit grabbed Hylas' hair and twisted the thin strands in his hand. The abbot winced in pain as the Estonian forced his face upwards.

'The Supreme God, the creator who blessed us with life. Bow and declare your allegiance to Him and I will let you go free.'

He released the abbot's hair and looked back at the shaking monk, pointing at Hylas.

'Your fate, boy, lies in his hands.'

He walked over to Rusticus who was holding his sword in readiness.

'Why the delay?'

Lembit shook his head. 'I have promised them their lives if the old man kneels and swears allegiance to Uku.'

Rusticus was appalled. 'You cannot let them go, lord.'

'Why?'

'It will look bad.'

'Will it?' said Lembit. 'Look at them, Rusticus, an old man and his three deluded followers. Have you no pity in your heart?'

'But you promised,' muttered Rusticus forlornly.

'I did promise,' said Lembit, 'to send them back to the bishop and I always keep my promises.'

'But if they swear allegiance to Uku,' protested Rusticus, 'then I will not be able to execute them.' He pointed his sword at the people standing in silence on the ramparts. 'They will be disappointed, lord.'

'You mean *you* will be disappointed. Well, console yourself with knowing that you can kill some prisoners later if the old man agrees to my terms.'

He walked back to Hylas as Rusticus muttered under his breath.

'Well, abbot,' said Lembit, 'what shall it be, life or death?'

'I do not fear death,' answered Hylas firmly, 'and will never abandon my god.'

Lembit nodded to the two wolf shields who shoved the young monk down on his knees in front of Hylas.

'Time to see if your sword is sharp, Rusticus,' said Lembit.

His deputy grinned with relish. He took a few steps forward, gripping the hilt of his sword with both hands, and then swung the blade at the monk's head, severing it in one blow. The ramparts erupted in cheers as the head rolled to the feet of Abbot Hylas, its eyes and mouth wide. The abbot nearly swooned but managed to stay on his feet. Lembit gestured to a wolf shield standing behind the priest who kicked at the back of his knees, sending him sprawling on the ground.

'It is inappropriate that you should be looking down on me, priest,' said Lembit.

The chief walked over to the headless corpse and took the wooden crucifix that had been around the young monk's neck. He placed the bloody necklace around the abbot's neck.

'A memento for you.'

Lembit ordered the next monk to be brought from the gates. 'I give you another opportunity, abbot, to save yourself and your two companions. Renounce your god and acknowledge Uku as the true supreme deity and I will let you live.'

'Blasphemer!' spat Hylas as the second monk, gaping wide-eyed at the headless corpse in front of him, was shoved down on his knees beside it.

Lembit sighed and nodded to Rusticus who lopped off the quivering monk's head with a single blow – wild cheering from the ramparts. Lembit once more retrieved the crucifix that had hung around the monk's neck and placed it around Hylas' neck. The latter was shaking with rage, his eyes bulging and his cheeks purple.

'You will rot in hell for your crimes,' he spat at Lembit. 'Oh Lord, strike down this heathen and show the disbelievers Your power!'

Lembit looked around him. 'It would appear that your god is not listening. That being the case, I'm sure he will not mind if you kneel and swear fealty to Uku.'

But Hylas had his eyes closed and was reciting a silent prayer, trying to shut out the horror that was unfolding before him. Lembit raised his arms to the ramparts.

'I have offered this priest his own and the lives of his followers in return for him paying homage to Uku and yet he refuses. Am I not merciful?'

Those on the ramparts cheered and whistled, the warriors banging their spear shafts against their shields. Lembit waved forward the last monk, who put up a mighty struggle before he was forced down onto his knees in front of Hylas. Rusticus gripped his sword and placed the bloody edge against the monk's thin neck. Lembit struck Hylas across the face with the back of his hand.

493

'Pay attention, you do not want to miss any of the entertainment. Rusticus, can you make it three out of three?'

Rusticus drew back the blade and then swung it forward to take the head off the last monk, a blow so speedy and expertly delivered that for a few seconds the severed head rested on the corpse's neck, until the body crumpled and the head rolled on the ground. Rusticus raised his hands to the applause showered upon him and stepped forward, smirking at Hylas.

'No, Rusticus,' said Lembit, retrieving the last monk's crucifix and placing it around Hylas' neck, 'not this one. This one will live to take my message back to the bishop.'

Rusticus was shocked. 'You will let him live?'

'Sort of.'

Lembit ordered Hylas be tied to a wooden frame and then had him flogged. Rusticus was allowed the honour after he had executed the other prisoners with his sword. He undertook the flogging with a whip made of cowhide, the blows biting deep into the abbot's back, tearing the flesh. At first Hylas cursed Rusticus after every blow but after twenty lashes his head hung down and he merely moaned with each strike.

'That is enough, Rusticus,' said Lembit, arms folded and standing on the other side of the frame so he was near Hylas' face.

'But I am just getting warmed up,' protested Rusticus.

Lembit held up a hand to his subordinate and leaned closer to the pale, pain-wracked face of the abbot.

'I have a surprise for you, priest. My deputy uses his right hand.'

Lembit waved forward one of his wolf shields, a stocky man shorter than Rusticus but powerfully built nonetheless.

'Give him the whip, Rusticus,' ordered Lembit.

He continued to speak to the abbot. 'But the next man to flog you is left handed and so the strokes across your back that he will make will cross the first set of cuts and mangle your flesh even more.'

He placed a hand under the abbot's chin and lifted his face. 'Enjoy.'

The second set of strokes resulted in the abbot passing out, only to be rudely awakened when Rusticus threw a bucket of water in his face. When his back had been cut to ribbons salt was rubbed into Hylas' wounds and then he was left to hang on the frame all night.

In the morning he was cut down and given water before all his fingers were broken with a hammer and his toenails were pulled out. He was then thrown on the back of a cart, together with a sack containing the severed heads of his monks tied to one of his ankles. The dozen riders who were instructed to take him back to Livonia and dump him near Wenden were ordered to given Hylas food and water should he request it, but on no account to harm him further and to ensure that he did not die of exposure on the journey.

Lembit stood at the entrance to Lehola as the cart trundled down the track south, Rusticus beside him.

'This signals the end of our peace with the crusaders,' said Lembit.

Rusticus rubbed his hands together. 'Good, your warriors grow restless with no blood to wash their blades in.'

Rusticus pointed at the cart. 'Why did you let him live?'

'So he can carry my message back to the Christians that their religion has no place in Estonia and if they send any more priests they can expect to receive the same treatment.'

'They will send an army, not priests,' said Rusticus.

Lembit nodded. 'I know. But of the two I would rather fight a crusader army than an army of their priests. At least you can see the men of iron.'

Rusticus looked confused. 'I do not understand.'

'The men of iron come with swords but their priests wage war with words and ideas, and once ideas are planted in people's minds it becomes almost impossible to remove them or prevent them from spreading. I do not wish to see the Estonians going the way of the Livs. I would rather see this land laid waste than fall to the religion of the Bishop of Riga.'

*****

'He must be over a hundred paces away, said Hans, staring at the wild boar with its snout to the ground.

Conrad placed a finger over his lips to quieten Hans and lifted up the crossbow that was hanging via a strap over his shoulder.

'If you miss him and waste a bolt there will be extra duties for you tonight,' whispered Lukas behind him as Conrad pulled back the bowstring with the claw on his belt and patted the neck of his horse. Ever since the arrival of the German settlers at Wenden and the building of their hovels beyond the north wall of the castle Master Berthold had organised daily patrols to safeguard the area. Usually the riders saw nothing aside from birds but each patrol always took along a crossbow on the chance that it might come across something to add to the stockroom of the castle's kitchens.

Today it was the turn of Lukas and the novices and now Conrad had the opportunity to kill a boar that was so busy sniffing for worms and insects that it did not spot the five stationary horsemen.

'Don't miss, Conrad,' said Anton. 'He'll make a fine meal.'

'Must weigh at least two hundred pounds,' added Johann.

Conrad took a bolt from his quiver and placed it in the groove in the crossbow's stock. The others fell silent as he raised the weapon and took aim. There was no wind so all he had to consider was elevation. He relaxed and slowed his breathing – his horse would sense any nervousness and might become skittish. He waited for the hog to turn so it was presenting its side before he released the trigger. The crack of the crossbow was followed by the squeal of the boar as the bolt hit it in the shoulder. Then there was a grunt and the animal collapsed.

The others cheered and Hans slapped Conrad on the arm.

'You got lucky,' said Lukas.

But it wasn't luck; it was the result of hundreds of hours of training that had turned these young men into skilled fighters and horsemen. He was proud of how they had turned out but frowned on their occasional displays of bravado. He was about to tell Conrad to go and fetch his prize when he saw movement in the trees to his right, and this was no animal.

'Ready!' he shouted, drawing his sword and bringing his shield up to cover his torso. The others did likewise. They were in a clearing with trees fifty paces on the right and brush thickets ahead and on their left.

They brought their horses in line with Lukas who had turned his animal to face the threat. They could all see him now, a lone figure who seemed to have halted just back from the treeline.

'Show yourself,' shouted Lukas but the figure did not move.

'Do you want me to shoot him, Brother Lukas?' asked Conrad.

Lukas pulled down his mail coif to hear better, listening for any sounds that might indicate more men in the trees.

'He's moving again,' said Anton, pointing his sword at the lone figure as it exited the trees.

They stared in disbelief at the half-naked man with torn breeches who staggered towards them and then collapsed. Lukas spurred his horse forward and the others followed. The brother knight sheathed his sword and dismounted when he reached the poor wretch, kneeling beside him and gently lifting his head off the ground. He saw the bloody crucifixes around his neck and the wounds to each of his toes, then caught site of the lacerated top of his shoulders.

'Water bottle.'

Johann threw him his waxed leather water bottle and Lukas uncorked it and tipped some of the contents into the man's mouth.

'Abbot Hylas,' he said gently, 'what in God's name happened to you?'

They took the abbot back to Wenden slung belly first over Lukas' horse so as not to aggravate the weeping wounds on his back. Conrad cut the rope that fastened the sack of what he thought was meat to his ankle and carried that back to the castle as well. In the excitement everyone forgot about the boar.

Hylas was transported to the Master's Hall where he was placed in Berthold's bedroom. Ilona was summoned to treat his wounds and Conrad saw her enter the hall carrying a box filled with herbs and potions. He still had the sack hanging from his saddle as he and the others dismounted in the courtyard.

'What have you there, Conrad?'

Conrad stopped to see Rudolf and Henke walking towards him.

'We found Abbot Hylas whilst on patrol.'

'He was in a bad way,' said Johann.

Henke looked at Rudolf and then at the sack hanging from Conrad's saddle. 'What's that?'

'It was tied to the abbot's ankle,' replied Anton.

Henke lifted the sack from the saddle and pulled his knife from its sheath.

'I was wrong about not seeing the missionaries again, Rudolf. I underestimated the Estonians.'

He sliced open the sack and emptied its contents at Conrad's feet. The novice jumped in alarm as three severed heads rolled onto the cobbles, their necks packed with salt and sealed with hide to prevent the sack being stained with blood.

'Looks like Lembit did not appreciate Christian missionaries on his land.'

'So the peace is over,' said Rudolf. 'Well, it was always going to come to this, I suppose.'

Henke stuffed the heads back in the sack and handed it to Conrad, who turned up his nose in disgust.

'Take these to Otto. He will arrange a proper funeral for them.'

'What about the rest of their bodies?' said Anton.

Henke shrugged. 'What about them?'

'Surely it is not proper to bury just the heads?' remarked an appalled Anton.

'You're right,' agreed Henke. 'You boys ride north and ask Lembit to give up the cadavers. I'll give you a fresh sack so he can put all your heads in it.'

'Just take their remains to Father Otto,' said Rudolf. 'They will be interred in the cemetery, along with others who will fall in the coming conflict no doubt.'

Conrad gave the reins of his horse to Hans and held the sack at arm's length as he walked towards the chapel. Henke came to his side and placed an arm around his shoulders.

'Do you feel bad, Conrad?'

'No. Why?'

'I was just thinking that if you had aimed that crossbow properly when you had Lembit in your sights then perhaps those monks might be still alive. A useful lesson for you: always aim before you shoot and never let any enemy escape.'

Rudolf must have told him about letting that Lithuanian boy go at the Dvina. Henke laughed and slapped him on the back. Sometimes he really disliked the brother knight.

The atrocities committed against Abbot Hylas and his monks prompted an emergency gathering at Riga. As the bishop had once more returned to Germany to recruit crusaders for the coming year the meeting was hosted by Archdeacon Stefan in the bishop's palace. Berthold took Rudolf to the assembly, both of them travelling by riverboat from Wenden down the Gauja before riding south to Riga. When they arrived at the town they found it crowded with crusaders, Livs and an increasing number of settlers from Germany, in addition to markets teeming with Russian and Lithuanian traders. The burning of the bridge of boats across the Dvina had allowed the waterway to once again become a highway for trade and so Riga's docks and markets filled with goods and the bishop's treasury filled with money.

Outside the town walls the tents of the crusaders were slowly being replaced with wooden huts so the soldiers and squires could live out the winter in a modicum of comfort, their masters being housed inside the town's defences. The castle was crammed with knights, much to the consternation of Grand Master Volquin. Berthold and Rudolf found him in his office, his desk piled high with papers. One of the two sergeants standing guard at his door showed them in, Volquin looking up and pointing to the chairs opposite his desk.

'You have become a librarian, grand master,' Berthold teased him.

'Bring some wine,' Volquin instructed the sergeant. He threw one of the parchments on the desk. 'The demands of my castellans are insatiable. Mail, helmets, horses, saddles and harnesses. The list is endless.'

He rifled through the papers. 'I have one from you as well, Berthold. Ah, here it is. Two tons of iron in addition to the usual annual request for weapons and armour.'

'My crossbowmen need iron tips for their bolts, grand master, especially after the Lithuanian assault.'

'You should have dug the used ones out of the bodies of the dead heathens,' suggested Volquin.

'We did,' replied Berthold.

'And we melted down their mail armour and helmets,' added Rudolf.

'And still you need more iron?' Volquin asked in amazement.

'Wenden will be a great fortress, grand master,' said Berthold, 'perhaps the greatest in all Livonia. As such it will need a well-stocked armoury and a large garrison. It is on the frontier with Estonia and must remain strong, the more so now the first settlers from Germany have arrived.'

'The bishop is most eager that they prosper,' said Volquin. 'Those that can be enticed here are usually granted land around Riga but the bishop hopes that those who were persuaded to go to Wenden will be the first of many to settle in the heart of Livonia.'

'Their homes are within sight of the castle walls and we send out regular patrols to the north to provide warning of Estonian war parties,' said Berthold.

'They can be brought within the perimeter wall quickly enough,' added Rudolf, 'which is just as well seeing as Lembit has made his intentions clear.'

'You think he will assault Wenden?' asked Volquin.

'He has neither the men nor the machines to batter Wenden into submission,' said Berthold. 'He has thrown down the gauntlet and awaits our response.'

'Archdeacon Stefan cries out for revenge,' remarked Volquin.

'And he will lead an expedition against Lembit in the bishop's absence?' enquired Rudolf.

Volquin smile wryly. 'I think that is very unlikely. The archdeacon likes soft living and playing the king in the bishop's absence. I doubt he has ever sat upon a horse. But he is most eager for Estonia to be conquered so Bishop Theodoric can take up his bishopric and Stefan can be rid of him. They do not get on.'

That was hardly surprising as the two were exact opposites: Stefan sly and cunning; Theodoric pious and forthright. But at the meeting that took place the next day they did at least see eye to eye. The gathering was held in the great hall of the bishop's palace where long tables covered with fine linen had been arranged in a great rectangle. At one end sat Stefan and Theodoric flanked by their abbots, half a dozen clerks sitting at desks behind them to record the proceedings for posterity. Along one side were seated the Sword Brothers: Grand Master Volquin in the centre with his castellans and their deputies around him. Opposite the order sat the leaders of the crusaders who had vowed to stay in Livonia for at least a year, though some like Sir Helmold had decided to make the new kingdom their semi-permanent home. He and Count Horton sat next to each other, their lords either side of them. While opposite the archdeacon and Theodoric sat Caupo, Thalibald and four other Liv chiefs. Thalibald had been at Treiden when the archdeacon's summons had arrived and rode directly to Riga in the company of his king.

The bishop's palace was now far removed from the plain, humble building it had resembled when Riga had been first established. In the subsequent years it had been extended and reworked. Now all the rooms had oak panelling, chairs covered with silk, stuffed with cushions and with grand tapestries adorning the walls. In the great hall itself a fire burned in a magnificent stone fireplace that was carved with scenes from the life of Christ, while above hung a huge silk banner bearing the cross keys symbol of Riga. Servants wearing scarlet tunics embroidered with the symbol of the town served wine to the guests in silver flagons and pastries in silver bowls.

When everyone had been seated the doors were closed and Archdeacon Stefan rose and invited Bishop Theodoric to say prayers. As one the whole assembly stood and bowed their heads as the deep voice of the bishop filled the chamber.

'Through God's strength to pilot me.

God's might to uphold me,

God's wisdom to guide me,

God's eye to look before me,

God's ear to hear me,

God's word to speak for me,

God's hand to guard me,

God's way to lie before me,

God's host to save me from snares of devils,

From temptations of vices,

From every one who shall wish me ill,

Afar and near,

Alone and in multitude.

I summon today all these powers between me and those evils,

Against every cruel and merciless power that may oppose my body and soul,

Against incantation of false prophets,

Against black laws of pagandom,

Against false laws of heretics,

Against craft of idolatry,

Against spells of women and smiths and wizards,

Against every knowledge that corrupts man's body and soul.

Amen.'

Once seated Archdeacon Stefan wasted no time in reporting the outrages committed against Abbot Hylas and his monks, which produced a wave of anger in the hall, particularly among the crusaders.

Stefan held up his hands. 'Brothers, we cannot allow such acts to go unpunished. The defeat of the Lithuanians and the presence of our brave crusaders from Germany,' he smiled at Sir Helmold and Count Horton, 'means that we can now undertake the conquest of Estonia, which I propose should commence immediately.'

The crusader lords banged the table to signal their agreement but Grand Master Volquin stood and folded his arms. Stefan frowned when he saw him staring in silence at the lords opposite, the din gradually dying down as they noticed him.

'You have something to say, grand master?' said Stefan.

Volquin unfolded his arms. 'We have recently and with some difficulty defeated a Lithuanian invasion that inflicted heavy casualties upon King Caupo's forces.' He extended a hand to the king.

'Furthermore,' continued Volquin, 'it will soon be winter and the land will be frozen, and whilst it is possible to campaign with small-sized forces in such conditions a large army will be difficult to maintain. We all remember the losses among our brave crusaders when the garrison of Wenden stormed Fellin.'

'And if the Sword Brothers had occupied that pagan fortress,' snapped Stefan, 'then likely we would not be in this predicament.'

There were murmurs of agreement from the crusader lords until Sir Helmold told them to be quiet. He at least knew the difficulties of campaigning in Livonia.

501

Volquin was unperturbed. 'Archdeacon, you may remember that the attack on Fellin was a raid only, designed to illustrate our strength to Lembit.'

'He seems to have forgotten the lesson,' remarked Stefan sourly, prompting laughter among the crusader lords.

Volquin sat down. 'And may I remind everyone that two years ago Livonia was in such straightened circumstances that the bishop had to negotiate a peace treaty with the Estonians and the Lithuanians.'

'The Lithuanians are no more,' said Stefan dismissively.

'Lembit cannot go unpunished, grand master,' said Theodoric.

'I know that, lord bishop.'

Stefan was going to say something but Theodoric stilled him. 'Then what do you propose?'

Volquin stood again. 'A winter raid into Estonia followed by an invasion of Lembit's territory in the spring when the bishop returns.'

His subordinates were nodding their heads, as were Caupo and his chiefs, but the crusaders were most unhappy.

Count Horton rose from his chair. 'We have three thousand soldiers sitting on their arses here and all you propose is a raid?'

Volquin smiled at Horton. 'My lord, you will find that the cold of Livonia can whittle down an army in a short space of time, the more so since it will have to sit in front of the walls of Lembit's fortresses in addition to forming a defensive screen to defeat any attempts at relief.'

'Lembit's fortresses, as you call them,' sneered Stefan, 'are nothing but timber forts that can be burned with ease.'

Horton and the other crusader lords laughed, though Sir Helmold was staring reflectively at the tabletop.

Volquin held up his hands. 'It is as you say, archdeacon, and as the bishop's representative the final decision rests in your hands. The Order of Sword Brothers will gladly ride beside you when you lead the army against the pagans. Give the order and I can assemble my forces at Riga in two weeks.'

Stefan blanched and it looked as though he was going to panic as all eyes turned in his direction. But his wits, probably his greatest asset, did not desert him. His eyes narrowed as he regarded the grand master and his calculating demeanor returned.

'We have been remiss,' he said, 'for in our thirst to punish Lembit we have allowed ourselves to become discourteous.'

The Sword Brothers and crusader lords looked at each other in confusion.

Stefan rose from his chair and held out his arms towards Caupo. 'It is only fitting that we hear from one who grew up in this land, a man whose opinion the bishop always seeks before he embarks upon a campaign, as will I.'

'That's news to me,' Volquin whispered to Berthold.

Stefan smiled at the somewhat surprised Caupo and sat down. The king could not remember a time when the archdeacon had even been civil to him, let alone seek his opinion. However, he took the opportunity that was being presented to him, slowly rising to his feet. He looked at the row of crusader lords, for it was they whom he had to convince.

'If you fight Lembit now, the snow will be on the ground before you are able to march. If you march in the winter your great warhorses will die from exposure, and after them your squires and then your foot soldiers. If, as Grand Master Volquin desires, you mount a properly organised raid into the enemy's lands, leaving your great horses behind and travelling light but with proper provisions, then you will achieve your aims and will live to take part in the bishop's great campaign when he returns in the spring.'

Sir Helmold smiled at the king as he sat down but his lords were silent as they weighed up his words. As Christian knights they were compelled to avenge the wrongs done to Abbot Hylas and his monks. However, the thought of losing their precious warhorses dampened their enthusiasm. Losing a squire was of less import.

'Once again your majesty illuminates proceedings with the light of your wisdom,' said Stefan, who then turned to the crusaders. 'I think it would be prudent, my lords, to leave the details of the raid to his majesty and the grand master, and to gird our loins for the great battle with the devil's servants in the spring.'

Volquin, feeling mischievous, raised a hand.

'Yes, grand master?' said Stefan.

'Does this mean that you will not be leading the army against Lembit?'

'Did you not hear his majesty, grand master?' said Stefan gruffly, 'to undertake a major campaign in the winter is to invite disaster. I have been charged with safeguarding the bishop's interests, not squandering his forces in an exercise in vanity. You surprise me, grand master.'

'And you never fail to amaze me, archdeacon,' replied Volquin.

The archdeacon heard the slight but let it go, though the other Sword Brothers could not resist smiling.

'So it is agreed,' said Theodoric, 'we raid the enemy this winter and wait until the bishop's return in the new year before finishing Lembit once and for all.'

'God willing,' said Volquin.

'Ay, God willing,' replied Theodoric.

'There is also the matter of Gerzika,' remarked Stefan, 'and more specifically how we are to deal with Prince Vsevolod.'

'He should die,' spat Sir Helmold.

'I am apt to agree with Sir Helmold,' said Caupo. 'Despite his apparent close relations with the bishop he did nothing to alert us of the invasion of the Lithuanians and, when they were butchering my people, he did not send troops to aid our cause.'

'We should march on his city right away,' shouted Count Horton, to thunderous applause from his fellow lords.

Volquin once again rose from his chair. 'My lords, noble though your intentions are Gerzika lies nearly a hundred miles to the east of this town. We cannot raid Estonia and assault Gerzika at the same time.'

'But Vsevolod must be punished for his treachery,' said Theodoric. the lords murmuring their approval.

'And he will be, lord bishop,' said Volquin, 'only not this year. He is, after all, not going anywhere.'

'He is not at Gerzika,' said Stefan, 'he is in Lithuania.'

Volquin was most surprised. 'Oh?'

'The river gossip talks of Vsevolod being in the stronghold of his dead father-in-law, along with his wife and children,' continued Stefan. 'He is now grand duke of the Lithuanian tribes, or at least those who have remained loyal to the memory of his wife's father. Vsevolod will not be able to keep peace among the Lithuanian tribes and resist an assault against Gerzika.'

'Then let us sail down the river and storm it,' suggested Count Horton.

'It is still garrisoned,' said Stefan, 'and its defences are strong and will require siege engines to breach.'

'You seem to know much about Gerzika, archdeacon,' remarked Volquin.

'I make it my business to know about the bishop's enemies, grand master,' replied Stefan.

'Be that as it may,' said Theodoric. 'Gerzika will have to wait until Lembit has been crushed. We deal with the Estonians first and then Prince Vsevolod. Does everyone concur?'

He looked at the crusader lords who said nothing, smiling at Caupo when he caught the eye of the king. Volquin's serious face nodded his approval and so the meeting was concluded with everyone standing whilst Theodoric asked for God's blessing on the decisions they had taken.

The next day there was a meeting in the grand master's office, which was crowded as his castellans and their deputies crammed into the room to petition Volquin on their requests for supplies. He told them that Stefan had refused to authorise the release of armour, weapons and supplies from the well-stocked storerooms and armoury in Riga's castle until the bishop had returned from Germany.

'We need the supplies now, grand master,' insisted Master Friedhelm.

'We also need money to pay our mercenaries,' said Master Berthold. 'We may fight for God but they kill for money and if they do not receive their wages then they will pack up and leave.'

'It is true, grand master,' added Master Griswold. 'My mercenaries are already complaining that they have not been paid in six months. They will not go another half year without pay.'

Volquin held up his hands. 'Brothers, I hear your pleas and have given a great deal of thought to the matter of money. Archdeacon Stefan believes that he has the Sword Brothers over a barrel but I will show him that our order is not the plaything of a jumped-up office boy.'

Volquin picked up a number of parchments from his desk and held them up.

'We all know that the Dvina is a highway along which goods flow to the markets in this town, and that merchants pay tolls for the privilege of trading here. They get rich and the bishop's treasury fills with gold. My brothers, it is time that we dipped our toes into the rich waters of the Dvina.'

He smiled and looked up to see a row of blank expressions.

'It is quite simple,' he said. 'Along the Dvina travel boats filled with fur, flax, timber, tar, corn and hides. And when these Russians and Lithuanians sail or row to Riga they have to pass the castles of the Sword Brothers.'

'Our castles along the Dvina provide security for the merchants,' said Master Gerhard.

'Indeed they do,' concurred Volquin. 'And now they will discover that security has to be paid for.'

'You wish us to plunder shipping on the river?' asked Master Friedhelm.

505

Volquin feigned shock. 'Plunder, Master Friedhelm? We are the knights of Christ. We do not plunder, we protect. No, no. We exact a small tax, that is all, in order to raise the funds that will allow us to supply our brother knights and sergeants and pay for our mercenaries. In doing so I do not have to trouble Archdeacon Stefan with petitions, thereby giving him more time to address matters of state, such as the colour of the seat covers in the bishop's palace.'

The others laughed.

'He will not like it,' warned Master Berthold.

'I will have to take that chance,' replied Volquin.

He handed one of the parchments to Master Griswold. 'This document authorises you to stop and search all vessels that pass by Kokenhusen. It also instructs you to levy a tax on any vessels carrying furs and hides, the precise amount stated on the document.'

He next handed a parchment to Master Aldous. 'Lennewarden will levy a toll on those vessels carrying flax.'

He handed the last two parchments to masters Friedhelm and Gerhard, telling them that Uexkull would tax vessels carrying timber and tar while Holm would impose a levy on boats transporting corn and other crops.

'In this way we will raise enough money to maintain our garrisons. All monies collected will be evenly divided between the castles along the Dvina and along the Gauja. And may God bless our enterprise.'

Berthold and Rudolf went back to Wenden in a far happier mood than when they had made their journey to Riga, though they and the other garrison commanders wondered about the reaction of Archdeacon Stefan when word reached him that the Sword Brothers were levying taxes on the Dvina's commerce.

'He came to this land the bishop's young nephew who had been taught to read and write,' said Berthold. 'And now he has the ear of Bishop Albert, is the governor of Riga and has the town garrison and militia at his command.'

'He made himself indispensible to the bishop,' remarked Rudolf, 'and has been richly rewarded. But to what end?'

'To what end? To our friend the archdeacon ambition is an end in itself. As his power and position grows so does the fear that he may lose it all. And that makes him dangerous.'

Rudolf thought of the pale-skinned, slightly portly archdeacon with his feminine hands and laughed. 'Dangerous?'

'Not all enemies wear armour and carry swords, Rudolf.'

The winter was the most severe that anyone could remember. The Dvina and Gauja froze solid and the lakes and smaller rivers and streams became as hard as iron. Christmas was celebrated at Wenden as usual and Master Berthold welcomed not only Thalibald and his family but also the German settlers who shivered in their newly built huts. And as usual Conrad and the other novices served the Christmas meal to the master and his guests in the dining hall. It had snowed nearly every day in December and the whole garrison had been employed in shovelling snow to clear the courtyard, track and walkways between huts, though Lukas always made sure that they did not neglect their training.

They undertook exhausting patrols on foot, wading through the deep snow with snowshoes fashioned from branches on their feet. When it stopped snowing the skies were clear and blue, the land an endless sea of pure white. When the sun shone it reflected off the snow and ice and could lead to snow blindness, so they wore eye protectors: wooden masks that were carved to fit the top half of the wearer's face. Tied behind the head with leather thongs, they had long, thin slits cut in them for the wearer to see through that allowed only a small amount of light to enter. Anton thought they looked ridiculous but Lukas told them that it stopped them going snow blind and such masks were worn by the hunters of the far north where the night never came.

It was bitterly cold but beautiful, though not as beautiful as Daina who graced the castle for three days at Christmas. Conrad was allowed to walk alone with her in the courtyard and within the perimeter, Rudolf informing him that her father held him and the other novices in high regard, but him especially as he had saved the bishop's life.

'Just remember that a knight thinks more of a maiden's honour than he does his own life.'

'I would never besmirch her honour, Brother Rudolf. But I'm not a knight.'

'You will be soon,' said Rudolf, 'a knight of Christ.'

But he was not thinking of being a knight as he walked with Daina in the courtyard towards the bridge across the moat.

'My father thinks highly of you, Conrad,' she told him. 'If you asked him for my hand in marriage he would say yes.'

His heart soared and he could not suppress a smile. 'He said that?'

She stopped and turned to face him, her green eyes sparkling with excitement. 'He does not have to. I know my own father.'

507

He wanted to grasp both her hands but resisted the temptation, aware that sergeants and brother knights were going about their business.

'I want nothing more, my love, but…'

A frown creased her forehead. 'But what?'

'In the new year the great campaign against Lembit will begin. I wish to be a part of it.'

Daina's frown was replaced by concern. 'You will go to war again?'

'Of course, that is why I was brought here all those years ago. Once Lembit is defeated there will be peace in Livonia and then we can be married.'

She was disappointed, he could see, but he could not desert his companions.

'Next year Hans, Anton and Johann will be made brother knights but I will choose to leave the order and marry you, Daina, if you will wait that long.'

She smiled at him and leaned closer. 'I will wait for you, my heart. Just ensure that you come back from your war.'

He felt like a conquering hero. 'I always come back. In any case, Brother Rudolf has said that such is the size of the army that will march against Lembit that he will probably give up without a fight.'

'And then we can be married?'

It was his turn to smile. 'And then we can be married, though I don't know where we shall live.'

'In my father's village, of course,' she replied. 'He will give us a hut and we will keep pigs and goats and share in the harvest. And in the winter we will hunt elk and wolves and wrap ourselves in wolfskins. And I will bear you strong sons and you will become the headman of your own village in time.'

'You have it all worked out,' said Conrad.

She brushed his nose. 'The winters in Livonia are long and hard and there is plenty of time to think.'

They walked on snow-cleared paths under a clear-blue sky and made plans for their future together. It was a happy time and war and death seemed far away. The north tower had a completed second floor and the foundations of the gatehouse had been built on. Wenden continued to grow, a physical indication of the rising power of the Sword Brothers and the defeat of paganism.

*****

Nigul stared out to sea, his blue eyes ringed with red from the bitter wind that was blowing from the north. He wrapped his fur-lined cloak made from the hide of a brown bear around his shoulders, his head covered by a fur-lined cap. Despite the layers of clothing he could not get warm. It was the bitterest winter he could remember in all his sixty years, made more unsavoury by the corpses that littered the beach. The sea along the shore had frozen, the light brown sand being fringed by a band of white ice that extended out for at least a hundred paces before the black waters of the Baltic began. Some of his people had attempted to flee to safety across the ice but had fallen through it and drowned in the raw sea, but most had been butchered on the beach. His men were going among the bodies to see if any still lived but he knew it was a fruitless search.

The crusaders had struck north from Treiden, moving across the frozen landscape with their Liv allies to enter western Saccalia and then Rotalia where they divided into small groups to attack villages. They came to burn, kill and steal and they carried out their aims with ruthless efficiency before disappearing before he could organise an effective response. Now all he could do was bury the dead.

'They are all dead, lord,' reported his deputy.

He nodded but said nothing.

'Will we take a war party south, lord?'

'My first responsibility is to my people,' said Nigul. 'The crusaders might return and until I am certain that they will not then my warriors will stay in Rotalia to guard them.'

He looked around at the corpses on the beach. 'I should have been here instead of drinking ale with Lembit.'

In the aftermath of the execution of the Christian missionaries and the return of their leader to the bishop's territory, Lembit had requested the presence of the Estonian chiefs at Lehola. There, amid great festivities, he had informed them that the final war against the Christians was about to begin and that in the spring they should bring their warriors to his stronghold so they could march south in a great army that would rid the world of the bishop and his followers once and for all. He had told them that the crusader kingdom was on its knees, having suffered a Lithuanian invasion that had only been defeated with difficulty. Their Oeselian allies would attack Riga from the sea while the Estonians would sweep through Livonia like a plague.

Nigul and the other chiefs had toasted their host and saluted his plan, getting drunk on copious amounts of ale in a smoke-filled hall that smelt of roasted meat and sweat. It had all seemed so simple then. He and the other chiefs had known that the bishop had begged Lembit for peace, and only weak men begged. And so they drank themselves into oblivion and dreamed of driving the Christians into the sea along with their Liv allies. And then the crusaders had attacked.

The survivors, those who had managed to hide in the woods or flee north to other villages through the snow, had told of hundreds of soldiers on ponies and on foot, of Caupo leading hundreds more Livs who razed villages to the ground after stealing food and livestock, butchering any who protested. Near the coast Rotalian settlements had always built and maintained watchtowers to warn of the approach of raiders, usually Oeselian longships. They had lit their beacons to warn of the approach of the crusaders but they had availed them little, the Christians shooting the tiny shield walls to pieces with their crossbows before the men of iron finished off the survivors. By the time Nigul had collected his army it had been too late.

'Too late,' he said to himself.

'Lord?'

He turned his back to the bitter wind and faced his subordinate. 'Evacuate the villages south of here and take their inhabitants to those settlements in the north, together with their food and livestock.'

His subordinate looked troubled. 'In these conditions, lord, many will die.'

'If they remain here and the crusaders return all will die,' snapped Nigul. 'Obey my orders.'

The man saluted and walked away, barking orders to his men to collect the bodies on the beach. Nigul's stag banner fluttered in the wind at the head of his bodyguard as he walked to his pony. He heard the voice of Lembit in his mind and his anger rose. Like a love-struck young boy he had been seduced by the Saccalian's honeyed words and had allowed himself to be deluded into thinking that the crusaders could be brushed aside with ease. This corpse-littered beach had disabused him of that notion. He would not be taking his warriors south to fight beside Lembit in the spring. Let the Saccalians and the other tribes shed their blood for once. He would rather have the old times back when his enemy was the Oeselians and no one had even heard of the Bishop of Riga and his crusaders.

Nigul spurred his pony forward back to the track that had led to the beach. His men were piling bodies onto carts for cremation on the pyre that was being built by the survivors from the nearby village. Flecks of snow swirled around in the air as the breeze continued to buffet the living and the dead on the beach. Nigul scowled; if anything it was getting colder. The sooner this dreadful winter ended the better for in the spring and summer the rivers, bogs and flood plain grasslands of southern Rotalia and western Saccalia created an excellent impediment to the movement of armies. Wagons, carts and horses sunk in the bogs and even the forests filled with four or five feet of floodwater every spring. But at present the area was frozen solid and gave easy access to his people's heartland. At least in two months' time the weather would get warm and the ice and snow would melt, as would his alliance with Lembit.

Chapter 19

At the beginning of May in the new year an army camped in the lush meadows around Wenden. The bishop had returned from Germany the previous month, bringing with him two hundred knights and the same number of squires to fight for his cause, plus four hundred lesser knights that were under obligation to serve their masters. In addition, the burghers of the city of Lübeck had paid for the raising and equipping of five hundred foot soldiers for the bishop to take back with him to Livonia. These men wore tan coloured brigandines – jackets with protective metal plates underneath that covered their torsos and groins – with the shield of the city of Lübeck sewn on the left-hand side of the chest. The design was a simple shield, the top half white, the bottom half red, but it awakened long dormant feelings within Conrad when he first saw it as the soldiers from his home city pitched their camp to the east of the castle, towards the quarry.

The Bishop of Riga arrived at the head of the army accompanied by Theodoric, a mounted bodyguard of twenty men, a hundred of his spearmen and an equivalent number of his crossbowmen. The two bishops were housed in the master's hall, which meant that Conrad and the other novices were ejected from their dormitory to make room for the priests attending the bishop, in addition to Master Berthold.

Two hundred knights, three hundred mounted retainers and two hundred squires accompanied Sir Helmold. Count Horton mustered a hundred knights, the same number of squires and two hundred mounted retainers. Their foot soldiers had been distributed among the castles along the Dvina to counter any new Lithuanian incursions into the crusader kingdom. Because of this threat the garrisons of Holm, Uexkull, Lennewarden and Kokenhusen remained at their castles, but the Sword Brothers from Segewold, Kremon and Wenden gathered at the latter place prior to marching north. It had been nearly a year since the Lithuanian invasion and during that time the order had replenished their garrisons with new recruits. This meant that there was a full complement of brother knights and sergeants, new members having come from among the crusaders who had arrived the previous year. Many of the knights had also donated funds to the order, which had helped to alleviate its parlous financial state. Together with those men Grand Master Volquin brought with him from Riga, the Sword Brothers at Wenden mustered forty-one brother knights, a hundred and fifty sergeants, one hundred and ten crossbowmen and an equal number of spearmen.

512

The final contingent of the army comprised Caupo, Thalibald and a thousand Liv warriors who camped around the latter's village, being eager to avoid the smell and filth of the three thousand men camped around the castle, together with their horses, mules and oxen. Dozens of two- and four-wheeled wagons littered the camp, draught animals held in corrals nearby. Squires and foot soldiers were sent into the forest to bring back firewood and materials to build animal pens to hold the cattle, goats, and chickens that provided a mobile source of milk and meat for the army. It was fortunate that Livonia was filled with lush meadows where animals could graze.

Nevertheless, Grand Master Volquin had planned this campaign very carefully, and so as well as living off the land the wagons contained barrels of salted fish and meat as well as thousands of crackers – twice-baked bread – that had been prepared in Riga's ovens and which reportedly lasted a hundred years if stored correctly. There were also barrels of mead made from the honey of the beehives that littered Livonia, though the knights from Germany had reportedly brought with them a cog filled with nothing but wine casks.

Though there were women with the army – mostly the wives of Lübeck's foot soldiers but also some whores – Master Berthold was very aware that the wives of Wenden's civilian workers and the females of the settlers might be vulnerable to assault and so he forbade anyone entering the castle grounds without permission and placed guards around the small village. He was also eager for the army to commence its march from Wenden as soon as possible to prevent pestilence breaking out, especially as the temperature was rising, as was the stench that he believed carried disease.

Conrad could not hear his friend's words.

'What did you say?'

Hans pulled down the mask covering the lower half of his face. 'I said you should wear a mask.'

Conrad laughed. 'Why?'

Hans, who had replaced his mask, pulled it down again. 'Because everyone knows that bad air carries pestilence.'

'You look ridiculous,' was all that Conrad said.

They had been instructed to go to the forest to chop some firewood, Conrad leading the mule that pulled the two-wheeled cart on which had been loaded the axes.

'Are you really going to leave the order?'

513

Conrad looked down. 'I don't want to, but I cannot marry Daina and become a brother knight.'

'It is a great honour to become a brother knight,' said Hans, who had forgotten about his mask. 'When I stood before the judge in Lübeck accused of theft I did not expect to end up here and about to become a brother knight. Who would have thought it, a lowly thief becoming a knight.'

Conrad halted and placed a hand on his shoulder. 'I can think of no one more worthy of the white surcoat, my friend.'

They heard a shout and men cursing and looked towards the trees fifty paces away. They had threaded their way through the sprawling camp to head for the woods to the northeast of the castle, leaving the tents and campfires behind as they led the mule across a meadow filled with grazing cows. They heard a woman's scream, then evil laughs and knew something was awry.

Conrad released the mule's reins and drew his sword. 'Come on.'

They ran to the trees and entered the forest, to see four men bent over a struggling figure on the ground. Conrad noticed an empty wicker basket nearby and knew that it was Ilona the men had pinned to the earth, who had foolishly left the castle without any guards. Two were holding her wrists, a third was holding her legs and attempting to lift up her dress while a fourth was standing over here, licking his lips. He tossed a rag on the ground.

'Put this in her mouth to shut the bitch up.'

One of the men, wearing the shield of Lübeck on his brigandine, took the cloth and shoved it into Ilona's mouth. She was struggling like a woman possessed but they were four soldiers against one woman and she probably knew that she would be raped at the very least.

'Let her go,' said Conrad.

'Piss off,' sneered the standing man.

Perhaps he thought the two young men, attired only in shirts, leggings and boots, were no match for him and his comrades, or perhaps he was so preoccupied with the idea of raping his victim that he gave them no thought at all.

'Forgive me, Brother Lukas,' said Conrad, who tossed his sword into his left hand, pulled his dagger from its sheath and then hurled it at the standing man. The long, thin blade plunged into his neck, a fountain of blood spurting from the wound as Conrad transferred the sword back to his right hand and thrust the point into the chest of one of the men who had been holding Ilona's wrists, the blade going through the brigandine, between the metal plates and between his ribs. His spluttered and tried to say something but though his mouth opened no words came out as Conrad pulled back the blade and stood facing the other two soldiers.

'Safeguard Ilona,' he said to Hans as he circled them, who kept glancing at their two dead comrades.

They were both armed with swords – the burghers of Lübeck had been generous – and they thought they were more than a match for him.

Conrad smiled, glanced behind him to ensure that Ilona was safe, and then focused on the task in hand.

'Do you want any assistance, Conrad?' queried Hans.

'That will not be necessary,' replied his friend as the first man lunged at him with his sword.

It was a clumsy, predictable strike that might have caught him three years ago, but Conrad could now wield a sword with dexterity and, more importantly, could anticipate what an adversary was going to do. He had already leapt to the left as the man was about to strike and so his thrust struck air. Conrad brought up his sword and slashed it down it a blur, severing the man's right hand at the wrist. He emitted a scream that was loud enough to waken the dead as the hand, still holding the sword, fell to the ground and blood gushed from the bloody stump. The man collapsed to his knees and moaned as he stared in disbelief at his severed hand.

Conrad spread his arms wide to present his torso as a target to the last would-be rapist, a portly, middle aged man who had no doubt spent many an afternoon in the ale house following a morning spent on the training field as part of Lübeck's city militia. There were beads of sweat on his forehead as he held his sword towards Conrad. The latter turned to Hans.

'Take Ilona back to the castle on the cart, Hans, I will finish affairs here.'

'Are you sure?' asked Hans.

Conrad smiled. 'Oh, yes, I am sure.'

Hans, his arm around Ilona's shoulders, led her from the trees to the cart.

'God bless you, Conrad,' she called to him.

'Are you going to use that sword or are we both going to die of old age?' he said to the chubby man.

The man said nothing but kept glancing at his whimpering comrade on his knees clutching his bloody wrist and at the trees to his left and right.

'If you run I will catch you,' Conrad told him, walking towards him. 'You are too fat to get away.'

The man suddenly lunged forward, swinging his sword at Conrad's head. The latter ducked to avoid the blow and then jabbed the point of his sword into the man's right thigh before springing back out of range. The man yelped in pain and hobbled backwards.

'Interesting things, swords,' remarked Conrad, circling the fat man like a wolf observing its prey. 'Did you know, for example, that a fighter should never parry a sword blow with the cutting edge of his own sword?'

Conrad sprang forward, made to swing at the man's head, causing him to bring his sword up to block the blow, before whipping the blade back, crouching low and stabbing the point into his left thigh. He jumped back as the podgy man cried out in pain and dropped his sword.

'It's true,' continued Conrad. 'Meeting a blow with a sword's edge results in chips and heavy gouges and will eventually fracture and split it. Imagine that.'

The portly man's sword was now lying on the ground in front of him, Conrad standing some five paces away.

'What do you want?' he said.

Conrad stepped away from him and struck the man whose hand he had severed across the face with the back of his left fist. The man had been attempting to stagger to his feet.

'Stay on your knees.'

He turned back to face the chubby man. 'What do I want? Firewood, that is what I am here for.'

He pointed at the man's sword. 'That is a nice sword. You should treat such a weapon with respect. Pick it up.'

The man hesitated.

'Pick it up!' shouted Conrad.

The man stooped down to retrieve his weapon and in a flash Conrad lunged forward to drive the point of his sword through the man's outstretched hand, pinning it to the ground. The man screamed in pain and stared wide-eyed at the sword blade embedded in his hand. Conrad stepped on his fingers and slowly withdrew his blade, the victim screaming again as pain shot through his arm. He fell to the ground and held his wounded hand to his chest in a futile attempt to comfort the injured limb. Then he began to sob, rocking to and fro like an old woman.

Conrad heard horses' hooves and turned to face what he thought were more attackers. He smiled when he saw Rudolf, Henke and Lukas walk from the meadow into the trees, all carrying swords and shields. Behind them came Hans and Ilona, the latter with a face like thunder when she saw her attackers.

'These are the ones,' she said, pointing at the dead bodies and the two wounded men.

She smiled at Conrad and linked arms with Hans. 'Two gallant knights came to my rescue.'

'So it would seem,' said Rudolf. 'You can put your sword away now, Conrad.'

Conrad wiped his blade on the brigandine of one of the dead men and slid it back in its scabbard. Henke stood over the man with the severed hand.

'Do you want me to kill them, Rudolf?'

Rudolf shook his head. 'No, we take them back to Wenden. They must be tried and convicted before a court.'

Henke was disappointed. 'They are going to be hanged so what is the difference?'

'The difference, my friend, is that justice must be seen to be done. Hans, go and fetch the cart.'

'This one might bleed to death first,' said Henke, looking at the severed hand.

Lukas went over to one of the corpses, removed the belt around its waist and used it as a tourniquet to staunch the loss of blood from the arm that no longer had a hand.

Henke looked around and nodded. 'You did well, Conrad.'

'Thank you, Brother Henke,' said Conrad.

'You taught him well, Lukas,' said Ilona as Henke hauled the two wounded men to their feet and bundled them towards the meadow.

'I've never seen his trick before.'

Lukas raised an eyebrow. 'Trick?'

'Yes. Swapping his sword from one hand to the next and throwing his dagger at one of my attackers. Look, the dagger is still in him. Such skill.'

Lukas folded his arms and Rudolf shook his head.

'Did I teach you to throw your weapons away or treat them like juggling balls?' said Lukas calmly.

Conrad's cheeks became red with embarrassment. 'No, Brother Lukas.'

Lukas wagged a finger at him. 'No I did not.' He looked at the corpse with the dagger in its throat.

'You had better retrieve your dagger, unless you have learnt a trick to make it jump back into its sheath.'

Conrad looked down and shuffled over to the dead man, pulling his dagger from his neck, wiping it and slipping it back into its sheath.

'You can put the dead bodies on the back of the cart when it arrives,' said Lukas curtly. 'If I find out about any more tricks your sword will be confiscated. Is that understood?'

Conrad was crestfallen. 'Yes, Brother Lukas.'

However, Rudolf slapped him on the arm and thanked him and Ilona kissed him on the cheek as they went back to their horses, and back at the castle Lukas had nothing but praise for him and Hans and commended their actions to Master Berthold. The two surviving attackers were hanged the next day in the middle of the Lübeck camp alongside the two corpses. Bishop Albert, who was appalled when he heard of the incident, ordered that the bodies were to be left hanging until they rotted. He assembled the great lords in the master's hall and impressed upon them that the aim of the forthcoming campaign was to liberate the Estonians from their wicked ways and to lead them to Christ's teachings. Theodoric had been created Bishop of Estonia and it was their solemn duty to make the bishopric a reality.

It was mid-May when the army marched from Wenden on a sunny spring morning. The meadows were filled with buttercups, ivy and blackthorns and hares peeked above the long grass to observe the great column of horsemen, men on foot, carts and wagons that wound its way northeast towards Estonia.

Caupo and Thalibald, together with the latter's two sons, rode with the two bishops, Count Horton, Grand Master Volquin, Sir Helmold and Sir Jordan, the latter leading the newly arrived crusaders from Germany. Caupo provided the forward screen for the army, two hundred of his men on ponies scouting ahead to guard against Estonian attacks. Two score of Liv warriors from Thalibald's village were moved into Wenden to garrison the castle in the absence of the Sword Brothers and mercenaries. The latter were in a good mood at the prospect of plunder.

'They say that this Lembit is king of all the Estonians,' said leather face, crossbow over his shoulder as he walked beside the wagon that held spare bolts, spare crossbows and the tents and supplies for his men.

'Really?' remarked Conrad walking beside him after having helped him and the other crossbowmen load it after striking camp, his boots splattered with mud. Livonia in spring had beautiful fresh mornings but it invariably rained in the afternoon and that meant the track along which the army travelled quickly became muddy and rutted, slowing the rate of advance to five miles a day at best.

Leather face grinned wickedly. 'And you know what kings have, don't you?'

'Crowns?' offered Conrad.

'Treasuries filled with gold.'

Conrad saw the mischievous glint in his eyes. 'There are many fine lords in this army. They will have first call on any treasure, will they not?'

Leather face tapped his nose with a finger. 'Rules of war, boy. Any plunder taken must be divided up, the great and the good getting the largest share, the rest divided up among the common soldiery. But taking a king's palace means that there will be a nice share for everyone. Master Berthold will take care of us.'

'Then you will be able to go back to Germany and buy your alehouse,' said Conrad, stepping over a muddy puddle.

'Perhaps.' He looked at Conrad. 'What about you?'

'My life is here, in Livonia,' he answered, saying nothing of his desire to marry Daina.

'A life of poverty and loneliness,' sniffed leather face.

'Loneliness?'

'No women. Once you take the vows of a brother knight that's it, no women for you.'

Conrad shrugged. 'The Sword Brothers have been good to me.'

'Ha! You'll think differently when you are old and shivering to death in some draughty castle with no woman to warm your bed.'

'If we survive this campaign,' remarked Conrad.

'No reason why we shouldn't, not with so many knights and crossbowmen with us. The heathens will either be cut to pieces or shot down where they stand. Should be over in no time at all.'

But he was entirely wrong concerning the tactics that would be employed by the crusaders.

When Fellin had been attacked and captured three years before the Bishop of Riga had led just over four hundred men in the siege. Now he sent the four hundred lesser knights that had sailed with Sir Jordan from Germany, together with the entire complement of Lübeck's foot soldiers, to besiege Fellin. They were accompanied by a hundred of Caupo's Livs who were to act as scouts to warn of the approach of any Estonian relief force. Should such a relief force approach the fort the crusaders were ordered to immediately march the few miles north to Lehola where the main crusader army was located.

*****

'They will be here in two days, perhaps three.'

Lembit leaned on the timber walls of Lehola and stared south, across the endless expanse of forest, lakes, rivers and meadows that filled Saccalia. The land looked so peaceful, the sky filled with white clouds and the occasional flock of corncrakes.

'Send orders to the local headmen to bring their warriors here,' he told Rusticus, 'together with what food they can carry, their livestock as well. Tell them to burn their villages after they have escorted the women, young and old to their forest hiding places.'

Rusticus was surprised. 'Burn the villages?'

Lembit continued to stare south. 'The crusaders will either use them as stables for their horses or barracks for their soldiers. I see no reason to furnish them with accommodation.'

The crusaders were moving slowly north, guarding their multitude of wagons that contained their infernal machines that could batter down timber walls that had stood for centuries. Their Liv allies scouted far ahead of the bishop's army, making it almost impossible to mount a surprise attack against the men of iron.

With the advent of spring Lembit had sent word to the other chiefs but only the Jerwen and Wierlanders had pledged troops, and his riders had informed him that they were still many miles away. Kalju of the Ungannians, alarmed that his land was between the crusaders in the west and the Novgorodians in the east, had refused to send any warriors, informing him that he needed every man to defend his own lands. The Rotalians had been attacked during the winter and their villages raided, thus Nigul refused to leave his kingdom or allow any of his warriors to fight beside Lembit.

'Where was Saccalia when my people were being raped and murdered and their homes torched?' Nigul had written in his letter.

For his part Alva, leader of the Harrien, sat in Varbola and trembled at the thought of the crusaders raiding his territory as they had done to Rotalia.

Rusticus articulated his thoughts. 'They will not arrive in time.'

'I assume you mean our allies, Edvin and Jaak?'

Rusticus spat over the ramparts. 'If they come at all.'

520

Lembit turned away from the south and walked to the steps that led to the ground level of his stronghold. 'You should have more faith in the other tribes.'

Rusticus trailed after him. 'Why?'

Lembit stopped halfway down the wooden steps and faced his deputy. 'Because they all know that if Saccalia falls then so do they.'

He continued down the steps and walked briskly to his hall, Rusticus following. Already Lehola was a hive if activity, his wolf shields manning the walls and towers and smiths hammering on anvils in the forge as they mended helmets and fashioned blades. The armoury was well stocked with spears, axes, shields and arrows. The menfolk of the villages would bring their own weapons and food, and together with the supplies held in the fort's storerooms Lembit hoped that he would be able to hold out until his allies relieved him. Even though only two of the tribes were coming to his aid he reckoned on each chief marching with at least a thousand warriors. His wolf shields numbered five hundred men and he could muster at least fifteen hundred warriors from the surrounding villages. And the fort of Fellin was also manned by two hundred of his men who would be a thorn in the side of the crusaders when they came. The Christians would not be able to besiege Lehola and fight off a relief force. They would eventually be forced to retire and when that happened he would follow and harry them every step of the way back to Livonia.

His plan rested on the crusaders' inability to take Lehola, the strongest fortress in all Saccalia. Built on a great mound that had a dry moat surrounding its entirety, it was three times the size of Fellin. Rectangular in shape, it measured four hundred yards in length and was two hundred yards wide. Its timber walls contained thirteen towers, two of which flanked the main gates positioned in the middle of the southern wall. Inside the perimeter were storerooms, a forge, stables and huts that provided living quarters for the garrison. In the northern sector of the fortress was an inner citadel – the original stronghold – that had its own timber wall, towers in all four corners and which contained Lembit's great hall, more storerooms, huts, stables and the armoury. No enemy had ever breached Lehola's high walls since the first chief of the Saccalians had built it hundreds of years before.

That afternoon Lembit led a hundred warriors south when a scout rode into the fort with news that the crusaders were less than ten miles away. With the headmen from the surrounding villages still on their way, he had to slow the bishop's advance else the Christians would be at Lehola's gates before they arrived.

The Estonians rode due south for half a mile before heading west into the forest for two miles and then moving south once more. The crusaders were moving along the ancient track that led from Lehola south towards Fellin, which meandered its way through deep woods that were seldom ventured into by travellers. However, there were more ancient trails through the forest and Lembit and his men rode along one now as they journeyed south.

They moved slowly, their ponies walking through the spruce and pine trees. No one spoke to maintain stealth, though there was little need for silence as the raucous noises on their left would have drowned out any voices. They were now parallel to the crusaders as the latter moved north, Lembit estimating the distance between them to be a quarter of a mile, perhaps less. He held up his hand to halt the column, removed his helmet and craned his neck to listen. He heard muffled shouts and chopping noises. The crusaders were collecting firewood. He smiled and replaced his helmet. He dismounted, pointed towards the noise and led his pony on foot towards it. His men did likewise, now advancing in a line towards the left flank of the crusader army. After a hundred paces the ponies were left in the care of every tenth man, Lembit leading the rest on as they moved slowly and silently through the undergrowth.

Each man carried a shield, two javelins and a sword at his hip. Dressed in varying shades of browns and greens they blended into the background perfectly as they approached the enemy.

*****

Conrad threw the bundle of firewood into the back of the cart.

'Any sign of the Estonians?' he asked Rameke.

'None.'

His father had been riding in the company of the bishops, Grand Master Volquin, Caupo and the crusader lords, but he had sent his men to scout ahead and on the flanks of the crusader army as it inched its way towards Lehola. Rameke, now nineteen years old, led his own company of a hundred men, his elder brother Waribule also commanding a similar number of warriors. Conrad still felt like a boy in his friend's presence despite their near similarity in age. Rameke had great responsibility whereas he was still a novice.

'They must have locked themselves in their fort,' said Conrad, slotting the two-handed axe into the rack fitted to the cart's side.

Rameke turned and looked at the wagons, carts, foot soldiers and horsemen that filled the track north and south as far as the eye could see.

'The bishop's army is too large and well armed for Lembit to risk meeting it in battle.'

Anton threw another pile of firewood into the cart. 'He prefers to starve to death rather than dying in battle.'

Other carts pulled by a single mule stood at the edge of the forest, ready to receive the wood collected by other foraging parties – it was as well that Estonia was blanketed with forests otherwise the army would have no fuel for its campfires.

Hans and Johann threw their loads into the cart, which was barely a quarter full. Warriors stood behind Rameke, their shields resting on the ground as they chatted among themselves. They and their leader had spent the whole morning patrolling the forest, cautiously moving through the undergrowth in search of the enemy. It was hot and airless among the trees and they were tired and thirsty. Even in the open the temperature was rising, Conrad and the others having taken off their helmets and mail shirts to lighten their load, leaving them on the front of the cart. They still carried their swords and daggers, of course, and had their shields slung on their backs.

'I had better report to my father,' said Rameke, 'and inform him that I have become well acquainted with Estonia's trees and wildlife.' He turned to his subordinate behind him.

'Give the order to the men.'

A piece of dead wood fell from the cart and he stooped to pick it up, just at the moment when a javelin flew through the air to hit his subordinate in the chest. There was a succession of thuds as other javelins struck the standing Liv warriors. One hit the mule harnessed to the cart, causing it to stumble and collapse.

'Ambush!' screamed Conrad as he grabbed Rameke and hauled him behind the cart, Hans, Anton and Johann also making a beeline for the safety of the cart. More javelins came from the trees and then there was a mighty roar as the enemy charged.

Rameke's Livs were the first to suffer the full brunt of the attack, many being speared and cut down before they had time to react. But the foraging parties – foot soldiers mainly – also stood little chance as the Estonians swept from the forest.

Rameke jumped up as the first Estonians appeared. 'To me, to me, rally to me.'

He drew his sword, brought up his large round shield to cover his torso and charged the enemy. Conrad and the others had no time to don their mail or helmets as they raced after him. Horns were blowing among the Livs and drums and trumpets were sounding up and down the column as the nearest companies became aware of the attack.

The best form of defence is attack, that was what Lukas had taught them, so Conrad and the other novices charged the enemy as Rameke's men formed a shield fort around their leader, fending off the Estonians with their spears as he organised a counterattack. Half a dozen Estonians diverted themselves from attacking the Livs to assault the novices, who came at them in a line. Conrad ran screaming at an opponent carrying a shield and wielding an axe above his head, no doubt hoping to split open Conrad's exposed skull. But the blow was too obvious, Conrad barging his shield into his enemy's and positioning his sword so that the man's forearm would slam into its edge as he attacked with his axe. This is what happened and the bone in his arm was shattered on the steel. Conrad ducked as the man's grip on his axe was broken and the weapon fell to the ground. He swiftly brought his sword down, flicked his wrist and drove an arm of its cross-guard into one of the Estonian's eye sockets. It was a neat trick, for which he mentally apologised to Brother Lukas.

The man crumpled to the ground where Conrad stepped over him. He saw another warrior coming at him, shorter than him but broader in the shoulders, long hair coming from under his gilded helmet. He saw Conrad and Conrad saw the scar on his left cheek and they both recognised each other.

Lembit, accompanied by four other warriors who attacked Conrad's companions, smiled at him. Conrad thought himself an accomplished swordsman but Lembit's attacks were deft and powerful and he had difficulty in standing his ground. He leapt aside when Lembit attempted a sideswipe with his sword, the edge of his blade ripping the fabric of Conrad's gambeson. His shield was splintered by a succession of strikes, the last of which he managed to stop with his cross-guard. He smashed his shield into Lembit's and then unleashed a series of powerful attacks that forced the Estonian back. But Lembit was quick on his feet and he managed to sidestep, duck and dodge the blows, though the last one cut away part of his shield.

'You are good, Conrad Wolff,' he said mockingly, 'but not that good.'

Conrad saw the Livs advancing against perhaps a score of the enemy and his three comrades holding their own against the Estonians, who now broke off their combat to come to their leader's side.

'We must leave, lord,' one said to him.

Conrad kept his battered shield and sword raised as trumpets sounded behind him and he heard horses' hooves. Lembit screamed in frustration and pointed his sword at Conrad as a party of knights trotted up, lances couched.

'Until we meet again, Conrad Wolff.'

The other Estonians were now beating a hasty retreat, Lembit following them as the knights rode into the trees to attempt a pursuit. But the branches were too low and the undergrowth too thick to risk the lives of expensive warhorses and so the Estonians made good their escape.

Rudolf arrived in the company of Henke and Lukas as the wounded Livs were helped to the surgeons. Conrad sat on the cart with the others as Rameke came to them and clasped each of their forearms.

'Praise God you are all unhurt,' he said, wincing when he saw the cut above Anton's right eye and Conrad's torn gambeson.

The brother knights dismounted and walked over to them.

'Are you hurt?' Rudolf said to Anton.

'It is nothing,' replied Anton, feeling the wound with his hand.

'Get it seen to,' ordered Rudolf.

Lukas saw the helmets and mail shirts draped over the cart's driver's seat.

'That is why we issue you with helmets and mail armour. Looks like latrine duties for you all.'

'But we were collecting firewood, Brother Lukas,' protested Hans.

'You think that the enemy should have allowed you the time to put on your armour and helmets, according to the code of chivalry?' said Lukas in mocking tone.

Hans was going to say yes but thought better of it.

'It was Lembit,' said Conrad.

Rudolf spun round. 'Are you certain?'

Conrad nodded and Henke laughed.

'And you let him get away? Really, Conrad, you are making a habit of allowing your enemies to escape.'

Rudolf walked over to Conrad and inspected his torn gambeson. 'A parting gift from Lembit?'

Conrad nodded and Henke laughed again.

'Not so easy to kill him, then?'

'He was very quick on his feet,' said Conrad sullenly.

'You don't become leader of all the Estonian tribes without being able to use a sword,' said Henke. 'Strange that he should lead a raid, though.'

But Lembit had achieved his aim and the crusader army halted its march, sent out patrols in all directions and then made camp, the tents and wagons ringed by guards standing ready to repel another attack. None came but the march to Lehola had been delayed and the next day, as the bishop's army packed away its tents and recommenced its march, hundreds of warriors arrived at Lehola and filed through its gates.

*****

Lembit had lost only a dozen men killed and four more wounded but he returned to his stronghold in a foul mood, almost beating a man unconscious when he failed to control his pony while leading it to the stables. Afterwards he sat in his great hall drinking copious quantities of beer as the new arrivals were shown to their sleeping quarters. Rusticus let him stew for a while and then went to see him.

Lembit pointed at the jug on the table. 'Help yourself.'

Rusticus filled a cup with beer and leaned against the table, facing Lembit in his high-backed chair.

'You remember that boy, Conrad Wolff?'

Rusticus shook his head. Lembit pointed at his scar.

'Oh, that boy. What about him?'

'He is with the crusader army. I came face to face with him.'

'Did you kill him?'

Lembit shook his head.

'You should have. Him still walking the earth is a bad omen, lord. No good will come of it. His fate is intertwined with yours.'

Lembit frowned. 'Are you a fortune teller now?'

Rusticus drained his cup and belched. 'No, lord, but I know a sign from the gods as well as the next man.'

'Get out,' snapped Lembit, knowing that his deputy was speaking the truth.

If the Estonian leader thought that he had outwitted the bishop he had reckoned without the talents of Master Thaddeus. The architect of the fall of Acre twenty-three years before had worked closely with Grand Master Volquin regarding the assault upon Lehola, Thaddeus having travelled to Riga in the weeks before the bishop's arrival to thrash out the details of how Lembit's stronghold would be taken. Volquin knew that the crusaders and the masters of his order would favour an immediate assault with siege towers but Thaddeus convinced him to adopt a different strategy.

Conrad, Anton, Hans and Johann had spent the hours after the Estonian raid digging latrine trenches as a punishment for discarding their mail and helmets, after which they had to feed and groom horses before finally erecting their tent at

526

well past midnight. They awoke three hours later to attend prayers in the chapel tent before eating breakfast and beginning the ritual of daily chores again. The army arrived before Lehola three hours later and once more they were issued with axes and saws as the first part of Master Thaddeus' plan was put into effect.

Lehola stood tall and imperious on its great mound, the ground having been cleared of trees and foliage three hundred paces from its base in all directions. The ramparts and towers were thronged with warriors when the crusaders arrived, wolf banners flying from every tower. Master Thaddeus, mounted on an old grey palfrey, trotted around the fort, occasionally stopping and looking up at the defences as dozens of pairs of eyes stared down at him from the timber walls. Grand Master Volquin, Master Berthold and Wenden's brother knights escorted him to ensure he did not stray too near the walls and thus risk being shot by an archer, who nevertheless did loose the odd hopeful arrow in their direction.

While this reconnaissance of the enemy was being carried out, the knights donned their full armour and their squires saddled their warhorses and the Sword Brothers arrayed their banners in front of the fort. The coats of arms of the lords of northern Germany fluttered in the breeze and were displayed on dozens of shields as the crusader army showed itself to the enemy in all its pomp and glory, the great banner of Riga flying behind the bishop of the town as he sat on his horse beside Theodoric in front of Lehola's main gates. Trumpets blew among his foot soldiers as they deployed in front of him with his mounted bodyguard behind. Sir Helmold arrayed his knights and their mounted retainers on the eastern side of the fort, Count Horton's men on the western side and the Sword Brothers on the northern side. Sir Jordan's depleted forces fell in beside the bishop.

It had been decided beforehand that the crusader camp should be located to the southwest of the fort. Volquin knew that the other Estonian chiefs would probably be summoned to Lembit's aid and would probably join forces in the north before marching south. All except the Ungannians whose lands were to the southeast and would approach from that direction. The force besieging Fellin further south would hopefully act as a breakwater in the event that Kalju led his warriors west. If not then Caupo's Livs would provide prior warning of their arrival and of the approach of any Estonians from the north. In any event the crusader camp, positioned to the southwest, would not be overrun.

The bishop's pavilion that he shared with Theodoric also doubled as the army's command tent, where Master Thaddeus explained his strategy to the lords assembled round a table. Thaddeus stood at the table and pointed to a rough sketch on parchment that showed Lehola and two lines drawn around it.

He pointed at the line that was nearest the forts' walls. 'Just as Caesar built lines of circumvallation and contravallation around Alesia so will we erect the same around Lehola, my lords.'

Count Horton, bored, stared out of the open tent flaps at the bustle of the camp outside. Sir Jordan looked perplexed.

'When do we attack?'

Thaddeus smiled. 'We do not, my lord.'

Count Horton turned back to the table. 'What did you say?'

The bishops were staring intently at the sketch map and Grand Master Volquin was observing everyone knowingly. Sir Helmold, seated between Caupo and Thalibald, maintained a polite silence.

'My engines will batter the fort into submission,' said Thaddeus, who again pointed at his map, this time at the outer line that encompassed the fort. 'Our lines of contravallation will prevent any relief of the fort, thus making its surrender inevitable.'

Count Horton was not happy. 'We did not come all the way from Germany to sit on our arses in this godforsaken place.'

'No place is forsaken of God, count,' Bishop Albert reprimanded him.

'Apologies, lord bishop,' grunted Horton.

'If we are not to assault the walls,' remarked Sir Helmold, 'then why do we have hundreds of men chopping down trees if not to make siege towers?'

Thaddeus nodded. 'An excellent question, my lord, and in answer I will again allude to Caesar and his strategy at Alesia.'

Count Horton sighed and rolled his eyes but Albert and Theodoric nodded. They at least were acquainted with ancient history.

Thaddeus continued. 'We dig a ditch to encompass our camp and siege works and, just as Caesar did at Alesia, we top it with a rampart. This will provide adequate defence against any Estonian relief force. Meanwhile, the siege engines and crossbowmen will require mantlets to protect them from any projectiles launched from the walls.'

'And how long do you anticipate the siege lasting?' said Sir Helmold.

'Five days,' replied Thaddeus.

Count Horton and Sir Jordan burst out laughing and even Sir Helmold found it hard not to smile. They were all veterans of wars and campaigns in Germany and had first-hand experience of siege warfare. They knew that it could take weeks to bring about the surrender of even a small citadel, and Lehola was a formidable prospect.

Bishop Albert brought his hands together. 'You are confident in your estimation, Master Thaddeus?'

Thaddeus bowed his head. 'Quite certain, lord bishop.'

'Ha!' scoffed Count Horton. 'More like five weeks. Is your eyesight poor, Thaddeus?' He pointed out of the tent. 'That is a big stronghold.'

Thaddeus, clearly intimidated by the big gruff knight, started to stammer but was saved by Volquin.

'I will strike a deal with you, count,' said the grand master. 'If, after five days, the fort has not fallen then you can lead your men against its walls.'

Count Horton thumped the table, making Thaddeus jump. 'Agreed.'

As the afternoon wore on the forest around the fort was filled with the sound of axes, saws and falling trees. Squires, crossbowmen, spearmen and sergeants were organised into parties and ordered to collect wood for the defence lines. There was a westerly breeze blowing and so Master Thaddeus gave orders that any unwanted freshly cut branches were to be deposited facing the western side of the fort. They were arranged in a long line and were then set on fire. Soon white smoke from the burning greenery was drifting over the ramparts of Lehola. Thaddeus ordered that the fires were to be fed as he went to site his siege machines.

Conrad and the other novices, after two hours felling trees, were ordered to assist Master Thaddeus and his engineers set up their siege engines, specifically the trebuchets. Thaddeus had had one such machine at Fellin three years before but now he had three that were positioned to the south of the fort, beyond the range of the archers on the walls and in the tops of the towers. The garrison, having jeered, whistled and bared their buttocks at the crusader army, had fallen silent after the lords and knights had dispersed back to camp and had been replaced by small groups of Livs, spearmen and crossbowmen that ringed the fortress. After a while they grew bored and drifted away. Grand Master Volquin was concerned that Lembit might launch a sally from the fort and so deployed the brother knights in front of the gates, reinforced by a hundred of the order's crossbowmen. But after two hours of inactivity he ordered the crossbowmen to assist the parties felling trees. The brother knights dismounted and sat on the ground in front of the trebuchets as the smoke from the fires drifted over Lehola to the accompaniment of hundreds of men hacking and sawing trees.

Carpenters sweated and cursed as they manoeuvred the various components of the trebuchets into place as Conrad stirred a cauldron of burning pitch being heated over a fire.

'That's right,' said Thaddeus, who wore a floppy hat on his head and looked more like a mathematician than a chief engineer. 'Don't let it get too thick.'

It was now late afternoon and the smell of smoke was permeating the entire area as the wind began to lessen.

'Will you heat it until morning, Master Thaddeus?' Conrad enquired.

Thaddeus shook his head. 'Not, we will wait until it gets dark and then we will commence our assault.'

'At night?'

Thaddeus tapped the cauldron with his cane. 'Keep stirring.' He turned to look at Hans, Johann and Anton who were also attending to cauldrons of pitch. 'You boys also keep stirring. Now, where was I? Oh yes, the assault.'

He turned to look at the fort. 'Now, young Conrad, you will notice that the shape of the Estonian fortress is rectangular. This means that projectiles launched into it from this, the narrow side, stand more of a chance of hitting something. You understand?'

Conrad did not really but nodded and pretended he did.

Thaddeus smiled and pointed his cane at the row of fires on the western side of the fort that were being allowed to die down.

'Now on the western side of the fort will be positioned five mangonels throwing stones, the machines on the other side also shooting stones over the eastern side of the fort. It would, of course, have been better if three trebuchets could have positioned to the north of the fort. In this way the enemy would have been assailed from four sides.'

He cast his head down. 'Alas, I can only work with what I have.'

Thalibald sent out parties to the north and east to search for any signs of the enemy but they returned before nightfall to report that there were no signs of a relief force. The mangonels had still to be assembled when the trebuchets commenced their work. Night had fallen and a yellow glow came from within the fort made by a host of Estonian campfires.

Conrad stood with Hans and the others as the burning pitch was poured into a small barrel that was placed into the sling of the first trebuchet. A priest stepped forward and blessed the projectile and Master Thaddeus turned to look at Bishop Albert and Theodoric, who had both come to watch the spectacle. Count Horton, Sir

Jordan, Sir Helmold and Grand Master Volquin were also in attendance. The bishop smiled, nodded and Thaddeus gave the order to release the throwing arm. The counterweight fell, the sling was drawn backwards, then whipped up and forward and the barrel left it. No one could see its flight but seconds later there was a muffled bang from within the fort.

'Excellent work, Master Thaddeus,' announced Bishop Albert, 'please carry on.'

He and the others retired to their tents, leaving the priest behind to bless each barrel before it was flung at the enemy. The rate of shooting was slow – one barrel every twenty minutes – but Thaddeus kept them working all night, and in the morning the trebuchets desisted when the mangonels took over.

Though tired and hungry, Thaddeus supervised their positioning and range and once more the bishop sent two priests to bless the stones that were launched into the fort: one for the mangonels on the eastern side, one for the machines facing Lehola's western walls.

And so began a day of hurling stones into the fort, each one blessed by a priest to improve its chances of smiting a heathen. Conrad spent the day felling trees and sawing their trunks and branches to fashion mantlets, logs for the top of the rampart and the fence around the camp, and sharpened stakes to go on the outward-facing side of the rampart and in front of the ditch. The latter was not very deep and the rampart was not very high, but together and with the stakes they presented a formidable enough barrier to any attacker. The knights thought felling trees beneath them and so spent the day in their armour riding up and down in front of the fort, hurling threats at the defenders. The latter were nowhere to be seen, the crossbowmen behind their mantlets shooting at any that showed their heads.

The squires, lesser knights, spearmen, crossbowmen, Sword Brother sergeants and brother knights, plus those Livs who were not patrolling the countryside, all took turns with axes and saws. By the end of the day hundreds of trees had been felled and it looked as though a giant had been at work with his scythe at the edge of the forest. Master Thaddeus, who had been ordered by Bishop Albert to sleep in his tent in the afternoon, was most pleased with the result. He conducted a tour of his lines of contravallation with the two bishops, arriving at the sector beyond the northern ramparts of the fort – held by the Sword Brothers – in the early evening.

Conrad sat on the earth rampart and picked up one of the water bottles lying on the ground. He had walked from the trees to collect water for the other three who were still toiling in the forest. He picked up four and slung their straps over his shoulder, uncorked another and took a great gulp.

'Don't gulp it down,' said Lukas. 'On campaign always treat water with care. You don't know where your next drink will come from.'

Conrad stopped drinking. 'From the nearby river, Brother Lukas.'

They were soaked in sweat but all of them wore their gambesons, helmets and mail armour, though Lukas, Henke and Rudolf had swapped their full-face protection for kettle helmets.

Lukas pointed his hammer towards the forest. 'If the Estonians attack and surround the army then you will not be able to get to the river and your only water will be in that bottle.'

'Let us pray that does not happen, brother.'

Conrad looked up to see a yellow mitre on top of a tall individual with a chiselled face. He and the others jumped to their feet when they recognised Bishop Albert and Grand Master Volquin. He smiled when Master Thaddeus raised his cane to him.

Rudolf, Henke and Lukas bowed their heads.

'Lord bishop,' said Rudolf, 'it is an honour to see you.' He saw Theodoric beside him. 'And you, Bishop Theodoric.'

Now nearly fifty, Bishop Albert's eyes were still alert but there were flecks of grey in his hair and he looked tired. Clearly the years spent travelling to and from Germany had taken their toll. His brother bishop had a similar lean, severe appearance but seemed less drawn.

'Master Thaddeus assures me that the fort will fall imminently,' said Bishop Albert as another stone launched from a mangonel crashed into Lehola. 'How are my brave brother knights from Wenden?'

'We are well, lord bishop,' answered Rudolf.

The bishop stared at Conrad for a moment and then recognised him. 'Conrad Wolff.' He turned to Theodoric. 'This is the young man who saved me at Riga two years ago. A most valiant individual.'

Theodoric examined Conrad. 'The church is in your debt, young man.'

'He is to be a brother knight, I seem to remember,' Bishop Albert said to Rudolf.

'He is, lord bishop, if he lives that long.'

Albert placed a hand on Conrad's arm. 'See that you do, young man. Livonia needs people like you to safeguard its Holy Church.'

'Thank you, lord bishop,' said Conrad, slightly overawed by the two bishops' presence.

'Well, I will leave you to your work,' said Albert. 'God be with you all.'

The two bishops continued on their tour of the outer works, accompanied by half a dozen of Riga's spearmen, Grand Master Volquin chatting to Rudolf before he too departed. Master Thaddeus spoke to Henke and Lukas before he left.

He pointed his cane to the freshly made tree stumps in front of the ditch.

'You need to cut down some trees so that they fall parallel to the ditch.'

'Why?' asked Henke.

'Because, Brother Henke, felled trees will impede the advance of an enemy towards these defences.'

'The tree stumps will do that,' sniffed Henke.

'They will,' agreed Thaddeus, 'but having to scramble over felled trees will further discomfort the enemy and impede his advance, giving your crossbowmen more time to shoot them down.'

'If they come at all,' remarked Lukas.

Thaddeus looked back at the fort and smiled when he saw another stone arching into the sky before falling inside Lembit's stronghold.

'They will come, for the other chiefs know that if Lehola, one of the greatest forts in all Estonia, falls then so will their own kingdoms.'

'Rameke has seen no sign of the enemy,' said Conrad.

'Neither did he when Lembit slipped by his men and nearly cut you into small pieces,' replied Henke. 'This is his land, not Rameke's, or Caupo's for that matter. He and his people know it and all its secret paths. Why do you think we've found no women and children?'

'They must be in the fort,' said Conrad.

Henke scoffed at the notion. 'No they ain't. Do you know what they call women and children caught inside a stronghold during a siege?'

Conrad shook his head.

'Useless eaters,' said Henke. 'Lembit is not stupid. He would have sent all those who can't hold a spear or axe away from the fort into the forest to hide until the fighting's done. There are only warriors inside Lehola.'

'I hope so,' said Thaddeus.

'You find the idea of the stones from your machines mangling women and little ones disagreeable, Master Thaddeus?' teased Henke.

'I deplore the killing of any innocents,' said Thaddeus gravely.

Henke roared with laughter. 'There are no innocents. Women bear children who grow up to become soldiers and children learn to wield a sword soon enough. Better to kill them all before they breed more of the enemy.'

'That's enough, Henke,' said Rudolf. 'Go and chop down some trees as Master Thaddeus has instructed.'

Henke winked at Thaddeus, picked up a two-handed axe and pointed at Conrad. 'Come on, otherwise your companions will die of thirst.'

Conrad picked up his axe and followed Henke, who called back to Master Thaddeus.

'When do your trebuchets begin their work again?'

'As soon as night falls, Brother Henke,' replied Thaddeus.

'The old fool thinks he can batter Lembit into submission,' Henke said to Conrad, 'but it would be better to build siege towers with all the wood we have cut and then we can launch an assault and kill all those inside the fort.'

'What if Lembit surrenders?'

Henke shrugged. 'Then we can chop off his head in front of his fort, it makes no difference.'

Conrad was surprised. 'Even if he has given himself up?'

'The bishop wants to make Estonia kneel to the church, but as long as Lembit is still alive the Estonians will not renounce their pagan religion or their allegiance to him. The sooner Bishop Albert realises that the better for all of us. If Bishop Albert wants Estonia then he will have to kill Lembit.'

*****

But Master Thaddeus was not a fool and inside the fort a crisis was unfolding. There were two thousand warriors in Lehola and they were discovering that there were few places to hide within its spacious confines. The first night of the crusader siege had resulted in fifty killed and nearly sixty wounded as a result of the barrels of burning pitch that had landed among the huts and other wooden structures. A stable had been hit and set alight, the ponies inside being overcome by smoke and flames before they could be evacuated. Then a dozen huts had been set on fire as the garrison was stood to arms to extinguish the flames when the barrels hit anything solid and split apart, their contents spilling out and igniting as they did so. Warriors tried to stamp out the flames but discovered to their horror that to do so was to get the sticky, flaming liquid on their boots and leggings, which then consumed the material and then their flesh.

Some barrels hit the ground and showered men with their burning contents, resulting in horrific, sometimes fatal, burns. Because the trebuchets had been positioned to the south of the fort's main gates Lembit's great hall had escaped the dreadful night of fireballs, the wounded being brought and laid out in rows on its floor, seemingly safe from the crusaders' machines.

The new dawn came and the trebuchets stopped and men, their eyes red, their faces unwashed and dirty and their clothes stinking of smoke, congratulated each other and thanked the gods for their salvation. Then the first stones fell from the sky. They were only small, weighing perhaps ten pounds or less, but they fell into the fort silently and with lethal forces, splitting skulls or smashing bones to pulp. Men fled for cover and soon discovered that the best place to hide was near the main gates or in the extreme north of the compound, between the wall that enclosed the great hall and the outer wall.

After a sparse meal of nuts and milk Lembit walked from his hall to speak to the men huddled at the foot of the northern perimeter wall, many of them sleeping under their cloaks as they attempted to grab some rest after the night of fire. But their sleep was fitful and interrupted by the stones that fell on the roofs of huts, storerooms and stables, the beasts inside screaming in fear, though in truth the thick thatch acted as an effective shield against the stones. Nevertheless, it all contributed to the general unease that permeated the fort as everyone's nerves were frayed further.

Lembit went among the men and casually chatted and reassured them, announcing that a relief force was nearing the fort. He then walked slowly through the centre of the fort to the main gates to show he had no fear of the crusaders or their machines. Rusticus walked beside him.

'The men's morale is fragile,' said Lembit.

'They need a victory to put some iron back in them,' remarked his deputy.

A stone suddenly smashed into the ground a few feet ahead of them. Rusticus looked up at the sky but Lembit, unconcerned, continued his stroll.

'I am open to ideas, Rusticus, what do you suggest?'

'We could raid the enemy camp tonight, send a party of wolf shields out of the gates to kill a few crusaders.'

They continued past the still smouldering ruins of huts that had been destroyed during the night.

'They would have to cut their way through the line of defences the enemy has erected around the fort,' said Lembit without enthusiasm. 'There are many enemy soldiers guarding the machines that throw the fireballs, which are unfortunately positioned directly south of the gates. If the crusaders became aware of any troops leaving the fort they would commit those guards.'

'What then?' said Rusticus.

'Our fate lies in the hands of the other chiefs.'

Rusticus spat on the ground. 'Saccalians do not rely on others to save their honour.'

Lembit stopped and looked at him. 'Saccalia is here, Rusticus, in this fort. If the men within its walls perish then there will be no more Saccalia. It will become the northern part of Livonia.'

'How do you know that the others will come to our aid?'

'Because they know,' replied Lembit, 'that if we fall then so do they.'

But that night no relief came and as darkness fell the infernal trebuchets once again began their deadly work, sending flaming barrels into the fort. This time the garrison knew the trajectory they would take and largely escaped injury, but the showers of burning liquid set alight more buildings that were allowed to burn. Lembit sent parties into the stables to slaughter the ponies and others to kill the pigs and fowl in their pens to stifle their awful screams and squeals that shredded men's nerves.

When morning came the fort was filled with more smoking ruins and men's mouths tasted of smoke and their eyes smarted. Rusticus came to the hall to find his master, shaking him awake in his chair.

'The gods are smiling on us,' beamed his hulking deputy. 'You had better come and see.'

Lembit rubbed his eyes and stood. His neck and back ached and his mouth felt dry and stale. He filled a metal bowl on a table with water from a jug and washed his face, then threaded his way through the moaning and sleeping sea of injured on the floor to follow Rusticus. They walked through the gates that led from the inner compound, both of them choking on the smoke that hung in the air, hastening to a ladder that led to the first floor of the tower in the northeast corner of the outer wall. They then ascended a second ladder that gave access to the tower's fighting platform.

'Keep your head down, lord,' Rusticus warned Lembit, 'the crusaders have some accomplished crossbowmen.'

On the platform Lembit crouched low as he shuffled to the wall and rested a hand on one of the great logs that had been used to build it. A warrior in a helmet beside him gave him a slight nod and then turned back to look towards the north.

'There, lord,' he said, pointing at a great column of dark smoke rising on the horizon.

Lembit clenched his fist. He slapped the man on the back and turned to Rusticus. His deputy nodded and leered. The signal was clear enough. His allies had answered his call and were nearing Lehola.

Salvation was at hand.

*****

Conrad sat on the ground cleaning the blade of his sword when the alarm was sounded. There was soon a great commotion in the crusader camp, near panic among those who were newly arrived from Germany, quiet determination among the Sword Brothers. Johann ran into the tent and threw kettle helmets to Conrad, Hans and Anton, all of them buckling on their sword belts and grabbing their other close weapons of choice as they slung their shields on their backs and made their way to the chapel tent. The brother knights and sergeants were likewise making their way there and soon the area around the temporary chapel was filled with men in white surcoats bearing the red cross and sword insignia. In other parts of the camp trumpets were blaring and men were already in the saddle and heading towards the siege works.

Conrad stood beside Hans, checking his belt was buckled and his dagger secure in its sheath. His sword hung on his left hip and his axe was tucked into his belt. He saw Rameke and called to him. The Liv came over and they shook hands, Thalibald's son also greeting the other novices.

'An Estonian army approaches,' he said. 'Our scouts ran into them earlier.'

'How many?' asked Conrad.

'Hundreds,' answered Rameke. 'They come to relieve the fort.'

Conrad slapped Hans on the arm. 'Chopping off Estonian heads is better than chopping down trees.'

'I must go and join my father. Take care that it is not your head that is lopped off, my friend,' said Rameke, bidding them all farewell as he took his leave.

Moments later Lukas appeared.

'You four are with me. An enemy relief force approaches and it is our task to ensure they do not break through our defences.'

Around them the brother knights and sergeants were being informed of their tasks by their masters who had come from the chapel where Grand Master Volquin had issued his orders. The mercenaries of each garrison followed their paymasters as the order made its way to the outer works in the northern sector, files of men following the banner of each garrison. By popular choice Brother Walter had been asked to carry Wenden's flag, which was a red cross over a red sword on a white background with the letter 'W' in the top corner next to the flagpole.

Conrad was in a confident mood for he knew, as did everyone else, that if this battle was won then Lembit would be defeated and Estonia would fall to the Bishop of Riga. He pulled the axe from his belt and tossed it up into the air, catching its handle as it fell to earth.

'No tricks today, Conrad,' said Lukas behind him.

'Tricks, Brother Lukas?'

'Don't get clever. You've done well so far. How many battles have you fought in?'

Conrad flashed a smile. 'Three, Brother Lukas.'

'Three?'

'If you count Fellin.'

'And not a scratch on you,' said Lukas. 'You've been lucky but luck doesn't last forever. What you were taught in training does, however, and if you cast your mind back you will recall that I did not teach you any tricks.'

'We do not need luck, Brother Lukas,' boasted Conrad, 'we have God on our side.'

'God doesn't like cocky young men, Conrad, always remember that.'

Grand Master Volquin had briefed the commanders of the army on his plan the day they had arrived at Lehola. Count Horton and Sir Jordan wanted nothing more than to lead a great charge against the enemy but Volquin knew that it would require more subtle tactics to defeat the enemy. Thus far his plan had worked perfectly but he had fulfilled but part of his scheme. For victory to be achieved everyone had to perform the tasks allotted to them. The crusader lords had at first bristled at being told what to do but the grand master was backed up by Bishop Albert and also by Sir Helmold, the latter now a veteran of campaigning in Livonia. And so they grumbled but acquiesced in Volquin's plan.

As Conrad trotted to the northern lines of contravallation Sir Helmold took his knights and squires to the outer defence lines to the east of the fort, where he was joined by Thalibald and five hundred Liv warriors. He was also reinforced by the hundred crossbowmen from Riga. All these men – Livs, knights, squires and crossbowmen – were on foot, their horses left in camp.

To the west of the fort, between the inner and outer siege works, were the knights, squires and retainers commanded by Count Horton. These troops were all mounted and formed the reserve, to be committed to any part of the field of battle where the pagans threatened a breakthrough. To the south where Master Thaddeus had placed his trebuchets, stood Bishop Albert and Bishop Theodoric surrounded by the horsemen and spearmen of Riga, Caupo and his remaining Livs and the crusaders led by Sir Jordan – nearly a thousand men. Their first duty was to haul back the wheeled trebuchets two hundred paces, so that their projectiles would fall in and around Lehola's gates when Lembit made his expected sally from the fort.

The Sword Brother crossbowmen who had been manning the mantlets that faced the fort were withdrawn and sent to the earth rampart to the north of Lehola manned by the sergeants and brother knights. This sector would bear the brunt of the Estonian attack as the enemy advanced south, intent on smashing through the crusader lines to relieve Lembit. This part of the outer siege works was around four hundred paces in length and was held by a paltry three hundred and seventy men in total. Of these, one hundred and ten were crossbowmen expected to inflict heavy losses on the enemy before they reached the ditch. If they failed then the spearmen and members of the Sword Brothers would try to prevent the enemy breaching the rampart, which was nothing more than a few stakes hammered into the top of an earth wall. Conrad looked up and down the line and behind him. It was a very thin white line.

He shook the hands of Hans, Johann and Anton in what had become a pre-battle ritual, each wishing the other good luck. Though they had lost Bruno in combat all of them had come to believe themselves if not invincible then at least difficult to kill.

'We win this one,' announced Anton, 'and the war is over.'

'Then there will be no one left to fight,' said Johann.

Henke overheard their conversation. 'Don't you worry about that. There's always someone left to fight.'

Walter planted Wenden's banner in the earth beside him and then knelt and began to pray, his eyes closed and his mouth reciting a private devotion. It was most strange. Brother Walter was as kind and considerate as the most pious monk, a gentle lamb, but in battle was a remorseless killer who believed salvation could only be achieved by washing his sword in the blood of God's enemies. Walter finished his prayers and rose to his feet. He caught Conrad's eye.

'God with be with, Conrad.'

'And with you, Brother Walter.'

Conrad stood at the log fence and stared at the tree stumps in front of the ditch and the felled trees lying parallel to the rampart.

'Remember what I told you,' Lukas appeared beside him. 'No tricks.'

'No tricks,' agreed Conrad.

He pointed ahead at the stumps daubed with white paint to indicate ranges: one hundred paces, two hundred paces, three hundred paces and the felled trees splattered with paint to show four hundred paces.

'Master Thaddeus is a clever man. I always thought he was an old fool but I was wrong.'

Lukas nodded. 'His machines, calculations and engineering feats will win us this war. Rudolf once told me that Thaddeus is worth a thousand soldiers. I laughed at the time but I now think he is worth ten times that number.'

Conrad heard shouts and sounds coming from the forest and the hairs on the back of his neck stood up.

Lukas laid a hand on his shoulder. 'Time to go to work.'

The noises got louder as the enemy approached, the sound of drums standing out as the forest resonated with the sound of hundreds of voices. Crossbowmen loaded their weapons and rested them on the top of the fence. Brother knights put on their helms to cover their faces and Conrad gripped the handle of his axe and slipped his left forearm through the straps on the rear of his shield.

Then he saw movement, fleeting shapes among the trees in the distance. The crossbowmen saw them as well and crouched down to take aim with their weapons. Master Berthold raised his sword.

'God with us!'

The call was answered by dozens of voices as the Estonians clambered over the felled trees and showed themselves – warriors dressed in brown, green and red hues carrying round shields and armed with spears. Dozens and then hundreds swarmed from the forest like a plague of rats. They picked their way through the tree stumps as the crossbowmen released their triggers and sent a hail of bolts in their direction. Conrad saw leather face hook the bowstring over the claw on his belt and draw it back, slipping another bolt in the stock of his weapon, taking aim and shooting once more. Conrad felt a tingle of excitement when he saw Estonians fall, only to be replaced by others from behind.

The crossbowmen were unleashing quarrels at a rate of four a minute, the thwacks of their bowstrings combining to produce a continuous scraping sound along the line. The Estonian advance was interrupted by the tree stumps but not halted as they poured forward. Bolts went through shields, helmets and into eye sockets. Within two minutes over eight hundred crossbow bolts had been shot at the enemy, but then the enemy were at the ditch and climbing the earth bank beyond.

Conrad did not know it but these were Edvin's Wierlanders and if he had had time to look more closely he would have seen a banner bearing a boar in the centre of the line where the Estonian chief was leading the attack. Over a thousand warriors poured out of the forest to assault the Sword Brothers. Three hundred were dead or wounded from crossbow bolts but now the rest smashed into the Christian warriors like a great wave striking a white cliff.

The crossbowmen fell back from the fence as the Wierlanders came up the bank and attempted to scale it, only to be met by a multitude of spears, axes, maces and swords. The Estonian front ranks were filled with the best-equipped and trained warriors, men in mail armour, helmets and armed with spears and swords. Conrad used his shield to brush aside a spear thrust and hacked at the helmeted brute who gripped it. The warrior brought up his own shield to block the blow as Conrad swung the axe to the left, against another warrior attempting to climb over the fence, the blade slicing into his left calf. The man screamed and collapsed belly first onto the fence, to be finished off by Anton beside him who rammed his sword into the warrior's back. His body remained draped over the fence as the Estonian tide pressed forward.

Conrad smashed the spear shaft in front of him as a warrior came hurtling through the air towards him. He ducked and the man tumbled down the earth bank behind him. He jumped to his feet and was shot in the belly by leather face. The bloody fight at the fence went on, Conrad dodging spear blades that were thrust at him. Arrows hissed through the air, shot by enemy archers in the rear, but he had no time to worry about them. Hans to his right was fighting like a demon, his skinny arms delivering powerful, well-aimed blows with a mace that caved in the chests and split the helmets of enemy warriors. He smashed one man in the face, his nose becoming a bloody pulp, and then went to step on the fence to follow.

'Hold your ground, Hans!' shouted Conrad as the edge of a sword hit his helmet.

He thrust his axe forward at his assailant, driving its top spike through the mail armour, into his chest and through his heart. He yanked back the axe but the dead warrior stayed upright, caught in the press of men behind and the fence in front. The latter had now been broken down in several places as the Estonians threatened to break though. But behind the Sword Brothers the crossbowmen were taking aim and picking off Edvin's men as they fought at the fence, such was their proficiency and ice-cool nerves.

The battle at the northern outworks was finely balanced as, to the east, the Jerwen assaulted the soldiers of Sir Helmold and Thalibald's warriors.

*****

Lembit had seen the Wierlanders come from the forest to the north and assault the accursed Sword Brothers. He had stood on the fighting platform of the tower and witnessed the Christian crossbowmen scything down Edvin's men but being unable to stop them reaching the crusaders' defences. The angled wooden shelters that ringed his fort, from behind which crossbowmen had expertly picked off some of his garrison, now stood deserted as the bishop's army tried to fight off the relief force. Rusticus was at the gates with his Saccalians, ready to lead them against the bishop's forces waiting for them outside. But not yet, for as the Wierlanders spilt their blood another tide of Estonians came from the forest to the east.

Jaak's Jerwen had come to crush the crusaders and their Liv allies.

Lembit scrambled down the ladders to reach the ground as the sounds of a new battle erupted to the east of the fort. He ran towards the gates where a phalanx of his warriors waited, passing charred huts, stables and dead ponies. His men cheered when he arrived, banging the hafts of their spears against their shields and chanting his name. He ran to their head, turned and raised his sword.

'For our gods, for our families, for our homeland, for our freedom. Kill the bishop. Open the gates!'

Rusticus came to his side as the massive beam of wood that secured the gates was removed.

'Fine speech.'

Lembit tightened the grip on his sword as the gates were pulled back.

'Kill the bishop!' screamed Lembit who led nearly eighteen hundred men forward as he ran through the gates with Rusticus beside him. It was not a disciplined assault with tightly packed ranks but a mad rush intended to overwhelm the bishop's soldiers.

Master Thaddeus gave the order for the trebuchets to shoot their projectiles before the first Estonians burst from the gates. He had estimated that as soon as the latter were opened the enemy would not delay but would immediately attack. The few seconds between when the gates opened and when the enemy charged would be all that would be needed for a volley of barrels of burning pitch. Once again his mathematical mind yielded a rich harvest, the barrels falling in the midst of the enemy warriors and bursting open to shower them with hot liquid. The momentum of their charge was not stopped, indeed barely interrupted, but at least fifty men were incapacitated when splashed with hot pitch.

Lembit charged at the line of spearmen barring his path, some of them sporting the arms of Riga on their shields, others being Caupo's Livs, and yet more carrying shields that bore strange devices and animal shapes. Behind him the rearmost ranks of his men flooded left and right to get to grips with the crusaders. Lembit hacked and thrust with his sword with Rusticus beside him as the ferocity of their assault began to push the crusaders back.

Bishops Albert and Theodoric rode up and down behind the line with Caupo, all of them shouting encouragement and promising that victory was at hand. But victory was not at hand and in the clatter of weapons and screams and shouts of men involved in mortal combat, it was clear to Grand Master Volquin sitting calmly on his horse that the fort's garrison was forcing the crusaders back. He knew there was fighting to the north, to the east and directly in front of him. The separate crusader formations were all isolated, desperately fighting for their lives. He wheeled his horse to the left and dug his spurs into its sides.

There was only one course of action to avoid a catastrophe.

*****

Conrad felt as though he had been fighting for hours but it was probably no more than thirty minutes. Even so, his reserves of energy were draining away fast as he battled to keep the Estonians at bay. The log fence was now broken and littered with dead, mostly Estonians but also mercenary spearmen and a few brother knights and sergeants. The pagan wave had crashed against the Christian breakwater and had buckled and dented it but had not broken it. Now, weariness began to grip both sides as the frenzy of bloodlust began to subside.

Conrad swung his axe at the helmet of a warrior who was attempting to skewer Hans with his spear, denting the metal but more importantly making him drop his shaft. He pulled a small axe that was tucked into his belt and swung it at

Conrad, but the latter had anticipated the move and smashed his shield into the man's face, bundling him over and causing his fall down the rampart's slope. And so it went on: Estonians scrambling up the bank to stab and hack at the Sword Brothers holding the fence. As men were killed and fell on and around the logs it became more difficult to get to grips with the enemy, the latter having to claw their way over the dead and dying.

Hans grinned at him as there was a lull in the fighting, Conrad taking the opportunity to catch his breath as the Estonians pulled back to regroup less than twenty paces from them. Their chiefs were going among them, cajoling and encouraging them to make one last effort to break the Christians. Conrad looked around and saw Johann prostrate, Rudolf and Hans kneeling over him.

'Anton,' he called, gesturing to the body of Johann behind the fence.

Forgetting their tiredness they rushed over to their friend. Johann's face was contorted with pain. At least he was still alive.

'He'll live,' said Rudolf, looking up at them. 'He has a broken ankle, that is all.'

'Some heathen fell on me,' said Johann, wincing in pain as Rudolf examined his ankle. 'He was dead and fell on my leg.'

'Take him from the rampart,' instructed Rudolf.

Conrad and Hans lifted Johann up and supported him between them as they slowly made their way down the bank and took him to a cart that was loaded with wounded. Another cart was taking more wounded back to camp.

'What's this?' asked a harassed surgeon with a balding head and both sleeves covered in blood.

'Our friend has broken his ankle,' said Conrad.

'Put him in the cart. He will have it bound back in camp.'

They assisted Johann into the cart where two other men – sergeants – were leaning against the sides, one with a head wound; the other with his left arm half hanging off. Both were pale and listless from shock and loss of blood.

'We will see you in camp,' said Conrad, shaking Johann's hand.

'God be with you,' added Hans.

'And you, my friends,' said Johann, his face creased with pain.

They returned to the rampart, Anton meeting them at its base. His gambeson was ripped and his mail shirt torn. He held out the water bottle to Conrad and looked up at the sky that was rapidly clearing of clouds. To the south and east the sounds of battle could be heard. Conrad took a sip and handed it to Hans.

'Get your arses back on this bank,' bellowed Henke, helmetless and clearly in a foul mood.

The three of them walked slowly up the mound and assumed their positions.

Walter checked that Wenden's banner was still firmly rooted in the ground before joining them.

'Brother Henke appears to be most annoyed.'

'Any particular reason why?' enquired Conrad.

'Probably because there are no Estonian girls to rape,' offered Hans.

Anton and Conrad laughed but Walter frowned. He disapproved of such remarks in much the same way as he deplored the language Henke employed when he decided to shout at the enemy.

'You sons of whores, come and fight instead of cowering behind your shields. I piss on your chiefs and your gods, you shit-eating maggots.'

'Brother Henke,' shouted Master Berthold, 'desist using such language at once. You dishonour the surcoat you are wearing.'

Henke sneered at the locked shields of the Estonians a few yards away and spat in their direction, but hurled no more insults. Conrad had to smile. Master Berthold stood with his sword smeared with blood while Walter's tunic was covered in enemy gore. But slaughtering the heathen was godly work whereas lewd language was a sign of a corrupt mind. Henke's mind was certainly corrupt and he revelled in slaughter, but as Lukas once told him there were few men that he would want by his side in battle beside Henke. Unfortunately the latter was frustrated beyond measure by the lull in the fight, especially with the enemy so close.

'Let me lead a sally against them,' he pleaded with Rudolf beside him.

'No, Henke, we will wait for them to attack and kill them here, at the fence.'

Henke picked up an enemy spear lying at his feet and hurled it at the Estonians, the front ranks parting when they saw it hurtling through the air. They whistled and jeered when it thudded harmlessly in the earth. This made Henke even angrier and Conrad thought he was about to launch a one-man assault against the enemy when Walter called out.

'Arrows! Take cover!'

Conrad looked up to see the sky filled with missiles and then threw himself against the fence, lifting up the torso of a dead Estonian slumped over it to use as cover. Seconds later arrows slammed into the ground and the corpse. He heard groans and yelps as crossbowmen standing away from the fence, who carried no shields for protection, were hit. And then there was a great roar and the Estonians attacked once more.

Conrad heard Rudolf's voice. 'Wait for the second volley.'

He remained crouched under the corpse, Hans huddle beside him, as another deluge of arrows struck their position, and then he sprang to his feet just as the first warriors were scaling the fence.

He had his shield on his back and his axe in his left hand as he drew his sword and thrust it into the stomach of a burly man with a huge black beard and stinking breath, who was shocked by the sudden appearance of the mail-clad individual in front of him and even more surprised when Conrad's sword point went through his leather armour into his belly. He collapsed head first over the fence as Conrad withdrew his blade and stepped on his back to fight the next warrior coming over the barricade. This was a spearman who wore no armour and attempted to run his lance through Conrad's guts. But the novice was too quick for him and jumped to one side so the warrior thrust into an empty space, lost his footing and sprawled onto the dead brute. Conrad jumped on his back and rammed his sword through his spine.

The battle raged all along the fence, Estonians attacking the thin line of Sword Brothers and mercenaries as they attempted to break through to the fort. But unbeknown to both sides the battle had already been decided to the south.

Grand Master Volquin had ridden to where Count Horton sat on his charger at the head of nearly four hundred horsemen. The count needed no persuasion to lead his men to the relief of the bishops, having been previously frustrated with his role as de facto commander of the reserve. And so he gave the order and trotted south at the head of his men, though not before he had granted Grand Master Volquin's request for the loan of a score of knights.

*****

Rusticus killed the spearman and stepped over his body to tackle the soldier behind. He could see the bishop now, surrounded by the traitor Caupo and horsemen in mail carrying lances. He stuck close to Lembit who was fighting like a forest demon, hacking and slashing with his sword as the wolf shields cut deep into the enemy's ranks. Their battle with the Livs was particularly vicious, drawing on the enmity between the two races that was hundreds of years old. The wolf shields fought in a tight formation, shield to shield as they had been taught, making it almost impossible for the enemy horsemen to break their ranks.

The wolf shields formed the centre of the Saccalian line, flanked by the village warriors whose ranks were more ragged. However, Lembit's warriors were methodically grinding their way forward in their desire to slay the bishop. The latter's spearmen were brushed aside with some ease and his crossbowmen had been sent away to reinforce Sir Helmold, so it was left to the horsemen under Sir Jordan to hold the line. Their commander and his most trusted knights stayed with the bishops, riding forward to jab their lances at the advancing shield wall. But though those horsemen on the flanks could ride among the Estonians easily enough, spearing some and killing others with their swords before withdrawing, they could make no impression on the warriors in the centre who sported a leering wolf design on their shields. The bishops would not ride from the field and so the knights and squires were forced to defend him, Caupo and Sir Jordan.

Rusticus picked up a discarded lance and thrust it into the horse that was in front of him, driving the point through the red caparison into its shoulder. The animal squealed and collapsed on the ground, trapping the leg of its rider underneath. Lembit stepped on the knight's full-face helmet and hacked down at his neck. There was a muffled cry, a spurt of blood and the wolf shields pressed on.

'Kill the bishop,' screamed Lembit, a call answered by those men around him.

Saccalians were being cut down on the flanks but their phalanx was still advancing. In the rear ranks of Lembit's men were archers, no more than forty, but they were able to shoot at the mailed horsemen who attempted to charge at their comrades in the front ranks. Their missiles hissed through the air to strike the Christian riders, killing a few but wounding more. In this battle of grim attrition and wills between Lembit and Bishop Albert the former was winning. The bishop grabbed the shaft holding his banner, resolved to die rather than flee.

And then he heard the blissful sound of trumpets.

Lembit did not hear them but he saw the crusaders in front of him raise their weapons and give a mighty cheer and felt a chill run down his spine. He heard shouts of alarm to his right and saw the warriors from the village begin to pull back.

He raised his arm. 'Halt!'

Rusticus glowered at him. 'On! They are beaten.'

'No, something is wrong.'

Then he too heard a blast of trumpets coming from the rear and knew that he was beaten. The men from his villages instinctively grouped around their chiefs who rallied their men around their banners: crude carved wolf heads on the ends of poles. Their warriors thrust the blunt ends of their spears into the earth, locked shields and awaited the crusader horsemen who were cantering towards them.

The rear ranks of the wolf shields turned to face the approaching horsemen, pointing their spears at the riders as the archers also turned and nocked arrows in their bowstrings. Count Horton led his men to within two hundred paces of the pagans and then halted and formed a long line of horsemen, sending riders to the bishop to present his compliments. No one noticed Volquin leading a party of knights through the open gates of Lehola in the rear.

Lembit shoved his way through his men behind him to gaze at the line of knights who sat on their horses to the rear of his men, then came back to stand beside Rusticus.

'We can fight our way back to the fort,' spat his deputy.

Lembit shook his head. 'There are too many of them.'

He sheathed his sword and unbuckled his sword belt.

'What are you doing?' said an incredulous Rusticus.

Lembit handed the belt to him. 'Saving my people.'

He walked from the ranks as the two sides eyed each other warily. Injured horses lay on the ground grunting and wounded men groaned as Lembit spread his arms and called to Bishop Albert.

He spoke in perfect German. 'Bishop Albert, if your soldiers will leave my lands then I will embrace your faith, for is it not better to live in peace than butcher each other?'

Sir Jordan removed his helmet and burst out laughing. 'A cornered rat will say anything to save his hide, it would appear.'

But the bishop was not laughing and neither was Caupo. Albert had been charged by the pope with the holy task of converting the pagans to the true faith. Caupo, formerly a foe, was now a servant of the Holy Church and had brought his people into the fold. Now Lembit, his most intractable foe, was standing before him offering to accept baptism. If Caupo's conversion was remarkable enough, this was nothing short of a miracle. The bishop closed his eyes and thanked God, for surely it was His hand that was at work here. He opened his eyes and nudged his horse forward.

'My lord bishop,' protested Sir Jordan but the bishop raised a hand to still him.

He rode through the horses of his bodyguard and dismounted, Lembit standing but ten paces away.

'You will travel with me to Riga and accept baptism into the Holy Church?' said the bishop.

Lembit nodded. 'I will.'

'Your chiefs must provide me with hostages as a sign of good faith,' continued the bishop.

'I will order it, bishop.'

'And you must permit my priests to travel freely through your lands to preach the word of God.'

Lembit swallowed and hesitated but then smiled. 'It shall be so.'

The bishop could not continue to hold the mask of severity he wore. He stepped forward and embraced a somewhat surprised Lembit.

'Then let us put away our swords,' said the bishop, 'and treat each other as brothers.'

Thus did Saccalia, most powerful among the Estonian kingdoms, accept the word of God and become an ally of the Bishop of Riga. The Estonians stared at each other and the crusaders in confusion, the latter also unsure what to make of it. But the bishop was seized with joy and ordered riders to be sent to all parts of the battlefield to announce that Estonian and Christian were now brothers and brothers did not harm each other.

While this outbreak of peace was occurring Grand Master Volquin calmly rode into Lehola and ordered the knights with him to scale the tower and cut down the wolf banners flying from them. This act had a demoralising effect on the Jerwen and Wierlanders battling to the north and east of the fort. Edvin and Jaak both saw the banners fall from the ramparts and assumed that it had fallen, which in reality it had. Soon horns were being sounded and bands of warriors were falling back to seek the sanctuary of the forest.

Saccalia had fallen and southern Estonia was at the mercy of the crusaders.

Chapter 20

Wenden's garrison had lost three brother knights wounded, five sergeants killed and a further two wounded. Among the mercenaries a dozen crossbowmen and six spearmen had been killed, most by Estonian arrows. The other garrisons had suffered similar losses, though the enemy had incurred many more casualties. Fresh water bottles were brought from camp to quench the raging thirst everyone was experiencing in the aftermath of the battle.

Walter, his helmet dented and his mail armour pierced in numerous places, took off his headwear and knelt beside a wounded enemy warrior who had been knocked unconscious when he had lost his helmet. He lay on the ground concussed, fear in his eyes and expecting to be killed by the Christians but grateful when Walter gently lifted his head and placed the water bottle at his lips. Everyone just stood and admired his piety and graciousness in victory.

'I truly hope that if the roles are reversed and Walter finds himself at the mercy of the enemy,' remarked Rudolf in admiration, 'that the foe will show him the same grace. But I fear it will not be so.'

He looked at Conrad. 'Not a scratch on you. You live a charmed life, Conrad.'

'Johann's ankle is broken.'

'He'll soon recover.'

Rudolf looked at the twisted and lacerated bodies that decorated the fence, ditch and tree stumps beyond. 'A grim harvest. Still, this battle should settle things. Lembit won't escape now. And with his death the other Estonian chiefs will no doubt submit.'

More carts were now arriving from camp to take away the dead and wounded and a herald arrived from the bishop. He saw Wenden's standard planted in the ground and rode over to it, Master Berthold standing beside it. The herald spoke to him and then wheeled away to report to the other castellans.

'To me,' called Berthold, 'all Wenden's brother knights and sergeants to me.'

'You three as well,' said Rudolf to Conrad, Hans and Anton.

The members of the order gathered round their master as the crossbowmen and spearmen remained at their posts at the fence.

'Lembit has surrendered to Bishop Albert,' said Berthold. The others cheered but the master raised his hands.

'There's more. Lembit has also agreed to be baptised. He will travel to Riga for the ceremony. It would appear that he is now our brother and ally.'

The brother knights and sergeants stood stony faced and silent at this news. Henke put their thoughts into words.

'So all this has been for nothing?'

'Not for nothing, Brother Henke,' said Berthold, 'for the bishop has secured the allegiance of the Saccalians and where they lead the other tribes will follow.'

But no one believed his words. They had spent years fighting Lembit and the other Estonian chiefs and felt cheated of victory. Henke was most aggrieved and mumbled to himself as the assembly dispersed. Another who was less than happy on receiving news of Lembit's decision was leather face. He stood at the fence, his crossbow resting on the back of the corpse of an Estonian hanging like carrion on the logs.

He spat towards the ditch. 'No plunder. Looks like another year of fighting for me at least, then.'

'What's wrong with that?' grinned Conrad, his strength returning after taking water.

'For a young pup like you, nothing,' replied leather face, 'but I'm not getting any younger and the cold and the wet of Livonia are beginning to take their toll. You've got a life of fighting to look forward to but I'm thinking about my retirement.'

He looked behind at the dead crossbowmen being thrown into the back of a cart.

'The thing about being a mercenary is that you can be killed at any time, and the longer you do it the more the odds lengthen against you staying alive.

'That Lembit's a slippery bastard, though. Just when you think you have him he escapes the noose. Now he would make a good mercenary. Knows when to call it a day and save his neck.'

'He is to accept baptism,' said Conrad sternly.

'I doubt that means much to him,' scoffed the grizzled dog of war. 'Just a way of buying more time. What do you think, Brother Henke?'

Conrad turned to see the brooding figure of Henke approaching, a face like thunder and still muttering to himself. He stopped and looked at leather face.

'What are you smiling about, you bag of old bones?'

Leather face grinned some more to reveal his broken, black teeth. 'I was just mentioning to the lad, here, that Lembit is a clever bastard.'

'I'm seriously considering going into that fort and slitting his throat myself,' snarled Henke.

'The bishop would burn you for that,' said Rudolf behind him.

'It would be worth it,' said an unrepentant Henke.

Rudolf put an arm around his shoulder. 'And I would lose a good friend and the order would lose a fine knight. Can't allow that to happen. Come on, let's go and find some of the badly wounded and slit their throats. You'll feel better afterwards.'

Henke was still grumbling as he followed Rudolf over the fence, down to the ditch and into the corpse-filled field of tree stumps. Already parties were going among the Estonian bodies to put those still living out of their misery. Better that than lying in agony staring at your guts that had been ripped open by a sword or axe, or waiting with smashed limbs for birds to come and peck your eyes out. Every soldier, pagan and Christian alike, prayed that they would be spared such horrors.

That night the bishop gave a great feast in his tent to celebrate Lembit's decision to embrace the Holy Church, though Count Horton, Sir Jordan and most of the crusader leaders sat in sullen silence, believing that they had been robbed of victory. Bishop Albert upbraided them for their uncharitable attitude, reminding them that they were in Christ's service and not in Livonia for personal gain or profit. He was delighted that Theodoric's title of Bishop of Estonia finally had substance.

Grand Master Volquin noticed the scowling faces of the crusaders, including Sir Helmold who was usually more sanguine than most, having known the mores of Livonia for some time now. For his part Caupo was also downcast, believing that Lembit had out-foxed Bishop Albert, but such was his love and respect for the prelate he kept his opinions to himself. Volquin understood the air of frustration that permeated the crusader army but believed that it could be banished by a symbolic victory. Not in Estonia, that much was certain. As he sipped at his wine the castle of Gerzika came into his mind.

Two days later the army began its slow crawl back to Livonia. The Christian dead were buried in what had been the crusader camp, the ground being consecrated by the bishop. Albert also insisted on the erection of a monument outside Lehola's gates where the monks of Abbot Hylas had been brutally murdered. Lembit sent back his warriors to their villages and ordered the chiefs to return, each with one of their sons. These would serve as hostages and would live in Riga until such time as the bishop thought fit to return them to their homes. In return the bishop agreed that no Christian soldiers would remain in Saccalia but Lembit agreed that missionaries would be allowed to travel freely throughout his land to live among his people and preach the word of God. The Estonian chief had no choice but to agree.

*****

Lembit stood before the doors of his hall in Lehola before the wolf shields drawn up in their ranks. A slight smell of smoke and charred wood still hung in the air and wolf banners no longer flew from the fort's towers. To one side stood a group of long-haired chiefs in full war gear with their sons who would accompany Lembit to Riga. The Estonian leader wore mail armour over a red tunic and a gilded helmet. He also carried a shield bearing his wolf insignia. The silence in the open space was deafening. He waved over Rusticus who stood in front of his men.

'You are in command in my absence,' he told him. 'The Christians will send their priests to spread their religion. See to it that they are not harmed, that is my command.'

'You killed the other priests to prevent them spreading their poison,' said Rusticus, 'and now you welcome them?'

'As long as there are no Christian castles or soldiers in Saccalia then there is still a chance to achieve final victory, Rusticus. We have suffered a temporary defeat but I am still hopeful that we might win the war.'

He walked over to his pony and hoisted himself into the saddle, pointing at the sons of his chiefs to do likewise.

Lembit smiled at the chiefs. 'If any of their fathers are mindful to rebel against my rule in my absence, kill them.'

A dozen of his wolf shields had been killed in the battle and a further twenty-five wounded, but that still left over four hundred and fifty of the best warriors in all Estonia, and they would make short work of any rebellion in Saccalia.

Lembit was about to ride from the compound when he had an afterthought. 'And Rusticus.'

'My lord?'

'I will return so please try to curb your more violent tendencies. Your task is to rule not terrorise. Work with the village chiefs and they will be your loyal servants, unless of course they step out of line.'

Rusticus nodded. 'What about the other tribes?'

'I will write to them explaining the situation.'

Rusticus was surprised. 'The Christians will allow you writing materials?'

Lembit smiled. 'Of course, they put great store in trust and forgiveness.'

'They betrayed us, all of them,' sneered Rusticus.

'Not all of them,' said Lembit, 'Jaak and Edvin came if none of the others did. For that they deserve our thanks not condemnation.'

He spurred his pony forward.

'Farewell, Rusticus. I will return.'

'The gods be with you, lord.'

He trotted from the compound with the hostages following, their heads down and one or two of the younger ones weeping. Outside Lehola's gates the Bishop of Riga and his bodyguard were waiting, along with Sir Helmold, Sir Jordan, Count Horton, Grand Master Volquin and fifty fully armed and armoured knights. It was an impressive show of strength, though the bishop was all smiles and courtesy as Lembit fell in beside him and the nervous hostages were escorted to the rear. Then the whole entourage trotted south to join the rest of the army on its way back to Livonia.

Though they had horses of their own Conrad, Hans and Anton held their reins as they walked behind the cart that held the injured Johann, his ankle now re-set and held in place by two wooden splints strapped to his leg. It was hot and humid and the air smelt of leather and horse dung, copious quantities of the latter being deposited along the churned-up track they had advanced upon and which they now used for their return journey.

Though peace had been agreed between the bishop and Lembit everyone still marched in their armour as a precaution against an assault by the Estonians who had attempted to relieve Lehola. Caupo himself organised the army's rearguard, had mounted patrols out every day to ensure security and the knights and brother knights remained fully armoured and mounted throughout the march. But there was no attack and the journey consisted solely of the monotony of everyday campaigning: digging latrines, cleaning weapons and equipment, cooking meals, grooming and mucking out horses and setting up and dismantling tents. At least in the order the sergeants and brother knights assisted with these chores; in the rest of the army the squires and foot soldiers were tasked with camp duties. The great lords and knights viewed such work as beneath them.

It was now approaching the longest day of the year and Conrad was daydreaming about Daina when there were shouts behind him.

'Make way for the bishop, make way for the bishop.'

He stopped and pulled his horse to the side as a great number of horsemen approached, pennants fluttering from lances with the bishop's great banner among them. Two heralds trotted past issuing their demands for wagons and men to get out of the way and then the bishop himself approached, wearing his priestly robes and accompanying a figure in a rich helmet, mail armour and a red cloak. Conrad looked admiringly at the bishop but then his jaw dropped as he recognised Lembit and the scar that he had inflicted on the pagan leader. The latter also identified him and brought his horse to a halt. There was a brief commotion as those following the bishop had to speedily stop their horses to prevent a collision.

Lembit turned his horse ninety degrees to face Conrad. The bishop, having discovered that his guest was no longer next to him, turned his horse around and retraced his steps. Lukas, Henke and Rudolf, who had been riding ahead of the cart that held Johann, placed their steeds between it and Lembit, the latter unconcerned by their presence. He leaned forward.

'Conrad Wolff.'

'You know this young man?' said the bishop, slightly perturbed by the unintended halt.

'Oh, yes, I know him,' said Lembit. 'We are old friends.'

The bishop looked quizzically at Conrad and then at Lembit.

'Young Master Wolff has distinguished himself since his arrival in Livonia. He is to be a brother knight in the Order of Sword Brothers.'

'I am well acquainted with his prowess in battle,' said Lembit.

'He was not proficient when he gave you that scar on your cheek,' said Henke loudly. 'He is much better with a crossbow now.'

Lembit glared at Henke who stared back unconcerned.

'Well,' said the bishop, 'pleasant though this interlude has been I think we should be on our way.'

'I told you we would meet again, Conrad Wolff,' said Lembit.

He leaned closer to Conrad. 'I have a debt to settle with you, *boy*.'

'Feel free to collect it any time,' remarked Conrad.

Lembit tugged on his reins to turn his horse. The bishop raised his hand to the brother knights who bowed their heads and he and the pagan chief continued their journey.

'Arrogant bastard,' spat Henke.

'Who, the bishop?' grinned Lukas.

'No good will come from letting Lembit live,' said Henke.

Rudolf prodded his horse forward and leaned over to speak to Conrad. 'Lembit holds a grudge against you, Conrad, you must take care.'

'I thought he was our ally now, Brother Rudolf.'

'In this world allies can turn into enemies in the blink of an eye. Watch yourself.'

But Conrad quickly forgot his chance meeting with Lembit when the army reached Wenden and the bishop and the pagan continued their journey on to Riga. The rest of the army followed, Caupo leaving it to take his warriors back to Treiden and Thalibald and his sons returning to their village.

He had other things on his mind as the garrison settled back into is daily routine of patrols and training, the brother knights and sergeants also attending the prayer sessions that divided their day. Johann was excused duties until his ankle healed, Ilona treating his injury with her herbal concoctions that seemed to aid his recovery to a remarkable extent. It had been the same with Abbot Hylas whose back had healed and who now had taken to sitting in the chapel most days mumbling to himself. He wore a fresh white habit but refused to take off the crucifixes that Lembit had placed around his neck after the execution of his monks. He thus wore four around his neck, which jangled whenever he walked anywhere. He was very fond of Ilona who had tended his wounds but rarely spoke to anyone else.

'His mind has gone,' she said as she left the dormitory after dressing Johann's ankle.

Conrad had offered to carry her box of potions as she made her way back to her hut below the castle.

'I can heal his wounds but not his mind. The ordeal that he was subjected to has destroyed his faculties. Poor man.'

They made their way across the courtyard to the large gatehouse that was now growing up from its foundations.

'He will never recover?' asked Conrad.

'It is in God's hands now.'

She sensed that Conrad was in a pensive mood by the way his mind seemed to be elsewhere, that and his eagerness to carry her medicines. She noticed that he kept glancing at her and then at the ground as though he was trying to summon up the courage to ask her something. After a few minutes she could bear it no more.

'What is on your mind, Conrad?'

He shook his head. 'Nothing.'

'Are you sure? There is nothing you want to ask me?'

He shook his head more vigorously. 'No. Well, yes, but…'

She stopped and faced him. 'Then ask me and put us both out of our misery.'

He stared at the ground to avoid her eyes. 'I was wondering if, well, if you would ask someone something.'

'Someone?'

He smiled furtively. 'Yes.'

'And does this someone have a name?'

'Brother Rudolf,' he whispered.

'Who?'

'Brother Rudolf,' he said more loudly.

'Rudolf.'

He nodded.

'This is like pulling teeth,' she sighed. 'I have things to do.'

With that she strode away, Conrad walking briskly after her.

'Ilona, wait.'

'What do you want me to ask Rudolf?'

'I wish to marry Daina.'

She stopped and turned to face him, a knowing expression on her face. 'So, we finally come to it. You are to be made a brother knight soon, along with Anton, Hans and Johann?'

He nodded.

'And if you take your vows you can never marry,' she continued. 'But you feel torn between your love for Daina and your desire not to let Rudolf and the order down.'

He said nothing but the anguish in his eyes told her that it was so.

'And you think that Rudolf's affection for me will soothe his anger if I tell him that you wish to marry the daughter of Thalibald.'

He nodded enthusiastically.

'I will not do it.'

His jaw dropped. 'But…'

'But, but, but? But what? What would Rudolf think of you if he learned that you had asked a woman to do your work for you, or the other brother knights for that matter?'

'I just thought it might be easier coming from you,' he muttered.

'This is no easy matter, Conrad. What you desire is a great thing. Daina is the daughter of a chief and you are but a novice.'

His heart sank at her words. He knew she spoke the truth but he could not give up on his dream.

'I will not give her up,' he said defiantly.

'That's more like it,' she said. 'We must strike while the iron is hot. Go to my hut and wait for me there.'

She turned and walked back towards the castle.

'Where are you going?'

'Just wait at my hut,' she instructed him.

Twenty minutes later he was pacing up and down in front of Ilona's small wooden dwelling, the children of the civilian workers running in a pack between the huts of their parents, when she and Rudolf appeared.

'Conrad has something to ask you, don't you Conrad?' she said, opening the door to her hut and beckoning them both inside.

The hut was a simple square abode with a bed against one wall, a table and two chairs against another and shelves fixed to another wall. There was no window. A candle stood in a metal dish on the table and baskets full of herbs rested on the floor. Ilona sat in one of the chairs and offered the other to Rudolf, leaving Conrad standing.

'Spit it out, then,' said Rudolf.

Conrad stood erect and swallowed. 'Forgive me, Brother Rudolf, but I wish to marry Daina.'

Rudolf said nothing as he looked at Ilona whose eyes flitted between him and Conrad. The brother knight then looked at the novice.

'I see.'

'The thing is, brother,' stuttered Conrad, 'I love her and...'

Rudolf lifted his hand to still him.

'If you are considering marriage I would hope that you do love your intended bride. What do you want of me?'

Conrad made to speak but discovered he had nothing to say. He had believed that if he broached the subject with Rudolf then.... Then what? Ilona rolled her eyes.

'Conrad saved my life a short while ago.'

'And mine on the ship that first brought him to Livonia,' added Rudolf.

'And since that time he has wounded Lembit and saved the life of the Bishop of Riga,' she continued. 'And yet now he dithers and acts like an imbecile.'

Rudolf laughed. 'He is very quick in battle. Perhaps you could administer one of your herbal cures.'

'There is no cure for what he has caught, I fear.'

Rudolf stood. 'This is what I am going to do, Conrad. I shall write to Thalibald requesting his presence at Wenden tomorrow, informing him of the reason why his attendance is vital, after which I shall inform Master Berthold that you wish to marry the chief's daughter. If Thalibald does not cut off your head then we shall see if the master will release you from your obligations.'

A tide of relief swept through Conrad. 'You are most kind, Brother Rudolf.'

Rudolf jabbed a finger in his chest. 'I am merely setting events in motion. I have no idea how they will turn out. Do not thank me yet.'

That evening Conrad went about his tasks with gusto, offering to clean the swords of his three companions after he had helped to muck out the stables. At vespers he prayed for his family, his friends, the order and also asked God to look favourably upon his desire for Daina's hand.

The next day Thalibald arrived, accompanied by his son and a dozen warriors armed with spears and swords and wearing helmets and mail armour. The chief himself was resplendent in steel lamellar armour, helmet, aventail, green tunic and rich leather boots. As Caupo's deputy he was expected to dress like a great warlord. Rameke had also come with his father to Wenden, no doubt having been told of Conrad's intentions. He had known for a while, of course, and Conrad prayed that he had not revealed so to his father. He also hoped that Daina had not been promised to another, for Thalibald was held in high esteem throughout Livonia and many a Liv chief would welcome an alliance between his family and that of Caupo's right-hand man through a marriage between Daina and one of his sons.

After their morning training session, during which Conrad and the other two novices had taken part in riding manoeuvres with the other brother knights, he told Anton and Hans of his intentions.

'Are you allowed to leave the order?' enquired Hans.

'I do not know,' said Conrad.

'If you are allowed to do so, where will you live?' asked Anton.

'In Thalibald's village, I assume,' replied Conrad, not knowing if he would even be made welcome there.

After he had taken his horse back to the stables, unsaddled it and brushed it down, a sergeant arrived with orders that he was to go the master's hall immediately, announcing that he had been ordered to escort him there.

Hans offered his hand. 'Good luck, my friend.'

Anton also proffered his support.

'The master is waiting,' snapped the sergeant.

Conrad, his face pale and his mouth dry, left the stables with his stony faced escort beside him. They walked across the cobbled courtyard, Conrad's mind racing with thoughts of what kind of reception was awaiting him. By the time the sergeant opened one of the thick oak doors that led to the interior of the master's hall he was sweating with apprehension.

The sergeant left him after he had been shown into the main chamber of the master's hall. The door was closed behind him and he looked nervously at those seated at the long oak table in front of him. In the centre was Master Berthold, flanked by Rudolf on his left and Thalibald on his right. Lukas was seated to the left of Rudolf and Rameke sat next to his father. The silence was oppressive as the master looked up at Conrad.

'Step closer,' he ordered.

Conrad took two paces forward and then stopped, hands by his side and his back as straight as a spear. He could feel his heart pounding in his chest. Berthold's brown eyes regarded him coldly.

'Brother Rudolf has informed me that you no longer wish to become a brother knight of our order, even though you would ordinarily have been a sergeant were it not for the beneficence of the Bishop of Riga.

'Furthermore, Brother Rudolf has also informed me that in your impertinence you desire nothing less than the hand of the daughter of Chief Thalibald in marriage.

'Is all that I have stated correct?'

Conrad was aware of a scribe seated at a desk to one side who was noting the exact words of Master Berthold.

'That is correct, master.'

Berthold stroked his beard. 'I should have you flogged for your brazenness. However, your great valour in battle merits your case being considered as opposed to being treated with contempt. I am aware that during your time at Wenden you have saved the life of the bishop himself.'

'And mine, master,' interrupted Rudolf.

'As well as the life of Daina herself,' added Rameke, which earned him a glare of rebuke from his father.

'Indeed,' said Berthold. 'Well, it would appear that you are quite the hero, Master Conrad. Brother Lukas, as the one who has been responsible for his training, what is your opinion of this novice?'

'Conrad would have made a fine brother knight, master. He is brave, intelligent and has a desire to learn.'

Berthold tapped his forefingers on the table. 'I would be remiss to lose such a soldier, would I not? Chief Thalibald, I would hear your words on the matter as it is your daughter that this young man is fixed upon.'

'My daughter needs a husband,' said Thalibald bluntly. 'I have seen this young man numerous times in my village assisting with the harvest and Rameke has informed me of my daughter's affection for him, though that is irrelevant. I know that he and others,' he nodded at Lukas, 'saved my womenfolk from Estonian raiders and I also know that there are several Liv chiefs who wish to see their sons married to my daughter.'

Conrad's heart sank and he knew his love was lost.

'Still,' Thalibald sniffed, 'if I deny them and give her to this young man I can save myself a hefty dowry. I assume the order will not require me to pay a dowry, Master Berthold?'

'Indeed not,' said Berthold.

Thalibald rubbed his nose. 'Then I leave the matter to you, Master Berthold.'

'Might I say something, master?' said Rudolf.

'By all means, Brother Rudolf,' replied Berthold.

'I would like to look beyond the immediate matter at hand to address the future of Livonia.'

Berthold's brow furrowed and Lukas looked surprised at his comrade but Rudolf continued.

'I believe I am correct in saying that at present there are no marriages between Livs and Germans in Livonia, or this region of it at least. Chief Thalibald, are any or your peoples' women married to Germans?'

Thalibald racked his brains for all of half a minute. 'Not to my knowledge.'

Rudolf smiled at him. 'Exactly. Would it not be therefore prudent to encourage marriages between native and settler to strengthen the bonds between the two and thus safeguard the future of Livonia? After all, that is what our order exists for.'

Thalibald looked confused and Lukas bemused and in truth it was a weak argument. However, Berthold was clearly bored by the whole matter and considered the aspirations of a novice hardly worth considering. But he did value the opinion of his deputy and for some reason Rudolf seemed to be championing this young man and so he gave way, or at least did away with his responsibilities.

'In this matter,' he announced, 'I fear I must play the part of Pontius Pilate and wash my hands of the matter. I hand over judgement to Chief Thalibald whose opinion I value above all others.'

'I think Conrad would make an excellent addition to your household, father,' said Rameke hurriedly.

'Well, I know he is good with a sword and I suppose I am in his debt,' said Thalibald. He pointed at Conrad. 'If I give you my daughter do you swear not to demand pigs, cows, ponies or land from me or my two sons?'

Conrad was beside himself with joy. 'I swear, lord. Of course, I swear never to make any demands on you or your household. I swear that I will be a faithful servant, I swear…'

'Thank you, Conrad,' said Rudolf. 'That is enough swearing for one day.'

Berthold, relieved that this inconsequential matter had at last been brought to an end, rose from his chair. 'You may go, novice Conrad.'

Conrad bowed to him and all the others, desperately trying to conceal the wide grin that was creeping over his face. He felt as though he was floating as he left the master's hall and went to tell his comrades that he was going to marry Daina. His time with the Sword Brothers was over.

He left Wenden two days later, saying his goodbyes to those who worked in the kitchens, the surly armourers and leather face. In the armoury he handed back his mail armour, gambeson and kettle helmet, unbuckling his sword belt and, with a heavy heart, handing it to the chief armourer, along with his axe and dagger.

'Hold,' came a voice behind him.

He turned to see Lukas approaching the armourer. 'I'll have those.'

'Make your mind up,' said the armourer, who like the others believed that the weapons and armour kept in the blockhouse were their personal property, to be jealously guarded.

Lukas took the belt, scabbard and sword and handed them to Conrad. 'Sir Frederick gave this sword to you, Conrad, so it should accompany you wherever you go.'

'It's the property of the Sword Brothers,' grumbled the armourer.

'And I say it belongs to him,' said Lukas firmly, 'unless you would rather I bring the master to confirm my order.'

The armourer mumbled something under his breath but did not protest.

'The axe and dagger too,' said Lukas.

The armourer sighed deeply and handed him Conrad's weapons. Lukas passed them to Conrad.

'Come Conrad,' he said, 'the air is objectionable in here.'

They walked into the courtyard, Conrad bucking his belt as they made their way across the cobbles, through what would eventually be the gatehouse and across the bridge.

'It will be a drawbridge when the gatehouse has finished,' said Lukas. He held out a hand to Conrad.

'Thank you, Brother Lukas,' said Conrad, taking the outstretched hand.

'You are a fine soldier, Conrad, and would have made an excellent brother knight.'

Conrad felt a pang of remorse. 'I hope you do not think ill of me.'

'Of course not. You have followed your convictions, and there are few men in this world who do that. I will see you at your wedding.'

Conrad walked down the track that led to the outer perimeter, through the ever-increasing spread of huts towards the open gates that led out of the castle and south to his new life. Spearmen and crossbowmen were practising drills and on his right two riders in full armour were galloping towards each other, lances couched. There was a bang and one of the riders toppled from his saddle, the other bringing his horse to a halt and removing his helmet. Conrad recognised the broad shoulders and powerful body as Henke drew alongside the brother knight he had just unhorsed and spoke a few words to him.

Conrad continued on, children and geese crossing his path as the wind brushed his face and the sun shone on his back. This summer had a glorious feel about it. He heard hooves behind him and looked round to see Henke approaching, drawing his warhorse alongside.

'So, you are to be a farmer.'

'I will battle the land now, Brother Henke, instead of the Estonians.'

Henke looked at Conrad's sword. 'I wonder what Sir Frederick would say if he knew that his sword was going to hang in a village hut?'

'I hope he would respect me for choosing wisely.'

Henke pulled up his horse. 'I remember that night when I first saw you, in Lübeck with your sister.'

Conrad stopped and looked up at him. 'As do I. I will always be grateful for your help, Brother Henke.'

Henke waved his hand at him. 'That is not my point. Afterwards Rudolf was convinced that you were sent to us by God and he has always bent my ear ever since, saying that your actions in battle are proof that God has marked you out to be one of His chosen warriors.'

'God has given me Daina.'

Henke leaned forward, his cold eyes fixing him. '*You* chose Daina, Conrad, but God has not finished with you yet, mark my words.'

He tugged on the reins, dug his spurs into his steed and went back to lance practice.

Despite his indifference in the master's hall Thalibald made Conrad welcome in his village. He gave his daughter away at the marriage that took place two weeks later where Otto was the priest. Conrad was delighted that Anton, Hans and Johann attended, all now brother knights and wearing the insignia of the Sword Brothers on their white surcoats. Rudolf, Lukas and Walter also attended and brought Ilona along, who gave Daina a silver necklace with silver ingots, upon which were etched good luck symbols: the Lifetree that celebrates the dawn, the crescent moon, the protector of warriors; Zalktis, the ancient serpent that brings well being; and Laima, the goddess of destiny and prosperity. Rameke and Waribule smiled when they saw it and Daina's eyes lit up at the beauty of the piece. Rudolf and Lukas saw it but said nothing, though they did advise Daina to hide it from Otto who might take exception to a display of devilry and pagan superstition on God's holy union of two of his lambs.

Conrad embraced Ilona and thanked her for her gift. He had grown immensely fond of her during his time at Wenden, this tall, raven-haired woman who had brought Rudolf back to life. Otto never spoke to her, believing her to be sent by the devil to tempt the brother knights. But for their part the sergeants and brother knights loved her and held her in high esteem, seeing her as a sort of lucky mascot, which increased Otto's wrath even more. But today his brutal features were all smiles as he stood before the couple in his white habit and sandals and read the sacred words from a bible.

Most Livs wore varying shades of brown or green but Daina, being the chief's daughter, wore a blue skirt and a white shawl adorned with bronze ornaments. Her white sash was also decorated with bronze and next to her Conrad looked like the poor farmer he was: a simple brown woollen tunic over a white linen shirt, brown leggings and boots. But he felt more prosperous at the feast afterwards when Thalibald gave the newlyweds the hut of a warrior who had been killed at Lehola. His childless wife was evicted to a smaller widow's hut in the village, Thalibald instructing Conrad that it was his responsibility to feed her from the produce of his animal stock. When Conrad enquired what stock, Thalibald informed him that he was giving him two cows, six pigs, four goats and a dozen chickens. In addition to the crops that the villagers harvested from the fields, a portion of which went to Wenden, which was shared out among the inhabitants, Conrad would also supplement his household's diet with what he caught hunting. Thalibald also gave Conrad a shield and a hunting spear so he could stalk boars.

Normally Otto restricted his diet to coarse bread, vegetables, herbs and beans in accordance to the rules set down by the Cistercian Order, though at Conrad's wedding he consumed vast quantities of pork, boar, duck and chicken, all washed down by copious amounts of *medalus*. His booming voice announced that as it was a special occasion it would be uncharitable to refuse Thalibald's hospitality. He eventually passed out and Rudolf and Lukas had to carry him outside where they dunked his head in a water trough before leaving him to sleep off his stupor.

The next morning, as Otto sat outside Thalibald's hall nursing his sore head and swearing never to partake of alcohol again, Conrad said his farewells. As they were not marching to war the brother knights wore their swords but not mail armour. Instead all of them sported tunics of dark cloth and on their heads wore dark-coloured soft caps. They could all have been mistaken for merchants had it not have been for the white lightweight cloaks – mantles – draped round their shoulders. On the left shoulder on their cloaks they wore the red cross and sword of their order. This was to symbolise martyrdom for they fought and died in the service of God.

Thalibald and his sons also gathered to say goodbye to their friends and allies, knowing that they would no doubt be marching to war together in the future.

Rudolf shook Conrad's hand. 'The next time we will be fighting together you will be one of Thalibald's warriors.'

'I hope that there will be no more fighting, Brother Rudolf,' said Daina, her arm tightly round Conrad's waist.

Rudolf nodded knowingly to Conrad. 'Let us hope that it is so, child.'

He kissed Daina on the cheek, said farewell to Thalibald and mounted his horse. Lukas shook Conrad's hand. He pointed to the sword at his hip.

'Keep it clean and sharp and do not forget how to use it.'

'I will not, Brother Lukas.'

'And treasure your wife more,' was Ilona's advice as she kissed them both on the cheeks before mounting the pony that she had been given by Rudolf.

Walter embraced him and then Daina, placing a hand on each of their shoulders and asking God to bless their union. It was a solemn moment and Conrad believed that one day Walter would be a saint of the Holy Church, such was his piety and purity. Walter walked over to where Otto was still seated on the ground, gently lifted him to his feet and escorted him to the waiting donkey that would take him back to Wenden. Conrad embraced Anton and Johann, both of them proud and strong in their new garbs. His embrace with Hans was the most earnest.

'We have come a long way since we first met in Lübeck, my friend,' said Conrad.

'Who would have thought that we would end up as we have,' grinned Hans.

Conrad was genuinely pleased for Hans, the orphan and thief whose neck had nearly been snapped on the gallows, had it not have been for the bishop's intervention. He had been dealt a cruel hand in life but had overcome adversity to become one of Christ's warriors. He was a living example of how good could triumph in the world.

'We are waiting, Brother Hans,' said Rudolf as the others sat on their horses. Hans grinned, embraced Conrad and Daina and mounted his horse. Otto weakly made the sign of the cross as he and the others trotted from the village to leave Conrad to begin his new life.

*****

Mindaugas was taller than Aras now. It was apparent as they stood beside each other and observed the scene of carnage that stretched out before them. Piles of twisted, bloody corpses littered the ground. The stench of death was already filling the air, crows were circling overhead and had taken up position in the surrounding trees in expectation of a gory feast. Aras' warriors were going through the dead, searching for anything of use that could be taken back across the Dvina when they returned to Lithuania. The smashed shields, broken spears and dented armour and helmets would be left behind but swords, functional crossbows and complete mail armour would be transported over the river in boats that were waiting less than a mile away.

Aras began walking among the dead and dying, the majority of the latter either trapped under their slain horses or wedged under piles of dead. Mindaugas followed him, aware that he was very much a spectator to the triumph that had been his tutor's. And what a victory it had been. Vsevolod had known that eventually the bishop would turn his attention to Gerzika. He knew that he would not be able to retain his stronghold in the face of a determined crusader assault. Years of peace had resulted in its defences being neglected and it would take a huge outlay of money to restore them to their former glory. He had neither the resources nor the time to do so, and in any case his army was small in comparison to the army that the bishop could send against him. So, despite Rasa's initial hostility, he had taken the momentous decision to abandon Gerzika and evacuate its population across the Dvina. Some had refused to go, especially among the outlaying villages where there was great hostility towards the Lithuanians. Many of the merchants had also refused to leave and so had been left behind to form a council that hoped to barter with the crusaders when they appeared before the walls.

Vsevolod had been denounced as a coward and a traitor by the Orthodox priests in Gerzika, but when the crusader army arrived the merchants found that the only terms acceptable to the bishop's servants was immediate surrender. And Gerzika's priests discovered that the only religion acceptable to the crusaders was that practised in Rome and so they were expelled from Gerzika and their houses of worship plundered.

Following their disappointment at Lehola the crusaders, led by Count Horton and Sir Jordan, had petitioned the bishop for a continuation of the war against the Estonians. They had reluctantly agreed that the Saccalians had sued for peace but there were other tribes. Surely they could despoil their lands? The bishop had strictly forbidden it. However, Grand Master Volquin had raised the matter of Prince Vsevolod and Gerzika. The prince's duplicity and support for Daugerutis meant that he had to face punishment. Why not let Count Horton and Sir Jordan take their men and storm Gerzika? And so it came to pass.

The two nobles led their forces south instead of west towards Riga, guided by Liv scouts provided by Thalibald and accompanied by Volquin's five brother knights and ten sergeants from his office in Riga. Sir Helmold and his knights accompanied the two bishops and their 'guest' Lembit but the force that attacked Gerzika was considerable. Not only did it comprise the bulk of the troops that had fought at Lehola, it also included the knights and foot soldiers who had besieged Fellin. The latter had suffered no casualties due to a lack of siege engines, which meant there was no assault. Count Horton and Sir Jordan had arrayed their forces before Gerzika's wooden walls, demanded its surrender and had been surprised when the gates were opened. After a week of rapine they had left a garrison to secure the stronghold and begun a leisurely march back to Riga with a host of wagons loaded with treasure.

After their great victory Count Horton and Sir Jordan had dismissed the Liv scouts. They did not share the bishop's or Sir Helmold's fondness for these heathens who dressed and looked like the pagans they had come to butcher. They did not need them to show them the fifty miles downstream to Kokenhusen, which was unfortunate because had the Livs remained they most probably would have learned that over three thousand Lithuanian warriors crossed the Dvina one night to set an ambush for the crusaders. Sprung equidistance between Gerzika and Kokenhusen, it had been spectacularly successful.

Aras stopped and turned to look at Mindaugas. 'Repayment for your father's death.'

Mindaugas said nothing as he looked down at a man lying face up whose legs had been crushed under a collapsed wagon. He was groaning faintly, his eyes full of pleading.

'He would have been pleased with you, Aras.'

The latter picked up a mace at his feet and walked over the injured man, the wagon's driver probably on account of his poor quality clothing and lack of armour.

'It was Vsevolod who gave permission for the ambush.' Aras stood over the wounded man and proceeded to smash in his head with the mace, reducing it to a disgusting bloody pulp that made Mindaugas grimace.

'My father believed he was a coward.'

Aras tossed the mace aside and continued walking among the crusader dead. He had launched his attack when the Christians were strung out along the track for miles, only a few of the knights wearing their armour in the summer heat. The attack achieved total surprise and overwhelmed the enemy before they had a chance to respond.

'I admit he's no warrior,' agreed Aras, skirting a heap of Christian dead, 'but he has a keen mind and is nobody's fool.'

Mindaugas caught up with him. 'He wants me to marry his daughter.'

They came to a wagon piled high with silver trays, cups and ornaments.

'Have this transported back to the river,' Aras ordered one of his subordinates who was guarding the plunder. 'Prince Vsevolod should have his cutlery returned to him.'

He took off his helmet and wiped his brow on his sleeve. It was unbearably hot.

'Is she pretty, his daughter?'

Mindaugas smirked. 'Yes.'

Aras replaced his helmet. 'Child-bearing hips?'

Mindaugas looked embarrassed. 'I suppose.'

'Well then, sounds like a decent proposition. You like her?'

Mindaugas shrugged. 'I don't dislike her.'

Aras nodded. 'That's a good start. Get the men back to the river!' he bellowed at a group of his officers examining a crusader banner. 'And leave those barbarian flags behind. They are probably bewitched.'

'My father warned me not to trust Vsevolod,' said Mindaugas.

Aras turned back to the boy. 'At the moment Vsevolod's interests are the same as yours. He wants to preserve the grand duke's territories, defeat the other dukes and keep the Christians this side of the river. I'd say you have nothing to worry about for the moment.

'Come on, let's get back across the river before the garrison at Kokenhusen sends out a patrol to find out where their crusader friends are.'

They walked towards the river as the Lithuanians began transporting their plunder back to the boats that awaited them. Mindaugas stepped over the body of a knight with a spear in its back. Had he stopped to turn it over he would have seen that it was Sir Jordan.

*****

The harvest around Wenden was excellent that year, the fields yielding a healthy bounty. Despite his change of lifestyle Conrad found that he took to the life of a farmer with relative ease. His life of a novice had been one of discipline, austerity and hard training; in Thalibald's village he found that his daily routine was also long and hard, but with the lovely bonus of sharing a bed with his wife every night. Daughter of a chief she may have been but Daina had to undertake her fair share of work like all the other women of the village.

In July she pulled up the flax and hemp in the garden at the back of their hut, laying them out in the sun before being retted, which involved her and the other women hauling them down to the nearest stream where they were placed in the water to rot away the fleshy parts of the plant. Once the fibres were clean they were beaten to separate them and hung up in strikes to dry them. The hemp was then ready to be wound into rope or cord and the flax placed on a distaff and spun into yarn.

At the end of the day, after all the chores had been attended to, Conrad always spent an hour practising with his sword, going through the routines that Lukas had taught him. Afterwards, exhausted, he sat on the edge of the bed watching Daina spinning yarn.

'Do you think that Master Berthold will summon you back to Wenden one day?'

He ran a cloth over the weapon's blade. 'That would be very unlikely.'

'Then why do you practise with it every day?'

He slid the blade back into the scabbard and placed it on the hooks above his head. 'Because I was taught how to use it and it would be an insult to Brother Lukas and Sir Frederick to forget the skills I was taught.'

She stopped her spinning and looked at him, the light of the candles catching the glint in her eyes.

'Who is Sir Frederick?'

'He was a crusader lord,' he said, 'who died of his wounds at Fellin three years ago. It was his sword. He carried the symbol of a unicorn on his shield and banner.' He pointed at the sword. 'There are unicorns carved into the pommel.'

'What's a unicorn?'

'A horse that has a horn on its head.'

'Do such things exist?'

He shrugged. 'I have never seen one but I believe they live in a faraway land.'

She went back to her spinning, a task that has been carried out by women for centuries.

'You will tire yourself out with all that swordplay. And you will need all your strength for the harvest. My father says that now the Estonians have accepted baptism there will be no more fighting. So you see, Master Berthold will not be calling on your services again.'

Berthold may not have been calling upon his services but he sent some of his men to assist in gathering in the wheat, rye, barley and oats that had ripened in the fields. Hans, Anton and Johann came and drank too much *medalus* as they celebrated with their friend and toasted his good fortune. Rudolf and Lukas also came and accompanying the latter were ten scrawny, pale-faced boys who looked as though they would break into pieces at any moment.

'Do you recognise them, Conrad?' asked Lukas as he harvested wheat with a sickle, wielding it with the same effortless skill as he did when holding a sword. Conrad shook his head.

'They are you.'

Conrad stopped and looked at the boys struggling in the summer heat. 'Me?'

'A few years ago. They are novices fresh from Germany, wastrels, orphans, thieves and the like. Brought here to be moulded into sergeants, perhaps even brother knights.'

Conrad looked at their pallid flesh and bony arms. 'Good luck with that, Brother Lukas.'

'I remember when I first clapped eyes on you,' said Lukas, cutting a great swathe with his sickle. 'You looked like them and Brother Hans was in a more parlous state. Look at you now, all muscle and strength. It is remarkable what good food and dry quarters can do.'

'And a good instructor,' smiled Conrad.

'I hope you are not letting your sword go to waste.'

'I practise with it every day, even though Daina informs me that I waste my time.'

Lukas stopped, stretched his back and looked over at Conrad's wife smiling and teasing Hans, Johann and Anton as she handed them ladles of water from the buckets she was carrying. 'Marriage suits her, and you. But always keep the edge of your sword sharp, Conrad, and your skills sharper. Peace never lasts forever.'

But that summer was gloriously peaceful and in the autumn the peas, beans and vetches were harvested and the oxen provided by Master Berthold were used to plough the fields for the sowing of the winter crops. The women collected wild fruit and berries and the wheat stubble was gathered in to mix with hay to create winter fodder. Rameke showed Conrad how to shoot a bow and together they went into the forest to hunt deer and elk. He also took part in the weekly gatherings of the village militia, which was when all able-bodied men aged sixteen and upwards gathered outside Thalibald's hall to undergo training. This involved nothing more then marching outside the village and forming up into a shield wall, though Conrad found it useful as it acquainted him with the various horn calls used by Liv war bands: alarm, muster, attack, retreat and form shield wall. Aside from the full-time warriors who attended Thalibald most of the village menfolk were poorly armed and equipped with shields, spears, axes and a few helmets. And not even Thalibald had a sword to rival Conrad's in terms of workmanship, balance and lightness.

571

He was conscious that his hut had formerly been the lodgings of a widow who had been evicted to make way for him and Daina and always made sure that she was provided for out of their food stocks. The widow was in fact a handsome woman in her late twenties named Elita. She missed her husband terribly and had no children to console her and so Daina insisted that she was a regular visitor to her former home. Conrad gave her half their chickens, a goat and two pigs, though there was no prospect of her starving as she ate at least three evening meals with them every week. Conrad did not mind as she was affable enough and it made Daina happy for her to be with them rather than sitting alone with her distaff. Elita was one of the first ones to be told that Daina would be having a baby in the new spring.

Thalibald was delighted and when he informed Master Berthold the latter sent Daina a silver crucifix as a present. The winter that gripped Livonia that year was, like the previous one, harsh, the rivers and lakes freezing over and the ground covered in deep snow. When the first snowflakes had begun to fall Conrad acquired a new companion when a stray dog wandered into the village. He found it one morning curled up shivering outside his hut and immediately took pity on it. He did not know why but perhaps the sight of anything abject and alone elicited feelings of compassion in him. The dog was a mangy, flea-bitten beast with sores on its back legs and a slight limp. Conrad took it in, fed it and left it asleep by the fire as he and Daina went about their daily tasks. They washed its wounds, filled its belly and combed the fleas from its coat. It loved Daina but had little time for Conrad, being content to lie at her feet and occasionally growl and bark at him when he showed his wife any affection. Bad tempered and rather affectionless, at least to him, Conrad named it Henke, which provided him with endless merriment.

Daina got the village blacksmith to make Conrad a silver ring that she gave to him one evening. It was a simple affair and he put it on a finger on his left hand.

'No, no, you must look at it first,' she implored.

He took it off and turned it in his hand.

'Look at the inside.'

He peered at the ring and saw strange markings on the inside.

'It is our names in our language,' she said with a girlish giggle. 'The blacksmith sent it off to an engraver in another village. It means that we are together for all eternity.'

He took her in his arms and gazed into her green eyes. 'I don't need a piece of metal to tell me that.'

She leaned forward and kissed him on the lips. 'It is silver not iron.'

'It is wonderful, thank you.'

Though winter was harsh life was made bearable by the feasts Thalibald gave, the swelling of Daina's belly and the company of Rameke and Elita. Waribule kept himself to himself but told Conrad he was pleased that he would soon have a niece or nephew to play with.

'It will be a boy of course,' Conrad told him.

'How do you know?'

'Elita dangled my ring on a strand of Daina's hair over her belly and it rocked to and fro, which means a boy apparently.'

When Thalibald heard of this he had a gold ring made that he presented to Daina, insisting she wear it at all times. He may have been baptised into the Christian faith but old habits die hard and Conrad found out from Elita that the old gods looked favourably upon women who wore a gold ring. It ensured that they and their infants would survive childbirth.

As Christmas came and went and the new year was born Conrad heard little of events beyond the village's confines. Thalibald told him that the Rotalians had raided south towards Treiden but Caupo and the Sword Brothers from Segewold and Kremon had chased them back to their own land. The spring came and Thalibald informed him that Lembit had been released from his luxurious confinement at Riga and he, along with the hostages that the bishop had taken, had gone back to Saccalia. An Oeselian fleet of longships sailed into the estuary of the Dvina but Riga's defences were too strong and they retreated after causing little damage. As the lichens and mosses began to appear on the ground and on trees as spring took hold and the forest filled with fungi, Daina went into labour.

As she had promised to do Ilona came from Wenden to be the midwife, throwing Conrad and Henke out of their hut while she and Elita tended to the expectant mother. Conrad spent hours either pacing up and down outside the hut or on his knees praying when he heard Daina's screams, while Henke pawed at the shut door or cried when he heard Daina in distress. Then it went quiet and he feared the worst, but wept like a child when he heard the cries of a small infant and Ilona came from the hut to inform him that he had a son. They called the child Dietmar.

At long last Conrad's life seemed to make sense. He had seen his life and family ripped apart, he and his sister being saved only when they had the good fortune to literally run into Rudolf and Henke. He had never questioned his fate in the intervening years, being resigned to becoming a member of the Sword Brothers. But now he realised that he had been brought to Livonia for a reason and that reason was to marry Daina and raise a family with her. He counted himself truly blessed that God had smiled on him and led him to the wonderful life that he was now living.

Chapter 21

It was an old trick but effective nevertheless. They had arrived two days before: four Saccalians who sailed down the Gauja in a riverboat with a cargo of grey squirrel pelts. They left their boat on the bank and walked inland to Thalibald's village, requesting an audience with the chief. The peace between their people and the Christians meant that trade could now be conducted along the Gauja and they told the chief that they had access to furs from Novgorod. Most trade was conducted along the Dvina but why not open an alternative route? The wealthy who lived in the cities and towns of Germany had an insatiable desire for furs and paid handsomely for those that came from Novgorod. Why bother paying the taxes levied by Riga when ships could pick up their valuable cargo at the mouth of the Gauja? Thalibald listened to their words and was convinced.

He feasted them in his hall and they told him that the furs they had brought with them were a gift. But they represented only a fraction of what could be purchased from Novgorod. Peace meant trade and trade meant riches. Both Livs and Saccalians would grow rich together and their peoples would prosper. Thalibald knew that Lembit had accepted baptism and had returned to his land a follower of Christ. The priests and missionaries of the bishop were now living among the Saccalians, preaching the word of God and being unmolested. Surely, they suggested, now was the time to put aside old grievances and embrace the new future. After all, did not Christ himself preach forgiveness?

Thalibald embraced them, drank with them and saw a future of prosperity and peace. While he, Waribule and his warriors got drunk with the traders he sent Rameke to Wenden to inform Master Berthold of these developments so he would not find out via a third party. Rameke was unimpressed and asked to stay but his father reminded him that he was a warrior and a warrior obeys his lord. And so, as Thalibald's hall echoed with the sound of drunken laughter, Rameke and a small escort rode from the village and headed to Wenden. The gates were shut behind him for although there was now peace with Lembit, Thalibald was not so naïve to believe that a warlord should sleep with the gates of his village open.

Henke began barking when he heard the sounds of revelry coming from the hall. Conrad's hut was not next to the chief's residence but the night was warm and still and the noise of drunken voices and cheers carried far.

'Shut up, Henke,' Conrad hissed, concerned that he would wake Dietmar in his cradle at the foot of the bed.

Sure enough the babe started grumbling and then crying as he heard the dog's bark. Conrad got out of bed and grabbed the mongrel by the scruff of the neck.

'You can sleep outside tonight,' he said irritably as he slid the bolt back, opened the door with his other hand and turfed the mutt outside, closing the door and slamming the bolt back into place. Daina, dressed in her nightshirt, picked up Dietmar and cradled him in her arms to soothe him. Outside Henke growled, snarled and scraped at the door.

'You can sleep outside, you bag of fleas,' Conrad shouted.

Dietmar began crying again.

'Shush, Conrad,' whispered Daina as she began walking up and down, rocking Dietmar in her arms.

After a few minutes she managed to quieten her son and laid him back in his cot. The sounds of merriment continued to come from Thalibald's hall. Daina rested her head on Conrad's chest.

'Your father will have a sore head in the morning,' he said.

'I think it is the morning,' she whispered.

Outside he heard a low snarl.

'I swear I'm going to strangle that dog,' he said in exasperation. 'If he wakes Dietmar again…'

There was a yelp and then silence. A shiver ran down Conrad's spine and the hairs on the back of his neck stood up. He jumped out of bed and pulled on his trousers, then his boots.

'Get up,' he ordered, 'and get Dietmar.'

Bleary eyed, Daina sat up in bed.

'Hurry!' he shouted, causing Dietmar to start wailing.

He felt sick as he heard screams and knew that the village was under attack.

They had sailed downriver at night, hauling their boats from the water before the dawn broke and concealing themselves and their vessels among the trees. They were particularly careful to remain hidden when they got to Wenden, knowing that the crusaders always sent men to the river to keep an eye on what was happening on the Gauja, or so their lord had told them. On the last night of their journey they had beached their boats on a sandy strip on the northern bank and pulled them into the dense forest that came almost to the water's edge. They had removed the telltale indentations caused by the boats and the marks left by dozens of boots and then waited. Waited until it was dark.

576

It was easy enough. While Thalibald and his men filled their bellies with meat and beer two of the merchants left the hall to take a piss. They quickly made their way to the watchtower next to the closed village gates, slit the throats of the guards before descending to the ground and lifting the oak beam that secured the gates. In they flooded, silent death dealers attired in mail armour, helmets and armed with spears, axes and swords. They did not come to plunder or rape, only kill. Kill quickly. Kill efficiently. Kill everyone.

Conrad tucked the axe in his belt, gripped the handle in the shield boss and clutched his sword.

'Stay close behind me,' he said to Daina.

She was trying to calm Dietmar but was herself in tears, frightened by the dreadful noises outside. He held his shield slightly behind him to cover them both as he edged towards the door. He saw the boar spear that Rameke had given to him as a present, sheathed his sword and picked it up just as the door was kicked in. Daina screamed as the snarling brute with a thick beard heard her and was stopped in his tracks as the blade of the spear was thrust into the nape of his neck. Daina stared wild-eyed in terror as blood sheeted out onto the earth floor of her hut and followed Conrad mutely as he held the spear in place and pushed the dead warrior back out of the door into the street. To witness chaos.

Some of the huts were already alight, the flames illuminating the scene of panic as women and children raced around in alarm before being cut down by warriors. He saw the body of Henke in the dirt and kicked the dead man off his spear, momentarily catching sight of the design on his shield. He saw a leering wolf's head and gritted his teeth. He had to get to Thalibald's hall. That was the place where the Liv warriors would rally. If they were still alive. He heard Daina's voice.

'Conrad!'

He turned to see Elita, half naked, running towards them, and following her was a wolf shield about to split open her skull with his axe. Elita's mouth opened in terror as Conrad threw the spear that missed her head by inches and thudded into the chest of her pursuer. He pulled the axe from his belt.

'Move Elita,' he shouted.

She rushed to Daina's side and kissed Conrad's wife.

'We have to get to the chief's hall,' he told them. 'Stay close. Move.'

The warriors were going into every hut and slaughtering all inside. Animals in pens behind dwellings were squealing and screeching as the sounds and smell of death reached their nostrils. Conrad's hut was less than a hundred paces from

Thalibald's hall but that short distance turned into the longest journey of his life as he tried to be ahead of the women, by their side and covering their backs. Two warriors came from a hut, their axes bloody and leers on their faces. Conrad swung the axe blade at one, cleaving his face in two, then whipped back the weapon to send the spike into the other man's eye. He clutched his face, screaming in pain, as he fell to the ground. Conrad bundled the women before him and shepherded them around a pen full of squealing pigs. He opened the entrance and the animals bolted into the street and into the path of a group of wolf shields that had seen him kill two of their comrades.

On they went, skulking by the sides of huts where women and children had been butchered. The air was filled with screams, cries and the smell of smoke as the village was torched. Conrad roughly shoved the two women into the shadows of a hut as half a dozen enemy soldiers raced by, heading towards the centre of the village. Daina was trying to hush the howling Dietmar, but such was the din that his noise was barely audible. Perhaps he should try to escape from the village and hide in the woods. But what sort of man would he be to abandon his wife's family in their hour of need? So he followed the wolf shields, herding the women between two animal pens and by the side of a hut to come into the small piece of open ground in front of Thalibald's hall. Just in time to see Waribule scythed down by a succession of axe blows.

'Noooooooo!' screamed Daina as she beheld her brother's death.

'Move!' screamed Conrad as he bundled them both towards where Thalibald and half a dozen of his men were still fighting, holding off an increasing number of Estonians with difficulty.

Conrad tucked the axe back in his belt, drew his sword and plunged it into the back of a warrior who was fighting his father-in-law. Thalibald saw him and then Daina and ran forward, grabbing his daughter and hauling her into the middle of his small circle of fighters. He said nothing to Conrad, merely nodding grimly and continuing the fight. Elita tripped and fell, jumped up, smiled at Daina and was then decapitated by an Estonian axe. Daina shook with horror as Conrad ran the man through, deflected an axe with his shield and severed its owner's arm at the wrist with his sword.

Thalibald's hall was on fire now, the flames roaring as they engulfed the building, sending sparks high into the night sky. The chief was wounded in the arm and then a spear blade pierced one of his hamstrings. He went down on one knee, holding his shield above his head to deflect the rain of blows that was directed at him. Conrad fought off his attackers and hauled him to his feet. Thalibald smiled at him and his expression went blank as a spear was thrust into his spine.

'Conrad.'

He heard the faint whisper of his wife's voice and turned to see her clutching Dietmar, an arrow lodged in the cloth that held him and blood staining the material. His eyes filled with tears as he witnessed his son's death but in his despair did not see another arrow lodged in Daina's stomach. She smiled weakly at him and collapsed to the ground, still holding the infant to her chest.

Conrad screamed with fury and helplessness as he hacked and thrust to keep the wolf shields away, standing over his wife as he cut down three enemy warriors. He saw Daina's mother fall and die not six paces from him, Thalibald's other warriors also being slain near their lord's wife. He caught an axe blade on his shield, stooped and thrust his sword under it to rip open the mail armour covering the belly of an Estonian, the broken metal rings being soaked in blood as he twisted the blade. Whipping it back he flicked the handle and sliced open the nose of an opponent with the point. The flames roared and he fought on, never moving from his wife and child. He heard Lukas' words.

'Keep moving. If you stand still you are dead.'

But he would not leave them.

He felt a jolt and looked down to see that a spear blade had been thrust through his side. But he did not feel anything. He felt another jolt as a sword point was thrust into the rear of his left shoulder blade. But he did not feel anything as he fell to his knees and dropped his shield as he still clutched his sword. He felt another jolt as an axe blade gashed the side of his head and he was knocked to the ground. He kept looking at the face of his beautiful wife as the darkness enveloped him and he faded away. But he did not feel anything.

*****

'Will he live?'

Rudolf stared at the unconscious, bandaged figure of Conrad on Ilona's bed and shook his head.

'That is in God's hands,' she said, tying off the dressing that covered that top half of Conrad's skull. 'I have done what I can.'

The glow of the flames of Thalibald's village had been spotted from the gatehouse in Wenden's perimeter wall and Master Berthold had been notified. He and Rudolf had been entertaining Rameke in the master's hall and were about to retire when they were informed that the Liv settlement appeared to be burning. The alarm was sounded and Rudolf, Lukas, Henke and a dozen sergeants rode south with Rameke and his men. The five-mile journey took an hour because it was pitch black and the riders had to take care lest their horses were injured on the pot-holed track. In addition, though no one said the words, the possibility that the village had been raided could not been discounted.

That fear became a reality when they reached the village, the paths choked with dead and many of the huts on fire. Terrorised, injured animals raced around, some on fire and others driven mad by the inferno. They left the horses outside the gates in the care of two sergeants and ventured inside with drawn swords but they saw no one alive. Reaching what remained of Thalibald's hall, Rameke held his head in his hands and wept when he saw the bodies of his father, mother and brother, surrounded by their faithful warriors. He did not see the corpses of his sister and nephew but Rudolf did, and he also recognised the figure lying beside them with a fine sword still in his hands. He and Henke examined the bodies and found that Conrad was still alive, though the ground around him was stained with his blood from his wounds. As Rameke railed, wept and vowed vengeance they bound the wounds and sent a sergeant back to Wenden to inform Berthold of what had happened and to fetch a cart to carry Conrad back to the castle.

The fires burned themselves out and after the dawn Master Berthold himself rode to the village to survey the damage, bringing with him half a dozen brother knights and ten sergeants. The area around the settlement was scoured for any signs of the raiders but nothing was found; indeed, inside the village itself there were no clues as to who had raided the village: no broken shields, dead bodies or discarded helmets to identify the attackers. Whoever they were they had carried out their mission with deadly efficiency. No one was left alive in the village, at least almost no one.

'Only he can provide an answer to this mystery,' remarked Berthold as he watched Anton, Hans and Johann place Conrad's body in the back of the cart.

He was taken to Ilona's hut where Rudolf assisted her in washing the body and cleaning the wounds with a lotion made from marigold, after which rosemary was placed in the cuts and dressings soaked in honey to prevent infection were wrapped around them. Ilona was most concerned about the gash on the right side of Conrad's head so she packed yarrow into the wound to staunch the flow of blood.

'Do you know who attacked the village?' she asked, washing Conrad's hands. Rudolf stood next to the door. 'Not yet.'

580

'It can only have been the Estonians,' she said.

'Daina and her child died in the village. We found Conrad next to them.'

He saw her head drop and momentarily stop what she was doing.

'They should be buried in the cemetery here, at Wenden,' she said. 'Conrad would want that.'

'If he lives.'

She finished cleaning his hands and stood up, holding the bowl of dirty water. 'If he dies then he can be buried alongside his wife and child.'

She passed him to go outside and empty the bowl. He followed her. She was crying.

'I hope the Sword Brothers will exact vengeance for this crime.'

'We cannot launch reprisals without the authority of the bishop,' replied Rudolf. 'To do so would spark a war.'

'You already have a war, Rudolf, whether you know it or not.'

They both saw Hans approach, his face etched with concern. In his arms he held a sword in a scabbard, a dagger in a sheath and an axe.

'These are his weapons,' he said. 'They should be with him when he wakes up.'

Ilona saw the dejection in his eyes and embraced him. Rudolf took the weapons.

'They will be the first things he sees when his eyes open. Thank you, Brother Hans.'

*****

Olaf nursed his injured arm as his men pulled on their oars to power the longship through the choppy waters of the Baltic. Long and slim, it cut through the grey sea with ease despite carrying nearly two hundred warriors. Fifty more had made the journey to Riga in this dragon ship, the greatest vessel in the Oeselian fleet, but they had fallen vainly trying to storm the high stone walls of the bishop's town. The crews of the ten longships that trailed his own boat had suffered similar losses in the abortive assault. The pain in his arm was nothing compared to the realisation that gnawed at him like a toothache, that Riga was now too strong a fortress to be taken. Gradually the crusaders were tightening their control over the eastern Baltic, once his and his predecessors' domain.

'We should be back on Oesel before nightfall, father,' said Sigurd.

Olaf growled a reply that his son did not hear. They stood near the stern of the vessel in silence for several minutes, sea spray brushing their faces as the ship with its great carved dragon at the prow cut through the water. On the port side was the coast of northern Kurland, the kingdom of the Lithuanian Duke Arturus, a man who had also tried and failed to seize Riga. Olaf glanced at the shoreline and looked for any signs of Lithuanian vessels. He would welcome an opportunity to slaughter some of Arturus' men and sink their vessels. At least that would be something to talk about in his longhouse that evening. But Arturus kept his men safely on dry land.

'You were right, Sigurd,' said Olaf at last.

'Father?'

'You among all of us saw the future accurately. That the strength of the crusaders would grow just as ours and that of the Estonians would decline.'

On his return to Saccalia Lembit had sent a missive to Sigurd alerting him to the fact that he would be renewing hostilities against the bishop, the sons of his chiefs having been sent back to their fathers as a sign of goodwill by Albert a few weeks before his own release. Burning with hatred against the Christians, Lembit's usual calm, calculating nature had abandoned him as he sought vengeance for the humiliation of having his head dunked under the waters of the Dvina by Bishop Albert when he was baptised into the foul Christian faith. Lembit promised endless war against the crusaders and pledged eternal friendship between the Estonian people and the Oeselians.

*****

Henke yawned. 'So what is to be done about Conrad Wolff?'

It was a legitimate question but no one was prepared to grasp the nettle. Everyone knew that Conrad had suffered grievous wounds that would have killed a lesser man and had been nursed back from the brink of death by Ilona's healing arts. He had been confined to his sickbed for six weeks. He had been in a state of delirium for two of those weeks, eventually waking and speaking his first words: 'wolf shields'. Everyone also knew that he was the only one who had survived the Estonian attack on the village and they thus regarded him as special, someone whom God had chosen for a specific purpose.

'And that is my point,' stressed Henke. 'If God spared him then he should be about his business, not moping about Wenden feeling sorry for himself.'

'Blasphemy!' snapped Otto. 'No mortal can know what the Lord is thinking.'

Henke waved a hand at him. 'Spare me the sermon.'

582

Otto's cheeks coloured with anger but Berthold prevented another outburst.

'Your words are intemperate, Brother Henke. Father Otto is correct, we must not question the Lord's plans.'

'Conrad attends to his duties diligently,' said Rudolf. He looked at Lukas. 'Including his practise at arms.'

Lukas scratched his beard. 'He trains well enough and the novices respond well to his presence. He has become something of an inspiration to them, though he never talks to them and they never exchange words with him.'

'You teach him what he already knows well enough,' said Henke. 'He has fully recovered from his wounds?'

'Ilona says so,' answered Rudolf.

Henke looked in turn at Hans, Anton and Johann. 'What about you three? You are his friends. What does he say to you?'

'Very little,' said Hans.

'He still feels the loss of his wife and child deeply,' added Johann.

'He believes that he should have died in Thalibald's village alongside them,' said Anton.

Henke looked up at the ceiling. 'Well, he didn't.' He pointed at Hans. 'You should tell him to get off his arse and either become a brother knight or join a monastery.'

Thus far Walter had kept his counsel but now his face wore a deep frown. 'You exceed your authority, brother. A man must come to the order voluntarily or not at all, else he cannot be a true warrior of Christ.'

Berthold could see that the exchange was going nowhere and so called a halt to proceedings.

'We will not be marching until the spring when the bishop returns so I see no need to make a decision now. The matter of novice Conrad is closed until I raise it again.'

But after the meeting Henke sidled up to Rudolf as they left the master's hall.

'You and I both know that Conrad's place is among us, as a brother knight. He saved the bishop's life, wounded Lembit and was the only survivor of a massacre. It would also be good for morale if he marched with us in the spring. Soldiers are superstitious, you know that. If he marches beside them they will fight twice as hard.'

'A fair point,' said Rudolf, 'and we will certainly need all the fighting men we can muster if we are to subdue Lembit. But you heard what the master said and we must respect his wishes. We must let Conrad find his own path.'

The winter passed slowly. The new settlers found life hard in the iron grip of the snow and ice and several of their children died of exposure despite Ilona's efforts. The temperature was so cold that the sea froze and Caupo led an audacious raid against the island of Oesel, but Olaf and his warriors were more than a match for the Livs and beat them off with ease. Life carried on at Wenden as usual: brother knights and sergeants trained, prayed, went on patrol and hunted in the woods. And every morning Conrad accompanied the novices onto the training field where Lukas gave them instruction in the martial arts. This day was no different, everyone's breath misting in the bitter cold, made worse by a biting wind that came from the east and not alleviated by the sun that shone from a cloudless sky. It was so cold that the boys had been issued with felt boots, woollen leg wraps under their leggings and fur-lined caps to keep their ears from freezing. They stood in a line before Lukas, Conrad on the end, each one armed with a waster and shield.

'Now remember,' Lukas told them, holding up his shield, 'a fighter carries a shield to protect himself from an attack but a shield should also be used as a weapon. It's the same with armour. A fighter wears armour in case he is hit, not so that he can be hit. Do you understand?'

He saw a row of blank faces. Conrad, not listening, was staring at crows circling in the sky, no doubt having spotted a dead or dying animal below and waiting patiently to satisfy their hunger.

Lukas carried on. 'No fighter purposely receives a blow on his armour. Rely on your wits, not your shield or armour.'

'What if a fighter's wits have deserted him?'

The boys turned to see Henke behind them, dressed in mail armour, felt boots and carrying a sword in a scabbard in his hand.

'What then, Brother Lukas?'

Lukas twisted up his mouth. 'Is there something I can do for you, brother?'

Henke walked on the freshly fallen snow to stand beside Lukas. Conrad saw him and gave him a disinterested stare, until he saw his sword in Henke's hand.

'That is my sword,' he spat, 'what are you doing with it?'

Henke feigned hurt. 'Your sword, are you accusing me of stealing it?'

Conrad marched over to him. 'Well if it is mine and you have taken it then draw your own conclusions.'

'Henke,' protested Lukas, 'this is not the time...'

'No, brother,' interrupted Henke, 'this is precisely the time.'

Conrad was now inches from Henke's face. 'Give me my sword.'

Henke stepped back and held out his hands in innocence. 'You know very well that personal property is not allowed in the Sword Brothers, poverty being one of our vows. So how can it be yours? In any case, don't you prefer to play with a wooden sword in the company of boys? The latter carries a severe penalty in the order, by the way.'

'Give me my sword, Henke,' hissed Conrad, 'and I will show you how it should be wielded.'

'No!' shouted Lukas as the novices glanced at each other nervously and backed away as Henke smiled and threw Conrad the scabbard holding his sword.

'This is between me and him,' Henke said to Lukas.

'If the master finds out you will be flogged,' Lukas warned him.

Conrad caught the scabbard, placed his waster on the ground and drew his sword.

Henke drew his own sword and slashed the icy air with it. 'A chance I'm prepared to take, my friend. This has been a long time coming.'

Conrad clenched the black leather of his sword's grip. It felt good to hold it again, the first time he had done so since that dreadful night that he had tried to block out of his mind. He had tried to block everything out of his mind in an attempt to keep the feelings of loss and pain from him. But now he was forced to recall everything he had learned over the past five years as Henke came at him. The brother knight was big and strong but exceedingly light on his feet, wielding his sword as though it was a feather-light stick.

He smiled triumphantly as Conrad jumped to one side but not before Henke's sword had ripped the right arm of his gambeson.

'This won't take long,' he announced loudly.

A side stroke, a lunge, an attack with his shield and Henke once more tore Conrad's clothing, this time on his left thigh. Henke flicked his wrist and whipped his sword point towards Conrad's exposed neck, missing his windpipe by inches. Henke jeered at him.

'Is this all you've got? No wonder your wife and child died.'

The words hit Conrad like crossbow bolts piercing his flesh and a steely determination rose within him. It was not anger but a cool conviction to avenge his loved ones. It infused every fibre of his soul and for the first time in weeks he felt alive, suddenly aware of every little thing that was going on around him. Phlegm dripped from one of Henke's nostrils; a look of fear was on the face of one of the young novices and Lukas' eyes watched the duel with a piercing gaze.

'You should be in a nunnery you…'

Henke did not have time to finish his sentence as Conrad set about him with a plethora of attacks, his sword moving with such speed that the brother knight had difficulty in blocking them let alone avoiding them. Conrad cut off a corner of his shield, severed the chainmail links on his shoulder and ripped open his surccat. Henke smashed his shield into Conrad's chest, knocking him to the ground. But before he had chance to drive his sword through Conrad, the latter swept back with his right leg to catch the back of Henke's right ankle, causing him to topple backwards. Conrad sprang to his feet as Henke rolled but recovered his balance quickly. And so it went on, each fighter delivering a dazzling variety of sword strokes that the other either parried or avoided.

Conrad, now utterly calm and in control, kept hearing Lukas' sage words in his mind: better to avoid a blow entirely that to block it with your sword. Henke was a big man and a fearsome fighter but he knew he had the measure of him. The brother knight was no longer smirking as he tried to finish the fight. But Conrad ducked, dodged and stepped aside to avoid his blade and shield, in turn delivering a blow on the latter that split it in two. He then launched a series of counter-strikes that forced Henke back. Had he been looking he would have seen Lukas smiling approvingly – his pupil was putting into practice what he had taught him. The novices stood, transfixed, as a master class in swordplay was enacted in front of them.

The fight continued, Henke brushing away Conrad's attacks with downward cuts and horizontal sideways blows. And all the time they moved around each other like wary wolves. Then they would close in to suppress each other's strikes. Henke was all strength allied with lightning-fast reflexes; Conrad's ultimate skill matched with supreme calm, and it would have been interesting to learn which combination was the superior. But it was not to be.

The bout had not only been seen by Lukas and his novices but also by nearby spearmen, crossbowmen and Brother Walter practising with his lance on the quintain. When he saw what was happening he immediately rode to the castle to raise the alarm, and returned accompanied by Rudolf and half a dozen mounted sergeants.

Rudolf placed his horse between the two fighters and levelled his lance at Henke's chest, Walter doing likewise with Conrad.

'Desist or die,' Rudolf ordered, the sergeants surrounding Conrad and Henke also pointing their lances at them. 'Surrender your swords.'

Henke, totally unconcerned, shrugged and handed his weapon to Rudolf, who swung in the saddle and fixed Conrad with an angry stare. Conrad also gave up his sword.

'Report to the master's hall immediately,' he commanded before wheeling away.

Henke said nothing as he followed the horsemen, Conrad retrieving his waster and handing it to Lukas before following. As he walked through the snow he heard Lukas's voice behind him.

'If you boys pay attention and practise diligently, one day you might be as good as they are. Now back to training; tournament's over.'

Conrad took in a deep breath. The air was freezing and he felt it seep into his lungs. And although he could have been killed fighting Henke he felt more alive than ever.

He felt less exuberant when he stood beside his nemesis in front of Berthold's table in the master's hall, Rudolf standing behind them with his sword in his hand.

'I think we can dispense with the sword, Brother Rudolf,' said Berthold at last. He looked up at the two miscreants.

'Fighting in public, with swords and in full view of novices and mercenaries. You bring disgrace upon our order.'

'We were not fighting, master,' said Henke calmly.

Berthold looked at him in surprise. 'Oh?'

'We were practising sword strokes, master,' continued Henke, 'so the young novices could copy the moves.'

Rudolf walked slowly from behind them to stand by the master's table. 'You will observe Brother Henke's ripped mail and novice Conrad's torn gambeson, master,' he said. 'Hardly indications of a practice bout.'

'Training should be as realistic as possible, brother,' replied Henke, his face a mask of sincerity.

'What do you say on this matter, novice Conrad?' asked Berthold. 'Is what Brother Henke says correct?'

Conrad felt a great pressure bear down on him. If he told the master that Henke was telling lies then the brother knight could be dismissed from the order. He himself would be flogged, though that was of little consequence. He realised that he held Henke's fate in his hands. Why would he do such a thing? It made no sense. Henke had provoked him and he had gladly risen to the bait, and in doing so had thrown off the cloak of doom that had covered him since the murder of his wife and child. He now realised that he had Henke to thank for that. Surely the brother knight had not purposely instigated the fight to shake him from his lethargy? Did the brutal Henke possess such foresight?

'I am waiting,' said Berthold impatiently.

'It is as Brother Henke says,' answered Conrad.

Rudolf folded his arms and stared at them both, a knowing look on his face. Conrad expected him to declare that they were both liars but he didn't, though his gaze became uncomfortable after a while.

Berthold shook his head. 'I've always known it. Soldiers cooped up in a castle all winter become bored and restless. What we need is a good, long campaign against the pagans to sweep away all our ill humours.'

He clenched a fist. 'To show them some Christian steel.'

'Indeed, master,' said Rudolf. 'But what are we to do with our master practitioners of the sword?'

Berthold snapped out of his vision of a mighty Christian army smiting the unbelievers. 'Mm? Extra guard duties should temper their enthusiasm, I think. See to it, Brother Rudolf.'

'And what of novice Conrad?' queried Rudolf.

Berthold brought his hands together and leaned back in his chair. 'Yes, thank you, Brother Rudolf. You have vexed myself and the brother knights of this garrison, novice Conrad, as to what to do with you. You cannot remain a novice forever so I must ask you what are your intentions.'

That was easy, mused Conrad: kill Lembit. He knew that the Sword Brothers did not approve of the notion of vengeance; they preferred to slaughter their enemies with no malice or impure thoughts in their hearts. And he knew that in the coming year the bishop would be leading them north against Lembit.

'To enter the order as a brother knight, master,' said Conrad, 'if you deem me worthy enough.'

A broad grin crept over Rudolf's face as Henke stared impassively ahead. For his part Berthold looked relieved.

'Most excellent. The ceremony will take place tomorrow morning. See to it, Brother Rudolf.'

'What about their extra guard duties, master?' queried Rudolf.

Berthold waved a hand at him. 'This is much more important. We must not keep God waiting for the creation of one of His holy warriors.'

Rudolf tilted his head towards the door. 'You two get out. I will see you both after prayers.'

Henke gave him an impish smile and Conrad bowed his head solemnly to Rudolf and Berthold.

As they left the master's hall and entered the courtyard Conrad breathed a sigh of relief.

'That was lucky.'

Henke nodded. 'I agree. If Walter and Rudolf had not appeared when they did your guts would have been spread all over the training field. You had a lucky escape.'

Conrad grabbed his arm. 'You don't really think that, do you?'

Henke yanked his arm free and sneered at him. 'You and I aren't finished.'

He marched away towards the armoury. Conrad was mystified. He had thought Henke's actions earlier had been made out of consideration, compassion even. But then he remembered that there was not a kind bone in Henke's body.

That evening, after night prayers had been celebrated, Master Berthold and Brother Rudolf escorted him to the chapel. There he was locked inside the building so he could pray and contemplate his future as a brother knight. At all times two sergeants would stand guard outside the chapel to ensure he did not leave and no one entered. Peace and solitude were essential in preparation for the solemn vows each individual would take.

It was cold in the stone building and Conrad shivered as he knelt before the altar and prayed to God. The walls of the chapel were sumptuously decorated with scenes from the life of the Blessed Virgin Mary, illuminated by the dozens of candles that flickered on their stands. Because it was still winter he was allowed to wear his felt boots, woollen leg wraps beneath his leggings and a woollen shirt under his padded jerkin. It was still bitterly cold, though, and after a while his fingers and toes were frozen. He thought about his life, his youth in Lübeck, and the terrible tragedy that had brought him to Livonia where he had found bliss, only for it to be cruelly snatched away. He subconsciously turned the ring on his finger that Daina had given him. To become a brother knight meant renouncing all worldly property but Rudolf had informed him that, notwithstanding Henke's declaration, he would be allowed to keep the sword bequeathed to him by Sir Frederick and his ring.

He closed his eyes and begged God to forgive him his sins but most of all to take care of the souls of his parents, his wife and his son. He also prayed for the safekeeping of his sister. For she was all alone in the world, like he was again.

'She is not alone, Conrad.'

He opened his eyes and saw a vision before him, a woman surrounded by a celestial light, a woman dressed in a pure white robe that glowed radiantly. Warmth filled the room as he struggled to comprehend what his eyes beheld.

'Are you the Virgin Mary?' he stuttered.

She smiled gently at him, her full lips parting to reveal perfect white teeth.

'Do you not know me, Conrad?'

Her voice was soft and calming, like a light breeze on a summer's day. He looked at her shoulder-length hair and saw bright green eyes.

'Daina?' he said with disbelief.

She smiled once again and grief tore at his stomach.

'I should be with you,' he said, choking back tears.

'You are with me and I am with you,' she replied. 'Just because you cannot see me does not mean I am not there. We are together always.'

'Dietmar.'

'He is safe and in the company of angels,' she replied.

'I should have died with him and you,' he said bitterly.

She looked at him with sympathetic eyes. 'It is not your destiny, my love. You must become what you were born to be.'

'What is that?' he asked.

'You must discover that for yourself. But in the dawn you will take the first steps to that new life.'

'I want to come with you,' he pleaded.

'A day, a year, a life. They are all fleeting, Conrad. You must make the most of what has been given to you. We will be together again, my love, that I swear. And remember, I am with you always.'

He was going to speak more words for he had so much to say but there was a dazzling white light that blinded him and then she was gone. The candles flickered, the air was still and silence returned to the chapel. He heard a key turning in the lock of the chapel door and knew that the dawn had come.

He said nothing to Berthold, Rudolf or Otto of what had happened during the night, nor to the witnesses summoned to the ceremony: Walter, Hans, Anton and Johann. It was personal to him and no one else's business. After Otto commanded everyone to kneel he proceeded to say prayers, calling upon God to bless Conrad and all his future actions. He noticed that Otto's face was very pale and his eyes ringed with red for it was a bitterly cold morning.

Master Berthold stood in front of the altar with Conrad kneeling before him, his four friends standing behind him and Rudolf standing next to the master with a new mantle in his arms. Berthold opened a small, leather-bound book that contained the rules and statutes of the order and read aloud a number of questions that Conrad had to answer.

'Are you married?'

'My wife died, master.'

'Do you owe anyone any money?'

'No, master.'

'Are you anyone's slave?'

'No, master.'

'Do you promise to obey your master, to abstain from sexual activity, to live without personal property, to uphold the traditions and customs of the Order of Sword Brothers, and to help conquer the holy land of Jerusalem?'

Conrad thought the last clause most odd but was happy to obey it anyway. 'Yes, master.'

Berthold smiled, placed his hands on Conrad's shoulders and raised him up. He turned to Rudolf who handed him the new mantle, Berthold placing it around Conrad's shoulders, fastening the laces that held it on. He also handed Conrad a woollen cord that he placed around his waist as a sign of chastity and a soft cap in the style worn by the brother knights of the order. Everyone then bowed their heads while the pallid Otto said another prayer, after which Berthold read out a summary of the customs and rules of the order. Finally, after enquiring whether he had any questions, Master Berthold dismissed him with a blessing.

Everyone shook his hand and embraced him as Conrad Wolff, brother knight of the Order of Livonian Sword Brothers, left the chapel to take the first steps of his new life.

*****

It was spring and the land was alive with a torrent of birdsong and the drumming of woodpeckers. The lush green forests were also filled with great reed warblers, sedge warblers and spotted crakes, the meadows, peat bogs and marshes covered with carpets of flowers providing food for newly emerged butterflies. The column of men on horseback, foot soldiers, wagons and draught ponies stretched for many miles as it threaded its way through the numerous lakes that gave the land its name: Latgale – 'The Land of Blue Lakes' – that lay between the Kingdom of Novgorod to the north and the Principality of Polotsk to the south. A land that bordered the great marshes to the east but which also contained many peat bogs and marsh areas itself, as well as ancient wetland oak forests that seemingly went on forever.

During the winter a message had arrived at Pskov from the new ruler of Polotsk: Prince Boris, son of Vladimir. The latter had been planning a campaign against the Bishop of Riga and his heretical supporters but had collapsed and died on the eve of the war – an ill omen that had stopped the operation in its tracks. Since then Gerzika had fallen to the Catholics and Boris, alarmed by the approach of the apostates, had extended the hand of friendship to Novgorod. Relations between the two kingdoms had traditionally been cool at best but Mstislav, also aware of the crusader threat, had accepted the offer to meet halfway between Pskov and Polotsk, at a spot beside a small river called the Ritupe.

The prince brought Domash, five hundred horsemen and the same number of foot soldiers to the meeting, the banners of Pskov and Novgorod fluttering behind them as they rode south. Also accompanying them was the irksome Gleb whose fame and influence had increased enormously after he had saved Domash outside Pskov. Mstislav thought him amusing, if a little seditious, but he recognised his influence among his common soldiers and citizenry, the majority of which still clung to the old beliefs as they gave lip service to the Orthodox religion.

Now in his sixties, Mstislav had a beard streaked with grey and hair that was almost white. But his wits and curiosity were as sharp as ever and the prospect of gaining at the expense of Polotsk was too good to miss.

'How do you know you will gain from our esteemed allies on the Dvina?' posed Gleb mischievously.

Mstislav did not rise to the bait. 'Because, my diabolical young demon, the Prince of Polotsk normally would not piss on me to put me out if I was on fire. Polotsk esteems itself the religious, learning and trading centre of northern Russia. Why then would it denigrate itself to seek an alliance with the barbarians of the north?'

'To kill you, perhaps?' Gleb shot back.

'And what good would that do them?' replied Mstislav smugly.

592

'Remove you two and the new ruler of Polotsk can march against both Pskov and Novgorod,' replied Gleb.

'It is as well you are a mystic and not a strategist, Gleb,' said Domash. 'If Novgorod is attacked then the Cumans will ride to its aid.'

'My wife, Princess Maria, is the daughter of Khotyan, leader of the Cuman people,' added Mstislav.

The Cumans were the wild nomads who lived to the east of Novgorod. Famed for their insatiable desire for rape and plunder, only a marriage alliance could keep their horseman from a ruler's borders.

'Domash, you should get yourself a wife,' said the prince. 'I'm sure my wife can find you a nice Cuman princess to keep your bed warm.'

'His bed is already warm with a constant supply of Pskov's most expensive whores,' stated Gleb, 'so you had better get him a bigger one to accompany his new bride.'

'One day, Gleb,' said Domash, 'you will convince me that your head would look better on the end of a spear instead of on your shoulders.'

Gleb grinned at Mstislav. 'Then I wouldn't be able to save you when you got yourself surrounded by the enemy. Like at Pskov. I remember it well, a half-dead boyar comes riding into the city blubbing like a small child, shouting "the mayor is dead, the mayor is dead". I was the only one to keep his head and organised a relief force, and then…'

'Shut up!' roared Domash.

Mstislav smiled. He liked Domash and his impish companion, even if his priests said he should be burnt at the stake for being a sorcerer.

'Returning to my original point,' said Mstislav. 'Polotsk is not interested in conquest. Its prince and city merchants desire riches and influence and they know that war can prove ruinous to both. No, they want my help, of that I am certain.'

'Perhaps they want to purchase your kingdom, lord,' offered Gleb.

'Perhaps we should sell them you, Gleb,' suggested Domash, 'though we may have to sell you at a bargain price.'

Gleb was unimpressed. 'Charming.'

But Mstislav was right and when the Novgorodians arrived at the designated spot – a large expanse of grassland by the gently flowing waters of the Ritupe – they found the soldiers of Polotsk already camped there. Brightly coloured tents of varying sizes dotted the grassland and men sat or stood around a countless number of campfires.

'You should have brought more men,' said Gleb as he surveyed the scene.

The prince saw a group of horsemen approach, at which his bodyguard deployed into line each side of him. He ordered them back into column.

'We are here to talk, not to fight.'

The Polotskian horsemen were an impressive sight: at least a hundred soldiers in lamellar armour, aventails, plumed helmets, almond-shaped shields painted red, green tunics and knee-high leather boots. Each rider carried a lance with a red pennant and at their head was a standard bearer carrying the banner of Polotsk: a great ship sailing the waters of the Dvina. The prince's men deployed into battle array behind him, the horsemen on the wings and the foot in the centre as he and Domash watched the brightly coloured horsemen approach. The banner of Novgorod flickered behind Mstislav, the golden snow leopard of Pskov behind Domash.

'Well, Gleb,' said Mstislav, 'we are about to find out if Polotsk desires peace or our heads.'

The column of riders slowed and halted, four men at its head continuing to walk their horses forward until they were around twenty paces from the ruler of Novgorod. One raised his hand and spoke to the prince.

'Greetings, Prince Mstislav, Lord of Novgorod and Pskov and ruler of the northern domains. I am Boris, prince of the city of Polotsk and I welcome you.'

Boris was around half the age of Mstislav and about half his weight, notwithstanding the rich lamellar armour that covered his torso. His open-faced helmet revealed a thoughtful visage with a long nose and pale brown eyes. Despite his warlike uniform and the soldiers at his back Mstislav could tell that the new ruler of Polotsk wanted to treat not threaten or bully.

'Greetings to you, Prince Boris,' replied Mstislav. 'Novgorod grieved when it heard of the premature death of your father and looks forward to amiable relations with Polotsk.'

The formalities over with, Boris invited Mstislav and his chief officers to a banquet in his pavilion once they had set up their camp and refreshed themselves.

The feast was a sumptuous affair, Boris having brought with him his personal cooks as well as his silver cutlery and bowls. Boris' lords and priests were richly attired in purple and white tunics worn beneath embroidered dalmaticas, fine leather belts around their waists. As was the custom no swords were worn in the pavilion, which made Domash feel a trifle nervous. But as the evening wore on and the wine flowed he relaxed and enjoyed the excellent hospitality of his hosts, in addition to the much stronger *stavlenniy myod*. Boris sat with Mstislav and talked about their two kingdoms. The former found, much to his surprise, that Novgorod's ruler was not the unwashed brute that the city council had told him to be wary of, and for his part Mstislav found Boris to be intelligent and interesting.

The omens were therefore propitious when formalities began the next morning, the venue being a large, oblong-shaped tent that had been pitched near the Ritupe on a stretch of lush grass. The weather was pleasant and the flaps at each end of the tent had been tied back to allow air to circulate within the tent, which unfortunately allowed a plague of midges to enter as well. Two parallel trestle tables had been arranged inside the tent to accommodate the rulers of Polotsk and Novgorod. Boris sat at one with two of his commanders and a stern-faced priest of the Orthodox Church. Opposite them were Mstislav, Domash, Gleb and the general of Novgorod's army.

Gleb looked bored as everyone stood and the priest said a prayer, calling upon God to bless the meeting, afterwards the priest giving him a hateful stare as the attendees retook their seats. Boris looked determined as he smiled at Mstislav and began proceedings.

'I asked for this meeting because both our kingdoms face a great peril. Every year the Bishop of Riga brings more crusaders to Livonia and they advance ever further east. Once the principalities of Kokenhusen and Gerzika paid homage to Polotsk but now they are garrisoned by the Sword Brothers. The banners of the church of Rome now fly less than fifty miles from the walls of my city.'

'What has this to do with Novgorod?' said Mstislav.

'A great deal,' replied Boris. 'My spies inform me that Lembit raises the banner of rebellion among the Estonian tribes and hopes to maintain the independence of his people, while the Oeselians also fight the crusaders.'

'You wish to join Lembit and the pirates against the bishop?' asked Mstislav, unsure of where the conversation was going.

Boris shook his head and batted away a group of midges as a servant poured wine into silver cups.

'I propose that Novgorod seizes Ungannia to halt the eastward expansion of the crusaders. You have fought the Ungannians before, I believe.'

'Many times,' said Domash, 'they provide good targets for our spears.'

'Why don't you conquer it?' said Mstislav bluntly.

'For one thing,' said Boris calmly, 'it is over a hundred miles from Polotsk and to conquer and hold it would require a great many soldiers. Soldiers that I will need to face the crusaders when they continue their march along the Dvina. But Ungannia lies next to Novgorod.'

He smiled at Domash. 'Just a short distance from Pskov.'

'I have no interest in Ungannia,' said Mstislav.

Boris swatted away more midges that were entering the tent in greater numbers. 'You will when Lembit is crushed by the bishop and you discover the Sword Brothers building stone castles on your border. Then, my lord, it will be too late.'

'The bishop would not dare attack Novgorod,' declared Domash, crushing a midge on the lip of his cup.

'They would not have to,' answered Boris. 'If they control the Gauja and Dvina then they also control the trade of both our kingdoms. In such circumstances they could stop goods being transported along both rivers or impose such heavy tolls upon them that Livonia would grow rich as we were impoverished.'

Mstislav sat back in his chair and looked at Boris. He may have been half his age and slight of build but he obviously had a brain and had given this matter a great deal of thought.

'What you say is only half true,' said Mstislav at length. 'You are right that if the crusaders control both the Dvina and Gauja then they can impose sanctions upon our goods. But you seem to forget that if they halt trade then they too will suffer. Riga itself will wither and die and in turn Livonia will be harmed.'

'The bishop cares not for riches or great cities,' answered Boris. 'He fights a religious war, lord, against those that his church has deemed pagans and heretics. The Orthodox Church that we love is viewed as heretical by the bishop and the Sword Brothers. They will not rest until it is erased from the earth.'

'It is as my prince states,' said the priest, his brow creased into a frown.

'And you would know about erasing religions,' Gleb shot at him.

'Polotsk did away with the *Skomorokhs* many years ago,' sneered the priest. 'They are the servants of the devil.'

Gleb laughed. 'And when the crusaders do away with you I shall be in Polotsk's city square to see you burn.'

The two officers seated either side of Boris jumped up and swore at Gleb, threatening him with death. Domash also rose and looked at them menacingly.

'Gleb is under my protection and I will have words with any man who threatens his life.'

Boris ordered his two officers to sit down as Mstislav indicated that Domash should do likewise.

'When you did away with my kind did you also get rid of the man who knew where the best place was to pitch tents?' remarked Gleb mischievously. 'I'm being eaten alive by these midges.'

'Silence, Gleb,' barked Mstislav as the priest glared at the imp who toyed with his golden moustache.

'If I was the Bishop of Riga,' said Boris calmly, 'I would be smiling at two of my enemies squabbling like small children.'

'Perhaps Lembit will defeat the crusaders and save us all the trouble,' suggested Mstislav.

'Do you really believe that, lord?' said Boris.

Mstislav did not, and nor did he believe that the crusaders would stop with the conquest of Estonia.

'If Novgorod makes war against Ungannia what will Polotsk do to support it?'

'I will give you two thousand horsemen as a sign of my goodwill, to serve under your command as you see fit,' said Boris.

Mstislav rubbed his beard. 'Five thousand.'

The two officers flanking Boris protested but he waved their remonstrations away.

'Very well, five thousand horsemen. When will you begin your campaign?'

'In two months,' answered Mstislav.

The journey back to Pskov was uneventful, Mstislav and Domash making plans for the forthcoming attack against the Estonians.

'As soon as Boris' horsemen reach Pskov,' Mstislav said to Domash, 'we will march west. This time we go to conquer, not to raid. So no burning villages. We will need the native population. Where is the Ungannian stronghold?'

'Odenpah,' answered Domash. 'Take that and Ungannia will fall into our laps like a ripe apple.'

'He is clever,' remarked Gleb idly.

'Who?' said Domash.

'The ruler of Polotsk. He gets you two to fight his battles for him.'

'I thought that at first,' replied Mstislav, 'but what he said about the crusaders was true. If we do nothing then they will be at Novgorod's borders so we might as well take the opportunity presented to us while the bishop is preoccupied with Lembit.'

'At least we will have an additional five thousand horsemen to assist us,' said Domash.

'You will need them,' remarked Gleb casually. 'The conquest of Ungannia will not be as easy as you think.'

'Did you see that in a vision?' enquired Mstislav.

Gleb cast him a sly look. 'Perhaps, perhaps not.'

*****

That summer war was visited upon the Estonian people. Bishop Albert was delayed in his journey back to Riga, but when he did land at the head of a great flotilla of cogs he was possessed of a great fury when Archdeacon Stefan and Grand Master Volquin informed him that Lembit had treacherously renounced the Christian faith and returned to his pagan ways. In a surprising move he had ejected the priests who had gone into Saccalia to preach the word of God rather than having them executed. Perhaps he thought that by doing so he would win the bishop's forgiveness but in this he was wrong. Lembit gathered his forces at Lehola and called upon the other chiefs to rally to him there. But Grand Master Volquin was above all a strategist and counselled deception against Lembit the deceiver. Troops were sent to Wenden and patrols were despatched from the castle north to give the illusion of a gathering army, but the real army was forming at Treiden. Reinforced by Caupo's warriors, the bishop and grand master marched directly north into western Saccalia, Rotalia and then into Harrien, plundering the countryside of its supplies and livestock. Alva and his warriors, gathered at Lehola, found out too late that their homes were being destroyed and by the time they returned home Harrien had been devastated. Nigul had not even bothered to acknowledge Lembit's summons but had instead mustered his warriors to meet the bishop. It did him little good, he and his men being brushed aside with ease by the men of iron and Nigul and half his men falling in battle. Afterwards Rotalia ceased to exist as an independent kingdom.

To the west Kalju and his people felt the full wrath of the Novgorodians as ten thousand Russians marching from Pskov assaulted Ungannia. They swept through Ungannia like a plague of rats, torching villages and crops in the fields, carrying off women and children and butchering livestock. To Domash it was like his raids of plunder years before when he and his horsemen had ridden through the lands of the Estonians and Livs at will, spreading terror and misery over the land, even crossing the Dvina to butcher Lithuanians. Then he had led but two hundred men at most but this time he commanded ten thousand. He cut a swathe of destruction through Kalju's kingdom but when he finally came before the great timber walls of Odenpah he found its battlements crowded with warriors and the banner of the golden eagle flying from its towers.

He rode up and down in front of the walls as his horsemen surrounded the fort in an impressive display of strength. But he had no siege engines to batter the Ungannians into submission and his men had destroyed all the food supplies and livestock in the area instead of capturing them. After a week of surrounding the fort he was forced to send foraging parties far and wide so he could feed his men. After three weeks his men grew mutinous at having to live off berries and what they could catch in the rivers and lakes or hunt in the woods, and so he gave the order to withdraw back to Pskov. He felt satisfied that he had cowered the Ungannians but Mstislav was furious at his mishandling of the campaign.

The Prince of Novgorod had achieved far more with but a tenth of the number of men under Domash's command. He had ridden west from the city to raid Wierland, the purpose of his expedition being to distract the Estonians and make Domash's capture of Odenpah easier. In the event Domash failed and Mstislav retreated but his incursion did cause Edvin to abandon Lembit at Lehola and take his warriors back to Wierland. As autumn approached Saccalia was largely undisturbed but at Lehola only Jaak's warriors still remained camped outside its walls, though a few others did appear at the end of September.

The 'rock' was tired and irritable when he slid off his pony in front of Lembit's great hall at Lehola. It had been a long ride and his pony cast its head down as it was led away to the stables, the beasts of his bodyguard similarly being led away.

'Treat them well,' he called after the stable hands, 'they've earned it.'

'Greetings, brother.' He turned to see Lembit, Rusticus and Jaak walk from the hall, their tidy, clean appearance contrasting to the dirt that covered his cloak, smeared his face and caked his boots.

'A hard ride?' asked Jaak.

'Hard enough,' snapped Kalju.

He looked at Lembit. 'I need warriors to ride back with me to Odenpah.'

Lembit smiled and placed an arm around his shoulder. 'Come, take refreshment with me.'

He led Kalju back into the hall, ordering Rusticus to see to the needs of the fifteen Ungannian warriors who had accompanied their leader. But a wash and a hearty meal did nothing to sweeten Kalju's mood as he paced up and down in front of Lembit as the latter sat in his chair listening to his words.

'Ungannia is a wasteland, Lembit, laid low by the Russians while I sat on my arse here waiting for an attack that never came.'

He stopped pacing and faced Lembit. 'They will return, of that I am certain. Therefore I ask you for a thousand men so I can strengthen my border forts to meet the next assault from Pskov.'

'A thousand men?' scoffed Rusticus. 'Do you think that we grow warriors in the fields?'

Kalju looked at Lembit's hefty subordinate. 'I think that the warriors of Saccalia drink and eat well while others battle Estonia's foes.'

Rusticus' nostrils flared at the insult but Lembit waved him away.

'I sympathise with your predicament, Kalju, but you must understand that Saccalia is also in peril. My scouts report a great army mustering at Wenden. I need every warrior here.'

'What of you, Jaak,' said Kalju, 'will you lend me some of your men?'

'Jerwen must stand with Saccalia,' the chief replied, his sly eyes narrowing.

'And who will stand with Ungannia?' said Kalju.

He received no reply to his question. Lembit continued to profess sympathy but reminded Kalju that the Russians had also attacked Wierland and that the Bishop of Riga had killed Nigul, scattered his army and had also ravaged Harrien and Rotalia. Kalju pointed out that not even the bishop could be in two places at once and the fact that he had campaigned in the west indicated that the forces at Wenden would probably not march against him, especially since autumn was here.

At this Lembit let his calm demeanour slip. 'Autumn? My fort at Fellin was assaulted by the crusaders in the depth of winter. And do you not remember that we battled the Russians with snow on our boots? It is a risk I cannot take.'

'And that is your final word on the subject?' fumed Kalju.

'It is.'

'Then there is nothing left to say.'

The Ungannian chief left the next morning, a keen easterly wind ruffling his cloak as he mounted his pony and trotted from the compound, his men following. He did not bother looking back to acknowledge Lembit and Jaak standing in the doors of the great hall.

'What will he do now?' asked a concerned Jaak.

'What can he do?' replied Lembit. 'He will sit and sulk in his hall and in the spring will bring his warriors to fight by our side, as will the other chiefs.'

Chapter 22

The days were getting cooler and the sky was filled with migratory birds flocking together as they embarked on their quest for warmer places to see out the winter. The leaves were turning pink and yellow and falling from the trees, the forests resounding to the mating calls of elk and red deer. Conrad pulled up his horse and surveyed the scene. It was quiet and peaceful – not the ideal conditions for a knight of the Sword Brothers who thirsted for Estonian blood.

'What is the matter?' asked Hans beside him who also halted his horse, the four sergeants behind doing likewise.

'Nothing,' said Conrad.

'Then why have you stopped, we still have two more miles to go before we head back?'

'Every day we go out on patrol and every day we see nothing except trees and lakes. Autumn is here and all we have done this year is wear out horse shoes.'

Hans shrugged. 'We obey orders, my friend.'

'And Lembit still lives,' hissed Conrad.

Hans said nothing. He and the others had been delighted when Conrad had decided to become a brother knight, but he never spoke of Daina or Dietmar and they never raised the subject. They knew he tended to their grave and laid fresh flowers upon it but he never mentioned it to anyone and his friends respected his privacy. They also knew that he longed to exact revenge on Lembit, even though Master Berthold and Walter told him that only God could decide who was worthy of life and death.

Because they were on patrol their horses were not wearing caparisons and Conrad and Hans were wearing kettle helmets instead of the fully enclosed helms traditionally worn by brother knights. Vital in battle, both found them restrictive and uncomfortable for patrolling. They did, however, wear full mail armour and white surcoats and cloaks bearing the insignia of the Sword Brothers, the pennants on their lances and those of the sergeants also sporting the symbol of the order.

'The sooner we finish our patrol the sooner I can get some food inside me,' said Hans. 'I feel hungry.'

Conrad smiled and shook his head. 'You're always hungry.' He nudged his horse forward and signalled to the sergeants behind to follow.

'So would you be if you had spent your childhood starving.'

'You were not a very good thief, then?'

'I only stole to stay alive,' said Hans, 'bread, mostly. They were going to hang me for a loaf of bread.'

'I know.'

'They hanged some of my beggar friends. I watched them standing around, the fine people of Lübeck, stuffing their fat faces with food and expensive wine as my friend was hoisted up and dangled in front of them.'

He turned to look at Conrad, his eyes moist. 'He was eight years old, Conrad.'

'There are many wrongs committed in this world, my friend. But it is my belief that the Sword Brothers exist to create justice and peace in Livonia. There are still many good men in the world, Hans.'

'I never want to go back,' said Hans.

'Where?'

He spat to the side. 'Lübeck.'

'Brothers!'

Conrad heard the call of the commanding sergeant and then saw them: a group of riders approaching, around four hundred paces away. Their round shields, green cloaks, brown leggings, helmets and spears told him they were not crusaders. They were now around seven miles east of Wenden and there were no Liv settlements nearby, certainly not one large enough to support a dozen or more heavily armed warriors.

'Ready,' ordered Conrad, lowering his lance and halting his horse. They had been riding through a long, thin strip of land between two great forests that was around fifty paces wide. The sergeants moved right and left to form line either side of Conrad and Hans. The warriors in front of them slowed but remained in their column formation as the sergeants closed in so as to present a solid wall of horseflesh when they charged. Conrad gripped the strap on the inside of his shield as one of the warriors broke ranks and began riding towards them.

'He must be tired of living,' opined Hans.

Conrad was about to signal the charge when he noticed that the warrior riding towards them was not holding a spear but a piece of evergreen. He was also shouting. Conrad heard the words; they were Estonian.

'We come in peace,' the man was shouting.

He was now two hundred paces away.

'That is far enough,' shouted Conrad in the warrior's native tongue.

He turned to Hans. 'Stay here. If he tries to kill me charge them.'

Conrad spurred his horse forward.

'Make sure you kill him first,' Hans called after him.

The warrior waited as Conrad approached, the sprig of evergreen still in his right hand. Conrad brought his horse to a halt ten paces in front of the warrior, who threw the sprig away and removed his helmet to reveal a middle-aged man with a hard expression, brown beard and long, thick hair. He wore a mail shirt, sword at his hip with a shield hanging from his saddle, upon which was painted an eagle insignia.

'You speak our language, crusader,' said the warrior.

'State your business,' snapped Conrad, looking behind the warrior to see if he and his men were but the vanguard of an army.

'I wish to see Master Berthold, commander at Wenden.'

'Why?'

'Among my people,' said the warrior, 'it is polite for each party to introduce themselves when they have a conversation.'

This took Conrad aback. Until now he was used to killing Estonians rather than engaging them in discourse. For a moment he was lost for words. He cleared his throat.

'My name is Conrad Wolff, knight of the Order of Sword Brothers.'

The warrior tilted his head. 'I am Kalju, chief of the Ungannian people and I have an offer for your master, so I would be grateful if you would escort me to him.'

During the ride back to Wenden Kalju did not reveal the nature of his mission nor why he was riding in enemy territory with so few warriors. But Conrad did probe him about Lembit.

'Have you seen him lately, lord?' said Conrad casually.

'Only a few days ago,' replied Kalju.

'At Lehola?'

'At Lehola, yes. You have been there?'

'Two years ago, when Lembit submitted to the bishop, accepted baptism and professed friendship to the Holy Church.'

Kalju chuckled. 'Warlords have no friends, boy.'

'My name is Brother Conrad,' said Conrad sternly.

'I meant no insult.'

When they arrived at Wenden Kalju and his men saw the great number of tents pitched to the south of the castle's outer perimeter, together with stacks of lances, racks of spears and wagons corralled in fenced-off parks. Flags flew from the tops of the largest tents and soldiers milled around within the campsite. It was an impressive sight but had Kalju tarried and looked more closely he would have discovered that half the tents were empty.

Conrad had sent a sergeant ahead to give Master Berthold prior warning of Wenden's unexpected guest, and the castellan stood in the courtyard in front of his hall when the patrol and the Ungannians trotted onto the cobbles. Rudolf, Henke and Lukas stood behind Berthold fully armed in their mail armour while a party of crossbowmen and spearmen stood to attention either side of the master. The Ungannians looked uneasy and kept glancing back at the half-finished gatehouse, no doubt estimating whether they could get out alive if the crossbowmen began shooting. But Berthold stepped forward and opened his hands to Kalju as the chief dismounted and Conrad escorted him over to the master. The latter did not speak Estonian and so Conrad had to translate.

'This is Kalju, master, lord of the Ungannian people.'

Berthold smiled. 'Welcome Kalju, eagle of the east.'

The chief laughed when Conrad relayed the master's words. Berthold offered Kalju and his men refreshments, suggesting that Lukas and Henke take the chief's escort to the dining hall and feed them while he talked with the Ungannian leader. Berthold began to lead him away but Kalju stopped and turned round to look at Conrad.

'What about you?'

Conrad held out a hand to Rudolf. 'Brother Rudolf speaks your language and will be able to translate.'

'You can speak my words,' said Kalju bluntly.

Conrad informed the master of this and was told that his presence would be welcome in the hall. Kalju ordered his men to follow Henke and Lukas to the dining hall and to keep their swords close in case the Christians tried to kill them. If they succeeded he would meet them all in the afterlife for he too would be dead. Conrad looked at Rudolf who understood the words but merely smiled at Kalju.

'We do not murder our guests, lord.'

Berthold ordered food and drink brought to his hall as he made Kalju welcome in his office just off the main anteroom. The chief took off his helmet and spread himself in the high-backed chair and drank the wine offered him by a novice, Berthold sitting opposite him as more novices brought bread, smoked fish and meats and set them on the desk. Rudolf stood beside the master, Conrad beside Kalju. The latter regarded the master and his deputy with his cold blue eyes. When he had sated his thirst and hunger he spoke to the master, Rudolf translating and Conrad relaying the master's words.

'I come with an offer for the bishop,' said Kalju. 'I will submit to his authority if he sends soldiers to help my people.'

Somewhat startled, Berthold sat and listened as Kalju informed him of the Russian incursion into Ungannia and Lembit's unwillingness to assist him.

'He is no friend of Ungannia and so I am no friend of his,' declared Kalju.

'If you become the bishop's friend,' Berthold warned him, 'you will earn the enmity of Lembit and the other Estonian chiefs.'

Kalju laughed. 'Nigul is dead, Alva wails like an old woman after the bishop raided his lands and Edvin is busy fighting the Russians.'

Berthold raised an eyebrow at this. 'The Russians?'

'Novgorod sent raiders into Wierland as well as Ungannia. The bear stirs and covets lands in the west just as your bishop desires his own conquests.'

'And what price does Ungannia place upon the bishop's friendship?' said Berthold.

'That my people remain free and Ungannia becomes an ally of Livonia, not a slave.'

'I cannot speak for the bishop,' said Berthold, 'but I am certain that he will welcome the hand of friendship that you have extended to him.'

'But will he send soldiers to aid me?' queried Kalju.

'I am sure he will,' said Berthold in a non-committal way.

Kalju looked around at the austere room. 'Lembit believes that Wenden will march against Lehola.'

Berthold nodded. 'The bishop will finish affairs with him, of that you can be certain. In his impudence he tried to assault this castle.' He pointed at Conrad. 'He failed and Brother Conrad scarred his face as a permanent reminder of his folly.'

Kalju looked up at Conrad. 'You did that?'

'Yes, lord.'

'Can I take him back with me to Odenpah?' he said to Berthold.

A courier pigeon was sent to Riga and a message came back with a another bird the next morning stating that the bishop was indeed interested in Ungannia's friendship but that Kalju would have to submit hostages as surety against treachery. These hostages were to be Kalju's sons and the sons of his chief elders. In exchange, the bishop promised to send soldiers to Ungannia to reinforce the chief's own warriors.

Kalju spent four days at Wenden, during which Conrad accompanied him at all times as his interpreter. He found the chief amiable, intelligent and concerned about the fate of his people. It was the latter consideration that was uppermost in his mind when he talked again with Berthold and Rudolf before he and his men departed the castle.

'Odenpah must be held at all costs,' he said. 'For five hundred years it has been the physical and spiritual home of my people. The Russians have tried to take it once; they will do so again.'

*****

The bishop sat with Stefan in the withdrawing chamber of his palace, tapping his fingers on the arm of his chair while he waited for the grand master to appear. He had always been a serious man but Lembit's betrayal had seemingly banished any light heartedness that may have resided within him. His chiselled features had become darker, more severe and he had become more determined than ever to subdue Estonia and rid the world of Lembit.

Volquin arrived at last to allow the meeting to start.

'What do you make of this Kalju?' said the bishop. 'Are we to accept his offer, to put our faith in the word of an Estonian after another of their race betrayed me so basely?'

'I would say no, lord bishop,' said Stefan. 'The Estonians, like all pagans, are untrustworthy.'

'I would not dismiss Kalju's offer,' said Volquin. 'He rode to Wenden of his own volition whereas Lembit was facing certain defeat when he submitted to Bishop Albert.'

'What is the difference?' asked Stefan.

'Lembit did what he did to save his own skin,' answered Volquin. 'Kalju is trying to preserve his people.'

'If we send soldiers to this fort what is to stop the pagans slaughtering them?' said Stefan.

'Nothing,' admitted Volquin, 'though what would that avail him? By doing so he would create enemies of the lord bishop as well as Lembit and the Russians.'

The bishop looked at Volquin. 'Your advice would be to send soldiers to this fort?'

Volquin nodded. 'To Odenpah? Yes, lord bishop.'

'Why?'

607

'We know that forces from Pskov have raided Ungannia. Indeed, years ago they raided Livonia before it became strong. If they conquer Kalju's kingdom then their soldiers will be on our border and I would rather have Ungannia as an ally than a hostile Novgorod bearing down on us.'

'If we did decide to aid the Ungannians,' said the bishop, 'what resources are available to us?'

Volquin frowned. 'In truth very few, lord bishop. The garrisons along the Dvina must be reinforced to prevent any more Lithuanian incursions.' He looked at Stefan. 'I don't suppose the garrison of Riga would be able to spare any soldiers?'

Stefan shook his head vigorously. 'Out of the question, grand master. We barely escaped with our lives when the Oeselian pirates attacked the city.'

Volquin remembered it differently and recollected the garrison and its engines seeing off the enemy raiders relatively easily. But he said nothing.

'Riga needs all the soldiers it can lay its hands on.'

'That just leaves the garrisons along the Gauja and the additional troops at Wenden, then,' said Volquin.

'The crusaders that came with me from Germany can reinforce those castles in the absence of their garrisons,' said Bishop Albert.

'Then I take it you are accepting Kalju's offer, lord bishop?' said Volquin. The bishop nodded.

Volquin smiled triumphantly at Stefan. 'Excellent, lord bishop. You will not regret it. With your permission I will make the arrangements immediately.'

He went to rise from his chair but the bishop stopped him.

'There is another matter I wish to speak to you about, grand master.'

Volquin sat back down.

'It has been brought to my attention that the garrisons of the Sword Brothers along the Dvina have been intercepting merchant vessels and imposing dues upon them before they reach Riga.'

Volquin looked at Stefan who had a smug expression on his face.

'This activity must cease,' ordered the bishop.

'With respect, lord bishop,' said Volquin, 'the Sword Brothers were forced into such drastic action by the reluctance of the treasury in Riga to furnish them with weapons and equipment with which to carry out your orders.'

Stefan raised an eyebrow at this but remained silent.

'The Sword Brothers will have whatever they need,' said the bishop, 'but the merchants must have confidence that their vessels can sail the Dvina unmolested.'

'Then can I take it that the ship that docked at Riga yesterday filled with weapons and armour will be made available to the Sword Brothers?' enquired Volquin.

'Those supplies have been purchased for the needs of the garrison of Riga,' said Stefan.

Volquin tried hard to maintain his composure. 'Why does the garrison need two hundred new crossbows, archdeacon, seeing as its armouries in the castle and city are already full?'

'The office of the grand master seems to know a great deal about the personal business of the Governor of Riga,' remarked Stefan.

'Would that the Governor of Riga knew a great deal about the needs of the Sword Brothers,' Volquin shot back.

'How dare you,' said Stefan.

The bishop, tired and irritable, had no time for such bickering. 'Enough! Grand master, you will order your masters to desist interrupting trade along the Dvina and in return you will draw up an inventory of your order's needs and I will sign it. Archdeacon Stefan, when I have authorised the grand master's requirements you will ensure that the armouries in Riga furnish him with everything that is on the list.'

Volquin smiled smugly at Stefan who glared at the grand master. The bishop saw the expressions.

'We are all here to undertake God's holy work. I find this constant bickering and political intrigue tiresome and unworthy of the Order of Sword Brothers and the office of Governor of Riga. Every year I see such boorish behaviour in the courts and castles of northern Germany and have no wish to see Livonia become infected with it.'

Volquin and Stefan mumbled their apologies and were dismissed by the bishop, who the grand master thought looked pale and drawn and not at all well. Albert had almost single-handedly created Livonia by his determination and religious fervour, and had for years travelled to Germany and back to enlist men to his cause. Everyone hoped that he would live to see the completion of the cathedral that was being constructed in his honour, the foundation stones of which had been laid the previous year, but Volquin feared that the burden of being the man who carried the weight of Livonia upon his shoulders would prove too great He would make an effort to reduce that burden, even if it meant trying to be more friendly to the toadlike governor of the city. But first he had much work to do assembling a force to be sent to Odenpah.

*****

It took two months to organise the expedition to Odenpah, during which time the weather got cooler and wetter as autumn set in. Wenden was the mustering point for the force that Grand Master Volquin gathered to aid Kalju. The latter, expecting an assault from Pskov at any time, sent riders to Wenden requesting clarification concerning the apparent delay in the arrival of the Sword Brothers at his stronghold. Master Berthold sent them back after explaining that it took time to organise an expedition but that it would be at Odenpah before the end of the year. To guard against an attack by Lembit at Lehola, Berthold decided to retain a significant garrison at Wenden. He was in the happy circumstances of having a full garrison and a superfluous number of brother knights. Since the acceptance into the order of Conrad, Hans, Anton and Johann he had four additional brother knights who ordinarily would be sent to other garrisons. However, the expedition to Odenpah put paid to that, at least for the present. He decided to send eight of his brother knights to Kalju – Rudolf, Henke, Lukas, Walter, Conrad, Hans, Anton and Johann – leaving seven others and himself to man Wenden. Accompanying them would be thirty sergeants, a score of crossbowmen and the same number of spearmen. Volquin sent Master Bertram from Segewold to join Berthold, who brought with him eleven brother knights, a score of sergeants, a score of crossbowmen and an equal number of spearmen. From Kremon came Master Mathias with eleven brother knights, twenty sergeants, thirty crossbowmen and the same number of spearmen.

When they heard of the march to Odenpah, even they had no idea where it was, all the crusaders who had spent the summer at Wenden in idle activity begged Berthold to be allowed to join it. The master tactfully informed them that Wenden was still in danger and only a percentage of their number would be able to join the Sword Brother expedition, otherwise Lembit might assault and overrun the castle. The crusaders were most unhappy but reluctantly acquiesced in the master's decision. Berthold told them they were going to defend a stronghold and so it would be better to leave their warhorses behind, though they did use them in a jousting competition that was held to decide which among them would go to Odenpah. In the end fifty knights were selected, plus their squires, and fifty crossbowmen that the lords had brought with them from Germany.

Curiously, their elected leader was a non-German, an Englishman by the name of Sir Richard Bruffingham. Taller than most, he had shaved his head and beard in an act of penitence before he had left England to crusade in Livonia. The eldest son of a powerful northern lord, Bruffingham had had the misfortune to fall in love with the woman who was to wed his best friend. His affections had turned into infatuation and he had pursued the poor woman until, beside herself with worry, she had taken her own life. This had cast Sir Richard into the pit of despair, his misery and guilt made worse when his best friend also killed himself rather than face a lifetime without his true love. Overcome with remorse, he had decided to go on crusade in an effort to seek God's forgiveness for his sins. He brought with him his squire, a man not much younger than himself whose vocation had been executioner before Sir Richard persuaded him that serving as his squire was more noble than stretching necks, torturing people and cutting off their heads. Tough, able to use a sword and ride a horse, squire Paul was a useful man to have in a tight spot.

The final component of the army that numbered just under four hundred men was Master Thaddeus, his engineers and the six mangonels that had been dismantled and packed onto wagons for the journey north. More wagons carried their ammunition and yet more spare weapons, armour, clothes, food, fodder and thousands of crossbow bolts. Each wagon had waterproof covers for autumn in Livonia was above all wet. There were actually more horses and draught animals than men when the army finally left Wenden on a wet, windy morning; the track north soon turning to mud as dozens of heavy wheels churned up the ground. The spearmen and crossbowmen marched beside the wagons, after a few hours piling their shields and weapons on them as the rain got heavier, the ground wetter and men had to haul the wagons out of the mud. The army covered a grand total of five miles that first day.

Joint command had been awarded to Sir Richard and masters Bertram and Mathias, though during the twenty days that it took the army to crawl through the rolling hills and forests of southern Estonia they followed the directions of the Ungannian guides sent to them by Kalju. Conrad often rode with the three leaders on account of his knowledge of the Estonian tongue, allowing them to liaise with the guides.

'You are a friend of this pagan chief?' Sir Richard asked him in flawless German.

'No, lord,' said Conrad. 'I was on patrol when he came to Wenden and was the first person he came across.'

'Is it true that they sacrifice babies?'

Conrad tried hard not to laugh. 'I have not heard so, lord.'

Sir Richard looked around at the trees that stretched for miles either side of the column of men and wagons behind them.

'It seems strange that we march to assist a pagan.'

'Better that he fights by our side, lord, than with Lembit against us.'

'Brother Conrad wounded Lembit a few years back, scarred his face,' said Master Mathias, 'when his warriors tried to take Wenden.'

Sir Richard looked at Conrad who was at least ten years younger than him. 'Perhaps you will get a chance to give him another scar soon.'

Conrad thought of his wife and child and the wolf shields who had killed them. 'If God wills it, lord.'

But he prayed that he would be given a chance to face Lembit on the battlefield.

After a thoroughly miserable and lengthy march, during which forty beasts had died of heart attacks due to excessive exertions pulling wagons through mud, peat bogs and marsh when the rear of the column inadvertently strayed off course, the crusaders finally reached Odenpah. The name meant 'bear's head' on account that the fort looked like the head of said animal when viewed from the side. It was sited upon a huge hill positioned in the middle of a large expanse of grassland surrounded by thick woods. The stronghold had two levels, an exterior timber wall extending all the way round the lower level and an inner wall encompassing a great hall on the higher, upper level. It was certainly an impressive stronghold.

Kalju himself rode out to greet the army as it made its way towards the twin gates that gave access to the fort's lower level. The chief galloped to where the two masters and Sir Richard sat on their horses, a great banner bearing a golden eagle carried by his bodyguard behind him. Both Rudolf and Conrad were in attendance when the chief halted before the Christian leaders as he had never before met Sir Richard, Bertram or Mathias.

He raised his hand to the knights wearing white surcoats, the masters sporting the insignia of the Sword Brothers. But Sir Richard wore no coat of arms because he thought his actions had disgraced his family's honour and he was therefore not fit to bear its heraldry.

'Welcome to Odenpah,' beamed Kalju, who spotted Conrad. 'And greetings to you, Conrad Wolff.'

Conrad bowed his head as Kalju invited the lords to a feast he would give in his hall in celebration of their arrival. All his soldiers were invited to attend but the lords were horrified at the idea and told him that the army would pitch its tents in front of the fort where it would remain until such time as the enemy appeared.

That night the first snow fell to herald winter in Estonia.

The next day, as the sky in front of the fort filled with the smoke of dozens of campfires, Kalju escorted the Sword Brother masters and Sir Richard on a tour of his stronghold. Also in attendance were Rudolf and Conrad to act as interpreters, and Master Thaddeus. Odenpah had been constructed in traditional style, with high timber walls and towers at regular intervals. The towers were roofed over with shingles and there was a walkway along the whole extent of the wall that connected all the towers, though it was not covered. Warriors in leather and mail armour and helmets manned the towers but the walkway was clear.

The higher, inner timber wall was shorter in extent but also contained towers. Between the two walls were huts, stabling areas and animal pens. As they walked along the wall Kalju noticed that Master Thaddeus kept looking at the area between the walls, the upper level of the fort and then beyond the outer perimeter to the grassland that surrounded three sides of Odenpah. On the northern side of the fort was a small lake that came right up to the slope of the hill on which Odenpah was built. There was a small gate in the northern wall that allowed the garrison to fetch water from the lake.

Kalju nodded towards Thaddeus who was mumbling to himself.

'Who is that old man?'

'Master Thaddeus,' replied Rudolf.

'One of our most important men,' added Conrad.

Kalju pointed at the doddering figure wrapped in felt boots, a padded jacket and fur-lined cloak who carried no weapons and talked to himself.

'Him?'

'He is our chief engineer,' said Rudolf, 'a man who can batter down walls with his machines.'

Kalju was not convinced but was happy enough to allow the old man to follow them as he showed the crusaders the walls, towers and then hall, barracks, stables and huts that were sited on the hill's upper level, within the inner wall. They were impressed by the fort's position, strength and layout, though not by the fact that it was filled with the old, women and children.

'I have gathered the elderly, women and children from the surrounding villages,' said Kalju when they sat with him in his hall, a cavernous wooden structure filled with huge oak pillars that supported the high roof. A fire raged in the stone hearth in the centre of the hall, filling it with smoke despite the openings in the ceiling.

'How many warriors do you have here,' asked Bertram.

'Just over four hundred,' replied Kalju.

'That few?' said Sir Richard, Rudolf translating for him.

Kalju shrugged. 'I have to garrison the other forts in my kingdom so they too can provide safe havens for my people when the Russians come.'

Thaddeus was squinting at Kalju, not understanding his words and becoming more frustrated.

'Are you ill, Master Thaddeus?' enquired Conrad.

'No, but you can speak my words for me, young Conrad,' said Thaddeus.

But before he spoke a woman entered the hall: tall, wearing a green woollen skirt and long-sleeved brown tunic. She had wild hair and as she came closer Conrad noticed that she had green eyes.

'Ah,' said Kalju, spotting her, 'this is my wife Eha and the mother of my two sons and three daughters.'

She smiled at the crusaders who rose and bowed their heads at her.

'Dusk,' said Conrad.

They all looked at him with amusement.

Kalju laughed. 'That is correct, Conrad, Eha means "dusk" in our language.' He pointed at Conrad. 'Eha, this is Conrad Wolff who speaks our language and has fought many battles in his short life.'

Eha smiled at him and tilted her head. 'I am pleased to meet you, Conrad Wolff.'

Master Thaddeus cleared his throat.

'Master Thaddeus would like to say something.'

Before he spoke Kalju ordered beer and food be brought to the hall, his wife sitting beside him at the table that was hastily arranged by servants, who proceeded to pile it with wooden bowls and platters loaded with meat, fish and bread. Other slaves brought strong honey beer that was served to Kalju, his wife and the crusaders. Conrad took a gulp and then stood as Master Thaddeus began talking, Conrad translating his words as the engineer began pacing up and down and wagging his finger at the others.

The fort was very strong and could be held against a far superior attacking force, notwithstanding the women and children who would eat up supplies very quickly during a siege. Thaddeus said that it would be better it they were sent away. Was there any possibility of this? Kalju said no. Thaddeus then asked him how many archers he had at Odenpah. Less than fifty. Thaddeus frowned but stated that the best course of action therefore would be to line the outer wall with all the crossbowmen and archers they possessed, but stockpile bolts and arrows along the inner wall in the event that the outer wall was taken by the foe. The latter would soon discover to their cost that missiles could be shot down on them from the high, inner wall.

He next addressed the issue of the moat.

'What moat?' said Kalju.

Odenpah was built on an oblong hill and below the outer wall was a sloping earth rampart but there was no moat.

'The one that your men and the soldiers that have marched here are going to dig,' Thaddeus told him.

Bertram, Mathias and Sir Richard looked at each other in confusion.

'That is correct, my lords,' said Thaddeus without the need for translation. 'Your men will assist in the creation of a moat that will surround the fort to add another layer to its defences. Please continue to translate, Conrad.'

Thaddeus told Kalju that he was amazed that no one had thought of the idea of creating a moat, especially as a nice-sized lake abutted the north side of the fort. He was now pacing up and down, lecturing those seated like a tutor before his students. Kalju was amused, the crusaders bemused as Thaddeus informed the chief that some of the huts and other buildings between the outer and inner walls would have to be demolished to accommodate his mangonels.

'What are they?' asked Kalju.

'Machines for throwing large objects,' answered Thaddeus. 'But the immediate priority is the construction of the moat.'

'The Russians could be here any day,' remarked Kalju.

Thaddeus stopped and stood to face the chief. 'Well, my lord, I suggest we begin digging as soon as possible.'

And so they did, hundreds of men sweating and cursing as they dug and hacked at the earth at the base of the fort's rampart under the watchful eye of Master Thaddeus and his engineers. Kalju sent out mounted patrols to keep watch for the enemy but they returned with the happy tidings that no Russians had been spotted.

As the snowfall grew steadily heavier and the ground harder, at Odenpah both Ungannians and Christians started to believe that the enemy would not come.

*****

'You will march against Odenpah immediately,' ordered Mstislav. 'You should have taken it earlier in the year but instead you amused yourself with burning and raping instead on focusing on taking the Ungannian stronghold.'

Domash bristled at the insult but kept his tongue. He knew better than to contradict the prince when he was in a rage, his predecessor having paid with his life for daring to stand up to Mstislav. The latter had returned in triumph to Novgorod following his foray into Wierland but had been enraged to discover that Domash, who had five thousand Polotskians as reinforcements, had failed to capture Odenpah. He had made a leisurely return to Novgorod but on his arrival had set out for Pskov. Mstislav had decided to execute Domash for his failure but before he left had received an interesting missive that made him change his mind.

'The year is old, lord,' said Domash. 'A winter march will be hard on the troops.'

Mstislav jabbed a finger in his face. 'When your men start bellyaching you can tell them they have been dragged out of their wives' beds because of the incompetence of their mayor. You will march west immediately.'

'The Polotskians have returned to their city,' said Domash. 'I will have too few men.'

Mstislav gave him a sly smile. 'Far from it. You will be pleased to know that when you arrive at Odenpah reinforcements will be awaiting you.'

Domash looked at Gleb, who shrugged his shoulders.

'Reinforcements, lord?'

'The leader of the Estonian tribes, Lembit, has contacted me with a proposal. In return for Novgorod leaving Wierland alone he will give me Odenpah. It seems that the Ungannians no longer accept the leadership of Lembit and have turned against them. As we speak he is mustering an army to march against them. So you see, your forces combined with his will be more than sufficient to take the fort.'

Domash was horrified. 'I am to fight beside the Estonians?'

Mstislav approached him until their faces were but inches apart. 'Better that than your head decorating the walls of this city, I think.'

'That's true,' said Gleb glibly.

'If it comes to that your head will be on a spike beside his, mystic,' sneered Mstislav.

It took Domash two weeks to muster seven thousand variably armed and equipped men. The élite were Pskov's *Druzhina*: five hundred fully armoured and trained horsemen, supported by three thousand men of the city militia, mostly spearmen and archers but also two hundred horsemen. The rest of his army were the *Voi*, who at least were wrapped in fur-lined hats and cloaks. They still wore bast footwear but Domash issued them all with boots from Pskov's warehouses. It was bad enough that he was campaigning in winter; there was no need to arrive at Odenpah with half his army afflicted by frostbite.

Retracing his steps from the earlier campaign, he marched due west and then north along the western shore of Lake Peipus, now a great expanse of ice and snow. Mercifully most days were sunny and free of the biting wind that cracked skin and froze fingers and toes. But the army still covered only six miles a day.

*****

Lembit left Lehola when his scouts reported back to him that Kalju was fortifying his hill forts and that the crusader army that had spent the summer camped around Wenden had dispersed. This meant that it was highly unlikely that the bishop would re-assemble an army to march against him when snow was on the ground, thus leaving him free to deal with Kalju. An example needed to be made of the Ungannian chief, else the fragile alliance of tribes would disintegrate. Nigul was dead and the Russians had raided Edvin's kingdom. If action was not taken Estonia would fall prey to foreign invaders, but Lembit believed he could play the foreigners off against each other and thus preserve the independence of his people. Well, most of them.

'Does it feel unusual to be far from the sea?' he asked Sigurd seated on the pony beside him.

'It may surprise you, lord, to learn that Oeselians spend more time on dry land than they do on the water.'

'Yes, I suppose they do,' said Lembit thoughtfully.

On his other side Jaak sat silently on his pony as it plodded through the snow. He had brought a thousand warriors to join the two thousand Saccalians that were marching to Odenpah, Sigurd having left Rotalia with a thousand Oeselians. Lembit had at first been alarmed when Nigul had been killed fighting the crusaders but then looked upon it as a sign from Uku himself. With Rotalia prostrate and without a leader he feared that the Bishop of Riga would seize it anyway, but before he could do so Lembit offered it to Olaf. The Oeselian leader thus sailed the short distance from his island to Rotalia and took possession of the most important hill forts. Most of the Rotalians fled to seek sanctuary in Saccalia rather than fight the sea pirates. Thus did the empty land of Rotalia become Oeselian territory. And the price was the loan of a thousand warriors to march with Lembit against Kalju.

Lembit could feel the tension in the air and the frostiness between Sigurd and Jaak that made the winter air seem mild by comparison but he did not care. He needed all the allies he could get and if that meant giving Olaf Rotalia then so be it. In any case he had too few warriors to defend that kingdom on his own and none of the other chiefs were inclined to send their warriors to garrison it. He knew that a Russian-occupied Ungannia was not an attractive prospect but hoped that by fighting alongside Mstislav he would win enough favour with the Russians to be able to influence their future policy. He also knew that a Russian-occupied Ungannia would bring them into direct conflict with the crusaders and hoped the two would soon be fighting each other instead of killing Estonians. He also hoped that the Oeselians in Rotalia would also come into conflict with the bishop's men. And with everyone fighting each other the freedom of the Estonian tribes might still be preserved.

'I do not understand why we march to assist the Russians conquer Ungannia,' said Jaak suddenly.

Lembit sighed. 'For one thing because Kalju has proved an enemy rather than a friend, and for another the Russians are assisting us, not the other way round.'

'In what way?' said Jaak incredulously.

'Because in return for Ungannia Mstislav will not attack Wierland, which means northern Estonia will be unmolested.'

He did not tell Jaak that he hoped the Russians and crusaders would start fighting each other once they found themselves on each other's border. Nor did he mention that the Oeselians would soon be fighting the crusaders next spring when the bishop renewed his hostilities.

'Kalju's treachery has proved most useful, Jaak, as you will soon see.'

'You are wrong, Lembit,' said Jaak. 'We should be fighting against the Russians not with them.' He cast a disparaging glance towards Sigurd. 'You are unwise in the choice of your allies and my view is not the only one in this.'

Rusticus riding a pony immediately behind Lembit snorted at this effrontery but Jaak was unconcerned with the opinions of Lembit's pet brute.

Lembit continued to stare ahead, speaking calmly after a few seconds had elapsed. 'The last time someone spoke to me like that was the last time they spoke. You are a fool, Jaak, a short-sighted fool. Do you think we can fight the Russians and crusaders at the same time? Nigul is dead and Kalju turns against us. You think we can conjure up armies in the spring when the crusaders advance north and the Russians sweep west to the north and south of Lake Peipus? What I do I do for the good of all Estonia and not for my own interests.

'No one forced you to march with me. If you feel so strongly you are free to return to your stronghold, there to await the spring and to see if it is the crusaders or the Russians who arrive at your gates first.'

Jaak snorted in contempt but kept his tongue. Sigurd noted the animosity between the two and the thought entered his mind that Rotalia might not be the only province that his people could acquire at the expense of the Estonians.

It was a relatively short distance from Lehola to Odenpah, a southeasterly march across a snow-covered land filled with villages that were now empty. Sigurd noticed with amusement that Lembit gave orders that these settlements were not to be torched as the army moved by them. He informed the Oeselian that their occupants had fled to the sanctuary of either the forests or the local hill fort if one was nearby. The villagers had taken their food and animals with them but their huts provided warm, dry shelter for the army's commanders and chiefs on the march. Lembit also explained that they would need them when they made the return journey after capturing Odenpah.

'You do not mind giving up this place to the Russians?' asked Sigurd.

'That is part of the agreement I have with their leader,' replied Lembit, drinking beer from a wooden cup in the long hut of a village elder who had fled with his people. The fire in the stone hearth crackled and spat and filled the hut with smoke.

'Don't put damp wood on the fire, you idiots,' Lembit barked to the two wolf shields tending the fire, his eyes smarting from the smoke. 'Otherwise I'll make you sleep outside in the snow with the others.'

'What of this Kalju, the leader of the Ungannian people?' said Sigurd. 'What will you do with him?'

'Better for him that he dies in the fighting,' said Lembit. 'He will discover what happens when he breaks an agreement with me. The defenders of Odenpah will also be put to the sword as an example to the rest of Ungannia.'

'And then that kingdom will belong to the Russians,' said Sigurd.

Lembit thought of the Russians fighting the crusaders and trying to hold a land that the Bishop of Riga desired.

'Can't be helped.'

*****

Lembit believed the Ungannians who had fled to the small hill forts that dotted Kalju's land to be lambs that could be left until Odenpah had been taken. They posed little threat to the thousands of warriors who tramped through the snow, many of them wearing snowshoes made from the supple branches of evergreens. Most of the hill forts were small affairs that could accommodate perhaps a hundred people behind their crude timber walls. They could have been stormed with ease but that would have taken time and Lembit wanted affairs concluded with Kalju long before the spring came. And so the long column of warriors, sleds and ponies loaded with supplies ignored the forts that sat on the hills where village elders and their people prayed to their gods for safe deliverance from the invaders.

But when it is not snowing Estonia is blessed with bright sunshine on cold winter days when the sun glinted off whetted spear points and burnished helmets. Lembit's army would not have detected the flashes of light coming from the hill forts as the elders and chiefs used polished silver to reflect the sun's rays to send signals to other strongholds on high ground. By the time Lembit was a week away from Odenpah Kalju knew the exact location and approximate strength of the invading army advancing from the west. That was Lembit's first mistake. And before the sky thickened with grey clouds holding thick snowfall he had also learnt of the size and composition of the Russian army marching from the east.

'They will be here in a week,' said Kalju after being told the latest news that had been relayed by his signalling system.

Once more Rudolf and Conrad acted as interpreters as the chief, Eha, two of Kalju's most senior men, Bertram, Mathias and Sir Richard gathered in his great hall to drink warm milk and take shelter from the biting cold. The mutual suspicion that had existed between the chiefs and crusaders had abated greatly since the latter's arrival at the fort, not least because all of them soon directed their hostility towards the man who seemed to have assumed command over all of them, and who, realising this, had turned into something of a taskmaster. The atmosphere in the hall was relaxed without his presence as chiefs and crusaders nodded and grinned at each other and drank their milk.

'That is a lot of men,' remarked Bertram.

'Perhaps we could attack at least one of the enemy columns before they combined,' mused Mathias. 'Take the brother knights and sergeants and hit them hard.' He smiled at Sir Richard. 'And your horsemen too, my lord.'

Rudolf translated the words to Kalju. 'Who would you attack?'

'The Russians,' answered Bertram. 'They are the larger force and will be more strung out.'

The doors opened and in swept Odenpah's taskmaster. Everyone groaned when they saw him.

'Ah,' said Thaddeus, taking a cup from a wooden tray held by one of the servants, 'warm milk. Excellent.'

He gulped it down and looked at the figures sitting round the large trestle table. He saw Conrad standing by Rudolf.

'Translate for me, Conrad.

'I have organised rotas for the scattering of the spoil from the ditch that has been dug, rather tardily I might add.'

Kalju looked confused. 'Rotas?'

Thaddeus smiled. 'Indeed, lord. Organisation may be a necessary evil but it is vital for success.'

'Why do we need to scatter the spoil?' asked Sir Richard.

'I would have thought that was obvious,' remarked Thaddeus. 'When the enemy arrive they must be convinced that there is no moat. If they see a great hump surrounding the fort even the simplest among them will discern that the earth has been dug. Quite obvious.'

'We have just learned that two enemy columns are a week away,' said Mathias, 'so you had better get your rotas to fill the moat with water.'

They all chuckled but Thaddeus was not amused. 'Why would I wish to fill the moat with water?'

This stopped their chuckling.

'Then why in the name of all that's holy did we dig it?' demanded Sir Richard.

Thaddeus began to pace up and down as he had done many times since his arrival at the fort, explaining that if the moat was filled with water it would freeze, which would provide a hard surface upon which to stand.

'The ice will break if anything heavy is rested on it,' said an exasperated Sir Richard.

621

Thaddeus smiled knowingly at him. 'Having spent a number of years in this land, my lord, I have knowledge of how the cold can turn water into thick ice. You must trust me in this.'

'Your lords are thinking of riding out to attack the Russians,' remarked Kalju.

Conrad translated and Thaddeus was horrified. 'Leave the fort? Out of the question. For one thing you will weaken the workforce and there is still much to do.'

'We did not come here to shovel dirt,' snapped Sir Richard.

'No, my lord,' replied Thaddeus calmly, 'you came here to defeat the enemy and if you do things my way your chances of doing so will increase substantially.'

Sir Richard looked away as Mathias looked at Bertram, who shrugged. Thaddeus brought his hands together in front of him and walked towards Kalju.

'I do not suppose, my lord, that you would reconsider your decision not to send the women, children and the old away.'

'You suppose right,' said Eha answering for her husband.

Thaddeus smiled most graciously at her. 'Then I would ask your husband to organise hunting parties to gather as much food as possible so we can withstand a siege.'

Kalju nodded. 'It shall be so.'

'And men to fish on the ice on the nearby lakes also,' added Thaddeus. 'This will require a slight alteration to the rotas, of course. Still, should be possible. A week before the enemy arrives, you say?'

Kalju nodded.

Thaddeus looked at the others sitting at the table. 'Then I suggest, my lords, that we all attend to our duties forthwith. Time is of the essence.'

He bowed his head to Kalju and Eha, turned on his heels and strode from the hall. A grumbling Sir Richard, Bertram and Mathias followed, Kalju sending his two chiefs after them. Conrad made to walk with Rudolf from the chief's presence when Eha called after them.

'Conrad.'

He turned. 'Lady?'

'That old man, Thaddeus, is he a holy man?'

'No, lady.'

'Then why do your lords obey him?'

'A question I have often asked myself,' said Rudolf.

622

'It is because he is very knowledgeable when it comes to defensive warfare and sieges, lady,' said Conrad. 'It was his wisdom that led to the fall of...'

He was going to refer to the fall of Lehola but knew that at that time Kalju was an ally of Lembit.

'Continue,' said Eha.

Conrad glanced at Kalju. 'It was Master Thaddeus' knowledge that resulted in the fall of Lehola.'

'To think that one old man could reduce such a mighty fortress,' said Kalju thoughtfully. 'He is truly powerful and wise.'

He rose from his seat and walked to the hall's doors.

'Where are you going?' Eha called after him.

'To see Master Thaddeus so I can receive his orders concerning the hunting and fishing parties.'

Eha laughed as he blew her a kiss and marched from the hall. She too went to rise, Conrad stepping forward and offering his hand to assist her. As she bent forward Conrad noticed the heavy silver necklace she was wearing, from which hung a large piece of amber. Eha saw him looking at it.

'A gift from my sister.'

She stood and he released her hand.

'She is in the fort?' he asked.

Her eyes filled with hurt. 'She is dead or at least I hope she is dead. She lived in a village on our southern border. It was raided one winter and all the menfolk were killed. The women and children were all taken. Slave traders, most likely.'

Conrad went pale. He felt physically sick as shame gripped him and he was unable to look Eha in the eye.

Conrad suddenly fell to his knees and took Eha's hand.

'I promise you, lady, that the enemy will not breach the walls of this fort and the women and children will be safe. This I swear in the name of God.'

Eha's eyes opened wide with surprise and looked at Rudolf in confusion.

'He is apt to make such gestures,' remarked the brother knight.

Eha, delighted, raised Conrad up to his feet and kissed him on the cheek.

'Many among my people believe that the crusaders are bloodthirsty barbarians but now I can see that this is false. There are obviously many fine warriors among them.'

Eha linked her arm in his and walked from the hall. She was smiling at him but he could have wept such was the self-reproach he felt.

That night, as he sat round the campfire with his companions, he told them of what had happened earlier.

'This is our punishment for what we did at that village,' said Conrad, staring into the fire.

'You do not know that it was Kalju's sister-in-law who was in the village,' said Hans.

Conrad rounded on him. 'Does that matter?' He tugged at his surcoat. 'We are supposed to be warriors of Christ, devoting our lives to truth and justice, not filthy slave traders.'

'Henke says that pagans do not count and so it does not matter how we treat them,' said Anton, trying to be helpful.

Conrad fixed him with a stare. 'Henke is an animal. Do you believe what he says, Anton?' He gestured at the fort bathed in moonlight. 'Are the women and children in the fort less deserving of protection because they are pagans? Will you defend them with less vigour when the enemy comes on the advice of Henke?'

Anton shook his head and looked at his feet.

Conrad remembered the mournful look on the woman's face as she was led away by the slave traders after the raid on the village.

'Eha's sister was among the captives we took; of that I am certain.'

'It is God's will we are here, Conrad,' said Johann.

'And God will ensure that we shall pay for our crimes,' replied Conrad.

The next day, as the sun beat down on dozens of men hacking at the soil around the fort, on the advice of Master Bertram one of the polished silver signal mirrors was used to send a message to the nearest hill fort to the south. Once received it would in turn be relayed to the Ungannian fort nearest to Wenden. From there scouts would ride to the Sword Brother stronghold with a message for Master Berthold: *enemy force very large, send reinforcements immediately.*

*****

'Our new allies,' said Gleb, resting his hands on the saddle's pommel. 'Not much to look at, are they?'

Domash said nothing but sighed heavily and waved forward one of his mounted officers. His scouts had made contact with Lembit two hours earlier and both sides had agreed to rendezvous by the frozen surface of the Leevi, a small river located around six miles north of Odenpah. It flowed from the uplands near the fort east to Lake Peipus.

624

'Come Gleb, let us meet our fellow conquerors.'

He nudged his horse forward, the officer and a dozen of his men falling in behind as Gleb also walked his horse forward.

'Give the order to make camp,' Domash called to another of his senior commanders. The foot soldiers escorting the sleds that carried supplies were at least two hours behind so it made sense to call a halt. There was flat ground either side of the river and the trees did not begin until around two hundred paces from the riverbank.

The Estonians were mostly on foot save for a group of warriors wearing helmets and mail armour, armed with spears, who sat on ponies directly ahead. One carried a standard of some sort but there was no wind and so it hung limply from its staff. His own horsemen filled the ground extending to the east but he could only see two relatively small groups of foot behind the mounted warriors, one carrying brightly coloured round shields, the other sporting wolf heads on their shields. As the foot soldiers moved to stand either side of the mounted men he saw blonde hair extending from beneath many of the helmets of the men with coloured shields. One of the men sitting on a pony took off his helmet and raised his hand. Shorter in stature than most of his companions, especially the oversized brute next to him, he had broad shoulders and long hair.

'Greetings, friends. I am Lembit, leader of the Saccalian people.'

Domash raised his hand and also removed his helmet before answering in Estonian. 'Domash Tverdislavich, Mayor of Pskov and deputy to Prince Mstislav of Novgorod.'

Both parties smiled politely and did their best to forget that they had spent more time fighting each other than being allies.

'This is all you have?' said Domash, looking at the warriors standing bored in the snow.

'Our camp is two miles to the west,' replied Lembit, who looked beyond the Russian to the horsemen standing in the snow. 'You bring many horse?'

'A few thousand,' remarked Domash casually.

'Not much use when storming a fort,' sneered Jaak.

Lembit maintained his polite smile. 'This is Lord Jaak, ruler of Jerwen, whose warriors will aid us in our assault.'

He then turned to Sigurd. 'And this is Prince Sigurd who commands a large body of Oeselians.'

'Oeselians?' said Gleb in surprise upon hearing the word. 'Are we going to eat any captives we take?'

The horsemen with Domash smiled but their commander was not amused and froze Gleb with a stare. Fortunately he had spoken in Russian and Lembit and his allies did not understand the language.

Domash nodded to Sigurd, who had removed his helmet, and to Jaak who had not.

'What of the Ungannians?' he asked.

'Cowering in their hill forts,' reported Lembit with satisfaction. 'Kalju has dispersed his forces rather than concentrate them at Odenpah. I doubt if he has even a few hundred men to defend his stronghold.'

Domash nodded contentedly. 'Will you give him an opportunity to surrender?'

Lembit laughed. 'You do not bargain with traitors, mayor, you execute them. We shall storm Odenpah to make an example of Kalju. I will send his head to Prince Mstislav as a present.'

'I am sure he will be touched,' remarked Domash.

His gross underestimation of the enemy was Lembit's second mistake.

*****

It snowed heavily during the night and early morning, so that by the time Lembit and his Russian allies arrived before Odenpah just after midday the ground all round the fort was a blanket of white. No sign of the crusader camp that had been dismantled the day before was visible, and the dry moat that encompassed three sides of the fort was also hidden from view. Kalju's scouts had alerted their leader of the approach of the Estonians and Russians once they had arrived within five miles of the fort, the enemy's progress having been exactly tracked by the signals from the other hill forts.

As soon as word reached Odenpah that the enemy was a day's march away Master Thaddeus put his plan into effect. The crusaders moved into the fort along with their wagons, horses and draught animals, pitching their tents between the inner and outer walls. It was very cramped, especially as Thaddeus' engineers had set up the six mangonels in the same area: two behind the outer western wall, two on the other side of the compound behind the outer east wall, and the other two directly behind the gatehouse in the outer southern wall. The elderly, women and children were all moved to the higher, inner stronghold where they would not only be more removed from immediate danger but also be kept out of the way to allow the soldiers to do their work.

There were eight square timber towers along Odenpah's outer perimeter wall and another four at each corner of the inner timber wall. The latter was reached by steps fashioned from great stone slabs that were positioned on the eastern side of the higher hill. These led to a single squat gate that gave access to the inner stronghold. The steps were steep and the gate deliberately narrow to prohibit horsemen from entering.

Master Thaddeus had given express orders that no crusaders, Sword Brothers or crossbowmen were to show themselves in the towers or on the battlements until he said so. Sir Richard grumbled at this but the chief engineer was insistent. He explained his reasoning as he stood with Kalju, Bertram, Mathias and Sir Richard in one of the towers that flanked the main gates as the enemy began to deploy around the fort. Conrad was in attendance in his role as translator for Master Thaddeus.

'We must give the illusion of weakness,' he said to Sir Richard whose unhappiness had increased at having to wear a fur-lined cap, thick woollen tunic and brown cloak so he resembled one of Kalju's men. Bertram, Mathias and Conrad were similarly attired.

Kalju looked at the hundreds of men deploying to the south, west and east of his fort. 'We *are* weak.'

His warriors filled the other towers but the battlements between them were empty.

Thaddeus shook his head. 'Have no fear, my lord, it is within our interests for the enemy to take our bait.'

'Bait?' said Sir Richard, flicking a louse off his cloak.

Thaddeus pointed at the empty battlements between the towers. 'What do you see, my lords?'

Sir Richard looked perplexed and Bertram confused.

'Nothing,' said Kalju.

'Exactly,' smiled Thaddeus. 'And that is what the enemy will see: nothing. They will deduce that if they mount a mass assault against the fort it will fall quickly. And that is what we want them to think for they will believe that victory is within their grasp. They will become over-confident and that will lead to their downfall.'

Sir Richard looked at the now thousands of men moving into position around the fort.

'Looks like they are preparing to attack.'

Mathias shook his head. 'Not today, lord. This display is purely for our benefit so we can behold their strength and dwell on it through the night. In this way the enemy hopes to demoralise us.'

He pointed at a large group of soldiers directly ahead, facing the main gates. 'There are no scaling ladders among their ranks, which indicates that they will not launch an attack today.'

Kalju looked into the sky. 'There are only two hours of daylight left.'

But in that time the enemy put on an impressive display. As they made no attempt to approach the walls the commanders decided to take a tour of the ramparts to observe their opponents more closely. Kalju pointed to the west where the Saccalians stood between the men from Jerwen and Sigurd's warriors.

'You see the men with red painted on their shields? Those are Lembit's wolf shields.'

Conrad clenched his fist at the mention of Lembit's name. Kalju pointed at the block of warriors standing to the right of the Saccalians.

'They are Jaak's warriors. The symbol painted on their shields is a bear.'

'What about the warriors on the left flank of the Saccalians?' asked Master Bertram.

Kalju stared at the wall of locked shields painted red, yellow, orange and blue and the dragon standards within their ranks.

'Oeselians?'

Mathias was surprised. 'Oeselians, here?'

'Our list of enemies grows longer,' remarked Bertram.

They walked to the western ramparts where more Russians were deploying. Their ranks presented a stark contrast between poorly equipped foot soldiers armed with spears and axes but wearing no armour, and the superbly equipped boyars of the *Druzhina* in their shining helmets, aventails and mail hauberks. They carried large, brightly coloured shields. Among their ranks were dotted red and blue banners carrying images of Russian and Byzantine saints and the Virgin Mary. The cloaks of the armoured horsemen were likewise brightly coloured whereas those worn by the levy foot soldiers were mainly hues of green and brown. Sir Richard noticed that very few of the thousands of Russian foot soldiers wore helmets. The exception was around a thousand men standing in well-dressed ranks wearing helmets and mail armour, with a small number of attached horsemen carrying banners showing a golden snow leopard on a blue background – Pskov's militia.

For an hour they watched the enemy move into position to the accompaniment of a great din produced by horn trumpets, metal trumpets and frame drums scattered among the Estonian and Russian ranks. The Oeselians began singing a stirring war song, their ranks swaying as they belted out its words, the Ungannians responding with their own song of death and glory.

'Brotherly business, killing each other,' remarked Thaddeus dryly.

As the light faded and dusk approached, the ranks in front of the fort thinned notably as parties were detached to pitch tents and organise the various camps. The singing and playing of instruments died away as campfires were lit, meals prepared and beasts of burden were fed, watered and quartered for the night. Kalju stood most of his men down, leaving guards in the towers and others to patrol the outer battlements. Inside the fort men were contemplative as they awaited the new day, one that they knew would be violent and bloody. Brother knights and sergeants went to the chapel tent to attend prayers, the crusaders filing into Sir Richard's tent to receive the blessing of his personal priest who had accompanied him from England.

Conrad slept little that night, the air outside his tent filled with the hushed conversations of men on the eve of battle. For some, the mercenaries of the order, it was but one of many engagements they had taken part in. As Hans and Anton snored around him he heard the distinctive voice of leather face, winning at gambling and seemingly unconcerned that the next night might see his head on an enemy spear. He got up, wrapped his cloak around him and went outside to warm himself at a brazier. His mail armour hung on a wooden frame next to the suits of the others with his full-face helmet perched on top. He buckled on his sword belt as he walked over to the brazier and held out his hands to the warmth.

'Can't sleep, Conrad?'

He turned to see Rudolf with Henke, his faithful dog, by his side.

'Guilty conscience?' leered Henke. 'Rudolf has a gift for you.'

'The battle positions have been agreed for tomorrow. The garrison of Wenden will defend the western ramparts.'

'Which means,' said Henke, still smiling dumbly, 'that we will face the Saccalians. So you might get your chance to kill Lembit.'

'It means,' said Rudolf, 'that we will defend the western wall whatever foe we fight, that is all.'

Henke held out his hand to the fire. 'Just think, Conrad, Lembit is but a short distance away, over that wall. You could slip out of the fort, scamper across the snow, slit his throat and be back before breakfast. All it takes is a bit of courage.'

Conrad looked at him. 'Talk is easy, Henke. But I will gladly do as you advise if you will accompany me. And afterwards we can see who is the better with a sword.'

'That's enough,' snapped Rudolf. 'You two can focus on the task in hand. There will be more than enough enemy soldiers to keep you both amused tomorrow. Master Thaddeus has estimated that we are outnumbered ten to one.'

'That's about right, then,' said Henke.

'What is?' asked Rudolf.

Henke spat on the brazier. 'One Sword Brother is worth ten Russians.'

He watched as a group of Ungannians walked by. 'And the same number of Estonians.'

Conrad laughed and even Rudolf smiled. Henke was a violent, uncivilised cutthroat but in battle you wanted him to be fighting by your side. He slapped Conrad hard on the arm as he and Rudolf walked away.

'Try not to let the wolf shields use your body for target practice. The last time that happened it took Ilona weeks to patch you up.'

Conrad smiled. 'Go with God, Henke, for surely no one else will.'

He managed to grab a couple of hours' sleep before the trumpet call for prayers woke him. Bleary eyed he and the others put on their fighting attire: quilted cotton-covered aketon, over which was worn a hauberk with integral mittens that had soft leather palms, and over the latter a quilted, sleeveless gambeson. A quilted linen coif was worn beneath the mail equivalent. A padded leather squab was worn on top of the mail coif to make wearing a helmet more comfortable. Conrad pulled on his mail chausses, beneath which was thick linen hose held up by leather laces to prevent his skin chafing on the metal and for warmth. The chausses also had thick leather soles. Then he put on his white surcoat and wrapped his cloak around his shoulders.

He buckled his sword belt that also held a sheath for his dagger and slung his shield on his back, tucking his axe into his belt and cradling his helmet in his right arm.

'Ready?' he said to the others.

He walked out into the freezing pre-dawn air, his breath misting in front of his face. He nodded to other brother knights and sergeants as they all made their way in silence to the chapel tent.

After prayers and a frugal breakfast of bread, warm milk and salted meat Rudolf gathered the garrison of Wenden around him for a final conference. Despite the great disparity in numbers between the two sides the mood within the fort was relaxed and confident, not least because everyone had been thoroughly briefed on their mission. The crusaders and Sword Brothers were greatly cheered by the fact that the Ungannians would be fighting in the fort's towers, and Kalju's warriors were delighted that they would be fighting by the side of their friends and neighbours. And everyone was emboldened by the thoroughness of Master Thaddeus' plans.

'You all know the plan and your role in it,' said Rudolf to the men standing in a semi-circle before him. 'For it to work we need to keep our nerve and our discipline. Above all, we must hold the outer wall. If that falls then Odenpah falls.'

He looked at the determined, hardened faces before him.

'God be with you all.'

Chapter 23

As a grey half-light slowly crept over the frozen landscape movement was detected among the enemy camps, the Russians to the south and east, the Estonians and Oeselians to the west. The latter had pitched their two-man tents near the lake and the sentries in the fort's northern towers reported that warriors were walking onto its frozen surface to test the thickness of the ice. This was merely a ruse, though, for already thousands of men were stamping their feet and shuffling into their battle positions to make their assault across the frozen ground in front of the fort.

Once again the horn trumpets sounded and the drums were beaten as chiefs and officers bellowed at their men to dress their ranks. Kalju's warriors embraced their families and made their way to the fighting platforms in the towers on the outer wall. The mercenaries, brother knights, sergeants and crusaders, meanwhile, climbed the ladders to the walkways behind the wall's ramparts where they made their way on all fours to their designated fighting positions. They moved slowly and cautiously, not wanting to reveal their presence to an eagle-eyed enemy commander who might be riding near to the fort. In the towers, meanwhile, the Ungannians began shouting insults at the enemy to attract the latter's attention as below them the battlements silently filled with soldiers.

At approximately an hour after dawn, with a few snowflakes in the air and a mild easterly breeze blowing, a sudden roar of noise erupted from the Russian ranks and the entire *Voi* moved forward, the front ranks carrying crude scaling ladders to allow them to conquer Odenpah's eastern wall. Pskov's city militia, a row of archers standing ahead of the front ranks, moved forward towards the southern wall, while to the west Lembit gave the signal for the assault against the west wall to commence. Sigurd also sent his men forward, their large shields locked over their heads as a precaution against enemy missiles. He had seen the empty battlements but his Oeselian instincts had told him that something was wrong.

The first to realise that the fort was going to be a tougher nut to crack than they had thought were the Russians, the undisciplined mass of *Voi* tramping through the snow towards the empty eastern wall. A few arrows were shot in their direction from the handful of archers in the towers but they killed only a tiny number before the Russians reached the slope of the hill, and fell headlong into the snow-filled moat. Instead of placing their ladders against the timber wall hundreds of men found themselves in head-high snow as hundreds more piled in on top and crushed them.

There were frantic shouts and orders as the commanders realised that their men had encountered an unexpected obstacle, but they were too late to prevent the *Voi*'s assault degenerating into chaos.

To the south of the fort it was the same, Pskov's militia advancing in a more orderly fashion with its archers providing covering arrow support. But when the front ranks reached the unseen moat they too were thrown into disorder. Master Thaddeus had a bird's-eye view of things from a tower in the inner perimeter wall, and when he saw that the Estonian attack to the west had also faltered he raised his hand.

A young squire holding a trumpet had been studying the old man intently and when he saw his hand signal he raised the instrument to his lips and blew it. The squires to his left and right likewise blew their trumpets. Rudolf heard the sound, picked up his helmet and stood up.

'God with us!' he shouted, placing his helmet on his head.

The battle cry was answered by the dozens of men who had been sitting on the walkways with their backs rested against the timber wall. They now stood up, turned and began raining death down on the hapless Estonians and Russians below.

Conrad placed his shield on top of the timber logs as the brother knights, sergeants and spearmen did the same. And then the crossbowmen loaded their weapons and began shooting down at the enemy through the gaps between the shields. They shot quarrels that were a foot long, made of hardwood with four-sided iron bodkin points that could punch through mail and leather armour with ease. Leather face and the other mercenary crossbowmen had also smeared theirs with hellebore, a fatal poison that would ensure a slow and lingering death for those wounded by their bolts.

There were forty crossbowmen on the west wall, the same number on the southern and eastern ramparts, and though those that had come with crusaders shot three or four bolts a minute, those in the pay of the Sword Brothers maintained a steady rate of two quarrels a minute. Partly to conserve ammunition, mostly to ensure every bolt struck a target.

Leather face loaded another quarrel, grinned at Conrad and pointed his weapon at the press of Saccalians below. He released his trigger and another man went down. Conrad held his shield in place as leather face reloaded. He pointed his weapon down at the warriors scrambling around in the snow, tripping over scaling ladders and dead comrades. Chiefs desperately tried to restore order, bellowing commands at their men to rally round them. Leather face saw one of them, sword in hand and shield tucked into his left side, holding his blade aloft as he tried to restore order. He released his trigger and saw the bolt slam into his shoulder, smashing his collarbone. The chief stood still for a few seconds before collapsing. A subordinate went to his side and attempted to lift him to his feet, slinging his shield on his back as he tried to raise his lord up, as a bolt went through the top of his helmet into his brain. Leather face looked at the crossbowman next to him who had killed him.

'Nice shot. You might be as good as me one day.'

Frantic horn blasts among the Estonian ranks restored some semblance of order as the scaling ladders were abandoned and Lembit and Jaak hurriedly pulled their men back. But the crossbowmen men had maintained their steady rate of shooting: forty men loosing eighty bolts a minute. In the ten minutes they had been shooting they had killed or wounded five hundred of the enemy – the Estonians had lost a quarter of their strength.

On the other side of the fort the Russians had fared far worse. Not only had they been subjected to a greater deluge of bolts from the crusader crossbowmen, once their attack had been halted many of the *Voi* stood still, unsure what to do. Mostly villagers led by their headmen, they instinctively clustered around their leaders and friends. They stood shoulder to shoulder with shields locked. But their enemy was not on the ground but above them, and shooting at densely packed groups of stationary men mostly devoid of helmets, the crossbowmen could not miss. Domash sent riders to the *Voi* to order them to fall back out of range, but not before over a thousand had been killed. Even the more disciplined soldiers of Pskov's militia had been surprised by the expert shooting of Kremon's crossbowmen, managing to retire in good order but not before three hundred of their number had been killed or wounded.

In the space of a few minutes the formality of an easy conquest of Odenpah had turned into a bloody disaster.

The only commander who had escaped the debacle was Sigurd, who had kept his men back and then diverted some of them onto the ice of the frozen lake when it became apparent that the walls were lined with crossbowmen. His men held their shields over their heads as they gingerly approached the fort's northern walls, advancing almost to base of the sloping earth rampart until driven away by a handful of archers in the fort's north-western tower.

Conrad took off his helmet and rested his shield against the wall.

'That was easy enough,' said leather face, checking the number of bolts in his quiver. 'Next time won't be, though. The cat's out of the bag now. They know the Sword Brothers are in the fort so that will make them more careful.'

'They might try to starve us out,' said Conrad.

Leather face screwed up his ugly features. 'They might, although their food might run out before ours. No, they will try another assault, most likely.'

He smiled at Conrad. 'When our ammunition runs out it will be down to you and your brother knights to earn their pay.'

'We don't get paid,' said Conrad.

'Ah, yes, that poverty thing again. I forgot. Very strange.'

*****

Domash urgently requested the presence of Lembit, Sigurd and Jaak at his tent after his men had returned to camp. They arrived as it was getting dark, the Russian commander still pacing up and down as Gleb sat on a stool sipping ale. Domash knew that he had to take Odenpah if he was to keep his head, the chances of achieving both rapidly diminishing following the calamity that had occurred earlier.

Lembit and Jaak wore dark expressions as a guard showed them into the tent, though Sigurd appeared relaxed as he took a stool and a guard offered him and the others ale.

'You neglected to inform me that Kalju had allied himself with the Sword Brothers,' said Domash to Lembit.

'That is because I did not know,' replied the Saccalian.

Domash sat down on a stool and eyed Lembit. 'This changes many things.'

Lembit winced at the bitter-tasting liquid he had been given.

'He thinks it is poison,' remarked Gleb, noticing Lembit's disparaging squint.

'What did he say?' asked Lembit, wondering who the strange figure always accompanying the Russian commander was. Domash shook his head. 'Nothing. I must inform the prince that to proceed with the operation against Odenpah will result in open war between Novgorod and the Bishop of Riga.'

'But you will still carry on with the siege?' said Lembit. 'That is, after all, what we are all here for.'

'I lost nearly a thousand men today,' snapped Domash. 'All for nothing.'

'We all lost men,' said Jaak.

Domash looked at Sigurd. 'And you?'

'A few,' replied the Oeselian.

Lembit had cheered up somewhat, it having dawned on him that what he desired – open conflict between the bishop and Novgorod – had materialised, notwithstanding the bloody nose he and the others had been given.

'The enemy's crossbowmen are very effective,' said Sigurd, 'but they presumably do not have an inexhaustible supply of ammunition.'

Domash looked up at the tent's roof. 'What do you suggest? We continue assaulting the walls in the hope that they run out of ammunition before we run out of men?'

'I am suggesting, lord,' replied Sigurd calmly, 'that we build siege towers. There is an abundance of wood in the nearby forests and we have thousands of men who can construct them. The garrison of Odenpah is not going anywhere, we have assembled a large army here and so I suggest we make the most of our advantages.'

'The Sword Brothers in the fort may be the vanguard of an army being assembled by the bishop in the south,' said Jaak.

'I will despatch horsemen south to ensure that we are not surprised again,' said Domash. He looked at Sigurd. 'We will try your strategy, Oeselian.'

During the following three days the besiegers established their siege lines and felled hundreds of trees to provide the building materials for the siege towers. They were crude affairs hurriedly built, moved forward on wheels hewn from great oaks, men sweating and heaving in the base of the towers as they pushed them towards the fort. There were six of them – two earmarked to assault each wall – each one three storeys in height with a ramp attached to the top storey that would fall forward onto the top of the wall once they had reached the ramparts. To allow the towers to be pushed up against the walls the moat had to be filled so they could cross it, and the earth slope beneath the wall had be dug away.

Domash ordered his commanders to attach overhanging log roofs to some of the wagons, members of the *Voi* pushing them forward to the moat and then filling the latter with logs carried on the wagons to build bridges for the towers to cross. It was difficult, dangerous work and dozens of Russians were killed by crossbowmen on the walls and in the towers. The *Voi* commanders pleaded with Domash to send archers forward to shoot at the crossbowmen but he refused. Poorly armed villagers were expendable; archers were not.

*****

The enemy worked not only in the day but also through the night, hammering nails into wood and cutting down trees by the light of torches and fires. Conrad stood in one of the inner perimeter's towers and heard the sounds coming from the enemy camp.

'They sound very close,' said Eha beside him.

'That is because sound travels further on a cold, clear night, lady,' he said.

It had been five days since the enemy's attack and since then the garrison had largely stood and watched the siege towers being built around five hundred paces from the walls. Kalju had wanted to launch a raid against them but Master Thaddeus, who had assumed the role of de facto chief military adviser, was adamant that the enemy should not be disturbed.

'Never interrupt your enemy when he is making a mistake,' he had told the chief.

Sir Richard was all for riding out to destroy the siege towers but Bertram and Mathias concurred with Thaddeus and pointed out to him that the Russians had many horsemen in the saddle at all times. Any raiding party would be quickly cut off and surrounded and the garrison would lose some of its most effective members for no result. Sir Richard bridled at his enforced inactivity in close proximity to the enemy but Thaddeus said that if he showed patience he would be rewarded. And so the garrison watched as the towers took shape.

Sir Richard did amuse himself by borrowing a crossbow and shooting at the poor wretches who were filling the moat and removing earth from the hill. He and his fellow knights and their squires looked upon it as great sport until Thaddeus prevailed upon Bertram and Mathias to persuade the knights not to waste precious ammunition. The culling of the enemy labourers was left to the expert marksmanship of the Sword Brothers' crossbowmen.

Eha, her handsome features highlighted by the torch that burned in its holder nearby, pointed at one of the towers being worked on.

'When they have finished they will push them against the walls?'

Conrad nodded.

'And then their soldiers will flood into the fort.'

'Not if Master Thaddeus can help it, lady. And even if they reach the wall they will not be able to take it.'

She noticed that he was toying with a ring on a finger of his left hand.

'That is a marriage ring, is it not?'

'It is, lady,' he replied.

'My husband told me that the Sword Brothers are not allowed to marry.'

'That is correct. I was married before I became a brother knight. My wife and child are dead.'

'I am sorry.'

He stared at the enemy siege towers. 'It is no concern if I am killed here because I know that I will join them in the next life.'

'I will pray that it is not so,' she said.

'How are the other women and children?'

She sighed. 'Fearful that they will be raped and taken as slaves after seeing their husbands butchered. My children will not suffer such a fate and neither will I.'

'Oh?'

She smiled, a cunning glint in her eye. 'I have enough poison to ensure we are all dead before the enemy violates our bodies.'

'My religion holds that it is a sin to take your own life.'

'Then I am fortunate,' she said, 'that I do not follow your god.'

They heard laughter coming from the enemy camp.

'It will not be long now,' said Conrad.

In fact it was the following morning when the enemy at last moved the siege towers forward. The alarm was sounded in the fort and the Ungannians and Christians calmly went to their positions. Conrad stood beside Hans, axe in hand, as his friend chewed on some biscuits. The crossbowmen had been redeployed in the towers so they could direct their bolts against the sides and rear of the towers, behind which were long columns of soldiers holding their shields above their heads.

Two towers approached the southern wall, two the eastern wall and the last two, operated by Estonians and Oeselians, were directed towards the western wall held by the men of Wenden and Segewold. Despite their heavy losses the Russian levies had filled the moat in six places and removed the soil from the earth slope so that the towers could be pushed against the walls. Then the ramps would be lowered and men would pour into the fort. The top platform of each tower held twenty men, with dozens more waiting on the ladders and platforms below. The front and sides of each tower were covered with thick logs to stop crossbow bolts and arrows, thus negating the defenders' most effective weaponry.

On each wall was one of Thaddeus' engineers who watched the approach of the siege towers carefully. When he was satisfied that the towers were at the correct distance he gave the signal to his comrades below. Seconds later barrels of burning pitch shot by the mangonels were arching into the grey sky.

'Supplies are running low,' remarked Hans as the first barrels landed on top of the tower directly ahead of him and Conrad with a muffled bang. Then flames shot into the air and hideous screams came from the tower as the warriors on the top level were covered with hot pitch. The Sword Brothers cheered but their acclamations were drowned out by the high-pitched yells of men engulfed in flames. Some threw themselves off the tower in desperation and fell to their deaths in the snow below as another barrel struck the tower, this time its front, to engulf the logs in flames. The tower came to a grinding halt as those pushing it forward heard the grisly screams of men above them and heard the calls of alarm from the warriors packed on the ladders at higher levels. A third barrel was shot by the mangonel and landed where the first had struck, setting the top of the tower alight and causing panic inside it.

The Sword Brothers cheered again and raised their shields and weapons as men began to flee from the tower, causing panic among the column of Saccalians behind them, the crossbowmen to the left of where Conrad was standing shooting at the warriors behind the siege tower and adding to their misery. The tower had been stopped less than a hundred paces from the wall.

Unfortunately the second siege tower, the one being propelled forward by the Oeselians, was still trundling forward. The mangonel allocated to stop it had malfunctioned, its skein having lost its torsion. A new one had been hurriedly fitted but by the time it had shot its first barrel the tower was too close to the wall and so the projectile landed among the column of warriors following it.

'God with us!' shouted Rudolf as the tower's ramp crashed down on the top of the wall and Oeselian warriors raced across it. Two sergeants standing in the path of the warriors killed four of them with their swords before they were literally barged aside by sheer weight of numbers, falling from the walkway to their deaths.

The walkway was two paces wide, which meant that the Sword Brothers could not be outflanked. But as Rudolf and Henke stood side by side, killing Oeselians with mace and sword, they were gradually forced back by weight of numbers, back towards the fort's tower behind them.

Conrad and Hans likewise stood together as a tide of Oeselians rushed them. He heard Lukas' words in his head but there was no room to manoeuvre and so he and his friend used enemy bodies as shields. The Oeselians carried one-handed axes that they swung over their shields in an attempt to split the Sword Brothers' helmets, but the blows were too clumsy and Conrad raised his shield and thrust his sword below the first Oeselian's shield and upwards, driving the point into his belly. The man groaned and his body went limp but Conrad pressed his shield forward to stop him from collapsing as other warriors behind the dying man pressed their shields into his back. Hans had also killed his man and the two brother knights kept the corpses in front of them upright, pushing forward to create a press of men on the walkway.

'Anton, Johann,' screamed Conrad, 'use your swords.'

He felt a weight on his shoulders as Anton barged his shield into his back and lurched up and forward, jabbing his sword over Conrad's head, over the dead Oeselian and into the eye socket of the warrior desperately trying to get the dead man in front of him out of the way so he could get to grips with Conrad.

On it went, Johann and Anton jumping up and lunging forward with their weapons to try and strike living Oeselians. But after a few minutes neither side could get at each other because there were at least three ranks of dead men between the living. Sergeants and brother knights gathered behind Johann and Anton and pressed forward.

Conrad was finding it difficult to breathe, pressed between dead Oeselians and live Sword Brothers, and he could not move his arms. He tried to turn his head, to no avail, but from his vision slits he saw that Hans was still beside him.

'Keep breathing, Hans,' he shouted at his friend. Hans did not move. Pray God he still lived.

The quick-thinking leather face located in the tower closest to the siege tower saved the day. He and his men shot their bolts at the Oeselians filing into the tower, loosing quarrels at a rate of four a minute, the iron heads going straight through wooden shields. Soon there was a great heap of Oeselian dead to the immediate rear of the tower, making it difficult for reinforcements to join their comrades on the battlements. The crossbowmen were shooting forty bolts a minute, the great majority of which hit flesh and bone. Not even the feared sea pirates of the Baltic could withstand such a deluge and soon they were streaming back to camp, leaving their comrades still fighting in the fort to their fate.

When the last Oeselians had been cut down and thrown from the battlements Conrad pulled off his helmet and sank to his knees, shoving the dead enemy warrior away. He gulped in the icy air to fill his lungs. He raised a hand to Hans who had likewise removed his headgear and looked deathly pale. Anton slapped him on the back.

'Still in one piece?'

640

He was so exhausted and short of breath that he could not answer, managing only a forced smile as Anton hauled him to his feet and Johann pulled Hans up. Conrad wiped his sword on his cloak and slid it back into its scabbard as feeling slowly returned to his arms and hands. Hans was leaning against the top of the wall, shaking his head.

'I thought we would be crushed to death. Another few minutes and I would have passed out.'

'Look lively!'

Conrad groaned as he heard Henke's voice and saw the brother knight picking up dead Oeselians and throwing them off the walkway out of the fort.

'Get this path cleared before they come again,' he barked.

Anton and Johann stepped forward and began tossing dead men from the battlements, assisted by a number of sergeants, as Conrad and Hans, still weak, watched.

But the enemy did not attack again that day. It began snowing as the dusk came, the wind producing swirling patterns of snowflakes in the dim light. The men on the battlements wrapped their cloaks around them as the temperature dropped and they stamped their feet and rubbed their hands to keep warm. Braziers were brought to the battlements and towers to warm the garrison. Henke suggested setting alight the siege tower that the Oeselians had used to enter the fort but Kalju was worried that to do so would cause the timber wall to catch fire, which Thaddeus thought unlikely. So that night Rudolf, Henke and a dozen sergeants went across the ramp and smashed the ladders and floorboards inside the tower. Finally they cut away the ramp itself and hauled it into the fort for firewood.

The fort had been assaulted by six siege towers in total, all of them now lying still beyond the walls. Three had been struck several times by barrels of burning pitch before they had reached the walls and had been abandoned. One had managed to reach the western wall where the Sword Brothers had managed to repel the attackers at minimum cost, though the two assaulting the eastern wall had managed to escape Master Thaddeus' mangonels to reach the ramparts. Fierce fighting had ensued as Sir Richard and Kalju fought desperately with their men to prevent the battlements being taken. Once more crossbowmen in the flanking towers had proved decisive and the Russians had been destroyed, but not before Kalju had lost fifty men and Sir Richard thirty knights and fifteen squires in the fighting. Fortunately Wenden had lost none of its brother knights.

That night, as a light snowfall covered the dozens of bodies in and around the moat and behind the siege towers, the Ungannian women brought those freezing on the battlements food. Eha cooked porridge over a brazier and handed it out to Conrad and his fellow brother knights and the sergeants.

'How are the children?' he asked as she filled his bowl with another ladle of thick porridge.

'Frightened,' she said, trying to smile, her eyes full of concern.

'The enemy threw their entire strength at us today,' he replied. 'They will need time to recover. Do not fear.'

'For myself I have no fear,' she said defiantly, 'but I could weep for the young mothers who may not see their babies take their first steps.'

'Is there any more?' said Hans, holding out his empty bowl.

Eha looked guilty. 'We have to ration the food, Master Thaddeus' orders.'

Hans looked at his empty bowl.

'Here,' said Conrad, handing him his, 'can't have you starving to death.'

Hans' eyes lit up. 'Your reward will be in heaven, my friend.'

'That's his third bowl,' said Anton. 'I think we should send Hans to raid the enemy's food supplies. He could eat them all up by himself.'

No one said anything more about food supplies, though the hundreds of men, women and children crammed into the fort would be consuming them at an alarming rate, especially as the freezing conditions increased the pangs of hunger.

After evening prayers Conrad returned to his place on the wall. He placed his blanket on the boards and wrapped himself in his cloak and attempted to sleep while Hans stood guard. It was still snowing lightly and the wind was still blowing from the east, an icy blast that made the eyes water. He was tired, though, and when he closed his eyes he instantly fell asleep. He slept for four hours, though when Anton's foot nudged him awake it seemed like he had been in slumber for a matter of seconds. He rose slowly, his neck aching from the cold. He immediately felt the cold blast of the wind on his face as he slowly rose to his feet.

'The wind's picked up.'

Anton, a thick fur-lined cap on his head, nodded. 'At least it's stopped snowing.'

It was two hours before dawn when Conrad began his watch. He tied the flaps of his own cap under his chin and began pacing up and down to try to keep warm, clutching his cloak around him. The walkway was filled with sleeping brother knights and sergeants, with others standing guard like him. After twenty minutes or so he felt snowflakes striking his face as the wind increased, rattling the shingle roofs of the watchtowers. The air suddenly filled with thick flakes as the wind began howling and he could see no more than ten paces in front of him. He put his chin to his chest and his back to the wind to avoid getting frostbite, for prolonged exposure of the skin in such conditions could lead to the loss of a nose. Fortunately he still wore his mail mittens and Rudolf had ordered that everyone wear a pair of felt boots to prevent their toes freezing. But he was still cold.

The time passed slowly. He stamped his feet, moved his arms around to maintain his circulation and squinted as he peered ahead into the whiteout beyond the fort. Nothing. Snowflakes went into his beard and eyes and he considered putting on his helmet when he spotted something out of the corner of his eye: movement on top of the wall. He rubbed his eyes. He was still tired and the blizzard made it almost impossible to see anything. He stared at the top of the seasoned timber, his eyes trying to focus as a multitude of snowflakes swirled in front of him. He could see the ends of two poles sticking up. How odd. Then his feelings of cold disappeared as his stomach churned in horror. A scaling ladder!

He gripped the handle of his sword and tried to pull it as he stepped forward. The sword was frozen solid in its scabbard!

'Get up!' he shouted at the figures of his three friends huddled in their capes against the wall. 'We are under attack! Get up!'

He kicked at the figures before taking his axe from his belt and peering over the wall where the scaling ladder was resting. He held up his shield to ward off the snow flurries and saw the top of a helmet, then a bearded face staring up at him. Then he split the man's skull with his axe. There was a scream and the enemy fell off the ladder into the snow-filled blackness. Another figure appeared, thrusting a spear up at him as he clutched a rung with his left hand. The point narrowly missed Conrad's face as he pulled back to avoid the blow, just as Hans and Johann pushed the top of the ladder away from the wall to send it collapsing to the ground.

Using the cover of the blizzard the enemy had mounted an audacious assault on the fort, on every side placing scaling ladders against the walls to capture Odenpah. The Oeselians walked across the frozen lake to scale the previously unmolested northern ramparts, as the Estonians once again threw themselves against the western wall and the Russians stepped over their own dead to try to storm the southern and eastern ramparts. There was renewed fighting all along the fort's outer wall, though the conditions that had allowed the attackers to approach the fort undetected also worked against them. Several parties of Oeselians got lost in the blizzard during their trek across the frozen lake and never reached the fort, twenty men freezing to death as they wandered around on the ice and never left the lake. Hundreds of *Voi* waited at the bottom of ladders as their comrades battled on the ramparts above, many, weakened from inadequate rations and deficient clothing, collapsing from exposure before they even climbed the ladders.

A wolf shield speared a sergeant who collapsed to the floor and then toppled from the walkway. Conrad swung his axe and smashed the man's jawbone, jumping forward to barge his shield into the legs of another of Lembit's warriors standing on the top of the parapet. The blow toppled him backwards over the wall and to his death as Conrad waited for the next wolf shield to appear, who was promptly skewered by Henke's spear. Conrad nodded to him and they both grabbed the top of the ladder and pushed it away from the wall.

Conrad turned to the man with the bloody jaw and began raining axe blows on the back of his neck – one, two, six, a dozen. He severed it from the torso and kicked it into the fort below. He saw the insignia on the shield, spat on it and tossed it over the battlements.

The fighting was over now, brother knights and sergeants standing resting on their shields and talking to each other. The wind had dropped markedly though it was still snowing heavily. The dawn broke cold and overcast, the dark grey clouds overhead ready to unload yet more snow on the earth. Visibility was once again reduced as the snow fell uninterrupted and once more men stood to arms on the battlements.

'For Lembit to send his best warriors against us can mean only one thing,' Rudolf said to Conrad as they stood looking out into the snowfall. 'His losses must be high.'

He looked round at the exhausted figures in their ripped surcoats and torn mail. 'Though he is not alone in suffering casualties.'

That morning a council of war was held in Kalju's hall. Conrad was ordered to attend and he noticed that the men who sat round the table in the smoky room all looked drained and listless. Sir Richard had thick stubble on his dirty cheeks, Rudolf had black rings round his eyes, Bertram had a hacking cough and Mathias a heavily bandaged left arm. For the first time since he had arrived at Odenpah, Thaddeus looked uncertain. Conrad acted as his translator as he listed the dire state of the fort's food supplies, which would last no more than two weeks.

'After that.' He spread his hands to indicate he knew not what would happen.

Kalju said that he would order the slaughter of the pigs, goats and ponies.

'I have already taken that into account, sir,' said Thaddeus.

'What about arrows and bolts?' asked Rudolf.

'We are down to twenty bolts for each crossbowman,' reported Thaddeus.

'That few?' said a startled Mathias.

'Repelling the siege towers expended a great deal of ammunition,' replied Thaddeus flatly. He looked at Kalju.

'Those of my archers still alive are in a worse condition.'

'We have enough men and ammunition to defeat one more enemy assault, then,' said Sir Richard.

No one spoke for a few seconds. Conrad looked around at the women, children and elderly who filled the hall: tired expressions, the look of fear in their eyes, like caged animals that know there is no escape.

Kalju looked at the Christians. 'I know that you came here because I asked you to, but I cannot ask you to stay and die if there is no hope. This is our home but it is not yours.'

Bertram looked kindly at him. 'You appealed for help, lord, and the Sword Brothers answered that call. We will not abandon an ally in his hour of need.'

'I've never run away from a fight in my life,' announced Sir Richard, 'and I don't intend to start now.'

Kalju's hard face cracked a smile. 'I thank you all. Let us get some rest before the next enemy attack.'

*****

'There will be no more attacks,' sniffed Domash as he sat huddled in his tent, drinking warmed ale, 'or at least no more Russian attacks.'

He cast Sigurd, Jaak and Lembit glances. 'You three may go your own way. I have lost too many men.'

'That is because you have more men to lose,' said Sigurd. 'One more assault and the fort will fall.'

Domash laughed. 'One more attack and I will have lost half my men.'

'We have all lost men,' said Lembit.

'We will starve them out,' hissed Domash. 'Not even the Sword Brothers can live without food.'

Sigurd stood. 'A long siege is not in Oeselian interests.' He looked at Lembit. 'I was led to believe that the fort would fall easily but instead I have lost a tenth of

645

the men I brought here and stand to lose many more waiting for Odenpah to surrender. In the morning I will be marching back to Oesel. I would suggest, Lord Lembit, that you accompany me.'

'Leave tonight,' sneered Domash. 'At least the garrison will not see you skulking away.'

Sigurd curled his lip at Domash and nodded to Lembit before exiting the tent. Lembit looked decidedly uncomfortable.

'That was unfortunate.'

Domash refilled his cup. 'We do not need him or his pirates. Kalju is not going anywhere and neither are the Sword Brothers. We will let hunger do our work for us.'

What he did not tell Lembit was that he had lost two thousand men killed and the tents of his army held another thousand wounded and sick. His *panje* ponies were hale but the horses of the *Druzhina* were suffering from respiratory infections caused by lack of fresh grass. They were also eating up the supplies of fodder at an alarming rate. If the fort did not fall within a fortnight he would have to head for home and face the wrath of his prince.

*****

Inside Odenpah they slaughtered the pigs, chickens and goats and cooked their meat, and by doing so they put an end to the supply of eggs and milk to feed the children. The Sword Brothers went on half rations as the inner fort was filled with the anguished cries of hungry babies. Kalju gave the order to kill the Ungannian ponies, which provided only a brief respite, giving what fodder remained to the mounts of the Sword Brothers. Rudolf, Mathias and Bertram believed that they too would have to slaughter their animals, but then word came from a lookout that Christian banners had been spotted to the south.

The masters, Sir Richard and Kalju rushed to the nearest watchtower and there, to the south, was a body of horsemen, the sun glinting off lance heads and helmets. The day was windless, bright and ice cold and visibility was excellent as they squinted in the sunlight to identify the banners that they caught glimpses of. A red cross on a white background perhaps, reds and oranges, horses covered in white and brightly coloured caparisons. They heard the alarm being sounded in the enemy camps and knew that a relief force was heading to their rescue. Mathias and Bertram clasped their hands together and said a silent prayer of thanks.

'Where are the rest of them?' said Sir Richard.

Bertram and Mathias looked at each other and then at Sir Richard.

'There can only be a couple of hundred, if that,' said Sir Richard.

Kalju heard the concern in his voice but did not understand the words but the two Sword Brothers did. They looked at the column of horsemen approaching and saw that it was indeed only a small number. They also saw dozens of Russian horsemen leaving the camp to the east of the fort and knew that there was a real danger of the relief force being destroyed.

They rushed down the steps in the tower and raised the alarm. Word had spread among the garrison that a relief force had been spotted, and Christians and pagans had climbed to the towers and ramparts to see for themselves. But now the Sword Brother masters called for the brother knights and sergeants to saddle their horses.

Rudolf had been late arriving at the tower and he informed Kalju that those inside the fort would have to support the relief force.

'You might also be cut off and destroyed,' Kalju warned him, observing dozens of Russian horsemen in armour riding south to cut off the relief force.

'We cannot stand idly by and watch our brothers be slaughtered,' said Rudolf.

Conrad was glad to be away from the freezing ramparts. He threw the saddle on his horse, buckled the straps and then led his mount from the stables to the assembly point behind the main gates.

He stroked the beast's neck. 'Stroke of luck for you, my friend. Another two days and you would have been killed for food.'

'Talking to your horse, Conrad,' said Hans behind him. 'First sign of madness.'

'The only chance of a sensible conversation, more like.'

Ungannian warriors were frantically moving aside the carts that had been piled up against the gates in case the enemy had used battering rams, also removing the long braces that had been place against them. Master Thaddeus had given instructions that the moat was not to be dug in front of the gates because it would only make exiting the fort inconvenient. Bertram had questioned his wisdom in this, pointing out that the first target of an enemy attack would be the fort's gates. Thaddeus replied curtly that any idiot knew that the main gates of a stronghold were heavily defended, in Odenpah's case with towers on either side, and so an attacker would generally avoid an initial assault against the gates. He had proved right, though Bertram had not forgiven him his insolence.

It was Bertram who addressed the horsemen as they sat on their horses waiting to ride out to link up with the relief force. The ramparts and towers were full of soldiers and warriors, the walkway of the inner stronghold thronged with women and children, all looking down on the knights, sergeants and squires. There were just over twenty brother knights and fifty sergeants of the order, the rest being either dead or wounded. Sir Richard had entered Odenpah at the head of fifty knights and the same number of squires. Now he commanded thirty knights and twenty-five squires. Not all had been killed: several were lying in the huts in the inner compound suffering from frostbite.

It was a minor miracle that Wenden had suffered no deaths among its brother knights, who now sat in a line before Bertram, helmets in the crook of their arms as the master spoke the words.

'Holy Michael, the Archangel, defend us in battle. Be our safeguard against the wickedness and snares of the devil. May God rebuke him, we humbly pray; Prince of the heavenly host, by the power of God cast into hell Satan and all the evil spirits who wander through the world seeking the ruin of souls. Let our lances be your holy weapons that scatter your enemies like dust to the wind. Amen.'

The horsemen replied 'Amen' as Bertram raised his lance.

'God with us!'

The assembly shouted 'God with us!', placed their helmets on their heads and the gates were opened. The spectators cheered, Eha catching Conrad's eye and smiling at him as he put on his headgear.

The mail-clad horses and horsemen trotted out into the snow, avoiding the bodies of dead Russians heaped in front of the gatehouse, bolts and arrows lodged in their frozen flesh. The sounds of battle filled the air, ahead Russian horsemen attacking the relief force as it desperately battled to reach the fort.

Once they had trotted a hundred paces from the fort a halt was called and the horsemen deployed into two lines: the knights and brother knights in the front rank, the sergeants and squires behind them. The brother knights from Wenden rode on the right flank, those of Segewold on their left and the men from Kremon next in line; Sir Richard's knights formed the left flank – fifty-five knights with a similar number of sergeants and squires behind.

Bertram spurred his horse forward and the two lines followed. Conrad glanced right at Hans and left at Anton and couched his lance. He peered through his vision slits at a swirling mass of horsemen wearing brightly coloured cloaks – Russians.

The horses moved slowly through the snow, breath at their nostrils misting in the freezing conditions. They broke into a canter as they closed the distance between them and the enemy to around three hundred paces. Conrad gripped his lance and felt his heart racing as he spotted an enemy horseman directly ahead locked in a duel with a knight in a red surcoat, their swords flashing in the sunlight. Forget everything else, concentrate on the target. He felt the power of the horse beneath him as it cantered forward. His eyes never left the target as the Russian swung his sword and knocked the shield out of the knight's hand at the moment Conrad drove the point of his lance into his side.

He let go of the shaft, took hold of his axe and swung it to the right, into the face of another Russian as he rode into the mêlée. There was a loud grating noise as the line of horsemen struck the Russians, unhorsing at least a score in the initial impact and then more than that as they cut into the soldiers of Pskov. But there were many of the latter and they began swarming around the Christian knights, the sergeants and squires turning their horses to battle enemy horsemen.

Conrad was between two Russians, both in full-face helmets and both trying to cut him down with their swords. He pulled his horse back to avoid the blows, deflecting some with his shield and others with his axe. He saw the banner of the Sword Brothers behind the Russians and then in front of him as the head of the relief force battled its way forward. Hans appeared at his side and ran through one of the Russians with his sword as the relief force continued to advance. As it did so the men who had ridden from the fort guarded its flanks, moving left and right in an attempt to fend off the swarms of Russian horsemen. Sir Richard moved to the left and the Sword Brothers to the right to create a gap through which the relief force could escape to the fort.

Trumpets sounded the retreat as the relief force galloped towards the gates, some horses tripping and falling in the snow, throwing their riders. The animals got up and ran off, leaving their riders stranded. Bertram and Mathias removed their helmets and shouted orders for the stragglers to be picked up, for now groups of Russian foot soldiers were marching towards the battle, and from the north came Lembit's Estonians. The immediate danger was Russian horsemen, though, who were reorganising themselves after the shock of the attack from the fort.

The horsemen that had ridden from Odenpah once more formed line as they faced the Russians, the latter now numbering several hundred despite the casualties they had suffered. Christian numbers, by contrast, had been further depleted. Sir Richard had been wounded in the right arm and it now hung limply by his side as squire Paul grabbed his reins and led him back to the fort, the knight shouting obscenities at him as he did so. It might not have adhered to the knightly code but it made sense: there was no point in his master dying unnecessarily.

Bertram and Mathias, their surcoats torn and their shields battered, gave the order to fall back to the fort once the relief force had reached safety. As the tired men and horses wheeled around and trotted back, the Russians charged. In the front rank were the *Druzhina*, encased in mail and lamellar armour, behind them the horsemen of Pskov's militia. This time the knights spurred their horses into the gallop, knowing that if the Russians caught them they would be slaughtered. Conrad saw the open gates of the fort and the last of the relief force disappearing inside. Then he could have cried with joy as warriors poured out of the gates to form a shield wall.

Kalju had seen his allies ride from Odenpah and engage the Russians, link up with the relief force and then cover the retreat of the latter. He now led his men out of the gates to form a wall of shields and spears to save the Christians.

He stood, sword in hand, in the front rank as his men stood shoulder-to-shoulder with their spears levelled.

'Let them through,' he shouted as the Christian horsemen thundered towards his men.

The warriors, who had formed a great semi-circle in front of the gates, ran left and right to create a gap through which the horsemen could pass. They brought their horses to a halt inside the fort as Kalju's men reformed to meet the Russians. The latter had failed to reach the Christians, their horses rearing up as they faced a row of locked shields and spear points. A few riders stabbed their lances at the Ungannians and leaned forward in their saddles to hack at them with their swords. But Domash ordered his élite soldiers to withdraw, trumpet blasts calling them back as a phalanx of Pskov's foot soldiers marched forward to get to grips with Kalju's warriors.

The latter were now trapped and outnumbered outside the fort as five hundred militiamen advanced in ordered ranks towards the Ungannians. Domash sat on his horse urging them on. He saw the open gates and knew that even if they were closed his men would destroy a large part of Kalju's garrison. He had caught sight of the chief's golden eagle standard and knew Kalju himself stood with his men. For over two weeks he had seen hundreds of his men die trying to take this miserable fort but now he stood on the brink of victory.

'On, on!' he shouted as the militia's trumpets sounded the charge.

And on the battlements above the fort's gates and from the towers on either side over a hundred crossbowmen stood up and began shooting at the Russians below.

The hail of bolts stopped the militiamen in their tracks, two hundred quarrels in the space of half a minute felling at least a hundred men in the front ranks. The next four volleys killed or wounded a further three hundred men in sixty seconds, throwing the Pskovians into chaos. They had expected an easy victory against the hairy, stinking pagans but instead were being shot to pieces by crusader crossbowmen. Their ranks faltered, halted and then disintegrated as death rained down upon them.

The Ungannians gave a mighty cheer and wanted to charge after them but Kalju kept them under iron control and ordered them back into the fort. He raised his sword to Master Thaddeus standing on the battlements above, the man who had organised the crossbowmen.

The gates were closed, the Ungannians cheered and whooped in triumph as the womenfolk led by Eha came from the inner stronghold to tend to the wounded, of which there were a great many.

The crossbowmen filed back to their positions as Conrad slid from his horse and took off his helmet. He immediately looked for his friends. He saw Hans and Anton, then Johann whose shield was hanging in two pieces from his arm. They embraced each other and grinned sheepishly at having survived another battle unscathed. Conrad saw leather face.

'Excellent shooting.'

'Don't look too pleased with yourselves,' he retorted, 'that little bit of sport used up the last of our ammunition.'

'Don't worry,' said Hans, 'Master Thaddeus stockpiled bolts in the inner stronghold.'

Leather face smiled. 'I know, we just used them all up.'

The four knights looked at each other and then at the wounded being helped from their horses. Other men took off their helmets and slid from their saddles, barely able to stand so weakened were they. The horses of the garrison and relief force were also exhausted. With no crossbow bolts, arrows or ammunition for the mangonels the enemy was now free to approach the walls unmolested.

Grand Master Volquin, who was wintering at Kremon when word reached the castle from Berthold that Odenpah was besieged, had led a scratch contingent of all the brother knights, sergeants, crusaders and anyone else he could collect. Caupo had given him fifty of his best warriors, most of whom had been killed outside Odenpah fighting the Russian horsemen. He had also brought all the novices from Wenden, Segewold and Kremon, half of whom had also fallen during the fighting. In addition, Bishop Theodoric had accompanied him, stating that Estonia was his domain and he should support those fighting to preserve it from the heathens. Less than two hundred men had made it into the fort and half of those were wounded. There had been no time to muster soldiers from those garrisons along the Dvina or at Riga and so Volquin had gambled that the appearance of a relief force, albeit a weak one, would be enough to break the siege. It was a gamble he lost.

Rudolf had embraced Master Berthold after the fort's gates had been closed and the master had collapsed into his arms, his stomach ripped open by a Russian lance. He was taken to Kalju's hall but lapsed into unconsciousness soon after and died later that night. For the men of Wenden it was a devastating blow. Berthold had been appointed castellan when the hill fort had fallen to the Sword Brothers eight years before. Conrad had been right. God had exacted a price for Wenden's taking of slaves, claiming the life of the man who had authorised it. As the news spread of his death among those sheltering behind Odenpah's walls a pall of gloom hung over the fort.

Otto said prayers over the body of Berthold as the Sword Brother grand master and masters, Theodoric, Master Thaddeus, Sir Richard, Kalju and his chiefs gathered in a cramped stone hut near his hall. The latter was filled not only with the elderly, women and children but also the wounded of the relief force, Eha and other women tending their wounds as Otto went among them to administer absolution. Thaddeus had searched out Conrad and once again asked him to be his translator.

There was a bench and a single bed in the hut, two candles providing a dim light to illuminate weary, filthy faces. Kalju ordered more stools to be brought so everyone could be seated.

'Apologies for the cramped conditions, bishop,' said Volquin.

'Our lord was born in a stable, grand master,' replied Theodoric, 'so what was suitable for Him is more than adequate for me.'

'We might be living in something far worse, or not living at all, if our predicament is not sorted,' complained Thaddeus, squashing a mite in his beard.

Theodoric frowned at the old man.

'This is Master Thaddeus, lord bishop,' said Rudolf hurriedly, 'Wenden's chief engineer and the man who has thus far masterminded the defence of Odenpah.'

Kalju looked at Rudolf and pointed at the stern-looking figure in the surcoat that bore the insignia of Riga.

'This man is your commander?'

Rudolf explained that he was a holy man, a bishop, and equivalent in rank to the Bishop of Riga himself.

'And yet he brings few warriors with him,' remarked the chief.

'Well, Master Thaddeus,' said Theodoric. 'How would you extract us from the predicament we find ourselves in?'

'A larger relief force would have helped,' replied Thaddeus without a hint of irony. Kalju laughed and slapped him on the back.

'However,' continued the engineer, 'we must work with what we have, which is not much. That said, the enemy has lost hundreds of dead and probably many more wounded during their abortive attacks and they too must be in a weakened state.'

'That does not help us,' remarked Volquin glumly.

'It might,' said Thaddeus. 'They do not know that we have no ammunition left and that our food supplies are dangerously low.'

'So?' said Bertram.

'So, Master Bertram,' answered Thaddeus, 'we request a parley and bargain with the enemy.'

'Out of the question,' said Kalju. 'I will not bend my knee to the invaders of my kingdom.'

Thaddeus waved a hand at Conrad. 'Translate for me, young Conrad.

'My lord, what would you say if I told you that we can persuade the enemy to leave your kingdom?'

'I would say that you are a miracle worker, Master Thaddeus,' replied Kalju, 'and if you made such a thing happen I would give you a young virgin girl to warm your bed, two if you so desired.'

Theodoric looked most uncomfortable when Conrad translated what Kalju had spoken, while Thaddeus smiled politely and Rudolf laughed.

'It is simple, lord,' said Thaddeus, slightly distracted by the prospect of a young woman to fill his lonely bed, 'give the enemy something he wants.'

'He wants Odenpah,' said Volquin in irritation.

'Then offer him something more,' replied Thaddeus.

Mathias scratched his lice-filled beard. 'What?'

Thaddeus shook his head. 'My lords, I am just an engineer not a diplomat. There must be something you can offer to tempt the enemy, especially one that has been mightily mauled before the walls of this fort.'

Theodoric clasped his hands together, making everyone jump. He offered his hand to Thaddeus.

'The Lord himself must have decided to bring you here, Master Thaddeus, for truly your words are full of wisdom. You are right, we will offer something that the enemy desires.'

Rudolf translated the bishop's words to Kalju, who remained sceptical.

'I will not yield this fort or any of my kingdom,' he growled.

The bishop smiled at him. 'I swear by Almighty God, lord, that Ungannia will remain free and undiminished.'

'A parley it is, then,' said Volquin.

They all stood and filed out of the hut. Thaddeus got Conrad to ask Kalju if he had been serious about the offer of the virgins.

The chief smiled. 'You can select them yourself, my friend.'

Kalju looked at Conrad. 'What about him?'

Conrad, mortified, translated the chief's words.

'Oh, no, lord. He has taken a vow of chastity. He is not allowed carnal relations with women, or men for that matter,' replied Thaddeus.

Kalju looked horrified. 'Never?'

Thaddeus nodded. 'I'm afraid so.'

'You are happy with this?' Kalju asked Conrad.

'Yes, lord.'

'Than you are a better man than I am.'

*****

'Another two hundred have deserted.'

Domash looked to see Yaroslav standing in his tent's entrance. Mstislav had sent his son-in-law to keep an eye on the mayor of Pskov and at first he had resented his presence. But Yaroslav had shown himself an excellent officer and, more importantly, had not questioned his orders. For the last five days increasing numbers of the *Voi* had absconded during the night, deciding that only a slow death in the snow or a quick death at the hands of the Sword Brothers awaited them at Odenpah.

Domash waved Yaroslav in and pointed to a chair opposite.

'Do you wish me to organise parties of horsemen to hunt them down?'

Domash closed his eyes and sighed. 'Send out a small mounted party. We must maintain the appearance of discipline.'

'The army is demoralised,' said Gleb. 'I have been among the *Voi* and they say that the appearance of the Sword Brothers was an ill-omen that you ignored.'

'Do they,' snapped Domash. 'And what would you suggest, Gleb? Crawl back to Pskov with our tails between our legs?'

Yaroslav looked at Gleb but said nothing. He had found the blue-shirted mystic amusing and irritating in equal measure, but he knew the power and influence he held over the simple-minded villagers who made up the bulk of the *Voi*. And even among the militia of Pskov he held great sway.

'Meet with the leaders of the crusaders,' said Gleb, 'tell them that you will retreat if the Sword Brothers do the same. Our strength diminishes by the day. What if the crusaders send another relief force, what then?'

'He speaks sense, lord,' said Yaroslav.

Domash smiled wanly. 'The prince would take a dim view of losing so many men for nothing.'

'He would take a dimmer view of knowing that the Sword Brothers have taken control of Ungannia,' replied Yaroslav, 'for it would mean that the crusaders are on his border.'

They heard a horse coming to a halt outside the tent, then voices and the tent flap opened and a guard entered. He stood in front of Domash and saluted.

'A horseman from Odenpah, highness, rode from the fort and spoke with our guards under a flag of truce. The garrison commanders wish to speak with you. The horseman waits at our siege lines for your response.'

'It would appear that the crusaders wish to bring hostilities to an end too,' observed Gleb. 'Now the question is, which side is the most eager to be away from this dreadful place?'

'Will you agree to talk with them, lord?' asked Yaroslav.

'I have little option,' replied Domash. He looked at the guard. 'Tell the messenger from the fort that I will meet his commanders tomorrow, at noon, halfway between our lines and their gates.'

The guard saluted and exited the tent.

Domash groaned and rose to his feet. 'Now I shall inform our Estonian allies of my decision, and no doubt feel their wrath for doing so.'

'Do you wish me to come with you, lord?' offered Yaroslav.

'No need. Organise that hunt for the deserters. We will hang a few as an example.'

'It would be better to hang a few Estonians,' remarked Gleb. 'I think you will find that once friend Lembit learns of your plans to negotiate with the enemy he will skulk back to his homeland, like a child who does not want to play any longer.'

'War breeds strange allies,' observed Yaroslav.

'And even stranger enemies,' said Gleb.

Gleb was right about Lembit, though far from flying into a rage the Estonian leader merely shrugged and told Domash that he must do what he had to. It was of no consequence to him, though he would take no part in the negotiations with the Christians, stating that they would probably try to kidnap him and take him back to Riga. The narrow face of Jaak, who sat with Lembit in his tent, had become more gaunt and his eyes were full of resentment when he could bring himself to look at the Russian leader. No wonder he was bitter: half his men were dead in the snow in front of Odenpah.

Domash asked that the Estonians array their men before the western ramparts of the fort the next day to impress the garrison, while his Russians would be drawn up to the east and south of the fort. He felt sure that the crusaders wished to surrender and seek passage from the fort. Lembit scoffed at such a notion and told Domash that he would be taking what was left of his men back to Saccalia. Jaak muttered that he would also be returning to his homeland. Domash pleaded with them to stay but to no avail. He therefore asked them to depart that night so that the garrison would not notice their absence. He rode back to camp hoping that he would never again have to fight by the side of Estonians.

*****

It snowed that night as hundreds of Estonian warriors dismantled their tents and trudged disconsolately west towards Saccalia and Jerwen. Three thousand had marched full of confidence to Odenpah; less then fifteen hundred made the return journey. When the dawn came it had stopped snowing and a bitter easterly breeze blew away the clouds to bathe the white land in brilliant sunshine. The heaps of dead around the fort were covered in snow and hidden from view as the gates were opened and the delegation rode out to meet with the enemy.

Since dawn riders had been sent to and from the fort to work out the details of the size and composition of both delegations to the parley. Eventually it was agreed that each side would comprise ten individuals. From the fort rode Bishop

Theodoric, resplendent in mail armour and red surcoat emblazoned with golden keys, Grand Master Volquin, Kalju in mail armour, helmet and green cloak, Sir Richard, two brother knights of the Sword Brothers and three of Kalju's most senior officers. The last of the party was Conrad, who attended as translator. At the last moment the bishop and grand master realised that they had no knowledge of the Russian tongue. They sent a courier to the Russian lines to ascertain whether Domash or one of his officers spoke Estonian, to which the reply was yes. Rudolf offered to be the translator but Volquin reminded him that he was now master of Wenden and as such it was unbecoming for one of the order's castellans to serve as a translator. So it was that Conrad was selected to be the official translator in the first negotiations between the Sword Brothers and the Principality of Novgorod.

As the intention was to talk rather than fight neither party carried lances as a sign of goodwill. Conrad rode beside the bishop in his armour and helm, sword at his hip and axe dangling from his saddle, just in case. The Russians then appeared from behind the line of wagons that had been placed around the fort following the arrival of the relief force. They looked magnificent in their gleaming lamellar armour, red cloaks and gilded helmets. Three figures rode at the head of the group, two wearing the uniforms of rich Russian boyars, the third in boots, brown leggings, fur-lined jacket and cap and ragged cloak. He was clearly neither a soldier nor a noble.

The Russians halted some twenty paces from the bishop, who wore his mitre on his head and a gold cross around his neck. He carried no weapons but sat tall in the saddle and his rich attire marked him out as a figure of authority. The Russian in the centre of the group took off his helmet. He had a handsome face, though it was etched with worry and fatigue.

'I am Domash Tverdislavich, mayor of Pskov and commander of the army before Odenpah,' he said in Estonian.

'Take off your helmet, Conrad,' said the bishop, 'so that we may hear your words.'

Conrad did so and announced the Russian's name and position to his party.

'I am Theodoric, Bishop of Estonia,' he held out a hand to the others beside him.

'This is Grand Master Volquin, commander of the Sword Brothers, Sir Richard Bruffingham, an English knight who leads the crusaders that have come to Odenpah, and Chief Kalju, Lord of all Ungannia, the land you currently trespass upon.'

That pleased Kalju because he smiled triumphantly at Domash.

'These are my senior officers,' said the governor of Pskov curtly. 'You requested this meeting, bishop, so I await your words.'

The bishop smiled politely. 'Not my words, governor, but the words of the prince of this land.'

He smiled again, this time at Kalju.

'It is quite simple,' said the chief, 'I demand that you leave my kingdom immediately.'

Domash tried hard not to laugh in the chief's face but before he could answer the bishop spoke.

'To do so would profit Novgorod enormously.'

Domash was suspicious of this priest who was head of a fictitious bishopric. That said, his army was severely depleted and his allies had deserted him. He could not afford to mount another assault against the fort for fear it would result in the destruction of his army. But if he continued with the siege he risked further desertions as his men rotted in the snow.

'How so?'

'Ungannia is an ally of Livonia,' replied the bishop. 'That being the case, Novgorod's goods can, with Lord Kalju's permission, be transported through his kingdom and then by boat down the Gauja, a river now controlled by the Sword Brothers.'

'The goods of Novgorod travel along the Dvina,' said Domash dismissively.

The bishop turned to Conrad. 'Make sure you translate the next bit accurately. It is very important.'

'Yes, lord bishop.'

'The Dvina is also controlled by the Sword Brothers,' continued the bishop. 'If you do not withdraw from Ungannia the Sword Brothers will deny the use of both rivers to the merchants of Novgorod. It is your choice, mayor. Take advantage of the hand of friendship offered to you by the Sword Brothers or see the trade of Novgorod, and Pskov, suffer.'

'The coffers of Riga would also suffer,' retorted Domash.

The bishop brought his hands together. 'Riga is God's town, mayor, established in His name. It is a holy place not a pit of money lenders.'

Domash regarded the bishop for a moment. Was he pretending or making promises he could not keep? The fur trade with Riga alone was worth a fortune and had made Novgorod rich. If that trade was interrupted or halted then Mstislav's wrath would be mighty indeed. But the prince wanted Odenpah. But at the expense of risking trade with Riga?

'I will need a few moments with my officers,' said Domash.

'Of course,' replied the bishop.

The Russians retreated out of earshot. The bishop and Kalju had hatched their plan after Thaddeus had planted the seed of the idea in Theodoric's mind. Kalju had agreed that he would allow Russian merchants to travel through his kingdom unmolested, in return for which the Novgorodians would agree to respect Ungannia's borders, which meant no further raids. Ungannia would become an ally of Livonia, though the bishop avoided any discussion of Kalju marching against Lembit and the other Estonian chiefs when Bishop Albert returned from Germany in the spring. Of course the whole plan would disintegrate if the Russians rejected the proposal, attacked the fort and put all those inside to the sword. But if they were martyred, the bishop told Kalju, the Sword Brothers would halt all Russian trade along the Dvina and Gauja and wage unceasing war upon Novgorod. It was a daring plan, especially as the crossbowmen and archers had no more ammunition and there was only two days' food left in the fort.

After explaining what the bishop was proposing Domash asked Yaroslav and Gleb for their opinions.

'Can we trust them?' asked Yaroslav.

'The bishop is a man of God,' said Domash.

'I wouldn't put much stock in that,' sneered Gleb.

'The prince would not wish for Novgorod's trade with the Catholics to be endangered,' said Yaroslav, 'not for the sake of a hill fort.'

Domash nodded. 'I am apt to agree with you. But we cannot retreat without the enemy making concessions also.'

'What concessions?' enquired Gleb.

Domash tapped his nose. 'Let's see if this bishop has the courage of his convictions.'

They returned to face the bishop, everyone in both parties pulling their cloaks about them as the wind picked up to increase the chill.

'We will retreat from Ungannia,' stated Domash, 'on condition that the Sword Brothers also leave the kingdom.'

Conrad translated the words and a look of triumph spread across the bishop's face. Kalju sat expressionless and Volquin looked relieved.

'In addition,' continued Domash, looking at Theodoric, 'you will accompany me back to Novgorod where you can pledge the agreement regarding the passage of trade through Ungannia and along the Gauja to Prince Mstislav himself.'

'Impossible,' spat Sir Richard, 'tell this barbarian that we will fight him today, on this ground, rather than meekly submit to his outrageous demands.'

Domash did not understand the words but he fathomed the raised voice and thunderous look from the mailed knight by the side of Kalju. Domash tilted his head towards Sir Richard.

'What did he say?' he asked Conrad.

'Sir Richard believes that if the bishop goes with you his life will be in danger.'

Domash looked hurt. He looked directly at the bishop. 'We are not barbarians. You will be treated as an honoured guest and not as a condemned criminal. This I pledge as a member of the Tverdislavich family.'

Volquin looked most alarmed. 'I would advise against such a course of action, lord bishop.'

'And if I accede to your demands,' Theodoric said to Domash, 'you and your army will leave Ungannia?'

'I give you my word,' stated Domash.

'I believe that this is one of those moments in life that requires a leap of faith,' said the bishop calmly. 'Conrad, inform the mayor that I will travel with him to Novgorod to arrange terms with his prince.'

Sir Richard was vehemently against the notion but his warnings were brushed away by the bishop. Theodoric knew that he ventured into the unknown but also knew that he had saved hundreds of souls inside Odenpah, and that alone was worth the sacrifice of his life if the Lord so decreed.

'My life is in God's hands,' he told Sir Richard, 'where it has always been.'

The formalities over, the two parties left each other. On the ride back to camp Domash breathed a huge sigh of relief. He had snatched a victory of sorts from the jaws of defeat and could return to Novgorod with the promise of a new trade route to the west.

Sir Richard was still grumbling when the bishop's party dismounted inside the main gates. Rudolf, Bertram and Mathias were informed of the agreement that had been reached, all surprised and concerned about Theodoric's impending journey. But the bishop waved away their worries. Kalju was all smiles. His great gamble had paid off: he had preserved his kingdom. Better still, his alliance with the Sword Brothers promised to halt Russian incursions into Ungannia.

'I never thought he would do it,' Thaddeus said to Rudolf as they stood watching the bishop trying to calm Sir Richard. He looked up at the battlements crowded with warriors and Christian soldiers, then at the walls of the inner stronghold thronged with women and children. 'No ammunition left, almost no food left, half the garrison either sick, dead or wounded and he convinces the enemy to retreat. Some would say it's a miracle.'

Rudolf smiled. 'Perhaps, Master Thaddeus, perhaps.'

'Well,' said Thaddeus, 'I best start dismantling my machines for the journey back to Wenden.'

He shook hands with Rudolf and ambled off to offer his congratulations to the bishop as a tangible wave of relief swept through the fort.

'Brother Rudolf,' Conrad called as he led his horse back to the stables.

'Conrad?'

'*Master* Rudolf, apologies,' said Conrad.

'I'm still getting used to the title myself. Congratulations, your translation skills have paid dividends, it seems.'

'The commander of the Russian army,' said Conrad, glancing at the new master.

'What of him?' queried Rudolf.

Conrad looked at the burn scars on the older man's neck. 'His name is Domash Tverdislavich. I remember that name being mentioned a while ago.'

Rudolf displayed no emotion. 'So he is still spreading misery and death.'

'He is the mayor of Pskov, so he said.'

'He rises in the world,' said Rudolf.

'As do you,' stated Conrad. 'Perhaps you are both destined to meet again in battle, each leading his own army.'

Rudolf laughed. 'Perhaps you should write poetry instead of wielding a sword.'

'Lembit has gone,' said Conrad glumly.

'Do not worry about that, brother. He owes Livonia a great debt and the Sword Brothers will collect it, that I promise.'

Chapter 24

It took three weeks to get back to Wenden, exhausted draught animals pulling wagons through deep snow and the occasional blizzard. Many collapsed and died, forcing the column to abandon valuable items such as Master Thaddeus' mangonels, though the engineer himself had been persuaded to stay at Odenpah, the weather being considered too harsh for his elderly constitution. At one stage the rate of advance was a mere three miles a day, a consequence of the inclement weather and the need to scour the forests for anything to eat, for the garrison of Odenpah could spare no supplies for the journey.

At the end of the first week Conrad's horse collapsed from under him and died. As it lay in the snow he called to the other brother knights within earshot and began hacking at the beast with his axe, chopping off its limbs and head. Soon others joined him and began slicing off pieces of still-warm flesh, handing it out to individuals who gathered round the carcass. In this way men could fill their bellies and stave off the hunger that had begun plaguing them even before they left Odenpah. Eating raw flesh was an abomination but a necessary one to preserve life.

Pitching tents in snow and ice further taxed the crusaders' strength but was better than no shelter at all and so at the end of every march camp was established and men huddled around fires, over which pots filled with horse blood boiled. Among Sir Richard's command the young squires were the first to succumb to fatigue, aside from squire Paul who was as strong as an ox. The Sword Brothers were fortunate in having Liv ponies to pull the majority of their wagons. These beasts, like the Russian *panjes*, were remarkably hardy and better suited to the climate than horses brought from Germany. But as the horses of the Sword Brothers and crusaders died a constant guard had to be placed around the ponies to prevent them being slaughtered and torn to pieces for food.

The crusaders were fortunate that they were accompanied by the Sword Brothers, whose knowledge of local conditions had resulted in them bringing along large quantities of additional clothing. The brother knights and sergeants wore woollen underwear, woollen leg wraps beneath their leggings and thick leather boots on their feet, over which they wore felt overboots to prevent the leather uppers of their boots from freezing. They retained their helmets but to save weight removed their mail armour and loaded it on the carts. By the end of the second week all of the crusader horses were dead and only the grand master, masters and a few brother knights still had mounts. But no one rode them so weakened were they.

By this time the food had all gone and the carts carried only armour, spare weapons, the order's dead to be buried in consecrated ground and the wounded. The felt capes kept the men of the order warm, their mercenary spearmen and crossbowmen also having been issued with them, but the crossbowmen who had travelled from Germany had no cloaks or caps and they suffered terribly from the cold. Their toes and fingers became blue and blotchy and hard to the touch. Those who could no longer walk rode on the wagons, which became increasingly heavy as more weight was loaded on them.

Grand Master Volquin, his beard frozen solid, ordered that those still capable of walking should assist in pushing the wagons through the snow to save the strength of the ponies. Conrad noticed that Hans shivered constantly. They were all cold, notwithstanding their layers of clothing, but his friend felt the conditions the most. Despite the years of eating like a fighting cock at Wenden he had never lost the lean, hungry look that Conrad remembered when he had first set eyes on him.

His teeth chattered as he sat in the tent vigorously rubbing pig grease into his boots to prevent them becoming brittle.

'Do you think we shall see Wenden again?'

Johann looked at him with bloodshot eyes. 'One of the Liv guards told me that we should be there within a week.'

Hans stopped rubbing. 'A week? I doubt if I can last another day.'

Anton, his face deathly pale, smiled weakly. 'You will make it, Hans. You are stronger than you look, which is just as well seeing as you look like a corpse.'

'Unlike the sick,' said Conrad, who had pins and needles in his face – a sure sign of frostnip. 'Most of them will not survive another day.'

Hans went back to his rubbing. 'Poor bastards. They survive a siege only to die of cold.'

'Master Berthold did not even survive the siege,' remarked Conrad glumly. 'I told you there would be a price to pay for slave trading.'

'At least we all survived,' said Anton.

But in the next few days they thought they might not as they trudged through the snow, heads down against the biting wind, taking short steps but always moving. Volquin, in consultation with the other masters and Sir Richard, had taken the decision to strike for Wenden as quickly as possible rather that travelling short distances each day and spending the rest of the time ice fishing or setting traps to catch game. The crossbowmen had no missiles with which to hunt and in any case many of them had frostnip in their fingers, making it difficult to aim their weapons accurately. The Livs informed the grand master that they could reach Wenden in three days, though the pace would be cruel.

The last of the fodder was given to the ponies and they were covered in caparisons as protection against the freezing wind. The scouts led them through trees covered in snow and in the lee of hillsides to protect the column from the merciless wind. At night they crammed bodies into tents so men could glean what warmth they could from their comrades. But in the morning there were always a few who did not open their eyes, having passed away during the night.

Rudolf barked orders to the men of Wenden, walking among them to encourage them to keep going. One foot after the other, focus on staying alert, don't daydream; a dull mind is your enemy. On the sixteenth day the wind dropped, the sun shone and men began to feel more optimistic. They were still tortured by hunger but at least their cold flesh was no longer being blasted by an icy wind.

Johann developed a limp and had to ride on a cart for long periods, while Hans' hands turned blue despite wearing two pairs of mittens. Conrad's lips became chapped and painful, the pins and needles spread to his hands and the reflection of the sun on the snow hurt his eyes. He still wore his sword and dagger and his axe tucked in his belt but he barely had the strength to buckle it each morning.

On the seventeenth day he had his arm round Hans' shoulder to assist him as they plodded through the snow, each step taking a mighty effort. They helped to push a wagon loaded with sick squires, though how much they assisted was hard to tell. Conrad could not feel his hands as he placed them against the side of the cart and attempted to push it. His eyes were mostly cast down as he pushed for ten minutes or so, then stopped as a trumpet call signalled a halt. The column of ghost-like individuals and exhausted ponies halted for what seemed like seconds, before another trumpet communicated the advance. On they tramped, through a white wilderness of undulating hills, thick forests and frozen waterways. He looked up and saw pairs of listless eyes staring at him from a gap in the canvas cover over the back of the cart.

On the eighteenth day Hans collapsed in the snow.

'Help me,' called Conrad as he struggled to lift his friend.

Hans was a dead weight and he had trouble raising him up. Then Henke and leather face appeared, grabbed one of Hans' arms each and dragged him towards the wagon.

'There is no room in there,' said Conrad.

Leather face, his visage barely visible under the huge fur-lined cap he was wearing, peered into the cart. He examined two of the squires and then pulled them off the cart, their frozen corpses falling into the snow with a dull thud.

'Now there is.'

'Quickly,' said Henke, as he and Conrad lifted Hans onto the wagon.

He looked at Hans' face. 'You'll live.'

Conrad nodded appreciatively at Henke and noticed that even Wenden's most fearsome soldier looking gaunt, his face pinched with cold.

That night another three quires and two knights died. The latter expired on guard duty, their reliefs discovering their frozen bodies in the snow. Like unthinking slaves the brother knights and sergeants attended prayers in the chapel tent before dismantling the ever-smaller camp and continuing the journey. The Livs scoured the forests for berries, sharing their meagre haul with the rest of the column, though it did nothing to dispel the hunger that tortured everyone.

It was the last day of February and Conrad had now lost all feeling in his feet, shuffling forward and leaning against the wagon that held Hans. The later had fallen asleep, though Anton and Johann, the latter using the former as a crutch, kept shouting at him and prodding him to prevent him falling into a slumber that he would not awaken from. The cart was near the front of the column and Conrad could see the stooped shapes of Volquin, Rudolf, Bertram, Sir Richard, taller than them all, and Mathias as they led what was left of their commands.

He put his shoulder to the wagon and attempted to lend his weight to the efforts of Walter, Lukas and Henke on the other side and Anton and Johann behind. The two ponies that were pulling it were almost spent, their heads cast down and their steps heavy and faltering. He looked up and saw the sun glint off something. He squinted and stared once more and saw helmets and lances ahead. He tried to open his mouth and shout but his lips were blistered and painful and his throat sore. But others had seen them now: two brother knights and two sergeants on horses wearing white caparisons and the insignia of the Sword Brothers on their white flowing cloaks. He closed his eyes and said thanks to God. They had reached home.

The last two miles of their journey was the hardest trek that Conrad had ever faced. Some were tempted to whip and beat the ponies to make the final leg of the ordeal pass as quickly as possible. They were severely rebuked by the masters and brother knights who knew that the animals were at the end of their physical limits. The scouting party from Wenden dismounted and hitched their animals to four of the wagons, those carrying the sick and injured, to ensure they at least reached the castle.

Conrad stumbled along in the snow as the wagon carrying Hans inched ahead of him. He walked on the other side of Johann, assisting Anton in supporting their friend whose limp had got worse. He could now put no weight on his injured leg and Anton's cough sounded dreadful.

Conrad suddenly laughed out loud. Johann and Anton looked at him quizzically and Lukas and Henke in front of them stopped and turned.

'What is so funny?' said Lukas.

Conrad looked at the thick woods to their right.

'I was just thinking that if Lembit and a few of his wolf shields came out of those trees he could probably put all of us to the sword with ease.'

Henke, his beard thick and frosted, shook his head. 'Lembit will be warming himself beside a big fire in Lehola. Only we are stupid enough to go trekking through Estonia in the middle of winter.'

'God would not allow Lembit to slaughter you, Conrad,' said Walter. 'He will ensure that when you do meet him to avenge the wrongs done to you, you will be both equally matched.'

Henke rolled his eyes and turned to continue the march. The sun was dipping rapidly in the west when they spotted the castle's northern tower at last. They skirted the eastern outer perimeter wall and walked through the gates, some falling to their knees and kissing the frozen track when they entered Wenden. Their ordeal was over.

Hans quickly recovered his strength after devouring copious quantities of hot broth and there was fortunately no lasting damage to Johann's leg. The remnants of Volquin's relief force, plus the depleted contingents from Kremon and Segewold, stayed at Wenden for a month, recovering their strength and waiting for the snow to melt as winter gave way to spring.

Conrad paid regular visits to the grave of his wife and child, which now had a headstone. One morning he stood with Ilona staring at it, unable to read the words.

'It says "Here lies Daina and Dietmar Wolff, wife and son of Conrad Wolff, Brother Knight of the Sword Brothers",' she told him. 'You should learn to read and write.'

'I have no need of it,' he said.

She looked at him, his blue-grey eyes full of sadness. 'You have lost weight.'

'It was a hard campaign.'

He looked across at the gravediggers trying hard to make an impression on the frozen ground with picks and shovels to dig Master Berthold's grave. He would have his own pit but the sergeants who had fallen at Odenpah would be buried in a mass grave. The brother knights and sergeants from Kremon and Segewold would also be buried at Wenden.

He looked back at the grave of his wife and child.

'It was good of Master Berthold to allow them to be buried here.'

'He was very fond of Daina,' said Ilona, 'we all were.'

Conrad looked around at the steadily increasing number of graves in the cemetery.

'When I first arrived at Wenden there were few graves. Now they prosper. And there will be more still come the summer when we finish business with Lembit.'

'Rudolf told me that he was at Odenpah.'

Conrad nodded. 'He crawled back to Saccalia before we left the fort. He should enjoy his freedom while he can. There are no sanctuaries for the enemies of Christ or for those who have betrayed the Bishop of Riga.' He smiled grimly at Ilona. 'Or me.'

*****

Lembit sat with his arms crossed, listening to the grievances of his chiefs and village elders as they stood before him in his hall at Lehola. Once the snows had disappeared and spring had arrived in all its glory he had summoned the leaders of his people to his stronghold. He had lost a thousand men at Odenpah and now the leaders, friends and relatives of those men stood in his hall and berated him, most of them clearly angry that he had been so profligate with Saccalian lives.

His wolf shields stood with spears in hand around the walls of the hall and Rusticus was at the side of his master, his knuckles white as he gripped the hilt of his sword, malice in his eyes. But Lembit sat calmly and listened to their remonstrations. He occasionally nodded and did his best to look earnest as fingers were pointed at him and the occasional fist was shook in the air in his direction. He went along with the drama, looking sorrowful when one elder with white hair, tears in his eyes, reported that half the menfolk of his village had been killed at Odenpah and the wail of their widows could be heard every evening. Lembit rose from his chair and embraced the man, telling him that he too heard the cries of grieving Saccalian women.

667

Eventually the hubbub burned itself out and the hall grew quiet. The visitors had satisfied their desire to be heard and now they looked down at the floor and shuffled uneasily on their feet. All wore leather or mail armour and held helmets in the crooks of their arms, though they had been required to leave their swords and other weapons outside the hall.

Lembit rose and raised his arms. 'My friends, when I agreed to shoulder the heavy burden of being leader of the Saccalian people I knew that the path would not be easy. This last winter has shown me how arduous is our task. Nigul died at the hands of the crusaders and Kalju betrayed our cause to throw himself into the arms of the Bishop of Riga.'

There were murmurs of agreement around the hall. Lembit began to slowly pace in front of the chiefs and elders, occasionally pointing and smiling at one he recognised as he continued to speak.

'I know as well as you that the bishop will once again march against us as soon as he lands at Riga. Perhaps he has already landed and is on his way, together with the traitor Caupo. I do not know. But what I do know is that I will not meekly stand by and let Saccalia become a slave to the foreigners.'

There were louder murmurs of agreement and nodding of heads.

'I know that many wives weep at the losses suffered at Odenpah but also know that we now stand on the verge of final victory over the bishop.'

There was a stunned silence and men looked at each other in confusion.

'You think that I delude myself?' asked Lembit. 'That I have spent too many nights drinking ale?'

There were a few yesses and he smiled.

'It's true, I have.'

They gave a great cheer. He raised his hands to quieten them.

'You think I do not want to avenge the deaths of so many fine warriors? You think that I am cowered by the crusaders? The reverse at Odenpah has merely increased my thirst for retribution. Lords Edvin, Alva and Jaak have pledged their warriors for the coming campaign.'

More cheers.

'But this time,' continued Lembit, 'this time the crusaders will not be able to use those things that have given them the advantage in the past. They will not be able to use their siege engines, their crossbows or their warhorses. This time, my friends, we will have the advantage. But before I put my plan into operation I have to ask you all whether you still want me as your chief?'

He stood before them with his head bowed as they gave a mighty cheer and began to chant his name. The rafters of the hall reverberating with 'Lembit, Lembit' as they came forward and all pledged their undying loyalty to him.

Afterwards, as slaves arranged benches and trestle tables in the halls in preparation for a great feast, Lembit pulled Rusticus to one side.

'That old idiot whom I was forced to embrace,' said the chief. 'Ensure he has an accident on the journey back to his flea-infested village.'

'What sort of accident?'

Lembit sighed. 'The fatal sort.'

'Fine speech earlier.'

'Thank you, Rusticus. People are like sheep, really. Tell them what they want to hear and mostly they will follow you.'

'Was that true about Alva, Jaak and Edvin?'

Lembit shrugged his shoulders. 'It will be. Jaak sulks at the moment and Edvin and Alva believe that they can sit out the coming war in the north, their borders secure and their neighbours peaceful. I will disabuse them of that notion.'

'And the bit about defeating the crusaders?'

Lembit's eyes lit up. 'That was true enough. I should have thought of it before but I was too busy defending forts and thus playing into the crusaders' hands. No more.'

He sniffed and turned up his nose, looking disparagingly at the chiefs noisily taking their places for the feast, a sea of thick beards and unruly hair.

'Leather and sweat,' remarked Lembit.

'Lord?'

'Have you ever noticed, Rusticus, that men stink? When they sit down together they stink of leather and sweat, and when they fight each other that odour is mixed with dung, piss and guts. But they still stink nevertheless.'

Rusticus belched and wiped his nose on his tunic. 'Can't say I've noticed.'

Lembit sighed again. 'Of course not.'

*****

With the spring came a resumption of building work at Wenden. The north tower was finished: a great stone structure having three floors and a fighting platform on top surrounded by crenellations. Work resumed in the quarry and construction commenced on the other two towers. Conrad had hoped that Rameke would return to the remains of his father's village but the settlement was left idle and nothing was heard from the son of Thalibald.

Brother Walter was chosen by Rudolf to be his deputy commander, an appointment that occasioned Walter praying and fasting for a week to cleanse his soul in preparation for his new role. Henke offered to be Walter's replacement when the brother knight collapsed and almost died from his exertions. But Walter did not die and he applied himself to his new duties diligently. Those duties included drawing up a list of Wenden's needs that would be submitted by Master Rudolf to the office of the grand master in Riga, subject to the approval of the garrison's brother knights.

Now they had attained that status Conrad, Hans, Anton and Johann were allowed to attend the weekly meetings of the brother knights held in the master's hall. There were now more than twelve brother knights at Wenden but Rudolf saw no reason to send any away to other garrisons, not with the prospect of war with Lembit looming.

'Not that this garrison will be in a fit state to march when it breaks out,' said Rudolf, sitting at the head of four tables arranged in a square formation, around which the brother knights sat. 'Walter, perhaps you could give the others an idea of our requirements.'

Walter picked up a long parchment and began summarising its contents.

'Horses, mules, oxen.'

'Oxen?' said Henke, 'have we been reduced to riding them to war instead of horses?'

Walter frowned. 'The oxen were all killed when Lembit raided Thalibald's village. If we are to plough and sow the fields around the village once more then we need oxen.'

'Who will sow and reap the crops?' asked Conrad.

'We are hoping that Rameke will return and rebuild his village,' said Rudolf. 'Have you had word from him since…?'

'Since the village was destroyed?' said Conrad. 'No. The last I heard he was with Caupo raiding Rotalia but that was months ago.'

Rudolf nodded. 'Please continue, Walter.'

His deputy read from the list. 'Long spears, short spears, four tons of iron for making crossbow bolt heads, saddles, harnesses, mail caparisons, padded caparisons, helmets, belts, boots, hauberks, chausses, mail coifs, surcoats, lances, daggers, swords, maces, axes, tools, wagons and so on. Not forgetting six new mangonels for Master Thaddeus.'

'We can send out a party to retrieve them now the snows have gone,' said Rudolf.

'The locals would have broken them up for firewood or building materials by now,' said Lukas.

Rudolf pursed his lips. 'Then let us hope that Grand Master Volquin's coffers are well stocked.'

Unfortunately they were not, at least not enough to fulfil the requirements of Segewold, Kremon as well as Wenden, in addition to the needs of the garrisons along the Dvina. The latter had briefly profited from levying dues on merchant vessels plying the river until they had been ordered to desist by Bishop Albert. Now the Sword Brothers were in danger of being impoverished as a result of their commitments and their recent campaign in Ungannia. And all the while the treasury in Riga filled with the proceeds of trade along the Dvina. The bitterness and resentment between the order and the governor of the city increased markedly as spring gave way to summer and both waited for the arrival of Bishop Albert to voice their grievances.

With the permission of Rudolf Conrad took one of the horses and rode south from Wenden, following the track that he had travelled upon in happier times. How long ago that all seemed now. He trotted across meadows and through trees until at last he came to the blackened, charred remains of Thalibald's village. The ditch that had surrounded it was now completely overgrown, as were the fields that circled it. He walked his horse across the broken wooden bridge and into the burnt-out settlement. He noticed there were no birds overhead and only the barest amount of vegetation on the areas of blackened earth where huts had once stood. He dismounted and led his horse across the eerily quiet ground. He saw the remains of smashed earthen pots, bleached animal bones and rusted spits and cauldrons. He stood in the centre of the desolation where he had been cut down by wolf shields while trying to protect his wife and child. He heard their screams, saw their faces and remembered the horror of that night. He suddenly felt vulnerable and totally alone, as he did that dreadful night in Lübeck all those years ago. Then he held his face in his hands and wept.

*****

Vsevolod held Rasa as they watched the young newlyweds ride from Panemunis, a hundred warriors grouped round them. His wife had been surprisingly emotional during the week-long wedding ceremony, like most Lithuanians believing that dead relatives and friends also joined in the celebrations. No doubt she thought her father and brother had been present to see the betrothal of her daughter to the son of Stecse. The prince had been popular among the people and Rasa's idea of marrying his son to Morta had been an astute one.

'You look ridiculous,' she said as the couple disappeared through the gates on their journey to a nearby hunting lodge in the hills.

As was tradition the guests wore white and wreaths of straw around their heads, which Vsevolod had found not only physically irritating but also degrading. But Rasa had insisted that all the customs should be observed, which meant the bride received presents of linen towels, woven belts and spindle whorls. These items were also the traditional gifts to Laima, the Goddess of Fate, Luck and Beauty, and were intended to bring blessings on the marriage. Vsevolod thought them fit only for throwing on a fire.

'And you look charming, my sweet.' He replied, kissing her tenderly on the lips. His white leggings and tunic made him resemble a scarecrow but her white linen dress and long red hair made her most appealing.

'Fine wedding, lord.'

He turned to see Aras, his usually tidy beard dishevelled and his tunic open to the waist. He bowed his head to Rasa.

'Lady.'

Vsevolod detected the aroma of mead coming from the newly appointed general, whose usual demeanour of calm seemed to have deserted him.

'Now that the newlyweds have departed,' said Vsevolod, 'get all these people out of Panemunis. They make the place look untidy.'

Aras stifled a belch and looked around at the dozens of individuals in various states of inebriation in the courtyard in front of the great hall.

'It's tradition to allow them to stay until they leave of their own free will.'

Vsevolod glared at him. 'Tradition? I have had a gutful of tradition. First of all they turn up unannounced, hundreds of the stinking parasites, before proceeding to help themselves to everything they can eat and drink.'

He turned up his nose in disgust at the piles of vomit that littered the courtyard.

'And then they commence turning my residence into a mirror image of their flea-infested hovels.'

He jabbed a finger into Aras' chest. 'Deal with them or I will order my guards to clear away the filth with their spear points.'

They were called *Kriukininkai*, uninvited guests who appeared at weddings, in this case a great crowd of them gathering at the gates of Panemunis. When news spread of the upcoming marriage the tracks and roads were filled with them, every man carrying a stick to symbolise that he would cause trouble if he was not admitted to the celebrations. It was a great Lithuanian tradition that the *Kriukininkai* were welcomed and feasted during the extent of the festivities. Vsevolod had been appalled but Rasa was delighted that the people had accepted the union of Mindaugas with a half-Russian girl.

Aras scratched his beard, his breath reeking of mead. 'You're sure you want to do that, lord? It would be considered an insult.'

Vsevolod stared, horrified, as a drunken man bent over and emptied the contents of his stomach in a horse trough.

'*That* is an insult,' said the prince loudly.

He then saw the white-bearded *Kriviu Krivaitis* approach, accompanied by two of his *Kriviai*. Even the most inebriated lowered their heads and staggered aside when the vessels of the gods approached.

'Marvellous,' groaned Vsevolod, 'just when I thought it could not get any worse.'

'Hail, Prince Vsevolod,' said the chief priest, opening his arms and embracing Vsevolod, who looked mortified. The priest stepped back and offered a hand to Rasa, who bowed her head, took it and kissed it.

'There were many among us who believed that your coming foretold misery for the late grand duke's people,' said the *Kriviu Krivaitis*. 'I am not too proud to tell you that I was one such individual.

'But you have displayed wisdom, temperance and respect for our traditions and religion since your arrival at Panemunis. I salute you. The Holy Fire burned brightly when I spoke to Perkunas about you.'

'You are most kind,' said Vsevolod, oozing false modesty.

The chief priest looked around at the clusters of people in the courtyard. 'You have embraced the people and they embrace you, Prince Vsevolod.'

Vsevolod smiled. 'I think it is important to respect people's traditions.'

The priest smiled at Rasa. 'The marriage will be a good one, child. The tree will flourish and Austeja will bless the union with a child.'

Rasa's eyes misted with tears. 'Thank you, Revered One.'

After they had been married by the *Kriviu Krivaitis* in the sacred grove, the couple planted a linden tree inside its boundary. The tree was traditionally associated with peace, truth and justice, qualities that the couple hoped would characterise the marriage. At the feast afterwards Morta had tossed her cup of mead upwards towards the ceiling to pay her respects to Austeja, the Goddess of Fertility. Most of the liquid had fallen on her father, which had done nothing to improve his humour.

'I will get on with clearing the courtyard, lord,' said Aras, clearly bored by it all.

The chief priest frowned at him and his two subordinates started to protest.

'What are you talking about, general?' said Vsevolod. 'Our guests must be allowed to partake of my hospitality as long as they desire.' He smiled at the *Kriviu Krivaitis*. 'That is the custom, after all.'

Aras was confused. 'But you said…'

Vsevolod raised a hand to silence him. 'Is there something you want, general?'

'There is someone to see you,' replied Aras. 'I kept him waiting until the couple had left. He says he is an ambassador from Duke Arturus.'

Vsevolod's eyes lit up. 'At last,' he muttered. He smiled at the chief priest. 'If you will excuse me, I have urgent business to attend to. Please feel free to treat my home as your own. My wife will accompany you.'

'Of course,' said Rasa, all smiles and happiness.

Vsevolod bowed his head to the priests and left them. 'You are with me,' he told Aras.

They walked between groups of drunken, raucous guests, their shirts dirty and smeared with mead.

'When the priests have gone get rid of the interlopers,' sneered Vsevolod.

'I thought you said they were welcome.'

'That was for the benefit of that decrepit senile idiot with the white beard,' said Vsevolod, angrily shoving aside a reveller.

'That old man holds great sway among the people,' said Aras.

'Which is precisely why I said to him what I did.'

They walked through the hall to the more private chambers located at its rear, the prince's Russian guards keeping any unwelcome guests out of this area. Aras led Vsevolod to a small room furnished with chairs and a table where the prince usually received visitors. The two guards outside the room brought their spears to their bodies as one and opened the door to allow them to enter.

Torolf was standing admiring a row of boar heads mounted on one wall. He turned and looked surprised at the two individuals standing before him. Aras realised that the ambassador must have thought they were servants or some sort of travelling entertainers with their simple attire and strange headwear.

'I am General Aras,' he said, extending an arm towards Vsevolod. 'And this is Prince Vsevolod, Lord of the Selonian and Nalsen people and son-in-law to the late Grand Duke Daugerutis.'

Vsevolod was suddenly aware of his attire. Mortified, he snatched at the straw wreath on his head and flung it on the table.

'Wine,' he called to the guards outside. 'Bring wine and refreshments for our guest.' He looked apologetically at Torolf.

'Please be seated.'

But Torolf bowed his head solemnly and handed Vsevolod a rolled parchment that had a red wax seal bearing the emblem of a seagull.

'I am Lord Torolf, appointed by Duke Arturus to be his ambassador and I thank you for your invitation to your kingdom.'

Vsevolod took the document and raised an eyebrow. Arturus had been tardy to say the least in replying to his requests for a meeting. He had wanted negotiations to start months ago but at least this was a start. He broke the seal and read the document that he was pleased to discover was in Russian. It confirmed Torolf's status and ended with Arturus' words that he hoped their future cooperation would be mutually beneficial.

'You must forgive our appearance, ambassador,' said Vsevolod, taking his seat behind the desk as Torolf sat down opposite with Aras next to him, 'we have been engaged in my daughter's wedding.'

Torolf, in stark contrast, wore a rich green tunic and red cloak that was fastened at the front by a huge gold brooch.

'To Mindaugas, son of the late Prince Stecse. Yes, I heard,' smiled Torolf, 'my congratulations.'

Slaves brought wine, meats, rye bread and fruit to the office, Torolf eating and drinking sparingly.

'My duke wonders why you solicit his aid,' remarked the ambassador, nibbling a grape.

'Lithuania is afflicted by civil strife,' replied Vsevolod. 'I would bring that strife to an end.'

'By subduing the other dukes,' said Torolf. 'My lord has no interest in being slave to a grand duke.'

Aras smiled. He remembered that Daugerutis had managed, more or less, to bribe, threaten and browbeat the other dukes to his will, all except the Northern Kurs. A fierce, warlike people, they went their own way and tended to kill first and ask questions later. But Arturus was not just a bloodthirsty brute. He realised that there was always a demand for hardy warriors and was not averse to offering the services of his warriors. At a price.

'I seek not to be a grand duke but to preserve my kingdom,' replied Vsevolod.

'You wish to hire warriors?'

'We have enough soldiers,' interrupted Aras, who had taken a dislike to this smooth-talking courtier.

Vsevolod frowned at his general but Torolf remained impassive.

'What I propose,' said Vsevolod, 'is the division of Semgallia. The son of Ykintas, Duke Vincentas, struggles to hold his father's kingdom against my assaults in the east and the Samogitians in the south. If Duke Arturus was to invade Semgallia from the west then Vincentas would be toppled from power easily.'

Torolf remained impassive.

'Unless the duke has his hands full with the Southern Kurs.'

Aras smiled as Torolf's mask slipped ever so slightly.

'It is only a matter of time before Duke Gedvilas submits to my lord,' replied Torolf icily.

Vsevolod leaned forward. 'I seek an alliance with Duke Arturus so that we may divide up the Lithuanian lands between us. While this land is divided the crusaders north of the Dvina laugh at us and make their preparations to cross the river to expand their empire. Like your lord I too do not wish to be a slave.'

Torolf sipped at his wine. 'You wish for the Northern Kurs to fight the Semgallians but what will you do for us?'

'A fair question,' replied Vsevolod. 'What I am proposing is a combined attack, my forces from the east, those of Duke Arturus from the west. Faced with such overwhelming force the Semgallians will collapse. After which I pledge warriors to aid your fight against the Southern Kurs.'

'You must understand that I have no authority to agree to your proposals,' said Torolf. 'I must report back to my lord.'

'But in theory you believe that the plan has merit,' probed Vsevolod.

Torolf took another sip of his drink. 'Any military cooperation will require proper planning and coordination, otherwise Vincentas will be able to march his forces east and west at will to stave off our assaults.'

'I promise that there will be full cooperation between us,' said Aras.

Torolf looked at the general. 'As I said I make no promises. However, I will report favourably back to my lord concerning what we have discussed. It would appear that our interests are the same regarding the future of Semgallia.'

'You must be tired after your journey,' said Vsevolod. 'General Aras will escort you to your quarters. I hope you will stay with us a while and enjoy our hospitality.'

It was a start and that was all that he wanted. One day he would recross the Dvina and take back his home from the accursed Bishop of Riga and the Sword Brothers. But for now he had to bide his time and apply his efforts to more pressing problems, which included subjugating the other Lithuanian tribes.

*****

It was the end of May before Bishop Albert returned from Germany. The twenty ships bringing crusaders and supplies docked at the great harbour at Riga, the sails of two of the cogs bearing the insignia of the Sword Brothers and carrying much-needed weapons and armour for the order's soldiers, though not enough to satisfy all their needs. The harbour itself was now protected by watchtowers, which were sited on the end of all the jetties. On the top platform of each tower was mounted either a stone-throwing mangonel or a ballista. The latter was a machine resembling a giant crossbow that could hurl iron-headed bolts over great distances. As the Oeselians had found to their cost, the defences of Riga and its harbour were now very strong. Under the careful nurturing of Archdeacon Stefan the garrison had increased to four hundred men, a small army in itself, in addition to the town militia that could muster five hundred men variously equipped and trained.

The harbour and streets leading from it to the bishop's palace were lined with soldiers of the garrison when the bishop stepped ashore from his ship, to be welcomed by Archdeacon Stefan, Grand Master Volquin, the castellans of the order, Caupo, Sir Helmold and Sir Richard. A fanfare of trumpets welcomed home the founder of the town; Albert was dressed in white robes and a white and gold mitre. A tall, fair-haired nobleman wearing a surcoat emblazoned with a white horse's head helped him from the gangplank. Onlookers gasped when they saw the knight, looks of horror momentarily on their faces before they composed themselves and clapped politely. For Count Albert von Lauenburg was horribly disfigured.

Now in his mid-thirties, the count was a Saxon who controlled the mighty fortress of Lauenburg, a stronghold on the River Elbe. He had fought many battles against the Danes and other German nobles, receiving severe wounds at the city of Stade two years before. Heralds spread the news of Count Albert's bravery and heroic deeds but did not relate that in the fighting his helmet had been knocked off his head during close-quarters combat. In the ensuring struggle half his nose was hacked off, the top of his right ear was severed and an enemy axe had slashed his face, leaving a deep scar that ran from just above his right eyebrow to his lower left jaw. It was fortunate that he was already married because it was thought that no woman would countenance a match with such a deformed individual, even accounting for his great wealth and power.

The reason that the bishop had been delayed on his journey back to Riga was that he had been involved in delicate relations with King Valdemar of Denmark, who controlled large areas of northern Germany, including the city of Lübeck. When Count Albert declared his intention to go on crusade in Livonia, Valdemar baulked at the idea of the Saxon lord marching a hundred knights, two hundred lesser knights, a hundred squires, a hundred crossbowmen and a hundred spearmen through his lands. Only the personal guarantee of the bishop that the Saxons would not plunder during their journey convinced the king to agree to the count's passage. He did, however, assign five hundred soldiers to act as an escort and insisted that the crusaders embark immediately once they reached Lübeck rather than loiter in the city.

The fleet that brought Count Albert to Riga also contained other knights who were either attracted to the crusade in Livonia or who had fallen on hard times and thought the prospect of being fed and housed by Bishop Albert for a year much more attractive than starvation. This category numbered fifty men.

Men of substance who expressed an interest in becoming brother knights of the order numbered twenty, while the bishop had collected a further fifty from Lübeck who would be inducted as sergeants, both groups being subject to the usual probationary period. Finally there were the waifs and strays and young criminals that the bishop had managed to save from the gallows: sixty boys who would be trained to be sergeants, some perhaps even attaining the coveted position of brother knight.

Every year the bishop had recruited mercenaries for the Sword Brothers, or at least the Cistercian Order throughout northern Germany had let it be known that salvation and regular pay awaited mercenaries prepared to serve in Livonia. This year was no different and accompanying the bishop were one hundred and fifty dogs of war for Grand Master Volquin.

The route from the harbour to the bishop's palace was thronged with Riga's citizens, all eager to acclaim the man who had single-handedly turned a collection of Liv villages into a prosperous, thriving port. The population had expanded to such an extent that dwellings had been built beyond the city walls, a new, wooden wall being erected to protect them. Indeed, such was the demand for timber for construction that several of Caupo's chiefs had become wealthy providing the town's carpenters and builders with wood.

While walking in the company of Volquin and the other masters of the order, Rudolf spotted Rameke among the chiefs with Caupo. He left the brethren and ambled over to the Livs, who now seemed strangers in their own land amid so many German Christians.

'Rameke,' he called, having difficulty hearing his own voice amid the tumult.

Rameke turned and recognised Rudolf. He smiled and they clasped forearms. He was still in his early twenties but he had a world-weary look that made him look ten years older.

'The new master of Wenden. It is good to see you.'

'And you,' said Rudolf as they followed the procession towards the palace. 'Wenden misses its chief.'

'Wenden's chief died,' he said bitterly, 'as should I.'

'You are a fool to think any blame attaches to you.'

Rameke shrugged. 'I am more useful being with my king than at Wenden.'

'Your place is at Wenden, Rameke, with your people and your friends. Conrad misses you; we all miss you.'

There was pain in Rameke's eyes. 'How is Conrad?'

'Well, though he would like to see his brother-in-law, I think.'

Rameke looked around at the procession of knights and Sword Brothers. 'This year Lembit will not escape.'

Rudolf nodded. 'His star wanes. The bishop will bring him to account this year, of that I have no doubt.'

'And I will be there to bring it about.'

None wore armour the next day when the bishop convened a war council in the audience chamber of his palace. It was a hot June day and the temperature inside the room was already warm when the meeting convened. The Sword Brothers wore their gowns and the lords surcoats over their tunics. Sir Helmold and Sir Richard chatted politely to Count Albert, doing their utmost not to stare at his disfigured face.

Servants brought wine as the guests were shown to their places at the four long trestle tables arranged in a square. The top table was earmarked for the bishop, the one opposite to Caupo and his chiefs. Volquin and his masters sat to the right of the bishop's table and the crusader lords to the left. The bishop and Stefan appeared shortly afterwards, everyone standing at they took their places and commanded that heads be bowed for prayers. When they again sat Rudolf noticed that Stefan had put on weight. He filled out his princely robes, his fingers looked bloated and a second chin was appearing under his jaw. But his eyes were alert as ever and they darted left and right as he surveyed the assembly of potential friends and foes.

All eyes were upon the bishop as he drank from his mazer before speaking. His hair was now heavily streaked with grey and his face thin and slightly haggard. Nearly twenty years of keeping alive the crusade in Livonia had taken their toll on the prelate.

'This year I intend to defeat the rebel Lembit once and for all and subdue the Estonians. His continual resistance insults the Holy Church and brings mockery upon my bishopric. Grand Master Volquin, how long before an army can be assembled to march against this servant of the devil?'

Volquin stood and bowed his head to the bishop. 'I anticipate that in two months' time we will be ready to launch your campaign against Lembit, lord bishop.'

'That long?' said Count Albert.

Volquin remained standing. 'Unfortunately, my lord, the order's winter campaign was most taxing and resulted in the loss of numerous siege engines.'

'Very remiss of the Sword Brothers,' smirked Stefan.

'The campaign was very successful and resulted in one of Lembit's allies deserting him and also in the retreat of the Oeselians and Russians,' continued Volquin, ignoring Stefan's condescension. 'We are still waiting for replacement horses from Germany.'

'They will be arriving within the month,' said the bishop. 'Thank you, grand master.' He looked at the row of lords.

'How are matters along the Dvina, Sir Helmold?'

Sir Helmold rose as Volquin took his seat.

'All is quiet along the river, lord bishop. The reports that we have received indicate that the Lithuanians fight among themselves. However, we know that Prince

Vsevolod is resident at Panemunis, just a short distance across the river from his former stronghold of Gerzika.'

'You think he will cross the river this year?' asked the bishop.

Helmold looked across to the castellans of Holm, Uexkull, Lennewarden and Kokenhusen. 'We have no way of knowing, lord bishop.'

'We have many soldiers tied up along the Dvina,' said the bishop, 'soldiers that would be put to better use fighting Lembit. Yet to strip the garrisons along the Dvina is to invite the Lithuanians to raid Livonia.'

Archdeacon Stefan leaned over and whispered something to the bishop, causing him to raise his eyebrows.

'And you are confident that this will bear fruit?'

'I am, lord bishop,' replied Stefan.

Albert smiled at Sir Helmold. 'It would seem that you and the masters of the garrisons along the Dvina may yet be able to join in our crusade against Lembit, Sir Helmold. Thank you for your report.'

Sir Helmold took his seat but the castellans were far from happy and looked at Volquin, who was also disturbed.

'Lord bishop,' he said, 'may I enquire as to why you feel confident that the Lithuanians will not cross the Dvina if we weaken our forces along the river?'

'Archdeacon Stefan has just informed me of certain developments that hopefully will work to our advantage.'

'And which for the moment have to remain confidential,' added Stefan, smiling triumphantly at Volquin. The grand master was far from amused.

'Nothing should be withheld from the Order of Sword Brothers, lord bishop, for we are the defenders of Livonia.'

'I thought God was the defender of Livonia, grand master,' said Stefan casually, 'unless you believe that you and your knights are higher than our Lord.'

Volquin jumped to his feet as his castellans shot hateful stares at Stefan. 'How dare you!'

The bishop raised his hands. 'Calm yourself, grand master, I am certain that the archdeacon meant no offence.'

'Of course not, my sincere apologies, grand master,' proffered Stefan, his voice laced with insincerity.

'Let us move on,' ordered the bishop.

'I would hear about the archdeacon's plans concerning the Lithuanians,' insisted the grand master.

'And you will be the first to be informed when there is anything of import to relate, grand master,' said Stefan.

Volquin was fuming but the bishop would hear no more on the topic and asked Caupo to report on matters to the north of Livonia, as he and his warriors had been raiding deep into Estonia during the winter and spring. Now nearly fifty years old, the Liv king still cut an impressive figure, though his hair was thinning slightly and his beard was flecked with grey. He rose and bowed his head to the bishop. Stefan rolled his eyes and began toying with his cross. He made no secret of the fact that he disliked and distrusted Caupo and his people, even if they professed to be Christians. Lembit made the same claim and everyone knew how that had turned out.

'It has been a year since Nigul was killed,' reported the king, 'and I hear that Rotalia has been wholly taken over by the Oeselians.'

Count Albert, perplexed, leaned over to speak to Sir Helmold who explained to him who Nigul was and where Rotalia was located.

'Doubtless,' continued Caupo, 'when we march against Lembit we will also have to fight his pirate allies.'

'But not the Russians,' interrupted Volquin, 'thanks to Bishop Theodoric.'

'Still held captive in Novgorod?' asked Stefan, examining his fingernails.

'Still conducting negotiations,' insisted Volquin. 'He is quite safe, the Russian commander gave his word.'

Rudolf raised an eyebrow but said nothing.

'Do we believe the word of an Orthodox,' remarked Stefan, 'a man who follows a false religion?'

Volquin was nearing the end of his patience. 'It was the bishop himself who volunteered to travel to Novgorod. The prince of that city has no wish to see his fur trade interrupted or harmed. And if I may add, lord bishop, we have also gained the allegiance of Chief Kalju and his Ungannians.'

'A pagan and his log fort. Riches indeed,' sneered Stefan.

'King Caupo,' said the bishop to halt the verbal duel between Stefan and Volquin, 'do you think that the Oeselians will fight beside Lembit this year?'

Caupo's brow creased. 'It seems highly likely, lord bishop.'

The bishop smiled at the king as he sat down. 'In two months' time, then, we will march against Lembit to put an end to his rebellion once and for all. I will write to the Prince of Novgorod requesting that he escort Bishop Theodoric back to Livonia, otherwise I will halt all Russian trade on the Dvina.

'Our aim is the subjugation of all Estonia to the Holy Church so that Theodoric may practise in his bishopric. Let us pray for God's help in this great enterprise.'

'Before we end the meeting, lord bishop,' interrupted Stefan. 'I have something else to say.'

There was a groan from the Sword Brothers and Volquin steeled himself for another bout of verbal jousting. Stefan picked up a parchment and held it towards Volquin.

'This is the list of supplies that you submitted to the bishop's office two weeks ago, grand master. I am happy to report that within six weeks a flotilla of ships will be arriving at Riga carrying all that is on this list. A token of appreciation from the citizens of Riga to the Order of Sword Brothers.'

Volquin was stunned into silence, his mouth opening and closing but no words coming out. The other masters were likewise taken aback. Until now the grand master had had to wage a constant battle with the archdeacon's clerks to release funds from the treasury to supply his garrisons. Indeed, Stefan seemed to have taken a perverse delight in obstructing every urgent request. But now, before the war council itself, he was promising everything Volquin had asked for.

'You should have doubled the quantity of everything on your list,' said Rudolf under his breath.

'He's up to something,' whispered Master Aldous.

'A word of appreciation is in order, I think, grand master,' said the bishop.

'Yes, well, I am indeed grateful, archdeacon,' stuttered Volquin. 'As are my masters.'

Stefan spread his arms magnanimously. 'It is the least I could do, grand master, seeing as you lost all your equipment during the winter.'

*****

Olaf stood on the shingle beach and admired the carpenters working on the new longship. Like most Oeselian vessels it had been constructed during the winter after the crops had been gathered during the autumn. Whenever possible vessels were made of oak, the shipbuilders being fortunate that Oesel produced enough tall oaks trees to provide the keels for the king's longships. The shipwrights did sometimes use other materials – ash, birch, alder, linden and willow – for various parts of a ship, but oak was the desired material. And no ship put to sea without an

683

'old woman' – the timber block on which the base of the mast rested – fashioned from oak.

Olaf looked to his right where two other ships were nearing the end of their construction, carpenters working furiously with chisels and hammers to carve the serpent heads that would be mounted on the prows.

He heard the rustle of mail armour behind him and footsteps on the pebbles. He looked round to see his three sons approaching.

Olaf continued to admire the work of his craftsmen. 'It must be important if all three of you have come to see me.'

'Lembit gathers his forces, father,' said Sigurd, 'and requests my presence by his side once more.'

'I wish to accompany Sigurd, father, to fight the crusaders,' stated Stark.

Kalf was similarly bullish. 'As do I, father, to take my place in the shield wall beside my brothers to avenge Eric.'

Olaf sighed. 'It is time to end our cooperation with Lembit. His wars have cost too many Oeselian sons.'

'We do have an alliance with the Estonians, father,' said Sigurd.

Olaf turned to face his sons. 'And I now choose to end that alliance Lembit uses us to further his own ends.'

'He gave us Rotalia, father,' said Kalf.

Olaf smiled at his eager young pup. 'Only because its leader was dead at the hands of the crusaders. Rotalia is an empty husk. No, we are done with Lembit.'

'You said that we would be stronger allied with the Estonians rather than standing alone, father,' said Sigurd, disappointment in his voice.

'You did well forging an alliance with Lembit, my son,' agreed Olaf, 'but times have changed. The Estonians are being slowly crushed between the crusaders from the south and the Russians from the east. Even his chiefs are deserting him, those that are not dead, that is.'

He looked at their eager faces. 'You have all heard the reports of our captains. Every month more and more ships dock at Riga full of warriors and supplies. You think that Lembit will be able to withstand such an onslaught?'

'With our help he could, father,' boasted Kalf.

Olaf saw Eric in his youngest son more and more.

'No,' said the king firmly, 'it shall not be.'

'Then what shall I inform the courier who waits for a reply to take back to Lembit?' asked Sigurd.

684

Olaf turned and looked at a carpenter fitting pivoted shutters to oar-holes to the topmost strake of the nearest ship. These shutters prevented water from coming through when the ship was at sea.

'Tell him that a thousand Oeselian warriors will march to fight by his side against the crusaders.'

Sigurd looked at his siblings in confusion. 'I do not understand, father.'

'You will command the warriors, Sigurd,' said Olaf. 'You will march at their head across Rotalia at a very slow pace, so slow in fact that you will reach Lembit only after he has fought the crusaders. His scouts will see your army and will report back to their leader that Oeselian warriors are on their way, thus fulfilling their terms of the alliance.'

'But father,' said Stark, 'we will not share in the victory over the crusaders.'

Lembit went to his son's side and place an arm round his shoulder. He pointed at the ships under construction on the beach and others moored in the bay.

'The gods gave us this island, Stark. They bestowed it with iron so that we could forge ploughs to grow our crops and make weapons and armour to defend ourselves. They covered it in forests so we would always have enough timber to build ships and they filled the seas around it with fish so we would not starve.'

He looked at the others. 'We have strayed from what the gods desire, which is to protect this island, and have suffered as a consequence. The death of your brother, the defeats at Riga and Odenpah; these things were divine retribution for ignoring the gods. I will not make the same mistake again.'

'But we now occupy Rotalia, father,' said Kalf. 'Perhaps we may march east and occupy other Estonian lands.'

'No,' said Olaf. 'If we were meant to live in Estonia we would be called Estonians. Sigurd, tell the courier what I have instructed and make your preparations to lead the thousand men.'

'I ask to accompany Sigurd, father?' asked Stark eagerly.

Olaf shook his head. 'You will stay here to conduct sea trials for the new ships when they are finished.' He glanced at Kalf. 'As will you.'

*****

At the beginning of August a great army began to assemble at Wenden. Ships from Germany brought a large quantity of horses and military supplies for the Sword Brothers and Archdeacon Stefan and Bishop Albert escorted Grand Master Volquin to Riga's docks to observe their unloading. True to his word the archdeacon signed them over to the grand master, who was forced to apologise for doubting him and then, to add insult to injury, was required to kiss his ring of authority as a sign of his piousness. Volquin seethed silently but the bishop was delighted to see his two senior subordinates being reconciled. Albert declared that he would not be accompanying the army north into Estonia as he had no wish to lay eyes on the heretic Lembit, and in any case he was still engaged in negotiations with the Novgorodians regarding trade and trying to secure the return of Bishop Theodoric.

The river was alive with merchant vessels bringing their wares to Riga and the town's treasury was filling with money. Volquin was still concerned about the Lithuanians but Stefan assured him that matters were in hand to neutralise the threat from across the Dvina. Once again the grand master queried the prelate on what actions he was taking to ensure security along the river, only to be informed that matters were on-going and it would be futile to elaborate further. The grand master, contemptuous of the archdeacon but delighted over the arrival of such a sizeable consignment of supplies, asked no more questions. But he would ensure that the order's castles along the Dvina were strong enough to repel a Lithuanian attack if it came.

In his office in the castle Volquin sent out a command that every order castle was to send ten brother knights, twenty sergeants, a score of crossbowmen and the same number of spearmen to Wenden, together with enough food and supplies to keep the men and horses fed for a month. In this way the garrisons of Wenden, Holm, Kremon, Uexkull, Segewold, Lennewarden, Kokenhusen and the newly established garrison at Gerzika would contribute a combined total of eighty brother knights, a hundred and sixty sergeants, a hundred and sixty crossbowmen and the same number of spearmen. A small cadre of the order's soldiers would be left at each castle, the strongholds along the Dvina being reinforced by the prospective brother knights and sergeants who had arrived with the bishop at the end of May, together with the mercenaries that had been hired by Albert and had also sailed to Riga with him. As the sun warmed Livonia and ripened the crops in the fields the various contingents made their way to Wenden.

Master Rudolf's castle was a hive of activity and just as he had done at Odenpah, the newly returned Master Thaddeus took charge of the logistical arrangements, reducing the garrison's brother knights and sergeants to couriers as he despatched orders on a daily basis. He had been given a small office in the master's hall where Conrad made his way one afternoon after a young novice had searched him out on the training field jousting with Walter.

686

'Saved in the nick of time, Conrad,' said Walter, staring down at the brother knight on the ground after being unhorsed by a well-aimed strike on his shield.

'I always make allowances for your senior position, Walter,' said Conrad as Hans helped him to his feet and handed him his sword belt.

Conrad turned to the novice, a boy no older than eleven or twelve who had arrived that spring. 'What does Master Thaddeus want with me?'

'Not to teach him how to joust, I'll warrant,' quipped Anton.

'How to fall off a horse graciously, perhaps,' suggested Johann.

'Go and fetch my horse,' Conrad said to the novice, pointing at his mount that was munching on grass.

Conrad dusted himself off and buckled his belt, Walter nudging his horse forward.

'I hope you did not make allowances for my rank, Conrad,' he said earnestly, 'that would not be right, not at all.'

The novice brought Conrad's horse to him and he lifted himself into the saddle.

'It was a jest, Walter.'

Walter still looked perturbed. 'Ah, I see. Brother Anton, perhaps you would like to tilt your lance.'

'It would be my pleasure,' grinned Anton, walking over to where the horses were tethered to a rack of lances.

Walter replaced his helmet on his head and rode away to the far end of the jousting range.

'Do you think Walter ever had a sense of humour?' Conrad asked Hans.

Hans puffed out his cheeks. 'Doubt it.'

'Come,' Conrad said to the novice, 'let us see what Master Thaddeus wants.'

He walked his horse up the track leading to the castle, the inner perimeter crowded with freshly made wagons, barrels of wine under canvas covers, tents that held the soldiers commanded by Sir Richard and animals pens filled with chickens, goats, sheep and cows. The stink made him turn up his nose as he rode across the bridge, through the half-finished gatehouse and into the courtyard. He dismounted and handed the reins of the horse to the novice.

'Stay here,' he ordered, 'I will probably need my horse after I have spoken to Master Thaddeus.'

'Yes, brother.'

687

Conrad heard Thaddeus before he saw him, his deep voice resonating through the master's hall as he barked orders at a pair of sergeants who emerged from his office with harassed expressions. They nodded to him as he knocked at the open door.

'Yes? Ah, Conrad, come in, come in. Take a seat.'

The office had rows of wooden pigeonholes on two of its walls, a desk in the centre of the room facing the door, behind which sat Thaddeus. Behind him was an iron candle holder with light, a small, square window set high in the wall and a wooden chest on the floor. There were parchments stuffed in all the pigeonholes, on the two chairs on the other side of the desk and on the floor. Conrad began moving the documents on one of the chairs.

'Please do not touch them,' snapped Thaddeus. 'I know where everything is and if you move them then you will ruin my timetable.'

He pointed at a large map spread out on the table, candle holders on two of its corners and iron paperweights on the other two. Thaddeus swept an arm over it.

'This is a map of Wenden and the areas designated for the different contingents that are gathering here, such as Sir Helmold, Count Albert and King Caupo. Do you see the problem?'

Conrad stared at the map. He recognised the shape of Wenden and its outer perimeter but did not know what the strange scribbles and symbols marked around the castle were.

'I cannot read,' said Conrad, slightly ashamed.

'Cannot read?'

Conrad shrugged. 'I have no need of it.'

Thaddeus looked shocked. 'No need of it? Would you not like to be able to read the classics, Conrad? Vegetius, Marcus Aurelius, Ovis, Horace and Virgil?'

The names meant nothing to Conrad. 'I am a soldier, Master Thaddeus, not a scholar.'

Thaddeus shook his head. 'That much is true.'

He picked up a parchment. 'Now, what we need to do is to ask Count Albert to move his men and horses to the south of the castle.'

He handed Conrad the now rolled-up parchment, fastened with a red ribbon. 'Please take this to the count. It is a sketch map of where he should be. These lords just turn up and pitch their camps where they wish. I have spent a considerable amount of time designating streams for watering holes for soldiers, lakes to water animals and meadows where they can graze them. The count's men are in the area allocated to Caupo and his Livs when they arrive.'

Conrad thought of Rameke and hoped he would see his friend and brother again.

'When will the Livs arrive?'

Thaddeus scratched his head. 'They should have been here yesterday. My itineraries are being ruined.'

He frowned at Conrad. 'Today would be a good time to speak to Count Albert.'

Conrad smiled at Thaddeus and left the office, walking through the hall and into the courtyard.

'Get yourself a horse from the stables,' he said to the novice, 'it will be instructive to see a crusader camp at close quarters.'

Five minutes later they were riding down to the gatehouse in the outer perimeter wall, making way for carts filled with weapons and supplies that had been ferried up the Gauja by riverboat. The armoury was being steadily filled with weapons, armour and crossbow bolts in preparation for the coming campaign.

Count Albert had brought six hundred men with him from Lauenburg and they were spread over a wide area to the west of the castle. Dozens of different-sized tents filled the grassland between the perimeter and the woods that bordered the river, the sound of men chopping wood greeting Conrad as he and his young companion rode into the crusader camp. To the east of the castle were pitched Sir Helmold's men and the Sword Brothers from the garrisons along the Dvina. The men from Kremon and Segewold had yet to arrive and were probably accompanying Caupo.

They rode through the perimeter guards and between a host of tents and temporary stables made of wooden poles and canvas sheets to the centre of the camp and the pavilion of Count Albert.

'Stay here,' Conrad said to the novice as they dismounted and he handed the boy the reins of his horse.

From the pavilion flew the flag of Lauenburg and the spearmen who guarded its entrance also carried the white horse motif on their shields. Two barred his way with their spears as he neared the entrance.

'State your business.'

'I am Brother Conrad from Wenden to see Count Albert on behalf of Master Thaddeus,' said Conrad.

'Wait here.'

One of the guards turned on his heels and disappeared into the tent, the other staring impassively at Conrad, still barring his way. Half a minute later the other guard came from the tent accompanied by a knight in mail armour and a rich red surcoat sporting the white horse crest. Whoever this knight was he had seen many battles for his face was horribly scarred. The maimed face twisted into a smile.

'I am Count Albert. Welcome to my camp, Brother Conrad. It is an honour to meet a member of the Sword Brothers.'

He did not know why but he expected the famous count to be handsome and aloof, but he bowed deeply to him nevertheless.

'Lord.'

'Come in, come in,' ordered the count, holding the heavy flap open for Conrad.

The pavilion was spartan but comfortable, with candle holders around the walls, a table, well-appointed chairs and, curiously, a makeshift altar upon which was a beautiful golden cross.

'Brother Conrad.'

Conrad turned to see Sir Helmold being served wine by a servant, a page in the livery of the count.

'Sir Helmold,' said Conrad, bowing his head, 'it is good to see you.'

'You know each other?' asked the count, who was also served with wine.

'Indeed, count. This is Conrad Wolff, the man who wounded Lembit and who saved the life of Bishop Albert in the great battle before Riga.'

'Wine for our hero,' ordered the count.

'Hardly that, lord,' said Conrad, embarrassed.

'How may I be of assistance?' queried Albert.

Conrad became more embarrassed. He handed the count the rolled parchment. 'Apologies, lord, but Master Thaddeus says that your camp is in the wrong place.'

Albert was perplexed. 'Master Thaddeus?'

'Wenden's chief engineer and something of a genius by all accounts,' reported Sir Helmold. 'It was he who masterminded the defence of Odenpah, I believe. You were there, were you not?'

'That is correct, lord,' said Conrad.

'What was it like fighting beside Estonians instead of fighting against them?'

'We were glad to have them by our side, lord,' replied Conrad.

Albert took his wine. 'I have heard of this place. A great Sword Brother victory.'

'One of many,' said Sir Helmold admiringly.

The page offered Conrad a silver goblet containing wine.

'To the Sword Brothers,' said Count Albert, raising his goblet.

Sir Helmold stood. 'The Sword Brothers.'

Albert looked at Conrad. 'Tell me, Brother Conrad, what is this Lembit like?'

Conrad sipped at his wine, which was of excellent quality. He thought of the wolf shields and the attack on Thalibald's village.

'Like a cockroach, lord. Difficult to kill.'

'And Conrad should know,' said Sir Helmold, 'he is one of the order's most accomplished soldiers and Lembit has even slipped through his fingers.'

'Hardly that, lord,' offered Conrad, his cheeks flushing.

The count untied the ribbon on the parchment and unrolled it. He examined it and smiled.

'Master Thaddeus clearly knows what he is about, Brother Conrad. Inform him that I will obey his request.'

'You are most gracious, count,' said Conrad.

He drained his goblet and placed it back on the tray proffered by the page.

'God be with you, my lords.'

Sir Helmold raised his goblet.

'I hope to fight beside you on the field of honour, Brother Conrad,' said the count.

Conrad smiled and left. It never failed to amuse him how even hardened knights referred to the battlefield as the field of honour. He himself had never seen much honour in men having their skulls smashed in or their bellies ripped open. The sight of dying men crawling on all fours, their bodies cut to shreds, others fouling their breeches in fear and sobbing uncontrollably had not invoked thoughts of honour, more like horror and disgust.

'What's this?'

He had walked to where his horse and the young novice were waiting, to discover the boy surrounded by half a dozen rough-looking men. One had taken the boy's waster and was tossing it in the air. Conrad guessed by their appearance – brigandines, poor quality leather belts and dirty tunics – that they were poor knights, perhaps dispossessed or cast out by their families and having to rely on their ill-maintained swords to put food in their bellies. The boy was clearly alarmed at being surrounded by these ruffians, all of them bare headed and their faces grimy.

They turned when they heard his voice, the one holding the waster grinning when he spotted Conrad's white surcoat and red insignia.

'Well look who we have here, boys, one of the famous Sword Brothers.'

He pointed the waster at the novice. 'Who's this, a boy to warm your bed?'

The others laughed mockingly as Conrad calmly walked up to the novice.

'Are you unharmed?'

'Yes, brother,' the boy said falteringly.

'Brother? So in addition to sodomy you are guilty of incest,' shouted the leader with the waster.

There was uproarious laughter from the others.

Conrad turned to face the leader, pointing at the waster. 'That is not yours, I believe.'

The man slashed the air with the waster, only inches from Conrad's face. 'I have heard many things about the Sword Brothers, how they are the finest soldiers in all Christendom. But what I have seen so far has left me sorely disappointed.'

The others nodded and shouted their agreement.

'A wooden sword for wooden soldiers,' sneered the leader. 'It's easy to butcher ill-armed savages and burn their wooden huts. You want to know about soldiering?'

He jabbed the point of the waster into Conrad's chest. 'Two days fighting the Danes on the Elbe. That's soldiering. Three campaigns in Franconia. That's soldiering. Holding the line against French horsemen in a field in Thuringia. That's soldiering.'

Conrad held his stare and said nothing. He was now surrounded by the lowly knights, their confrontation having aroused the interests of others nearby who began to drift over.

The leader smiled at the others and jabbed the wooden point again into Conrad's chest.

'What's the matter, cat got your tongue, I…'

In a lightning-fast movement Conrad grabbed the waster with his left hand, stepped back and smashed his elbow into the man standing directly behind him. There was a loud crack as the man's nose was broken and he was knocked over. Conrad transferred the waster to his right hand and swung it right to strike the side of the man's head to his right. The knight groaned in pain as his head took the full

692

force of the blow and he staggered away, semi-conscious. The man on Conrad's left drew his sword and thrust it forward but the brother knight had anticipated his move and jumped back. The sword lunge missed but Conrad grabbed the man's right wrist before he could withdraw it, yanked him forward and smashed the wooden pommel down hard on the back of his head. The man fell like a dead weight, unconscious.

The other three had also drawn their swords but Conrad was too quick for them, leaping forward to parry the strike delivered by the man standing to the right of the leader and head-butting him in the face twice in quick succession. He moaned in pain as Conrad grabbed him and shoved him at the leader who was forced to bundle him out of the way. This gave Conrad time to deal with the other man who raced forward, gripping his sword with both hands and swinging it wildly at him. Conrad ducked to avoid the blow, turned the waster in his hand and swung it to the left so the man's face connected with the flat of his blade. His nose was squashed against the hard wood and he collapsed to his knees, Conrad delivering a fearsome blow with the edge against the side of his skull that knocked him unconscious. Now only the leader remained.

This idiot was more cautious than the rest, though whether as a result of him seeing what had happened to his rash comrades or because he was a more accomplished swordsman Conrad did not know. But he allowed himself a tiny smirk as he saw a trace of alarm in the man's eyes. Focus! As his comrades groaned and bled the leader came at Conrad with a series of great scything strikes that looked impressive but which were easy to dodge. And as his blows failed to connect he became more frustrated and enraged, screaming as he swung left and right to slice the impudent brother knight in half. But after at least a score of these grandiloquent strikes Conrad was unharmed and the knight was breathing heavily.

Brother Lukas would not have approved but as the man screamed once more and came charging at him like a man possessed, Conrad jumped to the right, spun on his left foot and swept the man's feet from under him with his right leg. He fell to the ground and Conrad was on him, raining a succession of blows on the back of his head with the waster's pommel.

'Respecting your allies. That's soldiering.'

Thud.

'Treating the young, old and vulnerable with respect. That's soldiering.'

Thud.

'Saving the fight for the enemy. That's soldiering.'

Thud.

He heard the alarm being sounded and rose to his feet, the man on the ground unconscious. A ring of guards closed round him, spears levelled as he calmly rested the waster on his right shoulder. Hearing uproar, Count Albert and Sir Helmold came from the pavilion, four guards forming round them.

'Hold!' shouted the count, shoving his way through the gathering crowd. He saw the men on the ground and others rubbing their bloody heads and being assisted to their feet, then saw Conrad with his wooden sword.

'What is going on here?' he demanded.

One of the knights, his nose a bloody pulp, pointed at Conrad. 'He started it, lord, attacked us he did.'

The count's eyes narrowed. 'Attacked all six of you?'

'Yes, lord.'

'With a wooden sword?'

'Yes, lord.'

'They stole the sword, lord,' said Conrad.

Sir Helmold grinned. 'I told you he was good, count.'

'Back to your duties,' shouted the count to the spectators. He walked over to Conrad as the six assailants were helped away, the unconscious ones being awakened by buckets of water. Conrad handed the waster back to its wide-eyed owner.

'I apologise for the conduct of my soldiers,' said the count. 'I shall have them hanged.'

'There is no need for that, lord,' said Conrad, waving forward the novice, 'not on my account. Some sword practice would be more useful. They underestimate the enemy and that is dangerous.'

'I will not make that mistake,' said Count Albert.

Conrad mounted his horse and raised his hand to the lords as he and the novice rode from the camp.

'Were you afraid, Brother Conrad?' said the novice, glad to be away from the barbarians.

'Afraid, why should I have been afraid?'

'There were six of them and only one of you and they had real swords.'

Conrad halted his horse and looked at the fresh-faced youth.

'What is your name?'

'Franz, Brother Conrad.'

'Well, Franz, you are lucky to have Brother Lukas as your instructor, just as I did. And you will soon learn that in a fight it is quality that mostly decides the outcome, not quantity.'

'Some say you are the best fighter in the Sword Brothers,' said Franz.

Conrad nudged his horse forward. 'Idle gossip is a sin, young Franz.'

'Yes, brother. But is it true?'

'I have no idea,' replied Conrad. 'As I said, it is nothing more than idle speculation.'

'Others say that Brother Henke is the best.'

Conrad did not reply but had to admit that it was a question he had often posed himself. Who was better: he or Henke?

Three days later Caupo and his Livs arrived.

Aside from a contingent of a hundred mounted warriors of his bodyguard, the king's army comprised the men raised from the villages around his stronghold of Treiden. Every man of the bodyguard was equipped with mail armour, a helmet and a large round shield but Caupo's foot soldiers were variously armed and furnished. Around half had armour, mostly mail though a few had leather breastplates, helmets, spears and axes. The rest had no armour to protect their bodies, though each man did have a helmet and a large shield. Weapons for these villagers turned temporary warriors comprised mostly spears, axes and knives, only the village elders having swords. Caupo also brought a hundred archers who wore no armour on their bodies or heads and carried long knives for their secondary weapons.

Conrad was standing in front of his wife's and child's grave the day they arrived. As usual freshly laid flowers adorned the mound of earth. Next to the grave were the final resting places of Thalibald and Waribule, their graves like the others well tended by Wenden's gardener. Despite the hundreds of soldiers around the castle and the bustle of their camps the cemetery was quiet and calm. Conrad liked coming here, not only to be near his family but also because it was a place where he could collect his thoughts. He stared at the words on the headstone even though he could not read them.

'We shall be marching north again soon.'

He turned the ring on his finger.

'So I will not be able to visit you as often as I would like. I pray that I will fall in the coming war so that I may be with you both. Hans has promised that if God decrees it so then I will be buried with you. I would like that.

'I miss you, Daina. I miss your smile and the days of happiness we shared together. The world is cold without your love to warm it.'

He choked back the tears as he saw his wife's green eyes and her smile.

'I hear that it has been a good year for the harvest, though no crops grow in the fields where we first met.'

He knelt down and placed a hand on the grave.

'I love you both.'

There was no wind and there was silence in the cemetery; even the birds had seemingly disappeared. He heard no sound but knew that he was not alone. He felt his heart beat in his chest and the hairs on the back of his neck stand up. He stood and turned, and saw Rameke pacing towards him.

They were the same age as near as damn it but Daina's brother looked careworn, his thick hair long and ragged and his eyes mournful. He was still stocky, though, and his heavy mail armour made him appear more so. He stopped when Conrad turned, his demeanour hesitant, uncertain of his reception. Conrad stepped forward and offered his hand.

'Brother.'

The doubts disappeared as Rameke took his hand and they embraced.

'Your family is waiting,' said Conrad.

They stood before the graves and Rameke read the inscriptions, Conrad then informing him of events at Wenden. At last Rameke spoke, his voice low.

'I was ashamed that I had lived and they had died, Conrad, so I took refuge with the king and rode north with his men. Then I was more ashamed that I had left you and so stayed away, and would still be away had it not have been for the gathering at Wenden. I ask your forgiveness, brother.'

'You should feel no guilt, my brother,' replied Conrad, 'what happened was God's will, of that I am certain.'

'And now we go to fight Lembit once more.'

Conrad smiled. 'This time he will not wriggle free. Rudolf has told me that the bishop wants him dead.'

Rameke laid a hand on his shoulder. 'Then we must do our utmost to ensure his wishes are fulfilled.'

Chapter 25

Seven days after the arrival of Caupo and the soldiers from Kremon and Segewold the army left Wenden. Volquin was eager for the march to begin as soon as possible, not least because the area around Wenden was quickly being covered with the filth and waste produced by hundreds of men and thousands of animals. The smoke of hundreds of campfires mixed with the sickly aroma of thousands of tons of horse dung hung in the summer air like a thick pall of nausea. The commanders knew that the lakes and ponds in the vicinity would soon be awash with piss and dung and the flies and fleas that were the faithful travelling companions of an army would soon create sickness among both men and animals. In addition, though Livonia in summer was lush, fifteen hundred horses, a thousand ponies and fifty oxen were stripping the land bare. On average twenty-five horses required an acre of grassland to graze upon each day and Master Thaddeus was losing what little hair he had trying to accommodate the insatiable demands of the crusader forces.

As a reward for his sterling service at Lehola and Odenpah, as well as the years spent at Wenden, Bishop Albert created Thaddeus quartermaster general for the campaign against Lembit. He sent him a special commission that the engineer had mounted on the wall of his cluttered office. The bishop also sent him a rather elegant red sleeveless tunic that bore the insignia of Riga on the chest. Thaddeus did not see the humour in Henke's remark that he should be dressed handsomely to receive the young virgins that were surely on their way from Kalju.

For weeks the kitchens and forges at Wenden had been hard at work producing supplies for the campaign, the former churning out thousands of hard biscuits that could be eaten, used as patches for shields or, in emergencies, hurled from siege engines against the enemy. Thaddeus' engineers had overseen the construction of six new mangonels to replace those lost at Odenpah to add to the brace of trebuchets that the army would be taking north. The woodworkers and carpenters of Riga had also been busy and as the spring gave way to summer a steady stream of carts had been ferried to the castle, to be stored inside the outer perimeter wall. On a daily basis riverboats plied the Gauja to ferry supplies to Wenden, and when Count Albert arrived they were used to transport his men, horses and a vast amount of armour, weapons, tents, canvas, tent poles and crossbow bolts. The armouries at Wenden had also been producing the latter to replace the prodigious expenditure at Odenpah, so that when the end of August approached the order's crossbowmen had enough bolts to fight the Estonians.

The riverboats brought barrels full of wine, mead and beer, Caupo also bringing with him ample supplies of *kvass* for his own warriors. The rivers and lakes were fished and the catch salted; Wenden's kitchens also producing cured meat for the order's soldiers. They would fare better than the crusader foot soldiers whose main diet would consist of pottage made from beans, peas and oatmeal. The knights, of course, would supplement their rations with whatever they managed to hunt, though when they reached Saccalia their hunting activities would be curtailed by the threat of ambush in the heavily wooded terrain.

On the last day of August every brother knight, sergeant and novice drawn from the eight garrisons of the Sword Brothers assembled in the courtyard of Wenden to ask for the blessing of God in their forthcoming crusade. Out of courtesy Grand Master Volquin directed that Otto, Wenden's resident priest, say prayers before the congregation. It was a beautiful summer's day, white puffy clouds filling the sky and a gentle easterly breeze blowing the stench of man and beast beyond the walls away from the castle. Otto commanded everyone to kneel as he said the Lord's Prayer, every man and boy repeating his words. They stayed on their knees with their heads bowed as Otto's deep, booming voice filled the courtyard.

'Lord, look favourably upon these, your beloved sons, the brethren of the Sword Brothers, who have renounced secular desires and surrendered their possessions to take up the cross. They are the ones who are striving to free this land of Lembit, the scourge of Livonia, and to expel the enemies of the Christian name. Give them strength, Almighty Lord, that they may smite Your enemies and cleanse this land with pagan blood. Let their armour be invincible and their lances as lightning bolts to scatter Your enemies. Amen.'

As one the congregation said 'amen' and Otto commanded them to rise to their feet. He held his arms aloft and commended them to draw their swords, looking up to the heavens.

'God with us!'

Conrad gripped his sword and raised it aloft, shouting 'God with us' along with the other brother knights, sergeants and novices. Walter, his face flush with religious fervour, was in a trance as he shouted the order's war cry again and again, his sword and shield held high in submission to the Almighty. Henke's face was filled with eager anticipation as he repeated the cry, bloodlust in his eyes, his tongue licking his lips like a wolf anticipating a meal of tender young lambs.

The next morning the Warriors of Christ led the army north towards Saccalia. The army moved slowly, all the foot soldiers fully armed and staying close to the wagons that carried a month's worth of food and supplies. The lords, grand master and his masters travelled near the head of the column of wagons that spread over three miles, the rate of advance being restricted by the lumbering oxen that pulled the carts containing the siege engines and their ammunition. The first target would be Fellin, around seventy-miles away, and after that Lehola a further twelve miles north. This time Lembit would be given no opportunity to surrender. Each fort would be stormed and their defenders put to the sword. Count Albert was desperate to engage Lembit in battle but Volquin informed him that the Estonian leader was no fool and preferred to avoid open combat, knowing the advantages crossbowmen and mailed horsemen gave the Christians. The grand master also knew that the Estonians had a detailed knowledge of their own land, which is why he insisted on the foot soldiers marching in formation fully armed, with knights riding in their armour. The latter would ride palfreys on the march, leading their warhorses behind them, but they would still be able to fight off any assault against the column. Security was heightened when the camp was pitched and dismantled – ideal times to spring an ambush when men's minds were more concerned with loading wagons and saddling horses than keeping watch for the enemy.

The Sword Brothers were in the van of the army, sending out mounted patrols ahead to scout the route and keep a lookout for the enemy. But the latter was conspicuous by their absence.

'Lembit will be hiding behind the walls of Lehola,' said Anton as he and his comrades trotted past a small lake in southern Saccalia.

The army was around five miles to the south and they had been scouting all day, Rameke joining his old friends on his hardy pony as they travelled through Lembit's kingdom. They had come across a small village on the other side of the lake but it had been abandoned, the huts and animal pens empty, the inhabitants having fled deep into the forest.

'There is no point in taking Fellin,' said Hans, 'we might as well march straight to Lehola and take it.'

Johann shook his head. 'The grand master would never leave an enemy stronghold along our line of march.'

'You should have burned the village,' remarked Rameke.

'This land belongs to the Bishop of Estonia now,' said Conrad. 'It is up to him what happens within its borders.'

'When Lembit is dead,' Rameke corrected him.

'That will be soon enough,' boasted Anton. 'He could not hold Lehola two years ago and then he was much stronger.'

'Do not underestimate him,' warned Rameke, 'he will surprise you yet.'

Conrad had noticed that Rameke was no longer the cheerful young man he had known before that terrible night at Thalibald's village. Now he was full of anger and possessed of a grim determination. But it was still good to be riding beside the only surviving member of his family.

They left the village behind and continued their journey north, passing fields that had been harvested of their crops and meadows bursting with colour, and never once did they see anyone.

On the tenth day out from Wenden Conrad and the others were again scouting ahead of the army, riding through a familiar landscape of forest, gently rolling hills and deserted villages. He was beginning to think that the whole of Estonia had been abandoned and they would be able to ride unhindered to the Gulf of the Finns when Hans called out.

'Look, on the hill.'

Framed in the sunlight were six figures on ponies on the top of a hill around three hundred paces away. Conrad saw they were all armed with spears and had round shields, though they made no attempt to flee as they sat on their mounts observing the four Sword Brothers and one Liv below. One appeared to be pointing down at them.

'The enemy shows his face at last,' said Rameke, drawing his sword.

Conrad clutched his lance as the six figures on the hill suddenly rode down the slope towards them.

'Brave,' remarked Johann, nudging his horse forward as the others deployed into line beside him, Rameke taking up position next to Conrad on the extreme left. They spurred their horses forward into a canter as the enemy riders continued to close on them, though curiously their spears were held upright. One was shouting at the brother knights.

'This will be easy,' smirked Hans as he donned his helmet, the others following suit. Conrad was just about to put on his helm when he shouted at the others.

'Stop, stand down.'

He tugged on the reins to halt his horse as Rameke pulled up his mount and the other three did the same.

'They are friends,' he shouted, pointing at the warriors who were now walking their ponies towards them.

'We are from Odenpah, Lord Kalju sent us,' shouted their leader.

Hans, Anton and Johann halted their horses and removed their helmets as the Ungannians stopped a few paces from them. In appearance they were not so different from the Livs with their green cloaks and brown tunics and leggings, though these men carried Kalju's golden eagle symbol on their shields.

'Greetings,' said their leader, who like Rameke had a thick beard, 'my name is Andrus and I bring news for Master Thaddeus.'

Conrad translated the words for the others. Hans laughed.

'Master Thaddeus should have stayed at Odenpah, he would have been a king by now.'

'I am Conrad Wolff and I am friends with your lord and his wife Eha.'

Andrus recognised the name. 'I know you. You were the crusader who spoke the words for Master Thaddeus at Odenpah.'

Conrad nodded.

'He is well?' enquired Andrus.

'He is,' answered Conrad, 'and is with the army not five miles from this spot. What is your message, Andrus?'

'Lembit has abandoned Fellin. His warriors and their families have left the fort and trekked north to Lehola. There are no Estonians between here and Lembit's stronghold.

'You believe him?' snarled Rameke, looking contemptuously at Andrus.

'An Estonian's word is his bond,' Andrus shot back.

Rameke laughed. 'Really? Do you include Lembit in that, your overlord, who embraced the Holy Church and then reneged on his pledge to the bishop?'

Andrus bristled at the insult and his men sniffed contemptuously at the impudent Liv in their midst.

'I fought beside Andrus at Odenpah, Rameke,' said Conrad curtly. 'I trust him with my life. This is no time for petty squabbles.'

Rameke looked away. 'If you say so.'

'Will you accompany us back to the army, Andrus, to relay your news to Master Thaddeus?'

Andrus looked at Rameke. 'If we are welcome.'

Conrad convinced him that he and his men would be more than welcome and so they agreed to ride back to the army with them. Rameke said nothing during the journey as he sank into a sullen mood. Conrad thought that it would be a long time before Liv and Estonian trusted each other, and perhaps Rameke would always bare a grudge against the northern people. But in the short term the news that the Estonians had brought meant that the campaign had suddenly got a lot easier.

*****

'He's here, sir.'

Stefan looked up from his dish of apple slices. He dabbed his mouth with a cloth and waved it towards one of the young monks standing by the wall of the withdrawing chamber.

'Excellent, show him in.'

'He has come with four of his men, sir,' said the commander of the garrison. 'He will want them to be present also.'

Stefan sighed. 'Very well, very well. Make sure you and some of your soldiers remain, though. I don't trust these barbarians.'

Manfred smiled and bowed his head. It was just as well that the archdeacon did not speak Lithuanian else he might insult his guests and end the meeting before it began. He exited the room and moments later returned with half a dozen guards that were ordered to stand either side of the archdeacon to reassure the governor. Then he brought in the guests. Stefan tried not to show his repugnance as the five bearded men entered the chamber and were introduced to the archdeacon, who remained seated in his chair. Not a good start.

The Lithuanians were all dressed in green tunics, baggy tan leggings and leather boots. They had been required to surrender their swords at the entrance to the bishop's palace, being reassured by the commander that they were in no danger. He had made several trips across the Dvina to convince the Duke of the Semgallians that it would be within his interests to accept the invitation to Riga to meet with Archdeacon Stefan.

Manfred Nordheim, sometime mercenary, pirate and smuggler, had not been born into privilege or had the patronage of a rich lord. He did, however, have the ability to make himself useful and that had endeared him to the archdeacon, especially when he had displayed that talent when the Northern Kurs and Oeselians had assaulted Riga. As the garrison had grown so had his authority until he had been appointed by Stefan to be commander of the town guards. Now he acted as translator for Duke Vincentas as the Lithuanian leader studied the effeminate-looking man in women's clothing sitting before him.

'Why did you wish to see me?' asked Vincentas bluntly, unhappy that he stood without weapons in this foreign fortress.

Stefan had beckoned forward a young novice holding a tray of wine but now waved him away.

Stefan smiled. 'The Kingdom of Livonia wishes to be friends with the Duke of the Semgallians.'

Vincentas was unimpressed. 'Why?'

'Because your enemies are our enemies and your battles are our battles,' replied Stefan. 'Perhaps you would like some wine?'

He waved forward the novice who proffered the tray to the duke. He took one of the silver goblets and handed it to one of his men behind. The man took a sip as Vincentas watched him closely. Stefan, bemused, looked at Manfred who nodded. The taster thought the wine delicious and told his lord so, and as he had showed no signs of being poisoned the duke took the goblet and drank from it. The nervous novice offered goblets to the other Lithuanians and then to the archdeacon.

Stefan smiled. 'It is well known that Grand Duke Daugerutis was a tyrant who deceived the other dukes into a ruinous war in Livonia, in which your valiant father, Duke Ykintas, fell.'

'You know much about Lithuanian affairs,' remarked Vincentas.

'Events south of the Dvina affect Livonia, duke,' said Stefan. 'I was saddened to hear that Prince Vsevolod, now leader of the Selonian and Nalsen peoples, wages war against you and we wish to assist you in your fight.'

Vincentas drained his goblet. 'Why?'

Stefan smiled again. This barbarian really was most taxing. 'Because if Vsevolod triumphs then he will make war upon Livonia, just as he did before we captured Gerzika.'

'Semgallia does not need any help to defeat its enemies,' sniffed Vincentas.

'Of course not,' said Stefan, 'but perhaps you will accept a present from your allies.'

He pointed at a novice holding a small casket, who walked forward to stand in front of the duke, opening the lid and taking out a solid gold crossbow bolt, which he offered the duke. The duke's companions gasped when they saw it and even he was impressed.

'A most generous gift.'

Stefan nodded at Manfred who walked over behind the archdeacon's chair and picked up a crossbow. He held it out for Vincentas as he translated the archdeacon's words.

'Livonia would like you to have two hundred of these, together with ammunition, to aid you in your war against Vsevolod. If you agree we will also provide you with soldiers to train your men in their use.'

Vincentas handed the golden bolt to one of his wide-eyed soldiers and took the crossbow, admiring its craftsmanship and power.

'Why should Semgallia, a kingdom that has co-existed peacefully alongside Livonia,' continued Stefan, 'become a slave state under the tyrant Vsevolod.

Vincentas looked at Stefan. 'You will give me two hundred of these?'

'Yes.'

'What do you want in return?'

'Nothing,' replied Stefan.

Vincentas' boyish features cracked a smile. 'I am not such a fool to believe that the Bishop of Riga gives away the contents of his armoury freely.'

'Naturally,' said Stefan. 'The price is friendship between Semgallia and Livonia.'

Vincentas handed the crossbow back to Manfred. He scratched his head and turned to his companions, talking in hushed tones to them. Stefan sighed and looked at his commander who gave him a reassuring nod. The duke at length turned back to face Stefan.

'I accept your offer. When can I have the crossbows?'

Stefan thought him an impudent wretch. 'As soon as my commander can arrange their passage across the river, duke.'

Stefan rose and offered his hand to Vincentas but the duke stepped forward and embraced him, much to the horror of the archdeacon. Manfred ushered them out of the room and returned to the withdrawing chamber after the Lithuanians had been escorted back to their boat at the docks. When he arrived Stefan was ordering incense to be brought to purify the air.

'Did you smell their breath? Unbearable.'

'I will arrange for the crossbows and instructors to be sent across the river tomorrow, archdeacon,' reported Manfred.

Stefan had a cloth to his nose. 'Excellent. Let us hope that the brutes do not waste them.'

'If Vsevolod discovers that you are aiding Duke Vincentas he might send raiding parties across the Dvina.'

Stefan removed the cloth and smiled. 'That will be for the Sword Brothers to deal with, not the garrison of Riga.'

'Why do you wish to aid the Semgallians, sir?'

'To prevent them from uniting under a single ruler, to gain influence across the river and to annoy the Sword Brothers,' replied Stefan. 'Our warriors of Christ grow too lofty in their ambitions and forget that they are mere servants of the church. When the bishop learns that Riga has influence among the Lithuanians he will begin to rely less on the Sword Brothers.'

'And more on you,' suggested Manfred.

Stefan held his gold cross. 'I am just a humble servant of the church.'

*****

The city was heaving with people, the guards having difficulty forcing a passage through them as they escorted the mayor and the leading boyars of Pskov to Trinity Cathedral to celebrate the Dormition of the Mother of God, the 'falling asleep' of Mary, the mother of Jesus. Pskov was glorious that summer; the people filled its white stone churches. A rich harvest of flax had been gathered from around its strong ramparts and its markets heaved with goods. The dreadful losses of the winter had been largely forgotten and Yaroslav had escorted Bishop Theodoric to Novgorod where Prince Mstislav was entertaining him. The latter, delighted that such an important figure of the Roman Church was in his city, had forgiven Domash for not taking Odenpah, viewing the prospect of a new trade route down the Gauja far more important. The air was fresh, the sun shone and the people were happy.

'I hate these occasions,' complained Domash as the guards halted when the crowd surged and blocked their progress.

Gleb smiled and touched a baby that was held up by its mother. 'You should thank your god that the people have forgiven you for leading them on a merry dance in Ungannia.'

'God has nothing to do with it,' replied Domash, 'it was the prince that ordered the campaign in Ungannia. But I will thank God for sending me Bishop Theodoric. He saved my neck.' He looked at Gleb. 'And yours.'

Gleb clutched the hands of citizens who were desperate to receive his blessing. 'I wouldn't be too quick to thank him. He and his crusaders will soon be knocking on the door of the prince's kingdom.'

Domash waved politely at the crowds and ordered the guards to use their spear shafts to increase the rate of advance.

'He has ordered a halt to all military aid to the Estonians so that's them finished. The prince will seize the lands of the northern Estonian chiefs to compensate for the loss of Ungannia.'

'A new power will rise in northern Estonia,' said Gleb.

'What power?' asked Domash.

Gleb shrugged. 'I have seen it in a vision, a red and white banner.'

'The Sword Brothers?'

Gleb shook his head. 'No. The army of another king.'

Domash wracked his brains but could think of no other power that would lay claim to Estonia. Lembit had written to Mstislav requesting aid but did not know that the prince had abandoned him. He smiled when he thought of the Estonian chief being in a state of ignorance as the prince and the Catholics carved up Estonia between them.

*****

Lehola was heaving with men, hundreds of them. They had been arriving for days, some hauling small carts behind them loaded with sacks of supplies and spare shields, spears and axes. The chiefs' bodyguards rode on ponies with their lords, which meant that the beasts also had to be accommodated within the great fort. But there was no room for their followers and so the area around the fort was covered with tents, campfires, and pens for ponies and carts. The chiefs and a score of warriors from their bodyguards slept in Lembit's great hall, his wolf shields occupying the huts inside the compound itself. The women and children had been sent away to the sacred groves deep in the forests with enough food to last them a month. They were cared for and watched over by the priests of the old religion to fortify their courage.

It was the height of summer and the days were warm and long, though in the hall the air was rancid with the smell of leather, stale sweat and ale as the chiefs gathered in a great circle round the stone hearth, which had been swept clean in preparation for the great feast that would be held that night. Lembit sat with Rusticus, the other chiefs being flanked by half a dozen of their men. Torches burned in brackets on the walls and light filtered in from the ventilation holes in the roof to illuminate proceedings. Lembit wore a plain tunic and leggings, Rusticus also casually attired. The other chiefs and their men sweated in their full war gear, though none wore their helmets. Nor did they have their weapons, the long table near the doors was stacked with swords and daggers, for these meetings were apt to get heated and when men's tempers were aroused blood could be spilt. Wolf shields at the doors and around the walls would ensure that proceedings did not become too raucous, though Lembit believed that they would all see the benefits of his plan and go along with it. In any case they were in no danger: it was considered the height of ill manners to murder guests in one's hall.

Lembit looked at his allies. They were certainly a strange bunch. There was Jaak whose eyes had become even more untrusting since the losses he had suffered at Odenpah; the cheerful Edvin with his mop of curly blonde hair; and the tall and painfully thin Alva. They might have lost Nigul and Kalju had turned traitor but he had still managed to amass six thousand warriors at Lehola, the largest army Estonia had ever seen. All he had to do now was to convince them that his plan was sound.

'It is a bad idea, Lembit,' growled Alva, 'the crusaders will cut us to pieces.'

'Our men are brave enough,' added Jaak, 'but they cannot withstand a charge of the men of iron.'

Lembit tried to remain calm. 'My friends, I know as well as you the strength of the crusaders. Their machines can batter down the strongest walls.' He gestured at the hall. 'Even this fort, Estonia's greatest stronghold, succumbed to their devilry. So I tell you that it will avail us nothing if we try to sit behind our walls.'

'Then how can they be beaten?' asked Edvin.

Lembit stood. 'As I have said, we use their own advantages against them.'

Jaak stroked his pointed chin. 'You really think that they will take your bait, Lembit? They are not stupid.'

Lembit smiled. 'Not stupid, no, but they are arrogant. They have tasted victory so many times that they have forgotten the bitter flavour of defeat. It is their arrogance that will be our chief ally in the coming battle.

'You have all seen the ground. It will be impossible for the crusaders to refuse battle in such a location. The Oeselians and Russians are marching to our aid, and after the battle has been won we will join with them and march south to lay waste Livonia.'

Edvin looked alarmed. 'You will not wait until they arrive before meeting the crusaders?'

Lembit took his seat. 'This needs to be a purely Estonian victory, to prove to our people and to the Oeselians and Russians that we do not need to rely on their spears to defeat the Bishop of Riga.'

'What of Kalju?' said Jaak.

Lembit shrugged. 'What of him? When the bishop's army is no more he will have no allies to hide behind. I think we can rely on Kalju crawling back to us in the near future.'

'What will you do with him?' queried Edvin.

'What will *you* do with him, my friend?' replied Lembit. 'He betrayed you as much as he did me. It is for all of us to decide the fate of Kalju, and Ungannia.'

He omitted to mention that he had promised the kingdom to the Prince of Novgorod. What they did not know would not alarm them.

'You have all answered the call of your forefathers,' said Lembit, 'by bringing your warriors to this place but I do not command, I only ask. I ask for your trust and your company in the battle line. If you wish to return to your kingdoms I will understand. For myself, I will fight the crusaders to preserve the freedom of my people. The decision is yours.'

None of them spoke as they shifted in their chairs and stared at the floor. At length Edvin looked at Lembit.

'Wierland stands with you.'

'As does Harrien,' said the 'elf warrior'.

'My warriors will be at Wolf Rock,' stated Jaak.

A surge of elation and relief swept through Lembit. He had not been surprised when the other chiefs had answered his appeal to muster at Lehola. After all, it was better for them to fight in Saccalia than in their own kingdoms. But his audacious battle plan had at first been met with disbelief and ridicule. But after their arrival he had taken them to the spot where he wanted to offer battle to the crusaders and he and Rusticus had worked hard to persuade them that it offered the best chance to halt the seemingly inexorable crusader advance.

He turned to Rusticus. 'Issue the orders. We leave at dawn.'

*****

In the heat Conrad and the other brother knights from Wenden now sported kettle helmets instead of the full-face helms they were supposed to wear. They sweated enough in their mail armour; there was no need to roast their heads in the summer heat as well.

'It looks deserted,' said Henke, swatting away a fly from his nose.

It had been thirteen days since they had left the castle and they had yet to see any Estonians. Every day patrols were sent ahead of the army as it lumbered its way

708

through the Estonian countryside, being assailed by hordes of midges as it threaded its way between rivers and lakes and through vast forests. Rudolf and Henke had decided to attach themselves to Conrad and his companions, having got bored of being in the saddle for hours being nursemaid to wagons, mules and foot soldiers. Either that or be in the company of Volquin and the crusader lords listening to their boring conversations.

'Why don't you ride up to the gates,' said Conrad. 'I'm sure any archers will make themselves known.'

'I hope you were not suggesting that I get myself killed, brother,' said Henke.

'The thought never entered my mind, brother,' replied Conrad.

'That's enough,' ordered Rudolf. 'We will all ride up to the gates. Just keep your eyes peeled and your shields high.'

They had ridden north and arrived at Lehola to find it seemingly deserted. As ever the surrounding villages had been abandoned and the fort's towers and battlements appeared empty. The gates were closed, though a closer inspection revealed them to be slightly ajar. As they neared them they halted their horses and looked up at the towers and tops of the walls, expecting to see them filled with warriors. But nothing happened.

Rameke sniffed at the still air. 'The fort is empty. There is no smell of dung or campfires.'

'Conrad, open one of the gates,' said Rudolf. 'Henke, you shift the other one.'

Conrad jumped down from his horse and applied his shoulder to the heavy oak gate, pushing it inwards with difficulty. The aged iron hinges creaked as the gates were opened and the Sword Brothers entered Lehola.

'You were right, Rameke,' said Rudolf as Conrad and Henke mounted their horses and followed the others into the fort. They walked their horses past abandoned forges, huts, stables and storerooms until they reached the inner compound, the gates to which were wide open. Inside it was a similar story: empty stables and huts.

They dismounted and tethered their horses before entering the great hall of Lembit himself, the images of wolves carved on the oak beams over the entrance. Inside it was dark and airless and without thinking they all drew their swords as they entered the feasting room. There was a sudden sound in one of the corners and they instinctively raised their swords and held their shields in front of them, only to see a scrawny rat scurrying across the floor.

'Well, no one can say that Lehola was not defended,' said Henke.

That night the army camped two miles from the fort and there was still no sign of the Estonians.

Grand Master Volquin had persuaded Caupo to garrison Fellin with a hundred of his warriors, adding ten of the order's crossbowmen for missile support. With the fall of Lehola he was forced to deplete the army further, asking Caupo for an additional hundred of his men, to which he added a further ten of the order's crossbowmen. He sat with the king and the lords in his tent a hundred paces from Lehola's gates. He did not wish to sleep inside the fort until it had been again cleansed with holy water, fearing the malign influence of hundreds of years of paganism. He did, however, assign a number of the order's soldiers to keep watch in the forts' towers.

The grand master sat round a small table in the company of Sir Richard, Count Albert, Master Thaddeus, Caupo and Sir Helmold. The flaps of the tent were open in a futile effort to entice fresh air to enter.

'Having expected to have to fight for Fellin and Lehola,' said Volquin, 'we now find ourselves in the rather unusual position of having taken both places without a single sword having been drawn. The question now is: what course do we follow hereafter?'

'Logic would suggest garrisoning both places strongly before retiring back to Livonia,' suggested Thaddeus.

'Impossible,' said the count. 'I came to Livonia to wage war against the pagan. If I had wanted to spend the summer wandering around the countryside then I would have stayed in Germany.'

'I agree with the count,' added Sir Richard. 'If we let Lembit go then he will be free to torment us for another year.'

'To say nothing of the other Estonian chiefs,' said Sir Helmold. 'They will be emboldened if we retreat back to Livonia.'

'Well, then, my lords,' remarked Thaddeus, 'you have the unenviable prospect of trying to find Lembit in this green wilderness. But you need to find him quickly before the weather changes and the autumn rain turns the land to a sea of mud.'

Though they did not know where Lembit was and could not agree on where to march to next, they were of the same mind when it came to Thaddeus' siege engines. They would be stored inside Lehola until after Lembit had been engaged. In this way, it was hoped, the army would be able to cover more miles a day in their quest to track down the Estonian leader.

Conrad rubbed his eyes and peered north into the gradually lifting gloom. He had been on watch for an hour in one of the towers on the fort's northern wall.

'See anything?' asked Hans.

'Nothing.'

Conrad sat down on the stool as his friend leaned on the top of the log and stared north and west. Not that he could see anything aside from the brooding black shape of the forest that surrounded Lehola. He pulled his cloak round him for it was cold and clammy before the sun warmed the earth.

'Looks like we will marching further north, Conrad.'

'Seems strange that Lembit has abandoned his homeland and his stronghold,' mused Conrad. 'It is like us abandoning Wenden.'

'Who knows how pagans think,' declared Hans.

'The same as us, my friend.'

Hans turned to face him as the first shards of sunlight pierced the eastern horizon.

'Really?'

Conrad nodded. 'Really. Pagan or Christian, all a man really wants is a warm bed, food in his belly and...'

He was going to say a family but he fell silent instead. He turned the ring on his finger and suddenly thoughts of Daina flooded his mind.

'And what?' queried Hans.

'Doesn't matter. If we are to march further north we will need more supplies. Master Thaddeus has said that there are only fifteen days' of food and fodder left. Hans?'

His friend had his back to him, staring to the north as it got lighter and the eastern sky was filled with red and yellow hues.

'We will not need any more supplies, Conrad.'

Conrad, perplexed, stood up and went to his friend's side. Ahead, around half a mile from the fort's northern ramparts, in a thin meadow through which a dirt track ran, sat hundreds of warriors on ponies.

Lembit had shown his hand at last.

The alarm was sounded and the camp sprang into life, knights barking orders at their squires to fetch their warhorses as they desperately put on their armour, spurs and buckled their sword belts. As the Livs in the fort kept watch on the still-stationary Estonians a trumpet called the brother knights to the chapel tent where Otto said prayers while everyone knelt and bowed their heads. There was not enough room in the tent and so priests from the other garrisons of the order went among the sergeants and brother knights to bless them and their weapons.

Conrad held up his sword for Otto to bless, the solemn shaven-headed priest clutching the blade and looking up to the heavens.

'Oh Lord, thou knowest how busy this knight will be this day. If perchance in the cauldron of holy combat he forgets You, I beseech You do not forget him.'

Afterwards, as novices scurried about to fetch the brother knights' warhorses, Conrad, Hans, Anton and Johann gathered in a circle. Conrad held out an arm. The others placed their hands on top to form a wheel.

'God with us,' said Conrad, 'kill Lembit.'

'God with us, kill Lembit,' they repeated before embracing and joining the others to collect their horses.

Like the knights of the lords, each brother knight rode a warhorse in battle, riding a palfrey for everyday duties, the difference being each knight owned his own horse whereas the horses of the Sword Brothers were owned by the order.

Before the army moved out of camp everyone ate a hearty breakfast. The cooking pots had already been bubbling when the enemy had been spotted, and as the Estonians had shown little inclination to move nearer or further from the fort Volquin issued orders that men and horses were to be fed. It might be a long day. He also gave orders that the novices, civilian drivers, carpenters, pages and anyone else incapable of using a weapon were to remain at Lehola, inside the fort. This did not include the priests, who would accompany the fighting men of the army when they marched. But it did include Master Thaddeus and his engineers, who after breakfast directed the wagons loaded with their siege machines to be driven into the stronghold. The tents were left where they stood.

It was two hours past dawn when Grand Master Volquin led the crusader army out to face the Estonians, the latter retreating immediately upon sighting the hundreds of mail-clad horsemen approaching. They fell back slowly into the gently rolling hills north of Lehola, now bathed in bright morning sunshine. The cool of the evening had disappeared and the temperature began to rise, though mercifully there was a gentle westerly breeze that ruffled the Christian pennants and standards. And as the army crawled forward the Estonians slowly retreated.

Count Albert sent fifty of his knights forward to try to goad the enemy into action, but the Estonians merely increased their rate of retreat, though always remaining visible to the crusaders. After two hours the Estonians suddenly melted into the trees. Volquin considered ordering a halt but then the air was filled with the sound of shouts and cheers, which appeared to be coming from the north. The order was given to close up and keep watch on the flanks as the march was resumed and the army entered an area of flatland bordered by a thick forest on the left and a brooding black lake on the right. The ground in between contained a few scattered pines but was flat and covered in lush grass – ideal terrain for horsemen. And ahead, around five hundred paces away, filling the horizon, was a great wall of warriors.

They had found the army of Lembit.

Frantic trumpet calls and drum rolls called forth the divisions of the Christian army as it moved from column into line to face the Estonians. As had been agreed at the start of the campaign, in any battles against Lembit it would comprise five separate 'battles' of varying sizes. On the right wing – the place of honour – stood Count Albert and his men. The count took up position in the centre of the front rank made up of two hundred knights and their squires. The same number of lesser knights was drawn up immediately behind, with the count's foot soldiers arrayed behind them.

In the centre of the Christian line stood three more 'battles'. On the right centre were Sir Helmold and his one hundred knights, one hundred squires and two hundred lesser knights. To the left of Sir Helmold's men stood the smaller number of Sir Richard's command – thirty knights, the same number of squires, fifty less knights and forty crossbowmen. On the left centre were arrayed the Sword Brothers, a 'battle' of white caparisons, surcoats, mail armour and silver helmets. And behind them stood the spearmen and crossbowmen of the order.

On the left wing stood King Caupo's Livs, seven hundred foot soldiers and a hundred riders of the king's bodyguard, Rameke among them. The Livs began singing one of their mournful war songs that told of a valiant young chief slaughtering hordes of Estonians in a time long ago, until the king in front of his great banner bearing a cross ordered them to stop. So his men took to whistling and jeering at the Estonians instead, the enemy replying in kind, some running forward and raising their spears and shields in the air – an invitation to single combat. Rameke offered to accept the invitations but Caupo told him to remain where he was.

The Christian army looked beautiful that morning, the knights and their squires wearing a profusion of colours and carrying gaudily coloured banners and flags sporting every heraldic device imaginable. Behind Count Albert a hulking knight carried his white horse head banner, the golden lion fluttering behind Sir Helmold and the red cross and sword insignia of the grand master of the Sword Brothers behind Volquin. The Livs cut a more sober appearance and similar to the Estonians in their greens and browns, their round shields adorned with red crosses to signify that their king fought for the Holy Church.

There was a great blast of trumpets and then the priests that accompanied the various 'battles' walked beyond the front rank of horsemen, made the sign of the cross at the Estonians, turned and raised their arms.

'Dismount,' ordered Rudolf as he left his saddle.

'I thought we had done all our praying,' complained Henke. 'We're up and down like a whore's robe.'

'This is the twenty-first day of September, Henke,' replied Rudolf as Walter rammed the end of his lance into the ground, sank to his knees, clenched his hands together and closed his eyes, 'the feast day of St Matthew.'

Otto walked forward and blessed the soldiers of Wenden, glaring at leather face and his crossbowmen who showed a marked reluctance to get their knees dirty. After the priests had called upon St Matthew to aid the army they retired behind the horsemen. Conrad scraped the earth with his foot.

'This ground is very soft, even though it's summer.'

'We are here to kill the enemy not plant crops,' said Henke derisively, hauling himself back into the saddle.

Conrad did the same and looked at the line of Estonians across from him. His instincts told him something was wrong but he did not know what. Another blast of trumpets brought him back to reality and he plucked his lance from the earth. The sun was climbing high into the sky now and it was getting warmer, though fortunately the breeze continued to blow. The gaps between the various 'battles' were suddenly filled with foot soldiers as the crossbowmen marched forward with their spearmen protectors to commence hostilities.

'It was kind of Lembit to arrange his army in a long line so our crossbowmen could shoot it to pieces,' said Henke loudly. The prospect of imminent slaughter always put him in an ebullient mood.

'Lembit is not stupid,' said Conrad, becoming increasingly anxious, though he did not know why.

Henke, to the left of Hans who was beside Conrad, leaned forward. 'Course he is. Just watch as half his army is cut down by crossbow bolts.'

Conrad saw leather face walking forward, crossbow on his shoulder, as though he was taking a stroll. Like every other knight Conrad waited until the last minute before putting on his helm and smiled at the crossbowman as he passed him.

'Don't you worry, boys,' leather face called to them, 'we'll soften them up nicely for you.'

The Christian army numbered two and half thousand men and over six hundred of them were now walking towards the enemy. They halted around three hundred paces from the enemy, close enough to kill but far enough away to get back to the knights if the Estonians decided to charge them. From behind a wall of shields two hundred and eighty crossbowmen and a hundred Liv archers began shooting at a rate of four bolts and arrows a minute to shred the Estonian line.

From where Conrad sat on his horse it sounded as though hundreds of twigs were being snapped as the crossbowmen worked feverishly to deluge the Estonians with a hail of iron-tipped missiles. The horsemen of Count Albert, Sir Helmold and Sir Richard began cheering and shouting as the missiles struck the enemy – over two thousand quarrels in two minutes. The Sword Brothers, more disciplined, remained silent in their ranks. Each crossbowman was carrying three full quivers and they did not stop shooting until two had been emptied – over eleven thousand bolts unleashed in ten minutes. And the Estonians just stood in their ranks and were shot down like dogs. The Livs shot at a slower rate but their arrows added to the mayhem that was being thrown at Lembit's warriors, eventually running out of arrows as they emptied their quivers and marched back to their king.

'They just stood there,' said Hans in disbelief.

'Did you see them fall?' asked Johann.

'This is the most one-sided battle we have fought in,' added Anton.

The crossbowmen were now falling back, covered by the spearmen, while in the distance what was left of the Estonian army still stood, rock like, in their positions.

*****

Jaak had taken some convincing when Lembit had asked him and his men to be the bait to entice the Christians to engage in battle. He had brought a thousand warriors to Lehola and after hearing Lembit's plan believed that he and they would never see Jerwen again. But now, as he and his warriors emerged from behind their log screens, he saw the merit of Lembit's plan. In the days after their arrival there had been feverish activity at Lehola as hundreds of women created three and half thousand scarecrows to plant in the ground in front of the great boulder known as Wolf's Rock.

No one knew where these great rocks came from but they were scattered throughout Estonia and had been around before man had walked the earth. In the days before the battle each scarecrow – a log hammered into the ground, to which was fixed a shorter pole at right angles to make the arms – was set in place in front of Wolf Rock. They were wrapped with twisted bundles of withies and covered with sacking to resemble tunics. Crude wooden shields were hung from the arms and sharpened sticks to resemble spears were fixed to the other arms, while white cloth stuffed with straw and topped with leather was used to create the illusion of faces and helmets.

The scarecrows were arranged in three lines, with ample space between them to accommodate Jaak and his men, who created a great tumult when the Christians arrived to make the Estonian army seem like a seething mass of men.

'They will send their crossbowmen forward first to soften you up,' Lembit had told him, and sure enough the Christian foot soldiers were advancing towards them. As soon as their spearmen had halted Jaak's men fell back to behind the last line of scarecrows and took cover under large rectangular shelters made of several logs lashed together. The crossbow bolts took fearsome a toll on the scarecrows, cutting the first two lines to pieces. But when they and the Liv archers had finished shooting Jaak's men emerged from under their log covers unscathed.

*****

Volquin raised his lance in the air, clutching his helmet in his left hand as he turned his horse to face the ranks of the Sword Brothers.

'God with us!'

The brother knights and sergeants repeated the cry as the former placed their helms on their heads, couched their lances and spurred their horses forward. The horsemen of the other 'battles' did the same as over eleven hundred riders trotted towards what was left of the Estonian line. The mighty warhorses grunted as their iron-shod hooves tore up the ground and the earth shook as death approached the Estonians. Conrad saw the enemy through the slits in his helmet, still standing and hurling abuse at the crusaders. The riders broke into a canter, the brother knights in close order and the sergeants behind them. Conrad gripped his lance and held his shield close to his body. He would spur his horse into the gallop at the last moment so as not to tire his mount and, more importantly, break formation.

716

Whereas the crusader knights and their squires were unused to fighting as part of a group the Sword Brothers trained incessantly to work as a cohesive unit in battle: to attack, turn and retreat as one. Thus would they become unstoppable, an impenetrable wall of mail and horseflesh that brushed aside their foes as dust to the wind.

They were less than three hundred paces from the enemy now, moving as one towards the pagans. Conrad could feel his heart pounding in his chest as he focused on the nearest group of enemy warriors, most of whom appeared to be dead though one or two seemed to be hanging limply from poles. But his musings on the enemy disappeared as his horse suddenly slowed and nearly buckled under him as the beast sank into mud.

If they had had the opportunity to reconnoitre the battlefield the crusaders would have discovered that there was a large bog in front of Wolf Rock that drained into the lake beyond the Christians' right flank. It was not particularly deep, perhaps four or five feet, but it was enough to stop the mailed horsemen in their tracks. Conrad tried to halt his horse as the sergeants behind also endeavoured to stop their horses riding into the bog. Some horses stumbled and threw their riders, the latter falling headfirst into the slime. To the right of the Sword Brothers it was a similar story as horses cantered into the mud and either panicked and threw their riders or attempted to carry on forward. The Estonians jeered and cheered as the horsemen struggled to retain their formation.

Conrad had managed to stay in the saddle and attempted to calm his horse. He took off his helmet as the beast struggled to keep its footing. That he had been right about the soft ground was scant consolation as brother knights fell into the mud, dropped their lances or failed to prevent their horses from bolting in all directions. It was a disaster.

Riders in Sir Richard and Sir Helmold's 'battles' attempted to continue their charge but it was futile as their horses sank in the mud.

'Back, back,' shouted Volquin, helmetless and pointing frantically at his masters. Conrad gently tugged on the reins of his horse to turn him when he heard a sound, or rather a succession of sounds. Horns! He looked at Hans and they both knew what they were. They had heard them before and knew that more Estonians had come to the field. They were right: from the forest charged five thousand Estonian warriors led by Lembit himself.

The Estonian leader had nullified three of the crusaders' most potent weapons – their siege engines, crossbowmen and mailed horsemen – and now he played his hand, throwing the might of Estonia against the rear of the Christian army.

It was not a disciplined attack of locked shields inching forward to hack and thrust at an opposing shield wall, but rather a mad rush of savage warriors intent on slaughtering those who had invaded their homeland. Lembit led the way, sword in hand at the head of his wolf shields as he ran towards the Livs. His two thousand Saccalians buckled Caupo's left flank, swept round his rear and within minutes had cut deep into his men.

Alva and Edvin ignored the Livs as they led their men across the rear of the Christian army to battle the crusaders' foot soldiers. The Sword Brother spearmen were the first to react, closing ranks and forming all-round defence as hundreds of Estonian warriors came screaming at them. The crossbowmen then began shooting, cutting down dozens of men as they released their triggers and reloaded from behind the relative safety of the spearmen. But they had only one quiver each and soon their ammunition began to run out.

The foot soldiers of Sir Richard and Count Albert – less than two hundred and fifty men – were quickly overrun and hacked to pieces when the Wierlanders and Harrien reached them. Alva and Edvin then rallied their men to finish off the accursed foot soldiers of the Sword Brothers as Caupo's Livs were being whittled down by the Saccalians and Lembit appeared to be on the verge of a great victory.

Volquin forgot about the Estonians on the other side of the bog, forgot about the other 'battles' and screamed his orders once his men had extricated themselves from the mud and wheeled about.

'Save the order's foot soldiers,' he bellowed, slamming on his helmet and then digging his spurs into his horse's sides.

Conrad gripped his axe and likewise spurred on his horse, the other brother knights and sergeants doing the same. All he could see were groups of drab-coloured warriors as his horse thundered back towards the beleaguered foot. There was no disciplined advance with couched lance, just a desperate desire to save as many foot soldiers as they could.

It took them less than a minute to reach the first group of Estonians, perhaps two score of spearmen who attempted to form a shield wall but who fled when they realised that four times that number of mailed horsemen was bearing down on them. Conrad swung his axe and split the helmet of one man who had dropped his spear and shield in an attempt to outrun the riders. Another turned, raised his spear and had the side of his face hacked off as Conrad caught him with an axe blow as he rode past.

The Sword Brothers speared, hacked and thrust their way through the enemy to reach their beleaguered foot soldiers, who gave a great cheer when their relief arrived. The Estonians fell back but did not break, instead reforming into a great shield wall some fifty paces away.

But on the left flank Caupo's men were surrounded and had lost nearly half their number. As Lembit's men methodically gouged through their ranks Caupo still lived, riding up and down in the ever-decreasing Liv circle, sword in hand and shouting encouragement to his warriors. But if he and they were not relieved soon then they would be slaughtered.

Volquin tore off his helmet. 'Dismount, dismount.'

The brother knights and sergeants alighted from their horses and closed round the grand master. As they had practised many times on the training field, every tenth sergeant began collecting the horses as the spearmen formed a defensive circle round the tightly packed press of men and beasts. Ideally it would have been better for the order's horsemen to have remained mounted, but the ground was littered with heaps of dead Livs and Estonians and between Caupo's warriors and the Sword Brothers were hundreds of Saccalians, to say nothing of the hundreds of Harrien in their shield wall directly south of the order's soldiers.

Volquin was like a man possessed, grabbing leather face and ordering him to marshal the crossbowmen to face the Harrien and begin shooting at them when he gave the order. He ordered the sergeants to release the horses back towards the bog.

'We can collect them later if we are still alive. Save Caupo, save the king. Wedge formation.'

As the crossbowmen began shooting at the Harrien, their bodkin heads slicing through the Estonian shields with ease, Volquin placed himself at the head of the wedge that would attempt to reach the king. The masters closed behind him, the brother knights behind them and the sergeants in the rear.

'God with us!' shouted Volquin and then charged forward.

Conrad, axe in hand, was on the right side of the wedge as it covered the hundred paces or so between the Sword Brothers and the Saccalians attempting to kill the Livs. On the other side of the wedge the crossbowmen were shooting their last few bolts, felling an enemy warrior with every quarrel but knowing that when they stopped the Harrien shield wall would charge them. And so it was.

The first Saccalians the Sword Brothers reached were taken by surprise as they waited behind their comrades for the Liv circle to break. Volquin and the masters reached them first after scrambling over dead bodies, thrusting their swords into their backs. But then a great mêlée ensued as the Saccalians realised that they were being assaulted and turned to face the Christian warriors desperately trying to break through to Caupo.

And at that moment there was a great roar as the crossbowmen ceased shooting and Alva led his men forward.

The Harrien chief had led fifteen hundred of his warriors into battle. Three hundred lay dead or dying but the rest screamed their war cries and raced towards the small group of Sword Brothers. The quick-thinking sergeants in the wedge faced left and took up position alongside the hundred and fifty spearmen who closed ranks and braced themselves for the pagan tide that was about to hit them. The crossbowmen drew their knives and axes and stood ready as hundreds of Estonians buckled the left side of the wedge.

Conrad heard the roar and the loud bang but had no idea what was happening beyond what he could see through his vision slits. An Estonian came at him with an axe but the blow was overhand and predictable. Ideally he would have jumped aside so the blade hit air but he could not desert his place in the formation so he raised his shield to stop the blow and then thrust his axe forward, the top spike going into the enemy's unprotected belly. It was enough to double him over and allow Conrad to split the rear of his man's helmet with another strike. But in the mêlée he did not have the space to wield his axe effectively so he shifted his shield onto his back, transferred the axe to his left hand and drew his sword. Much better.

On they went, more and more Estonians filling the ground in front of him as the Sword Brothers continued to hack their way towards the king. Anton was on his left and Hans behind him as he stepped over a dead warrior. He saw Henke dash out from the ranks to cave in the skull of an opponent with his mace, retreating back after he had done so. He too stepped forward as a man armed with a spear ran at him. He had to be careful and act quickly, for to merely parry the blow might result in Hans or Anton being speared. So he thrust his sword into the ground transferred his axe to his right hand and hurled it at his attacker.

'Apologies, Brother Lukas.'

The axe blade embedded itself in the man's face and he collapsed to the ground. Conrad darted forward to retrieve it, yanked his sword from the ground and retook his position in the wedge, which was on the verge of being overwhelmed.

The spearmen and sergeants had done well to withstand the charge of Alva's men but the sheer number of the latter meant they were forced back as the Estonians hacked and thrust at them with axes, spears and swords. The wedge was about to fragment and dissolve completely but then the earth shook with thunder of hooves.

Salvation had arrived in the shape of Sir Helmold and Sir Richard.

The two lords commanded only just over five hundred horsemen but they struck the right flank of Alva's warriors just as the Harrien were about to overrun the Sword Brothers. Immediately the chief issued orders to reform a shield wall to repel the riders, but not before the lords and their men had cut down two hundred of his warriors. Alva managed to rally his men and place them in all-round defence but the Sword Brothers, having suffered dozens of casualties, had survived. The Christian horsemen lapped round the Harrien, who threw a deluge of spears and axes at the mailed riders, unhorsing at least fifty and killing a score more. Sir Richard and Sir Helmold led charge after charge at the Harrien, spearing some in the front ranks but being unable to break their shield wall.

The battle was now fragmenting into isolated pockets of combat. Alva and his warriors fought Sir Richard and Sir Helmold, Lembit was trying to slaughter the Livs and on the right, near the lake, Count Albert was engaged in his own private war with fifteen hundred Wierlanders. The latter had butchered the count's foot soldiers and all his priests, plundering and mutilating the bodies and ignoring the horsemen extricating themselves from the bog. By the time they heard the furious horn calls they were scattered over a wide area and had no time to rally round their chiefs as four hundred horsemen hit them. The charge had been disciplined and methodical, the long line of horsemen literally riding through small groups of Wierlanders, killing them with lances and swords. But the core of Edvin's forces was a band of five hundred warriors who now closed ranks round their lord and began shuffling east. There were fifty archers among these men and they commenced shooting at the knights, aimed shots that killed a score of the count's men and wounded a score more. And all the time Edvin marched towards the southern shore of the lake. The chief knew that he could not defeat mailed horsemen, hundred of whom were now riding round his men. He also knew that Lembit's great gamble had failed. He cared not. His only concern now was to get as many of his men back to Wierland as possible.

Conrad's eyes were stinging as sweat ran into them. He stopped an Estonian sword on his axe and thrust his own blade over the top of a shield and into a man's face. He caught sight of the design on the shield as the warrior tumbled backwards. Wolf shield.

Then he saw him, standing beside the great brute he had encountered before, his wolf banner being held behind him. Lembit, the murderer of his wife and child and the instigator of all the misery that had been inflicted upon Livonia. Ever since he had come to Wenden Lembit had been a thorn in the side of the order, Bishop Albert and the population of the crusader kingdom.

'Death to Lembit,' he shouted, though he doubted anyone heard him in his helmet.

But before he had even moved he saw the big warrior lift up a spear and hurl it forward. He swung his axe to the right to smash the blade into the side of the head of a warrior who was attacking Hans and looked back to see Caupo slump in the saddle as the spear went into his belly. He was wearing mail armour but the throw had been strong enough to pierce the iron links. There was a great groan among the Livs as they saw their king fall from the saddle. The Sword Brothers had reached their allies but now the Saccalians were filled with renewed vigour.

Masters Aldous and Gerhard were dead. Cut down as they tried to protect the grand master, who himself was wounded in the shoulder. As the Sword Brothers linked up with what was left of the Livs the wounded were dragged into the centre of the circle that was surrounded by the Saccalians. They included Lukas who had been speared in the leg and Walter, whose helmet had been knocked off and subsequently rendered unconscious by a blow to the head. It was chaos, a swirling mass of men trying to cut each other to pieces in the frenzy of combat.

Conrad saw Lukas being dragged inside the circle and saw two sergeants become separated and hacked to death by half a dozen wolf shields. He saw Lembit again, barely fifty paces away, perhaps less, urging his men on. But even the Saccalians were tiring, groups of them withdrawing to catch their breath and drink from their wooden water bottles. Many were wounded, even among the wolf shields, but the Livs and Sword Brothers were in a worse state. The fight lessened in intensity as a sort of mutual parley broke out all around the circle.

Rudolf, his surcoat torn and his mail armour ripped, came to Conrad's side. He lifted his helmet. His face was streaked with sweat.

He pointed at Lembit. 'You want that bastard?'

'With every bone in my body.'

He nodded. 'Very well. The only way to win this battle is to kill him and that means taking the fight to him.'

'Sword Brothers!' shouted Rudolf. 'Follow me. Kill Lembit.'

He pulled the helmet back over his face and ran forward, shield held in front on him, sword in hand, Henke on his left side. Conrad heard the shout 'kill Lembit' as he forgot his tired limbs and raced forward beside Rudolf, his mind possessed by a burning desire for vengeance. The depleted garrison of Wenden formed the vanguard of the desperate assault, the wolf shields who surrounded Lembit being taken completely by surprise by this daring move. Within seconds Rudolf, Henke and Conrad were among them, cutting down warriors attempting to protect their chief. Conrad, now free to duck and move as he pleased, feinted right with his sword before whipping back the blade and thrusting it into the belly of a wolf shield. Half the blade disappeared into the enemy warrior before Conrad yanked it back. The wolf shield fell to the ground and then he was face to face with Lembit himself. Henke and the brute that was Lembit's shadow were locked in their own fight to the death as the Saccalian leader came at him.

He was shorter than Conrad, broader and surprisingly light on his feet, weaving left and right to avoid his blows as the brother knight directed a series of rapid sword strikes against him. Lembit moved around him, probing for weaknesses but keeping his shield tight to his body. He thrust, hacked and swung his sword, moving it with great agility as though it was a feather. Conrad fended off the blows but Lembit kept circling and attacking, darting in and out like a wasp delivering a sting. He cut the mail on Conrad's left arm and dented the side of his helmet, Conrad splintering the wood of Lembit's shield with an overhead axe swing. They forgot about the battle, the dead bodies at their feet and the screams of men being sliced open as they continued their personal duel. Conrad screamed and attacked Lembit with a succession of sword and axe strikes, crouching and lunging as he sought to find a way through Lembit's defences, to no avail.

Lembit's eyes were full of hate as Conrad leaned back and then lunged forward to graze the Estonian's right arm. But the pagan barged his shield into the brother knight and swung low with his sword, slicing open the mail chausses covering his left leg and cutting the flesh beneath. Lembit grinned when he saw the blood.

'Come on, Christian,' he shouted, 'where is your god now?'

They circled each other once more, jabbing with their swords, looking for any openings in their opponent's defence. It was as if they were the only two people in the world as they exchanged another series of blows and strikes, Lembit's shield almost disintegrating as Conrad swung his axe at the Estonian's head again and again.

Lembit delivered a side swing that sliced open the mail covering Conrad's belly and grazed his flesh. He was breathing heavily now and it felt as though his head was being roasted inside his helmet. His arms and legs ached and his sword felt heavy. But he suddenly thought of Daina and Dietmar and ran at Lembit, brushing aside his battered shield and locking cross-guards as their swords came together. He swung his axe to the right and struck the side of Lembit's helmet, sending the Saccalian crashing to the ground.

Disorientated, Lembit staggered to his feet and pulled the dented helmet off his head. He faced Conrad and held his sword unsteadily. The Sword Brother could not breath inside his helmet. It felt as though his lungs were on fire. He pulled off his helmet, threw it aside and faced Lembit. The Saccalian recognised his attacker; the boy whom he believed had been killed long ago, the youth whom Rusticus had told him was a bad omen. His face registered shock and surprise and he hesitated.

'You?'

Conrad dropped his sword, gripped his axe with both hands and screamed as he swung it. And lopped Lembit's head clean off.

The headless body stood for what seemed like an eternity before collapsing to the ground. Conrad shouted in triumph and hurled himself at Lembit's standard bearer holding the wolf banner, grabbing the warrior's neck and wrenching off his helmet. Like a wild beast he then proceeded to sink his teeth into the man's nose and bit down hard. The man screamed as he tumbled to the ground with Conrad on top of him, the brother knight tearing at his nose in an effort to tear it from his face. As he did so he slipped his dagger out of its sheath and plunged it into the man's neck. He was covered in blood as the wound sheeted liquid and the standard bearer gurgled, gasped and then went limp. Conrad stopped biting his nose and started to stab at the neck wound frantically, plunging the narrow blade into the torn flesh again and again.

He felt a hand on his shoulder. 'He's dead, Conrad.'

In a rage he rolled off the corpse, spun round and faced the owner of the voice, ready to attack. It was a helmetless and bloody Hans. Conrad regained a semblance of composure and nodded at his friend, who offered him a hand and hauled him to his feet. At that moment there was a loud shriek and they turned to see the brute that had been Lembit's closest companion die.

Rusticus had been more than holding his own against Henke until he had seen his master fall, killed by his nemesis seemingly returned from the dead. He had looked on helplessly as the youth decapitated his lord and cried out in anguish. And that few seconds allowed Henke to deliver a crushing blow with his mace that split his helmet. It would have floored an ordinary man but Rusticus stayed on his feet, only to be run through by Rudolf, Johann and Anton who sprang at him. Three swords stabbed him repeatedly but he still managed to stay on his feet until Rudolf raised his sword above his head with both hands and plunged it into Rusticus' heart. Thus did he join his master in the afterlife.

Like a plague sweeping through a city the news of Lembit's death spread quickly among his Saccalians and soon they were fleeing for the safety of the forest. The wolf shields were the last to leave, the survivors forming a shield wall that shuffled back to the sanctuary of the trees as they stayed in their ranks and prepared to meet an attack that never came.

Brother knights and sergeants removed their helmets and gasped for air, some with hands on their knees as fatigue suddenly gripped them. Others shook uncontrollably as after-battle nerves took possession of them. A few sank to their knees and thanked God for their safe deliverance.

Conrad and Hans looked down at the head of Lembit.

'He looks small, insignificant,' said Conrad.

'He was big enough,' replied Hans.

Johann and Anton came over and all four embraced each other. Their surcoats were ripped and splattered with blood, their mail armour was cut and all had been wounded. But they were alive and the air they breathed in was the sweetest they had ever tasted.

'The bastard's dead, then,' remarked Henke as he jabbed the head with his bloody sword. He looked at Conrad and grinned. 'You got your revenge.' He patted him on he shoulder. 'Well done.'

Seeing the Saccalians leaving the battlefield, Alva had given orders for his men to do the same, the men from Harrien making a desperate run for the trees to reach safety. And on the other side of the battlefield Edvin had managed to withdraw with his Wierlanders, though Count Albert's horsemen had killed around five hundred of his warriors before he did so. It would have been more but the count gave orders to ride to the relief of those Christians still in peril. And beyond Wolf Rock Jaak was already leading his men back to Jerwen.

'What now, lord?'

Vetseke had led his men into the forest in the wake of the Saccalians who were now splintering into small groups as they fled in every direction through the green wood. He and his men had been with a group of a hundred Saccalians that had been battling the Livs, though such was the press of men that they had seen no actual combat.

'North,' replied Vetseke. 'There is nothing left for us in Estonia. Novgorod will offer us a home. Give the order to move out.'

Scattered groups of Estonians were still making their way off the battlefield as Volquin gave the order to collect the warhorses that had made their way to the edge of the bog and had their heads down, grazing. But first everyone knelt as Otto said prayers and gave thanks to God for their great victory. When he rose to his feet Conrad saw Rameke, pale and grief stricken but unharmed. He embraced his brother.

'The king is dead,' said Rameke flatly.

'He will be missed. What will you do now?'

Rameke looked around at the corpse-strewn ground. 'I do not know.'

'Come back to Wenden. You can rebuild your father's village.'

'First I have to travel back to Treiden to bury the king. After that?' He shrugged indifferently. 'And you?'

Conrad looked at the groups of Estonians disappearing in the distance.

'This war is only half won. There is a lot of fighting left to do.'

Epilogue

To His Holiness Pope Honorius III from Brother Albert, Bishop of Riga, and your humble servant, with due and devoted respect.

'Holy Father, I am glad to report that the army of the Lord has recently triumphed over the Estonian pagans led by the servant of Satan himself, Lembit. The noble crusaders from Germany, combined with your servant King Caupo and the Order of Sword Brothers, did battle with the enemies of the Holy Church on the Feast of Matthew's Day and scattered the enemy as Samson slew the Philistines. Though they be outnumbered and sorely tested by the trickery and deceit of the enemy, the Lord saw fit to reward His humble servants with a great victory. The triumph was not bought cheaply and it saddens me to report, Holy Father, that King Caupo and Sir Helmold, along with many score of other brave men, have joined those others who have been martyred during the holy crusade in Livonia.

'I am happy to report to Your Holiness that southern Estonian has now been subdued and that the Sword Brothers are poised to spread the word of God north to the waters of the Gulf of the Finns. I am currently eagerly waiting for the return of the Bishop of Estonia from the Principality of Novgorod, who has these last few months been concluding a treaty with the prince of that city. His return is greatly anticipated by the people of Livonia.

'One matter I must bring to Your Holiness' attention, and that is the conduct of one Conrad Wolff, a Sword Brother from the garrison of Wenden. In the recent battle it was his weapon that struck down the heathen Lembit, just as David cut down Goliath. This brother knight saved my own life a number of years ago and I can only conclude that God has marked out this holy warrior to be the instrument of His will in Livonia.

'It just remains for me to say that the Holy Church in Livonia stands strong and resolute in its aim to carry the word of God to the pagans and convert them to His ways.

'Given this twenty-ninth day of September in the year of our Lord one thousand, two hundred and seventeen and the second year of your pontificate.'

Printed in Great Britain
by Amazon